STEPHEN [...] d. He is the winner of three Wo[...] [W]riters Association Bram Stoker Awards and three International Horror Guild Awards as well as being a seventeen-time recipient of the British Fantasy Award and a Hugo Award nominee. A former television producer/director and genre movie publicist and consultant (the first three *Hellraiser* movies, *Night Life, Nightbreed, Split Second, Mind Ripper, Last Gasp* etc.), he is the co-editor of *Horror: 100 Best Books, Horror: Another 100 Best Books, The Best Horror from Fantasy Tales, Gaslight & Ghosts, Now We Are Sick, H.P. Lovecraft's Book of Horror, The Anthology of Fantasy & the Supernatural, Secret City: Strange Tales of London, Great Ghost Stories, Tales to Freeze the Blood: More Great Ghost Stories* and the *Dark Terrors, Dark Voices* and *Fantasy Tales* series. He has written *Stardust: The Visual Companion, Creepshows: The Illustrated Stephen King Movie Guide, The Essential Monster Movie Guide, The Illustrated Vampire Movie Guide, The Illustrated Dinosaur Movie Guide, The Illustrated Frankenstein Movie Guide* and *The Illustrated Werewolf Movie Guide*, and compiled *The Mammoth Book of Best New Horror* series, *The Mammoth Book of Terror, The Mammoth Book of Vampires, The Mammoth Book of Zombies, The Mammoth Book of Werewolves, The Mammoth Book of Frankenstein, The Mammoth Book of Dracula, The Mammoth Book of Vampire Stories By Women, The Mammoth Book of New Terror, The Mammoth Book of Monsters, Shadows Over Innsmouth, Weird Shadows Over Innsmouth, Dark Detectives, Dancing with the Dark, Dark of the Night, White of the Moon, Keep Out the Night, By Moonlight Only, Don't Turn Out the Light, H.P. Lovecraft's Book of the Supernatural, Travellers in Darkness, Summer Chills, Exorcisms and Ecstasies* by Karl Edward Wagner, *The Vampire Stories of R. Chetwynd-Hayes, Phantoms and Fiends* and *Frights and Fancies* by R. Chetwynd-Hayes, *James Herbert: By Horror Haunted, Basil Copper: A Life in Books, Necronomicon: The Best Weird Tales of H.P. Lovecraft, The Complete Chronicles of Conan* by Robert E. Howard, *The Emperor of Dreams: The Lost Worlds of Clark Ashton Smith, Sea-Kings of Mars and Otherworldly Stories* by Leigh Brackett, *The Mark of the Beast and Other Fantastical Tales* by Rudyard Kipling, *Clive Barker's A-Z of Horror, Clive Barker's Shadows in Eden, Clive Barker's The Nightbreed Chronicles* and the *Hellraiser Chronicles*. He was a Guest of Honour at the 2002 World Fantasy Convention in Minneapolis, Minnesota, and the 2004 World Horror Convention in Phoenix, Arizona. You can visit his web site at *www.stephenjoneseditor.com*

CONTENTS

CONTENTS

Constable & Robinson Ltd
3 The Lanchesters
162 Fulham Palace Road
London W6 9ER
www.constablerobinson.com

First published in the UK by Robinson,
an imprint of Constable & Robinson, 2008

A copy of the British Library Cataloguing in Publication
Data is available from the British Library

UK ISBN 978-1-84529-833-3

1 3 5 7 9 10 8 6 4 2

First published in the United States in 2008 by Running Press Book Publishers

US Library of Congress number: 2008931718
US ISBN 978-0-7624-3397-1

Running Press Book Publishers
2300 Chestnut Street
Philadelphia, PA 19103-4371

Visit us on the web! www.runningpress.com

Printed and bound in the EU

THE
MAMMOTH BOOK OF
BEST NEW
HORROR

VOLUME NINETEEN

Edited and with an Introduction by
STEPHEN JONES

ROBINSON

RUNNING PRESS
PHILADELPHIA · LONDON

ACKNOWLEDGMENTS

I would like to thank David Barraclough, Kim Newman, Hugh Lamb, Rodger Turner and Wayne MacLaurin (*www.sfsite.com*), Peter Crowther, Gordon Van Gelder, Mandy Slater, Andy Cox, Ray Russell, Brian Mooney, Andrew I. Porter, Amanda Foubister, Sara and Randy Broecker and, especially, Pete Duncan and Dorothy Lumley for all their help and support. Special thanks are also due to *Locus*, *Variety*, *Ansible* and all the other sources that were used for reference in the Introduction and the Necrology.

13 O'CLOCK copyright © Mike O'Driscoll 2007. Originally published in *Inferno*. Reprinted by permission of the author.

STILL WATER copyright © Joel Lane 2007. Originally published in *Supernatural Tales 11*, Spring 2007. Reprinted by permission of the author.

THUMBPRINT copyright © Joe Hill 2007. Originally published in *PostScripts* Number 10, Spring 2007. Reprinted by permission of the author and the author's agent, The Choate Agency, LLC.

LANCASHIRE copyright © Nicholas Royle 2007. Originally published in *Phobic: Modern Horror Stories*. Reprinted by permission of the author.

THE ADMIRAL'S HOUSE copyright © Marc Lecard 2007. Originally published in *At Ease with the Dead*. Reprinted by permission of the author.

MAN, YOU GOTTA SEE THIS! copyright © Tony Richards 2007. Originally published in *Going Back*. Reprinted by permission of the author.

THE FISHERMAN copyright © David A. Sutton 2007. Originally published in *The Fisherman*. Reprinted by permission of the author.

THE CHILDREN OF MONTE ROSA copyright © Reggie Oliver 2007. Originally published in *Dark Horizons* #51, Autumn–Winter 2007 and *Masques of Satan*. Reprinted by permission of the author.

THE WITCH'S HEADSTONE copyright © Neil Gaiman 2007. Originally published in *Wizards: Magical Tales from the Masters of Modern Fantasy*. Reprinted by permission of the author.

CALICO BLACK, CALICO BLUE copyright © Joel Knight 2007. Originally published in *Strange Tales Volume II*. Reprinted by permission of the author.

THIS RICH EVIL SOUND copyright © Steven Erikson 2007. Originally published in *PostScripts* Number 10, Spring 2007. Reprinted by permission of the author.

MISS ILL-KEPT RUNT copyright © Glen Hirshberg 2007. Originally published in *The Twilight Limited: The Rolling Darkness Revue 2007*. Reprinted by permission of the author.

DEADMAN'S ROAD copyright © Joe R. Lansdale 2007. Originally published in *Weird Tales* Issue 343, February-March 2007 and on *Subterranean.com*, Spring 2007. Reprinted by permission of the author.

A GENTLEMAN FROM MEXICO copyright © Mark Samuels 2007. Originally published in *Summer Chills: Strangers in Strange Lands*. Reprinted by permission of the author.

In memory of the
Popular Book Centre
Rochester Row, London SW1
where I discovered horror fiction
more than forty years ago.

INTRODUCTION

Horror in 2007

FOLLOWING German media conglomerate Bertelsmann's $150 million purchase of the remaining fifty per cent share in Time Warner's Bookspan, which included the Book-of-the-Month Club, the Science Fiction Book Club, and around forty other book clubs, SFBC editor-in-chief Ellen Asher was persuaded to take early retirement and senior editor Andrew Wheeler was let go. They were replaced by Rome Quezada.

Bertelsmann also announced that it would lay off 280 employees – around fifteen per cent of Bookspan's entire staff – and integrate the company with its direct marketing group, BMG Columbia House.

In February a US court decided that Perseus Book Group would take over most of the clients affected by the Publishers Group West (PGW) bankruptcy at the end of 2006. Despite a counter offer by the rival National Book Network, the judge made his decision in Perseus' favour, with the result that the company would represent more than 300 independent publishers.

Perseus announced that it was eliminating the Carroll & Graf and Thunder's Mouth imprints following its acquisition of Avalon Publishing Group. Twenty-four people were let go, while others were offered different positions within the company. Both imprints published their fall 2007 lists (including the previous volume of this series from C&G).

Meanwhile, in a separate judgment, book distributor Baker & Taylor was allowed to purchase American Marketing Services, which had owned PGW until the sale to Perseus.

After its purchase by French company Hachette Livre from the Time Warner Book Group, the Warner Books imprint announced that it would be changing its name to Grand Central Publishing. In a related decision, Hodder Headline changed its name to Hachette Livre UK in August.

Hachette's UK imprint Little, Brown Book Group purchased independent imprint Piatkus books from owner Judy Piatkus, who retired at the end of the year.

Small press imprint Meisha Merlin Publishing, Inc. announced in April that it was going out of business after eleven years. Co-founder Stephen Pagel blamed "major distribution problems".

In July, Ballantine paid literary novelist Justin Cronin a reported $3.7 million for a new trilogy about a viral pandemic carried by a rare species of bat that turns humans into vampires. The first book, *The Passage*, is due for publication in the summer of 2009.

According to a survey published in March, forty-two per cent of British readers found books too boring to finish. Despite the average person spending more than £4,000 on books during a lifetime, over half remain unread. Among the top fiction books left on the shelf, *Harry Potter and the Goblet of Fire* came second, just ahead of James Joyce's *Ulysses*.

Harry Potter and the Deathly Hallows, the seventh and final book in the series by J. K. Rowling, was released to worldwide hysteria at midnight on 21 July. The eagerly anticipated novel, which featured the final showdown between the seventeen-year-old boy wizard and his evil nemesis Voldemort, included the deaths of no less than seven significant characters and an epilogue set in 2020.

Child helplines brought in extra volunteer counsellors to cope with an expected surge of phone calls from young fans suffering from feelings of loss and bereavement after reading the book. Unfortunately, spoiler reviews in the *New York Times* and other newspapers gave away crucial plot points before the novel was published, and various Internet sites posted what they claimed to be pages scanned from the book.

In London, Potter fans from all over Europe (many in costume) queued for up to three days outside Waterstone's in Piccadilly to be at the front of the line. *Deathly Hallows* became the fastest-selling book ever, with sales of 8.3 million copies in the US and almost 2.7 million copies in the UK during the first twenty-four hours. It was published simultaneously in more than ninety countries.

Among concerns that copies of the book being sold at half-price or less would harm smaller independent bookshops, British supermarket chain Asda almost lost 500,000 copies when publisher Bloomsbury cancelled its entire order in a dispute over unpaid bills. The retailer settled its invoice at the eleventh hour and sold ninety-seven per cent of its stock at just £5.00 a copy, down from the recommended retail price of £17.99.

Author J. K. Rowling hosted a public "Moonlight Reading" and signing session at one minute past midnight at London's Natural History Museum for 1,700 fans chosen in an online draw. She signed 250 copies an hour, and the event was broadcast across the World Wide Web to millions.

Anybody who might be concerned about the number of forests destroyed to produce the latest *Harry Potter* volume would have been pleased to learn that Bloomsbury's UK edition was printed on part-recycled paper and paper from sustainable sources.

However, it was revealed later in the year that the publisher spent so much on marketing and distribution costs for the seventh and final *Potter* book that, despite a thirty-six per cent rise in first-half revenues, pre-tax profits were only up seven per cent.

Rowling and Warner Bros. sued a Michigan publisher over its plans to publish a book edition of the "Harry Potter Lexicon", a fan website hosted by a middle-school librarian. Although Rowling gave it a fan site award in 2004, she claimed that plans to publish its content would interfere with her own intention to produce "a definitive Potter reference book".

Meanwhile, in June, a rare first edition of *Harry Potter and the Philosopher's Stone*, the first book in the series, sold at auction at Bonhams in London for £9,000, almost double the original estimate. However, just four months later, another copy sold at Christie's for £19,700. Only around 500 copies were initially printed in 1997. A copy of the publisher's proof was also sold at the Christie's auction for £2,250.

Rowling's *Potter*-related collection of fairy stories, *The Tales of Beedle the Bard*, was only published in a leather-bound edition of seven copies, six of which were given to friends. The remaining copy was auctioned on 13 December at Sotheby's with a starting price of £30,000. The hand-written and illustrated volume was purchased by Amazon.com for a record-breaking £1.95 million, and proceeds were donated to the Children's Voice, the author's charity for vulnerable children in Europe.

After having controversially revealed to an audience of schoolchildren that Dumbledore was a closet gay character, in another interview Rowling explained that she couldn't kill off Arthur Weasley because "he is the father everyone would wish for", including herself.

*   *   *

Discovered in 2006 among his papers in the University of Maine Library and published under his deceased "Richard Bachman" alias, *Blaze* was a revised 1973 trunk novel by Stephen King about a baby kidnapper guided by the voice of his dead partner. It also included a reprint short story, "Memory", and a Foreword by King.

The author donated all royalties and subsidiary income from the book to The Haven Foundation, an organization that helps freelance artists who are down on their luck.

In June, Stephen King became the first non-Canadian to be presented with a Lifetime Achievement Award by the Canadian Booksellers Association. Meanwhile, the author's novella, "The Gingerbread Girl", appeared in the July issue of *Esquire* magazine.

On 12 December, Terry Pratchett revealed to the media that he was suffering from a rare form of early onset Alzheimer's. The fifty-nine-year-old writer discovered he had the incurable degenerative brain disease after suffering a phantom "mini-stroke" earlier in the year. "I think there's time for at least a few more books yet," quipped Pratchett in an upbeat statement, adding: "I am not dead. I will, of course, be dead at some future point, as will everybody else."

Clive Barker's latest novel, *Mister B. Gone*, was told in the form of an autobiographical memoir written by a demon.

Ray Bradbury's *Now and Forever: Somewhere a Band is Playing & Leviathan '99* contained an original short novella begun as a film treatment for Katherine Hepburn in the 1950s, about a young writer who stepped off a train into the *too* perfect Arizona village of Summerton, along with a prose version of a 1966 BBC radio play.

Bradbury was briefly interviewed in the November issue of United Airlines' in-flight magazine *Hemispheres*, where he admitted to "appreciating" *Harry Potter*, and the author received a special citation from the 2007 Pulitzer Prize committee for his "distinguished, prolific and deeply influential career as an unmatched author of science fiction and fantasy".

On 23 June, Dean Koontz became the first author to sign at London's Waterstone's Piccadilly branch from his home in California using LongPen technology. "I used to fight the label 'horror writer'", Koontz told a newspaper, "because I never considered myself one. I didn't write about vampires."

"I used stuff from every genre," continued the author, before going on to explain that his publisher had complained that his vocabulary was too large.

Koontz's avatar appeared in the online virtual world Second Life in March to promote his novel, *The Good Guy*, about a man mistaken for a hired killer. The author read from the book and mixed with (virtual) fans in the Bantam Dell Book Café.

The author's second novel of 2007, *The Darkest Evening of the Year*, was a thriller with supernatural elements, about a woman who aided dogs that have been abused.

Something monstrous was killing the crews of two ships frozen into the Arctic ice in Dan Simmons' chilling historical novel *The Terror*, based around the doomed Franklin expedition of 1845.

Set in eighteenth-century New York, Robert McCammon's historical serial killer novel, *The Queen of Bedlam*, was a sequel to *Speaks the Nightbird* and once again featured hero Matthew Corbett.

Frank Balenger had to hunt for a puzzling 100-year-old time capsule in David Morrell's *Scavanger*, a follow-up to the author's Bram Stoker Award-winning novel *Creepers*, and a fourteen-year-old girl raped by her stepfather was being stalked by him from beyond the grave in John Farris' *You Don't Scare Me*. Unusually, the final chapter was written in screenplay format.

The unsolved murder of a Seattle mother and son and the disappearances of a former cop's wife and a ten-year-old girl were revealed to be related in *The Intruders*, the latest urban thriller from Michael Marshall (Smith).

Meanwhile, a rookie female detective was lured into a cat-and-mouse game with a psychopathic killer driven by delusions of superhuman supremacy in Paul McAuley's *Players*. The author's second novel of the year, *Cowboy Angels*, involved an idealistic serial killer using covert American technology to go on a murder spree through various alternate realities.

Christopher Golden's *The Borderkind* was the second volume in the "Veil" series, and *Homeplace* was a haunted house novel by Beth (Elizabeth) Massie.

"Deliverance Consultant for the Diocese of Hereford" Merrily Watkins investigated the mysteries behind the renovation of a medieval mansion on the Welsh Border, and discovered murder and hidden secrets in Phil Rickman's *The Fabric of Sin*, which included references to M. R. James and the Knights Templar.

Unbroken was written by Rick Hautala under the pseudonym "A. J. Matthews", while supernatural police procedural *Nowhere* was the work of Matt Costello writing as "Shane Christopher".

A former Catholic psychologist ended up summoning Satan in Jeff Rovin's *Conversations with the Devil*, while a woman believed she was carrying the Devil's child in Andrew Neiderman's *Unholy Birth*.

A priest attempted to exorcise troubled teenagers at a boarding school in John Saul's *The Devil's Labyrinth*.

Sarah Langan followed her acclaimed debut novel, *The Keeper*, with the sequel, *The Missing* (aka *Virus*), about a contagious plague in a remote and affluent Maine community that turned its victims into inhuman creatures.

Echoing a nineteenth-century outbreak, men started murdering their families in Bentley Little's *The Vanishing*, while a curse returned every seven years in *Blood Brothers* by Nora Roberts.

John Aubrey Anderson's interracial horror novel *Abiding Darkness* was set in 1945 Mississippi and was the first volume in the "Black and White Chronicles". *Dead Man's Song* was the sequel to Jonathan Maberry's Bram Stoker Award-winning debut *Ghost Road Blues*, once again set in the haunted town of Pine Deep, and *Not Flesh Nor Feathers* was a Southern Gothic by Cherie Priest in which the city of Chattanooga was invaded by the walking dead.

Matthew Smith's *Tomes of the Dead: The Words and Their Roaring* was the second historical zombie novel in the shared-world series from Abaddon Books.

Set in 1808, Chris Roberson's *Set the Seas on Fire* was about a shipwrecked crew stranded on an island with an ancient, Lovecraftian evil. A group of disparate characters in the Appalachian Mountains were attacked by leathery-winged vampire creatures in *They Hunger* by Scott Nicholson, Bigfoot was out for revenge in Matthew Scott Hanson's *The Shadowkiller*, and people were transformed into flesh-eating monsters by alien spores in R. Patrick Gates' *'Vaders*.

A sheriff's lieutenant investigated the kidnap of a girl and the murder of her family in Jeffrey J. Mariotte's supernatural thriller *Missing White Girl*. The survivor of a car crash was pursued by an unknown killer in Tom Piccirilli's *The Midnight Road*, and a psychopathic killer menaced trapped hospital workers in Joe Schreiber's *Eat the Dark*.

African voodoo came to an English town in *Unmarked Graves*, the latest gore-fest from Shaun Hutson.

A woman discovered that her son may have inherited her psychic abilities in *Eye of the Beholder* by Shari Shattuck, and a five-year-old boy was helped by demons to get revenge in Mary Ann Mitchell's *The Witch*.

A Pulitzer Prize-winning author discovered that fallen angels were creating trouble in Jack Cavanaugh's Christian supernatural thriller *A Hideous Beauty*, the first volume in the "Kingdom Wars" series.

The inhabitants of a small rural town started dying mysteriously with the arrival of a strange little man in *Something Bad* by Richard Satterlie, and nineteenth-century murderers were accidentally revived by a history student in *Gossamer Hall* by Erin Samiloglu.

Howard Mittelmark's *Age of Consent* was about a house with a dark history, while a spiritualist was hired banish evil spirits in *Angelica* by Arthur Phillips.

An archaeologist and a ghost investigated a Manhattan burial ground in *The Dead Room*, and a dead detective was summoned by a Ouija board to investigate an unsolved fifteen-year-old serial killing case in *The Séance*, both by Heather Graham.

PI Harper Blaine, who has the ability to see the paranormal, became involved in a university research group's attempts to create an artificial "ghost" in Kat Richardson's *Poltergeist*, the sequel to *Greywalker*.

Sarah Pinborough's *The Taken* involved the vengeance-seeking ghost of a little girl. The author was joined under the Leisure Books banner by a number of fellow British writers:

In Tim Lebbon's *The Everlasting*, a man received a letter thirty years after his grandfather killed himself, which lead to a mysterious set of books that would allow him to resurrect a vengeful ghost.

Something nasty lived in the water of a flooded England in Mark Morris' *The Deluge*, a big cat was loose on the Norfolk moors in Stephen Laws' *Ferocity*, a woman was invited to a terrifying party in *Demon Eyes* by L. H. and M. P. N. Sims, and a man was under attack by his doppelgängers in *This Rage of Echoes* by Simon Clark.

Not to be outdone, Leisure's roster of American authors included Al Sarrantonio, whose *Halloweenland* grew from his novella "The Baby", which was also included in the book, along with notes by the author.

House Infernal was the third volume in Edward Lee's "City Infernal Saga", and a teenager inherited a farmhouse with a mysterious history in *Dead Souls* by Michael Laimo.

High school girls summoned dark forces in Deborah LeBlanc's *Morbid Curiosity*, a vampire scientist created an addictive drug in Jemiah Jefferson's *A Drop of Scarlet*, and Bryan Smith's *The Freakshow* was about a travelling carnival.

Set in the mid-1980s, Timmy Graco and his pals discovered a flesh-eating creature living in their local graveyard in *Ghoul* by Brian Keene. Meanwhile a group escaping from zombies took to the ocean in *Dead Sea*, from the same author.

Gary A. Braunbeck's *Mr Hands* was expanded from the novella of the same name and also contained the award-winning story "Kiss of the Mudman". A creature fed on its victims' fear in Mary SanGiovanni's debut novel *The Hollower*, while another small town was beset by evil forces in Thomas Tessier's *Wicked Things*.

Also from Leisure, *The Beast House* was a 1986 reprint from the late Richard Laymon. Ray Garton's *Night Life* was a vampire novel from 2005, *Edgewise* was another reprint by Graham Masterton, and the publisher also reissued the "definitive" edition of Jack Ketchum's *Offspring*.

A woman helped ghosts solve their problems in *Dead Girls Are Easy* by Terri Garey, a man whose fiancée committed suicide found he'd bought a haunted house in Jude Deveraux's paranormal romance *Someone to Love*, and *What's a Ghoul to Do?* was the first volume in Victoria Laurie's "Ghost Hunter" mystery series about supernatural sleuth M. J. Holliday.

A ghost asked Jade Nethercott to protect his lover from his murderer in Jocelyn Kelley's paranormal romance *Lost in Shadow*, and a young woman learned dark magic to avenge her boyfriend's death in Natasha Rhodes' *Dante's Girl*, the first in the "Kayla Steele" series.

Joanna Archer pretended to be her dead sister to uncover a supernatural conspiracy in Las Vegas in *The Scent of Shadows*, the first volume in Vicki Pettersson's "Sign of the Zodiac" series. It was followed by *The Taste of Night*, in which Joanna attempted to prevent her own father destroying Las Vegas by plague.

A woman tried to escape the supernatural by moving to a small Texas town in Catherine Spangler's *Touched by Darkness*, the first in the "Sentinel" series. It was followed by *Touched by Fire*.

The Dream-Hunter and *Upon the Midnight Clear* by Sherrilyn Kenyon (aka "Kinley MacGregor") were the first two volumes in a spin-off paranormal romance series set in the "Dark-Hunters" world. The author's initial series continued with *Devil May Care*, which was also released as an unabridged nine CD audio book read by Holter Graham.

Karen Marie Moning's *Bloodfever* was the second book in the "Fever" paranormal suspense series featuring MacKayla Lane, who was searching for an ancient book of black magic while trying to escape from an inhumane enemy seeking revenge.

Tombs of Endearment by Casey Daniels (Connie Lux) was the third volume in the "Pepper Martin" mystery series, about a cemetery tour guide who can talk with ghosts, while *Demons Are*

Forever by Julie Kenner was the third book in the "Confessions of a Demon-Hunting Soccer Mom" series.

Christine Feehan's *Deadly Game* was the fifth volume in the "GhostWalkers" paranormal romance series about genetically-modified soldiers. *Safe Harbor* was the latest volume in the same author's "Drake Sisters" series, while *Dark Celebration* and *Dark Possession* were the latest titles in the busy Feehan's "Carpathian" series.

Servant: The Awakening by L. L. Foster (Lori Foster) was the first in a series about demon-slayer Gabrielle Cody, Jackie Kessler's *The Road to Hell* was the second book in a trilogy about a succubus transformed into a human, and *The Nightwalkers: Elijah* was the third in the series by Jacquelyn Frank.

A new recruit joined the Otherworld Crime Unit in Vivi Anna's *Blood Secrets*, while Eileen Wilks' *Blood Lines* and *Night Season* were the third and fourth entries in the series about special FBI agent Lily Yu.

A woman inadvertently conjured up a demon in *Night Mischief*, a paranormal romance by Nina Bruhns in the "Dark Enchantments" series, while Lisa Cach's *A Babe in Ghostland* involved a woman with psychic powers renovating a haunted house and fending off the advances of an over-amorous ghost.

Yolanda Celbridge's *Sindi in Silk* was an erotic post-Apocalyptic vampire version of *Cinderella*, and *The Master of Seacliff* was a gay Gothic pastiche by Max Pierce.

Borne in the Blood by Chelsea Quinn Yarbro was the twentieth novel in the long-running series about the undead Count Saint-Germain. The book was set in 1817 Switzerland, and involved the scientific experiments of the Graf von Ravensberg, who used blood to determine a man's nature.

Laurell K. Hamilton's *The Harlequin*, the fifteenth title in her "Anita Blake, Vampire Hunter" series, debuted at number two on the *Publishers Weekly* fiction bestseller list in June with 250,000 copies in print.

In *All Together Dead*, the seventh "Sookie Stackhouse" novel from Charlaine Harris, the telepathic waitress attended a vampire convention and once again became involved in a murder mystery. From the same author, *Ice Cold Grave* was the third book in the "Harper Connelly" paranormal mystery series, in which the "dead-dowser" found herself on the trail of a small town serial killer.

Professional wizard Harry Dresden had to clear his vampire half-brother Thomas of a series of murders in the ninth volume in Jim

Butcher's "The Dresden Files", *White Night*. This book plus the previous title, *Proven Guilty*, were collected in the Science Fiction Book Club omnibus *Wizard Under Fire*.

Cristopher Moore's humorous novel *You Suck: A Love Story* was a sequel to the author's popular *Bloodsucking Fiends: A Love Story* and once again featured fledgling vampires Tommy and Jody and the evil ancient vampire encased in bronze in their apartment.

Valerie Stivers' *Blood is the New Black* was another humorous vampire novel, set in a fashion magazine publishing company run by bloodsuckers. In M. Christian's comic horror novel *The Very Bloody Marys*, undead gay cop Valentino found himself tracking the eponymous gang of Vespa-riding vampires through San Francisco.

Following *Monster Planet*, the third volume in his zombie trilogy, David Wellington tackled vampires with his thriller *13 Bullets*, the first in a new three-book series set in a world where the undead had been hunted to near-extinction. It was followed by *99 Coffins*.

Movie stuntwoman Dawn Madison investigated the mysterious disappearance of her estranged PI father and discovered an underground society of supernatural creatures in *Vampire Babylon: Night Rising*, the first in Chris Marie Green's Hollywood vampire trilogy.

Lara Adrian's *Kiss of Midnight*, *Kiss of Crimson* and *Midnight Awakening* were the first three books in the "Breed" series, in which psychic Elise Chase hunted vampires.

A demon-hunting knight confronted a demonic Lilith in contemporary San Francisco in *Demon Angel* by "Melijean Brook" (Melissa Khan), the first in a new paranormal romance series.

Demon's Kiss was a Harlequin vampire romance by "Maggie Shayne" (Margaret Benson). The same author's *Immortal Desire* contained the 2001 novel *Destiny* and a new novella.

An investigative TV reporter discovered more than expected about an Eastern European criminal in *Fangland*, John Mark's reworking of *Dracula*, while an Egyptian pharaoh was revived as a vampire in Las Vegas in *Night Life* by "Elizabeth Guest" (Suzanne Simmons Gunfrum).

In *Taken by the Night* by Kathryn Smith, a vampire was on the trail of a murderer. *The Rest Falls Away* by Colleen Gleason was the first in the "Gardella Vampire Chronicles", about a female vampire-slayer, and CIA assassin Jaz Parks had a vampire boss in *Once Bitten, Twice Shy* and *Another One Bites the Dust*, both by Jennifer Rardin.

Vampire bounty hunter Anna Strong featured in Jeanne C. Stein's *Blood Drive*, a sequel to *The Becoming*. It was followed by *The*

Watcher, in which Anna joined the eponymous group of super-natural enforcers.

Vampire-killer Cat teamed up with a vampire bounty hunter named Bones in *Halfway to the Grave*, a paranormal romance in the "Night Huntress" series by Jeaniene Frost, and Shiloh Walker's *Hunters: Heart and Soul*, a sequel to *Hunting the Hunter*, featured two linked novellas about a bounty hunter and vampires

A journalist encountered two very different vampires in Catherine Mulvany's *Something Wicked*, and a female psychologist became involved in the vampire underworld in Lynda Hilburn's *The Vampire Shrink*. An undead female FBI agent was on the trail of a vampire slayer in *Eternal* by "V. K. Forrest" (Colleen Faulkner).

A paranormal researcher teamed up with a sexy vampire professor in *Real Vamps Don't Drink O-Neg* by Tawny Taylor, while a paranormal investigation business was under threat in Minda Webber's humorous vampire romance *Bustin'*.

A thousand-year-old vampire found her powers waning in *The Vampire Queen's Servant* by Joey W. Hill, the first in the "Vampire Queen" series.

A woman in nineteenth-century London was infected by a vampire's blood in Susan Squires' *One with the Night*, the first volume in a new series. It was followed by *One with the Shadows*.

The undead Jon Hyde-Whyte tried to cure his vampirism in Dawn Thompson's Regency romances *Blood Moon* and *The Brotherhood*, while Julia Templeton's historical vampire romance *Return to Me* was set in the Scottish Highlands.

A vampire opened a boutique in Texas in Gerry Bartlett's *Real Vampires Have Curves* and its sequel, *Real Vampires Live Large*, and Delilah Devlin's erotic vamprom *Into the Darkness* was set in New Orleans.

Patrice Michelle's *Scions: Resurrection* was the first in a new vampire romance trilogy. *The Last of the Red-Hot Vampires* was another paranormal romance by "Katie MacAlister" (Marthe Arends, aka "Katie Maxwell").

Anne Frasier's *Garden of Darkness* was a sequel to *Pale Immortal* and once again featured haunted medical examiner Rachel Burton, who became involved in the public display of a mummified vampire and the discovery of a mass grave in Wisconsin.

Claimed by Shadow was the second volume in Karen Chance's vampire romance series featuring Cassie Palmer, while *X-Rated Bloodsuckers* was the second in Mario Acevedo's humorous series about vampire detective Felix Gomez.

Fanged & Fabulous, Michelle Rowen's sequel to *Bitten & Smitten*, was about new vampire Sarah Dearly, while Richelle Mead's *Succubus on Top* was the sequel to *Succubus Blues* and once again featured Seattle succubus Georgina Kincaid.

Coyote shape-shifting mechanic Mercedes "Mercy" Thompson had to stop a vampire possessed by a demon in *Blood Bound*, the second in Patricia Briggs' series after *Moon Called*.

Dead Sexy, the sequel to *Tall, Dark & Dead* by "Tate Hallaway" (Lyda Morehouse), once again involved witch Garnet Lacey, her vampire boyfriends, the goddess Lilith, zombies and the FBI.

Be Still My Vampire Heart by Kerrelyn Sparks was a sequel to *How to Marry a Millionaire Vampire*, while a witch and a vampire found themselves under a love spell in Michele Hauf's *Kiss Me Deadly*.

Michele Bardsley's *Don't Talk Back to Your Vampire* was the sequel to *I'm the Vampire, That's Why*, again featuring undead single mother and librarian Eva LeRoy.

Midnight Brunch was the sequel to Marta Acosta's humorous vampire romance *Happy Hour at Casa Dracula*, Alexandra Ivy's *Embrace the Darkness* was the second book in the "Guardians of Eternity" series, and Colleen Gleason's *Rises the Night* was second in the "Gardella Vampire Chronicles".

The Queen of Wolves was the third volume in Douglas Clegg's fantasy/vampire series *The Vampyricon*, and *Half the Blood of Brooklyn* was the third in Charlie Huston's series about undead New York private investigator Joe Pitt.

Raven Hart's *The Vampire's Secret* and *The Vampire's Kiss* were the latest volumes in the "Savannah Vampire Chronicles" series that began with *The Vampire's Seduction*.

Jennifer Armintrout's *Blood Ties Book Three: Ashes to Ashes* involved an attempt to turn the world into a vampire paradise.

Beneath the Skin and *In the Blood* by "Savannah Russe" (Charlee Trantino) were the third and fourth books in the "Darkwing Chronicles", while *Tempted in the Night* and *Lord of the Night* were the third and fourth volumes in the "Night Slayer" romance series by Robin T. Popp.

Bled Dry and *Sucker Bet* were the third and fourth volumes in the "Vegas Vampires" series by Erin McCarthy (aka "Erin Lynn"). From the same writer, *My Immortal* and *Demon Envy* were other paranormal romances published under various pseudonyms.

The half-undead Christopher Csejthe encountered drowned zombie vampires in New Orleans in Mark Wm. Simmons' humorous *Dead Easy*, the fourth in the "Half Life" series.

In the sixth "Betsy the Vampire Queen" novel, *Undead and Uneasy*, author MaryJanice Davidson threw everything into the long-awaited wedding, including the Wyndham Werewolves.

Secrets in the Shadows and *Shadows on the Soul* were the latest titles in Jenna Black's "Guardians of the Night" series. Meanwhile, *The Devil Inside* by the same author was the first volume in "Morgan Kinsley, Exorcist" series.

The Wicked and *The Cursed* were the most recent volumes in the "Vampire Huntress Legends" series by L. A. Banks (Leslie Esdaile Banks).

Lover Revealed and *Lover Unbound* were new books in the "Black Dagger Brotherhood" series by "J. R. Ward" (Jessica Bird), while Lynsay Sands continued her "Argeneau Vampires" series with *Bite Me If You Can* and *The Accidental Vampire*.

A werewolf and a vampire fell in love with each other in Morgan Hawke's *Kiss of the Wolf*, while a werewolf was pursued through New York by a hunter and a vampire in Melina Morel's *Devour*.

Touch of Madness was the sequel to C. T. Adams and Cathy Clamp's *Touch of Evil*, in which Kate Reilly and her werewolf boyfriend investigated the killing of young vampires. It was followed by *Moon's Fury*.

In Patricia Briggs' *Blood Bound*, the follow-up to *Moon Called*, Coyote shape-shifting mechanic Mercy Thompson helped her un-dead friend Stefan deliver a message to an evil vampire/sorcerer.

A pack of man-hungry female werewolves were searching for mates in Kimberly Raye's *Dead and Dateless*, the second in the "Dead End Dating" vampire romance series. It was followed by *Your Coffin or Mine?*, in which a vampire match-maker became involved with a reality TV show.

Keri Arthur's *Kissing Sin*, *Tempting Evil*, *Dangerous Games* and *Embraced by Darkness* were the latest volumes in the "Riley Jenson, Guardian" series, about a half-vampire, half-werewolf hybrid em-ployed by the US government.

Kathy Love's *My Sister is a Werewolf* was a sequel to *Fangs for the Memories*, while *Chasing Midnight* by Susan Krinard was about a female vampire meeting a werewolf in 1920s Greenwich Village.

Carole Nelson Douglas' *Dancing with Werewolves* was the first in a new mystery series featuring paranormal investigator Delilah Street and set in a Las Vegas controlled by werewolves.

Having been outed as a shape-changer on national television, werewolf Kitty retreated to a mountain cabin in Carrie Vaughn's

Kitty Takes a Holiday, the third in the series. Unfortunately, trouble followed in the shape of a werewolf hunter and a monstrous creature with blazing red eyes. This novel and the previous two books were collected by the Science Fiction Book Club in the omnibus volume, *Long-Time Listener First-Time Werewolf*. Kitty subsequently returned to Denver in *Kitty and the Silver Bullet*.

The Silver Collar by Mathilde Madden was the first volume in the erotic "Silver Werewolves" series, published by Black Lace.

A lycanthropic landscape architect was saved by a female werewolf from another dimension in *New Moon* by Rebecca York (Ruth Glick). The same author was responsible for the paranormal romance *Beyond Fearless*, which featured nightclub psychic Anna Ridgeway in search of a Caribbean treasure.

A series of murders threatened to expose lycanthropic supermodel Lou Kinipski in Ronda Thompson's romance/mystery *Confessions of a Werewolf Supermodel*, while Christina Dodd's *Scent of Darkness* and *Touch of Darkness* were the first two books in the "Darkness Chosen" series about a family of cursed shape-shifters.

Kresley Cole's *Wicked Deeds on a Winter's Night* was the third book in the "Immortals After Dark" romance series and involved a werewolf protecting the witch he had sworn vengeance upon.

Awaiting the Fire was the third volume in Donna Lea Simpson's werewolf romance series that began with *Awaiting the Moon*.

For a Few Demons More by "Kim Harrison" (Dawn Cook) was the fifth volume about PI witch Rachel Morgan, who found herself being pursued by werewolves and demons trying to get hold of a magical artefact. The paperback edition added a bonus story set in the same series.

A female doctor accidentally raised the spirit of a warrior shape-shifter in *The Lure of the Wolf* by "Jennifer St Giles" (Jenni Leigh Grizzle), the latest title in the "Shadowmen" series. From the same author, *Silken Shadows* was a paranormal romance in which psychic Gemini Andrews investigated a murder on a ship.

Lucy Monroe's *Moon Awakening* was the latest volume in the "Children of the Moon" werewolf historical romance series. *Touch of the Wolf* was another werewolf romance novel by Karen Whiddon about "The Pack", while Lori Handeland's *Hidden Moon* and *Thunder Moon* were new titles in the "Nightcreatures" series.

Although undoubtedly popular among a certain readership (which does not necessarily crossover into the rest of horror literature), it surely cannot be too long before the whole vampire/werewolf/paranormal/humorous/romance bandwagon implodes under its own weight and goes the way of horror's "boom and bust" period of the 1980s.

Without doubt, one of the most impressive debut novels of the year was Joe Hill's remarkable *Heart-Shaped Box*, which concerned a malignant ghost bought over the Internet by an ageing heavy metal rock star with a ghoulish hobby. Beautifully published on both sides of the Atlantic by Morrow and Gollancz, the latter imprint's first edition hardcover was a work of art in itself.

Hill himself was profiled on both sides of the ocean in the March issues of *The New York Times Magazine* and *The Times Books* supplement.

God's Demon from artist and film concept-designer Wayne Barlowe was billed as a modern sequel to John Milton's *Paradise Lost*. It involved one Fallen Angel's attempt to change his fate by rebelling against the forces of Hell to win his redemption.

A woman working on an uncompleted biography of Isaac Newton discovered a connection between a series of seventeenth-century murders and a number of contemporary killings in Rebecca Stott's mystery *Ghostwalk*.

A recently purchased bed-and-breakfast appeared to have ghosts in Richard Taylor's *The Haunting of Cambria*.

The ghost of a teenage murder victim was prevented from moving on by a lonely fifteen-year-old boy in Christopher Barzak's coming-of-age debut *One for Sorrow*, which the cover copy compared to *The Catcher in the Rye*.

Steve Berman's first novel, *Vintage: A Ghost Story*, involved a couple of disparate teenagers and the malevolent spirit of a boy who died in the 1950s.

A woman had visions of murders in *The Dark Gate* by "Pamela Palmer" (Pamela Poulson), while Virginia Baker's debut *Jack Knife* was a time-travel novel featuring Jack the Ripper.

Adrian Phoenix's debut *A Rush of Wings* was a serial killer/vampire novel set in New Orleans.

A first novel about a former boyfriend who would not stay dead, *Uninvited* was a young adult vampire romance by Amanda Marrone. Heather Brewer's *The Chronicles of Vladimir Tod: Eighth Grade Bites* was a first novel for young adults about a boy who was half-vampire.

Lucy Swan's short debut novel from Savoy Books, *The Adventures of Little Lou*, was set in David Britton's "Lord Horror" mythos.

*   *   *

There was more than a touch of *Something Wicked This Way Comes* to Will Elliott's humorous and macabre *The Pilo Family Circus*, about a boy forced to join a centuries-old carnival that hid a terrible secret.

Translated from the Swedish by Ebba Segerberg, *Let the Right One In* (aka *Låt den rätte komma in/Let Me In*) by John Ajvide Lindquist was about a troubled young boy who discovered that the mysterious girl who lived next door was actually a 200-year-old vampire.

Set in 1718, Clare Clark's Gothic mystery *The Nature of Monsters* involved a pregnant maid working for an opium-crazed apothecary with a bizarre theory about the development of embryos.

A woman made a bargain for eternal life in Miranda Miller's *Loving Mephistopheles*, while a worker in a funeral home encountered something unexplainable in Alan Lightman's *Ghost*.

From publisher Alfred A. Knopf, *Red Spikes* was a collection of ten original stories by Australian writer Margo Lanagan, ostensibly aimed a younger readers.

Toby Barlow's *Sharp Teeth* was a novel-length poem about werewolves, written in blank verse.

Published by Penguin Classics, a new deluxe edition of Mary Shelley's *Frankenstein* featured an Introduction by Elizabeth Kostova, John Polidori's story "The Vampyre" and a fragment by Lord Byron.

Bram Stoker's *Dracula's Guest and Other Weird Stories*, also from Penguin, contained the 1911 novel *The Lair of the White Worm*, along with an Introduction and notes by editor Kate Hebblethwaite.

From the same publisher, *American Supernatural Tales* edited by S. T. Joshi was an anthology of twenty-six classic stories from Stephen King, H. P. Lovecraft, Joyce Carol Oates, Edgar Allan Poe and others, along with an Introduction and suggested reading list by the editor.

Gollancz's impressive "Fantasy Masterworks" series reached its fiftieth volume under series editor Jo Fletcher with *The Mark of the Beast and Other Fantastical Tales*. Containing fifty classic fantasy, horror and SF stories by Rudyard Kipling, the book also included an Introduction by Neil Gaiman and a historical Afterword by editor Stephen Jones.

Edited by Rusty Burke, *The Best of Robert E. Howard Volume 1: Crimson Shadows* and *Volume 2: Grim Lands* each collected sixteen stories and twelve poems covering the whole range of Howard's fiction, including tales of Conan, Solomon Kane, Kull and Bran Mak Morn. Artists Jim and Ruth Keegan supplied a Foreword to the first volume and the disappointing black and white illustrations.

Containing twenty-four collaborations and revisions between H. P. Lovecraft and other writers, *The Horror in the Museum* from Ballantine Books/Del Rey was an expanded and revised edition of the 1944 Arkham House volume, with a new Introduction by Stephen Jones, plus notes on the texts by S. T. Joshi and August Derleth from the 1970 printing.

Paizo Publishing's Planet Stories imprint brought back into print a number of important novels and collections by such authors as Michael Moorcock, C. L. Moore, Henry Kuttner, Leigh Brackett, Robert E. Howard, Otis Adelbert Kline and others. Each paperback volume featured a new Introduction by contemporary writers, including Moorcock, Joe R. Lansdale, Samuel R. Delany, Suzy McKee Charnas, Ben Bova, C. J. Cherryh and Roy Thomas.

In China Miéville's inventive young adult novel *Un Lun Dun*, a young girl found herself in a surreal parallel-London where inanimate objects and ideas had lives of their own. The book was nicely illustrated by the author himself.

Neil Gaiman teamed up with Michael Reaves for *Interworld*, a novel about a fourteen-year-old boy who walked into an alternate reality filled with magic and multiple versions of himself.

F. E. Higgins' debut novel *The Black Book of Secrets* was shortlisted for the Waterstone's Children's Book Award. It involved a young runaway in Dickensian times who worked for a mysterious pawnbroker.

Set in 1906 London, a young girl had the ability to see the magical dark powers surrounding her father's museum artefacts in R. L. LaFevers' *Theodosia Throckmorton and the Serpents of Chaos*.

A twelve-year-old girl inherited her horror writer uncle's estate and teamed up with the eponymous skeletal detective to solve a suspected murder in Derek Landy's *Skullduggery Pleasant*.

Blood Beast and *Demon Apocalypse* were the fifth and sixth books in "The Demonata" series by "Darren Shan" (Darren O'Shaughnessy).

A group of young people were involved with a writing contest held in a haunted mansion in Andrew Nance's *Daemon Hall*, illustrated by Coleman Polhemus.

Wishes went wrong for three children in Frances Hardinge's

Verdigris Deep (aka *Well Wicked*), while a small town was terrorized by bikers from Hell in Justine Musk's *Uninvited*.

A teenage boy discovered New York's ghostly Underworld of the dead in Katherine Marsh's *The Night Tourist*, loosely based on the myth of Orpheus and Eurydice.

Dead girls related their stories in *Wicked Dead #1: Lurker* and *#2: Torn*, the first two volumes in a ghostly new series by Stefan Petrucha and "Thomas Pendleton" (Lee Thomas).

A girl's soccer team named the Weregirls found they had some powerful enemies in the first book in another new series, *Weregirls: Birth of the Pack* by Petru Popescu.

Following on from *Wuthering High*, Cara Lockwood's *The Scarlet Letterman* was the second in the "Bard Academy" supernatural romance series about a school where all the teachers were ghosts of famous authors.

Evil forces menaced a high school dance in Rosemary Clement-Moore's *Prom Dates from Hell*, while the similarly titled anthology *Prom Nights from Hell* collected five paranormal stories by Kim Harrison, Stephanie Meyer, Meg Cabot, Michele Jaffe and Lauren Myracle.

Caroline B. Cooney's *Enter Three Witches* was inspired by Shakespeare's *Macbeth*. Mary Downing Hahn's *Deep Dark and Dangerous* was about ghosts, and a group of children accidentally freed spirits trapped in library books in *The Phantom Isles* by Stephen Alter.

A boy on a camping trip encountered a legendary Native American creature in Joseph Bruchac's *Bearwalker*, illustrated by Sally Wern Comport. Meanwhile, another boy allowed one of his demon charges to escape while distracted by a girl in Royce Buckingham's humorous novel *Demonkeeper*.

Eclipse, the third in thirty-three-year-old Mormon mother of three Stephanie Meyer's YA vampire/werewolf "Twilight" series from Little, Brown, which included *Twilight* and *New Moon* and already had a combined 1.6 million copies in print, reportedly sold 150,000 copies on its first day. After an announced first printing of one million copies, the publisher quickly went back to press three times. "I'm *waay* too chicken to read horror," admitted the author.

Cynthia Leitich Smith's *Tantalize* was about a vampire-themed restaurant, while Adele Griffin's *Vampire Island* was a humorous novella about three vampire children who turned into fruit bats.

A teenage vampire plotted revenge on undead jocks in Julie Kenner's *The Good Ghoul's Guide to Getting Even*. It was followed by *Good Ghouls Do*.

A vampire princess found herself trapped in a menacing school in *Vampire Academy* by Richelle Mead, and a vampire slayer tried out for the cheerleading team in Mari Mancusi's *Girls That Growl*, the third book in a series.

Tiffany Trent's *Hallowmere: In the Serpent's Coil* was the first in a teenage historical series featuring vampire fairies. *Bloodline Book Two: Reckoning* was the second volume in Kate Cary's YA sequel series to Bram Stoker's *Dracula*, while *Masquerade* by Melissa de la Cruz was a sequel to *Blue Bloods*.

A teenager discovered that she was turning into a vampyre in *Marked* by P. C. Cast and Kristin Cast, the first volume in the "House of Night" series. It was followed by *Betrayed*. Another teen discovered she was half-vampire and went looking for her human mother in *The Society of S* by Susan Hubbard.

The Dead Girls' Dance and *Midnight Alley* were the second and third volumes, respectively, in the "Morganville Vampires" series by "Rachel Caine" (Roxanne Longstreet Conrad).

Serena Robar's *Dating4Demons* was the third in another young adult vampire series, while *Dance with a Vampire* was the fourth volume in Ellen Schreiber's YA romance series that started with *Vampire Kisses*.

Vampire Beach: Ritual and *Vampire Beach: Legacy* were the third and fourth titles in the series by "Alex Duval" (Laura Burns and Melinda Metz).

James McCann's *Pyre*, a sequel to *Rancour*, was about a vampire-hunting werewolf, and an orphaned teenager discovered his lycanthropic heritage in *Werewolf Rising* by R. L. LaFevers.

Neil Gaiman's *M Is for Magic* was a selection of ten previously published stories and a poem aimed at younger readers, illustrated by Teddy Kristiansen. Alongside the HarperCollins trade edition, Subterranean Press issued a 1,000-copy signed edition illustrated by Gahan Wilson and a twenty-six copy lettered edition at $350.00, housed in a custom traycase with an original remarque by the artist.

Robert D. San Souci's *Triple-Dare to Be Scared* contained thirteen original stories, illustrated by David Ouimet, and *The Curse of the Campfire Weenies and Other Warped and Creepy Tales* contained thirty-five stories (two reprints) by David Lubar.

Neal Shusterman's *Darkness Creeping: Twenty Twisted Tales* collected one poem and nineteen stories (four original), while *Hauntings* collected fifteen stories by Betsy Hearne.

The Restless Dead edited by Deborah Noyes contained ten original horror stories by Kelly Link, Nancy Etchemendy, Holly Phillips and others, including the editor.

Joyce Carol Oates, Christopher Pike, T. E. D. Klein, Chet Williamson, P. D. Cacek and Bentley Little were among the authors who contributed eighteen stories to the Scholastic anthology 666: *The Number of the Beast*.

Scary Stories included nineteen stories and a poem, illustrated by Barry Moser, and *Fendi Ferragamo & Fangs* collected three linked stories by Julie Kenner, Johanna Edwards and Serena Robar in which teenagers entering a modelling contest ended up as vampires.

Joe Hill's remarkable debut collection, *20th Century Ghosts*, was reissued in mass-market hardcover editions by William Morrow in the US and Gollancz in the UK with an added story, "Bobby Conroy Comes Back from the Dead", not found in the 2005 PS Publishing edition.

Christopher Fowler's tenth volume of short fiction, *Old Devil Moon*, collected twenty-two eclectic stories (at least fifteen original), along with a Q&A with the author and a Foreword quoting from recent news stories that was equally as horrifying as any of the tales in the book.

Midnight Bazaar: A Secret Arcade of Strange and Eerie Tales contained eight stories (two original) by Simon Clark, including the previously-published novella "She Loves Monsters".

From Chaosium, *The Spiraling Worm: Man versus The Cthulhu Mythos* collected seven linked Lovecraftian stories by David Conyers and John Sunseri, with an Introduction by C. J. Henderson and an Afterword by the authors.

Edited with an Introduction by Peter Haining, *The Demanding Dead: More Stories of Terror and the Supernatural* collected eight stories by Edith Wharton, along with material from an unfinished novel.

Inferno: New Tales of Terror and the Supernatural was a non-themed anthology of twenty original stories edited by Ellen Datlow. Although contributors included K. W. Jeter, Stephen Gallagher, Christopher Fowler, Mike O'Driscoll, Mark Samuels, Joyce Carol Oates, Lucius Shepard, Conrad Williams, Pat Cadigan, Glen Hirshberg and Terry Dowling, among others, the stories relied more on their literary value than their ability to disturb the reader.

Edited by Del Howison and Jeff Gelb, *Dark Delicacies II: Fear* contained nineteen original stories and a Foreword by Ray Harryhausen. Among the contributors were Barbara Hambly, Joe R.

Lansdale, Peter Atkins, Gary Brandner, John Farris, Glenn Hirshberg, Caitlín R. Kiernan and a number of media names.

Summer Chills: Strangers in Strange Lands edited by Stephen Jones contained twenty tales (six original) of holiday horrors by Clive Barker, Harlan Ellison, Ramsey Campbell, Brian Lumley, Robert Silverberg, Dennis Etchison, Michael Marshall Smith, Christopher Fowler, Karl Edward Wagner, Kim Newman, Glen Hirshberg and Basil Copper, among others. From the same editor and also featuring many of the same contributors, *The Mammoth Book of Monsters* collected twenty-two stories (five original) by David J. Schow, Scott Edelman, R. Chetwynd-Hayes, Thomas Ligotti, Gemma Files, Robert E. Howard, Jay Lake, Tanith Lee, Joe R. Lansdale, Robert Holdstock and others. Randy Broecker supplied the interior illustrations.

The Mammoth Book of Modern Ghost Stories: Great Supernatural Tales of the Twentieth Century edited by Peter Haining featured forty-four stories by Ray Bradbury, Philip Pullman, M. R. James, Rudyard Kipling, Lord Dunsany and others.

As usual edited by Jeff Gelb and Michael Garrett, *Hot Blood XIII: Dark Passions* contained twenty erotic horror stories from a list of authors that included Thomas Tessier, Chelsea Quinn Yarbro and David J. Schow.

Published by Hero Games, *Astounding Hero Tales: Thrilling Stories of Pulp Adventure* edited by James Lowder included sixteen original tales in the "pulp" tradition by such authors as Lester Dent, Will Murray, Darrell Schweitzer, David Niall Wilson, John Pelan, Robert Weinberg and the late Hugh B. Cave, who also supplied the biographical Foreword.

Edited by Kelly Link and Gavin J. Grant, *The Best of Lady Churchill's Rosebud Wristlet* reprinted almost fifty pieces from the slipstream fanzine.

Whispers in the Night edited by Brandon Massey was an anthology of nineteen original stories by black authors, including Tananarive Due.

Edited by Darrell Schweitzer, *The Secret History of Vampires* included thirteen original stories by Tanith Lee, Chelsea Quinn Yarbro, Brian Stableford and others.

Many Bloody Returns edited by Charlaine Harris and Toni L. P. Kelner contained thirteen original tales of birthdays with a bite aimed at middle-aged women who read non-scary vampire stories. Christopher Golden, Kelley Armstrong, Jim Butcher, P. N. Elrod, Jeanne C. Stein and Tanya Huff were among the authors included, along with the two editors.

Edited by Lindsay Gordon, *Love on the Dark Side* was an anthology of fifteen original erotic paranormal romance stories by women writers.

In a marketplace swamped with multiple "Best of" anthologies (mostly covering the fantasy and science fiction fields) from various publishers, the 2007 edition of the venerable *The Year's Best Fantasy and Horror* edited by Ellen Datlow, Kelly Link and Gavin Grant celebrated its *Twentieth Annual Collection*. It showcased thirty-four stories, seven poems and multiple annual summaries by various contributing editors, including Edward Bryant, Jeff VanderMeer, Charles de Lint and Jim Frenkel.

The Mammoth Book of Best New Horror Volume Eighteen edited by Stephen Jones collected twenty-four stories and novellas, along with the usual annual round-up, necrology and list of useful contacts.

The only crossovers between the two volumes were stories by Geoff Ryman and Gene Wolfe, although authors Glen Hirshberg and Nicholas Royle were also represented with fiction in both books.

In November Amazon launched the Kindle, an electronic reader that was capable of downloading new books, newspapers, magazines and websites to a six-inch display. The company claimed that the screen "looks and reads like real paper". Weighing the same as an average paperback and selling for around £200 each, Amazon planned to initially offer more than 88,000 titles via a high-speed mobile network rather than wi-fi.

In June, Matt Schwartz announced that his online horror bookstore Shocklines would be closing once it had sold off remaining stock. Unfortunately, the associated message board would continue to operate.

Subterranean began phasing out its magazine version and moved to online publishing. Issue #6 had Edward Miller as the featured illustrator, while the following issue was guest-edited by Ellen Datlow and included fiction by Lucius Shepard, Jeffrey Ford and Lisa Tuttle.

Published electronically by Screaming Dreams, *Estronomicon* was a nicely produced e-zine edited by Steve Upham. The Halloween Special included fiction from Amy Grech, Garry Charles, Gary McMahon, Peter Tennant and others, along with impressive artwork by Michael Bohbot, Vincent Chong, Les Edwards, Paul Mudie and Upham himself.

The consortium that now owns Hammer Films announced that it was producing a new horror film, *Beyond the Rave*, that would be available in 2008 in twenty-minute webisodes through the social networking site MySpace. Directed by Matthias Hoene, the contemporary vampire story featured a brief cameo by Sadie Frost.

Stargate's Amanda Tapping portrayed a doctor hunting down monsters in the Web series *Sanctuary*, while Sam Raimi developed *Devil's Trade*, about a cursed object belonging to a teenage boy. It aired over seven episodes, ranging from three to five minutes each, on Fearnet.com.

Richard A. Lupoff's mystery novel, *Marblehead: A Novel of H. P. Lovecraft*, which was set in 1927 and featured HPL, Frank Belknap Long and Vincent Starrett as characters, finally appeared after thirty years from print-on-demand (POD) publisher Ramble House after being cut in half, completely re-written, and published by Arkham House in 1985 as *Lovecraft's Book*.

An archaeological dig released something evil by the sea in Philip Haldeman's *Shadow Coast*, from Hippocampus Press.

Following the suicide of one of their group, three best friends discovered that he may have been a savage ritual serial killer in Greg F. Gifune's *The Bleeding Season*, available as an on-demand trade paperback from Shane Ryan Staley's Delirium Books.

Also from Delirium, Weston Ochse's *Recalled to Life* was the first book in the "Cycle of the Aegis" and limited to 250 hardcover copies and a twenty-six copy lettered edition.

A small town was overrun by monsters in Jason Brannon's *The Cage*, available as a print-on-demand book or online from KHP Industries/Black Death Books.

Christine Morgan's novel *Tell No Tales* from Sabeldrake Enterprise revolved around a historical-themed reality game show, *Pirate Adventure*, and the ghostly spirits that reached out from the grave to punish those who had invaded their resting-place.

A recovering alcoholic started hearing voices in Karen E. Taylor's *Twelve Steps from Darkness*, a dark fantasy romance from Wildside Press/Juno Books.

Dark Moods was a POD vampire novel by Charlee Jacob from Warren Lapine's Wilder Publications. From the same author and publisher, *The Indigo People: A Vampire Collection* contained twenty-two reprint stories and twenty-three poems about the undead.

Mortal Touch was the latest title in the "Vampires of New England" series by Inanna Arthen from By Light Unseen Media.

Vampires protected the humans they used as livestock from

zombies in D. L. Snell's *Roses of Blood on Barbwire Vines*, from Permuted Press.

The Vampire Gene – Book 1: Gabriele Caccini from AuthorHouse was the first volume in a proposed supernatural romance trilogy by new British author "Paigan Stone" (Samantha Goldstone). It involved a seventeenth-century vampire who fell in love with one of his victims.

A series of mysterious deaths surrounded an attempt to stage *Faust* in 1899 Paris in Brian M. Stableford's *The New Faust and the Tragicomique*, from Black Coat Press. For the same publisher, Stableford translated and introduced Pierre-Alexis de Ponson du Terrail's 1852 novel *The Vampire and the Devil's Son* (*La baronne Trépassée*), Marie Nizet's 1879 novella *Captain Vampire* (*Le Capitaine Vampire*), plus *Anne of the Isles and Other Legends of Brittany*, which collected four Gothic fantasy stories based on Breton folklore by French writer Paul Feval.

From Gary Fry's Gray Friar's Press, the "Gray Matter Novella" series kicked off with Conrad Williams' *Rain*, about a man who moved his family to France and found his life falling apart. It came with an Introduction by Nicholas Royle. The second volume in the series, Steve Vernon's *Hard Roads*, contained two new novellas and an Introduction by Norman Partridge. Both titles were available in 300-copy paperback and 100-copy hardcover PoD editions.

Dirty Prayers from the same publisher collected twenty-nine stories (sixteen original) by Gary McMahon, with an Introduction by Joel Lane and a brief Afterword by the author.

Canadian author Michael Kelly's first collection, *Scratching the Surface*, debuted at the 2007 World Horror Convention from Crowswing Books. The PoD trade paperback contained twenty-six psychological ghost stories (nine original) plus an Introduction by John Pelan.

Apple of My Eye from Two Backed Books collected thirteen stories (two original) by Amy Grech.

Issued in paperback by Mythos Books, *Dark Wisdom: New Tales of the Old Ones* was edited and introduced by Robert M. Price and collected twelve new Cthulhu Mythos stories by Gary Myers, who also supplied the photographic illustrations. From the same PoD publisher, *In the Yaddith Time* was a Mythos sonnet sequence by Ann K. Schwader, extensively illustrated by Steve Lines with an Introduction by Richard L. Tierney.

Edited by Ken Asamatsu with an Introduction by Robert M. Price, *The Dreaming God: Lairs of the Hidden Gods Volume Three* was the fourth anthology of Lovecraftian stories and essays from Kurodahan Press, originally published over two volumes in Japan in 2002.

Published by Welsh print-on-demand imprint Mortbury Press, *The Black Book of Horror* was a tribute to the *Pan Book of Horror* series of the 1960s and '70s and featured eighteen stories (two reprints) selected by Charles Black. Authors included Mark Samuels, Gary Fry, D. F. Lewis (twice), David A. Sutton, Paul Finch, John L. Probert, Gary McMahon, David A. Riley and the editor. Paul Mudie supplied the excellent cover art.

Edited by Jason Sizemore and Gill Ainsworth, *Gratia Placenti: For the Sake of Pleasing* was an original anthology of thirteen stories from Apex Publications. David Niall Wilson, J. A. Konrath and Bev Vincent were among the authors who contributed stories about individuals going to any lengths to get what they wanted (or, more likely, deserved).

Available in a limited edition of 600 copies from Silverthought Press, *A Dark and Deadly Valley* edited by Mike Heffernan contained twenty weird World War II stories by David J. Schow, Elizabeth Massie, Scott Nicholson and others, with an Introduction by John Skipp.

From Australian PoD imprint, Equilibrium Books, editor James Doig unearthed twenty-three rare stories for the fascinating compilation *Australian Gothic: An Anthology of Australian Supernatural Fiction 1867-1939*. The editor also included useful introductory material to the nineteen, mostly obscure, authors represented.

After fifty-two years, pulp magazine *Thrilling Wonder Stories* was re-launched in July as a print-on-demand trade paperback under new editor/publisher Winston Engle. The first issue contained classic reprints by Jack Williamson, Ray Bradbury, Raymond F. Jones and Isaac Asimov, plus an interview with Forrest J Ackerman.

Although Robert Morgan of Sarob Press initially announced that *Monster Behind the Wheel* by Michael McCarty and Mark McLaughlin would be the final title to appear from the Welsh small press, the book was subsequently rescheduled to appear from Corrosion Press (an imprint of Delirium Books). Meanwhile, Morgan and his wife Sara took early retirement and relocated to a small farm in northern France.

Available from Earthling Publications, Michael Marshall Smith's ghostly young adult novel *The Servants*, about an eleven-year-old boy coming to terms with responsibility in a haunted house by the wintry seaside, was published in both trade and signed, limited hardcover editions.

Glen Hirshberg's acclaimed debut novel, *The Snowman's Children*, was reissued by Earthling in an edition of 250 numbered and fifteen lettered copies. With a new Introduction by Elizabeth Hand and an original Afterword by Gary A. Braunbeck, this attractive leather-bound hardcover was illustrated by Alex McVey.

From the same imprint, *The Haunted Forest Tour* by James A. Moore and Jeff Strand was the third volume in Earthling's "Halloween Series". It was limited to 500 numbered and fifteen lettered copies, signed by the authors.

Featuring an Introduction by Michael Marshall Smith, Ramsey Campbell's latest novel, *The Grin of the Dark*, from PS Publishing was about a film critic whose life inexorably unravelled as he researched the life of a mysterious silent film comedian named Tubby Thackeray. It was available in a 500-copy signed edition and a slipcased edition of 200 signed by Campbell and Smith.

Meanwhile, Campbell's 2005 novel *Secret Stories* finally saw publication in America under the truncated title *Secret Story*, doubtless to prevent it from being confused with a short fiction collection by US readers.

Also available from PS, Elizabeth Hand's *Illyria* was a haunting novella about growing up and the power of theatre.

Introduced by Graham Joyce, *The Scalding Rooms* by Conrad Williams was a novella set in a mutant-filled post-Apocalyptic world. It was available in a 500-copy signed edition in illustrated boards and a 300-copy dust-jacketed edition signed by both Williams and Joyce.

Dead Earth: The Green Dawn by Mark Justice and David T. Wilbanks was an Apocalyptic zombie novella set in the New Mexico town of Serenity. With an Introduction by Gary A. Braunbeck, the book was published in three states, including a twenty-six copy lettered and slipcased hardcover signed by all the contributors along with cover artist Glenn Chadbourne.

Gary Fry's *Sanity and Other Delusions* was the first volume in the "PS Showcase" series. It collected six stories (four original) along with an Introduction by Stephen Volk.

The Collected Ed Gorman featured two hardcover reprint collections, *Out There in the Darkness* and *The Moving Coffin*, introduced by Max Allan Collins and Lawrence Block, respectively. PS issued both books in a deluxe slipcased set.

The eagerly awaited 50th Anniversary Edition of Ray Bradbury's classic "fix-up" novel *Dandelion Wine* from PS Publishing did not disappoint. Issued in three handsome states, the book included all the original illustrations that accompanied the individual stories when they were originally published. The special deluxe slipcased set (£375.00 and limited to just 100 copies) was signed by both Bradbury and Stephen King, who supplied the new Introduction. It came with a bonus book, *Summer Morning, Summer Night*, that included all the other Greentown, Illinois, stories and vignettes, seventeen of which were previously unpublished.

PS also issued Stephen King's 2005 crime novel *The Colorado Kid* in three different hardcover editions, each individually illustrated by "Edward Miller" (Les Edwards), J. K. Potter and Glenn Chadbourne. The books were available in a bewildering array of variant editions, ranging in price from £25.00 for a 10,000-copy trade hardcover to £375.00 for a ninety-nine copy leather-bound traycased edition signed by the author and all three artists.

From Hill House Publishers, *Anansi Boys* was one of the most impressive book productions of the year. A stunning limited edition of Neil Gaiman's 2005 novel, it was beautifully designed and illustrated by Dagmara Matuszak. Available in signed editions of 750 numbered and fifty-two lettered copies, the double slipcase also included *Anansi Boys: Additional Material Notebooks*, which featured an interview with the author, the original outline for the novel, script pages, a deleted scene and notebook extracts.

As a special gift limited to those subscribers to the delayed edition of Ray Bradbury's *The Martian Chronicles: The Definitive Edition*, Hill House sent out a framed "The Martian Chronicles Triptych" containing prints of three of the eight original pieces of art created by Edward Miller and signed by both author and artist.

A follow-up to the previous World Fantasy Award-winning anthology, *Strange Tales Volume II* from Tartarus Press was a handsome-looking volume that contained seventeen original stories by such authors as Joel Knight, Quentin S. Crisp, Mark Valentine, Adam Golaski, Simon Strantzas, David Rix, Rhys Hughes, Barbara Roden, Roger Dunkley, Christopher Harman and others.

From MonkeyBrain Books, Kim Newman's *The Secret Files of the Diogenes Club* collected seven stories (one original) featuring members of the titular British intelligence service founded by Sherlock Holmes' smarter brother. The author also included a couple of useful appendices for American readers.

Copying the format of the *Night Visions* series, *Five Strokes to Midnight* from new imprint Haunted Pelican Press collected 20,000 words of original fiction each by Tom Piccirilli, Deborah LeBlanc, Christopher Golden and co-editors Gary A. Braunbeck and Hank Schwaeble, along with an Introduction by Tim Lebbon and impressive artwork by *Hellraiser* actress Ashley Laurence.

From Gray Friar Press, *Stains* was a nice-looking hardcover collection of eight stories (including three new novellas) by Paul Finch limited to just 250 copies. Simon Clark supplied the Introduction.

Lucius Shepard's short novel *Softspoken* from Night Shade Books was a Southern Gothic about a haunted ancestral mansion. It was also published as a signed, limited edition with extra material.

The Imago Sequence and Other Stories from the same imprint was the first collection of Laird Barron's Lovecraftian-inspired stories and featured nine linked tales (one original) based around a monstrous entity named Belphegor. An extra story was included in the signed limited edition.

Hart & Boot & Other Stories was a collection of thirteen excellent stories (three original) by Tim Pratt. The author discussed the origin of each tale in his story notes. *Balefires* collected twenty-four stories by David Drake with extensive notes by the author. A signed, limited edition also included an extra bibliography.

Edited with story notes by Scott Connors and Ron Hilger, *The Collected Fantasies of Clark Ashton Smith Volume 1: The End of the Story* and *Volume 2: The Door to Saturn* were the first two titles in a proposed five-volume series from Night Shade Books. Presenting the "definitive" manuscript texts in chronological order, the two books included Introductions by Ramsey Campbell and Tim Powers, respectively.

Joe Hill's *Heart-Shaped Box* was available from Subterranean Press in a 500-copy signed and limited edition, a 200-copy deluxe edition with an added section, and a fifteen-copy leather-bound and lettered traycased edition, which all sold out before publication.

Stephen Gallagher's novel *The Painted Bride* and his collection of eleven stories (one original), *Plots and Misadventures*, were both available from Subterranean in signed editions of 750 copies.

Joe R. Lansdale's novel *Lost Echoes*, about a man who could see ghosts in sounds, was available in a 400-copy signed edition and fifteen traycased copies.

God of the Razor collected the same author's 1987 novel *The Nightrunners* and six connected stories (one original). Illustrated by Glenn Chadborne, it was also available in a 150-copy signed and slipcased edition that sold out before publication. *The Shadows Kith and Kin* contained eight stories (one original) by Lansdale. It was available in a signed, limited edition and a traycased lettered edition ($250.00) of just fifteen copies.

Charles de Lint's short novel, *Promises to Keep*, was set in an alternate world where the dead continued to live on.

Currency of Souls by Kealan Patrick Burke was available in a limited edition of 750 copies and a fifteen-copy lettered traycased edition for $250.00.

Published by Subterranean in a 1,500-copy signed hardcover edition illustrated by Mark Geyer, Cherie Priest's *Dreadful Skin* contained three tales about a pistol-carrying former Irish nun and an English shape-shifter (who was actually Jack the Ripper) pursuing each other across the United States during the years following the American Civil War.

Peter Crowther's collection, *The Spaces Between the Lines*, contained twelve reprint stories, along with an introduction by Jack Dann and an afterword by the author. It was limited to 750 signed and numbered copies.

Caitlín R. Kiernan's *Tales from the Woeful Platypus* was a small-sized hardcover containing eight erotic stories, illustrated by Vince Locke. The limited edition, which sold out before publication, included an extra vignette and a chapbook of exclusive material.

Subterranean Press also looked set to become Brian Lumley's major publisher in the US with a reprint of the author's 1998 collection *A Coven of Vampires*, limited to a signed edition of 1,000 copies with an accompanying chapbook. A new collection, *The Taint and Other Novellas: Best Mythos Tales Volume One*, contained seven previously published Cthulhu Mythos novellas, plus a new Introduction and story notes by the author. It was available in a deluxe hardcover edition signed by Lumley and illustrator Bob Eggleton.

Basic Black: Tales of Appropriate Fear from Cemetery Dance Publications collected eighteen stories (two original) from Australian writer Terry Dowling, with an Introduction by Jonathan Strahan.

Chet Williamson's *The Story of Noichi the Blind* was supposedly a "lost" novella by Lafcadio Hearn, introduced by Williamson with an Afterword by Alan Drew. It was available in a signed edition limited to 1,500 copies.

Thrillers 2 edited by Robert Morrish contained nine original stories by Caitlín R. Kiernan, Gemma Files, Tim Waggoner and R. Patrik Gates.

Edited by Tom Piccirilli and limited to 1,500 signed and fifty-two lettered copies from Cemetery Dance, *The Midnight Premiere* was an anthology of eighteen original horror stories about Hollywood. Authors included Jack Ketchum, Gary A. Braunbeck, Thomas F. Monteleone, Brian Hodge, Ed Gorman, Al Sarrantonio, Mick Garris and others.

CD also reissued Simon Clark's 1996 novel *Darker* in 1,000 signed and twenty-six traycased and leather-bound editions.

Michael Cisco's novel *The Traitor* from Wildside Press/Prime Books featured a spirit-eater as its protagonist. From the same imprints, *The Bone Key* was a collection of ten related stories (one original) by Sarah Monette featuring museum archivist and paranormal investigator Kyle Murchison Booth.

Edited by Paul Herman with an Introduction by Damon C. Sasser, *Beyond the Black River* was the seventh volume in Wildside's "The Weird Works of Robert E. Howard" series. It included five stories (three featuring Conan).

Also published by Wildside/Prime, *Weird Tales: The 21st Century: Volume One* was an anthology of twelve stories selected by editors Stephen H. Segal and Sean Wallace from the vastly inferior recent incarnation of the iconic magazine. Among those authors represented were Holly Phillips, Gerard Houarner and Carrie Vaughn.

Available from Gauntlet Press, *Somewhere a Band Is Playing* by Ray Bradbury not only contained the new novella of the title, but all sorts of extra material, including related story fragments and an unfinished screenplay. Also from Gauntlet, *Bloodline* was the eleventh volume in F. Paul Wilson's "Repairman Jack" series.

The same author's 1988 historical supernatural novel *Black Wind* was reissued by Borderlands Press in a signed and numbered edition limited to just 350 copies. From the same publisher, Peter Straub's *5 Stories* contained exactly what it said in the title.

Nightshadows from Fairwood Press/Darkwood Press collected twenty-three recent stories by William F. Nolan, one original.

Published by Manchester's Comma Press, *Phobic: Modern Horror Stories* edited by Andy Murray was one of the better anthologies of the year. Published in trade paperback with assistance from the Arts Council England North West and Literature Northwest, the book contained fifteen stories (two reprints) by Jeremy Dyson, Nicholas Royle, Conrad Williams, Paul Cornell, Chaz Brenchley, Ramsey Campbell and others.

Screaming Dreams was a classy new British small press imprint founded by artist Steve Upham. *The Midnight Hour: 14 Tales of Dark Imagination* collected the short stories (five original) of Neil

Davies, while *Phantoms of Venice* was an attractive trade paperback reprint of the 2001 anthology edited by David A. Sutton, with stunning new cover artwork by Edward Miller.

Thomas F. Monteleone, Scott Nicholson and Kealan Patrick Burke were among the authors who contributed thirteen stories to *Legends of the Mountain State: Ghostly Tales from the State of West Virginia* from Woodlands Press. Edited by Michael Knost, it included a Foreword by Rick Hautala.

Guy Adams' *Deadbeat: Dogs of Waugh* was the second volume in the comedy-thriller series from British imprint Humdrumming. It once again involved drunken ex-theatricals Tom Harris and Max Jackson and was set in a London populated by the walking dead.

Humdrumming's *You Are the Fly: Tales of Redemption & Distress* collected sixteen stories (at least four original) by British writer James Cooper, with an Introduction by Greg F. Gifune and an Afterword from the author's frequent collaborator, Andrew Jury.

From the same imprint came attractive "printed paper case editions" of Mark Morris' first two novels, *Toady* and *Stitch*, which featured new Introductions by the author. *Stitch* also included exclusive bonus material, along with an interview with Morris and a reprint short story.

Morris also supplied the Introduction to *The First Humdrumming Book of Horror Stories*, a tribute to the old *Pan Book of Horror* (complete with copied logo) selected by Ian Alexander Martin. The twelve original stories were all by Humdrumming authors, including James Cooper (twice), Gary McMahon, Garry Kilworth, Gary Fry, Rhys Hughes and Guy Adams.

Alex Hamilton's *The Attic Express and Other Macabre Stories* from Canada's Ash-Tree Press contained twenty-eight tales, mostly taken from the author's first three collections, along with an original story. It was published in an edition of 500 copies.

Francis Brett Young's supernatural novel *Cold Harbour* was reprinted with a new Introduction by John Howard. It was limited to 400 copies.

At Ease with the Dead was an all-original anthology of thirty stories from Ash-Tree, the fourth to be edited by Barbara and Christopher Roden. It included work by John Llewellyn Probert, Melanie Tem, Gary McMahon, Mark Valentine, Kealan Patrick Burke, Steve Duffy, Joel Lane, John Whitbourn, Robert Morrish, Chet Williamson, Paul Finch, Don Tumasonis and others, including co-editor Barbara Roden. With a cover by Jason Van Hollander, the book was available in both trade paperback and 400-copy hardcover editions.

A strange brown mist rising from the water in the Florida Keys created a world of zombies in Del Stone, Jr's novella *Black Tide*, from Telos Publishing.

Issued in a handsome hardcover edition of just 300 copies, as were the previous two volumes, *Phantoms At the Phil: The Third Proceedings* from Side Real Press in conjunction with Northern Gothic contained two new stories each by Sean O'Brien, Gail-Nina Anderson and Chaz Brenchley.

Elizabeth Hand's *Generation Loss* from Small Beer Press was a serial killer novel about a washed-up alcoholic photographer and the ritual murders of teenagers on a small island off the coast of Maine.

Containing a bonus novella and a new Afterword by the author, Thomas Tessier's 1979 novel *The Nightwalker* was reprinted by Millipede Press in cloth and leather-bound editions. The latter was limited to twenty-two numbered copies ($275.00) signed by Tessier and Jack Ketchum, who supplied the Introduction.

From the same imprint, a new edition of Mary Shelley's *Frankenstein* featured an Introduction by Patrick McGrath, a frontispiece by Berni Wrightson, and a selection of critical essays by Judith Halberstam, Brian Aldiss and Radu Florescu, among others. A twenty-two copy leather traycased edition was signed by various contributors.

Lawrence Santoro's debut novel, *Just North of Nowhere*, appeared from Annihilation Press in trade paperback with a cover painting by Alan M. Clark. Set in and around the haunted town of Bluffton, it comprised a number of linked stories, four of which had previously been published by Twilight Tales Books.

Published by Florida's The Spectre Library in a hardcover edition of just 200 copies, *The Tracer of Egos* collected twelve stories by Victor Rousseau about Greek-born occult detective Dr Phileas Immanuel, with an Introduction by Morgan A. Wallace.

From Mythos Books, Canadian writer Richard Gavins' *Omens* collected twelve stories (seven original) with cover art by Harry O. Morris.

New British imprint JnJ Publications, in conjunction with Rainfall Books, issued the trade paperback anthology *Cthulhu's Creatures* edited by Steve Lines and John B. Ford. Available in a signed and numbered edition limited to 100 copies, it featured nineteen stories and six poems (one original of each) by Joseph S. Pulver Sr, Stanley C. Sargent, Jeffrey Thomas, C. Henderson, Robert M. Price, Tim Curran, Franklyn Searight, Joel Lane, Richard L. Tierney and the two editors. Simon Clark supplied the Introduction.

Edited by William Jones, *High Seas Cthulhu* was an anthology of twenty Mythos sea stories (one reprint) by Alan Dean Foster, Darrell Schweitzer, John Shirley and others, from Elder Signs Press. A ship was lost on the *Dead Sea* in Tim Curran's novel from Elder Signs Press/Dimensions Books.

John R. Little's novelette, *Placeholders*, from Necessary Evil Press, was about a man who kept returning from death. Limited to 275 signed and numbered copies, Thomas F. Monteleone provided the Introduction.

Available from Doorways Publications, *Voyeurs of Death* collected fifteen stories (four original) by Brit author Shaun Jeffrey.

Zencore! Scriptus Innominatus was the latest anthology in the "Nemonymous" series from Megazanthus Press. It contained seventeen stories by Scott Edelman, Reggie Oliver, Patricia Russo, Mark Valentine and others. As usual, the authors were not credited with their contributions until the next volume.

From California's Dark Regions Press, *Over the Darkening Fields* collected twenty-six often quite short stories (fifteen original) by Scott Thomas, while *Doomsdays* featured twenty-two apocalyptic stories (four new) by Jeffrey Thomas, including a collaboration with his brother Scott.

Darker Loves: Tales of Mystery and Regret from the same imprint collected fourteen stories (two original) and ten poems by James Dorr, with an Introduction by Brian A. Hopkins, and Michael A. Arnzen's career-spanning *Proverbs and Monsters* contained twenty-nine tales (one original) and thirty-four poems (two new).

Tango in the Ninth Circle: The Selected Poetry of Corrine de Winter was a collection of twenty-seven macabre poems with an Introduction by Denise Dumars and illustrations by Matt Taggart. Also available from Dark Regions Press in trade paperback, *Vectors: A Week in the Death of a Planet* by Charlee Jacob and Marge Simon charted the end of the world through a series of linked verses.

Edited by Andy W. Robertson, *William Hope Hodgson's Night Lands Volume II: Nightmares of the Fall* was an anthology of eleven stories (one reprint) from Three Legged Fox Books/Utter Tower.

Going Back was a new collection of fourteen stories (one original) by Tony Richards, from Elastic Press. Published by Welsh imprint Pendragon Press, *No-Man* and *Other Tales* contained four novellas (two original) by the same author.

Sharing an oddly italicised title, *New Writings* in the *Fantastic* was a substantial trade paperback anthology from the same imprint, edited and introduced by the redoubtable John Grant. Containing forty-one original stories, contributors included Andrew Hook, Paul Finch, Scott Emerson Bull, Cyril Simsa and Gary McMahon.

Also from Pendragon, Paul Kane's *Dalton Quayle Rides Out* contained two humorous tales of the eponymous psychic investigator and his good friend, Dr Humphrey Pemberton. Tom Holt supplied the brief Introduction. Published by Australia's Tasmaniac Publications, Kane's *The Lazarus Condition* collected the title zombie novella and a bonus story about the walking dead, introduced by Mick Garris. Published in a 185-copy edition illustrated by Dion Hamill, it was also available as a fifteen-copy hardcover signed by all the contributors.

Read by Dawn Volume 2 edited by Adele Hartley and *Classic Tales of Horror Volume 2* edited by Jonathan Wooding were both available from Bloody Books.

The Animal Bridegroom from Canada's Tightrope Books collected thirty-seven poems by Sandra Kasturi, along with a very brief Introduction by Neil Gaiman and cover blurbs from Peter Straub and Phyllis Gotlieb.

Published by Space & Time, *Being Full of Light, Insubstantial* contained 100 mostly previously unpublished poems by Linda D. Addison with photography by Brian J. Addison.

Published in a softcover edition given away in the delegate bags at World Horror Convention in Toronto, *This is Now* was a handsomely produced chapbook from Earthling Publications that contained three stories (one original) by Michael Marshall Smith, with cover art by Edward Miller. A twenty-six-copy lettered hardcover was also available.

As usual, Earthling also published *The Twilight Limited*, an attractive chapbook of three stories (one reprint) and linking material tied in to The Rolling Darkness Revue 2007. Authors Peter Atkins, Glen Hirshberg and Dennis Etchison toured California bookstores in October performing their work to a musical accompaniment.

Number eleven in the Gothic Chapbooks series from Gothic Press, *The Fisherman* was an original short story by David A. Sutton with illustrations by Marge Simon.

Edited by Benjamin Szumskyj, *Black Prometheus: A Critical Study of Karl Edward Wagner* was a welcome collection from Gothic Press featuring eight essays by John F. Mayer, John Howard, Darrell Schweitzer, Garry Hoppenstand and others, including Wagner himself. Unfortunately, many of the articles simply recapitulated the plots of Wagner's stories and it was very obvious that some of the contributors never actually knew the late author (he would never have drunk Jim Beam).

Waiting for October from Dark Arts Books collected three stories each (two originals and a reprint) by Jeff Strand, Adam Pepper, Sarah Pinborough and Jeffrey Thomas, along with an Introduction by Bill Breedlove.

From Bad Moon Books, Weston Ochse's *Vampire Outlaw of the Milky Way* was signed by the author and Brian Keene, who supplied the Introduction. Meanwhile, Ochse contributed the Introduction to John Urbancik's novella *Wings of the Butterfly*, which included an extra story, from the same imprint. Both trade paperbacks were limited to 300 perfect-bound copies and twenty-six lettered hardcovers.

The Distance Travelled: A Little Slice of Heaven was a comedic horror novella by Brett Alexander Savory and Gord Zajac, published by Canada's Burning Effigy Press. The chapbook came with praise from Christopher Moore, Michael Marshall Smith and Stewart O'Nan. From the same imprint, Brian Keene, David Wellington and Sarah Langan gave glowing quotes to *General Slocum's Gold* by Nicholas Kaufman. It was about the search for a cursed treasure on a deserted island in New York's East River.

Published by Zen Films to commemorate the UK release of editor Robert Pratten's companion film *London Voodoo, Love and Sacrifice: Touching Stories About Troubled Relationships* was a paperback anthology of twelve original stories by Gary McMahon, James S. Dorr and others. A reading by *Hellraiser* actor Doug Bradley of Mike Davis' contribution "Stepping Off" was available on the publisher's website.

Rainfall Books' series of laminated-cover chapbooks continued with a whole raft of titles. Robert M. Price's *Witch-Queen of Lemuria* expanded the exploits of the late Lin Carter's Thongor the Barbarian, and *Sirens & Silver* collected the poetry of Michael Fantina. *E'ch Pi El* #2 contained three Lovecraftian stories by Ran Cartwright, Joseph S. Pulver and Clinton S. Green, while Tim Curran's *The Slithering & Others* collected three further tales inspired by Howard Phillips Lovecraft. *Pearls & Pyramids* and *Temples & Torments* contained Clark Ashton Smith-inspired fiction from Simon Whitechapel.

Also from Rainfall, *Thrilling Tales of Fantastic Adventure* #1 featured pulp-inspired stories by Gary McMahon, Franklyn Searight and Michael Fantina, among others. *Weird Worlds* #2 included four heroic fantasy tales, while issues 2–4 of *Strange Sorcery* contained

"Weird Stories of Lost Worlds of Space & Time" by many of the above authors. All these publications were edited by John B. Ford and Steve Lines, with the latter also contributing most of the art-work.

Ed McFadden resigned as the editor of *Fantastic Stories of the Imagination* after problems with Warren Lapine's DNA Publications concerning the erratic publishing schedule of the company's magazine titles. Meanwhile, DNA's website was taken offline.

As usual, PS Publishing's hardcover *PostScripts* magazine produced four excellent issues in 2007, not least a bumper 350-plus page special edition for the World Horror Convention in Canada. Available in three states – trade, signed and slipcased – the tenth issue not only featured an extensive section devoted to the fiction of Author Guest of Honour Michael Marshall Smith, but also a stellar line-up of contributors that included Stephen King, Ramsey Campbell, Lisa Tuttle, Nancy Kilpatrick, Lucius Shepard, Joe Hill, Christopher Fowler, Steven Erikson, Stephen Gallagher, Tim Lebbon, Peter Atkins and Mark Morris, among many others. Artist Guest John Picacio supplied the cover artwork.

The remaining three issues of the year also included superior work from Kealan Patrick Burke, Forrest Aguirre, Christopher Harman, Patrick O'Leary, Paul Jessup, Iain Rowan, Brian Aldiss, Scott Edelman, Christopher Fowler and others. Guest editorials were by Stephen Jones, Paul Di Filippo, Lisa Tuttle and Graham Joyce (who really needs to learn how to spell Stephen King's name!). Each issue of *PostScripts* was also available in a 200-copy edition signed by all the contributors.

Subscribers to *PostScripts* also received a special hardcover holiday chapbook for Christmas. *The Saved* by Joe Hill was a Depression-set fable, originally published in an obscure literary magazine in 2001. Slipcase subscribers received signed copies.

Boasting a "skullful" cover by Edward Miller, the February-March issue of *Weird Tales* was a special Joe R. Lansdale edition, featuring two stories (one reprint) and an interview by Chet Williamson. Other contributors included Michael Shea and Holly Phillips.

With the next bi-monthly issue, publisher Wildside Press made the mistake of dumping the magazine's distinctive logo after eight decades. Despite non-fiction contributions from Caitlín R. Kiernan and Michael DeLuca, an excellent book review column by Scott Connors, interviews with George R. R. Martin, Lisa Tuttle, Mike Carey and Sèphera Girón, plus fiction from Kurt Newton, Gerard

Houarner, Carrie Vaughn, Jay Lake, Tanith Lee, Darrell Schweitzer and others, *Weird Tales* lost its final link with the past and became just another small press title fighting for space on the magazine racks.

Meanwhile, following the reorganization of its entire editorial staff at the end of 2006, Ann VanderMeer was named as the new fiction editor of *Weird Tales*, beginning with the September-October edition.

The fourth issue of Wildside's companion title, *H. P. Lovecraft's Magazine of Horror*, featured a conversation with very un-Lovecraftian author Laurell K. Hamilton and a couple of whimsical mystery stories by Esther Friesner and Ron Goulart. There was also fiction from Darrell Schweitzer, Ken Rand, Jay Lake, Morgan Llywelyn and others, columns by Craig Shaw Gardner, Peter Cannon and Ian McDowell, plus some Really Bad Poetry.

A much better tribute to the pulp tradition was editor John O'Neill's *Black Gate: Adventures in Fantasy Literature*, which managed to get two attractive issues out in 2007. These included heroic fantasy and horror stories by Iain Rowan, Mark Sumner, Martha Wells and others, along with some of the best black and white artwork to appear in any contemporary fiction magazine. Rich Horton contributed interesting articles looking at the smaller fiction magazines of the 1970s and some neglected SF stories.

After three years and various production delays, Andy Cox's *The Third Alternative* was finally reincarnated as *Black Static*. However, based on the two monochromatic issues published by TTA Press in 2007, it may not have been worth the wait. Among those supplying the fiction were Simon Avery, Joel Lane, Lisa Tuttle and Steven Utley, F. Brett Cox, Scott Nicholson, Steve Rasnic Tem and Lynda E. Rucker. Along with reviews of books and films, there were also opinion columns by Stephen Volk, Mike O'Driscoll, Christopher Fowler, John Paul Catton and Peter Tennant.

Black Static's companion title, *Interzone*, celebrated its 25th Anniversary and managed six far more attractive issues featuring SF and fantasy fiction from Jay Lake, Paul Meloy, Hal Duncan, M. John Harrison, Gwyneth Jones, Alastair Reynolds, Chris Roberson and others. Along with interviews with Elizabeth Hand, Neil Gaiman, Susanna Clarke, Hal Duncan, Kim Stanley Robinson, Stephen Baxter and Charles Stross, there was also a nice article by Harlan Ellison about his friendship with Theodore Sturgeon. Issue #211 was a Michael Moorcock special.

Copies of *Cemetery Dance* #57 were apparently marred by production problems. The issue included new fiction by David Prill,

A. R. Morland and others, along with all the usual columns and an interview with Colorado novelist Michael McBride.

Gordon Van Gelder celebrated his eleventh year as the editor of *The Magazine of Fantasy & Science Fiction* with contributions from Neil Gaiman (a reprint), Bruce Sterling, the late John Morressy, William Browning Spencer, Fred Chappell, Ron Goulart, M. Rickert, Michael Swanwick, Ian R. MacLeod, A. A. Ananasio, Don Webb, Charles Coleman Finlay, Lucius Shepard, Ray Vukcevich, Esther M. Friesner, Gwyneth Jones, Robert Silverberg and Frederic S. Durbin.

There were the usual review columns by Charles de Lint, Elizabeth Hand, Paul Di Fillipo, John Kessel, James Sallis, Lucius Shepard, Michelle West, Kathi Maio and David J. Skal, while Graham Andrews, F. Gwynplaine MacIntyre, Douglas A. Anderson, David Langford, Bud Webster and Don D'Amassa all contributed to the "Curiosities" section.

The April edition of *F&SF* was a "Special Gene Wolfe Issue".

The fifth issue of Adam Golaski and Jeff Paris' paperback magazine *New Genre* included five stories and an essay.

As a result of personal changes between issues #34 and #35, the always entertaining *Talebones: Science Fiction & Dark Fantasy* lost co-editor Honna Swenson, and Patrick Swenson took full control of the attractive digest-sized magazine. William F. Nolan, Darrell Schweitzer, Carrie Vaughn, Jason Stoddard, G. O. Clark and Cardinal Cox were among those contributing fiction and poetry, while Richard Pellegrino provided a superb cover painting for the second issue of the year.

The three issues of Jason B. Sizemore's nicely-produced *Apex: Science Fiction & Horror* featured fiction from Kevin J. Anderson (a Frankenstein story), Lavie Tidhar, William F. Nolan, Bev Vincent, Ian Creasey, Gary A. Braunbeck and Daniel G. Keohane, along with interviews with Anderson, Nolan, Braunbeck, Liz Smith, Cherie Priest and Bryan Smith.

The two issues of James R. Beach's continually improving *Dark Discoveries* featured fiction by Tony Richards, Elizabeth Engstrom, John Maclay, Tim Waggoner, Jay Lake, John Everson and others. There were also interviews with Maclay, Waggoner, Lake, Everson, T. M. Wright and Brian Hodge, along with book reviews and columns on Harlan Ellison, the late Charles L. Grant, and Stephen King's signing tour.

The ninth issue of Trevor Denyer's *Midnight Street: Journeys Into Darkness* included stories and verse by Peter Straub, Allen Ashley and Ken Goldman, along with interviews with Straub, Sarah Pin-borough and Donna Taylor Burgess.

Issue #11 of William Jones' *Dark Wisdom: The Magazine of Dark Fiction* was full-colour throughout. Contributors included Alan Dean Foster, John Shirley, Robert Dunbar, C. J. Henderson and Douglas Smith. There was also a regular column from Richard A. Lupoff and an interview with Jack Ketchum.

Christopher M. Cevasco published the eleventh issue of *Paradox: The Magazine of Historical and Speculative Fiction*, which included a number of contributions by Darrell Schweitzer.

From Ireland, the two issues of *Albedo One* featured fiction from Brian Stableford, Uncle River, Andrew McKenna and others, along with interviews with Christopher Priest, Geoff Ryman and Sam Millar.

Eric M. Heideman's annual *Tales of the Unanticipated* #28 was a special "Heroes" issue with fiction and poetry from Terry Black, Uncle River, Martha A. Hood, Stephen Dedman, Mary Soon Lee, Laurel Winter and many more.

Canada's *Rue Morgue* magazine celebrated its tenth anniversary with eleven issues (including a bumper Halloween edition) in 2007. The full-colour glossy of "horror in culture and entertainment" included interviews with authors Jemiah Jefferson, Mick Garris, Michael Laimo, Sarah Langan, Clive Barker and F. Paul Wilson, artists Mike Mignola and Les Edwards, Earthling publisher Paul Miller, film-makers Don Coscarelli, Tom Savini, William Lustig, Alejandro Jodorowsky, Lamberto Bava, Eli Roth, Fred Dekker, Rob Zombie, Dan O'Bannon, Rob Bottin and Frank Darabont, and actors Angus Scrimm, Ron Perlman and Kurt Russell (twice), along with the usual articles and reviews.

Overlooking an appallingly trivial interview with forgotten 1970s Brit actress Judi Bowker, the eight issues of *Video Watchdog* included Kim Newman's thoughtful appraisals of the second Charlie Chan and German Edgar Wallace boxed sets, David J. Schow's look at the first two seasons of *The Wild Wild West* on DVD, Ted Newsom's tribute to director Freddie Francis, a fascinating guide to Greek Fantastic Cinema, and an interview with genuine cult actor Tony Russel, along with plenty of reviews and the usual columns. Unfortunately, during 2007, publishers Tim and Donna Lucus seemed more concerned with their long-awaited Mario Bava book than with the contents of the magazine.

Steven Puchalski's long-running magazine about cult movies, *Shock Cinema*, produced two well-researched issues, featuring interviews with actors Ronny Cox, Tim Thomerson, Michael Ironside, Austin Pendleton, Belinda Balaski and director Steve Carver, among the copious obscure film reviews.

The November issue of *Total Film* contained a thirty-two page "History of Horror", with decade-by-decade retrospectives and guest editorials by Eli Roth, Neil Marshall and other movie directors.

YA author R. L. Stine had a new short-short story in the 22–28 October issue of *TV Guide*. "A Tasty Halloween Treat" was tied in to the TV movie *R. L. Stine's The Haunting Hour: Don't Think About It* on the Cartoon Network.

Stephen King cut back on his "The Pop of King" columns in *Entertainment Weekly*, but he still found time to talk about such eclectic subjects as the curse of celebrity, how publishers bury their books, what it was like in rehab, violence in movies and his recent trip to Australia. Besides regularly plugging *Deathly Hallows* in his column, King also contributed the article "J. K. Rowling's Ministry of Magic" to the 17 August issue of the magazine, in which he defended the *Harry Potter* series and R. L. Stine's *Goosebumps* books.

Charles N. Brown's newszine *Locus* entered its forty-first year of publication. Despite the magazine's increasingly Bay Area bias, it included interviews with Ace/Roc editor Ginjer Buchanan, Tim Powers, Guy Gavriel Kay, Kelly Link, Elizabeth Hand and newcomer Holly Phillips. Cory Doctorow continued his bi-monthly column about alternative publishing technologies, and there was the usual mix of reviews, listings and convention reports.

The May issue of *Locus* was another "Horror" special, with Edward Bryant's report of the World Horror Convention in Toronto, an interview with Joe R. Lansdale, a round-table discussion between Peter Straub, John Clute and Gary K. Wolfe, and short opinion columns by Peter Crowther, William K. Schafer, Edward Bryant, Ellen Datlow, Ramsey Campbell, Caitlín R. Kiernan, Elizabeth Hand, Laird Barron, Paula Guran and Jeremy Lassen.

With its eleventh and twelfth issues, David Longhorn's *Supernatural Tales* returned to a twice-yearly schedule. Authors included Joel Lane, Gary McMahon, John L. Probert, Gary Fry, William I. I. Read, Michael Chislett and others, while Adam Golaski contributed a short article on the late Charles L. Grant. The editor announced that the small press magazine would return to a stapled booklet format with the next issue.

From F&M Publications, the three issues *One Eye Grey: Stories From Another London* were an attempt to revive the tradition of the old "Penny Dreadful" publication for a contemporary readership. Each issue contained a number of short stories, all written by Carl Gee and Chris Roberts, which were based on traditional folktales and ghost stories set in and around London.

Edited by Gavin J. Grant and Kelly Link, the two issues of *Lady Churchill's Rosebud Wristlet* contained slipstream stories, non-fiction and poetry by Karen Joy Fowler, Carol Emshwiller and others.

The two issues of Heather Shaw and Tim Pratt's *Flytrap* included contributions from Ray Vukcevich, Leslie What, Sonya Taaffe and Nick Mamatas, along with three poems by Jay Wentworth.

John Benson's *Not One of Us* also produced two more issues, which featured the usual mix of fiction and poetry. From the same publisher, the annual special was titled *Mindrash* and included poems and prose by Sonya Taaffe, Terry Black and others.

Along with the usual concoction of stories and poetry, issue #15 of *Whispers of Wickedness* contained a report from World Horror Convention 2007 by Gary McMahon.

Editor Gwilym Games' *Machenthology* featured tributes to the author by Jerome K. Jerome, M. P. Shiel, Lady Cynthia Asquith, Michael Powell, Gerald Suster, Iain Sinclair, Tanith Lee, Mark Samuels, Simon Clark, Tim Lebbon, Gwyneth Jones, China Miéville and others, along with some obscure journalism by Machen himself.

Edited by S. T. Joshi and Jack M. Haringa, *Dead Reckonings* was launched by Hippocampus Press as a bi-annual literary review magazine.

The Ghost Story Society produced two bumper volumes of *All Hallows* in 2007, adding up to more than 600 pages of news, reviews, articles and original fiction. Along with interviews with veteran editor E. F. Bleiler and writers Dan Simmons and Stephen Volk, retrospectives of *Devil Doll* (1964) and *The Queen of Spades* (1949), and the always entertaining "Ramsey Campbell, Probably" column (on Val Lewton and Japanese film-maker Hayao Miyazaki), there were forty-seven stories by John L. Probert, Gary McMahon, James Cooper, Gary Fry, Rhys Hughes and others.

The British Fantasy Society produced four editions of its newsletter, *Prism*. Jenny Barber was responsible for a double issue in the spring, and the editorial team of Jay Earles and Selina Lock took over for two attractively designed issues before handing over to Lee Harris to end the year with a full-colour edition. With the quality regularly improving, there were columns by Ramsey Campbell, James Barclay,

Mark Morris and Eric Brown, along with several reports on the 2006 FantasyCon and the usual news and reviews.

Under the guidance of new editorial team Peter Coleborn and Jan Edwards, the Society's *Dark Horizons* passed its fiftieth issue with stories and poetry by Joyce Carol Oates, H. P. Lovecraft, Karl Edward Wagner, Reggie Oliver, Mike Chinn, Ian Hunter, Allen Ashley and Anne Gay, non-fiction from David A. Sutton and Juliet E. McKenna, plus interviews with Oates, Ellen Datlow, John Connolly and artist Anne Sudworth.

As a Christmas present to BFS members, the December mailing included a special non-fiction chapbook, *H. P. Lovecraft in Britain: A Monograph* by Stephen Jones. Detailing the history of how Lovecraft had been published in the UK, the booklet was limited to 750 copies signed by the writer and artist Les Edwards, who provided the interior illustrations and a full-colour cover.

Sides from Cemetery Dance collected numerous non-fiction pieces by Peter Straub, mostly drawn from introductions, afterwords, essays and speeches, along with pseudo-critical commentary by the author's fictional alter ego and avowed *bête noire*, "Putney Tyson Ridge, Ph.D". The book was available in a signed, slipcased edition of 350 copies, and a traycased lettered edition of fifty-two copies ($200.00).

American author John Lauritsen claimed in his controversial book *The Man Who Wrote Frankenstein* that Mary Shelley was a fraud, and that poet Percy Bysshe Shelly was actually the author of the novel. "I go further than denying her authorship," said the Harvard-educated Lauritsen, "I deny that she was even a good writer."

Even the paranormal romance field started getting its own reference books. *The Dark-Hunter Companion* (aka *Sherrilyn Kenyon's Dark Hunter Handbook*) by Sherrilyn Kenyon and Alethea Kontis was about the series of books by Kenyon (aka "Kinley MacGregor"), including a travel guide around New Orleans and recipes.

Available as a print-on-demand volume from Hippocampus Press, *Warnings to the Curious: A Sheaf of Criticism on M. R. James* collected twenty-eight essays on the ghost story author, edited by S. T. Joshi and Rosemary Pardoe. From the same publisher, *W. Paul Cook: The Wandering Life of a Yankee Printer* edited by Sean Donnelly collected six articles about H. P. Lovecraft's friend and fellow amateur journalist, along with thirteen articles and twenty-five poems written by Cook under the pen name "Willis T. Crossman".

From McFarland & Company, *Horrifying Sex: Essays and Sexual Difference in Gothic Literature* edited by Ruth Bienstock Anolik collected sixteen essays about the work of Clive Barker, Edgar Allan Poe, Ann Radcliffe and others, along with author bibliographies and a general index.

McFarland's *Plagues, Apocalypses and Bug-Eyed Monsters: How Speculative Fiction Shows Us Our Nightmares* was a look at specific themes in societal fears by Heather Urbanski. Available from the same imprint, the title of *Robert E. Howard: A Collector's Descriptive Bibliography of American and British Hardcover, Paperback, Magazine, Special and Amateur Editions, with a Biography* pretty much summed up Leon Nielsen's study.

Jess Nevins' *Pulp Magazine Holdings Directory: Library Collections in North America and Europe* was an alphabetical index of titles and bibliographic information along with details of library holdings.

Edited by Benjamin Szumskyj, *Fritz Leiber: Critical Essays* collected eleven articles by Justin Leiber, S. T. Joshi and others, with a Foreword by John Pelan.

Published in two hardcover volumes ($175.00) by Greenwood Press, *Icons of Horror and the Supernatural: An Encyclopedia of Our Worst Nightmares* edited by S. T. Joshi looked at twenty-four major classic monsters and supernatural beings with alphabetically arranged essays by Mike Ashley, Brian Stableford, Stefan Dziemianowicz and Darrell Schweitzer, among others.

For those writers looking for new ideas, *Chambers Dictionary of the Unexplained* may have held the answer. A group of specialist contributors revealed the truth behind everything from life on Mars to the mystery of the *Mary Celeste* in more than 1,250 alphabetical entries.

The movie tie-ins of the year included *Ghost Rider* by Greg Cox, *Spider-Man 3* by Peter David, *Fantastic 4: Rise of the Silver Surfer* by Daniel Josephs, *Resident Evil: Extinction* by Keith R. A. DeCandido and *Memory* by Davlin Bennett.

Alan Dean Foster's *Transformers: Ghosts of Yesterday* was the official prequel to the movie *Transformers*, which he also wrote the novelization of.

Predator: Flesh and Blood by Jan Michael Friedman and Robert Greenberger was based on the Twentieth Century Fox movie series.

From Dark Horse Books, *The Bride of Frankenstein: Pandora's Box* by Elizabeth Hand and *The Wolf Man: Hunter's Moon* by Michael Jan Friedman were based on the classic Universal movies.

Richard Matheson's seminal SF vampire novel, *I Am Legend*, was reissued in a film tie-in edition with ten other stories. Stephen King's novella *The Mist* was published as a stand-alone movie title, while King's 2002 collection *Everything's Eventual* was also reissued to tie-in with the movie *1408* and went back into the US bestseller charts.

Based on the screenplay by Neil Gaiman and Roger Avary, *Beowulf* by Caitlín R. Kiernan included an Introduction by Gaiman.

Meanwhile, Gaiman's novel *Stardust*, based on his 1998 graphic novel with Charles Vess, appeared in the US in two different movie tie-in editions, one including eight pages of colour stills and the other featuring additional material. The original graphic novel was also reissued by DC Comics/Vertigo in a new edition that added around thirty pages of sketches and the original proposal for the book.

In *Doctor Who: Sting of the Zygons* by Stephen Cole, the Doctor and Martha travelled back to the Lake District in 1909, where a village was being terrorized by a giant, scaly monster.

Martin Day's *Doctor Who: Wooden Heart*, Jacqueline Rayner's *Doctor Who: The Last Dodo*, Mark Morris' *Doctor Who: Forever Autumn*, Paul Magrs' *Doctor Who: Sick Building*, Mark Michalovski's *Doctor Who: Wetworld*, Simon Guerrier's *Doctor Who: The Pirate Loop*, James Swallow's *Doctor Who: Peacemaker* and Trevor Baxendale's *Doctor Who: Wishing Well* all featured TV's tenth Doctor.

Also available in BBC Books' hardcover line were Andy Lane's *Torchwood: Slow Decay* and *Torchwood: Border Princess* by Dan Abnett, while Peter Anghelides' *Torchwood: Another Life* had the team of paranormal investigators tracking a serial killer through a rain-flooded Cardiff.

Supernatural: Nevermore by Keith R. A. DeCandido and *Supernatural: Witch's Canyon* by Jeff Mariotte were both based on The CW series, while several episodes of the NBC series formed the basis of Aury Wallington's *Heroes: Saving Charlie*.

Craig Shaw Gardner's *Battlestar Galactica: The Cylons' Secret* was the second novelization of the new series. It was followed by *Battlestar Galactica: Sagittarius is Bleeding* by Peter David and *Battlestar Galactica: Unity* by Steven Harper. *Stargate Atlantis: Entanglement* by Martha Wells was the sixth in that series.

Tanya Huff's 1990s "Victory Nelson" novels *Blood Price*, *Blood Trail*, *Blood Lines*, *Blood Pact* and *Blood Debt* were reissued to tie-in with the Lifetime TV series *Blood Ties*.

Buffy the Vampire Slayer: The Deathless by Keith R. A. DeCandido, *Dark Congress* by Christopher Golden and *One Thing or Your Mother* by Kristen Beyer were all based on the cancelled vampire TV show.

Scott Ciencin's *Charmed: High Spirits* was a young adult novelization based on another cancelled series.

Hellboy: The Dragon Pool by Christopher Golden was based on the movie and comic series created by Mike Mignola, while *30 Days of Night: Immortal Remains* by Steve Niles and Jeff Mariotte was based on the vampiric graphic novel series created by Niles.

Initially announced for spring 2001 publication, Tim Lucas' *Mario Bava: All the Colors of the Dark* finally saw print some six years late as a hernia-inducing 1,125-page hardcover. With a brief Introduction by Martin Scorsese and a Foreword by the late Riccardo Freda, this beautifully produced and designed volume told you more than you ever needed to know about the legendary Italian director and his work. Although arguably not worth the long wait, there was still no denying that it was probably the most impressive movie-related book of 2007.

However, a close runner-up for that title was also *Nightmare USA: The Untold Story of the Exploitation Independents*, from FAB Press, in which author Stephen Thrower took an incisive look at American independent film-makers of the 1970s and early 1980s.

Jonathan Rigby's *American Gothic: Sixty Years of Horror Cinema* was a welcome follow-up to the author's earlier volume *English Gothic: A Century of Horror Cinema* also published by Reynolds & Hearn. Profusely illustrated with black and white stills and posters, along with an impressive colour section, the book focused on many classic titles from the silent era up to the mid-1950s.

Paul Kane's *The Hellraiser Films and Their Legacy* from McFarland & Company took an illustrated look at the series created by Clive Barker, with an Introduction by Doug ("Pinhead") Bradley.

Universal Horrors: The Studio's Classic Films, 1931–1946 was a welcome updating of Tom Weaver, Michael Brunas and John Brunas' definitive study, originally published in 1990.

David Deal's *Television Fright Films of the 1970s* examined almost 150 made-for-TV features.

In McFarland's *Grimm Pictures: Fairy Tale Archetypes in Eight Horror and Suspense Films*, Walter Rankin explored the fairy tale motifs and themes in such movies as *Rosemary's Baby* and *Alien*.

Published by Collectable Press, *Bela Lugosi: Dreams and Night-mares* was written by Lugosi scholar Gary D. Rhodes with Richard Sheffield who, as a teenage horror fan, befriended the *Dracula* actor during his final years.

Issued as a hefty trade paperback by Telos Publishing, *Zombie-mania: 80 Movies to Die For* was a profusely illustrated guide by Dr Arnold T. Blumberg and Andrew Hershberger that included an extensive index of more than 550 titles and a brief Afterword by *Shaun of the Dead* actor Mark Donovan.

A 500-copy limited edition of the 2005 tie-in book of *MirrorMask*, signed by Neil Gaiman and Dave McKean, was published by Sub-terranean Press at $125.00. The twenty-six copy lettered and tray-cased edition ($500.00) even came with an original drawing by McKean.

Beowulf: The Script Book included both the motion-capture movie's first and final scripts by Neil Gaiman and Roger Avary, along with a sampling of some early concept artwork and story-boards, plus commentary by the writers.

Published by Titan Books, *Stardust: The Visual Companion* looked behind the making of the fairy tale fantasy movie based on the graphic novel series by Neil Gaiman and Charles Vess. Written by Stephen Jones, with an Introduction by Gaiman, the oversized volume also included the shooting script by Jane Goldman and director Matthew Vaughn.

Titan also issued revised and updated oversized hardcover editions of *Starring Sherlock Holmes: A Century of the Master Detective on Screen* by David Stuart Davies and *The Hammer Story: The Authorised History of Hammer Films* by Marcus Hearn and Alan Barnes.

Sinclair McKay's *A Thing of Unspeakable Horror: The History of Hammer Films* was an official history of the House of Hammer from Aurum Press, using new interview material from surviving cast and crew.

Published by Duke University Press, *Undead TV: Essays on Buffy the Vampire Slayer* edited by Elana Levine and Lisa Parks collected eight critical essays, a bibliography and a filmography.

British aristocrat Lord Henry Baltimore encountered an ancient evil on the bloody battlefields of The Great War, and his story was told from various points-of-view in *Baltimore, or, The Steadfast Tin Soldier and the Vampire*, a novel by Christopher Golden and Mike Mignola that included more than 150 black and white illustrations by *Hellboy* creator Mignola.

The Devil's Rose was an illustrated novel by (Gerald) Brom about a group of escapees from Hell terrorizing Texas.

Published by Feral House, *Mexican Pulp Art* was a full-colour collection of the weird, wild and just plain wacky paintings used for pulp novels and comics published South of the Border during the 1960s and 1970s. Maria Christina Tavera supplied a short, but informative, Introduction.

From NonStop Press, *Emshwiller: Infinity x Two* was a profusely-illustrated biography of the late pulp artist with text by Luis Ortiz and introductions by his widow Carol Emshwiller and art consultant Alex Eisenstein.

Edited and written by J. David Spurlock and Dean Motter, *Mythos: The Fantasy Art Realms of Frank Brunner* collected the work of the under-appreciated comics artist.

John Gunnison's *Walter Baumhofer: Pulp Art Masters* from Adventure House showcased the work of the acclaimed pulp illustrator of the 1930s and 1940s.

Vampyre: The Terrifying Lost Journal of Dr Cornelius Van Helsing was credited to "Cornelius Van Helsing and Gustav de Wolff" (Mary-Jane Knight) and was an illustrated young adult journal for vampire-hunters.

Spectrum 14: The Best in Contemporary Fantastic Art edited by Cathy Fenner and Arnie Fenner contained work by more than 300 artists, along with a profile of Grand Master Award recipient Syd Mead.

From the same editorial team, *Spectrum Presents: Rough Work by Frank Frazetta* featured sketches and conceptual designs by the legendary illustrator.

In July, British lawyer David Enright complained to his local Borders chain about finding a copy of Hergé's *The Adventures of Tintin in the Congo* for sale on their shelves. In a letter to the store, Enright said that he was "utterly astonished and aghast" at the book's depiction of black African people. As a result of his protest, specialist hate crime officers from the Hertfordshire police logged it as a "racist incident" and the bookstore agreed to move the volume from its children's section to the adult "graphics" area.

In a statement, Borders said that it "cannot and will not act as moral judge and jury in deciding what material we sell to our customers". Written in 1930, *Tintin in the Congo* was the second book by Belgium cartoonist Hergé about his popular boy detective, and although published in thirty-five languages around the world, it has only been available in the UK since 2005 and includes a warning about its subject matter.

Sixty-six years after he was created by Joe Simon, Captain America was killed off by Marvel Comics in March when the character was shot by an unknown sniper on the steps of a court house.

Written by Robin Furth and Peter David, with art by Jae Lee and Richard Isanove, *The Dark Tower: The Gunslinger Born* from Marvel Comics was a seven-issue miniseries based on the novel cycle by Stephen King that looked at the back story of hero Roland Deschain. The entire saga was subsequently collected as a graphic novel, with an Introduction by Ralph Macchio and an Afterword by King.

The Nightmare Factory from HarperCollins/Fox Atomic Comics adapted four stories ("The Last Feast of Harlequin", "Dream of a Mannikin", "Dr Locrian's Asylum" and "Teatro Grottesco") by Thomas Ligotti into graphic format, with introductions to each tale by the author.

The same imprints also issued *28 Days Later: The Aftermath*, Steve Niles' four-story graphic collection set in a world overrun with zombies, with art by Dennis Calero, Diego Olmos and Nat Jones.

Neil Gaiman's Neverwhere collected the first nine issues of the DC Comics/Vertigo adaptation of Gaiman's dark fantasy novel, written by Mike Carey and illustrated by Glenn Fabry.

Following on from *Batman and The Monster Men*, DC Comics' "Dark Moon Rising" graphic novel series continued with *Batman and The Mad Monk*, which collected the six-volume series written and edited by Matt Wagner. Another early adventure of the Dark Knight, it pitted Batman against a sacrificial vampire cult.

From DC's WildStorm Productions, *Supernatural: Origins* was a six-issue prequel series to The CW television show created by Eric Kripke. Writer Peter Johnson and artist Matthew Dow Smith charted the adolescent exploits of brothers Sam and Dean Winchester and their father John's quest to discover who or what killed his wife Mary.

Also from WildStorm, *Heroes: Volume One* collected the first thirty-four chapters of the online graphic series. Illustrated by Tim Sale (who produces Isaac's paintings in the show), with an Introduction by actor Masi Oka, the hardcover compilation was available in two editions, with different covers by Alex Ross and Jim Lee.

WildStorm also published graphic novel compilations of its *Friday the 13th*, *The Texas Chainsaw Massacre* and *A Nightmare on Elm Street* titles.

Comics writer turned *Lost* producer Brian K. Vaughan reworked a failed direct-to-DVD project featuring renegade Slayer Faith into a four-issue arc of Dark Horse's *Buffy the Vampire Slayer Season 8*. Created by Joss Whedon, the comics series was launched in March and continued the narrative several months after the TV show finished, with Buffy leading a team of potential new slayers.

From Marvel, *Anita Blake Vampire Hunter: Guilty Pleasures Volume 1* collected the six-issue comic series adapted from Laurell K. Hamilton's books by Stacie Ritchie and Jess Ruffner-Booth and illustrated by Brett Booth.

Vampire Kisses: Blood Relatives, Volume 1 was a graphic novel based on the YA vampire series by Ellen Schreiber.

The late Frank Hampson's classic spaceman hero, Dan Dare, was once again reincarnated for a new audience with his own title from Virgin Comics.

Edited by Tom Pomplun, *Graphic Classics Volume Fourteen: Gothic Classics* from Eureka Productions featured six illustrated adaptations of classic works, including J. Sheridan Le Fanu's "Carmilla", Mrs Ann Radcliffe's *The Mysteries of Udolpho* and Jane Austin's *Northanger Abbey*.

Published by Fantagraphics Books, *The Grave Robber's Daughter* was an original graphic novel by Richard Sala. This odd little fable featured short-tempered girl sleuth Judy Drood trapped in the cursed town of Obidiah's Glen, which had been taken over by demonic clowns.

With Rob Bowman, Ridley Scott, James Cameron, Michael Bay and Guillermo del Toro all previously attached to direct, and at one time set to star Tom Cruise, Michael Douglas or the current Governor of California, Arnold Schwarzenegger, Francis Lawrence's dull $100 million-plus *I Am Legend*, the third version of Richard Matheson's classic 1954 SF/vampire novel, featured Will Smith as the last man on earth, battling CGI zombies in New York. The film broke *The Lord of the Rings*' record for a US December weekend opening with a take of $76.5 million and went on to earn around $200 million before the end of the year. In the UK it went straight to #1.

Shia LaBeouf spied on his neighbours in *Disturbia*, a teen version of *Rear Window* that debuted in the US at #1 with a surprisingly low gross of $22.2 million. However, the twenty-year-old actor enjoyed a far bigger success later in the year playing a geeky teenager who discovered that his new car was actually a transforming Autobot in Michael Bay's big, loud and stupid *Transformers*, inspired by the

1980s children's TV cartoon series. Executive produced by Steven Spielberg, it had the biggest non-sequel opening ever in the US, debuting at #1 with a gross of $155.4 million. The film went on to make more than $300 million in America and shifted an impressive 8.3 million units in its first week on DVD.

An alien entity possessed Peter Parker (Tobey Maguire) and turned him into the black-suited "Venom" in Sam Raimi's dreary *Spider-Man 3*.

Gore Verbinski's *Pirates of the Caribbean: At the World's End*, the third in the overblown Walt Disney franchise, was better than the first sequel but still did not make a lot of sense.

Although Christopher Lee's singing cameo was cut when filming shut down in March after star Johnny Depp's daughter became seriously ill, Tim Burton's pared-down version of Stephen Sondheim's Broadway musical *Sweeney Todd: The Demon Barber of Fleet Street* still featured an impressive supporting cast that included Helena Bonham Carter (as pie-maker "Mrs Burton"), Alan Rickman, Timothy Spall and Sacha Baron Cohen.

In *Next*, based on a story by Philip K. Dick, Nicolas Cage's Las Vegas magician helped Julianne Moore's FBI agent prevent a nuclear attack on LA by seeing two minutes into the future. Much more successful, at the box-office if not in content, was *Ghost Rider*, in which the actor was miscast as Johnny Blaze, the flame-headed Marvel supernatural superhero. It set a President's Day opening record, taking $52 million in the US over its first weekend, passing the $100 million mark in just four weeks, and going on to amass a worldwide gross of more than $200 million.

Although the first film didn't deserve a sequel, *Fantastic Four: Rise of the Silver Surfer* opened at #1 in the US and eventually made $130 million.

David Slade's unimaginative *30 Days of Night* was based on the 2002 graphic novel by Steve Niles and Ben Templesmith, which used the hoary old idea about vampires existing in Alaska, where there is no sunlight for thirty days each winter. Stealing its ideas from *Dracula*, *Salem's Lot*, EC comics and a (much better) 1980s *Twilight Zone* episode, Josh Hartnett played the sheriff who discovered that the walking dead had come to his little town. It still managed to top the US box-office charts in October with a meagre $16 million gross.

Jim Carrey's obsessed dog-catcher was driven mad by a mysterious book in Joel Schumacher's mind-bending *The Number 23*, while John Cusack's travel writer checked himself into the titular haunted Manhattan hotel room in *1408*, based on the story by Stephen King.

Thomas Jane led a band of small-town survivors battling monstrous creatures in Frank Darabont's *The Mist*, based on King's 1980 novella with a surprisingly downbeat dénouement. Despite being one of the best Stephen King film adaptations ever, the film barely scraped into the US top ten during its opening week.

Kevin Costner's urbane family man *Mr Brooks* was really a serial killer goaded on by his dark alter-ego (played by a cackling William Hurt), and Sandra Bullock's perfect housewife couldn't work out whether her husband (Julian McMahon) was dead or not in *The Premonition*. Despite poor reviews, the film was Bullock's best opening ever, taking $17.8 million in its first week.

Hugh Jackman played an immortal conquistador and Rachel Weisz his dying wife in Darren Aronofsky's ludicrously pretentious fantasy *The Fountain*.

Although the character was dead, Tobin Bell's "Jigsaw" reached out from the grave through flashbacks in Darren Lynn Bousman's redundant *Saw IV*. It became the third entry in the sequel franchise to top the US charts with an opening weekend gross of $31.8 million.

Again presented by Quentin Tarantino, Eli Roth's "torture-porn" *Hostel Part II* failed to do much on either side of the Atlantic, despite making his victims women this time.

Soon-to-be-divorced couple Luke Wilson and Kate Beckinsdale ended up in a creepy motel in Nimorod Antal's neat little chiller *Vacancy*, and a catwalk model (TV actress Elisha Cuthbert) was abducted and tortured by a hooded tormentor in *Captivity*, based on a script by Larry Cohen and directed in Russia by a slumming Roland Joffé (Oscar-nominated for *The Killing Fields*).

Despite opening at #1 over the Labor Day weekend with a record-breaking $30.6 million, Rob Zombie's reworking of the classic slasher *Halloween*, with Malcolm McDowell in the Donald Pleasence role, came and went long before that iconic night. However, it still managed to become the third highest-grossing film in that particular series, behind the 1978 original and *Halloween: H20* (1998).

Although it co-starred Nicole Kidman and Daniel Craig, Oliver Hirschbiegel's $65 million *The Invasion*, the fourth screen version of Jack Finney's 1955 classic *Invasion of the Body Snatchers*, had the summer's third-lowest major opening in the US, taking just $6 million. Following a couple of title changes and an on-set car accident involving Kidman, German film-maker Hirschbiegel's original cut failed to impress producers in 2006. Andy and Larry Wachowski were reportedly brought in to re-write around a third of the movie, while James McTeigue directed an extra seventeen days of shooting at an added cost of $10 million.

Sean Bean took over the role of *The Hitcher* from Rutger Hauer for David Meyers' pointless remake of the 1986 classic.

Michael Caine (who was in the 1972 original with Sir Laurence Olivier) played a cat-and-mouse game with Jude Law in Kenneth Branagh's reworking of *Sleuth*, scripted by Harold Pinter and based on Anthony Shaffer's play.

Following the murder of his family by a crazed Craig Fairbrass, Nathan Fillion discovered he could see dead people and other people's auras in the workmanlike sequel *White Noise: The Light*.

A group of National Guard soldiers found themselves battling nuclear mutants in the disappointing sequel *The Hills Have Eyes 2*, and who knew we even needed the appalling inept *Alien vs. Predator: Requiem*?

The third entry in the video game franchise, Russell Mulcahy's *Resident Evil: Extinction* went straight into the US #1 slot at the end of September, taking $23.7 million over its opening weekend. This time, Milla Jovovich's moody heroine Alice briefly battled zombies in a ruined Las Vegas.

Despite being based on a novel and script by creator Thomas Harris, the misconceived prequel, *Hannibal Rising*, took just $13.1 million during its US opening weekend, apparently putting an end to the tired franchise.

When released in American movie theatres in April, audiences didn't really understand that they were getting two "B" movies for the price of one with *Grindhouse*, a homage to the exploitation double-bills of the 1970s. As a result, Quentin Tarantino's psycho road movie *Death Proof* and Robert Rodriguez's superior zombie sci-fi flick *Planet Terror* were subsequently re-cut and re-issued in extended versions on DVD, but without most of the fake trailers (directed by Rodriguez, Edgar Wright, Eli Roth and Rob Zombie) and reel "damage" that made the initial cinema experience so special.

Lindsay Lohan found time between her various trips in and out of rehab to star in *I Know Who Killed Me*, which took just $3.5 million during its opening weekend.

From the makers of the *Saw* movies, the excellent *Dead Silence* attempted to turn a cursed ventriloquist's dummy into a new franchise character.

Hilary Swank experienced the "Curse of Oscar" when she starred as a debunker of miracles investigating a Louisana town beset by the ten plagues of Egypt in *The Reaping*. Meanwhile, Adam Green's derivative "slasher" *Hatchet* was located in a Louisiana swamp and hyped as "old school American horror".

Directed by Hong Kong twins Danny and Oxide Pang, *The Messengers* was a derivative Asian-style horror movie set in a haunted North Dakota farmhouse.

Primeval featured a giant CGI crocodile attacking a US TV news crew in war-ravaged Burundi, and Lucy Liu played a victim turned vampire assassin is *Rise: Blood Hunter*.

A team of astronauts had to reignite a dying sun in Danny Boyle's low budget *Sunshine*, while American troops claimed control of a virus-infected London as survivor Robert Carlyle tried to protect his family from the scourge of the walking dead in Juan Carlos Fresnadillo's zombie sequel *28 Weeks Later*.

Carrie Anne Moss and Billy Connolly starred in the low-budget Canadian zombie comedy *Fido*, and Ron Perlman battled the elements, literally, on an Alaskan oil-drilling station in Larry Fessenden's "B" movie chiller *The Last Winter*.

Brit actress Emily Blunt played an American college girl menaced by a possible psycho and something creepy in the woods in Greg Jacobs' atmospheric *Wind Chill*, produced by George Clooney and Steven Soderbergh.

From New Zealand, *Black Sheep* was a silly low-budget movie in which genetically modified killer sheep went on a bloody rampage, while college kids on a remote island were terrorized by wild dogs in *The Breed*, executive produced by Wes Craven.

The impressive ensemble cast of David Fincher's intricate *Zodiac* investigated the real-life Bay Area serial killings of the late 1960s and early 1970s.

Based on an Off-Broadway play, Ashley Judd played a woman who shared her boyfriend's paranoid hallucinations about invisible insects in William Friedkin's *Bug*.

David Lynch's three-hour *Inland Empire* starred Laura Dern as an actress who lost all sense of reality – apparently much like the director. Gael Garcia Bernal couldn't tell dreams from real life in Michel Gondry's equally perplexing *The Science of Sleep*.

Brad Dourif played an alien working for the CIA in Werner Herzog's baffling *The Wild Blue Yonder*, and Francis Ford Coppola only managed to alienate audiences with his self-indulgent *Youth Without Youth*, about a Hungarian linguistics expert (Tim Roth) who mysteriously grew younger after being hit by lightning.

Despite a cast that included Dwayne ("The Rock") Johnson, Sarah

Michelle Gellar and Justin Timberlake, the futuristic flop *Southland Tales* indicated that Richard Kelly's debut success, *Donnie Darko*, might have been a fluke.

A photographer was haunted by the woman whose death he caused in the Thai ghost story *Shutter*, and teenagers were menaced by zombies and psychos in *Zibahkhana (Hell's Ground)*, shot in a month in Pakistan.

The Russian-made *Day Watch* was the second in the contemporary vampire trilogy, following *Night Watch*, while people battled their zombie doubles in a haunted Russian mansion in *The Abandoned*.

Vincent Cassell portrayed a homicidal shepherd preying on a group of French teens in a ruined château in Kim Chapiron's *Satan (Sheitan)*.

After her mother was murdered in her own home, Emilie Dequenne's TV sound engineer started recording sounds from the past to discover the culprit in Alante Kavaite's *Ecoute Le Temps*.

Building on its Christmas 2006 release, *Night at the Museum* took more than $200 million in just five weeks at the US box-office.

Morgan Freeman's God told Steve Carell's everyman to build an ark in the flop comedy sequel *Evan Almighty*, while Vince Vaughn played the bitter older brother of Santa Claus (Paul Giamatti) in the Christmas comedy *Fred Claus*.

From the same team behind the overrated *Shaun of the Dead*, *Hot Fuzz* was an enjoyable British comedy that owed more than a nod to *The Wicker Man* and the Italian *giallo* genre.

Harry Potter and the Order of the Phoenix was the best in the series to date, with the boy wizard leading a Hogwarts resistance movement against Lord Voldemort (Ralph Fiennes) and the forces of evil and repression. David Yates' darker fifth instalment in the *Harry Potter* franchise had its premiere in Tokyo in June. When the film opened the following month in forty-four territories, it was #1 in every market in which it played, making it the biggest-ever opening for a Warner Bros. picture. Although it took $77.4 million in the US and Canada across its debut weekend, it still opened behind *Spider-Man 3*, *Shrek the Third* and the latest *Pirates of the Caribbean*. However, *Order of the Phoenix* ended up grossing nearly $1 billion dollars worldwide, and in some territories the climactic battle scene was shown in 3-D in IMAX cinemas.

Christopher Lee had a blink-and-you'll-miss-him moment in Chris Weitz's *The Golden Compass*, based on the "His Dark Materials" trilogy by Philip Pullman, which also reunited stars Nicole Kidman and Daniel Craig. Despite costing New Line an estimated $250–300 million to make and market, the film only took $25.8 million on its opening weekend in the US, although it did debut at #1 on both sides of the Atlantic.

Michelle Pfeiffer's wicked witch was on the trail of a fallen star (a miscast Clare Danes) in Matthew Vaughn's fantasy adventure *Stardust*, based on the graphic novel written by Neil Gaiman and illustrated by Charles Vess. Despite a disappointing US opening weekend gross of just $9.2 million, mostly positive reviews and good word-of-mouth resulted in it taking almost £15 million in the UK, where it was the #1 movie, and grossing more than $125 million worldwide.

The first entry in a proposed series loosely based on Susan Cooper's superb series of award-winning children's fantasy books, *The Dark is Rising* was released in America under the pointless title *The Seeker*. Despite a cast that included Ian McShane and Christopher Eccleston, it quickly died at the box office on both sides of the Atlantic.

Based on a Swedish young adult novel, *The Invisible* involved a poetic high school student (the likeable Justin Chatwin) returning as a spirit to haunt and ultimately fall in love with the delinquent classmate (Margarita Levieva) who was responsible for nearly killing him.

Agnes Brucker played a teenage werewolf in Bucharest in *Blood and Chocolate*, adapted from a YA novel by Annette Curtis Klause.

Dakota Fanning teamed up with a talking spider (voiced by Julia Roberts) to save a pet piglet in *Charlotte's Web*, the second film version of E. B. White's classic 1952 children's book.

A young boy (Daniel Magder) befriended a Canadian lake monster in *Mee-Shee: The Water Giant*, while two Scottish children in 1940s Scotland discovered a mysterious egg that hatched into a friendly sea monster in *The Water Horse: Legend of the Deep*, directed by Jay Russell (not to be confused with the horror author of the same name).

Bob Shaye's *The Last Mimzy* was a children's film based on the 1943 SF story by "Lewis Padgett" (Henry Kuttner and C. L. Moore), and two children created their own fantasy world in the disappointing *Bridge to Terabithia*.

Natalie Portman inherited a magical New York toyshop from an eccentric 243-year-old magician (Dustin Hoffman) in the family fantasy *Mr Magorium's Wonder Emporium*.

Susan Sarandon's evil queen banished a cartoon fairy-tale princess (the impressive Amy Adams) to real-life New York City in Walt Disney's delightfully referential live-action and animated spoof *Enchanted*. It opened at #1 in the US with a take of $49.1 million.

Filmed in the "performance capture" technique previously used for *The Polar Express*, a digitally-enhanced Ray Winstone battled a hideous monster (voiced by Crispin Glover) and its sexy demonic mother (Angelina Jolie) in Robert Zemeckis' *Beowulf*, scripted by Neil Gaiman and Roger Avery and based on the tenth-century Anglo Saxon saga. During its November opening weekend in America, when it went to #1 with a below-expectation gross of $28.1 million, the filmed earned twice as much from IMAX theatres equipped with digital 3-D projectors than it did in all the other cinemas combined.

Disney/Pixar had to explain to audiences how to pronounce the title of *Ratatouille*, about a French rat that became a gourmet cook. Peter O'Toole was among those who supplied the voices. Meanwhile, Disney's loud and frenetic animated time-travel comedy *Meet the Robinsons* had seven credited scriptwriters.

The busy Shia LeBeouf and an iconic Jeff Bridges supplied the voices of surfing penguins in Columbia's animated *Surf's Up*.

The CGI-created *TMNT* (Teenage Mutant Ninja Turtles) did better than anyone expected, topping the US box-office with a $24.3 million gross when it was released in March. Made for under $40 million, with most of the animation being produced in Hong Kong, Sarah Michelle Gellar and Patrick Stewart were among the voice cast.

Jason Lee played songwriter David Seville, creator of *Alvin and the Chipmunks*, in Tim Hill's CGI film about the high-pitched rodents from the 1960s. The film opened at a healthy $44.3 million in the US and even managed to take more than £7 million in the UK.

Robert De Niro, Madonna, Snoop Dog, David Bowie and Harvey Keitel were among some of the surprising names that contributed their voices to Luc Besson's CGI fantasy *Arthur and the Invisibles*.

The third and fourth books in Ursula K. Le Guin's classic fantasy series were adapted by Japanese animator Goro Miyazaki as *Tales from Earthsea*, featuring the voices of Timothy Dalton, Willem Dafoe and Mariska Hargitay.

A psychiatric researcher entered the dreams of her patients as the eponymous *Paprika* in Satoshi Kon's adult *anime*.

DreamWorks' *Shrek the Third* may have suffered from the curse of "threequels", but that did not stop the CGI fairytale opening at #1 on both sides of the Atlantic and taking more than $300 million at the US box-office.

Co-writer Jerry Seinfeld and Renée Zellweger were among the voice cast of *Bee Movie*, from the same studio.

Blade Runner: The Final Cut was the seventh(!) version of Ridley Scott's 1982 movie.

How times have changed. Hammer's classic *Dracula* starring Peter Cushing and Christopher Lee was reissued theatrically in the UK for Halloween and provoked a debate in the media when it received a BBFC warning lower than the *Harry Potter* movies. When initially released in 1958, Terence Fisher's film carried a "X" certificate, restricting it at that time to those over sixteen years of age. For its latest remastered outing on the big screen, it was given a "12A" rating along with a "mild horror" advisory, allowing anyone twelve years or older to see it, or younger children accompanied by an adult. While sharing the same certification, the most recent *Potter* films were considered to contain "moderate horror".

The 79th Annual Academy Awards were hosted by Ellen DeGeneres in Hollywood on 25 February. Among a decidedly mixed bag of nominees, *Pirates of the Caribbean: Dead Man's Chest* won the Visual Effects award and George Miller's *Happy Feet* was the winner in the Animated Feature category. Guillermo del Toro's *Pan's Labyrinth* picked up three Oscars, for Make-up, Cinematography and Art Direction, but missed out on the more prestigious award for Foreign Language Film.

London's annual FrightFest fantasy film festival opened on 23 August with New Zealand director Jonathan King's comedy gore movie, *Black Sheep*. Other films screened over the weekend included Mexico's *KM 31*, about two sisters with a telepathic link, the Norwegian serial-killer thriller *Cold Prey*, and *Shrooms*, in which a group of American college students encountered Irish magic mushrooms and yet another crazed killer. When released in November, the latter took a pathetic £31,000 at the UK box-office.

For the second year, *Horrorfest* was screened in more than 350 American movie theatres for ten days in early November. It again included eight new "Films to Die For".

The wet summer in Britain resulted in the largest number of cinema admissions in forty years. Numbers were up twenty-seven per cent over the previous summer to 50.8 million, with a record £904 million taken at the box office. This was the third-highest since records began in the 1990s.

Harry Potter and the Order of the Phoenix was the UK's top movie, with a gross of nearly £50 million. With a combined income of more than £2.2 billion ($4.47 billion), it was announced in September that the *Harry Potter* films have now officially taken more in worldwide box-office sales than the twenty-two *James Bond* movies and the entire *Star Wars* series (but only if you don't adjust those films' grosses for inflation).

Britain's other highest-grossing films included *The Golden Compass* (£23.52 million), *Hot Fuzz* (£20.99 million) and *Stardust* (£14.85 million).

In early November, the first strike by movie and television writers since 1988 shut down the industry for the rest of the year. Writers were joined by many actors on picket lines outside Hollywood and New York studio facilities as they demanded a large increase in what they are paid for use of their work on digital distribution systems.

Scott Thomas' *Flight of the Living Dead: Outbreak on a Plane* was an enjoyable direct-to-DVD movie featuring Kevin J. O'Connor and Dale Midkiff and involving flesh-eating zombies at 30,000 feet.

William Atherton starred in Gregory Wilson's adaptation of Jack Ketchum's *The Girl Next Door*, co-scripted by Daniel Farrands and Philip Nutman, which went straight to DVD.

Ignoring the clever premise of its predecessor, *Wrong Turn 2* was about a group of reality TV contestants being picked off in the woods by a family of inbred hillbillies. Henry Rollins' former marine was one of the first casualties.

Return to the House on Haunted Hill was a direct-to-DVD sequel to the 1999 remake, but without any of the original cast members, and Richard Matheson was thankfully not credited on the belated sequel *Stir of Echoes 2: The Homecoming*, starring Rob Lowe.

Genre veterans Kane Hodder and Michael Berryman starred in the direct-to-DVD *Ed Gein: The Butcher of Plainfield*.

Species: The Awakening featured a slumming Ben Cross, James Denton starred in the zombie Western *Undead or Alive*, and Adrienne Barbeau and *Buffy*'s Nicholas Brendon were top-billed in *Unholy*, about a occult Nazi legacy.

Dougray Scott played a 300-year-old genetically-engineered vampire who teamed up with Saffron Burrows' police detective in *Perfect Creature*.

Blade: House of Chthon was an unrated, extended feature-length version of the vampire TV series pilot, which also included a documentary and commentary by the writers and director.

Network's first commercial release of the dull 1979 TV version of M. R. James' *Casting of the Runes*, featuring Jan Francis and Iain Cuthbertson, was thankfully supplemented with *Mr Humphreys and His Inheritance*, a rarely-screened James adaptation made for ITV schools programmes in 1976, and the excellent 1995 documentary *A Pleasant Terror*.

In February, 20th Century Fox Home Video released *The Mr Moto Collection Vol.2* featuring Peter Lorre as the wily detective in *Mr Moto's Gamble*, *Mr Moto in Danger Island*, *Mr Moto Takes a Vacation* and *Mr Moto's Last Warning*.

Released for Halloween, *Fox Horror Classics* contained three 1940s films from the studio, *The Lodger*, *The Undying Monster* and *Hangover Square*, all directed by John Brahm. The set also included informative documentaries on Brahm, the making of *The Lodger* and star Laird Cregar, plus two radio show adaptations featuring Vincent Price.

Issued by Fox under the "M-G-M Scream Legends" banner, the *Vincent Price* boxed set contained *Tales of Terror*, *Twice Told Tales*, *The Abominable Dr Phibes*, *Dr Phibes Rises Again*, *Theater of Blood*, *Madhouse*, *Witchfinder General* and a "Disc of Horrors" containing three new documentaries. *Witchfinder General* was also available on a separate "Midnite Movies" disc with an audio commentary and documentary.

The second half of the second season of 1960s Irwin Allen TV series *Voyage to the Bottom of the Sea* was also available from Fox.

Monsters and Madmen from Criterion was a four-disc set containing the Richard Gordon-produced movies *The Haunted Strangler* (aka *Grip of the Strangler*), *Corridors of Blood*, *The Atomic Submarine* and *First Man Into Space*.

Warner Bros' four "Cult Camp Classics" boxed sets each included three movies with selected commentaries. Best of the batch was "Sci-Fi Thrillers" that featured *Attack of the 50 Foot Woman*, *Queen of Outer Space* and *The Giant Behemoth*.

Kino's masterfully restored version of F. W. Murnau's silent *Nosferatu* was available on a two-disc set that included a documentary about the film's creation and a version with German intertitles.

Helen McCrory's Dr Victoria Frankenstein used stem-cell research to create a sympathetic Monster (Julian Bleach) from the DNA of her dying son in writer/director Jed Mercurio's updated adaptation of *Frankenstein*, made for British television and shown in October.

Scottish actor Dougray Scott played contemporary versions of *Dr Jekyll and Mr Hyde* in yet another redundant variation on the story, this time filmed in Canada.

Dan Castellaneta portrayed Hollywood director Cecil B. DeMille in the Sci Fi Channel's *Sands of Oblivion*, in which an ancient Egyptian curse haunted the set of the 1923 movie, *The Ten Commandments*. Stars Morena Baccarin and Adam Baldwin were reunited from *Firefly*.

A group of teenage partygoers desecrated a graveyard during a friend's wake and released three vengeful ghosts in *Gravedancers*, while the dead rose from their watery graves in a flooded town in *Beneath Still Waters*.

Kevin Sorbo's unlikely environmental activist priest found himself battling a slimy subterranean entity in *Something Beneath*, and backwoods locals (including veteran Richard Moll) tried to sacrifice seven stranded teenagers to the *Headless Horseman*, in another variation on the *Sleepy Hollow* plot.

Adrian Paul returned as the immortal Duncan MacLeod, searching for the origin of his power in Sci Fi's TV movie sequel *Highlander: The Source*. Featuring an unlikely Cloris Leachman, *Lake Placid 2* was a big croc sequel to the 1999 original, while *Pumpkinhead 4: Blood Feud* was shot in Romania with Lance Henriksen briefly reprising his role as a ghost.

The actor didn't fare much better as a crazed jungle doctor using a sacred cave full of spiders to facilitate his organ-harvesting operation in *In the Spider's Web*.

Oscar-winner F. Murray Abraham was definitely slumming as a crazed anthropology professor attempting to capture a breed of intelligent prehistoric ape in *BloodMonkey*.

Gary Busey's Southern sheriff was on the hunt for an escaped tiger that shared a mystical connection with a young boy (Ty Wood) in *Maneater*, and a group of dumb college kids who ran over a bear cub were justifiably eaten by its revenge-seeking mother in David DeCoteau's awful *Grizzly Rage*.

James Van Beek's ocean scientist teamed up with a local sheriff (Alexandro Castillo) to battle a giant squid threatening a small fishing community in Gary Yates' better-than-it-had-any-right-to-be *Eye of the Beast*.

Sean Patrick Flanery's small town sheriff had to deal with ravenous ravens in *Kaw*, a surprisingly effective homage to Alfred Hitchcock's *The Birds* that also featured that film's star, Rod Taylor.

Patrick Muldoon's ex-marine turned ski instructor and Vanessa Williams' scientist encountered six escaped giant mutant arachnids in Sci Fi's *Ice Spiders*. Roger Corman executive produced *Supergator*, in which a slumming Kelly McGillis' bio-engineered alligator snacked on Hawaiian tourists.

The crew of a World War II American bomber was forced down behind enemy lines in France, where they discovered that sinister Nazi forces had reanimated an ancient race of monsters in Ayton Davis' action-packed *Reign of the Gargoyles*.

Stephen Baldwin's museum guard was transported to the Dark Ages in *Stan Lee's Harpies*. *Buffy*'s Amber Benson turned up in *Gryphon* as a princess who battled a flying monster conjured up by a wizard, while Nicholas Brendon, another veteran of the vampire slayer's show, played a fire-fighter who found himself confronted by an alien creature unleashed as a result of a solar flare in *Fire Serpent*, created by executive producer William Shatner.

Chris Bruno starred in *Grendel*, based on the epic poem *Beowulf*, and Tom Wopat's brain was taken over by alien-controlled ants in *The Hive*.

Zooey Deschanel, Alan Cumming and Richard Dreyfuss starred in a futuristic deconstruction of *The Wizard of Oz* in the Sci Fi Channel's three-part miniseries *Tin Man*.

The Gathering was a two-part Lifetime miniseries about a Manhattan doctor (Peter Gallagher) searching for his missing wife (Kristin Lehman), who became involved with a New York coven of witches controlled by Peter Fonda's charismatic leader.

Teenagers Alexz Johnson and Magda Apanowicz made a date with a book that brought demons to life in the LMN's *Devil's Diary*, which also featured Brian Krause. On the same channel, Victoria Pratt feared she had given birth to Satan's offspring in *Hush Little Baby*, a psychiatrist treated a patient literally plagued by demons in *They Come Back*, and Antonio Sabato Jr was one of the passengers aboard a plane overrun with killer ants in *Destination: Infestation*.

Also on LMN, *The Haunting of Sorority Row* was set during Pledge Week and starred Leighton Meester.

In the BBC's feature-length *Empathy*, Stephen Moyer played a former convict who used his empathic powers to help a pair of police detectives catch the murderer of two teenage girls.

Tiffani Thiessen and French Stewart starred in the three-hour *Pandemic* on Hallmark, and Valerie Bertinelli's eponymous widowed clairvoyant attempted to solve a series of local murders in *Claire*, from the same channel.

Following *The Ruby in the Smoke*, Billie Piper returned as Victorian financial consultant/amateur detective Sally Lockhart in the BBC's *The Shadow in the North*, based on the novel by Philip Pullman. This time Sally was involved with stage magicians, seances, psychics, ghosts and murder. There was also a nice in-joke involving Bram Stoker.

From BBC Scotland, John McKay's Edinburgh-set *Reichenbach Falls* was based on an original idea by crime writer Ian Rankin (who turned up in a cameo). While investigating an ancient mystery, Alec Newman's police detective found himself haunted by the literary ghosts of Professor John Bell (John Sessions) and Sir Arthur Conan Doyle (Richard Wilson).

Eddie Kaye Thomas' animal-control officer kept a lycanthropic secret from his fiancée (Autumn Reeser) in the ABC Family werewolf comedy *Nature of the Beast*.

A girl (Emily Osment) found a strange book that took her into a macabre cartoon world in *R. L. Stine's The Haunting Hour: Don't Think About It* on the Cartoon Network, and nine-year-old Roxy Hunter (Aria Wallace) discovered that her new home was haunted in Nickelodeon's *Roxy Hunter and the Mystery of the Moody Ghost*.

Tia and Tamera Mowry were reunited as the twin witches searching for their missing father on the Disney Channel's *Twitches Too*.

Hellboy: Blood & Iron was the second animated feature from the Cartoon Network, based on the characters created by Mike Mignola. Ron Perlman, John Hurt and Selma Blair were among the voice artists who contributed to this muddled tale involving Countess Bathory.

The first episode of the 2007 season of the BBC's increasingly popular *Doctor Who* had more than a nod to *Dracula* as David Tennant's space and time-traveller encountered new companion Martha Jones (Freema Agyeman) on the Moon, where they battled a blood-sucking alien.

Subsequent episodes featured a young William Shakespeare (Dean Lennox Kelly) and a trio of witches, another appearance by The Face of Boe (whose surprising origin was revealed), and a Daleks' invasion of 1930s Manhattan.

Based on his 1995 novel, Paul Cornell's two-part episode, which found the Doctor hiding in pre-First World War England, having lost his memory and menaced by an army of creepy scarecrows, was not only the best episode of the year, but one of the best television dramas of 2007. Almost as good was "Blink", a stand-alone episode by Steven Moffat in which teenager Sally Sparrow (Carey Mulligan) was menaced in a dilapidated house by living statues. The Doctor and Martha were barely featured.

Although the final three episodes included the return of companion Captain Jack Harkness (John Barrowman) and a welcome guest appearance by Derek Jacobi, John Simm's much-anticipated turn as The Master was sadly misjudged as he overplayed his role as a Tony Blair-like megalomaniac.

Following on directly from the season finale, Tennant's new Doctor encountered his 1980s incarnation (Peter Davison) in an original bridging sequence scripted by Steven Moffat for the BBC's *Children in Need* fundraiser shown on 16 November.

This vignette led into the annual *Doctor Who* Christmas special. Despite featuring Australian singer Kylie Minogue as a waitress and a bunch of murderous robot angels aboard a *Titanic* space-cruiser, Russell T. Davis' *Voyage of the Damned* was a disappointing rehash of clichés from *The Poseidon Adventure*. At least the supporting cast featured such stalwarts as Clive Swift, Geoffrey Palmer and Bernard Cribbins.

Meanwhile, the first season of spin-off "adult" show *Torchwood* limped to an end in January with an episode in which Barrowman's bisexual Captain Jack and Naoko Mori's Tosh travelled back in time to a World War II dance hall, while a demonic "Beast" came through the Rift and threatened to destroy the Earth in the apocalyptic season finale "End of Days".

Another *Doctor Who* spin-off show, aimed at children, was much better. *The Sarah Jane Adventures* kicked off on New Year's Day with an hour-long pilot in which the Doctor's former companion from the 1970s, Sarah Jane Smith (Elisabeth Sladen), teamed up with her thirteen-year-old neighbour Maria (Yasmin Paige) and others to confront alien menaces. Ten half-hour shows followed. After dealing with ludicrous aliens the Slitheen, Sarah Jane and her young friends encountered an order of creepy nuns that protected Medusa, Sarah Jane's life was usurped by an embittered dead schoolfriend (Jane Asher), and robot dog K-9 returned to save the Earth in the season finale.

James Nesbitt overacted as Dr Tom Jackman, a descendant of the infamous *Jekyll*, in writer Steven Moffat's BBC series of the same name. After Jackman discovered that he was the product of a decades-spanning conspiracy, the final show (retitled *Hyde*) cleverly tied everything into Robert Louis Stevenson's original novel, but then spoiled it with a silly "shock" revelation. The excellent supporting cast included Gina Bellman, Denis Lawson, Meera Syal and new Bionic Woman Michelle Ryan.

John Simm returned in February as police detective Sam Tyler, thrown back in time to 1973 in the BBC's second – and presumably final – series of *Life on Mars*. After doing his best to convince his remarkably un-PC boss DCI Gene Hunt (the wonderful Philip Glenister) to clean up his act, Tyler finally made it back to the twenty-first century in the enigmatic last episode but had to choose where his future lay. *Ashes to Ashes*, a follow-up series set in the 1980s, was announced.

The second season of Showtime's darkly comic *Dexter* saw Michael C. Hall's sympathetic serial killer under suspicion by various characters, including Keith Carradine's laconic FBI Agent Lundy and sexy stalker Lila (Brit actress Jaime Murray), as his murderous past was discovered decomposing on the Miami seabed and the police started hunting among their own for the "Bay Harbor Butcher".

After ABC's *Lost* hit an all-time ratings low in February, the producers optimistically announced that the increasingly dull show would eventually end in 2010 with the next three seasons reduced from twenty-two to sixteen episodes apiece. Meanwhile, Jack (Matthew Fox) and Kate (Evangeline Lilly) were shown together in the future, and Dominic Monaghan's Charlie was the series' latest fatal casualty in the two-hour season three finale in May. Season four kicked off with a number of new characters joining the already overburdened cast on the island, plus even more flashbacks and flashforwards.

Meanwhile, NBC's equally meandering *Heroes* featured guest appearances by *Star Trek*'s George Takei, *Doctor Who*'s Christopher Eccleston (as "Claude", an invisible man) and comics guru Stan Lee, introduced the evil Sylar's mother, and then decided to confuse viewers even further with a "possible future" episode. The second season opened with Hiro (Masi Oka) trapped in ancient Japan. *Star Trek*'s Nichelle Nichols subsequently turned up as a kindly New Orleans grandmother who looked after two heroes, while Kristen Bell (star of the cancelled *Veronica Mars*) joined the cast as an electrical-powered Company operative after turning down a role in *Lost*. The premature December finale (a result of the writers' strike) left a number of heroes in perilous situations.

The second season of Showtime's *Masters of Horror* anthology series ended with Rob Schmidt's "Right to Die", David J. Schow's adaptation of John Farris' "We All Scream for Ice Cream" directed by Tom Holland, Stuart Gordon's clever reworking of "The Black Cat" featuring regular collaborator Jeffrey Combs as a psychotic Edgar Allan Poe, Peter Medak's silly version of Bentley Little's cannibal story "The Washingtonians", and Norio Tsuruta's atmospheric J-horror treatment of Koji Suzuki's ghost story "Dream Cruise", filmed in Japan.

Hosted by Stephen Hawking's voice (although it could have been anyone), ABC's *Masters of Science Fiction* ran for just four one-hour episodes in August. Based on original stories by John Kessel, Howard Fast, Robert A. Heinlein and Harlan Ellison (who turned up in a cameo in his episode, "The Discarded"), the dull *Outer Limits*-style show featured such actors as Sam Waterston, Judy Davis, Terry O'Quinn, William B. Davis, Malcolm McDowell, Anne Heche, John Hurt and Brian Dennehy.

After encountering an imaginary friend, a bank-robbing shape-shifter, apparent angels, a highway ghost, a female werewolf (Emmanuelle Vaugier), Hollywood horrors, a wish-granting Djinn and their dead dad (Jeffrey Dean Morgan), Sam Winchester (Jared Padalecki) was transported to a ghost town by the Yellow-Eyed Demon in the two-part Season Two finale of *Supernatural*, where Dean (Jensen Ackles) had to make the ultimate sacrifice for his brother.

Despite US audience figures dropping below three million, The CW decided to continue *Supernatural* for a third season, as Dean enjoyed his last year of life and two tough new female characters (played by Katie Cassidy and Lauren Cohan) were introduced. In the season opener, the brothers confronted the demonic Seven Deadly Sins, which they had inadvertently released from Hell. For the Halloween episode they investigated a series of Grimm fairy tale killings connected to the Crossroad Demon (Sandra McCoy), and a Christmas special involved pagan cannibalism.

Bill Patterson returned as Dr Douglas Monaghan in a special two-part *Sea of Souls* on BBC in April. Now apparently working alone and possessed of psychic powers, Monaghan investigated a strange painting found in a haunted Scottish manor house that was apparently linked to the occult group The Golden Dawn.

Following on from such serious TV shows as *Brimstone* and *The Collector*, The CW's comedy horror *Reaper* found Bret Harrison's warehouse worker Sam Oliver discovering on his twenty-first birthday that his parents sold his soul to an urbane Devil (a mahogany-tanned Ray Wise). In return for a life-lesson every week, he had to track down escapees from Hell with the help of his goofy friend (Tyler Labine). The pilot episode was directed by Kevin Smith.

NBC's sci-spy comedy *Chuck* was about another nerdy warehouse employee (the likeable Zachary Levi) who became a reluctant secret agent after a database full of government secrets was downloaded into his brain.

From the same network, *Journeyman* channelled such shows as *Quantum Leap* and *Early Edition* as San Francisco newspaper reporter Dan Vasser (Brit actor Kevin McKidd) mysteriously bounced back and forth through time helping people while encountering his dead former fiancée (Moon Bloodgood). In the final episode, Dan met fellow time-traveller Evan (Don McManus) from the not-too-distant past.

Meanwhile, after debuting in its slot earlier in the month at #1 with thirteen million viewers, the horror movie-themed Halloween episode of the quirky *Pushing Daisies* set a new low (8.6 million) for the ABC series, in which pie-maker Ned (Lee Pace) used his magic touch to return the dead to life or send them back beyond the veil. Created by Bryan Fuller and Barry Sonnenfeld, Anna Friel co-starred, Paul Reubens guest-starred and veteran Jim Dale supplied the cute storybook narration.

Co-produced by actor Nicolas Cage and based on the popular novels by Jim Butcher, the first season of Sci Fi Channel's entertaining *The Dresden Files* featured likeable British actor Paul Blackthorne as sorcerer-turned-PI Harry Dresden and Terrence Mann as his talking skull/mentor Bob. Together with Valerie Cruz's Chicago police detective, they found themselves involved with monsters, ghosts, werewolves, vampires and rival magicians.

Based on Tanya Huff's popular series of "Vicki Nelson" novels, *Blood Ties* from Lifetime Television turned out to be a clichéd collection of old horror ideas dressed up for the post-*Buffy* generation. Christina Cox played the former police detective-turned-PI who investigated the supernatural with 450-year-old vampire Henry Fitzroy (a miscast Kyle Schmid) and former partner Detective Mike Celluci (Dylan Neal).

It's hard to imagine how a show dealing with voodoo curses, psychic children, revenge-seeking ghosts, incubi, Windigos [sic], Gorgons, Egyptian gods and brainwashing cults could be so tedious, but *Blood Ties* managed it every time. The only real surprise was why an obviously slumming Julian Sands guest-starred in a two-part episode as obsessed vampire-hunter Javier Mendoza.

The subsequent season was an improvement, with Danny Trejo turning up as a revived Mayan Mummy sorcerer, and Vicki reliving the same day over and over again. However, the second season finale was pulled by Lifetime from its broadcast schedule and was only available to US viewers on the station's website.

After almost completely reworking and recasting the original pilot episode, CBS came up with its own new vampire private investigator show with *Moonlight*, starring Australian actor Alex O'Loughlin as undead LA detective Mick St John who could literally smell the past. *Angel* creator David Greenwalt left the anaemic series after only a couple of episodes.

If vampires weren't enough, Angels were also spreading their wings all over the US TV schedules. Leon Rippy's tobacco-chewing angel Earl watched over Holly Hunter's abrasive Oklahoma detective on TNT's *Saving Grace*. ABC Family aired three new episodes of *Fallen* in early August, about Aaron Corbett (Paul Wesley), a Nephilim charged with returning all the fallen angels to Heaven. Bryan Cranston turned up as Lucifer.

Although Austin Nichols' enigmatic character in HBO's cancelled *John from Cincinnati* was never identified as such, he definitely had divine powers in David Milch's drama about a dysfunctional California surfing family.

Julian Sands was back in the two-part second season finale of CBS's much improved *Ghost Whisperer*, as Melinda (Jennifer Love Hewitt, always in an impressive array of low-cut tops) learned that she may have an evil half-brother and that there was a darkness inside her waiting to be released. For the new season, things turned even creepier as Melinda's parents (Anne Archer and Martin Donovan) returned with a dark family secret, she once again encountered her evil counterpart, Gabriel (Ignacio Serricchio), and blogging university student Justin Yates (Omid Abtahi) was introduced.

Eric Stoltz guest-starred as a serial killer with intuitive powers in NBC's *Medium*, while in a three-episode story arc featuring guest stars Neve Campbell and Jason Priestley, the third season ended with Alison's (Patricia Arquette) psychic ability being revealed in public.

In the final episode of Sci Fi Channel's *Painkiller Jane*, based on the comic book series, Kristanna Loken's indestructible DEA agent investigated a mass escape of Neuros (humans with genetically enhanced brains) from a secret facility.

Jennifer Finnigan (as fellow psychic Alex Sinclair) returned in the sixth and final season of the USA Network's *The Dead Zone*, while Anthony Michael Hall's Johnny tried to discover what his friend Walt Bannerman was investigating before he died. Tom Skerritt – who played Bannerman in the 1983 movie – turned up again as

Johnny's late father, who was revealed as also possessing psychic powers.

Douglas Henshall's Professor Nick Cutter discovered that mysterious "anomalies" were allowing CGI prehistoric creatures to come through to the present time in the enjoyable six-part British series *Primeval*. In the first season finale, Cutter and his team of researchers not only had to deal with creepy mutant bat-monsters from the future, but also Cutter's scheming wife, Helen (Juliet Aubrey).

In June, CBS' cancelled post-apocalyptic drama *Jericho* was given a mid-season second series of seven episodes following a fan campaign that flooded the network's offices with more than an estimated twenty tons of peanuts (inspired by a line delivered by star Skeet Ulrich in the first season finale). Esai Morales joined the cast as an emissary of America's new government, based in Cheyenne, Wyoming.

Joe Dante directed the Halloween episode of CBS' *CSI: NY*, set in the town of Amityville and featuring Bruce Dern as a gravedigger. Gill Grissom (William Petersen) and his team were called onto the set of a slasher film in the Halloween *CSI: Crime Scene Investigation*, and Joe Mantegna's Agent David Rossi debuted in "About Face", the Halloween edition of CBS' *Criminal Minds* (whose plot bore a very close resemblance to Kim Newman's 2001 short serial killer movie *Missing Girl*). The show topped the night's ratings with 14.7 million viewers.

The 100th episode of CBS' *NCIS* was also a Halloween special set aboard a drifting ghost ship, complete with a mysterious corpse and bleeding rats.

Nathan Fillion's Adam dressed up as the Universal Frankenstein Monster for a Halloween fancy dress party on ABC's *Desperate Housewives*, while the wedding episode of the network's *Ugly Betty* went *Wicked* with a visit to the stage musical.

Following the creation of a nascent Justice League, a guest appearance by former Wonder Woman Lynda Carter as Chloe's superpowered mother, and a silly 1940s "dream" episode, the sixth season of The CW's greatly improved *Smallville* ended with the usual life-or-death cliffhangers and the introduction of a Bizarro Superboy.

The seventh season opener introduced Clark Kent's cousin, supergirl Kara (Canadian actress Laura Vandervoort), who had been stuck in suspended animation, and the revelation that Lana (Kristin Kreuk) wasn't dead after all. Super-veterans Dean Cain (as a mad scientist after Chloe's heart) and Helen Slater (as Clark's Kryptonian mother, Lara) guest-starred in subsequent episodes.

Despite the return of his ex-wife (Olivia D'Abo), clueless Sheriff Jack Carter (the likeable Colin Ferguson) continued to become involved in the lives of the scientific geniuses who lived in the eponymous small town of *Eureka* (aka *A Town Called Eureka*) on Sci Fi. The second season wrapped up with an episode in which an aggressive Franken-virus infected the town.

Eric Johnson starred as the titular *Flash Gordon* in the same channel's low rent reinvention of the classic sci-fi hero, who was now searching for his missing father while battling Ming the Merciless (a miscast John Ralston) and other menaces from Mongo. The 1980 film Flash, Sam J. Jones, had a small role in the episode titled "Revelations".

After a shaky start, the third season of Sci Fi's *Battlestar Galactica* kicked into gear with the trial of Gaius Baltar (James Callis) and the surprise revelation of their true identities by four of the final five Cylons. With its fourth and final season not airing until 2008, a two-hour special episode was shown in November before being released as an extended-cut DVD. The grim *Battlestar Galactica: Razor* was set during the second season and detailed the first mission of the Pegasus under the command of Lee Adama (Jamie Bamber), with flashbacks to when the crazed Commander Cain (Michelle Forbes) was in charge.

Brit actress Michelle Ryan was the upgraded Jaime Sommers, who clashed with Katee Sackhoff's unstable earlier model in David Eick's re-imagined version of *Bionic Woman*. After a debut audience of nearly fourteen million viewers, that number quickly halved and producers brought in a new creative team to try to save the show. However, the writers' strike resulted in a two-part re-launch not being filmed, and NBC declined to pick up any additional episodes.

After ten seasons (making it the longest-running, continuous SF series on American television), Amanda Tapping's astrophysicist Samantha Carter headed over from the cancelled *Stargate SG-1* to replace an infected Dr Weir (Torri Higginson) as the new boss of *Stargate Atlantis*, which enjoyed its fourth season on the Sci Fi Channel.

The enigmatic Jordan Collier (Billy Campbell) had to deal with the consequences of distributing the drug Promicin, which gave people superpowers or killed them in USA's *The 4400*. After an episode involving killer clowns, the show ended its fourth and final dull season in September with hundreds of people (including a few series regulars) being killed by a deadly virus in a chaotic Seattle, while others were imbued with new abilities.

ABC Family's teen-without-a-belly-button (Matt Dallas) returned for a second season in *Kyle XY*. This time he discovered he wasn't clone alone when he met the mysterious Jessi XX (Jaimie Alexander). The series ended mid-season, with the remaining episodes scheduled to air in 2008.

The Disney Channel's *The Wizards of Waverly Place* featured three teen siblings living in New York who were sorcerers.

After being cancelled by NBC in August, the sexy supernatural soap opera *Passions* moved over to satellite station DirectTV in September with a cliffhanger episode, multiple murders and re-formed witch Tabitha returning to her evil ways, which led to her inviting Death to the town of Harmony.

Halloween proved a ghostly time on American soaps with the spirits of dead characters returning to *General Hospital, The Young and the Restless, Guiding Light* and *All My Children*.

An attempt to guerrilla-promote the Cartoon Network's *Aqua Teen Hunger Force* in Boston went disastrously wrong in January when electronic billboards placed around the city resulted in a major security alert and the closure of roads and bridges because police mistook them for home-made bombs. The network's owner, Turner Broadcasting System, agreed to pay $2 million compensation to state and local agencies, while the head of the Cartoon Network, Jim Samples, was forced to resign.

Lucy, the Daughter of the Devil debuted on the Cartoon Network, as Satan's little girl started dating a DJ named Jesus.

Scooby-Doo and his pals were unwisely "pimped up" for a new generation in *Shaggy and Scooby Get a Clue*, in which Shaggy inherited a billion dollars and those "meddling kids" were pitted against the evil Phineus Phibes.

After Fox's cartoon series *The Simpsons* celebrated its 400th episode earlier in the year, the disappointing *Treehouse of Horror XVIII* spoofed such films as *E. T.* and, bizarrely, *Mr And Mrs Smith* with the stories "E. T. Go Home", "Mr and Mrs Simpson" and "Heck House". Jack Black and reclusive comics writer Alan Moore added their voices to another episode, based around a new comic-book store opening in Springfield.

Meanwhile, the same channel's much more cutting-edge *Family Guy* continued to sprinkle cultural genre references into most episodes as it passed its 100th episode and entered its sixth season. Shows included spoofs of *Back to the Future* (featuring Death and Molly Ringwald) and *Star Wars*.

Over on The CW's *The Batman*, the cartoon caped crusader teamed up with the Martian Manhunter and Green Lantern (voiced by Dermot Mulroney), and the fifth season kicked off with the creation of The Justice League. Meanwhile, the same channel's *Legion of Super Heroes* featured a grown-up Superman teaming up with the 31st-century group of super-powered characters.

Produced by Britain's Road House Films/B7 Media and shown on Canada's Space network, Michael MacDonald's *Famous Monster* was an affectionate hour-long tribute to #1 film monster fan and editor Forrest J Ackerman. Along with archival footage and movie clips, the show featured interviews with Ray Bradbury, Ray Harryhausen, George Clayton Johnson, John Landis, Joe Dante, Roger Corman and many others.

On Fox Reality they were looking for a new "hand-maiden" (okay, assistant) for the high-haired horror host in *The Search for the Next Elvira*, while Spike's *Scream Awards 2007*, broadcast in October, honoured rock star Alice Cooper (Vincent Furnier) with a Career Achievement Award.

John Carpenter, John Landis and Cheech Marin were among those featured in the Starz! documentary *Bloodsucking Cinema*, in which Richard Roeper looked at vampire movies.

Although James Runcie's hour-long documentary *J. K. Rowling: A Year in the Life* was spoiled by too many interjections by the self-serving producer/director, Rowling herself came across extremely well, as cameras followed her up to the launch of the final *Harry Potter* book in July.

BBC 2's irritatingly downmarket *British Film Forever* documentary series included a feature-length episode devoted to *Magic, Murder and Monsters: The Story of Horror and Fantasy*. Along with many choice clips, there were interviews with the inevitable Kim Newman, Anne Billson, Jonathan Rigby, Mark Gatiss, Simon Pegg, Jimmy Sangster, David McGillivray, Tudor Gates, John Landis, Roy Ward Baker, Pete Walker, Freddie Francis, Ken Russell, Michael Winner, Terry Gilliam, John Boorman, Danny Boyle, Neil Marshall, Barbara Shelley, Jenny Agutter, Anna Massey, Ian Ogilvy, John Hurt, Sir Anthony Hopkins, Richard Todd, Sylvia Syms, Ingrid Pitt, Madeline Smith, Martin Stephens and others, including archive footage of Michael Powell, Roman Polanski, David Lynch, Sir James Carreras, Yutte Stensgaard, Christopher Lee and Peter Cushing.

On Friday nights in October, Turner Classic Movies in the US honoured "Classic Horror Directors" with retrospective screenings of key films by Jacques Tourneur, William Castle, Tod Browning and Roger Corman. On Halloween, TCM hosted a night of seven Boris Karloff films that included the station's premiere of *The Ghoul* (1933).

*   *   *

Developed by Spain's Mercury Stream and featuring photo-realistic graphics, *Clive Barker's Jericho* was based on an original game concept and story by the author. The first-person player could lead the eponymous strike team trained in occult warfare into a flaming ruined city where an ancient evil had broken through a dimensional rift into our world.

Harry Potter and the Order of the Phoenix was hailed as one of the best movie-to-games ever made, with the eponymous boy wizard moving around a remarkably detailed Hogwarts, recruiting fellow students to Dumbledore's Army.

The incredibly popular Wii platform put players right into the zombie action in *Resident Evil 4*, although *Fantastic Four: Rise of the Silver Surfer* was as dull as the movie that inspired it.

Celebrating the first decade of the successful video game franchise, *Tomb Raider: Anniversary* combined new technology with a nice retro feel.

Neil Gaiman's novel *Anansi Boys* was broadcast by BBC World Service in November as an hour-long drama starring Lenny Henry and Matt Lucas.

BBC Radio 4's *M. R. James at Christmas* broadcast five fifteen-minute adaptations of the author's work by Chris Harrald, each introduced by Derek Jacobi as James. The series comprised "Oh, Whistle, and I'll Come to You", "The Tractate Middoth", "Lost Hearts", "The Rose Garden" and "Number 13".

Meanwhile, Robin Brooks' radio play *A Warning to the Curious* involved a feminist film-maker and her crew visiting the Suffolk coast to make a documentary about James and his work.

Radio 4 also adapted Roald Dahl's *The Witches* as two two-hour dramas, featuring Margaret Tyzack and Amanda Lawrence.

Produced by The H. P. Lovecraft Historical Society and Dark Adventure Radio Theatre, the CD of *At the Mountains of Madness* presented Lovecraft's novella as it might have been adapted for radio in the early 1930s. Recorded in "Mythophone", the package also included various documents pertaining to the story, including a newspaper clipping, pencil sketches and never-before-released photographs.

From Rainfall Records and The Society of the Yellow Sign, *The King in Yellow* CD was inspired by the story by Robert W. Chambers and included words and music by Chambers, Richard L. Tierney, Robert M. Price and Steve Lines, among others.

*   *   *

While the writers' strike crippled the US movie and TV industries, theatre stagehands also went on strike for the first time in November, closing down more than twenty-five Broadway shows over the Thanksgiving holiday, including *The Little Mermaid*, *Phantom of the Opera* and *Wicked*. However, having signed a separate agreement with the union, *How the Grinch Stole Christmas* was given special dispensation by a judge to remain open until the dispute was settled the following month.

London's Theatre Royal, Drury Lane, was closed for four months prior to the opening of the £25 million, three-hour stage production of *The Lord of the Rings* on 9 May so that a £1 million revolving stage could be built. Unfortunately, it jammed during the first performance. As if that was not bad enough, during previews a performer playing a Ranger injured himself on stage in front of an audience of 2,300 people. The actor was thought to have got his leg caught in the hydraulic machinery that controlled the spectacular stage designs, and two performances were cancelled. During its initial six-month run in Toronto, Canada, *The Lord of the Rings* lost millions of dollars and was heavily panned by the critics.

From the same creative team who came up with *The Producers*, Mel Brooks' *Young Frankenstein* arrived on Broadway in November following previews the month before. The stage musical, based on the 1974 movie spoof, starred Roger Bart as the hysterical Dr Frederick Frankenstein, Megan Mullally as Elizabeth, and Shuler Hensley as the tap-dancing Monster.

Meanwhile, *Frankenstein* was a rival Off-Broadway musical starring Hunter Foster as mad scientist Victor and Steve Blanchard as the Creature.

Xanadu was an unlikely stage adaptation of the 1980 musical fantasy movie, with Kerry Butler mimicking the Australian accent of Olivia Newton-John's original roller-skating heroine.

The Peepolykus production of *The Hound of the Baskervilles* was a clever spoof version of Sir Arthur Conan Doyle's classic novel that had a limited run at London's Duchess Theatre. Javier Marzan gave a thick-accented performance as a Spanish Sherlock Holmes.

Patrick Stewart and Kate Fleetwood starred in Rupert Goold's new production of *Macbeth*, which reset Shakespeare's play in a 1940s Stalinist state. The critically-acclaimed production transferred from Chichester's Minerva studio to London's Gielgud Theatre at the end of September.

Audiences sang along with *The Buffy Musical*, which presented the "Once More With Feeling" episode from the TV series' sixth season on big screens in a number of US cities, until Fox abruptly pulled all its TV shows from theatrical exhibition over licensing issues in early October.

A Matter of Life and Death at London's National Theatre was based on the 1946 Powell and Pressburger film, while the Lyric Hammersmith mounted a production of *Don't Look Now* inspired by the Daphne Du Maurier short story and Nicolas Roeg's movie.

Kenneth Cranham, Rosamund Pike and Andrew Woodall starred in The Old Vic production of *Gaslight*, based on a Victorian stage play by Patrick Hamilton.

Over Christmas, London's Almedia theatre staged an adaptation of Catherine Storr's classic 1950s children's book *Marianne Dreams*.

The Edgar Allan Poe-inspired *The Masque of the Red Death*, was an interactive experience created by Felix Barrett of London's Punchdrunk theatre group at the Battersea Arts Centre. Audience members were asked to put on masks and then guided through various Gothic rooms in which a bizarre Victorian vaudeville was being performed. The show was so popular that its run was extended until April 2008.

Doctor Who merchandise such as the Cyberman Voice Changing Helmet and the radio-controlled Dalek were the hit toys of Christmas 2006, resulting in a thirty-five per cent increase in sales for manufacturer The Character Group.

After Jakks Pacific dropped the Universal Monsters licence, Toy Island stepped in with five action figures of the Frankenstein Monster, Dracula, The Wolf Man, The Mummy and Creature from the Black Lagoon. Each set came with pieces for a "Build-a-Franken-stein" figure.

Meanwhile, *The Bride of Frankenstein Premium Figure* was eighteen inches high and hand-painted.

For fans of 1950s "B" movies, Ultratumba Productions released display models of the monsters from *Angry Red Planet* and *It Conquered the World*, limited to just 150 and 200 pieces, respectively.

Lovecraft fans could keep their feet warm in winter with a pair of Cthulhu plush slippers from Toy Vault.

"The Village of Horror Classics" from Hawthorne Village included sculptures of "842 Elm Street", "The Hewitt House" and "Camp Crystal Lake Cabin" from the New Line Cinema movies *A Nightmare on Elm Street*, *The Texas Chainsaw Massacre* and *Friday the 13th*. Each mail-order set came with free figurines.

Hallmark created a series of musical birthday cards based on *Bride of Frankenstein*, *The Munsters*, *King Kong*, *Beetle Juice*, *The Twilight Zone* and, best of all, *The Birds* ("A little birdie told me it's your birthday . . . Actually, it was like a million little birdies, and they kind of screamed it. You might want to stay indoors. Anyway, Happy Birthday!").

In June, a 1933 German poster for *King Kong* sold to a mystery buyer at the London branch of Christie's for £60,000. Designed by Josef Fenneker, only two copies of the poster are known to exist.

That same month, the original costume worn by the late Christopher Reeve in *Superman* (1978) sold at Bonhams in London's Knightsbridge for £8,400.

In October, the original cape worn by Christopher Lee in Hammer's 1958 version of *Dracula* was discovered in a London fancy dress shop. The shop called upon the actor to verify that the item was authentic. Apparently missing for thirty years and worth an estimated £24,000, the cape was discovered during an annual stock check at Angel's Fancy Dress, who had been hiring it out to customers for Halloween. The long overcoat worn by Peter Cushing's Van Helsing in the film was found at the same time.

Available from Black Phoenix Alchemy Lab, The Neil Gaiman Scent Collection ("a tribute to the literary corpus of the inimitable master of fiction") consisted of seven scents "based" on the author's characters. Proceeds from every bottle went to the Comic Book Legal Defense Fund.

Britain's Royal Mail issued a series of seven "Harry Potter" stamps on 17 July to commemorate the publication of the final volume in the series. Each of the stamps featured a book cover from the series, and they were also available as postcards. An additional set of five stamps included the badges of the different houses and school crests at Hogwarts. Pre-orders totalled a record-breaking 340,000 sets.

For the first time since it was founded in 1991, the World Horror Convention was held outside the United States from 29 March – 1 April in Toronto, Canada. Celebrating "The Diversity of Horror" as a theme, the international line-up of Guests of Honour included authors Michael Marshall Smith and Nancy Kilpatrick, artist John Picacio, publisher/author Peter Crowther, editor and pulp magazine expert Don Hutchison, and scriptwriter Peter Atkins. Author Joe R. Lansdale was the popular recipient of the 2007 Grand Master Award, and veteran cartoonist Gahan Wilson was the Special Horror Writers Association Guest.

Many other major names from both sides of the Atlantic attended the up-market event, and the convention produced a hardcover souvenir book that was limited to just 600 copies.

The Horror Writers' Association Bram Stoker Awards were presented at a glitzy banquet at World Horror on the evening of 31 March. Mistress of Ceremonies Sèphera Girón hosted the event, and various guest presenters revealed the winners. The previously-announced Life Achievement Award went to Thomas Harris. PS Publishing picked up the Specialty Press Award, and Poetry Collection went to Bruce Boston's *Shades Fantastic*. Non-Fiction was a tie between Michael *Largo's Final Exits: The Illustrated Encyclopedia of How We Die* and *Gospel of the Living Dead: George Romero's Vision of Hell on Earth* by Kim Paffenroth.

Anthology was another tie between *Mondo Zombie* edited by John Skipp and *Retro Pulp Tales* edited by Joe R. Lansdale. Gary Braunbeck's *Destination Unknown* (from Cemetery Dance Publishing) won for Collection, the Short Fiction Award was presented to Lisa Morton for "Tested" (*Cemetery Dance Magazine*), and Norman Patridge's *Dark Harvest* (also published by CD) won for Long Fiction. Jonathan Maberry's *Ghost Road Blues* picked up the First Novel Award, and Stephen King's *Lisey's Story* won the Novel category. Donna Fitch also received the special Silver Hammer Award for services to the HWA.

All of the winners, except for Harris, King and Fitch, were present to collect their trophies.

The British Fantasy Society's FantasyCon 2007 returned to Nottingham over the weekend of 21–23 September. Guests of Honour were Terry Brooks, Michael Marshall Smith and Stephen Jones, and Peter Crowther was Master of Ceremonies.

The winners of the annual British Fantasy Awards were announced at the impressive Banquet on the Sunday afternoon. Ellen Datlow was the recipient of The Special Karl Edward Wagner Award, and Joe Hill was named as the winner of the inaugural Sydney J. Bounds Best Newcomer Award, which came with a cheque for £100.00.

The Best Non-Fiction Award went to Mark Morris' *Cinema Macabre* from PS Publishing, and Peter Crowther's imprint also picked up the Small Press Award. Vincent Chong won Best Artist.

Neil Gaiman's *Fragile Things* was voted Best Collection, and the Best Anthology award went to *Extended Play: The Elastic Book of Music* edited by Gary Couzens. Best Short Fiction was Mark Chadbourn's "Whisper Lane" (from *BFS: A Celebration*) and Best Novella was Paul Finch's "Kid" (from *Choices*). *Dusk* by Tim Lebbon won The August Derleth Fantasy Award for Best Novel.

The 2007 World Fantasy Convention, held over 1–4 November in Saratoga Springs, New York, was the largest in the event's history. Guests of Honour were authors Carol Emshwiller, Kim Newman and Lisa Tuttle and French artist Jean Giraud ("Moebius"), with Canadian writer Guy Gavriel Kay as Toastmaster.

The 2007 International Horror Guild Awards were given out at a lacklustre ceremony on 1 November, when many people had not yet arrived for the convention. Presenter John Picacio nearly had to accept from himself when *Cover Story: The Art of John Picacio* tied with Aeron Alfrey's online *Exhibits from the Imaginary Museum* for the Art award. Lewis Trondheim's *A.L.I.E.E.N.* won Illustrative Narrative, Bill Schafer's *Subterranean* topped the Periodical category and the Non-Fiction award went to *Icons of Horror and the Supernatural* edited by S. T. Joshi.

After the judges refused to give any awards in the category in 2006, *Lords of the Razor* edited by William Sheehan and Bill Schafer was the welcome Anthology winner, while Collection was a tie between Terry Dowling's *Basic Black* and Glen Hirshberg's *American Morons*. Stephen Gallagher's "The Box" (from *Retro-Pulp Tales*) won the Short Fiction, Mid-Length Fiction went to "The Old North Road" by Paul Finch (from *Alone on the Darkside*), and Norman Partridge's *Dark Harvest* won Long Fiction.

The Novel award went to Conrad Williams' *The Unblemished*, although nobody had bothered to inform the winner. At least Ramsey Campbell was on hand to collect his long overdue Living Legend Award from British editor Jo Fletcher.

The World Fantasy Awards were announced at the crowded Sunday afternoon banquet. The Special Award, Non-Professional went to *Locus* reviewer Gary K. Wolfe, and the recipient of the Professional Award was Ellen Asher for her outstanding work at the Science Fiction Book Club. Australian illustrator Shaun Tan won Best Artist, M. Rickert's *Map of Dreams* was awarded Best Collection and *Salon Fantastique* edited by Ellen Datlow and Terri Windling picked up Best Anthology.

M. Rickert was also the winner of the Best Short Fiction award for her story "Journey Into the Kingdom" from the *Magazine of Fantasy & Science Fiction*. Jeffrey Ford's "Botch Town" (from *The Empire of Ice Cream*) won for Novella, and Gene Wolfe's *Soldier of Sidon* was presented with the Best Novel award. The author had celebrated his 55th wedding anniversary the day before.

Previously announced Life Achievement Awards went to publisher
Betty Ballantine and children's author Diana Wynne Jones.

In 2007 I was involved in the running of the very successful World
Horror Convention in Toronto, Canada. I would like to say that,
overall, it was an enjoyable experience, but in fact it wasn't.

This was mostly due to a small – but vocal – minority in the horror
community who decided to attack the event before we had even
announced most of our plans.

I attended the first World Horror Convention in Nashville, Ten-
nessee, in 1991. Since then, I have probably been to more of them
than many people. For the most part, they have been well-organized
events but, over the past decade, it has become obvious that the
convention has been struggling, with some reportedly having problems covering their costs.

Also, for a so-called "world" event, the convention had never even
been held outside the United States before Toronto.

This was why, somewhat reluctantly at first, I agreed to become
involved in the Canadian bid. It was obvious to me, and others, that
the convention needed to be put on a much more professional
footing. Otherwise it was in danger of eventually failing altogether.

With the rising cost of air travel, hotel rooms and other ancillary
expenses, it no longer made sense to have a number of different literary
horror events held throughout the year across North America. The key
was to bring everything under one umbrella organization.

To this end, we decided to hold the convention in a major
metropolitan city just across the US border. We brought on board
the Horror Writers Association Bram Stoker Awards, which had
previously been held as a separate event. Chicago's respected Twilight Tales group was asked to oversee the reading programme, while
our distinguished line-up of guests drew upon the best writers, artists
and editors from three countries.

As a result, for the first time in years, attendance numbers
increased dramatically. We attracted some of the biggest names in
the genre, along with publishers, editors, agents and enthusiastic fans
from all over the world. The extra revenue allowed us to sponsor
parties, publish a handsome hardcover souvenir book, refund groups
and individuals, and award bursaries to various book-related organizations. In short, we achieved everything that any well-organized
convention should.

Unfortunately, all this was not good enough for a vociferous group
which continued to criticise the event in hateful terms on such

seditious message boards as Shocklines. This group of people was disgruntled that the convention was being held for the first time in a country other than America. They were surprised that, like everybody else, they were expected to pay a modest admission fee for the various talks, panels and other scheduled entertainments. But, most of all, they were outraged that they would not *automatically* be given programming slots, even though most of them had few or no professional credits to speak of.

Therefore, they not only used the Internet to spread false rumours, but a few people were also downright abusive and threatening in the months running up to the convention. I was left feeling ashamed that these individuals were even a part of the horror community.

In the end, of course, none of it really mattered, and the vast majority of those who actually attended the convention had a great time, with many considering it one of the best World Horror Conventions they had ever participated in. That, at least, was gratifying after two years of ceaseless hard work by everybody involved.

Unfortunately, what that small group of troublemakers did not realize was that they were not just attacking the convention, but the very genre itself. Whereas all we had wanted to do was revitalize the convention so that it would continue for many years to come, this group was only interested in having a good time and selfishly promoting themselves and their work.

These people simply could not care less about the bigger picture, and they had no interest in meeting or listening to the advice of their peers. No matter how desperately some of them may have needed that guidance.

For these people, it became a "them" or "us" situation, where the self-published and self-promoted considered themselves equal – or even superior – to those who make their living professionally working in the genre. This is a problem that has already infected some of the award processes within our field, and it would be a tragedy if conventions were also ultimately hijacked by such groups, who have little experience and even less credibility.

As a result of their continuous complaining and sniping, they managed to suck much of the energy and a little of the lustre from what should have been a valedictory event.

In the end, we get the conventions – like governments – that we deserve. The horror field is no different. What the future holds for the World Horror Convention rests in the hands of the fans and those hard-working volunteers who are willing to put one together for little reward or recognition.

If the people who attempted to sabotage the 2007 event ever manage to gain control, not only are they unlikely ever to become the kind of professional horror writer that most of them claim to aspire to, but they may also find they are left without a convention at which to enjoy their success.

And that would be a very bad thing for the genre indeed.

The Editor
May 2008

MICHAEL MARSHALL SMITH

The Things He Said

MICHAEL MARSHALL SMITH'S first novel, *Only Forward*, won the August Derleth and Philip K. Dick Awards, and his next two – *Spares* and *One of Us* – were both optioned by major Hollywood studios. His "Straw Men" books, written under the name "Michael Marshall", were *Sunday Times* and international bestsellers, and his most recent urban thriller, *The Intruders*, is currently in development as a series with the BBC.

The year 2008 saw the publication of a short supernatural novel, *The Servants*, under yet a further pen name, "M. M. Smith". He has also worked extensively as a screenwriter for clients in London and Hollywood, both individually and as a partner in Smith & Jones Productions. He lives in North London with his wife, a son, and two cats.

As the author explains: "One of the things I love about horror stories – and it's something that people who look down on horror simply don't understand – is how effective and honest they can be at examining the reality of how people respond to extreme circumstances: showing both our capacity for equally extreme responses, but also the way in which we will often just get on with things, make the best of it, adjusting our lives and standards to the new conditions. In the end, whatever the state of the world, sometimes every day is just another day . . ."

M Y FATHER SAID SOMETHING to me this one time. In fact he said a lot of things to me, over the years, and many of them weren't what you'd call helpful, or polite – or loving, come to that. But in the last couple months I've found myself thinking back over a lot of them, and often find they had a grain of truth. I consider what he said in the new light of things, and move on, and then they're done. This one thing, though, has kept coming back to me. It's not very original, but I can't help that. He was not an especially original man.

What he said was, you had to take care of yourself, first and foremost and always, because there wasn't no one else in the world who was going to do it for you. Look after Number One, was how he put it.

About this he was absolutely right. Of that I have no doubt.

I start every day to a schedule. Live the whole day by it, actually. I don't know if it makes much difference in the wider scheme of things, but having a set of tasks certainly helps the day kick off more positively. It gets you over that hump.

I wake around 6:00 a.m., or a little earlier. So far that has meant the dawn has either been here, or coming. As the weeks go by it will mean a period of darkness after waking, a time spent waiting in the cabin. It will not make a great deal of difference apart from that.

I wash with the can of water I set aside the night before, and eat whatever I put next to it. The washing is not strictly necessary but, again, I have always found it a good way to greet the day. You wash after a period of work, after all, and what else is a night of sleep, if not work, or a journey at least?

You wash, and the day starts, a day marked off from what has gone before. In the meantime I have another can of water heating over a fire. The chimney is blocked up and the doors and windows are sealed overnight against the cold, so the fire must of necessity be small. That's fine – all I need is to make enough water for a cup of coffee.

I take this with me when I open the cabin and step outside, which will generally be at about 6:20 a.m. I live within an area that is in the shade of mountains, and largely forested. Though the cabin itself is obscured by trees, from my door I have a good view down over the ten or so acres between it and the next thicker stretch of woods. I tend to sit there on the stoop a couple minutes, sipping my coffee, looking around. You can't always see what you're looking for, though, which is why I do what I do next.

I leave the door open behind me and walk a distance of about three hundred yards in length – I measured it with strides when I set it up – made of four unequal sides. This contains the cabin and my shed, and a few trees, and is bounded by wires. I call them wires, but really they're lengths of fishing line, connected between a series of trees. The fact that I'm there checking them, on schedule, means they're very likely to be in place, but I check them anyway. First, to make sure none of them needs re-fixing because of wind – but also that there's no sign something came close without actually tripping them.

I walk them all slowly, looking carefully at where they're attached to the trees, and checking the ground on the other side for signs anything got that far, and then stopped – either by accident or because they saw the wires. This is a good, slow, task for that time in the morning, wakes you up nice and easy. I once met a woman who'd been in therapy – hired a vacation cottage over near Elum for half a summer, a long time ago this was – and it seemed like the big thing she'd learned was to ignore everything she thought in the first hour of the day. That's when the negative stuff will try to bring you down, she said, and she was right about that, if not much else. You come back from the night with your head and soul empty, and bad things try to fill you up. There's a lot to get exercised about, if you let it. But if you've got a task, something to fill your head and move your limbs, by the time you've finished it the day has begun and you're onto the next thing. You're over that hump, like I said.

When that job's finished, I go back to the cabin and have the second cup of coffee, which I keep kind-of warm by laying my breakfast plate over the top of the mug while I'm outside. I'll have put the fire out before checking the wires, so there's no more hot water for the moment. I used to have one of those vacuum flasks and that was great, but it got broken. I'm on the lookout for a replacement. No luck yet. The colder it gets, the more that's going to become a real priority.

I'll drink this second cup planning what I'm going to do that day. I could do this the night before, but usually I don't. It's what I do between 7:30 and 8:00 a.m. It's in the schedule.

Most days, the next thing is going into the woods. I used to have a vegetable patch behind the cabin, but the soil here isn't that great and it was always kind of hit-and-miss. After the thing, it would also be too much of a clue that someone is living here.

There's plenty to find out in the woods, if you know what to look for. Wild versions of the vegetables in stores, other plants that don't actually taste so good but give you some of the green stuff you need. Sometimes you'll even see something you can kill to eat – a rabbit or a deer, that kind of thing – but not often. With time I assume I may see more, but for now stocks are low. With winter coming on, it's going to get a little harder for all this stuff. Maybe a *lot* harder.

We'll see. No point in worrying about it now. Worry don't get nothing but worry, as my father also used to say.

Maybe a couple hours spent out in the woods, then I carry back what I've found and store it in the shed. I'll check on the things already waiting, see what stage they're at when it comes to eating. The hanging process is very important. While I'm there I'll check the walls and roof are still sound and the canvas I've layered around the inside is still watertight. As close to airtight as possible, too.

I don't know if there are bears in these parts any more – I've lived here forty years, man and boy, and I haven't seen one in a long time, nor wolves either – but you may as well be sure. One of them catches a scent of food, and they're bound to come have a look-see, blundering through the wires and screwing up all that stuff. Fixing it would throw the schedule right out. I'm joking, mainly, but you know, it really would be kind of a pain, and my stock of fishing wire is not inexhaustible.

It's important to live within your means, within what you know you can replace. A long game way of life, as my father used to say. I had someone living here with me for a while, and it was kind of nice, but she found it hard to understand the importance of these things, of playing that long game. Her name was Ramona, and she came from over Noqualmi way. The arrangement didn't last long. Less then ten days, in fact. Even so, I did miss her a little after she walked out the door. But things are simpler again now she's gone.

Time'll be about 10:30 a.m. by now, maybe 11:00, and I'm ready for a third cup of coffee. So I go back to the cabin, shut and seal up all the doors and windows again, and light the fire. Do the same as when I get up, is make two cups, cover one to keep it semi-warm for later. I'll check around the inside of the cabin while the water's heating, making sure everything's in good shape. It's a simple house. No electricity – lines don't come out this far – and no running water.

I got a septic tank under the house I put in ten years back, and I get drinking and washing water from the well. There's not much to go wrong and it doesn't need checking every day. But if something's on the schedule then it gets done, and if it gets done, then you know it's done, and it's not something you have to worry about.

I go back outside, leaving the door open behind me again, and check the exterior of the house. That does need an eye kept on it. The worse the weather gets, the more there'll be a little of this or that needs doing. That's okay. I've got tools, and I know how to use them. I was a handyman before the thing and I am, therefore, kind of handy. I'm glad about that now. Probably a lot of people thought being computer programmers or bankers or TV stars was a better deal, the real cool beans. It's likely by now they may have changed their minds. I'll check the shingles on the roof, make sure the joints between the logs are still tight. I do not mess with any of the grasses or bushes that lie in the area within the wires, or outside either. I like them the way they are.

Now, it's about midday. I'll fill half an hour with my sculpturing, then. There's a patch of ground about a hundred yards the other side of the wires on the eastside of the house, where I'm arranging rocks. There's a central area where they're piled up higher, and around that they're just strewn to look natural. You might think this is a weird thing to do for someone who won't have a vegetable patch in case someone sees it, but I'm very careful with the rocks. Spent a long time studying on how the natural formations look around here. Spent even longer walking back from distant points with just the right kind of rocks. I was born right on this hillside. I know the area better'n probably anyone. The way I'm working it, the central area is going to look like just another outcrop, and the stuff around, like it just fell off and has been lying there for years.

It passes the time, anyway.

I eat my meal around 1:00 p.m. Kind of late, but otherwise the afternoon can feel a little long. I eat what I left over from supper the night before. Saves a fire. Although leaving the door open when I'm around the property disperses most of the smoke, letting it out slowly, a portion is always going to linger in the cabin, I guess. If it's been a still day, then when I wake up the next morning my chest can feel kind of clotted. Better than having it all shoot up the chimney, but it's still not a perfect system. It could be improved. I'm thinking about it, in my spare time, which occurs between 1:30 and 2:00 p.m.

The afternoons are where the schedule becomes a tad more free-form. It depends on what my needs are. At first, after the thing, I would walk out to stock up on whatever I could find in the local towns. There's two within reasonable foot distance – Elum, which is about six miles away, and Noqualmi, a little further in the other direction. But those were both real small towns, and there's really nothing left there now. Stores, houses, they're all empty and stripped even if not actually burned down. This left me in a bit of a spot for a while, but then, when I was walking back through the woods from Noqualmi empty-handed one afternoon, I spied a little gully I didn't think I knew. Walked up it, and realized there might be other sources I hadn't yet found. Felt dumb for not thinking of it before, in fact.

So that's what I do some afternoons. This area wasn't ever home to that many vacation cabins or cottages, on account of the skiing never really took off and the winter here is really just kind of cold, instead of picturesque cold – but there are a few. I've found nine, so far. First half-dozen were ones where I'd done some handy work at some point – like for the therapy woman – so they were easier to find. Others I've come upon while out wandering. They've kept me going on tinned vegetables, extra blankets. I even had a little gas stove for a while, which was great. Got right around the whole smoke problem, and so I had hot coffee all day long. Ran out of gas after a while, of course. Finding some more is a way up my wish list, I'll tell you, just below a new vacuum flask.

Problem is, those places were never year-round dwellings, and the owners didn't leave much stuff on site, and I haven't even found a new one in a couple weeks. But I live in hope. I'm searching in a semi-organized grid pattern. Could be more rigorous about it, but something tells me it's a good idea to leave open the possibility you might have missed a place earlier, that when you're finished you're not actually finished – that's it and it's all done and so what now?

Living in hope takes work, and thinking ahead. A schedule does no harm, either, of course.

Those lessons you learn at a parent's knee – or bent over it – have a way of coming back, even if you thought you weren't listening.

What I'm concentrating on most of all right now, though, is building my stocks of food. The winter is upon us, there is no doubt, and the sky and the trees and the way the wind's coming down off the mountain says it's going to land hard and bed itself down for the duration. This area is going to be very isolated. It was that way before the thing, and sure as hell no one's going to be going out of their way to head out here now.

There's not a whole lot you can do to increase the chance of finding stuff. At first I would go to the towns, and had some success there. It made sense that they'd come to sniff around the houses and bins. Towns were a draw, however small. But that doesn't seem to happen so much now. Stocks have got depleted in general and – like I say – it's cold and getting colder and that's not the time of year when you think hey, I'll head into the mountains.

So what I mainly do now is head out back into the woods. From the back of the cabin there's about three roads you can get to in an hour or so's walking, in various directions. One used to be the main route down to Oregon, past Yakima and such. Wasn't ever like it was a constant stream of traffic on it, but that was where I got lucky the last two times, and so you tend to get superstitious, and head back to the same place until you realize it's just not working any more.

The first time was just a single, middle-aged guy, staggering down the middle of the road. I don't even know where he'd come from, or where he thought he was going. This was not a man who knew how to forage or find stuff, and he was thin and half-delirious. Cheered right up when he met me. The last time was better. A young guy and girl, in a car. They hadn't been an item before the thing, but they were now. He believed so, anyway. He was pretty on the button, or thought he was.

They had guns and a trunk full of cans and clothes, back seat packed with plastic containers of gasoline. I stopped them by standing in the middle of the road. He was wary as hell and kept his hand on his gun the whole time, but the girl was worn out and lonely and some folks have just not yet got out of the habit of wanting to see people, to mix with other humans once in a while.

I told them Noqualmi still had some houses worth holing up in, and that there'd been no trouble there in a while on account of it had been empty in months, and so the tide had drifted on. I know he thought I was going to ask to come in the car with them, but after I'd talked with them a while I just stepped back and wished them luck. I watched them drive on up the road, then walked off in a different direction.

Middle of that evening – in a marked diversion from the usual schedule, but I judged it worth it – I went down through the woods and came into Noqualmi via a back way. Didn't take too long to find their car, parked up behind one of the houses. They weren't ever going to last that long, I'm afraid. They had a candle burning, for heaven's sake. You could see it from out in the back yard, and that is the one thing that you really *can't* do. Three nights out of five I could have got there and been too late already. I got lucky, I guess. I waited until they put the light out, and then a little longer.

The guy looked like he'd have just enough wits about him to trick the doors, so I went in by one of the windows. They were asleep. Worse things could have happened to them, to be honest, much worse. There should have been one of them keeping watch. He should have known that. He could have done better by her, I think.

Getting them back to the cabin took most of the next day, one trip for each. I left the car right where it was. I don't need a car, and they're too conspicuous. He was kind of skinny, but she has a little bulk. Right now they're the reason why the winter isn't worrying me quite as much as it probably should. Them, plus a few others I've been lucky enough to come across – and yes, I do thank my luck. Sure, there's method in what I've done, and most people wouldn't have enjoyed the success rate I've had. But in the end, like my father used to say, any time you're out looking for deer, it's luck that's driving the day. A string of chances and decisions that are out of your hands, that will put you in the right place at the right time, and brings what you're looking for rambling your way.

If I don't go out hunting in the afternoon, then either I'll nap a while or go do a little more sculpting. It only occurred to me to start that project a few weeks ago, and I'd like to get some more done before it starts to snow.

At first, after the thing, it looked like everything just fell apart at once, that the change was done and dusted. Then it started to become clear it didn't work that way, that there were waves. So, if you'd started to assume maybe something wasn't going to happen, that wasn't necessarily correct. Further precautions seemed like a good idea.

Either way, by 5:00 p.m. the light's starting to go and it's time to close up the day. I'll go out to the shed and cut a portion of something down for dinner, grab something of a plant or vegetable nature to go with it, or – every third day – open a can of corn. Got a whole lot of corn still, which figures, because I don't really like it that much.

I'll cook the meat over the day's third fire, straight away, before it gets dark, next to a final can of water – I really need to find myself another of those vacuum flasks, because not having warm coffee in the evening is what gets me closest to feeling down – and have that whole process finished as quick as I can.

I've gotten used to the regime as a whole, but that portion of the day is where you can still find your heart beating, just a little. I grew up used to the idea that the dark wasn't anything to fear, that nothing was going to come and do anything bad to you – from outside your house, anyway. Night meant quietness outside and nothing but forest sounds which – if you understood what was causing them – were no real cause for alarm. It's not that way now, after the thing, and so that point in the schedule where you seal up the property and trust that your preparations, and the wires, are going to do their job, is where it all comes home. You recall the situation.

Otherwise, apart from a few things like the nature of the food I eat, it's really not so different to the way life was before. I understand the food thing might seem like a big deal, but really it isn't. Waste not, want that – and yes, he said that too. Plenty other animals do it, and now isn't the time for beggars to be choosers. That's what we're become, bottom line – animals, doing what's required to get by, and there isn't any shame in that at all. It's all we ever were, if we'd stopped to think about it. We believed we had the whole deal nailed out pretty good, were shooting up in some pre-ordained arc to the sky. Then someone, somewhere, fucked up. I never heard an explanation that made much sense to me. People talked a lot about a variety of things, but then people always talked a lot, didn't they? Either way, you go past Noqualmi cemetery now, or the one in Elum, and the ground there looks like Swiss cheese. A lot of empty holes, though there are some sites yet to burst out, later waves in waiting.

Few of them didn't get far past the gates, of course. I took down a handful myself, in the early days.

I remember the first one I saw up here, too, a couple weeks after the thing. It came by itself, blundering slowly up the rise. It was nighttime, of course, so I heard it coming rather than seeing anything. First I thought it was someone real, was even dumb enough to go outside, shine a light, try to see who it was. I soon realized my error, I can tell you that. It was warmer then, and the smell coming off up the hill was what gave it away. I went back indoors, got the gun. Only thing I use it for now, as shells are at a premium. Everything else, I use a knife.

Afterwards I had a good look, though I didn't touch it. Poked it with a stick, turned it over. It really did smell awful bad, and they're not something you're going to consider eating – even if there wasn't a possibility you could catch something off the flesh. I don't know if there's some disease *to* be caught, if that's how it even works, but it's a risk I'm not taking now or likely ever. I wrapped the body up in a sheet and dragged it a long, long way from the property. Do the same with any others that make it up here from time to time. Dump them in different directions, too, just in case. I don't know what level of intelligence is at work, but they're going to have to try harder at it if they ever hope to get to me – especially since I put in the wires.

I have never seen any of them abroad during the day, but that doesn't mean they aren't, or won't in the future. So wherever I go, I'm very careful. I don't let smoke come out of my chimney, instead dispersing it out the doors and window – and only during the day. The wires go through to trips with bells inside the cabin. Not loud bells – no sense in broadcasting to one of them that they just shambled through something significant. The biggest danger is the shed, naturally – hence trying to make it airtight. Unlike just about everything else, however, that problem's going to get easier as it gets colder. There's going to come a point where I'll be chipping dinner off with a chisel, but at least the danger of smell leaking out the cracks will drop right down to nothing.

Once everything's secured for the night, I eat my meal in the last of the daylight, with the last hot cup of coffee of the day. I set aside a little food for the morning. I do not stay up late.

The windows are all covered with blackout material, naturally, but I still don't like to take the risk. So I sit there in the dark for a spell, thinking things over. I get some of my best ideas under those conditions, in fact – there's something about the lack of distraction that makes it like a waking dream, lets you think laterally. My latest notion is a sign. I'm considering putting one up, somewhere along one of the roads, that just says THIS WAY, and points. I'm thinking if someone came along and saw a sign like that, they'd hope maybe there was a little group of people along there, some folks getting organized, safety in numbers and that, and so they'd go along to see what's what.

And find me, waiting for them, a little way into the woods.

I'll not catch all of them – the smart guy in the car would have driven straight by, for example, though his girl might have had something to say on the subject – but a few would find my web. I have to think the idea through properly – don't know for sure that the others can't read, for example, though at night they wouldn't be able to see the sign anyway, if I carve it the right way – but I have hopes for it as a plan. We'll see.

It's hard not to listen out, when you've climbed in bed, but I've been doing that all my life. Listening for the wind, or for bears snuffling around, back when you saw them up here. Listening for the sound of footsteps coming slowly towards the door of the room I used to sleep in when I was a kid. I know the wires will warn me, though, and you can bet I've got my response to such a thing rigorously worked out.

I generally do not have much trouble getting off to sleep, and that's on account of the schedule as much as anything. It keeps me active, so the body's ready for some rest come the end of day. It also gives me a structure, stops me getting het up about the general situation.

Sure, it is not ideal. But, you know, it's not that different on the day-to-day. I don't miss the television because I never had one.

Listening to the radio these days would only freak you out. Don't hanker after company because there was never much of that after my father died. Might have been nice if the Ramona thing had worked out, but she didn't understand the importance of the schedule, of thinking things through, of sticking to a set of rules that have been proven to work.

She was kind of husky and lasted a good long time, though, so it's not like there wasn't advantages to the way things panned out. I caught her halfway down the hill, making a big noise about what she found in the shed. She was not an athletic person. Wasn't any real possibility she was going to get away, or that she would have lasted long out there without me to guide her. What happened was for the best, except I broke the vacuum flask on the back of her head, which I have since come to regret.

Otherwise I'm at peace with what occurred, and most other things. The real important thing is when you wake up, you know what's what – that you've got something to do, a task to get you over the hump of remembering, yet again, what the world's come to. I'm lucky that way.

The sculpting's the one area I'd like to get ahead of. The central part is pretty much done – it's coming up for three feet high, and I believe it would be hard to get up through that. But sometimes, when I'm lying in the dark waiting for sleep to come, I wonder if I shouldn't extend that higher portion; just in case there's a degree of tunnelling possible, sideways and then up. I want to be sure there's enough weight, and that it's spread widely enough over the grave.

I owe my father a lot, when I think over it. In his way, through the things he said, he taught me a great deal of what it turned out I needed to know. I am grateful to him for that, I guess.

But I still don't want to see him again.

SIMON KURT UNSWORTH

The Church on the Island

SIMON KURT UNSWORTH LIVES IN Lancaster in the north of England with his wife Wendy, young son Benjamin, two dogs and an apparently immortal fish. He has been a lecturer at university, a policy officer for a couple of local authorities and a support worker, but he currently works as a self-employed trainer and consultant specializing in health and social care, which kills the time between bouts of writing.

His only publication previous to "The Church on the Island" was in a BBC online anthology of work inspired by M. R. James, although four of his stories have been accepted for publication in *All Hallows*, the journal of The Ghost Story Society.

"'The Church on the Island' was almost entirely written during the course of a wonderful two-week holiday with Wendy on a small Greek island," recalls Unsworth. "The view from the hotel took in a half-mile sweep of golden-sanded beach with a ruined temple at one end, a glorious blue bay and, in the middle of the bay, a tiny island with a small blue and white church on it.

"Everyone I heard talking about the church said how beautiful it was, how nice it would be to go to a service there, or even better, to get married there. My first thought was, if the end of the world's going to happen, it'll start in somewhere just like that.

"I have no idea if this is normal or not."

C HARLOTTE PULLED HERSELF onto the beach and pushed her hair back off her face in a cascade of water. She took a couple of deep breaths, quietly pleased by the fact that she was not more affected by her swim. As she let her heart rate and breathing settle, she untied the string from around her waist and freed her plastic sandals; they had spent the swim bobbing along at her side, gently tapping her thighs every now and again as if to remind her of their existence. Now, she let them fall to the floor and slid her feet into them. Water squeezed under her feet and around her toes, spilling out onto the wet sand. Then, walking away from the sea, she let her eyes rise to the object of her visit: the little blue and white church.

Charlotte had seen the church the first time she had looked out from her hotel room window. Perhaps half a mile out from shore, nestling into the vibrant blue sea, was a tiny island. It seemed to be little more than an upthrust of grey rock from the ocean, its flanks covered in scrubby green foliage. Its lower slopes looked gentle, but there was a central outcrop of rock that appeared almost cubic, as though cut by some giant hand with a dull knife. This mass was settled on to the centre of the island as though the same hand that had cut it had placed it down, forcing it into the earth like a cake decoration into icing. Its sides were almost vertical and striated with dark fissures and it looked to be fifty or sixty feet tall, although Charlotte found it hard to judge this accurately and changed her mind every time she gazed at it.

The church was in front of the outcrop, tiny and colourful against the doleful grey of the rock face. Its walls were a startling white with blue edging, the roof a wash of the same blue. By squinting, Charlotte could just make out a door in the front of the building and a cross, set at the front of the roof. At night, the church was lit by a pale yellow light that flickered in time with the wind; Charlotte assumed that oil lamps hung around its exterior. The light made its walls shimmer and stand out starkly against the grey stone mass behind it. The mass itself loomed even more at night, rearing and blocking out the stars in the Greek darkness. It gave the impression of being man-made; the crags and fissures became the battlements of a castle, abandoned and decaying but resisting a final collapse with bleak force. It, too, appeared lit at its base by the same yellowing illumination. Charlotte never saw anyone light the lamps.

In fact, as hard and as often as she looked (and she spent long periods of time simply staring at the island, to Roger's irritation), she only ever saw one person at the church, and then only for a fleeting moment. A shadow framed in the doorway, seen in the corner of her eye as she turned away, that was gone by the time she turned back. It had to be a person, she told herself. Someone lights the lamps, and the church is well cared-for. Its sides (the two that she could see from her hotel balcony, at least) were the white of freshly painted stone or brick, and the blue roof and trim were neat and well defined. The low wall that surrounded the church corralled ground that was clear of plants or noticeable litter. It was curiously entrancing, this little blue and white building with its domed roof and dark doorway, and Charlotte studied it for hours.

It was Roger that put the idea in her head. "Why don't you swim out there?" he asked on about the third day of their holiday. "If you see it up close, you might stop staring at it all the time."

Charlotte could hear the irritation in his voice, but also the joking tone. She knew he was simply trying to draw her attention back to him and their break together, but the idea took hold in her mind and would not let go. The next day, she said to him, "It's not that far, is it? And the sea's fairly calm around here."

"You're serious?" he asked.

"Of course," she said, and couldn't help adding, "It was your idea, after all."

Charlotte planned the Great Swim (as Roger had taken to sarcastically calling it) for the second week of their break. It gave her time to get used to swimming in the sea, to feel the way it pulled and pushed at her. It also gave her the opportunity to ask around about the little church, but no one seemed to know anything about it. The holiday company representative merely shrugged, and the locals looked at her blankly when she asked. One said, "It is just an old church," and looked at Charlotte as though she were mad, but it *wasn't*. It was not old, not to look at anyway. This apparent disinterest in the church, which made Roger more dismissive of her plan, only strengthened her resolve and by the morning of the swim, she was determined to reach it, to feel its stonework for herself.

The path from the beach to the church was steeper than it had looked from the mainland and Charlotte had to scramble and grasp at plants and roots to support her on her ascent. The climb was more tiring than the swim and she reached the top grateful that she had not needed to go further. Grit had worked its way into her sandals and her feet felt hot and scratched by the time she reached her destination and her hands were grimy and sore. When she placed her hands on the top of the low wall and felt the heat of the sun on the rock and saw the church, however, all her aches were forgotten.

Close to, the building was even prettier than she expected. She wanted to walk straight to it, to marvel at its simple beauty, but before she could she had to deal with Roger. Standing by the wall, she turned back towards the beach. Across the strip of blue sea (I swam that, she thought proudly), the wedge of golden sand gleamed in the late morning sun. She located Roger's tiny, frail form by finding the hut that sold fresh fruit and cold drinks and looking just in front of it, the way they had arranged. There, besides a family group, sat Roger. She raised one arm in greeting and saw him do the same in return. At least now he would not worry and might even start to relax a little.

Ah, Roger, she thought, what are we going to do with you? Back home, his constant attentiveness was flattering. Here, its focus unbroken by time apart for work and without the diluting presence of other friends, it had become claustrophobic. She could not move, it seemed, without him asking if she was all right or if she wanted anything. The Great Swim had appealed, in part at least, because it gave her time away from him. He was neither a strong enough swimmer nor adventurous enough to want to do it with her, and although she felt a little guilty at taking advantage of his weakness, she revelled in the freedom that it gave her. She could not see their relationship continuing after they returned home and although this made her sad, it was a distant sadness rather than a raw grief.

Roger hopefully placated, Charlotte turned again to the church. The path up from the beach had brought her out directly facing the door, which hunched inside a shadowed patch surrounded by a neat blue border. There was a simple wooden step up to the door. Around it, the wall was plain, white-painted stonework. Instead of approaching, however (worried that she might find the door locked and that her little adventure would end too soon and in disappointment), Charlotte went around to the far side of the building.

As she came around the church's flank, Charlotte saw that one of her assumptions about the place had been wrong; she had expected that it was built on a little plateau (possibly man-made?) and entirely separate from the rocky outcrop that glowered behind it. It was not: the rear of the church was built up against the base of the natural cliff. Going closer, she saw that the mortar that joined the church's wall to the cliff was spread thickly so that no gaps remained. Under the skin of the paint, different sized stones had been used to ensure that the wall fitted as snugly as possible; she could see the irregular lattice of them.

The wall itself was plain except for a single dark window of quartered glass set just below the roof. The window was low enough for Charlotte to be able to see through if she went close, as the building was only single-storey. Along from the window, a metal and glass lamp hung from a bracket, and she gave a little private cheer. Her assumption about the night-time lights had, at least, been correct. She resisted the temptation to look through the window for the same reason that she had not tried the door; she wanted to save the inside of the building for as long as possible. Instead, she turned away from the church to look at the land around it.

It was beautiful. What appeared to be scrub from half a mile's distance was actually a thickly knotted tangle of plants and small trees. The air was heavy with the smell of jasmine and curcuma and other unidentifiable but equally rich scents. Butterflies chased each other around the branches and lazy bees drifted somnambulantly from flower to flower. Their buzzing came to Charlotte in a sleepy wave, rising and falling in pitch like the roll of the sea. Under it was the sound of crickets and grasshoppers, an insistent whirring that was at the same time both frantic and curiously relaxing.

The press of plants and insects, and the birds that darted and hovered in irregular patterns above it all, were held back by the stone wall surrounding the church. In places, the wall bulged and roots pushed their way between the rough stones. The only break in the stonework was a rusted iron gate. Past the gate, there was a gap in the flora and an earthen track that led away along the base of the cliff. Here, the dark green leaves and branches and the blooming flowers had been cut and pushed back so that they formed an archway over the gate and made living, breathing walls for the path.

Charlotte stood, breathing in the scented air and luxuriating in the quiet. If Roger were there, she thought, he'd be taking photographs, pointing out interesting creatures or sounds, asking if I was *okay*, if I *wanted anything*. Being there allowed her to just *be*, unfettered by expectation or implication or demand. It was the most relaxed she had felt for her entire holiday.

Finally, Charlotte walked back around to the front of the church. She intended to try the door, but instead she carried on walking, going to the right side of the building. It was, as she expected, the same as the other side, only in reverse. The window was dark and the lamp's brass fittings were shiny with age. There was another gate in the surrounding wall, also rusted (although, looking closely, she saw that the hinges were well-oiled and clean) and another path along the base of the cliff. She wondered if it was simply the end of the path that started around the other side and which travelled all the way around the base of the great ragged cube, and decided that it probably was. She smiled at the simplicity of it and its unrefined, functional beauty.

Through the window, Charlotte thought she could see a light inside the building. She went close, brushing away a thin layer of sand and dust from the glass and peering through into the interior of the church. What she saw disappointed her.

Other Greek Orthodox chapels that Charlotte had visited, both large and small, had been extensively decorated, with pictures of saints lining the lower part of the walls, scenes from the life of Jesus above them ("As a teaching aid," Roger had told her pompously in a church they had visited earlier in the week. "Remember, the peasants couldn't read and so the pictures could be used by the priests as illustrations to what they were saying." She had remained silent after he spoke, not trusting herself to say anything pleasant to him, so irritated was she at his thoughtless condescension). Icons, frequently of the Holy Mother and Child, lined the walls of these other churches, their silver and gold plate ("To protect the picture beneath" – more from Roger) shining in the light from the devotional candles that burned in trays of sand. The little blue and white church, however, had none of this. The walls were bare of pictures, painted or framed. There were no candles or chairs or tapestries here. Indeed, the only decoration seemed to be mirrors in ornate frames. There was one above the door, one behind the altar and one opposite her to the side of the window. The altar, which she expected to be bedecked with, at the very least, a delicately stitched altar cloth, was a simple table partly covered in what looked like a plain white strip of material. Two candles in simple silver candlesticks burned, one at each end. Behind the altar was an open doorway. Seeing the open doorway made Charlotte nod to herself; whilst it was, in other respects, odd, the church was at least conforming to some of what she knew about the Greek Orthodox Church, where Chapels had a narthex, a central area where worshippers gathered and a private area for the priests behind the altar. Presumably, this was what lay beyond the doorway.

Charlotte stepped back from the window, still confused. The inside of the church was so plain that it might belong to some dour Calvinist chapel and she wanted to know why this was so different from the exuberant stylings she had seen in other Greek churches. She went back around to the door, confident that she could enter: that candles were burning made her sure that there must be a priest there, and that the church should be unlocked. Before she entered, however, she went once more to the top of the path up from the beach. She was experiencing a little guilt about her feelings towards Roger and wanted to wave to him, show him some affection. It would make him feel good, and might stop him worrying. When she looked, however, she could not find him. There was the fruit and drink stall, there was the family, but Roger was nowhere to be seen.

Maybe he had gone to get some shade, she thought. He was paranoid about becoming sunburnt or dehydrated, another little thing about him that irritated her. Maybe he'd got angry waiting for her and taken himself off for an early beer; in a funny way, she hoped that this was the case. It would be a spark of adventurousness, a small reminder of the Roger she first met and liked, who'd made her laugh and surprised her and paid attention to her.

Swallowing a surprisingly large hitch of disappointment, Charlotte turned back to the church. As the sun rose higher, the church's shadows were creeping back towards it like whipped dogs, and its white walls gleamed. The domed blue roof was bright in the sun and the reflections of the light off the white walls were so sharp that she had to narrow her eyes as she approached the door. Whilst she expected it to be open, there was still a part of her that wondered if it might resist her push, but she never had the chance to find out. Even as she reached for the handle, the door swung open to reveal an old man who looked at her silently.

The man was dressed in a simple black robe, tied at the waist with belt of rope. His beard was a pepper of white and grey and black and a white cloth was draped over the crown of his head. Under the cloth, Charlotte saw long hair that fell in ringlets past his shoulders. He wore sandals and his toenails were long and curled.

"Welcome to the Island of the Church of the Order of St John of Patmos. My name is Babbas," the man said, and bowed. He straightened up slowly and walked by Charlotte without another word. As he went, she caught an unpleasant whiff of sour body odour and another, sweeter smell that was, if anything, even less pleasant.

Babbas was fully eight inches shorter than she was and as he walked by, she could see the top of his head with its cloth covering. What she taken for white, she saw, was actually a dirty yellow. It was stained with countless greasy rings, all overlapping like cup stains on an unvarnished table. With a little jolt of disgust, Charlotte realized that the rings were marks from his hair, from where it pressed against the linen. She took an involuntary step back from him, shocked and surprised in equal measure. Why doesn't he wash? she thought, and took another step away. He stopped and turned to her.

"This is a small church, with few facilities," he said, as though reading her thoughts. "Come, I will show you around and explain what needs to be done." His English was excellent, but she could still detect an accent there. Greek, almost definitely. Babbas spoke slowly, as though thinking about each word before he uttered it, and she wondered if this was because he was speaking a language that was not his own. His eyes were a faded blue, circled by wrinkles and overhung by heavy, grey eyebrows. He looked at her intently and then span around again and walked on. His walk was not an old man's shuffle, precisely, but Charlotte saw that he did not pick his feet far up off the ground and his steps were not long.

"Each day, before sunset," Babbas said, walking around to the left of the church, "the lamps must be lit. There are six. One here, one on the other side of the church and four at points around the island. The path will take you there; it goes all the way around this rock and comes out on the other side of the church." Silently, Charlotte gave herself another cheer. One point for me, she thought, I already worked that out!

Babbas was looking speculatively along the path and Charlotte stopped next to him. She was pleased to find that the scents from the plants and flowers covered the old man's own odour.

"It looks beautiful, does it not?" asked Babbas, but did not wait for a response. "It is, now. But it can be a long walk around the island, even in good weather. In winter, it is treacherous. The path becomes slippery when it is wet, and the wind can be harsh, but the work is vital. All four sides of this rock must be lit with light from a flame throughout every night. Each morning, the lamps must be extinguished and filled in preparation for being lit again that forthcoming night. This means that the morning walk is often the harder, as you must carry the oil with you in a can." He sighed.

Standing next to the old man gave Charlotte the opportunity to study him more closely. His face was deeply lined and his skin was the deep brown of someone who spent a great deal of time outdoors. Except for his dress, which seemed too simple, he acted as though he were in charge here. He must be the priest, she thought. Why else would he be here? Perhaps this parish isn't well off enough to afford to buy nice robes or icons for the church. I mean, it can't have many regular parishioners, can it? Even as she thought this, her eyes were taking in more details about him. His beard hung down to his chest and his hands were ridged with prominent veins. There was something else about him, though, something harder to identify. It took her a moment to recognize it, but when she did, Charlotte was a little surprised: he seemed sad.

The two of them stood in silence, looking down the path along the base of the cliff for so long that it began to make Charlotte uncomfortable. She wanted to ask the man something, but did not know what. Besides, he did not give the impression of wanting to talk. True, he had started tell her about the church, but not in an especially welcoming way. It reminded her of the lectures she had attended at university, given by tutors who saw teaching as a chore.

"Come," said the priest suddenly, making Charlotte jump, "there is much to show you."

Babbas walked back towards the church, not looking at Charlotte as he went. She followed, halfway between amused and irritated by the man's brusque manner. As he walked into the church, however, she stopped.

"Wait a minute, please," Charlotte said, "I can't come in dressed like this, can I?" She gestured down at her bikini, her naked legs and belly and shoulders now prickling in the sun. She wished she had brought sunscreen and a sarong with her; she could have tied them in a waterproof bag and towed it along with her sandals.

"Why?" asked the old man.

"Don't I have to cover my shoulders and legs out of respect? I've had to do that for the other Greek churches I've been in."

The priest looked at Charlotte as though seeing her properly for the first time. He let his gaze drop from her face down her body and she began to wonder if she was safe here alone with him. Before she had time to pursue this thought, however, he raised his gaze to her face again and sighed, as though terribly tired.

"God made both skin and cloth and loves you equally in both," he said. "He is with you dressed and undressed. He is in your clothes, and so always sees you as naked. He is God and sees us all as naked all the time. What use are clothes to Him? Religion, churches and chapels and monasteries, often forgets that God sees beyond the covers that we put around the world. They forget that the ceremonies they perform have function, have purpose beyond simply tradition or habit or worship. When ceremonies and rules become all-important, then God is forgotten. Here, the ceremonies are about a purpose. They have a function. They are not about simply the look or the sound or the history of things. You may enter this church of the Order of St John of Patmos dressed however you wish, as long as you respect the work that is done here and not just the ceremony that surrounds it." He stopped and sighed again, as though exhausted by his speech. Charlotte, unsure as to whether to be embarrassed by her lack of clothes or by the fact that she had asked about her lack of clothes and so drawn attention to it, simply nodded and followed him into the church.

The inside of the small building was not as plain as it had appeared from the outside. There was decoration of a sort, but it was delicate and subtle. A black strip was painted along the base of the walls, stretching about three inches up from the floor. The top of the back strip was irregular, dipping and rising as it went around the room. When Babbas closed the door behind her, Charlotte saw that it had been painted across the bottom of the door as well. Above the black strip, the walls were painted a light yellow. There were small streaks of orange in the yellow, along with tiny flecks of blue and green. The church was lit by the candles on its altar and by the sunlight coming in through the two windows. The mirrors on the walls (and there was one on each wall, she saw) caught the light and reflected it all around, catching the streaks of colour on the walls and making them dance in the corner of her eyes. It was like being at the centre of a vast, calm flame and it was magical in a way she had not expected. The air had a warmth that held her softly and she laughed in delight at it. The old man, hearing this, smiled for the first time and did not seem so sad.

"It is wonderful, is it not?" asked Babbas.

"It's beautiful," Charlotte answered, although this did not do justice to how beautiful or wonderful it was.

"The Order of St John of Patmos, here and elsewhere, is charged with the maintenance of the light of God, and we try to love the light wherever possible. It is not an easy life here on the island; there is only one delivery of food and equipment a week, and between these times, it can be lonely. These altar candles must always be aflame, as must other torches that we will come to soon. There must always be enough fuel, enough candles, enough torches, and this takes planning, so that the necessary items can be ordered at least a week in advance, to come in with the following week's delivery. But when it is hard and when the life I have had given to me seems tiring, I need simply stand in here and feel the beauty and power of God and His love, and I know that I am valued, that I am playing my part in the worship of the light over the darkness." He stopped talking and his face fell into sadness and tiredness once more. Charlotte wondered why Babbas was telling her these things, but dared not ask. Wasn't this what she had come here for, after all? And besides, it was interesting, listening to this old man. Such single-mindedness, she thought briefly. I'm not sure I could do what he does, day in, day out.

As if reading her thoughts again, Babbas said, "It is not always so. Sometimes, there are more here than just me. In past years, this place has housed four or five of the called at a time and we would split the daily tasks between us."

"Jesus, you mean there's just you by yourself?" exclaimed Charlotte, startled, and fast on the heels of this startler, embarrassed at having sworn in church. Babbas seemed not to notice, however, but simply sighed again and turned away. He walked to the rear of the church, going behind the altar. He went to the doorway and stopped, calling back over his shoulder, "Come."

This time, Charlotte did not move. It was not just the peremptory way in which he had called her, although that was irritating to be sure. No, it was also that the idea of going behind the altar, of entering the place where only those who served God as priests or higher could go that made her uncomfortable. Whilst her own faith was, at best, questionable, she had been raised in a family that respected even if it did not believe. She found it hard to disagree with members of the clergy and even thinking critical or dismissive thoughts about the church's ceremonies or regulations made her feel guilty. She sometimes felt it was this inability as much as anything that stopped her from taking the final step and dismissing the teaching of the church as simple superstition, and that this was a weakness in her that she should try to overcome, but she did not. Hard though it was to admit it even to herself, she liked that the church had mysteries, and revealing them would be akin to stripping away layers of her upbringing and replacing them with something smaller and infinitely more miserable. Seeing behind the altar would solve one of those mysteries, and the thought of it made her sad. She could not articulate this, knowing it made little sense. Rather, she remained still and hoped that the old man would return, would show her something else instead of what lay in the private inner sanctum.

"Come, now!" said Babbas from the darkness, and he no longer sounded old or tired, but implacable. He loomed into the light briefly, waving her towards him and saying in the same tone of voice, "There is much to show you." Miserably, feeling far worse than when she thought of losing Roger, she followed him.

She had expected to find a small chamber beyond the doorway, but was surprised to find a long passage cut into rock, lit by candles set into carved recesses. These recesses were at head height and occurred every five or six feet along the passage. The smell of smoke and old flames was strong but under it, the same sickly, corrupt odour from before caught in Charlotte's nose. Babbas was already some distance down the passage, walking in that stooped half-shuffle that she had begun to recognize. Wondering what other surprises were in store, she hurried after him.

The slap of her sandals echoed around her as she walked, the sound coming at her from all angles. She saw as she passed that behind each candle, painted on the back of the recesses, were portraits of people. There were both men and women, all unsmiling and serious-looking. All were wearing a white cloth over their heads, and all had dates across the base of the portraits. In the flickering light of the candles, their eyes seemed to follow her and their lips pursed in disapproval. As much to break the silence and to draw her attention from their gaze as anything, Charlotte called ahead to the old man, "Who are the people in portraits?"

"The previous leaders of the Order here."

"But there are women," she said before she could stop herself. Babbas turned back to her. There was light from somewhere ahead and for a moment, he was simply a silhouette in the passage. He stretched his arms out, placing his palms against the walls. Leaning forward, he let his arms take his weight. His face came into the light and Charlotte saw his teeth, gleaming a terrible ivory. He stared at her and smiled, although there was no humour in it.

"This is not a branch of the Orthodox Church," he said, "and we have always known that God gave women the same role to play in the struggle between good and evil as men. He cares not whether it is a man or a woman who lights the candles and lamps and torches, as long as they are lit. Try to understand, this place has a function, a purpose, beyond simply mouthing words and performing ceremonies, the reason for whose existence most have forgotten. To these walls, men and women are called equally to play their role as God intended." He glared fiercely at Charlotte and then whirled about, his belt ends and the hem of his robe flailing around him. Charlotte, against her better, more rational, judgment, followed.

The passage opened out into a cave that took Charlotte's breath away. It looked as if the whole of the huge outcrop of rock in the island's centre had been hollowed out. Looking up, she saw a roof far above her that was ragged with gullies and peaks, like a sonar map of deep ocean floors. Here and there, chisel marks were visible and she realized that this must have been a natural opening in the rock, and that man had expanded what nature (God? She wondered fleetingly) had begun. The floor was inlaid with white marble and the walls painted the same yellow and orange as in the church, although there was no black stripe around the base of the walls. At either side of her, doorways were set into the wall, carved rectangles of darker air. The nearest one, she saw, opened into a small carved room that appeared to contain nothing but a bed. He lives here as well! she thought in surprise, and then her eyes were drawn to what lay in the centre of the cavern.

There was a large opening in the floor.

Charlotte walked to the opening, beckoned on by Babbas who had gone to stand at its edge. It was roughly square and at each corner was a burning torch set on top of a metal stand. Lamps burned around the walls, she noticed, and then she was looking into the hole.

It was pitch black. Charlotte stared down and immediately felt dizzy, as though she were having an attack of vertigo and, in truth, it was like looking down from a great height. The darkness in the hole seemed to start just feet below its rim, as if it was filled with inky water. *Why doesn't the light go into it?* she had time to think and then Babbas' hand was on her shoulder and he drew her gently away. He guided her back to where she had been standing, to where the floor was all around her, gleaming and white.

"There is the function of the Order of St John of Patmos," he said in a soft voice. "We keep the light burning that holds the darkness at bay, and it is what you have come here to do."

Charlotte stood, breathing deeply to overcome her dizziness. The old man stood looking at her kindly. His eyes glimmered with . . . what? Expectation? Hope? She could not tell and then the thing that he had said last of all lurched in her memory and the individual words connected, made a sentence, gained meaning.

"I'm not here to do anything!" she said loudly. "I just wanted to look around!"

"Of course you did not," said Babbas, and the sadness was there again in his voice, the sound of a teacher coaxing a particularly slow child. "You were called here, as I was before you and the others were before me. No one comes here to look; we come because God needs us."

"No," Charlotte said as emphatically as she could, "I wanted to see the church. Now I've seen it, I'll go. Thank you for showing it to me." She took a step back, moving towards the passageway. Babbas did not move, but simply said, "You may leave, if you wish, of course. I shall not stop you, but you will find that the world has already forgotten you."

Charlotte opened her mouth to say something, to say anything to counter the oddly threatening madness that was coming from the old man's mouth, but nothing came. She wanted to tell him that he was insane, that the place she had made for herself in the world was as secure as it had ever been, but instead, the thought of Roger popped unbidden into her mind. Or rather, the memory that Roger had been gone when she looked for him a second time. Could he have forgotten her? Gone back to their hotel room because she no longer existed for him? No, it was madness, she was real, she had a home, a job, a boyfriend.

"He has forgotten you," said Babbas, once more guessing at what she thinking, seeing her thoughts and fears reflected in her expression. "Already, the skin of the world is healing over the space you have left in it. In a few days, no trace of you will be left. Now, your place is here."

Charlotte stared at the old man and took another step back towards the passage. He was looking at her with that calm, lecturer's assurance again, confident in the absolute truth of what he was saying. She wanted to say, that's impossible, but she dared not speak. Saying anything would be an admittance of the fact that, just for a moment, she had wondered, and in her wondering, Babbas' words attained a sort of reality. But he couldn't be right, could he? It was an absurdity spouted by an old man driven mad by solitude and religious extremism. Wasn't it? How could he believe it? she asked herself, and in that moment, she realized that she did not want to leave yet. She had to persuade him of his folly, make him see that he was wrong. Frantically, she went through the things she could say that might puncture his reality and let hers in. Finally, she came across what she felt was the perfect argument.

"But I can't," she said, "I don't believe, and how can I have been called if I don't believe?"

Babbas did not reply and Charlotte thought, for the shortest time, that she's done it, had made him see his error. But then, the sad little smile never leaving his face, he said, "Believe in what? This church, this place? It is all around you, more solid than your own flesh can ever hope to be. God, perhaps? Well, he does not care, he exists outside of your beliefs or mine and He does not need your faith or mine to continue. Ah, but I see that it is not Him that you do not believe in, but the function of this place. You think, maybe, that all here is ceremony without purpose, or that the purpose itself has become obsolete, like the act of watering a dead plant?"

Babbas' smile widened into a grin that showed his teeth. Under his eyebrows, his eyes were lost in pools of flickering shadow. "This is no place of idle ceremony," he said. "Watch."

Babbas took hold of Charlotte's arm in a grip that was gentle but unyielding and pulled her to one corner of the pit in the floor. Nodding at her, he took hold of the torch and removed it from the bracket in the floor. Holding it high over his head like a lantern, he retreated to the far side of the cavern and stood in the entrance to the passage. With the torch above him, the light danced more frenziedly around him. The walls, their colours melting and merging, were flames about Charlotte's skin and felt herself try to retreat from them, wrapping her arms tightly around her stomach. She made to step away, but with his free hand, Babbas gestured to the pit by her feet. She looked down.

The surface of the darkness was writhing and bucking. Even as she gasped in surprise and fear, Charlotte imagined some great creature roiling and thrashing just below the surface of inky water. There were no reflections within the pit or the boiling darkness.

Charlotte never knew how long she watched the moving darkness for; it may have been one minute or one hour. She only knew that she was mesmerized by the rippling thing that moved before her. There was no light in it, but there *were* colours, things she could neither name nor even recognize, flashes and sparks and flows that moved and swirled and came and went. She felt herself become trapped in it, like a fly in amber, and it was only with an effort that she pulled herself away, brought her mind back in to herself.

The darkness in the corner of the pit nearest her had risen.

The black, moving thing had crept up and was lapping at the edge of the pit and tiny strands of it had slithered out onto the marble floor. It no longer looked like a liquid to Charlotte, but like some shadowed thing slowly reaching out tentacles, sending them questing across the marble floor. They reminded her of tree roots groping blindly through the earth for sustenance. Even as she watched, the first tendril had found a patch of shadow, cast by the holder that Babbas had removed the torch from. The tendril (or root? or feeler? she did not know how to explain what she was seeing) writhed furiously as it reached the shadow, thickening and pulsing. The shadow itself seemed to bulge and sway and then it was solid, more solid than it ought to be. She could not see the floor through it. More tendrils found other shadows, moving with a greedy hunger, and with them came a sound.

It was the noise of insects in the night-time, of unidentifiable slitherings and raspings, of rustling feet and creaking, ominous walls. Claws tickled across hard floors and breathing came, low and deep. There was the whisper of saliva slipping down teeth as yellow and huge as the bones of long-dead monsters, of hate given voice and pain that hummed in the blood.

Charlotte tried to scream as the noise slipped about her but the air became locked in her throat as she looked at her feet and saw that the questing tendrils had reached her. They caressed her gently and then the shadows between her toes thickened, became as impenetrable as velvet. When she tried to lift her foot to kick them away, she felt them cling with a warm tenacity that nuzzled gently at her instep and the back of her ankle. It was soft, like the touch of a lover, and it pulsed with a rhythm all of its own, and then she screamed.

Charlotte stumbled back as she screamed, and it seemed to her as she stumbled that her own shadow felt different, had a weight and a solidity that it had never had before. She felt it hold on to her knees and ankles, slipping across her skin like rough silk. She kicked out, knowing the irrationality of being frightened of your own shadow but kicking nonetheless, and then her back hit something else, something warm and she screamed even louder. The warm thing wrapped itself around her and she caught a flash of light at her side. She recognized the same sweet, sickly smell as she had caught before and then Babbas was saying in her ear, "It is alright. Do not panic."

The old man had the torch in front of Charlotte, its flaming head close to the floor. He swept it around in great arcs, forcing it into the shadows and using it as though he were driving an animal away. He was breathing hard, the air coming from his mouth in heavy puffs across her cheek. It was warm and moist and made her want to cringe. The heat of the torch flashed near her foot and she yelped in surprise and pain. She started to cry, helpless in his arms, tears of frustration and fear and anger rolling down her face. She closed her eyes and waited, useless, until the old man let her go.

"It is gone," he said simply. Charlotte heard the rattle of the torch being placed back onto its stand. Trembling, she opened her eyes.

The cavern was normal again or at least, as normal as it had been when she first saw it. The walls still seemed to move with a fluid, balletic grace around her, the light from the torches giving the colours life. Now, the vibrancy she felt was a blessing, something that pinned the contents of the pit down with its warmth and vitality.

"What was that?" she asked, hearing the idiocy of the question but having to ask anyway.

"Darkness," said Babbas. "There are places where darkness gets into the world, through pits and caverns and sunless spots. The Order of St John of Patmos is dedicated to finding these places and to keeping in them the light of God, to keeping the darkness at bay. It has been my job on this island for many years, and now it is yours."

Babbas went past Charlotte and stepped through one of the openings carved into the cavern's wall. Charlotte, terrified of being left alone near the pit, scurried after him. At the doorway, she stopped, peering through into the shadowed beyond. There was a flare of a match igniting and then the softer glow of a lantern spread around in tones of red and orange, revealing a small room.

The walls were lined with shelves, and the shelves bristled with leather-bound book, their spines black despite the light. The far wall was curtained off and in front of the curtains was a desk. Its scarred surface held an open journal and a pen.

"This is where the records are written," said Babbas, gesturing first at the open journal and then at the books lining the shelves. "The activities of each day are listed, written in confirmation of their completion."

Charlotte, interested despite herself, said, "Are these the records for the whole order?"

"No, only this church. The Order has churches in other places and they keep their records as they see fit."

"How many other churches?"

"I do not know. People are called, and the order receives them. We do not move around. There are many places where darkness can escape into the world, and when the Order discovers them, it takes in light to combat it. That there is still darkness means that we have not found all of the places. Now, we must go. There are things to do."

Charlotte wanted to refuse, to tell him that she could not leave her life behind, but the sheer size and complexity of the loss she was facing meant that the words would not fit around it. No more saunas, she thought. No more work or going out at lunchtime with my friends. No more nights curled up on the sofa with a bottle of wine watching a movie. No more pizza or restaurants, no more telephone calls. No more life. I can't, she thought hopelessly, I can't do it. And yet, as she thought, she heard again that slithering, chitinous noise and remembered the darkness slipping across her foot like the warm kiss of some terrible, moistureless mouth, and she could not turn him down. Instead, she said, "Why can't you carry on?" A question, she knew, to avoid her own final acceptance.

"I'm dying," Babbas said. "I have something growing inside me and it is killing me. I cannot carry the oil for the lamps any more. I am slow. I have not yet, but one day I will slip and fall, or forget something, and then? It will escape. I can stay and teach you, but I cannot carry the responsibility any longer. It is why God called you." He removed the stained white cloth from his head and came towards her, holding it out in front of him reverently. She saw the marks of the old grease that stained it like tree-rings denoting age, and smelled the sickly scent of his decaying, dying flesh.

"We wear this, those of us who carry the burden," Babbas said. "It is, perhaps, our only symbolic act, the only thing we do that is devoid of true function. This is the mantle of light."

So saying, Babbas draped the cloth over Charlotte's hair so that it hung down, brushing her shoulders. It smelled old and sour. Babbas smiled at her and stepped back as the weight of centuries settled on Charlotte's head.

CHRISTOPHER FOWLER

The Twilight Express

CHRISTOPHER FOWLER LIVES IN King's Cross, London. He is an award-winning novelist best known for his dark urban fiction. He has written seventeen novels and over 120 short stories collected in ten volumes. After his latest "Bryant & May" mystery novel, *The Victoria Vanishes*, comes an autobiography, *Paperboy*. He then plans to return to suspense and horror.

About the following story, he says: "I wanted to create a timeless, dream-like feel in a piece of short fiction, and always loved the more disreputable funfairs and amusement parks because they expose your inner child, your excitement and fears.

"The ghost train on Brighton Pier bothered me as a kid, because it depicted a train carriage filled with nodding, skeletal passengers. But fairs also leave you feeling regretful and disappointed – so I wanted to catch that as well. The result is 'The Twilight Express'."

THE FUNFAIR BLEW IN one hot, windy night in early July, while everyone's doors and windows were sealed against the invading desert dust. Billy Fleet knew it was coming when he heard the distorted sound of a calliope drifting faintly on the breeze, but he didn't think then that it might hold the answer to his problem.

He leaned on his bedroom sill, watching the soft amber light move across the horizon of trees, beneath a velvet night filled with pinhole stars. The country dark was flushing with their arrival. On another night he might have climbed the trellis in his peejays and sat on the green grit of the tarpaper roof to watch the carnival procession, but tonight he had too much on his mind. The fair had travelled from

Illinois to Arizona, and somehow made the detour here. There were a few dates yet that weren't played out, small towns with bored kids and fathers jingling chump change, but soon the carnies would be looking to put down roots before the dying summer cooled the hot sidewalks and families grew more concerned with laying in stores for winter than wasting good money on gimcrack sideshows and freak tents.

Billy turned restlessly under his sheets, wondering what it would take to clear his troubles, and the more he thought, the more desperate he became. His mother would cry, his father would beat him, and then a subtler meanness would settle over his life as friends and teachers pulled away, shamed by his inability to do what was right. It was a town that put great store by self-discipline.

But it wasn't cowardice that would prevent him from pleasing them, it was preservation. He wasn't about to throw his life away just because Susannah's period was late. No matter how hard she pushed, he wouldn't marry her. Hell, he wasn't sure he even liked her much, and would never have gone up to Scouts' Point if she hadn't complained that all the other girls had been taken there. The entire bluff was crowded with creaking cars, and though the scent of rampant sex excited him, it all felt so tawdry, so predictably small town. He had no intention of staying in Cooper Creek for a day longer than he had to, for each passing moment brought him closer to stopping forever, just as his father had done, and boy, the family had never heard the end of that.

He couldn't just up and leave without money, qualifications, some place to go, and with just three weeks left before his graduation, it was a matter of pride to stay. He imagined the door to a good out-of-state college swinging open, taking him to a bright new future. But by the time summer break was over Susannah's belly would be round as a basketball, and the trap would have closed about him. He knew how the girls in the coffee shop talked, as if finding the right boy and pinning him down was the only thing that mattered. Mr Sanders, his biology teacher, had told him that after babies were born, the male stopped developing because his role in the procreation cycle was over. It wasn't right that a girl who came from such a dirt-dumb family as Susannah should be able to offer him a little dip in the honey-pot and then chain him here through the best years of his life, in some edge-of-town clapboard house with a baby-room, where the smell of damp diapers would cling to his clothes and his loveless nights would be filled with dreams of what might have been.

There had to be another solution, but it didn't present itself until he went out to the field where the Elysium funfair was pitching up in the pale gold mist of the autumn morning, and watched as the roustabouts raised their rides, bolting together boards and pounding struts into the cool earth. There was a shop-soiled air about the Elysium, of too many tours without fresh paint, of waived safety permits and back-pocket accounting. The shills and barkers had not yet arrived, but Billy could tell that they, too, would be fighting for one more season before calling it a day and splitting up to go their separate ways. Funfairs rarely stopped at Cooper Creek; there wasn't enough fast money to be made here, and although the local folks were kind enough to passing strangers, they didn't care to mix together.

Billy sat on the back of the bench and watched as the gears and tracks were laid behind the flats. He saw missing teeth and caked oil, mended brake-bars and makeshift canopies, iron rods bound with wire over rope, and wondered how many accidents had forced the Elysium to skip town in the dead of night. That was the moment he realized he would be able to kill Susannah's baby.

He saw the question as simply one of survival. He had something to offer the world, and the only obstacle that waited in his path was a wide-eyed schoolgirl. As the yellowing leaves tumbled above his head, Billy felt the first chill decision of adulthood.

The funfair ran its cycle through Labor Day, but only passed by Cooper Creek for a week. He felt sure that convincing Susannah to come with him would be easy, but before that evening he needed to find a way inside the ghost train. He had watched the canvas flats of hellfire and damnation being put together to form a righteous journey, devil snakes and playing cards lining the tunnel through which the cars would roll. Now he needed to befriend the woman who was helping her old man set up the ticket booth, the one the roustabouts called Molly. He knew how to use seventeen years of healthy boyhood on a thirty-five-year-old overweight woman. Girls flirt with attractive men, but boys flirt with anyone.

When he approached her, she was bending over a broken step, and all he could see was the wide field of blue cornflowers that covered her dress. He stood politely until she rose, hands on hips, a vast acreage of sun-weathered cleavage smiling at him. Her small grey eyes no longer trusted anything they saw, but softened on his face.

"Help you, boy?"

"Ma'am, my name's Billy Fleet, and I'm raising money for my college education by trying to find summer work. I know how to fix electrics, and it seems to me you need someone to work the ghost train, 'cause you got some shorts sparking out in there, and I ain't seen no one go in to repair 'em."

"What are you, town watchdog? Got nothing better to do than spy on folks trying to earn a decent living?" Molly's bead-eyes shrank further.

"No Ma'am. I meant no disrespect, I just see you setting up from my bedroom window and know you're shy a man or two. This town's real particular about health and safety, and I figure I can save you a heap of trouble for a few bucks."

The woman folded fat arms across her considerable bosom and rocked back to study him. "I don't take kindly to blackmail, Billy boy." Her eyes were as old as Cleopatra's, and studied him without judgment. "Fairs don't take on college kids. It don't pay to be too smart around here."

"Maybe so, but in this town a fair is a place where a guy gets a rosette for keeping a pig. This is a real carnival. It's special."

"Ain't no big secret to it. You take a little, give a little back, that's all." She saw the need in his eyes and was silent for a moment. "Hell, if the town is so dog-dead you got to watch us set up from your bedroom at nights maybe we can work something out. Let me go talk to Papa Jack."

That was how Billy got the job on the Twilight Express.

The night the fair opened, white lights punched holes into the blue air, and the smell of sage and dust was replaced with the tang of rolling hotdogs. Susannah had planned to go with her girl-friends, to shriek and flirt on the opalescent Tilt-A-Whirl, holding down their skirts and tossing back their hair with arms straightened to the bar, bucking and spinning across the night. She agreed with just a nod when Billy insisted on taking her, and he wondered whether she would really be fussed if he just took off, but he couldn't do that. He couldn't bear the thought of people bad-mouthing him, even though he wouldn't be there to hear it. So he took Susannah to the fair.

He couldn't bring himself to place his arm around her waist, because the baby might sense his presence and somehow make him change his mind. Babies did that; they turned tough men into dishrags, and he wasn't about to let that happen. She wore a red dress covered in yellow daisies like tiny bursts of sunlight, and laughed at everything. He couldn't see what was funny. She was happily robbing him of his life and didn't even notice, pointing to the fat lady and the stilt-walkers, feeding her glossy red mouth with pink floss as if she was eating sunset clouds.

He thought she would want to talk about the baby and what it meant to them, but she seemed happy to take the subject for granted, as if she couldn't care whether there was something growing inside her or not.

At the entrance of the ghost train, Molly watched impassively as he passed her without acknowledgment. Susannah balked and tried to turn aside when she reached the steps to the car. "No, Billy, don't make me go. It's dark in there. Let's take the rope-walk instead."

"Don't make a big deal of it, Susannah, the ghost train's a few devils and skeletons is all." He had stood inside the ride beside the flickering tissue-inferno, breathing in the coppery electric air, watching the cars bump over soldered tracks that should have been scrapped years ago, lines that could throw a rider like a bronco.

She saw the pressure in his eyes and gave in meekly, took her ticket and bowed her head as she passed through the turnstile, as if she was entering church. The car was tight for two adults; he was forced to place his arm around her shoulder. Her hair tickled his forearm. She smelled as fresh-cut as a harvest field. With a sudden lurch, the car sparked into life and a siren sounded as they banged through the doors into musty darkness.

He knew what was coming. After a few cheap scares of drifting knotted string and jiggling rubber spiders, the car would switch back on itself and tilt down a swirling red tunnel marked Damnation Alley, but just before it dropped into the fires of hell it would swing again, away to the safer sights of comically dancing wooden skeletons. The track was bad at the switch; a person could tip out on the line as easy as pie. The next car would be right behind, and those suckers were heavy. Papa Jack had fallen into a bourbon bottle a couple of nights back, and told him about a boy who had bust his neck when the cars had stalled in Riverton Fields, Wichita, a few seasons back. The Elysium had hightailed it out of town before their Sheriff could return from his fishing trip, had even changed its name for a couple of years. A second accident would get folks nodding and clucking about how they suspected trouble from the carnie folk all along. He would make sure Susannah didn't get bruised up, he wouldn't want that, but she had to take a spill, and land good and hard on her stomach.

As the car hit its first horseshoe she gripped his knee, and he sensed her looking up at him. He caught the glisten of her eyes in the flashbulbs, big blue pupils, daybreak innocent. They tilted into the spiralling tunnel and she squeaked in alarm, gripping tighter, as close now as when they had loved. The moment arrived as they reached the switch. The car lurched and juddered. All he had to do was push, but she was still holding tightly onto him. In an effort to break her grip, he stood up sharply.

"Billy – what—"

The car twisted and he tipped out, landing on his back in the revolving tunnel. Susannah's hands reached out toward him, her fingers splayed wide, then her car rounded a black-painted peak and was gone. The cylinder turned him over once, twice, dropping him down into the uplit paper fires of damnation, scuffing his elbows and knees on the greased tracks.

And then there was nothing beneath his limbs.

When he opened his eyes again, he found himself in the fierce green fields behind the house. Judging by the smell of fresh grass in the morning air, it was late spring, but he was wearing the same clothes. The sun was hot on his face, his bare arms. The voice spoke softly behind him. He could only just hear it over the sound of the crickets and the rustling grass.

"Oh Billy, what a beautiful day. If only it was always like this. I remember, I remember—" She was lying in the tall grass near the tree, running a curving green stem across her throat, her lips. Her print dress had hiked around her bare pale thighs. She stared into the cloudless sky as though seeing beyond into space.

"What have you done with the baby, Susannah?"

"I don't know," she replied slowly. "It must be around here somewhere. Look how clear the sky is. It feels like you could see forever."

The day was so alive that it shook with the beat of his heart, the air taut and trembling with sunlit energy. It was hard to concentrate on anything else. "We have to find the baby," he told her, fighting to develop the thought. "We went to all that trouble."

He looked up at the sun and allowed the dazzling yellow light to fill his vision. When he closed his eyes, tiny translucent creatures wriggled across the pink lids, as mindless and driven as spermatozoa.

"I forget what I did with it, Billy. You know how I forget things. Will you make me a daisy chain? Nobody ever made me a daisy chain. Nobody ever noticed me until you."

"Let's find the baby first, Susannah."

"I think perhaps it was out in the field. Yes, I'm sure I saw it there." She raised a lazy arm and pointed back, over her head. Her hair was spread around her head in a corn-coloured halo. She smiled sleepily and shut her eyes. The lids were sheened like dragonfly wings. "I can see the stars today, even with my eyes closed. We should never leave this place. Never, ever leave. Look how strong we are together. Why, we can do anything. You see that, don't you? You see that . . ." Her voice drifted off.

Her watched her fall asleep. She looked a little older now. Her cheekbones had appeared, shaping her face to a heart. She had lost some puppy fat. Light shimmered on her cheeks, wafted and turned by the tiny shields of leaves above. "I have to go and look, Susannah," he told her. "There are bugs everywhere."

"You just have to say the name," she murmured. "Just say the name." But her voice was lost beneath the buzzing of crickets, the shifting of grass, the tremulous morning heat.

He rose and walked deep into the field, until he came to a small clearing in the grass. Lowering himself onto his haunches, he studied the ant nest, watching the shiny black mass undulating around a raised ellipse in the brown earth. The carapaces of the insects were darkly iridescent, tiny night-prisms that bustled on thousands of pin-legs, batting each other with antennae like blind men's canes. He shaped his hands into spades and dug them into the squirming mass of segmented bodies, feeling them tickle over his hands and wrists, running up his arms. They nipped at his skin with their pincers, but were too small to hurt. Digging deeper until his fingertips met under the earth, he felt the fat thoraxes roll warmly over his skin. Carefully he raised the mound, shaking it free of insects. A baby's face appeared, fat and gurgly, unconcerned by the bugs that ran across his wide blue eyes, in and out of the pouted lips. Raising the child high toward the fiery summer globe, he watched as the last of the ants fell away, revealing his smiling, beautiful son.

"Tyler," he said, "Tyler Fleet."

And he set off back towards his sleeping wife.

"Billy. Billy, you came back." Her lank hair hung over his face, tickling. Her plucked eyebrows were arched in a circumflex of concern. She had been crying.

"What's your problem?" he asked slowly, feeling the words in his mouth. He was lying on the cool dry dirt in front of the ghost train ride. A few passers-by had stopped to watch.

"You fell out of the carriage is what's the problem," she said, touching his cheek with her fingers. "You cut your forehead. Oh, Billy."

"I'm fine. Was just a slip is all." He raised himself on one elbow. "No need to get so worked up." He rubbed the goosebumps from his arms.

"I was so frightened in there, I thought I'd lost you, I panicked," she told him. "Look." She held up her palm and showed him the crimson dot. "It's my blood, not yours. I started late, that's all. I'm not pregnant, Billy. I'm sorry."

He realized why she had been so unconcerned at the fair. She had been happy to place her trust in him unquestioningly. It had never crossed her mind that things might not work out. He studied her face as if seeing her for the first time. "I'm so sorry," she said again, searching his eyes in trepidation.

"Don't worry," he told her, pulling himself up and dusting down his jeans. "Maybe we can make another one." He offered his arm. "Give me your hand." He sealed his fingers gently over the crimson dot. She pulled him to his feet, surprisingly strong.

Molly looked up as he passed the ticket booth to the Twilight Express. There was no way of knowing what she was thinking, or if she was thinking anything at all. "Hey Billy, Papa Jack wants you to work with him tomorrow night," she told him. "You gonna need to put that money by. The baby'll be back, and maybe next time you'll be ready for him."

Then she went back to counting the change from the tickets.

The moon above the Elysium funfair shone with the colours of the sideshow, red and blue glass against butter yellow, as the calliope played on, turning wishes into starlight.

The Twilight Express was gone. It had been replaced by the Queen of The South, a Mississippi riverboat ride where passengers seated themselves on cream-coloured benches and watched as their paddle steamer slipped upriver, not past the real southland of jute factories and boatyards and low-cost housing, but an imagined antebellum fantasy of filigreed plantation houses glimpsed through Spanish moss. The candy-coloured deck looked out on pastel hardboard flats and painted linen skies that creaked past on a continuous roll as birds twittered on the tape loop.

Molly was still here at the Elysium, working the riverboat ride now. She watched him approach without pleasure or sorrow shaping her face. He supposed carnie folk saw too much to care one way or the other. To her, he was just another small-town hick.

"So you didn't leave," she said, sweeping coins from her counter without looking up.

"Did I say I was going?" he asked defensively.

"Didn't have to." She stacked dimes to the width of her hand, calculating the value, then swept them into a bag. "You should bring your wife here."

"You don't know I married her," he said, kicking at the dry dirt in annoyance.

"Don't I, though." Her expression never changed.

He left her counting the gate money, and resolved not to bring Susannah to the Elysium. But he did, that Friday night.

He breathed in the smell of hot caramel, sawdust and sugar-floss, fired a rifle at pocked metal soldiers and hooked a yellow duck for Tyler, but wouldn't go near Molly's ride. "I don't need to go on that," he told his wife, watching as she held their baby to her breast. "Not after last time."

Susannah jiggled the baby and stood looking up at the painted riverbank. "That was more than three years ago, Billy. The Twilight Express is gone. It's not a ghost train anymore. No one's gonna fall out of the car." She smiled at him bravely, as if it was all that could protect her from his simmering impatience.

Billy still wasn't sure what had happened that time. The accident had changed something between them. All he remembered was that she had freed him and he had elected to stay, but part of him remained regretful. He loved his boy, but the smell of the infant had lingered too long on his skin, reminding him of his responsibilities, removing any pretence of freedom. There was never time to be alone and think things through.

He worked in his uncle's feed store now, and made a decent living, but it wasn't what he had imagined for himself. Sometimes strangers passed through the local bar and talked of harsh cities they'd seen, strange lands they'd visited, and he wanted to beg them; *let me come with you.*

He loved his son, but knew there could have been a better life. The carnival had changed all that. It took a little and gave a little back, that's what Molly had once told him.

"Come with me," said Susannah. "We're a team. We do things together."

"You two are the team. Go have fun," he said, placing a hand firmly in the small of her back, propelling her toward the steps of the Queen of The South, its minstrel music piped through speakers set on either side of the great painted boat that seemed to move forward but never travelled anywhere. "Show Tyler the Mississippi. I'll be here when you get off."

Susannah passed reluctantly through the turnstile, balancing the boy on her hip. From within the ticket booth, Molly caught his eye for the briefest of moments, and he read something strange in her expression. His wife looked back, the dying daylight shining in her eyes. Her glance pierced his heart. She gave a brief nervous smile and stepped inside the boat. He wanted to run forward and snatch her back before she could take her seat, to tell her he knew what he had and it was real good, but even as he thought this he wondered what else he might be missing, and then the banjo music had started, the ply-board trees were shunting past, and the steamer was gradually lost from view.

The ride was long. He grew bored with waiting and tried to knock a coconut from its shy, even though he knew it was probably nailed in place. When he returned to the ride it had already emptied out, but there was no sign of his young family. He asked Molly where they had gone, but she denied ever having seen them. None of the barkers would be drawn on the subject. He vaulted into the back of the riverboat ride, clambering through the dusty sunlit diorama, trying to see how they might have escaped through the pasteboard flats, but was pulled out by Papa Jack.

Billy yelled and stamped and made a fuss, finally called the Sheriff, but everyone agreed that Susannah had gone, taking their child with her. People looked at him warily and backed away.

The heatwave broke on the day the Elysium carnival trundled out of town. As rain darkened the bald dirt-patch where the tents had stood, Billy watched the trucks drive off, and knew that he had failed the test.

The lilting sound of the calliope stole away his dreams and faded slowly with them, leaving him under clouded skies, filled with bitter remorse. Twilight died down to a starless night, and there was nothing left inside it now, just the empty, aching loss of what he might have had, who he might have been, and the terrible understanding that he had been looking too far away for the answer to his prayers.

Somewhere in another town, another state, the Twilight Express showed the way between stations for those passengers who were strong enough to stay on the ride.

RAMSEY CAMPBELL

Peep

RAMSEY CAMPBELL is probably the world's most respected living horror author. A multiple award-winning writer and editor with numerous books and short stories to his credit, he has just completed his most recent novel, *Creatures of the Pool*.

Publications in 2008 include *Thieving Fear*, his latest novel from PS Publishing, and *The Grin of the Dark*, which launched Virgin Books' new horror line in the UK. *The Influence* from Millipede Press includes new illustrations by J. K. Potter, while *Inconsequential Tales* is a volume of uncollected stories from Hippocampus Press.

"I've been revisiting a good deal of my early life and its prologue lately," explains Campbell, "reading the correspondence between my parents, mostly from before I was born. In due course all this will be the basis of an essay.

"Among the random memories I've dredged up in recent years from the depths of my ageing brain was one of my mother playing the game the present story takes as its basis.

"There was nothing macabre about it, but you know me – it quickly suggested some of the events in the tale that follows."

I'M LABOURING UP THE STEEPEST section of the hill above the promenade when the twins run ahead. At least we're past the main road by the railway station. "Don't cross—" I shout or rather gasp. Perhaps each of them thinks or pretends to think I'm addressing the other, because they don't slow down until they reach the first side street and dodge around the corner.

"Stay there," I pant. They're already out of sight, having crouched below the garden wall. I wonder if they're angry with me by association with their parents, since Geraldine wasn't bought a kite to replace the one she trampled to bits when yesterday's weather let her down. They did appear to relish watching teenage drivers speed along the promenade for at least a few minutes, which may mean they aren't punishing me for their boredom. In any case I ought to join in the game. "Where are those children?" I wonder as loudly as my climb leaves breath for. "Where can they be?"

I seem to glimpse an answering movement beyond a bush at the far end of the wall. No doubt a bird is hiding in the foliage, since the twins pop their heads up much closer. Their small plump eight-year-old faces are gleeful, but there's no need for me to feel they're sharing a joke only with each other. Then Geraldine cries "Peep."

Like a chick coming out of its shell, as Auntie Beryl used to say. I can do without remembering what else she said, but where has Geraldine learned this trick? Despite the August sunshine, a wind across the bay traces my backbone with a shiver. Before questioning Geraldine I should usher the children across the junction, and as I plod to the corner I wheeze, "Hold my—"

There's no traffic up here. Nevertheless I'm dismayed that the twins dash across the side street and the next one to the road that begins on the summit, opposite the Catholic church with its green skullcap and giant hatpin of a cross. They stop outside my house, where they could be enjoying the view of the bay planted with turbines to farm the wind. Though I follow as fast as I'm able, Gerald is dealing the marble bellpush a series of pokes by the time I step onto the mossy path. Catching my breath makes me sound harsh as I ask "Geraldine, who taught you that game?"

She giggles, and so does Gerald. "The old woman," he says.

I'm about to pursue this when Paula opens my front door. "Don't say that," she rebukes him.

Her face reddens, emphasizing how her cropped hair has done the reverse. It's even paler by comparison with the twins' mops, so that I wonder if they're to blame. Before I can put my reluctant question, Gerald greets the aromas from the kitchen by demanding, "What's for dinner?"

"We've made you lots of good things while you've been looking after grandpa."

The twins don't think much of at least some of this, although I presume the reference to me was intended to make them feel grown-up. They push past their mother and race into the lounge, jangling all the ornaments. "Careful," Paula calls less forcefully than I would prefer. "Share," she adds as I follow her to the kitchen, where she murmurs, "What game were you quizzing them about?"

"You used to play it with babies. I'm not saying you. People did." I have a sudden image of Beryl thrusting her white face over the side of my cot, though if that ever happened, surely I wouldn't remember. "Peep," I explain and demonstrate by covering my eyes before raising my face above my hand.

Paula's husband Bertie glances up from vigorously stirring vegetables in the wok he and Paula brought with them. "And what was your issue with that?"

Surely I misunderstood Gerald, which can be cleared up later. "Your two were playing it," I say. "A bit babyish at their age, do you think?"

"Good Lord, they're only children. Let them have their fun till they have to get serious like the rest of us," he says and cocks his head towards a squabble over television channels. "Any chance you could restore some balance in there? Everything's under control in here."

I'm perfectly capable of cooking a decent meal. I've had to be since Jo died. I feel as if I'm being told where to go and how to act in my own house. Still, I should help my remaining family, and so I bustle to the lounge, where the instant disappearance of a channel leaves the impression that a face dropped out of sight as I entered. Gerald has captured the remote control and is riffling through broadcasts. "Stop that now," I urge. "Settle on something."

They haven't even sat on the furniture. They're bouncing from chair to chair by way of the equally venerable sofa in their fight over the control. "I think someone older had better take charge," I say and hold out my hand until Gerald flings the control beside me on the sofa. The disagreement appears to be over two indistinguishably similar programmes in which vaguely Oriental cartoon animals batter one another with multicoloured explosions and other garish displays of power. I propose watching real animals and offer a show set in a zoo for endangered species, but the response makes me feel like a member of one. My suggestion of alternating scenes from each chosen programme brings agreement, though only on dismissing the idea, and Geraldine capitulates to watching her brother's choice.

The onscreen clamour gives me no chance to repeat my question. When I try to sneak the volume down, the objections are deafening. I don't want Paula and her husband to conclude I'm useless – I mustn't give them any excuse to visit even less often – and so I hold my peace, if there can be said to be any in the room. The cartoon is still going off when we're summoned to dinner.

I do my best to act as I feel expected to behave. I consume every grain and shoot and chunk of my meal, however much it reminds me of the cartoon. When my example falls short of the twins I'm compelled to encourage them aloud – "Have a bit more or you won't get any bigger" and "That's lovely, just try it" and in some desperation "Eat up, it's good for you." Perhaps they're sick of hearing about healthy food at home. I feel clownishly false and even more observed than I did over the television. I'm quite relieved when the plates are scraped clean and consigned to the dishwasher.

I'd hoped the twins might have grown up sufficiently since Christmas to be prepared to go to bed before the adults, but apparently holidays rule, and the table is cleared for one of the games Gerald has insisted on bringing. Players take turns to insert plastic sticks in the base of a casket, and the loser is the one whose stick releases the lid and the contents, a wagging head that I suppose is meant to be a clown's, given its whiteness and shock of red hair and enlarged eyes and wide grin just as fixed. I almost knock the game to the floor when one of my shaky attempts to take care lets out the gleeful head, and then I have to feign amusement for the children's sake. At first I'm glad when Gerald is prevailed upon to let his sister choose a game.

It's Monopoly. I think only its potential length daunts me until the children's behaviour reminds me how my aunt would play. They sulk whenever a move goes against them and crow if one fails to benefit their twin, whereas Beryl would change any move she didn't like and say "Oh, let me have it" or simply watch to see whether anyone noticed. "Peep," she would say and lower her hand in front of her eyes if she caught us watching. My parents pretended that she didn't cheat, and so I kept quiet, even though she was more than alert to anyone else's mistakes.

Eventually I try conceding tonight's game in the hope the other adults will, but it seems Paula's husband is too much of a stockbroker to relinquish even toy money. The late hour enlivens the twins or at any rate makes them more active, celebrating favourable moves by bouncing on the chairs. "Careful of my poor old furniture," I say, though I'm more dismayed by the reflection of their antics in the mirror that backs the dresser, just the top of one tousled red head or the other springing up among the doubled plates. I'm tired enough to fancy that an unkempt scalp rendered dusty by the glass keeps straying into view even while the twins are still or at least seated. Its owner would be at my back, but since nobody else looks, I won't. Somewhat earlier than midnight Bertie wins the game and sits back satisfied as the twins start sweeping hotels off the board in vexation. "I think someone's ready for bed," I remark.

"You go, then," says Gerald, and his sister giggles in agreement.

"Let grandpa have the bathroom first," says their mother.

Does she honestly believe I was referring to myself? "I won't be long," I promise, not least because I've had enough of mirrors. Having found my toothbrush amid the visiting clutter, I close my eyes while wielding it. "Empty now," I announce on the way to my room. In due course a squabble migrates from the bathroom to the bunks next door and eventually trails into silence. Once I've heard Paula and her husband share the bathroom, which is more than her mother and I ever did, there are just my thoughts to keep me awake.

I don't want to think about the last time I saw Beryl, but I can't help remembering when her playfulness turned unpleasant. It was Christmas Eve, and she'd helped or overseen my mother in making dozens of mince pies, which may have been why my mother was sharper than usual with me. She told me not to touch the pies after she gave me one to taste. I was the twins' age and unable to resist. Halfway through a comedy show full of jokes I didn't understand I sneaked back to the kitchen. I'd taken just one surreptitious bite when I saw Beryl's face leaning around the night outside the window. She was at the door behind me, and I hid the pie in my mouth before turning to her. Her puffy whitish porous face that always put me in mind of dough seemed to widen with a grin that for a moment I imagined was affectionate. "Peep," she said.

Though it sounded almost playful, it was a warning or a threat of worse. Why did it daunt me so much when my offence had been so trivial? Perhaps I was simply aware that my parents had to put up with my mother's sister while wishing she didn't live so close. She always came to us on Christmas Day, and that year I spent it fearing that she might surprise me at some other crime, which made me feel in danger of committing one out of sheer nervousness. "Remember," she said that night, having delivered a doughy kiss that smeared me with lipstick and face powder. "Peep."

Either my parents found this amusing or they felt compelled to pretend. I tried to take refuge in bed and forget about Beryl, and so it seems little has changed in more than sixty years. At least I'm no longer walking to school past her house, apprehensive that she may peer around the spidery net curtains or inch the front door open like a lid. If I didn't see her in the house I grew afraid that she was hiding somewhere else, so that even encountering her in the street felt like a trap she'd set. Surely all this is too childish to bother me now, and when sleep abandons me to daylight I don't immediately know why I'm nervous.

It's the family, of course. I've been wakened by the twins quarrelling outside my room over who should waken me for breakfast. "You both did," I call and hurry to the bathroom to speed through my ablutions. Once the twins have begun to toy with the extravagant remains of their food I risk giving them an excuse to finish. "What shall we do today?" I ask, and meet their expectant gazes by adding, "You used to like the beach."

That's phrased to let them claim to have outgrown it, but Gerald says "I've got no spade or bucket."

"I haven't," Geraldine competes.

"I'm sure replacements can be obtained if you're both going to make me proud to be seen out with you," I say and tell their parents, "I'll be in charge if you've better things to do."

Bertie purses his thin prim lips and raises his pale eyebrows. "Nothing's better than bringing up your children."

I'm not sure how many rebukes this incorporates. Too often the way he and Paula are raising the twins seems designed to reprove how she was brought up. "I know my dad wouldn't have meant it like that," she says. "We could go and look at some properties, Bertie."

"You're thinking of moving closer," I urge.

Her husband seems surprised to have to donate even a word of explanation. "Investments."

"Just say if you don't see enough of us," says Paula.

Since I suspect she isn't speaking for all of them, I revert to silence. Once the twins have been prevailed upon to take turns loading the dishwasher so that nothing is broken, I usher them out of the house. "Be good for grandpa," Paula says, which earns her a husbandly frown. "Text if you need to," he tells them.

I should have thought mobile phones were too expensive for young children to take to the beach. I don't want to begin the outing with an argument, and so I lead them downhill by their impatient hands. I see the scrawny windmills twirling on the bay until we turn down the road that slopes to the beach. If I don't revive my question now I may never have the opportunity or the nerve. "You were going to tell me who taught you that game."

Gerald's small hot sticky hand wriggles in my fist. "What game?"

"You know." I'm not about to release their hands while we're passing a supermarket car park. I raise one shoulder and then the other to peer above them at the twins. "Peep," I remind them.

Once they've had enough of giggling Geraldine splutters, "Mummy said we mustn't say."

"I don't think she quite meant that, do you? I'm sure she won't mind if you just say it to me when I've asked."

"I'll tell if you tell," Gerald informs his sister.

"That's a good idea, then you'll each just have done half. Do it in chorus if you like."

He gives me a derisive look of the kind I've too often seen his father turn on Paula. "I'll tell mummy if you say," he warns Geraldine.

I mustn't cause any more strife. I'm only reviving an issue that will surely go away if it's ignored. I escort the twins into a newsagent's shop hung with buckets and spades and associated paraphernalia, the sole establishment to preserve any sense of the seaside among the pubs and wine bars and charity shops. Once we've agreed on items the twins can bear to own I lead them to the beach.

The expanse of sand at the foot of the slipway from the promenade borders the mouth of the river. Except for us it's deserted, but not for long. The twins are seeing who can dump the most castles on the sand when it starts to grow populated. Bald youths tapestried with tattoos let their bullish dogs roam while children not much older than the twins drink cans of lager or roll some kind of cigarette to share, and boys who are barely teenage if even that race motorcycles along the muddy edge of the water. As the twins begin to argue over who's winning the sandcastle competition I reflect that at least they're behaving better than anybody else in sight. I feel as if I'm directing the thought at someone who's judging them, but nobody is peering over or under the railings on the promenade or out of the apartments across it. Nevertheless I feel overheard in declaring, "I think you've both done very well. I couldn't choose between you."

I've assumed the principle must be to treat them as equally as possible – even their names seem to try – but just now dissatisfaction is all they're sharing. "I'm bored of this," Gerald says and demolishes several of his rickety castles. "I want to swim."

"Have you brought your costumes?"

"They're in our room," says Geraldine. "I want to swim in a pool, not a mucky river."

"We haven't got a pool here any more. We'd have to go on the train."

"You can take us," Gerald says. "Dad and mum won't mind."

I'm undismayed to give up sitting on the insidiously damp sand or indeed to leave the loudly peopled beach once I've persuaded the twins not to abandon their buckets and spades. I feel as if the children are straining to lug me uphill except when they mime more exhaustion than I can afford to admit. They drop the beach toys in my hall together with a generous bounty of sand on the way to thundering upstairs. After a brief altercation they reappear and I lead them down to the train.

Before it leaves the two-platformed terminus we're joined by half a dozen rudely pubertal drinkers. At least they're at the far end of the carriage, but their uproar might as well not be. They're fondest of a terse all-purpose word. I ignore the performance as an example to the twins, but when they continue giggling I attempt to distract them with a game of I Spy: s for the sea on the bare horizon, though they're so tardy in participating that I let it stand for the next station; f for a field behind a suburban school, even if I'm fleetingly afraid that Gerald will reveal it represents the teenagers' favourite word; c for cars in their thousands occupying a retail park beside a motorway, because surely Geraldine could never have been thinking of the other syllable the drinkers favour; b for the banks that rise up on both sides of the train as it begins to burrow into Birkenhead . . . I don't mean it for Beryl, but here is her house.

Just one window is visible above the embankment on our side of the carriage: her bedroom window. I don't know if I'm more disturbed by this glimpse of the room where she died or by having forgotten that we would pass the house. Of course it's someone else's room now – I imagine that the house has been converted into flats – and the room has acquired a window box; the reddish tuft that sprouts above the sill must belong to a plant, however dusty it looks. That's all I've time to see through the grimy window before the bridge I used to cross on the way to school blocks the view. Soon a station lets the drinkers loose, and a tunnel conducts us to our stop.

The lift to the street is open at both ends. It shuts them when Geraldine pushes the button, her brother having been promised that he can operate the lift on our return, and then it gapes afresh. Since nobody appears I suspect Gerald, but he's too far from the controls. "Must have been having a yawn," I say, and the twins gaze at me as if I'm the cause. No wonder I'm relieved when the doors close and we're hoisted into daylight.

As we turn the corner that brings the swimming pool into view the twins are diverted by a cinema. "I want to see a film," Gerald announces.

"You'll have to make your minds up. I can't be in two places at once. I'm just me."

Once she and her brother have done giggling at some element of this Geraldine says, "Grumpo."

I'm saddened to think she means me, especially since Gerald agrees, until I see it's the title of a film that's showing in the complex. "You need to be twelve to go in."

"No we don't," they duet, and Gerald adds "You can take us."

Because they're so insistent I seek support from the girl in the pay booth, only to be told I'm mistaken. She watches me ask, "What would your parents say?"

"They'd let us," Geraldine assures me, and Gerald says, "We watch fifteens at home."

Wouldn't the girl advise me if the film weren't suitable? I buy tickets and lead the way into a large dark auditorium. We're just in time to see the screen exhort the audience to switch off mobile phones, and I have the twins do so once they've used theirs to light the way along a row in the absence of an usherette. The certificate that precedes the film doesn't tell me why it bears that rating, but that's apparent soon enough. An irascible grandfather embarrasses his offspring with his forgetfulness and the class of his behaviour and especially his language, which even features two appearances of the word I ignored most often on the train. The twins find him hilarious, as do all the children in the cinema except for one that keeps poking its head over the back of a seat several rows ahead. Or is it a child? It doesn't seem to be with anyone, and now it has stopped trying to surprise me with its antics and settles on peering at me over the seat. Just its pale fat face above the nose is visible, crowned and surrounded by an unkempt mass of hair. The flickering of the dimness makes it look eager to jerk up and reveal more of its features, though the light is insufficient to touch off the slightest glimmer in the eyes, which I can't distinguish. At last the oldster in the film saves his children from robbers with a display of martial arts, and his family accepts that he's as loveable as I presume we're expected to have found him. The lights go up as the credits start to climb the screen, and I crane forward for a good look at the child who's been troubling me. It has ducked into hiding, and I sidle past Geraldine to find it. "You're going the wrong way, grandpa," she calls, but neither this nor Gerald's mirth can distract me from the sight of the row, which is deserted.

Members of the audience stare at me as I trudge to the end of the aisle, where words rise up to tower over me, and plod back along the auditorium. By this time it's empty except for the twins and me, and it's ridiculous to fancy that if I glance over my shoulder I'll catch a head in the act of taking cover. "Nothing," I say like Grumpo, if less coarsely, when Gerald asks what I'm looking for. I bustle the twins out of the cinema, and as soon as they revive their phones Gerald's goes off like an alarm.

In a moment Geraldine's restores equality. They read their messages, which consist of less than words, and return their calls. "Hello, mummy," Geraldine says. "We were in a film."

Her brother conveys the information and hands me the mobile. "Dad wants to speak to you."

"Bertie. Forgive me, should we have—"

"I hope you know we came to find you on the beach."

"Gerald didn't say. I do apologise if you—"

"I trust you're bringing them home now. To your house."

I don't understand why he thinks the addition is necessary. "I'm afraid we're in trouble," I inform the twins as Geraldine ends her call. I have to be reminded that it's Gerald's turn to control the lift at the railway station. At least our train reaches the platform as we do, and soon it emerges into the open, at which point I recall how close we are to Beryl's house. As the train passes it I turn to look. There's nothing at her window.

The tenant must have moved the window box. It does no good to wonder where the item that I glimpsed is now. I'm nervous enough by the time we arrive at the end of the line and I lead the twins or am led by them uphill. They seem more eager than I feel, perhaps because they've me to blame. I'm fumbling to extract my keys when Paula's husband opens the front door as if it's his. Having given each of us a stare that settles on me, Bertie says "Dinner won't be long."

It sounds so much like a rebuke, and is backed up by so many trespassing smells that I retort, "I could have made it, you know."

"Could you?" Before I can rise to this challenge he adds "Don't you appreciate my cuisine and Paula's?"

"Your children don't seem to all that much," I'm provoked to respond and quote a favourite saying of Jo's. "It isn't seaside without fish and chips."

"I'm afraid we believe in raising them more healthily."

"Do you, Paula? In other words, not how your mother and I treated you?" When she only gazes sadly at me from the kitchen I say, "It can't be very healthy if they hardly touch their food."

"It isn't very healthy for them to hear this kind of thing."

"Find something to watch for a few minutes," her husband tells them. "Maybe your grandfather can choose something suitable."

I feel silenced and dismissed. I follow the children into the lounge and insist on selecting the wildlife show. "I've got to watch as well," I say, even if it sounds like acknowledging a punishment. They greet the announcement of dinner without concealing their relief, although their enthusiasm falls short of the meal itself. When at last they've finished sprinkling cheese on their spaghetti they eat just the sauce, and hardly a leaf of their salad. Though I perform relishing all of mine, I have a sense of being held responsible for their abstinence. I try not to glance at the mirror of the dresser, but whenever I fail there appear to be only the reflections of the family and me.

Once the twins have filled up with chocolate dessert, it's time for games. I vote against reviving the one in which the pallid head pops up, which means that Gerald vetoes his sister's choice of Monopoly. Eventually I remember the games stored in the cupboard under the stairs. The dark shape that rears up beyond the door is my shadow. As I take Snakes and Ladders off the pile I'm reminded of playing it with Paula and her mother, who would smile whenever Paula clapped her hands at having climbed a ladder. I've brought the game into the dining room before I recall playing it with Beryl.

Was it our last game with her? It feels as if it should have been. Every time she cast a losing throw she moved one space ahead of it. "Can't get me," she would taunt the snakes. "You stay away from me, nasty squirmy things." I thought she was forbidding them to gobble her up as if she were one of her snacks between meals, the powdered sponge cakes that she'd grown more and more to resemble. Whenever she avoided a snake by expanding a move she peered at me out of the concealment of her puffed-up face. I felt challenged to react, and eventually I stopped my counter short of a snake. "Can't he count?" my aunt cried at once. "Go in the next box."

Once I'd descended the snake I complained, "Auntie Beryl keeps going where she shouldn't."

"Don't you dare say I can't count. They knew how to teach us when I was at school." This was the start of a diatribe that left her panting and clutching her chest while her face tried on a range of shades of grey. "Look what you've done," my father muttered in my ear while my mother tried to calm her down. When Beryl recaptured her wheezing breath she insisted on finishing the game, staring hard at me every time she was forced to land on a snake. She lost, and glared at me as she said, "Better never do anything wrong, even the tiniest thing. You don't know who'll be watching."

Of course I knew or feared I did. I wish I'd chosen another game to play with Paula and her family. Before long Gerald pretends one of his throws hasn't landed on a snake. "Fair play, now," I exhort, earning a scowl from Gerald and a look from his father that manages to be both disapproving and blank. Perhaps Geraldine misinterprets my comment, because soon she cheats too. "If we aren't going to play properly," I say without regarding anyone, "there's no point to the game." Not addressing somebody specific gives me a sense of including more people than are seated at the table, and no amount of glancing at the mirror can rid me of the impression. I've never been so glad to lose a game. "Will you excuse me?" I blurt as my chair stumbles backwards. "I've had quite a day. Time for bed."

My struggles to sleep only hold me awake. When at last the twins are coaxed up to their room and the adults retreat to theirs, I'm still attempting to fend off the memory of my final visit to my aunt's house. She was ill in bed, so shortly after the game of Snakes and Ladders that I felt responsible. She sent my mother out for cakes, though the remains of several were going stale in a box by her bed. There were crumbs on the coverlet and around her mouth, which looked swollen almost bloodlessly pale. I thought there was too much of her to be able to move until she dug her fingers into the bed and, having quivered into a sitting position that dislodged a musty shawl from her distended shoulders, reached for me. I took her hand as a preamble to begging forgiveness, but her cold spongy grasp felt as if it was on the way to becoming a substance other than flesh, which overwhelmed me with such panic that I couldn't speak. Perhaps she was aware of her overloaded heart, since she fixed me with eyes that were practically buried in her face. "I'll be watching," she said and expelled a breath that sounded close to a word. It was almost too loose to include consonants – it seemed as soft as her hand – but it could have been "Peep." I was terrified that it might also be her last breath, since it had intensified her grip on me. Eventually she drew another rattling breath but gave no sign of relaxing her clutch. Her eyes held me as a time even longer than a nightmare seemed to ooze by before I heard my mother letting herself into the house, when I was able to snatch my hand free and dash for the stairs. In less than a week my aunt was dead.

If I didn't see her again, being afraid to was almost as bad. Now that she was gone I thought she could be anywhere and capable of reading all my thoughts, especially the ones I was ashamed to have. I believed that thinking of her might bring her, perhaps in yet worse a form. I'd gathered that the dead lost weight, but I wasn't anxious to imagine how. Wouldn't it let her move faster? All these fears kept me company at night into my adolescence, when for a while I was even more nervous of seeing her face over the end of my bed. That never happened, but when at last I fall uneasily asleep I wake to see a shock of red hair duck below the footboard.

I'm almost quick enough to disguise my shriek as mirth once I realize that the glimpse included two small heads. "Good God," Bertie shouts from downstairs, "who was that?"

"Only me," I call. "Just a dream."

The twins can't hide their giggles. "No, it was us," cries Geraldine.

At least I've headed them off from greeting me with Beryl's word. Their father and to a lesser extent Paula give me such probing looks over breakfast that I feel bound to regain some credibility as an adult by enquiring "How was your search for investments?"

"Unfinished business," Bertie says.

"We were too busy wondering where you could have got to," Paula says.

"I hope I'm allowed to redeem myself. Where would you two like to go today?"

"Shopping," Geraldine says at once.

"Yes, shopping," Gerald agrees louder.

"Make sure you keep your phones switched on," their father says and frowns at me. "Do you still not own one?"

"There aren't that many people for me to call."

Paula offers to lend me hers, but the handful of unfamiliar technology would just be another cause for concern. At least we don't need to pass my aunt's house – we can take a bus. The twins insist on sitting upstairs to watch the parade of small shops interrupted by derelict properties. Wreaths on a lamppost enshrine a teenage car thief before we cross a bridge into the docks. I won't let the flowers remind me of my aunt, whose house is the best part of a mile away. The heads I see ducking behind the reflection in the window of the back seats belong to children. However little good they're up to, I ignore them, and they remain entirely hidden as we make for the stairs at our stop.

The pedestrian precinct appears to lead to a cathedral on the far side of the foreshortened river. The street enclosed by shops is crowded, largely with young girls pushing their siblings in buggies, if the toddlers aren't their offspring. The twins bypass discount stores on the way to a shopping mall, where the tiled floor slopes up to a food court flanked by clothes shops. Twin marts called Boyz and Girlz face each other across tables occupied by pensioners eking out cups of tea and families demolishing the contents of polystyrene cartons. "I'll be in there," Geraldine declares and runs across to Girlz.

"Wait and we'll come—" I might as well not have commenced, since as I turn to Gerald he dodges into Boyz. "Stay in the shops. Call me when you need me," I shout so loud that a little girl at a table renders her mouth clownish with a misaimed cream cake. Geraldine doesn't falter, and I'm not sure if she heard. As she vanishes into the shop beyond the diners I hurry after her brother.

Boyz is full of parents indulging or haranguing their children. When I can't immediately locate Gerald in the noisy aisles I feel convicted of negligence. He's at the rear of the shop, removing fat shoes from boxy alcoves on the wall. "Don't go out whatever you do. I'm just going to see your sister doesn't either," I tell him.

I can't see her in the other shop. I'm sidling between the tables when I grasp that I could have had Gerald phone for me to speak to her. It's just as far to go back now, and so I find my way through an untidy maze of abandoned chairs to Girlz. Any number of those, correctly spelled, are jangling racks of hangers and my nerves while selecting clothes to dispute with their parents, but none of them is Geraldine. I flurry up and down the aisles, back and forth to another catacomb of footwear, but she's nowhere to be seen.

"Geraldine," I plead in the faded voice my exertions have left me. Perhaps it's best that I can't raise it, since she must be in another shop. I didn't actually see her entering this one. As I dash outside I'm seized by a panic that tastes like all the food in the court turned stale. I need to borrow Gerald's mobile, but the thought makes me wonder if the twins could be using their phones to play a game at my expense – to co-ordinate how they'll keep hiding from me. I stare about in a desperate attempt to locate Geraldine, and catch sight of the top of her head in the clothes store next to Girlz.

"Just you stay there," I pant as I flounder through the entrance. It's clear that she's playing a trick, because it's a shop for adults; indeed, all the dresses that flap on racks in the breeze of my haste seem designed for the older woman. She's crouching behind a waist-high cabinet close to the wall. The cabinet quivers a little at my approach, and she stirs as if she's preparing to bolt for some other cover. "That's enough, Geraldine," I say and make, I hope, not too ungentle a grab. My foot catches on an edge of carpet, however, and I sprawl across the cabinet. Before I can regain any balance my fingers lodge in the dusty reddish hair.

Is it a wig on a dummy head? It comes away in my hand, but it isn't all that does. I manage not to distinguish any features of the tattered whitish item that dangles from it, clinging to my fingers until I hurl the tangled mass at the wall. I'm struggling to back away when the head jerks up to confront me with its eyes and the holes into which they've sunk. I shut mine as I thrust myself away from the cabinet, emitting a noise I would never have expected to make other than in the worst dream.

I'm quiet by the time the rescuers arrive to collect their children and me. It turns out that Geraldine was in a fitting room in Girlz. The twins forgot most of their differences so as to take charge, leading me out to a table where there seems to be an insistent smell of stale sponge cake. Nobody appears to have noticed anything wrong in the clothes shop except me. I'm given the front passenger seat in Bertie's car, which makes me feel like an overgrown child or put in a place of shame. The twins used their phones to communicate about me, having heard my cries, and to summon their parents. I gather that I'm especially to blame for refusing the loan of a mobile that would have prevented my losing the children and succumbing to panic.

I do my best to go along with this version of events. I apologise all the way home for being insufficiently advanced and hope the driver will decide this is enough. I help Paula make a salad, and eat up every slice of cold meat at dinner while I struggle to avoid thinking of another food. I let the children raid the cupboard under the stairs for games, although these keep us in the dining room. Sitting with my back to the mirror doesn't convince me we're alone, and perhaps my efforts to behave normally are too evident. I've dropped the dice several times to check that nobody is lurking under the table when Paula suggests an early night for all.

As I lie in bed, striving to fend off thoughts that feel capable of bringing their subject to me in the dark, I hear fragments of an argument. The twins are asleep or at any rate quiet. I'm wondering whether to intervene as diplomatically as possible when Paula's husband says "It's one thing your father being such an old woman—"

"I've told you not to call him that."

"—but today breaks the deal. I won't have him acting like that with my children."

There's more, not least about how they aren't just his, but the disagreements grow more muted, and I'm still hearing what he called me. It makes me feel alone, not only in the bed that's twice the size I need but also in the room. Somehow I sleep, and look for the twins at the foot of the bed when I waken, but perhaps they've been advised to stay away. They're so subdued at breakfast that I'm not entirely surprised when Paula says "Dad, we're truly sorry but we have to go home. I'll come and see you again soon, I promise."

I refrain from asking Bertie whether he'll be returning in search of investments. Once all the suitcases have been wedged into the boot of the Jaguar I give the twins all the kisses they can stand, along with twenty pounds each that feels like buying affection, and deliver a token handshake to Paula's husband before competing with her for the longest hug. As I wave the car downhill while the children's faces dwindle in the rear window, I could imagine that the windmills on the bay are mimicking my gesture. I turn back to the house and am halted by the view into the dining room.

The family didn't clear away their last game. It's Snakes and Ladders, and I could imagine they left it for me to play with a companion. I slam the front door and hurry into the room. I'm not anxious to share the house with the reminder that the game brings. I stoop so fast to pick up the box from the floor that an ache tweaks my spine. As I straighten, it's almost enough to distract me from the sight of my head bobbing up in the mirror.

But it isn't in the mirror, nor is it my head. It's on the far side of the table, though it has left even more of its face elsewhere. It still has eyes, glinting deep in their holes. Perhaps it is indeed here for a game, and if I join in it may eventually tire of playing. I can think of no other way to deal with it. I drop the box and crouch painfully, and once my playmate imitates me I poke my head above the table as it does. "Peep," I cry, though I'm terrified to hear an answer. "Peep."

TIM PRATT

From Around Here

TIM PRATT'S STORIES HAVE appeared in *The Year's Best Fantasy and Horror*, *The Best American Short Stories* and other nice places, and have been collected in two books, *Little Gods* and *Hart & Boot & Other Stories*.

His work has been nominated for various awards, including the Nebula and the Mythopoeic, and in 2007 his story "Impossible Dreams" won the Hugo Award, much to his surprise.

The author's first novel, *The Strange Adventures of Rangergirl*, appeared in 2005 and won the Joshua Norton Award. More recently, he has been working on an urban fantasy series under the byline "T. A. Pratt". He is a senior editor at *Locus* magazine and co-edits a tiny 'zine called *Flytrap*. Pratt lives near a lake in Oakland, California, with his wife Heather Shaw and their son, River.

"I don't believe in fate," he admits, "but I do believe in synchronicity – the appearance of seemingly related events that don't have a causal relationship. One day, many months ago, I was in a Starbucks coffee shop (I know, I know, I'm ashamed, but I was craving a caramel apple cider). I noticed these weird little java jackets on the counter, each of which bore a single strange word, with pronunciation marks and a definition.

"The one I picked up said 'Autochthonous'. Later, I realized the coasters were part of a promotion for the spelling bee movie *Akeelah and the Bee*, but at the time I just thought, 'Hey, Starbucks, way to increase my word power'. Later that same day, John Klima sent me an invitation to submit a story to *Logorrhea*, an anthology of stories based on winning spelling bee words, and when I saw 'Autochthonous' on the list of available words, I submitted to the whims of synchronicity and chose that one. (It means 'indigenous' or 'native' or 'occurring where it is found'.)

"I'd been thinking a lot anyway about the role of place and setting in my work, and about my own shifting notions of home, and hit on the idea to write about a *genius loci* who'd lost his *loci* – my protagonist is a little god, native to a particular island in the Pacific that sank a long time ago. Deprived of his own home, he travels the world, trying to save the homes of others. Naturally, he occasionally encounters local resistance. The story is about yearning, and rootlessness, and nostalgia, and weird serial killers.

"So basically, a typical Tim Pratt story."

I ARRIVED ON A FERRY made of gull cries and good ocean fog, and stepped from the limnal world into Jack London Square, down by Oakland's fine deep-water port. I walked, pre-dawn, letting my form coalesce from local expectations, filtered through my own habits and preferences. I stopped at a plate glass window downtown by the 12th Street train station and took a look at myself: dreads and dark skin, tall but not epic tall, clothes a little too raggedy to make robbing me worth a mugger's time. I walked on, feeling the thrums and creaks of a city waking up or going to sleep or just keeping on around me. I strolled past the houses of sex offenders, one-time killers with high blood pressure, altruists, guilty activists, the good-hearted, the fearful, and all the rest of the usual human lot. I was looking for the reek of the deeply crazy, the kind of living crack in a city that can swallow whole neighbourhoods and poison the well of human faith in a place utterly. The kind that could shatter lives on an afternoon spree or corrode them slowly over decades.

After a while, I found a street like that, and then I went to get some breakfast.

It was the kind of diner where you sit at a counter and the menus are sticky with the last customer's pancake syrup and you hope for the best. There were no other customers – I was between morning rushes, which made me lonely – and when the waitress came to take my order she was frazzled, like nobody should look at five in the morning. I said, "I don't have any money, but maybe we can work something out." Either she was from around here, and I'd get some breakfast, or she wasn't, and I'd get thrown out.

She got that faraway look like they do, and said, "Let's work something out."

I nodded. "Where you from?"

"Grew up in Temecula."

"Ah. The Inland Empire. Pretty black walnut trees down that way."

She smiled, the way people do when you prod them into a nice memory.

People have different ideas about what "home" means. For her, home meant a good chunk of California, at least, since Temecula was down south a ways. I'd never been there, but I'd probably go eventually. For some people, home just means one town, and if they stray from there, they feel like foreigners in strange territory. For others, home is a neighbourhood, or a block, or a street, or one room in one house where they grew up. And for some, home is *nowhere*, and me, I have a hard time talking to people like that.

"What can I offer you?" I said. My stomach rumbled. I'd never eaten before, at least, not with these teeth, this tongue, this stomach. I couldn't even remember what food tasted like. Things of the body are the first things I forget.

She told me, and I knew it was true, because I wasn't talking to her conscious mind, the part that's capable of lies and self-deception. I was talking to the deep down part of her, the part that stays awake at night, worrying, and making bargains with any gods she can imagine. She had a son, and he was in some shitty public school, and she was afraid he'd get hurt, beat up, hassled by the gangs, maybe even *join* a gang, though he was a good kid, really.

"Okay," I said. "Give me breakfast, and I'll make sure your son is safe."

She said yes, of course, and maybe that seems like a lopsided bargain, keeping a kid safe through years of school in exchange for a plate of eggs and sausage and toast and a glass of OJ, but if it's in my power to give, and doesn't cost more than I can afford, I don't worry much about parity.

The waitress snapped out of that deep down state and took my order, knowing she'd pay for it, not sure why, but probably not fretting about it – and for the first time in however long, she wasn't worried about her boy getting stabbed in the school parking lot.

Breakfast was fine, too. Tasted as good as the first meal always does, I imagine.

The neighbourhood I settled on wasn't in the worst part of Oakland, or the best – it was on the east side of Lake Merritt, maybe a mile from the water, in among a maze of residential streets that mingled million-dollar homes and old stucco apartment complexes. I walked there, over hills and curving streets with cul-de-sacs, through little roundabouts with towering redwoods in the middle, tiny triangular parks in places where three streets all ran into one another, and past terraced gardens and surprise staircases providing steep shortcuts down the hills. A good place, or it could have been, but there was a canker along one street, spiderwebbing out into the neighbourhoods nearby, blood and crying and death somewhere in the near past, and lurking in the likely future.

First thing I needed was a place to stay. I picked a big house with a neat lawn but no flowers, out on the edge of the street that felt *bad*. I knocked, wondering what day it was, if I was likely to find anyone home at all. An old man opened the door and frowned. Was he suspicious because I was black, because I was smiling, because of bad things that had happened around here? "Yes?"

"I'm just looking for a room to rent for a few weeks," I said. "I can make it worth your while, if you've got the space."

"Nope," he said, and closed the door in my face.

Guess he wasn't from around here.

I went a little closer to the bad part, passing a church with a sign out front in Korean, and was surprised to see people sitting on their stoops drinking beers, kids yelling at one another in fence-hidden backyards, people washing their cars. Must be a Saturday or Sunday, and the weather was indeed springtime-fine, the air smelling of honeysuckle, but I'd expected a street with bars on the windows, people looking out through their curtains, the whole city-under-siege bit. This place *pulsed* with nastiness, the way an infected wound will radiate heat, and I knew other people couldn't feel the craziness the way I could, but shouldn't there have been some external sign? I wasn't sensing some hidden moral failings here – this was a place where violence had been done.

I looked for a likely house, and picked a small adobe place near a corner, where an elderly Chinese woman stood watering her plants. I greeted her in Cantonese, which delighted her, and it turned out she *was* from around here, so it only took a few minutes to work something out. She took me inside, showed me the tiny guest room, and gave me a spare key, zipping around the house in a sprightly way, since I'd gotten rid of her rheumatism and arthritis in exchange for bed and board. "We'll just tell everyone you're my nephew," she said. "By marriage. Ha ha ha!" I laughed right along with her, kissed her cheek – she was good people – and went out onto the street.

I strolled down the sidewalk, smiling and nodding at everyone I met. The street was long and curving, cut off at either end by a couple of larger cross streets. There were some apartment houses near one end, with younger people, maybe grad students or starving artists, and some nice bigger houses where families lived. The residents were pure Oakland variety – Koreans, Chinese, whites, blacks, Latinos of various origins. Even the cars on the sidewalks were diverse, with motorcycles, beaters held together with primer and care, SUVs, even a couple of sports cars. I liked it. It felt neighbourly. But it also felt *wrong*, and I couldn't pinpoint the badness. It was all around me. I was *in* it, too close to narrow it down further.

A pretty woman, probably half-Japanese, half-black – I'm good at guessing ethnicities and extractions, and the look is a unique one – sat on the steps of a three-storey apartment house with decorative castle crenellations on the roof, sipping an orange cream soda from a bottle and reading a slim book. There was something about her – ah, right, I got it. I was in a body again, and she was beautiful, and I was attracted.

"Afternoon," I said, walking up to the steps and nodding a greeting. "You know Miss Li?"

"Down on the corner?" she said. "Sure."

"I'm her nephew. I'll be staying with her for a while, maybe a few weeks, while I get settled."

"Nephew, huh?" She looked up at me speculatively. "By marriage, I'm guessing."

"You guessed right," I said, and extended my hand.

"I'm Sadie." She shook my hand. "Welcome to the neighbour-hood." There was no jolt of electricity, but she wasn't giving me go-away vibes, either, so I gave it a try.

"Are you from around here?"

"Me? No. I'm from Chicago, born and raised. Just came out here for school."

I grinned wider. I couldn't have a dalliance with someone from around here – it would be too easy to steer them, compel them, without even intending to, too easy to chat with their deep down parts by accident. But she had a different home, so we could talk, like people. I was a person now, for the moment, more or less. "I could use someone to show me around the neighbourhood, help get me oriented."

She shrugged. "What do you want to know?"

I sat down, not too close. "Oh, I don't know." *How about "Why aren't you terrified? Don't you sense the presence of something monstrous in this place?*" "Who's that guy?" I pointed at a young Latino man tinkering on a motorcycle in the garage across the street.

"Hmm. I think his name's Mike? I don't really know him. He goes on motorcycle rides most weekends."

"Okay. How about him?" This time I pointed at a big man in an unseasonable brown coat, walking up the hill dragging a wire grocery cart behind him. He was middle-aged, and had probably been a real bruiser in his prime.

"That's Ike Train," she said. "Nice guy, but kind of intense. He's a plumber, and he fixes stuff for people in the neighbourhood for free sometimes, but he likes to hang around and talk for a while afterward, and he gets bad BO when he sweats, so not a lot of people take him up on it. He's got a deal with whoever owns my building, though, and he does all the plumbing stuff here."

"How about her?" I said. A woman in sunglasses, attractive in a blonde-and-brittle-and-gym-cultured way, was walking a little yipping dog.

"Martha." Sadie rolled her eyes. "Put your trash cans out on the curb a day early and you'll catch hell from her. I think she's in a hurry for this neighbourhood to finish gentrifying. So why all the questions?"

"I just like talking to you," I said, which was the truth, but not the whole truth. "Asking about people passing by seemed like a good way to do that."

She laughed. "You never told me your name."

Why not? No one ever even remarked on the name – except to say it was weird – unless I was on a Pacific island, and even then, it meant so many things in so many different languages, no one ever guessed. "I'm Reva," I said.

"Interesting name. Where you from?"

"I was born on a little island in the Pacific," I said. "You wouldn't have heard of it. But I didn't stay there long. I've lived all over since then." I thought this was going well, but we were reaching the point where the conversation could founder on the rocks of nothing-in-common. "You said you're here for school? What do you—"

Someone shouted "Sadie!" A short man with wispy hair, dressed like an IRS agent from the 1950s – black horn-rimmed glasses, white shirt, narrow black tie – bustled over from the house across the street, an ugly boxy two-storey with heavy drapes in the windows. He reached our side of the street and said "Vocabulary word: 'Obstruction'."

"Oh, Christ," Sadie muttered.

"Something that gets in the *way*," he continued. "Another: 'Obstinate'. Unreasonably stubborn; pig-headed."

"The back bumper of my car's only in front of your driveway by an *inch*, Oswald," she said. "The car in front of me is too far back, I'm sorry, it's not like it's actually in your *way*."

"In my way, and in the *red*," Oswald said, not even glancing at me, staring at Sadie with damp-looking eyes magnified behind thick lenses. "The police have been notified."

"Whatever," Sadie said. "Fine, I'll move it." She stood up, glared at him, looked at me apologetically, and walked over to a well-worn black compact that was, maybe, poking two inches into the little driveway that led to Oswald's garage. She got in and drove away.

I nodded at Oswald. "Beautiful day," I said.

He squinted at me, then turned and went back to his house, up the steps, and through the front door.

I glanced at the book Sadie had left on the steps. It was a monograph on contraceptive methods in the ancient world. I wondered what she was studying. A few moments later she came walking up the sidewalk and returned to her place on the steps. "Sorry," she said. "Oswald's a dick. He never even opens his garage. As far as I know he doesn't even have a car." She shook her head.

"Every neighbourhood has a nasty, petty person or two."

"I guess. Most people here are pretty nice. I've only been here a year, but I know a lot of people well enough to say hello to, and Oswald's the only one I really can't stand. Him and his 'vocabulary words'. Somebody told me he's an English teacher, or used to be, or something. Can you imagine being stuck in a class with *him*?"

"I'd rather not think about it. So. Am I someone you'll say hello to in the future?"

"You haven't given me a reason not to yet," she said. "Look, it's nice meeting you, but I've got studying to do."

"What subject?"

"I'm getting my master's in human sexuality. Which, today, means reading about how ancient Egyptians used crocodile shit and sour milk as spermicide."

I wrinkled my nose. "Did it work?"

"Actually, yeah. But it can't have been very much fun." She rose, picked up her drink, and went into the apartment building.

I love a woman who can toss off a good exit line, I thought.

The next morning I ran into Sadie, and she invited me to brunch at a café down near the lake. We ate eggs and drank mimosas on the restaurant's patio, where bougainvillea vines hung all around us from pillars and trellises. She wanted to know things about me, and I was game, telling her a few stories from my travels. She was from Chicago, so I told her about the month I'd spent there, leaving out my battle in the train yard with a golem made of hogmeat. I told her a bit about my months working on a riverboat casino on the Mississippi, though I didn't mention the immortal singer in the piano bar who'd once been a pirate, and wanted to start plundering again, before I convinced him otherwise.

"So you're basically a drifter," she said, sipping her second mimosa.

"We prefer to be called 'people of no fixed address,'" I said.

"How long do you think you'll stay here?"

"Oh, I don't know," I said, leaning across the table, looking at her face, which seemed to fit some ideal of faces I'd never before imagined. "I'm like anybody else, I guess. Just looking for a place to call home."

She threw a napkin at me, and it bounced off my nose, and I thought I might be falling in love.

Sadie had to study, so I spent the rest of the lovely Sunday meeting people in the neighbourhood. It's not hard, once you overcome their initial reluctance to talk to strangers, and hearing I was Miss Li's nephew made most folks open up, too – the lady was well-liked. I visited the closest park, just a few blocks away, where some guys from the neighbourhood were playing basketball. I got in on the game, and didn't play *too* well, and they liked me fine. I got invited to a barbecue for the next weekend. I helped an older guy wash his car, and then spent an hour with Mike, who was rebuilding the carburettor on his motorcycle – I didn't know much about machines, but I was able to hand him tools and talk about California scenic highways. I chatted with mothers pushing strollers, young kids riding scooters, surly teens, and old people on afternoon walks.

And every time I got someone alone, if they were from around here, I talked to their deep down parts, and I asked them what was wrong with this place.

I didn't find out anything unusual. Oh, there were crimes – this *was* a big city, after all, even if a residential neighbourhood. There were occasional break-ins, and a mugging or two, though none right around here. A couple of car thefts. But nothing poisonously, unspeakably bad. Maybe my senses were out of whack, or I was picking up the irrelevant psychic residue of some long-ago atrocity.

I have trouble adapting my mind to the shortness of human time scales, sometimes.

It was late afternoon when I went past Ike Train's place. He had a tidy little house, and a bigger yard than most. His porch was shadowed, but I could see the big man sitting on a creaking wooden swing, messing with something in his hands. I was going to hello the house, but Ike hailed me first. "You're new!" he shouted. "Come over!"

"Mr Train," I said, delighted, because I do love meeting people, especially ones who love meeting me. "I've heard about you." I passed through the bushes, which overgrew his walk, and went up to his porch. He held a little man-shaped figure made of twisted wire and pipe cleaners in his hands. He set the thing aside and rose, reaching out to shake my hand. His grip was strong, but not a macho show-off strong, just the handshake of a man who wrestled with pipe wrenches on a regular basis.

"You're staying with Miss Li," he said, sitting down, and gesturing for me to take a cane chair by his front door. "Her nephew?"

"I'm Reva. More of a grand-nephew from the other side of the family, but yeah."

"What brings you to town?" He went back to twisting the wire, giving the little man an extra set of arms, like a Hindu deity.

"I've been travelling for a few years," I said. "Thought I might try settling here." Maybe I would, for a while, if I could find a way to get rid of the bad thing making the whole street's aura stink. Being in a body again was nice, and even on our short acquaintance there was something about Sadie I wanted to know better, like she was a flavour I'd been craving for ages.

"It's a nice enough place," Ike said.

"So tell me," I said, leaning forward. "Are you from around here?"

Ike's hands went still, the wire forgotten. "Oh, yeah," he said, and his voice was different now, slower and thicker. "This is my home. Nobody knows how hard I work to keep it clean, how filthy it gets. The whole fucking city is circling the drain. Dirty, nasty, rotten, wretched . . ."

I frowned. That was his deep down self talking, but it didn't sound like him. "Ike, what do you—"

"We have to twist their heads all the way around," he said, his voice oddly placid, and turned the little wire man in his hands, twisting its round loop of a head tighter and tighter until it snapped and came off in his fingers. "Break them and sweep them up. Clean up the trash, keep things clean. Yeah. I'm from *around* here."

"Ike," I said, careful, because there were sinkholes in this man's mind, and I didn't know how deep they were, or what might be hidden inside them. "Maybe you and me can work something out."

"*No*," he said, and crushed the little man. "There's nothing to work out. Everything's already been worked out." He stared at me, through me, and his eyes were wet with tears. "There's nothing you can offer me."

I stood up and stepped back. He was from around here, I was talking to his deep down self, but Ike wouldn't work something out with me. I didn't understand this refusal. It was like water refusing to freeze in winter, like leaves refusing to fall in autumn, a violation of everything I understood about natural law. "Don't worry about it, Ike. Let's just forget we had this talk, huh?"

Ike looked down at the broken wire thing in his hands. "Nice meeting you, ah, buddy," he said. "Say hi to Miss Li for me."

I headed back down the street towards Miss Li's, thinking maybe Ike was crazy. Maybe he had something to do with the badness here. Maybe he *was* the badness. I needed to know more. I asked Miss Li about him, over dinner that night, but she didn't know much about Ike. He'd lived on the street longer than anybody, and his parents had owned his house before him. He was seriously from around here. So why had talking to his deep down self been so strange and disturbing?

"Hey, Reva," Sadie said when I answered the door. "You busy?"

It was Monday, and the street was quiet, most everybody off about their business. "Not for you," I said, leaning against the doorjamb.

"Could you come up to my place and help me with something?"

I grinned, and grinning felt good; I'd forgotten that about bodies, that genuinely smiling actually caused chemical changes and improved the mood. "I'm at your service." I pulled the door shut and followed Sadie down the steps and up the street. I didn't bother locking the door – nobody would rob the place while I was staying there.

"What do you know about spiders?" she said, leading me into the lobby of the apartment building. The floor was black tile with gold flecks, and there was a wall of old-fashioned brass and glass mailboxes. I liked it. The place had personality.

"Hmm. Eight legs. Mythologically complex – sometimes tricksters, sometimes creators, sometimes monsters, depending on who you ask."

She looked at me, half-smiling, as if she wasn't sure if I was joking. She opened a door, revealing an elevator with a sliding grate. We went inside, and she rattled the gate closed. Back in the old days there would have been a uniformed attendant to run the elevator. This must have been a classy place in its day. "Can you recognize poisonous spiders? I've heard there are some nasty ones out here, black widows and brown recluses, stuff like that. There's a spider in my tub and it's freaking me out a little."

"It's probably gone by now, right?" The elevator rattled and hummed as it ascended.

"I don't think it can get out. It keeps trying to climb the sides of the tub and sliding back down."

She was standing a little closer to me than she had to. I wondered if I should read anything into that. "So you want me to get rid of it?"

"If it was a snake or a rat or something, I'd do it myself. Most things like this don't bother me. But spiders . . ." She shuddered. "Especially when I don't know if they're poisonous or not. I heard the bite of a brown recluse can make your skin rot away. Bleah. Vicious little things."

I shrugged. "They're just trying to get by. Besides, there aren't any brown recluses in California."

She frowned. "But everybody says there are."

"It's a common misconception. Only a handful of brown recluses have ever been found here, and they all came with shipments from the south or midwest. They aren't native anywhere west of the Rockies. Hundreds of people go to their doctors in California every year saying they've been bitten by recluses, but the bites are always from some other bug, or they're just rashes or something." The fear of brown recluse spiders in California was an oddly persistent one. I'd once seen a billboard in San Francisco, with a several-million-times-life-size depiction of a fiddleback spider, and a strident warning in Spanish. People do tend toward the fearful, even without cause.

Sadie gave me a new, appraising look. "No shit? You're, like, a spider expert or something?"

I laughed. How could I explain that I just had a *really good sense* for where things came from? "Nah, just something I read about. Anyway, whatever kind of spider it is, I'll take care of it for you. There are lots of black widows out here. Not to mention scorpions."

"My hero," she said, and touched my arm. It was the first time I'd been touched in this body, other than a handshake and Miss Li's friendly embrace, and I had to stop myself from taking Sadie in my arms right then. Having a body again was wonderful. Why had I gone without for so long?

She let me into her apartment, which was furnished in student-poverty-chic, mismatched furniture and beat-up bookcases overflowing with texts, prints of fine art hung alongside real art of the student-show variety. The apartment was big, though, for a single person in Oakland, with a nice sized living room, a little kitchen separated by a counter, and a short hallway leading to other doors. "This is a nice place."

"I know!" she said, and I liked how sincere she sounded. "It's crazy cheap, too. I looked at a lot of apartments when I first moved here, and they were all way more than I could afford, but this one's half as much as other apartments this size. I've got a bedroom *and* an office. I guess the owner doesn't live around here, and doesn't realize how rents have gone up these past few years? I don't know, but it's my good luck."

"You don't know the landlord?" I disapprove of absentee landlords on principle.

"Nah, I just mail rent checks to a PO box. There's a tenant on the first floor who gets even cheaper rent than the rest of us for managing the place, making sure leases get signed, interviewing people, all that. If she ever moves out, I might try to get that gig. It can be a lot of work, though – there's a lot of turnover here. Because it's so cheap, we get plenty of people who are down on their luck, and some them just take off without paying their last month's rent. I guess that's what deposits are for, though. Two or three girls have skipped out since I moved in, just leaving their stuff here. Not that they had much. They were all on drugs, I heard. Sometimes this place is like a halfway house."

"Huh," I said, thinking. "How are the pipes? You said Ike Train is the plumber here?"

"Yeah. I don't know if he's a lousy plumber or if the place just has shitty pipes, but it seems like he's over here all the time – somebody's always got a leak or a bad drain or something. But, hey, at these prices, we don't expect perfection. Anyway, speaking of bathrooms . . ." She led the way down the hallway, opening the door onto a nice big bathroom, with an old claw-footed tub.

I looked into the bathtub. "That," I said, "is a daddy longlegs." Specifically a *Spermaphora*, but why show off?

"Aren't they, like, the most poisonous spider in the world? But their fangs are too short to bite humans?"

"Another myth," I said. "They're pretty much harmless. They can bite, but it wouldn't do much to you." I reached down, picked up the spider by one of its comically long legs, and walked over to the open window. I set the spider on the sill, and it scurried off down the exterior wall. I looked back at Sadie, who stood by the door, looking at me.

I hadn't been in a body for long, but I knew that look. "You're not afraid of spiders at all, are you?"

"I needed *some* excuse to get you up here," she said, taking a step toward me. "I wasn't sure if you liked me, but the way you looked at me in the elevator . . ."

"I guess I'm not subtle." But I *was* lucky.

"That's okay. Games can be fun, but there's nothing wrong with the direct approach, either." She stepped in close and kissed me, putting the palm of her hand on my chest, over my heartbeat. I kissed back, my body responding in that wonderful way that bodies do.

"Mmm," I said after a moment. "So you're a student of human sexuality, huh?"

"Sure," she said. "But there are some things you can't get from a book."

Afterwards, as she brewed tea in her kitchen and I sat, feeling loose-limbed and glorious, on a stool at the counter, she said, "Look, I don't want you to get the wrong idea . . ." She had her back turned to me, and that was too bad, because she wasn't saying anything she couldn't say to my face.

"Don't worry," I said. "It was what it was. And it was very nice. But I don't think it gives me a claim on you. Which doesn't mean I'd object if you wanted to do it *again*."

Now she turned, and she looked relieved. "Sometimes I just want to be with somebody. You seem nice, and *god* you're pretty, but I'm not looking for a boyfriend or anything right now. I'm so busy with school, you know?"

That gave me a little pang, I admit, because of course I wanted to be seen as irresistible boyfriend material, even though I *know* I'm no more constant than a bank of fog blowing through. But she was being honest with me, at least. A lot of bullshit in this world could be avoided if people just told the truth, however inconvenient it might be. And maybe, if I could get rid of the nastiness on this block, I could settle down here, and become more constant, and win Sadie over. I was pretty low-maintenance. Hadn't I rambled around this world enough? Maybe it was time to pick a home and stick with it for a while.

I had an idea about the source of the badness here now, anyway. It's not like I'm a great detective or anything, but I can see how things fit together, when it's right in front of my face. I wondered why no one else had ever figured it out.

"Want to go out again sometime?" I asked. "I haven't taken in much of the local scene yet."

"Sure," she said, placing a cup of steaming tea on the counter before me. She looked me right in the eye. "We can do something this weekend. Or we could just stay in all weekend having sex. I've got toys in my bedroom I didn't even *show* you."

My heart went pitter-pat, and other parts of me did other things. Having a body was so wonderful, I wasn't sure what had ever possessed me to leave my last one.

Ike Train's back yard had a nine-foot wooden privacy fence, overgrown with vines that made it seem even higher. The lock on his gate was nothing special, though, so I popped it open pretty easily that night. He had a big garden back there, lots of tomato plants, the earth all churned up. I checked his back windows again – still dark, and he was probably deeply asleep, like the rest of the block. I found a shovel and a likely mound of earth, near the back fence, and started digging. I didn't worry about Ike waking up and noticing me. I wasn't going to get noticed unless I wanted to be. I was in a body, but that didn't mean I'd given up all my powers.

Ike had dug a good grave. I went about five feet down before I found the girl, wrapped in cloth sacks and sprinkled liberally with some kind of lye-based drain cleaner, though not enough to dissolve her body completely – that takes a *lot* of lye, even more than a plumber would have on hand. She was mostly just bones, at this point. I couldn't unwrap the burlap completely, because the lye could have burned my skin; that was one disadvantage to having a body. How many other girls were buried here? Lonely women with no families, women with drug problems who jumped at the cheap rents in the apartment house on the corner, who opened their doors to that nice plumber Ike Train and found out he wasn't so nice after all. I wondered if he lured them to his house, or somehow took their bodies out of the apartment building. I couldn't imagine how he'd gotten away with something like this – in a city, someone is *always* awake, and witnesses are a problem – but serial killers can be lucky motherfuckers.

Well, Ike didn't have good luck anymore. Now he had me instead.

"Here's my problem, Ike," I said, after he woke up, and realized he couldn't free himself. He tried to yell at me, but he was gagged pretty good, and still woozy from the chemicals I'd knocked him out with, and it was just muffled noise. I leaned back in the chair I'd dragged over by the couch where he was bound. "I could just call the cops, and let them know about the bodies in the backyard. I can be really convincing, especially if the cops are from around here. You'd get arrested and put away for a long time. But that would be bad for the neighbourhood. People here don't realize there's a monster like you in their midst. Everybody knows you. You've been in most of the *houses* on this street at once time or another. To find out you've been killing women and burying them in your back garden . . ." I shook my head. "Most of these people wouldn't trust anyone ever again. There'd be news reporters all over. Property values would plummet. People would move away. I'd hate to see that happen."

He made furious noises. I removed the gag. He tried to bite off my fingers. I couldn't blame him. "Make a fuss and I'll knock you out again," I said. "You've got lots of nice chemicals under your sink I can mix up."

His voice was low and intense. "You don't understand. This used to be a nice place, when I was a kid. Now all that trash lives on this street. Spics, chinks, whores and junkies. Jabbering away in Spanish and Chinese, trying to cadge change off people so they can by drugs, all that bullshit. This whole place is a toilet now. I wish I could flush them all."

I raised my eyebrow. "What about black folks? Want to flush us too?"

"I got nothing against black people," he said, wounded, as if I'd slandered him. "And there's decent Chinese people, like your aunt, and some Mexicans I don't mind, but the kind of garbage that rents rooms down at the castle apartments, they're just *worthless*, they—"

"So killing them has got nothing to do with your sexual gratification, then?"

"That's sick," Ike spat. "You're disgusting. I do what I do to keep this neighbourhood *nice*, to keep it safe. A piece of shit like you couldn't possibly understand that."

"You're no prize yourself, Ike. You know it's all over now, right? You're finished."

"You can't mess with me," he said, his eyes shining, as they had when I'd spoken to his deep down parts before. "This is *my* place."

"It's my place now. And you don't have a home here anymore." I put the rag of chemicals over his face again until he passed out.

I held a hammer in my hand with every intention of caving in Ike Train's skull, then disposing of his body out in the desert somewhere, but I couldn't do it. He was a *person*. I'd expected a monster, and yes, Ike was a monster too, but I couldn't see past his humanity. In my more natural state, without a body, I would have found executing Ike Train as simple as flicking an ant off a tablecloth. But for now I was wearing a human form, and Ike was one of my tribe, albeit a crazy, dangerous one. I couldn't smash his head in, not if I wanted to keep functioning in this body. Such an act would tear me apart. I put the hammer down.

Still, Ike had to die, and disappear, if I wanted to save this neighbourhood from imploding. They could never know this monster had been in their midst – such a revelation would poison the wellspring of camaraderie and human kindness I'd found here. I had to do something fast, though. He was a big man, and he would wake up soon, and I couldn't bear talking to him again.

Sometimes, back in the old days, I'd watched people drown, disappearing beneath churning waves. Losing those people hurt me – diminished me – but it felt more natural, somehow, with the elements taking their lives, instead of a human hand.

I'm not stupid. I know killing is killing, even if some natural phenomenon is the murder weapon. If you cast someone into a churning sea, and they die, you've murdered them, even if it's the water that ends their lives. But maybe you can sleep a little easier, since the blood isn't on your hands. Maybe.

Ike Train was a man who prepared for things. There were several gas cans in the garage, by his emergency generator. They sloshed full when I picked them up.

Fortunately, Ike didn't wake, even when I piled pillows around the perimeter of the living room and doused them with fuel. The smoke would kill him before the fire touched him. A mercy, and more than he'd offered his victims. But I'm not about vengeance. I'm about finding bad homes and making them good again.

When I felt tears on my face, I tried to believe they were just stinging from the gas fumes.

House fires aren't exactly good for neighbourhood morale, but they tend to make a community pull together. Everybody came out and watched Ike Train's house burn. The fire trucks got there pretty quickly, but not quickly enough. The roof collapsed while they were still hooking their hoses up, but Ike was surely gone by then.

Nobody paid any attention to me, not even Sadie, though she stood only a few yards away. Everyone was watching the flames. I needed to get cleaned up, and shower off the mud from Ike's back yard. Maybe I'd visit Sadie later, and see about making myself into boyfriend material. This could be a nice place now.

"Vocabulary word," said Oswald, walking over from his house down the block and joining the spectators. " 'Conflagration': a large fire. Also a conflict or war."

"Shut the fuck up, Oswald," someone said wearily. "We think Ike Train died in there."

"Another," Oswald said softly. " 'Cothurnus'. A tragedy. Also the costume worn by an actor in a tragic play."

Then he looked at me, for a little too long, like he had something to say, but some people just have eyes like that, intense and too direct. I slipped away from the neighbourhood crowd, though being among them was all I wanted. I knew the ugly burned-out lot in the middle of their street would be better than the ugliness that Ike Train had caused. I'd used fire to cauterize something much worse. But I still felt guilty. A shower would help, a little. You have to start getting clean somewhere.

I was on my way to visit Sadie the next Saturday, for our weekend of sex or tourism, when Oswald hailed me from his front yard, where he was brutalizing a patch of unkempt grass with a weed whacker. "Mr Reva!" he said, turning off his buzzing yard tool.

"It's just Reva," I called back.

"I wonder if I might have a word with you," he said.

"What, vocabulary words?" I called back, trying to sound cheerful, because even a miserable little guy like this probably had some good in him somewhere. But I really just wanted to see Sadie.

"Very droll," he replied. "Please? Just a moment? I have something inside that might interest you."

Was this a come on? Was Oswald so cranky because he was closeted and gay? I'd seen that sort of thing before. I wasn't interested in him, but maybe, if he was from around here, I could talk with his deep down self, and help him relax, and be a better neighbour. "Sure," I said, and went up the steps, following him to his front door. He opened the door and gestured for me to enter. I did, and it was dark inside – very dark – so I paused just inside the door. "Maybe we should turn the lights on—" I began, and then he shoved me, hard, and I stumbled forward into empty air, falling hard on what felt like a mound of rubble and broken glass. "Fuck!" I shouted, and turned over, my eyes starting to adjust. There was no *house* inside his house – it was scooped out and hollow, just a few beams to support the roof and walls, otherwise an open pit of dirt and rocks.

I realized, then, that I'd seriously misinterpreted the situation on this street.

Oswald leapt down from the little scrap of flat floor just inside the door, landing in a crouch on the dirt before me. He moved more like a spider than a man, which made sense; he wasn't a spider, but he wasn't a man, either. I started to rise up, and he threw a rock at my head, hard enough that I don't remember the impact at all, just the coming of the darkness.

"Vocabulary word," Oswald said later, tying up my wrists with lengths of wire. I was naked, and the rocks in his house were cutting into my skin. "'Chthonic'. Dwelling under the earth. Gods of the underworld. _Me_."

"Oswald," I said, alarmed at the slur in my voice. How hard had that rock hit my head? Way too hard, judging by the pounding in my skull. "We can work something out."

"Another: 'Autarch'. Absolute ruler. Tyrant. Me, here, in this place." He wired my legs together.

"You don't have to do this." I tried to twist, to kick, but he was agile, and I wasn't, and he didn't even stop talking while he dodged my flailing.

"Another: 'Autochthonous'. Originating where it is found. Native. From _around here_. Me, me, _me_." He kicked me in the chest on the last word, and darker black dots swam into my vision against the darkness inside his housepit, and I gasped for breath.

"This is my place," Oswald said, "and Ike Train was my man. He made the proper sacrifices to me, kept me fed, kept me _happy_. And you spoiled that, stranger, outside agitator, you _ruined_ it, and now I have to cultivate another man. But you'll die. Not a sacrifice to me. Just somebody who got in the way." He gnashed his teeth, and they clacked together like gemstones. "You didn't have to burn Ike. He wouldn't have killed that little bitch Sadie you like so much. She has too many friends. We only kill the ones no one will miss. Well, _usually_. Someone might miss you, but I don't care."

Oswald was the reason Ike Train's deep down self had been so strange. I couldn't make a deal with Ike, because he'd _already_ made a bargain with a creature like me. Well, _sort of_ like me. Oswald and I had the same means, but different methods and motivations. That explained why nobody had ever discovered Ike Train's murders – Oswald had used his powers to protect him, and he probably did other things, too, like keeping the neighbourhood safe from danger, but the price he demanded was just too high.

As far as Oswald knew, I was just a *guy*, somebody who came to town and discovered his lackey's secret. He didn't know what he was dealing with. Fortunately.

Oswald stood up, letting his human shape drop, revealing the shambling earthen thing underneath, the creature of the dark and deep who'd lived here, on this spot, for centuries. Oswald was a local spirit, tied to this place, but he was an ugly one, who chose to live off pain instead of prosperity. He reached out to me with arms of darkness, endless limbs that stank of minerals and stale air. "Vocabulary word," he hissed, in a voice that could never be mistaken for human. 'Decapitate'. To cut off a head. Another: 'Decedent'. One who has died. *You*."

Then he killed me.

While I was dying, I remembered the problem with having a body. The problem is pain.

I wasn't able to return for a few days. My new body was Korean, older, shorter, dressed in a plaid shirt and khaki pants. I'd needed to pick up some supplies, and they were tricky to get, since I didn't have money, and had to rely on the kindness of locals. I traded a lucky gambling streak for the truck, and the miraculous regeneration of some missing fingers for the stun gun.

I knocked on Oswald's door, late that evening. He opened the door, scowled at me, and I hit him with the stun gun. He was fully in his body then, so he went down shuddering, and I bundled him up and got him in the back of the truck, one of those little moving vans you can rent, though this one belonged to me for as long as I wanted it. I drove fast, hitting the highway and racing, because if Oswald woke up too close to his neighbourhood, he would shed that body like a baggy suit and come crashing right through the roof, and then we'd have the kind of epic fight that leads to waste and desolation and legends. Lucky for me Oswald didn't wake until we were miles and miles away from the place he called home, and he couldn't do anything but kick the wall behind the driver's seat with his very human feet.

I went north and east for miles and miles until I reached a good remote spot, down some dirt roads, out by a few old mines. It seemed appropriate, for Oswald's end to come in a place with underground tunnels. I couldn't abide him to live, but I could respect his origins. I parked, cut the lights, and went around back to slide open the door. Oswald was on his side, still tied up. "Vocabulary word," he said, voice thick and a little slurry. " 'Fucked'. What *you* are, once I get loose."

"You don't remember me, Oswald?" I said, climbing into the truck. "It's me, Reva. Last time you saw me, I had a different body, and you tore it to pieces and buried it in your lair. That wasn't very pleasant. I doubt this is going to be very pleasant for you."

He looked up at me from the floor. "Oh," he said, after a moment, then frowned. "You're like me. But you shouldn't have been able to take me, not in my place, so far from *yours*."

"It's true," I said, kneeling beside him. "I'm a long way from the place I began. I've got a vocabulary word for you. 'Reva'. It means habitation, or firmament, or water, or sky, or abyss, or god. Sometimes it's 'rewa' or 'neva' or other things, depending on where you are. It's a word from the islands, where I'm from. I used to be the spirit of an island, just a little patch of land in the sea, a long time ago. But you know what happened?"

I leaned in close to him. "The island *sank*. All the people who lived on it left, and I was alone for years. I could have just dissolved into the sea, but I made myself a body, and found myself a boat, and went with the currents."

"You abandoned your *place*," Oswald said, and tried to bite my face. "You're worthless."

"I didn't abandon it, it just disappeared, so I had options, Oswald. My people were travellers, and I became a traveller too. Anywhere I go is home, because I treat every place I go as home." I shook my head. "You're a monster. You poison the place you should protect."

"I *do* protect it. I keep it safe for the ones who belong there. I keep the trash out."

"You and me have different philosophies," I said, reaching over to open the toolbox I'd brought. There were lots of tools there, which I planned to use for purposes they weren't meant for. "My philosophy wins. Because you're so far away from home that you're just a man in a body now, and you don't have a choice."

He fought me, but he didn't know much about fighting without his usual powers, since he'd never left his street. I didn't try to cause him suffering, but I didn't go out of my way to prevent it, either.

By the time I was finished, he was altogether dead. Even if his spirit did manage to pull itself together again over the next decades, seeping out of the pieces of his corpse to reassemble, there was nothing around here but played-out mines, no people for him to make suffer, no sacrifices for him to draw strength from. I'd just made his neighbourhood a better place for the people who lived there. They wouldn't have Oswald's protection anymore, it was true, but the price he demanded for that protection was too high. I didn't regret a thing.

I buried Oswald in about ten different places, left the truck where it was, and started walking the long way back to the neighbourhood I now called home.

I didn't have any illusions about Sadie recognizing the real me in this new body, but I thought maybe I could be charming, and make her care about a middle-aged Korean guy. Stupid idea, but love – or even infatuation – lends itself to those. The thing was, once I knocked on her door, and she answered it, she didn't look the same. Or, well, she *did*, but the way she looked didn't do anything for me. My new body wasn't interested in her, not at all – this brain, this flesh, was attracted to a different kind of person, apparently. I always forgot how much "feelings" depend on the particular glands and muscles and nerve endings you happen to have at the moment. Having a body makes it hard to remember the limitations of being human.

"Can I help you?" she said.

"Ah," I said. "Reva asked me to give you a message. He said he had to leave town unexpectedly, and he's really sorry."

"Huh," she said. "Well, if you talk to him, tell him he doesn't have to be sorry. He doesn't owe me anything." I could tell from her face that she was hurt, and angry, and trying to hide it, and I *wished* she was from around here so I could talk to her deep down parts, and make amends, give her something, apologise. But she wasn't, and I couldn't.

"Okay," I said. "I'll tell him."

She shut the door in my face.

I walked downstairs, and stood on the sidewalk, and looked up the street. I felt as hollow as Oswald's house, as burned-out as the lot where Ike Train had lived. Why had I wanted to stay here? I wasn't needed anymore. I'd made things better. This wasn't my home, not really, no more than any other place.

Maybe I'd go south, down to the Inland Empire, to see those pretty black walnut trees. I could make myself at home there, for a while, at least.

GARY McMAHON

Pumpkin Night

GARY McMAHON LIVES, works and writes in West Yorkshire, England, where he shares a home with an understanding wife and their weird and wonderful boy-child. McMahon's fiction and non-fiction has appeared or is scheduled to appear in countless magazines in the UK and US, as well as such anthologies as *Poe's Progeny, At Ease with the Dead, The Black Book of Horror, The Humdrumming Book of Horror Stories* and *The Year's Best Fantasy and Horror.*

McMahon is the author of the British Fantasy Award-nominated novella *Rough Cut*, and his other books include *All Your Gods Are Dead*, and a collection of short fiction, *Dirty Prayers*. A novel, *Rain Dogs*, is published by Humdrumming, *Different Skins* is a double-novella collection from Screaming Dreams, and he has edited an anthology of novelettes called *We Fade to Grey*.

"It has always been my belief that horror fiction has the potential to be the most serious type of literature of all," explains the author, "and that it should be used to examine the most serious themes, ideas and issues.

"Because of its confrontational nature, and by way of an armoury of outlandish metaphor, horror stories are well suited to staring into the mirror of society and reporting back on what is found there, twisting away into darkness.

"'Pumpkin Night' was written in belated response to the tragic events that occurred in Soham, Cambridgeshire, in 2002. A school caretaker was arrested for the brutal murders of two ten year-old girls and his live-in girlfriend was accused of covering up evidence of the crimes by repeatedly lying about her movements at the time of the deaths – she was eventually jailed for three-and-a-half years for conspiring to pervert the course of justice; he got forty years for the murders.

"It seems that the woman's loyalty blinded her to the fact that her lover had committed these terrible acts, and only when she was arrested did she allow herself to confront the reality of what he had done.

"I was unable to get this terrible and misplaced act of love out of my head, and the story is my attempt to look at the potential extremes of such a situation, through the lens of a horror story. My heart breaks for every child killed, and for the families left behind to cope with the fall-out. The loss of a son or a daughter is surely a horror of the very worst kind, one that, sadly, never goes away."

> *"Men fear death as children fear to go in the dark;*
> *and as that natural fear in children is increased with tales,*
> *so is the other."*
>
> —Sir Francis Bacon, "Of Death"
> *Essays* (1625)

T HE PUMPKIN, FACELESS AND EYELESS, yet nonetheless intimidating, glared up at Baxter as he sat down opposite with the knife.

He had cleared a space on the kitchen table earlier in the day, putting away the old photographs, train tickets, and receipts from restaurants they had dined at over the years. Katy had kept these items in a large cigar box under their bed, and he had always mocked her for the unlikely sentimentality of the act. But now that she was dead, he silently thanked her for having such forethought.

He fingered the creased, leathery surface of the big pumpkin, imagining how it might look when he was done. Every Halloween Katy had insisted upon the ritual, something begun in her family when she was a little girl. A carved pumpkin, the task undertaken by the man of the house; the seeds and pithy insides scooped out into a bowl and used for soup the next day. Katy had always loved Halloween, but not in a pathetic Goth-girl kind of way. She always said that it was the only time of the year she felt part of something, and rather than ghosts and goblins she felt the presence of human wrongdoing near at hand.

He placed the knife on the table, felt empty tears welling behind his eyes.

Rain spat at the windows, thunder rumbled overhead. The weather had taken a turn for the worse only yesterday, as if gearing up for a night of spooks. Outside, someone screamed. Laughter. The sound of light footsteps running past his garden gate but not stopping, never stopping here.

The festivities had already started. If he was not careful, Baxter would miss all the fun.

The first cut was the deepest, shearing off the top of the pumpkin to reveal the substantial material at its core. He sliced around the inner perimeter, levering loose the bulk of the meat. With great care and dedication, he managed to transfer it to the glass bowl. Juices spilled onto the tablecloth, and Baxter was careful not to think about fresh blood dripping onto creased school uniforms.

Fifteen minutes later he had the hollowed-out pumpkin before him, waiting for a face. He recalled her features perfectly, his memory having never failed to retain the finer details of her scrunched-up nose, the freckles across her forehead, the way her mouth tilted to one side when she smiled. Such a pretty face, one that fooled everyone; and hiding behind it were such *unconventional* desires.

Hesitantly, he began to cut.

The eyeholes came first, allowing her to see as he carried out the rest of the work. Then there was the mouth, a long, graceful gouge at the base of the skull. She smiled. He blinked, taken by surprise. In his dreams, it had never been so easy.

Hands working like those of an Italian Master, he finished the sculpture. The rain intensified, threatening to break the glass of the large kitchen window. More children capered by in the night, their catcalls and yells of "Trick or treat!" like music to his ears.

The pumpkin did not speak. It was simply a vegetable with wounds for a face. But it smiled, and it waited, a noble and intimidating presence inhabiting it.

"I love you," said Baxter, standing and leaning towards the pumpkin. He caressed it with steady hands, his fingers finding the furrows and crinkles that felt nothing like Katy's smooth, smooth face. But it would do, this copy, this effigy. It would serve a purpose far greater than himself.

Picking up the pumpkin, he carried it to the door. Undid the locks. Opened it to let in the night. Voices carried on the busy air, promising a night of carnival, and the sky lowered to meet him as he walked outside and placed Katy's pumpkin on the porch handrail, the low flat roof protecting it from the rain.

He returned inside for the candle. When he placed it inside the carved head, his hands at last began to shake. Lighting the wick was difficult, but he persevered. He had no choice. Her hold on him, even now, was too strong to deny. For years he had covered-up her crimes, until he had fallen in line with her and joined in the games she played with the lost children, the ones who nobody ever missed.

Before long, he loved it as much as she did, and his old way of life had become nothing but a rumour of normality.

The candle flame flickered, teased by the wind, but the rain could not reach it. Baxter watched in awe as it flared, licking out of the eyeholes to lightly singe the side of the face. The pumpkin smiled again, and then its mouth twisted into a parody of laughter.

Still, there were no sounds, but he was almost glad of that. To hear Katy's voice emerging from the pumpkin might be too much. Reality had warped enough for now; anything more might push him over the edge into the waiting abyss.

The pumpkin swivelled on its base to stare at him, the combination of lambent candlelight and darkness lending it an obscene expression, as if it were filled with hatred. Or lust.

Baxter turned away and went inside. He left the door unlocked and sat back down at the kitchen table, resting his head in his hands.

Shortly, he turned on the radio. The DJ was playing spooky tunes to celebrate the occasion. "Werewolves of London", "Bela Lugosi's Dead", "Red Right Hand" . . . songs about monsters and madmen. Baxter listened for a while, then turned off the music, went to the sink, and filled the kettle. He thought about Katy as he waited for the water to boil. The way her last days had been like some ridiculous horror film, with her bedridden and coughing up blood – her thin face transforming into a monstrous image of Death.

She had not allowed him to send for a doctor, or even call for an ambulance at the last. She was far too afraid of what they might find in the cellar, under the shallow layer of dirt. Evidence of the things they had done together, the games they had played, must never be allowed into the public domain. Schoolteacher and school caretaker, lovers, comrades in darkness, prisoners of their own desires. Their deeds, she always told him, must remain secret.

He sipped his tea and thought of better days, bloody nights, the slashed and screaming faces of the children she had loved – the ones nobody else cared for, so were easy to lure here, out of the way, to the house on the street where nobody went. Not until Halloween, when all the streets of Scarbridge, and all the towns beyond, were filled with the delicious screaming of children.

There was a sound from out on the porch, a wild thrumming, as if Katy's pumpkin was vibrating, energy building inside, the blood lust rising, rising, ready to burst in a display of savagery like nothing he had ever seen before. The pumpkin was absorbing the power of this special night, drinking in the desires of small children, the thrill of proud parents, the very idea of spectres abroad in the darkness.

It was time.

He went upstairs and into the bedroom, where she lay on the bed, waiting for him to come and fetch her. He picked her up off the old, worn quilt and carried her downstairs, being careful not to damage her further as he negotiated the narrow staircase.

When he sat her down in the chair, she tipped to one side, unsupported. The polythene rustled, but it remained in place.

Baxter went and got the pumpkin, making sure that the flame did not go out. But it never would, he knew that now. The flame would burn forever, drawing into its hungry form whatever darkness stalked the night. It was like a magnet, that flame, pulling towards itself all of human evil. It might be Halloween, but there were no such things as monsters. Just people, and the things they did to each other.

He placed the pumpkin in the sink. Then, rolling up his sleeves, he set to work on her body. He had tied the polythene bag tightly around the stump of her neck, sealing off the wound. The head had gone into the ice-filled bath, along with . . . *the other things*, the things he could not yet bring himself to think about.

The smell hit him as soon as he removed the bag, a heavy meaty odour that was not at all unpleasant. Just different from what he was used to.

Discarding the carrier bag, he reclaimed the pumpkin from the sink, oh-so careful not to drop it on the concrete floor. He reached out and placed it on the stub of Katy's neck, pressing down so that the tiny nubbin of spine that still peeked above the sheared cartilage of her throat entered the body of the vegetable. Grabbing it firmly on either side, a hand on each cheek, he twisted and pressed, pressed and twisted, until the pumpkin sat neatly between Katy's shoulders, locked tightly in place by the jutting few inches of bone.

The flame burned yellow, blazing eyes that tracked his movements as he stood back to inspect his work.

Something shifted, the sound carrying across the silent room – an arm moving, a shoulder shrugging, a hand flexing. Then Katy tilted her new head from side to side, as if adjusting to the fit.

Baxter walked around the table and stood beside her, just as he always had, hands by his sides, eyes wide and aching. He watched as she shook off the webs of her long sleep and slowly began to stand.

Baxter stood his ground when she leaned forward to embrace him, fumbling her loose arms around his shoulders, that great carved head looming large in his vision, blotting out the rest of the room. She smelled sickly-sweet; her breath was tainted. Her long, thin fingers raked at his shoulder blades, seeking purchase, looking for the familiar gaps in his armour, the chinks and crevices she had so painstakingly crafted during the years they had spent together.

When at last she pulled away, taking a short shuffling step back towards the chair, her mouth was agape. The candle burned within, lighting up the orange-dark interior of her new head. She vomited an orangey pulp onto his chest, staining him. The pumpkin seeds followed – hundreds of them, rotten and oversized and surging from between her knife-cut lips to spatter on the floor in a long shiver of putrescence. And finally, there was blood. So much blood.

When the stagnant cascade came to an end, he took her by the arm and led her to the door, guiding her outside and onto the wooden-decked porch, where he sat her in the ratty wicker chair she loved so much. He left her there, staring out into the silvery veil of the rain, breathing in the shadows and the things that hid within them. Was that a chuckle he heard, squeezing from her still-wet mouth?

Maybe, for a moment, but then it was drowned out by the sound of trick-or-treaters sprinting past in the drizzly lane.

He left the door ajar, so that he might keep an eye on her. Then, still shaking slightly, he opened the refrigerator door. On the middle shelf, sitting in a shallow bowl, were the other pumpkins, the smaller ones, each the size of a tennis ball. He took one in each hand, unconsciously weighing them, and headed for the hall, climbing the stairs at an even pace, his hands becoming steady once more.

In the small room at the back of the house, on a chipboard cabinet beneath the shuttered window, there sat a large plastic dish. Standing over it, eyes cast downward and unable to lift his gaze to look inside, Baxter heard the faint rustle of polythene. He straightened and listened, his eyes glazed with tears not of sorrow but of loss, of grief, and so much more than he could even begin to fathom.

Katy had died in childbirth. Now that she was back, the twins would want to join their mother, and the games they would play together promised to be spectacular.

SIMON STRANTZAS

The Other Village

SIMON STRANTZAS WAS BORN in the dead of the Canadian winter and has lived in Toronto for nearly forty years. He has sold more than twenty short stories to various periodicals and anthologies, including *At Ease with the Dead*, *Strange Tales Volume II* and *Bound for Evil*, as well as the World Fantasy Award-winning *Cemetery Dance* magazine.

His first collection of short fiction, *Beneath the Surface*, is now available from Humdrumming, and he is currently compiling another. One thing he has not written yet is a novel, due in no small part to his intense lack of interest in doing so. This fact baffles every writer he has ever known.

"The origins of 'The Other Village' are a bit of a mystery, even to me," admits Strantzas. "I wrote the story during the summer of 2007, while juggling at least five other tales. Even my past blog entries reveal no notes towards its origins.

"I know it was inspired by a quite enjoyable cruise my mother and sister once took together, and was then combined with stories of other not-so-enjoyable vacations my friends have shared with me over the years. Once I put my two ladies into their exotic locale, they managed to find the rest of the story on their own without my help.

"I do remember one thing, however – my immense pleasure at how the ending worked itself out. Whenever I re-read it a shiver still creeps down my spine."

"SOMETHING DIFFERENT, you want?"

The man spoke to Monica, but kept his eye on the tour guide, not wanting to be overheard. His skin was dark, the colour of slick black olives, and his yellow shirt was unbuttoned halfway down his chest, revealing the ring of tiny deep-brown stones that lay in relief around his neck. A few dozen similar necklaces of a lighter shade were lined up on the table before him.

"God, yes," said Jessica. "This has been the worst vacation ever. We want to see something *different*, don't we Monica?"

But Monica knew Jessica didn't really care what she had to say, and hadn't since they left Toronto three days earlier. Going away together proved to be a huge mistake, and Monica wished there were some way she could step back in time and correct it. She closed her eyes and prayed, but when she opened them again she was still in the hot Mediterranean bazaar, and the dark-skinned merchant was looking straight at her.

"I know place. Not like here. This place, not so many people come see. Like *real* place." There was a sense of pride when he said that, yet it felt as though he were selling the experience. Monica suspected this happened a lot – everyone trying to poach the members of tour groups to extract money from them. It was probably why he didn't want anyone hearing his offer. Jessica, though, didn't seem concerned.

"Listen, buddy. If you can tell us where to go where there's less people like us and more like you, I'm sold."

He smiled large and nodded quickly, like some wind-up toy, and Monica felt uneasy. She whispered into Jessica's ear. The larger woman exploded.

"Who cares if we already paid them? They aren't showing us anything we couldn't see on television. Besides, this guy says we'll be back tonight. There's plenty of time to join up again with all the old ladies tomorrow. I'm tired of walking between the ropes; let's go behind the scenes!"

Jessica was starting to sweat with excitement, her doughy skin flushed. The merchant continued to smile, and waved a young man to his side.

"My friend. He will take you," he said, then turned and spoke something fast and guttural. The young man smiled as well, and nodded. He looked at Monica, and she stepped back into the sun.

"You give this," the merchant said, and handed Jessica a piece of paper. Then he picked one of the necklaces from his table. "You buy necklace now?"

Jessica laughed. "Not me. But Monica, you do it. It's not like you can't afford it."

Monica, resigned in irritation, opened her pocketbook again.

They followed the young man for what seemed like an hour, and the more distance they put between them and their tour group, the deeper Monica's dread became.

"Do you really think this is a good idea?"

"Stop being a baby. It's going to be fine. You *wanted* an interesting trip. I'm just finally making it happen."

"An *interesting* trip, yes," she said quietly, hoping the dark-skinned man in front of them couldn't hear, "but not a *dangerous* trip. Haven't you heard about what happens? About people being kidnapped and sold as slaves?"

Jessica snorted. "Have you looked at yourself? No one's going to buy you." She laughed, and their guide turned for a moment and laughed, too. Monica hoped he hadn't understood the joke.

And it wasn't that funny a joke. Considering the size of Jessica, Monica felt positively svelte. She could stand to lose a few pounds, true, but she thought she still looked as thin as she had back in her school days. Jessica, on the other hand, had ballooned since then.

Monica frowned, trying to keep her anger in check. She was sorely tempted to leave, but didn't want to deal with Jessica's whinging. It had been so far unbelievable, the amount that she complained about everything. The two of them had planned their trip out over a year before, at a time when both their lives had fallen into a funk. During that intervening year, however, Jessica had managed to find herself a new job and circle of friends, and as the months passed the two of them had grown distant. If not for the trip, Monica doubted they would have continued talking. And, yet, even after Monica gave the woman chance after chance of pulling out of their shared vacation, Jessica wouldn't do it. She spoke of how much closer it was going to bring them, how it was going to reignite their friendship, and Monica didn't know if it was her loneliness or something else but for some reason she let herself be convinced. Yet, her worrying seemed all for naught; everything went fine . . . until their plane left the runaway. As though a switch were flipped, Jessica's attitude turned, and Monica was blamed for taking her away from all her new friends – as though Monica should feel guilty, and at the same time privileged, that Jessica was spending this time with her. Halfway through their trip, when Jessica finally stopped talking and started sleeping, Monica contemplated how easy it would be to grab a pillow and hold it down over Jessica's face. She doubted any court would convict her once the evidence was presented.

They were walking past boats lined upon along a pier, the dark men on board juggling nets and equipment and staring at the two pale women walking past, when Monica heard the tinny electronic sound of a Latin rhythm. The young man produced a cellular telephone from one of his many pockets, and spoke a few words into it that Monica couldn't understand. Jessica seemed oblivious to the eyes that scoured them, and pointed skyward at a pair of large grey gulls circling overhead. The young man shut his telephone and motioned towards the end of the pier, to a small ship docked there. Monica's fears eased somewhat. Then, he held out his hand impatiently.

Jessica looked and said, "You're the one who gets paid the big money, not me."

Monica sighed and produced a few more bills from her shrinking wallet. She gave them to the young man who nodded, then jogged away.

"Don't worry, Monica. You're going to love this. Have I ever steered you wrong?"

Monica bit her tongue.

The ship was far from being the dirty boat Monica had expected. It was at least one hundred feet long, and on its deck was a handful of other North American tourists. When Jessica and Monica reached the ramp, a young native man in a white sailor suit came to greet them, and spoke further words Monica didn't understand. Jessica stepped up, holding the note she'd been given. "We were supposed to show this to you," she said. The steward read the note, and then studied the two of them. Monica felt the needles of worry. He turned to Jessica and held out his hand.

Jessica smiled and turned to Monica.

Monica sighed and paid the man more of their money, and then he disappeared up the ramp.

"I hope this works," Jessica said. "Or else I'm going to wring that guy's – oh, there's the captain."

The man approaching from the ship could be no one *but* the captain. His face was broad and weathered, trimmed with a thick white beard that contrasted his tanned skin. When he reached them, Monica could tell right away he wasn't originally a local.

"I'm Captain Lethes, and you two must be our new special guests. Please, come aboard. We'll be leaving momentarily."

As they followed him up the ramp, Monica saw the crew working on the pier, untying the long ropes, untethering the ship from what held it.

Up close, it was clear that the ship had seen its share of travels. There were signs of rust on the metal railings, and they stained the peeling white paint. Nevertheless, none of the other few passengers seemed to mind. In fact, they looked quite contented, chatting amiably amongst themselves as they sauntered across the deck or lounged in deckchairs. There was a sudden awful scream and it made Monica jump, before she embarrassingly realized it was the sound of the ship's whistle. The crew ran past with a practised step, and after a moment there was the smell of burning oil. Then the ship jolted forward and the pier where it had been docked slipped slowly away.

"Isn't this exciting?" Jessica said. "I bet you're glad I decided to take us on this detour. What would you do without me?"

Monica gritted her teeth, and wondered how hard it would be to push Jessica over the railing. Or, better yet, feel that fat loose skin between her fingers. She shook her head, surprised at herself.

"I'm going to take a walk around the ship," she stammered. "Maybe take some photos."

"Good idea. I'm just going to sit down here for a minute." Jessica eased herself into a vacant lounge chair. "My head is starting to hurt."

It felt good to get away from Jessica, if only for a few minutes. Monica walked past a couple holding hands and she smiled, At least someone was having a good vacation. They looked like newlyweds, and for a moment Monica wondered what it would have been like to be in that position. She was struck with the urge to take a picture, but faltered, knowing it was the last thing of which she wanted to be reminded. She didn't mind being alone, of course, but as time went on it felt less and less by choice.

She stopped at the prow of the ship, and looked ahead to where they were travelling. She could see an island there, its peak raised from the deep blue water, pointing toward white clouds. It looked like something from a postcard. She reached into her bag for her camera and came up empty-handed. She must have left it behind at the hotel, and cursed herself for being so forgetful, especially as it was one of the few things over the last week she *wanted* to remember. She sighed and checked her watch. It would probably take another fifteen minutes to reach the island. Perhaps she should stay there for a little while longer and try to commit the sight to memory.

"Hiding, are you?"

Monica turned upon hearing the voice. Beside her stood Captain Lethes, his smile highlighting the creases that covered his face. He cleared his throat, and then spoke conspiratorially. "It's okay, I won't tell."

She smiled, and then looked about her to make sure Jessica wasn't in sight. Even so, she kept her voice down. "I'm just taking a break, enjoying the view."

"Yes, it's beautiful, isn't it? I absolutely adore it. Once I came down here, I never wanted to go back home again. There's something about this place that makes it easy to forget about the ghosts of your past. It's a wonder, sometimes, we don't get more passengers. I dislike having to poach them."

Monica looked back at the sparkling water, the sun reflecting off its surface.

"I suppose it's the cost. No one ever has enough money."

"This is sadly true. One can work forever and only accrue troubles. Isn't that right?"

Monica nodded, and he looked out beatifically at the waters ahead of them. Around his neck, she noticed a familiar dark brown necklace.

"Those seem quite popular around here."

He seemed confused until she pointed at his neck. "Oh yes. It's an island custom of which I must admit I've grown quite fond. You should get one."

"I have one," she said, and retrieved the link of shiny tan stones from her pocket. "I'm just not wearing it."

"It won't do you much good like that."

"I suppose not," she said with a laugh, and fastened the string around her neck. Already, she was forgetting how irritating her trip had been thus far.

That relief, though, didn't last long.

"It seems your friend has found you."

"Pardon?"

Captain Lethes smiled and cocked his head. Jessica rushed towards them, waving urgently.

Monica closed her eyes for a moment to steel herself.

"Monica! Where have you been?"

"I've just been talking to the captain."

He smiled and nodded. Jessica eyed him with suspicion.

"Shouldn't you be steering the ship? We're almost at the island."

"We are?" said Monica, and looked to the water to see the island had grown tremendously in size. Yet, it was still quite small by most standards – one could easily walk its length in an hour or so. The colour of it was a deep gorgeous green, trees growing high amid plants below, and all that tropical scenery surrounded a small village filled with bright off-white stone roofs.

"Oh, I have a crew who take cares of the steering." The captain's smile didn't falter, which impressed Monica. "Besides, we'll be mooring at the village on the other side of the island. You don't want to stop at this one."

"What's wrong with it?" Jessica said.

"Look at it. It's deserted, for one."

He was right. Monica couldn't see anyone there. Even the plants had begun to invade its space. She saw some movement in the corner of her eye, but that was most likely the reflection of the trees in the empty windows. She saw no people in the streets.

"What happened to everybody?"

"What *ever* happens to people? Those that could eventually moved on. You see that a lot around here. Nothing seems to be permanent. We should be veering away from it at any moment."

And, as if by cue, the ship began to turn. He smiled as though pleased with his moment of forecast. "As your friend suggests, I ought to get back to ensure everything goes smoothly from here to the end. We should reach the pier in ten minutes, in case you needed anything."

"No," Jessica said, watching the village shrink into the trees. "We have all our baggage right here."

He smiled again and walked away.

Jessica turned to her friend after he left. "I see you're wearing that necklace now," she said, though the tone of her voice said something different.

It did not take long for the ship to make its way around the lush island. When the second pier came into sight, Monica heard the ship's engines cut out, and they began to coast towards their destination. The crew, hitherto unseen during the trip, emerged from hiding and began to dash across the ship to prepare for its impending mooring. Monica was amazed as she watched them work. It was as though they were so familiar with their jobs they could do them without thought.

Jessica, too, watched the crewmen, and then leaned close and said, "They all look the same, don't they?" Monica was horrified, yet recognized there was some truth to what Jessica had said. Beyond the issue of race, the crew all had the same haircut, the same uniform, the same build; from behind, they were indistinguishable. Yet, Monica could not admit it. If she did, it would be all the excuse Jessica needed to complain anew. So Monica said nothing and tried to forget Jessica was there beside her.

As the second village came into view, Monica was surprised to see it looked virtually identical to the one they had passed a few minutes earlier. Here were the same deep green trees surrounding the same off-white stone roofs. Except within *this* village people were milling about, some looking out at the approaching ship with hands above their eyes to block the noonday sun. True to the merchant's words, the island's inhabitants did seem more *authentic* than those back on the mainland.

The bulk of the people Monica could see looked to be natives, with only a few pale westerners among them. One of that minority stood farther away than the rest, among the trees just outside the village, and as the ship approached, the figure seemed to be waving fiercely. Monica looked back at the other passengers, including Jessica, as they waved in return. Monica did the same, before she realized that person on the island was gone, swallowed by the motion of the dark green leaves.

As the ship pulled alongside the peer, crew members leapt over the sides to moor the vessel. Their dark arms moved quickly, tying the ropes off and securely knotting them. Then, the captain walked onto the deck and said something in their language, waving them forward.

Jessica put on her backpack.

"Let's make sure we stay together now. I don't want us to get separated when everybody gets off."

Yes, Monica thought, picking up her own bags. That would be a shame.

Jessica and Monica were the last of the passengers in line to disembark. Captain Lethes had moved to the bottom of the ramp almost immediately, and insisted on offering a hand to each woman whether she needed it or not. Monica stopped to ask him what time the ship was going back to the mainland.

"As long as you're back here by six, you shouldn't have any troubles."

Monica thanked him and casually looked over at Jessica who already seemed displeased.

"This place is *just* like where we came from. Look!" She pointed at the rows of houses. What had been unclear from the ship was that each of the buildings had a large hole cut in its wall and from it sprouted a merchant-operated table or display. It was another bazaar like the one from which they had been recruited, except smaller and no doubt pricier. "What a waste! This vacation keeps getting worse."

"You know—" Monica said, then bit her tongue. She was embarrassed by Jessica's behaviour in front of Captain Lethes, yet she had to remember that there were still five days left to spend with her, and if there was one lesson learned so far, it was saying anything contrary would only cause another eruption. Instead, Monica tried to remain positive.

"It's only for a few hours. Maybe one of these places has food." She looked around, and saw a short distance away a group of the ship crew, sitting on chairs in front of another house. They were all laughing, and periodically lifted their drinks together.

"I'm afraid the food here isn't the primary attraction," said the captain.

Jessica rolled her eyes. "Then why *do* people come here?"

"Some appreciate the opportunity to relax in a place where they might leave their troubles behind. There once were walks around the island, as well, but that ended a few years ago. Nowadays, most confine their activities to the village."

"What about the other one? Have you been there?" Monica asked, and for a moment the captain didn't speak.

"Once, some time ago, but since then I've had no reason to return."

Jessica, however, immediately seized the idea.

"That's where we're going, then. Let's go, Monica." She hitched up her pack to secure it, and walked away.

"Wait. Where?"

She didn't slow. "You don't have to come, but I want to see that other village. It can't be worse than staying here."

"But—" was all Monica said before Jessica was too far to speak to without yelling. She looked around and saw the islanders had stopped and were watching her. Captain Lethes simply shrugged.

"Are you sure you want to go, too? It's quite a journey."

Jessica was already at the edge of the jungle beyond the rows of houses.

"If I don't, I'll never hear the end of it."

He smiled, sympathetically. "You should leave your baggage behind." He pointed at her pack. "You won't be needing it, and I'll make sure it's kept safe for you."

Monica thanked him, and gave him her backpack. Then, she jogged to catch up with her friend.

Jessica had stopped just outside the village to wait for Monica to catch up. When they were together, Jessica looked back at the village and said, "I'm not going to let that guy tell me where I can and can't go on my own vacation."

The walk through the plants and trees quickly turned humid. The two women trudged along the worn trail, aimed towards the other end of the island. Jessica did not seem especially prepared for the journey, and the sweat that soaked her pink shirt also turned it the darkest shade of red. She stopped periodically and took a drink from the bottle of water in her bag. She looked ready to collapse. Flies circled her, and she could barely wave them away.

"Maybe we should turn back," Monica suggested.

"No, we're practically there," Jessica said as she gasped for air. "If you want to chicken out and go back, that's fine with me. I came to see something different and that's what I'm going to do."

"You don't look well, Jessica. We shouldn't have come out here."

"Don't be stupid. You don't think I can do this, do you? 'Poor fat Jessica can't walk a few feet'." Her face was twisted as she used a shrill singsong voice. Monica's muscles clenched. Jessica was on the edge of her last nerve. If she said one more thing—

"I'm surprised someone so well off is such a quitter."

Monica snapped.

"Listen, I've put up with enough of your garbage. Why did you even come on this trip? We haven't been in the same room together in months. What makes you so – so vengeful – that you had to come here with me and ruin the only vacation I've had in years? Just what is your problem, exactly? Don't those friends of yours make you happy? Or, do they hate you as much as I do?"

The white-hot fury in Monica's eyes faded, and she saw Jessica again standing there, a shocked and disbelieving look on her face. Instantly, Monica regretted what she'd said. Nothing would be the same for the long days that were sure to follow.

"Well," Jessica said, curtly. "I think I'm ready to go on now." Jessica hitched her bag over her back and walked off in the direction of the other village. Monica was tempted to turn around. Instead, she followed.

She didn't want to apologise – that was the *last* thing she wanted to do – but she had to say *something*.

"I didn't mean that, Jessica. Please, stop for a minute." But instead the woman kept walking, pushing through heavy vegetation. The trees blocked sight of anything before them beyond a few hundred metres. "Jessica, please. Just talk to me."

"There's nothing more to say. I know how you feel now. But I'm not going to let it ruin things. I've spent money on this trip, too, if you'll remember – money that doesn't come as easily for me – and I *thought* I spent it so we could spend time together like we used to. I suppose I should have realized you were going to be like this."

"Be like what?"

"You know."

But Monica didn't. And Jessica wouldn't tell her.

They walked in silence for a few minutes more, until they stepped through a wall of vegetation that was blocking their path and, out of nowhere, found themselves in the centre of the other village. The place was surrounded by dense southern jungle and ocean, and it was amazing how much it looked like the village they had landed in, right down to the wooden walls and grey slate roofs. Yet, there was no one on the streets or in the windows there. The empty village had a feel to it that Monica couldn't quite understand, as though it were full of hiding people ready to pounce.

"Do you think this place is *really* deserted?"

"What do you care?"

Tables were laid out exactly as in the village on the other shore, though no products were upon them. Monica saw shadows moving behind the windows of the small houses that she was sure weren't cast by people, but they moved so fast it was hard to tell.

"What—?" she started, but Jessica hushed her.

"Do you hear that? It sounds almost like someone crying."

Monica didn't hear anything. She didn't even hear the birds she knew had to be close by.

She shivered, despite the humidity that weighed the air down, yet couldn't quite put her finger on what was wrong. Something in the back of her memory tried to wriggle away, some shadow that should never see the light.

"Jessica, let's go back now."

"No. I'm not ready." And she walked farther in, investigating the buildings. Monica stood where she was, absently fidgeting with her necklace. She could see greyish rocks on the ground, more of the shingles that roofed the houses, and she picked one up. Imprinted upon it, barely visible in the fading light, was the fossil of some ancient creature as wide as her hand. Its tiny ribs made grooves in the shingle, and its head a rough circle. She saw what looked like a wing, though folded over upon itself until it was only a series of lines. She dropped the piece to the ground and it shattered. She brushed the dust off her hands and then looked up.

Jessica was gone.

Monica called out for her repeatedly as she walked the edge of the village, but there was no answer. In the windows shadows moved, and for a moment she thought she saw a child's face, small and round, pressed against the glass, but it disappeared so quickly the image blurred in her memory. Monica called Jessica's name again.

She didn't know what to do but wait. She walked up to one of the empty tables and sat down. Surely there was no reason to worry – Jessica must be punishing her for what she'd said, but she couldn't ignore Monica forever. Eventually, she would have to show herself, if for no other reason than to return to the ship. Monica checked her watch. It was already past four o'clock.

"We don't have much time left," she yelled, and something responded with a noise that couldn't have been whimpering. She stood. Had there always been shutters on so many of the village windows? She couldn't recall, but things looked different from how they had previously. She checked her watch again, and though only a few minutes had passed, already the sky was losing its light. She looked up. Clouds had gathered, racing to cover the sun. She wondered if a storm was coming.

"Jessica! Where are you?"

Still, there was no answer. She looked at her watch again, not knowing what to do. Shadows of the clouds overhead surrounded her, and as she looked at their pattern there came a noise from within the trees, a noise that sounded like a cry, and Monica realized with cold anger what had happened.

Jessica had left without her.

Jessica, the woman who was supposed to be her oldest friend, had left her alone in the abandoned village while she returned to the ship that had brought them to the island. What was she doing? Did she think she could leave Monica behind, like a piece of refuse? Abandon her on an island where she didn't even speak the language? Monica started to run, eager to catch up with Jessica. She couldn't have travelled far, after all. Not with the weight she was carrying.

At first, Monica thought she heard footsteps ahead of her, Jessica's footsteps as she ran to keep ahead, but soon the echoes multiplied, until it sounded like many running with her towards the ship. With each step she felt the plants wrapping around her feet, like the fingers of many hands clawing at her as they gave chase. Yet, at no point did she actually *see* Jessica. After a few minutes Monica had to slow to catch her breath, and though the air continued to race by her, none of it wanted to fill her lungs. She gasped, trying to get her breath back, and for a moment forgot about Jessica and her betrayal. Monica panted, her hands on her knees, waiting for the stars in her eyes to clear.

The storm clouds were turning the sky into night, and the path became more difficult to follow, but it didn't matter. The island was small, and Monica knew as long as she headed straight ahead, she would end up where she needed to be.

She wiped the sweat from her forehead. Why was she running? Jessica's plan had failed, Monica still had time to reach the ship, and when she did she would give the heavy woman a piece of her mind. What she had said before would seem gentle compared to what was coming. Monica's whole body felt flush with anger, her skin so hot it was blistering. Even the stones around her neck had become like fiery coals, searing into her flesh. She stormed forward for the final confrontation.

But when she reached the village, Jessica wasn't to be seen.

At the small set of tables, Captain Lethes sat with his crew, a sweating drink in his hand. He looked up as the confused Monica returned, and he stood to meet her. Behind him his crew also stood, but then ran with a light jog towards the ship.

"Are you okay?" the captain asked her, looking her over. "Where's your friend?"

"I – I thought she would be here already. She should have been right in front of me."

He nodded. Then nodded again. The other passengers who had come to the island had started lining up by the ship when the crew returned to it. Monica looked at their pale lost faces, but none of them were Jessica.

"We have to wait for her. I think—" She paused for a moment, unsure of what she wanted to say. "—I think I must have left her back there someplace."

"It's okay, it's okay. Don't worry. We won't leave without her. But we can't just stand here waiting. I have other passengers I have to worry about, too. We have to be ready to leave when she arrives. You can wait here if you'd like, but you'll probably be more comfortable on the ship."

She looked behind her, back at the path she had just come from, and was unsure of what to do. It was getting so hard to think. She rubbed the sweat off her brow again.

"Okay, but we won't leave without her, right?"

"Of course not." He smiled reassuringly and led her back to the ship.

She stood on the deck, looking back at the island as the other passengers boarded. She was still quite tired from running, and underneath the heat she found her mind becoming muddled.

She watched the trees though, watched them swaying underneath the wind as though shaken by hundreds of hands, all trying to get her attention. But why they'd want her attention, she wasn't sure. She wasn't sure of anything anymore except that she was looking forward to getting back to the mainland, back to her tour group. It was silly, in hindsight, to have left it for a trip to the island, but she didn't think she regretted it. It was good to do different things on a vacation, and she wasn't sure if that was something she'd really understood until that moment. Perhaps the rest of her vacation would improve now that she had uncovered the secret to enjoying it. Already, she felt better.

When the crew had finished unmooring the ship and the vibrations of the engine were making the deck hum underfoot, Captain Lethes came down to stand with Monica as they pulled away from the island.

"You were right about that village," she said to him, as she watched the people on the island getting smaller. "I'm glad I saw it, but I can't imagine ever wanting to go back to it."

"True. Still, it looks like it's done you some good."

She smiled, and played with the stones around her neck. Their dark brown colour stood out in contrast against her pale skin, yet they seemed strangely cool under her fingers.

"I can't remember why I was so miserable before we arrived. I suppose we all need to put our troubles behind us sometimes. Oh look!" she said, pointing. "There's someone waving goodbye to us from the island."

She lifted her arm high and waved happily back at the shrinking figure.

"Goodbye!" she cried out.

MIKE O'DRISCOLL

13 O'Clock

MIKE O'DRISCOLL'S FIRST collection of short fiction, *Unbecoming*, was published by Elastic Press in 2006, and his story "Sounds Like" was filmed by Brad Anderson for the second season of Showtime's *Masters of Horror* TV series.

Other stories have appeared in *The Year's Best Fantasy and Horror*, *The Mammoth Book of Best New Horror*, *The Dark*, *Inferno*, *Poe's Progeny*, *Subtle Edens*, *Interzone* and *The 3rd Alternative*. O'Driscoll also writes a regular column on horror and fantasy, "Night's Plutonian Shore", for *Black Static*.

"The germ of '13 O'Clock' was born one night, some years ago in hospital, where I was recovering from a post-op infection," remembers the author. "I had spent the best part of twenty-four hours in the grip of a horrible fever and when it finally broke, some time in the early hours, I lay in the quiet stillness trying to make sense of what I had been through.

"Though exhausted, I couldn't sleep. I remembered at some point – probably when the fever was at its peak – wanting to die. Had I really wanted that, I wondered? Or had I just dreamed it in fever-induced delirium? I couldn't say for sure, but the possibility that I had desired death scared me and that, I think, was why I was so reluctant to let myself sleep in the aftermath.

"I found a pen and paper in my locker and scribbled some notes about what I was feeling. Eventually I did fall asleep. When I woke later that day I saw the words 'thirteen o'clock' among the notes I'd written. I thought then it might work as a story title.

"I spent the next couple of days thinking about it, mulling over ideas about dreams and nightmares, trying to remember the nightmares I'd had when I was a kid. I could recall one or two, but not much of their detail or narrative, and nothing of the terror I imagined must have accompanied them. Why? What was it that kept them at bay? I made some more notes, and then stashed them away in a folder and forgot about them until trying to come up with an idea for a new story. I dug out the folder and rummaged through the countless scraps of paper, searching for some inspiration.

"When I saw those two words again, something clicked, and over the course of the next couple of days I discovered how to tell the story that had been waiting inside them."

T HE DAYS WERE BEGINNING to stretch out. Another couple of months and it would be surf and barbecue, cold beer out on the deck listening to Bonnie "Prince" Billy. Play some silly tunes on the guitar for Jack, teach him his first chords. Make some other kind of music for Polly. The sweet kind for which the diminishing nights left barely enough time.

The cold still hung in the air at this hour though. Caleb Williams could feel it on his face as he followed Cyril across the rising field. He bent down, scooped up the mostly black mongrel terrier and boosted him up the stone ditch. He climbed up and over while the dog, resenting the indignity of having to be lifted, scrambled down by itself.

They crossed the dirt track to the garden, where Caleb paused to lean against the unpainted block wall. The sun was a ball sinking below Cefn Bryn, leaving the mid-April sky streaked with red.

Gazing up at the house, he felt a sudden, unaccountable yearning. The otherness of dusk made the cottage seem insubstantial. Shrugging off this unexpected sense of isolation, he opened the back gate and let Cyril bolt through. They got the dog two years ago for Jack's birthday, but whether Jack had tired of it, or the dog had tired of the boy, it had ended up attaching itself to Caleb. Only now was he getting used to the idea of himself as a dog person.

In the living room, Polly was curled up on the sofa, dark red hair breaking in waves over her shoulders, ebbing across her blouse. She was channel hopping as he came in, and had opened two small bottles – stubbies, she called them – of San Miguel. "Saw you coming from Jack's room," she said, her grey eyes lucent with mischief. "You looked like you need one."

Caleb took the beer and sat next to her. "Is it me," he said, "or is the climb up from the bay getting steeper?"

His wife swung her feet up into his lap. "It's decrepitude," she said.

"Good. For a moment there I thought I was getting old." He tapped his bottle against hers and took a sip.

She smiled for a moment, then her expression changed. "You didn't hear Jack last night?"

"No. What?"

"I meant to tell you this morning. He had a bad dream." She frowned. "More than that, I guess. A nightmare."

"There's a difference?"

"Of course there is, fool." She jabbed a foot playfully into his thigh. "This was a nightmare."

"How could you tell?"

"I'm serious, Cale. He was petrified. He screamed when I woke him."

"Was he okay?"

"After a while, yes."

"What did he dream?"

"He was alone in the house at night. That's scary enough for most eight-year-olds."

"Poor Jack. How is he tonight?"

"He's fine. Has been all day. I was half-expecting him to say something but he never mentioned it. I guess he's already forgotten."

"Good," Caleb said, feeling a vague sense of guilt. Should have been there for him, he thought.

Polly sighed and rubbed her foot across his belly. "So, how was your day?"

Caleb said nothing. He was thinking about Jack's nightmare, trying to imagine how he must have felt. A yellow woman moved across the TV screen. He wondered where nightmares came from. What caused them?

Polly wiggled her toes in his face. "What's the matter? Got the hots for Marge Simpson?"

He laughed and grabbed her foot. "It's the big hair that does it for me"

She yanked her foot free. "There you go, making me jealous," she said, sliding along the sofa.

He drained his bottle and pulled her close. "I always thought blue would work for you," he said, before kissing her. He didn't think about Jack's dream again until after they had made love, and then only for a short while, until sleep took him.

Caleb taught basic literacy skills to young adult offenders, most of whom were serving community sentences for alcohol and drug-related crimes. Twice a week he held a class in Swansea Jail for those whose crimes were more serious. In all the time he had worked as an English teacher in a city comprehensive, he had seen countless faces just like theirs. The faces of disaffected boys who had never willingly picked up a book, or lost themselves in words. After ten years he had walked away. Now, watching these young men begin to find pleasure in reading, he felt he was finally doing something that mattered.

All the more maddening then, not being able to comprehend his son's terror. As he moved from one student to the next, his thoughts kept drifting back to Jack. He'd had another nightmare last night, worse than before. Hearing him, Polly had woken Caleb. When he'd gone to his son's room, the look of terror on Jack's face had shocked him. After he'd calmed the boy and returned to his own bed, he'd lain awake for hours, trying to comprehend the extent of Jack's fear. His inability to understand the dream left him feeling helpless, and this in turn had added to his confusion and guilt.

At lunchtime, he called Polly on her mobile. "Hi Cale," she said. "What's up?"

"You busy?"

"On my way to town. Got work to drop off at McKays." She worked part-time, auditing small business accounts. "Can I get back to you?"

"It's okay," Caleb sighed. "I was just wondering about Jack. How he was this morning."

"Okay, I guess." Caleb heard the doubt in her voice. "He dreamed about a stranger. He, uh—"

"He what?"

"He said a stranger was coming to our house."

Caleb tried to imagine his son's nightmare.

"We spoke at breakfast and he was all right. I think he forgot most of it. He's tough, you know, resilient."

"You're right," Caleb said. "I'll stay with him tonight, till he's asleep."

"He'll like that, Cale. Really." She broke the connection.

I hope so, Caleb thought, as he flipped the phone shut. Despite Polly's reassurances, he felt there was more he should be doing. Like being able to explain the dream to Jack, stealing its power through interpretation. Take away that ability to rationalize and he was no better than the most illiterate, most brutalized of his students.

In the evening Caleb put his son to bed and read him a chapter from *The Wind in the Willows*. Jack liked it when he put on different

voices for the characters. High-pitched and squeaky for Rat, pon-
derous and slow for Mole. Toad was his favourite. He always
laughed at Caleb's braying, exaggeratedly posh voice, but tonight
there was no Mr Toad, just the softer, more subdued notes of Rat
and Mole as they searched the river for young Portly, the missing
otter. He found himself strangely moved by the animals' mystical
quest, experiencing an emotion akin to the yearning regret that was
all the memory Rat and Mole were left with of their encounter with
Pan. He closed the book and forced a smile, trying to hide his mood,
but his melancholy was mirrored in Jack's eyes.

"What's wrong, Dad?" Jack asked.

"I was thinking about the story."

Jack nodded. "Me too. About the friend and helper." He frowned.
"Why did they forget him?"

Caleb hadn't read the book since he was a child himself, and he'd
forgotten how mysterious, how at odds with the rest of the tale, the
"Piper at the Gates of Dawn" chapter had been. "So they wouldn't
feel sad," he said, after a while.

"But he helped them find Portly."

Caleb nodded. "Yes, but there are things . . ."

"Why?"

Caleb wondered what it had felt like when he had first become
aware of his own mortality. Choosing his words carefully, he said,
"Sometimes people know things they're better off not knowing."

"Things in dreams?"

"Yes." Something resonated in Caleb's memory. He couldn't quite
grasp it, though he suspected his feelings were an echo of Jack's
empathy for Rat and Mole. "You remember anything about your
dream last night?"

Jack shook his head.

"If you're scared, Jack, if something's troubling you, I want you to
tell me."

"Are you okay, Dad?"

Caleb wondered why Jack would ask that question. It disturbed
him, but he managed a smile and said, "Course I am."

"Right," Jack said, but the look of concern remained on his face.
"I'll say a prayer."

"Why?"

"You're s'posed to," Jack said. "Mrs Lewis said you have to pray
to Jesus to look after your family."

Mrs Lewis was Jack's teacher. Caleb had nothing against religion,
but he was troubled by the notion of Jack taking it too seriously.

"You don't need to pray for me, son. I'm fine, really. Sleep now, okay?"

"'Kay," Jack said, closing his eyes.

Caleb woke from a fretful sleep, scraps of memory gusting through his troubled mind. Though a film of sweat coated his body, he felt cold and vulnerable. A shaft of moonlight fell through the gap in the curtains, cloaking familiar objects in odd, distorting shadows that, in his drowsy state, unsettled him. He struggled to claw back the fragments of a dissipating dream and the sounds that had slipped its borders. A minute passed before he understood that he had followed them out of sleep, that he was hearing the same muffled cries from somewhere in the house. He sprang out of bed and crossed the landing to Jack's room. His son was whimpering softly, making sounds unrecognizable as words. As Caleb approached the bed, Jack's body spasmed and an awful scream tore from his throat. Caleb hesitated, unnerved by the intensity of his son's fear. He wrapped his arms around the boy and felt the iron rigidity in the small, thin body. Downstairs, Cyril began to bark.

"It's okay, Jack," he whispered. "I'm here." Jack's eyes opened, and in his disoriented state he struggled in his father's arms. Caleb made soothing noises and stroked his face. Jack tried to say something, but the tremors that seized his body made him incoherent. "Ssshhh," Caleb said. "It's over."

"Duh-duh, Dad," Jack cried.

"I'm right here," Caleb told him.

Jack struggled for breath. "He-he was here. He knew you wuh-were gone."

Caleb shuddered involuntarily at the words, and felt the lack of conviction in his voice when he said, "Nobody's here Jack. Just you and me."

Jack shook his head and looked beyond his father. "He came in the house. He was on the stairs."

Caleb held the boy in front of him and looked into his eyes. "There's nobody here. It was a nightmare. You're awake now." Cyril barked again, as if in contradiction.

"His face – it's gone," Jack said, still disoriented.

It was the same nightmare, Caleb realized with disquiet. Polly had said Jack had dreamed of an unwelcome stranger in their house. How common was it for kids to have recurring dreams? He wondered if it signalled some deeper malaise. "I'll go and check downstairs," he told his son, in an effort to reassure Jack.

"Please Dad," Jack said, his voice fragile and scared. "Promise you won't go."

A tingling frost spread over Caleb's skin, numbing his brain. His thoughts stumbled drunkenly, dangerously close to panic. He wondered if what he was feeling was, in part at least, a residue of his son's fear. He needed to be strong. "All right, Jack. You come sleep with us tonight, okay?"

Jack nodded, his gaze still flitting nervously about the room. Caleb picked him up and carried him back across the landing. He laid him down in the middle of the bed, next to Polly. She stirred and mumbled something in her sleep. He put a finger to his lips, signalling Jack to keep quiet. Then he left the room and went downstairs to the kitchen.

Cyril was standing at the back door, sniffing. Caleb crouched beside the dog and petted him for a few moments. "What's wrong boy? You having bad dreams too?" The dog licked Caleb's hand. He pointed to Cyril's basket, stood up and glanced through the kitchen window above the sink. Moonlight silvered the garden. Nothing was out of place. When he went back upstairs and climbed into bed, Jack turned and clung to him for a while, until fatigue loosened his hold and sleep reclaimed him.

The radio clock's LED screen pulsed redly in the darkness, as if attuned to the rhythm of Caleb's agitated mind. Vaguely disturbing thoughts had taken root there, but an unaccountable sense of guilt made him reluctant to examine them. They seemed born out of nothing. The darkness robbed him of reason, made his fears seem more real than they had any right to be.

What could he do for Jack? Explain that his nightmares were the product of his own unconscious fears? As if reason could ever outweigh terror in the mind of a child. As if it could account for what seemed to him a strange congruence between Jack's bad dreams and his own fragile memories. He felt powerless and bewildered. Though he believed he would do anything for his son, he was plagued by a small but undeniable doubt. He couldn't escape the feeling that he was in some way responsible for Jack's terror, that it was connected to some weakness in himself.

Caleb strummed his guitar listlessly, his chord changes awkward and slow, like they had been when he'd first started playing. Maybe, once you got past forty, it was too late to take it up. The fingers were too stiff and the willingness to make a fool of oneself was not so strong as it had been. Yet, he didn't feel that way about himself.

When Polly had bought the guitar for his birthday and told him it was time to stop talking and learn to play, it hadn't seemed such a crazy idea. And still now, after a year, the desire to play competently some blues and country tunes was as strong as ever. It was something else distracting him.

He leaned the guitar against the table, got up and walked to the sink. Polly glanced up from the book she was reading. "Not there today, huh?"

Caleb shrugged and watched his son through the kitchen window. Jack was playing in the garden by the recently dug pond that still awaited its first Koi Carp. He was manoeuvring his Action Men through the shallow water as if it were a swamp.

"You okay?"

Caleb looked at her. She'd put her book down on the table and was staring intently at him. He didn't want to talk. He knew already what she'd say. "I'm fine," he said, turning back to the window.

"It's Jack, isn't it?"

The boy was manipulating two of his soldiers into a fight. He paused suddenly, and cocked his head to one side, as if listening. Slowly, he swept his gaze across the garden. He seemed nervous, wary of something. After a moment or two, he continued with his game, but more guarded, as if aware that he was being observed. Caleb felt uneasy. He leaned closer to the window and let his gaze wander around the garden and down to the rear wall that backed onto the lane. Nothing appeared out of the ordinary.

"He's okay, Cale," Polly was saying. "He'd be even better if you'd stop fretting."

"I was trying to help him," Caleb said, still watching Jack.

"By interrogating him?"

"Talking about it will help him." Jack was shielding his eyes from the watery sun as he gazed south towards the bay. "Expose the irrational to the cold light of day and it loses its power. Making Jack talk about the dream will weaken its hold over him."

"Oh sure. After all, he's eight years old."

She didn't seem to get it. "What do you suggest we do?"

"Ignore them. They'll pass of their own accord if you stop bringing them up. Jesus Cale, all kids have bad dreams sometime or other."

"I never did. Not like his."

"We all have nightmares. Why should you be different?"

He looked at her and heard himself say, "I just never did."

"Or you forced yourself to forget."

Maybe she was right. He turned back to the garden. Jack had laid one Action Man face down in the water. He was draping strings of pondweed over the doll. He paused and glanced up towards the house, before turning his attention once again to his game.

Polly came up behind Caleb and slipped her arms around his waist. "You just need to give him a little time," she said, pressing her lips against the back of his neck.

How much time, Caleb wondered, feeling an ache of tenderness as he watched Jack rise up onto his knees. The same nightmare four times in one week. How much time before reason was exposed as a hollow lie? He would not let it happen.

As if feeling his isolation, Polly pulled away. He was about to reach for her when he saw what Jack was doing. The boy was kneeling over the pond where the Action Man floated, covered with strands of weed. His hands were clasped together, his head was tilted skywards and his lips were moving. Caleb's flesh tingled with disquiet. What kind of game was it that necessitated prayer?

Jack and Gary raced into the dunes ahead of Caleb and Cyril. A stiff breeze blew in from the east, across Oxwich bay, unleashing small, foam-flecked waves to snap at the shore. Caleb followed the terrier up the steep, sliding bank of a dune.

The boys were waiting for him atop the grassy ridge. Jack looked skinny and frail next to his friend, who, though only a month older, was a good six inches taller and a few pounds heavier. Sometimes Caleb feared for his son when he watched the rough and tumble of their play, but he was glad too that Jack had such a friend. Gary seemed to him indomitable, and he hoped that some of that strength would rub off on Jack. No nightmare last night. Third dreamless night in a row. Perhaps Polly had been right after all.

"We're gonna hide now," Jack said. "You gotta count a hundred."

Caleb nodded. He called Cyril to him and held on to the dog while the two boys took off. He began counting out loud as he watched them scramble further up through the tough marram grass. Cyril whined and struggled to chase after them, but Caleb held him until he had reached fifty. Then, still holding the dog by his collar, he crawled up the slope and peered over the crest of the dune.

Jack and Gary were sixty or seventy yards ahead, running through the small dip towards another rise. He waited until they had disappeared around the side of the hill, then called out that he was coming.

Letting Cyril race ahead of him, he followed their path, before cutting across and up the dune at a steeper angle. Crouching as he came over the crest of the hill, he scanned the dune slack below, searching the bracken and coarse grasses for anything other than wind-induced movement. He spied a patch of yellow moving beyond the pink and white trumpets of a bindweed-choked tree, and quickly chose a route that would allow him to get ahead of the two boys.

Soon after, he popped up from behind a thick mound of marram grass and made booming noises as he shot them with his forefingers. After yelping in surprise, the boys collapsed spectacularly into the scrub.

By the time they had picked themselves up and started counting, Caleb was already heading deeper into the dunes.

He ran for about a hundred yards, found cover in a clump of bracken, and lay on his back to watch the cirrus clouds race across the sky. He could hear the sea rolling in over the long flat stretch of the bay, the screech of gulls and the wind whistling through the dune grass.

He closed his eyes for a moment and heard voices carrying on the breeze. He was surprised at how much distance and the wind distorted the sounds, made them indecipherable, barely recognizable as human. The vastness of the sky overhead instilled in him a sense of isolation, which added to the strangeness of the voices. Despite the coolness of the breeze, he felt trickles of sweat on his back as the words shaped themselves in his head. Something about time.

He listened more intently, made out Jack's voice, frightened, asking what happens at thirteen o'clock. A sudden rush of panic swept through Caleb. He sprang up from the bracken and spun round, searching the immediate vicinity for his son. There was no sign of either boy. He was about to call out when he heard Jack shouting from the top of a dune some sixty yards away. The boy waved to him, then followed Gary and the dog down the slope.

"You're s'posed to hide, Dad," Jack said, as they arrived, breathless, beside him. "That was too easy."

"We would have found you anyway," Gary said. "Cyril had your scent."

There was nothing in either boy's faces to confirm what Caleb had heard. He had imagined it, he told himself. The wind and his own anxiety about Jack. Understandable, if foolish. He thought the boy looked a little pale, but he seemed untroubled. "Okay," he said. "I think it's time to go."

"Not yet," Jack said. "We only had one go of hiding."

Gary nodded, and without waiting for Caleb to agree, he tore off up the nearest slope. Caleb felt a surge of anger but he suppressed it. He gestured to Jack. "Get going," he said. "Make it good."

Jack sped off after his friend. Cyril stayed with Caleb of his own accord. It was getting on for seven and a chill lingered in the late April air. As he watched them disappear over the top of a high dune, he regretted letting them go again and considered calling them back. But they were gone now, and despite his sense of unease, he didn't want to spoil their fun.

He counted slowly to fifty, then set out on their trail. He climbed the dune and scanned the nearby hollows for any trace of them. "Where they go boy?" he said, more to himself than the dog, who had stopped to investigate a few pellets of rabbit shit. Caleb shrugged, scrambled down the dune towards a trail that skirted the copse separating the dunes from the marshlands beyond.

He followed this path to the end of the trees, then climbed up the nearest slope to get a better view. From the top, he saw the grey ocean and a thin line of sand, separated from him by the expanse of green, cascading dunes. A sudden, intense fear bloomed inside him as his eyes searched the wind-swept slacks. "Jack," he cried out. "Time to go son."

No voice came back to him, just the moan of the insistent breeze through the coarse grass and brittle sea holly. He moved in a shore-wards direction, clambering down one dune and up the next, calling Jack's name. He felt a tight knot in his stomach as he forced himself up the yielding slope. It sapped his strength and robbed him of breath. He reached the top, light-headed and panting. Cyril scampered up the path behind him, tongue lolling out of his mouth. He stopped abruptly and turned, just as a figure burst out from the scrub.

It was Gary. Caleb's relief dissipated when he saw the boy was alone. "Dammit Gary," he snapped. "Where the hell is Jack?"

Gary's grin slipped. "I – I'm sorry Caleb. We didn't mean to—"

Caleb saw that he had frightened the boy unnecessarily. "It's all right. Just tell me where he's hiding."

"I didn't see," Gary said.

Caleb's fear intensified. "Which way did he go?" he said, trying to keep his voice calm.

Gary looked around, then pointed back towards the marsh. Caleb took his hand, and together they headed down the slope. The sweat chilled his body as he raced over damp scabious, calling out.

The minutes ticked by and dusk began to roll in from the bay. Odd terrors clawed at the frayed edges of his mind, and his limbs shook with fatigue as he searched through the trees. What had he been thinking, especially after what Jack had been through? Please, please, let him be okay.

A whispered sound caught his attention. He turned and saw the dog running along another path back into the dunes. "There," he shouted at Gary, a sharp pain piercing his side. He staggered after the boy and dog. Beyond them, he caught a glimpse of yellow through the scrub, lost it, then saw it again, unmoving on the ground behind a stunted tree. His heart was pumping furiously and the cry of despair was on his lips as he came round the tree and nearly crashed into Gary, who stood over the motionless form.

Jack was grinning up at them. "What took you so long?" he said.

For a second, Caleb teetered on the edge of rage, then he fell to his knees and hugged Jack tightly to his chest.

Caleb turned into the school car park. Beside him, Jack stared blankly ahead. He'd not spoken in the six-minute drive from the doctor's surgery to the school.

After a dreamless week, the nightmare had returned to ravage the boy. Caleb had heard him cry out some time after midnight. He'd run to Jack's room and had found him sitting upright, his gaze fixed on nothingness.

Traces of whatever haunted his dreams lingered in his eyes even after Caleb had woken him, but he had been unable to ascribe it a material substance or meaning. And all the doctor had had to say was that there was nothing physically wrong with Jack. Jesus Christ – what did he expect? Broken bones? A gaping wound? Caleb had wanted answers, not fucking platitudes. Tell him why Jack was having these nightmares, what was scaring him. Instead, he'd had to listen to bullshit reassurances about Jack's overactive imagination and how they should maybe monitor his TV viewing and ease up on the bedtime stories.

Polly would be relieved, even if she had more or less predicted what the doctor would say.

Caleb turned off the ignition, his body tense with anger and concern. He glanced at his son in the passenger seat. Jack looked too fragile, he thought, too lost inside his own head. He wanted desperately to hug the boy, to let him know that he would do anything for him, but he was afraid that Jack would somehow see the truth.

"You sure you want to go to school?" he said. "I can take you home if you want."

"I'm okay," Jack said.

Caleb felt sick with anguish. He didn't want to quiz his son but felt he had no choice. "Jack, the other day, when you asked Gary about thirteen o'clock, what did you mean?"

"About what?"

Caleb forced a smile. "When we were down at Oxwich. You asked him what happens at thirteen o'clock."

Jack seemed confused. "I don't know what you mean, Dad."

Caleb wondered if his son was being evasive. "Maybe, like Rat and Mole, you feel that it's better to forget some things?"

Jack shook his head, making his uncertainty evident. "I never heard of it."

Caleb believed the boy. He leaned over and hugged him, trying to squeeze strength into his son. "I love you, Jack. You know that?"

"Yes."

"I won't let anything hurt you."

"Dad," Jack said, his voice muffled against Caleb's chest. "I don't want you to go."

Caleb stifled a sob and patted him on the back. "I got work, Jack."

The boy pulled away from him. "I didn't mean—" He stopped then, kissed his father and got out of the car. Caleb waved after him as he ran across the schoolyard, but Jack didn't look back.

Alone, his eyes watered, and he felt overwhelmed. His love was compromised by a sense of powerlessness, of having failed his son. He felt guilty too, at being afraid, not for Jack but for himself. He was ashamed of his weakness and angry at what he saw as the failure of his reason.

He caught sight of something in the rear-view mirror, a child's bewildered face staring at him from the back seat. Jack's, he thought at first, but after a moment he realized it was his own, as it had been thirty years ago. The cheeks were pale, the lips thin and trembling, the eyes haunted. Caleb felt the glacial creep of fear across his skin. Wanting to connect with the abandoned child, he reached up, touched the mirror, and saw the child's features blur and reassemble themselves into his own, harrowed face.

Discordant sounds frayed Caleb's nerves and a harsh chorus of jeers echoed from the far end of the bar. He realized Polly wasn't really listening to what he was saying. Her attention was elsewhere; on the football match playing on the big screen television, or maybe on the people gathered in front of it. As if sensing his scrutiny, she returned her gaze to him and said, "I'm sorry, Cale. It's just that I thought we could, you know, talk about something else."

"Something else?"

She sighed. "We don't often get the chance to go out for a night. We've both been under a lot of strain lately, I thought it would do us good to be alone together."

Caleb frowned, frustrated at what he perceived as a lack of concern. "You don't think we owe it to Jack to—"

"Please don't play the guilt thing on me," she snapped. "Of course I'm concerned, but Jesus Christ, Cale, we just have to be patient."

"I think we should take him to see a specialist."

"If they continue, yes, maybe we should take him back to Dr Morgan and get him to refer Jack to someone. But just for tonight, can't we talk about something else?"

It was a reasonable request, he knew. Jack's problem had taken its toll on them both. And yet, he was wary of looking away. "All right," he said. "Let me just say something, then we'll talk about whatever you want."

Polly's lips tightened and she leaned back in her seat, away from him.

"The common thing is a stranger," Caleb said. "Think about what that means. For a kid it signifies danger, right? What are kids told all the time? Be wary of strangers, and this is drummed into their unconscious." He spoke quickly, trying to flesh out his still sketchy interpretation, how Jack's fear of strangers was manifesting itself in his dreams as someone coming to kidnap him.

Stories were in the papers and on the TV about kids being abducted and murdered. That young girl found strangled in the woods outside Cardiff a couple of months ago, and more recently, the teenage boy whose naked body was found beaten to death on the sands along Swansea foreshore. Kids weren't impervious to things like that, he said. They made connections, even if they weren't conscious of doing so. In bad dreams, the most irrational things became real.

Polly finished her bottle of Corona. She tried to sound reasonable but Caleb could hear the frustration in her voice. "It's not that what you're saying isn't plausible, Cale. Maybe it is, I don't know. I'll read up on it. But I think you're becoming obsessed with this. What chance has Jack got of forgetting the bloody dreams if you keep on about them?"

"Ignoring it isn't going to make it stop."

"It sounds to me like you don't want them to."

"Shit, Polly, what the hell is that supposed to mean?"

She got up from her seat. "I want to go," she said. "I can't talk about this anymore."

Caleb grabbed her arm and said, "This is Jack we're talking about."

She pulled her arm free. "No it isn't. It's you." She hurried from the bar.

He sat there for a few moments, immobilized by panic and fear. How could she not sense the threat to their son? Slowly, his panic subsided and he followed her out onto the street. He saw her crossing the main road to the car park. A mild rain was falling and the lights of Mumbles flickered on the dark bay like fragile memories. Caleb felt alone as he walked after her, distanced from everything he held dear. How does a man get back what he's lost, he wondered, puzzled at the question. He wasn't even sure what he had lost. Some memory, or maybe some part of his self-belief.

Anna, the babysitter, was watching *The O.C.* when they got home. Jack was fine, she said. Not a peep since she'd put him to bed at nine. Polly asked Caleb to check on him while she ran Anna home.

Alone, Caleb headed upstairs. A wave of relief swept through him when he saw Jack was sleeping soundly. The muscles in his legs quivered, and fearing he would collapse, he went and sat on the edge of his son's bed.

Wan light edged into the room through the open door, falling on Jack's slippers and a couple of Play Station games at the foot of the bed. A Manchester United poster was on the wall over Jack's head, and other posters around the room depicted Bart Simpson and scenes from the *Harry Potter* movies. Caleb felt a surge of tenderness. The sight of *The Wind in the Willows* on the night table filled him with sadness and a deep sense of regret.

I'm sorry, Jack, he thought, as he stood up to leave. The boy stirred and rolled onto his back. Caleb's breath caught when he saw Jack's eyelids were flickering crazily. His lips moved as if he were trying to speak, but no words came out, only the muted sibilance of dreams. "Jack," Caleb said, but the sound was less than a whisper.

He turned, saw the small armchair beneath the dormer window. He pulled it a little closer to the bed and sat in it. Jack continued to make soft, indecipherable noises on the bed, one hand above the sheet, the fist clenching and unclenching.

Caleb wondered what his son was seeing. He tried to will himself inside Jack's head, to witness the slow unfurling terror. "Stay with it, Jack," he said to himself. "Be strong."

Jack began to toss and turn on the bed, his legs kicking sporadically beneath the sheets. His voice grew louder, but Caleb was still unable to recognize the sounds as words.

His movements became more agitated, more violent. Caleb leaned forward in the chair, peering intently at his son. He anticipated some kind of revelation, as long as he didn't weaken and let his attention falter. That was the mistake he had been making, he realized, as Jack started to scream. Waking the boy too soon. Have to let him go further into it, see what he needed to see. Maybe then it would end. Recalling it in the daylight hours, his reason would overcome the nebulous fear.

Jack was writhing now, his lips pulled back in a rictus grin as scream after scream tore from his throat. As awful as it was, Caleb felt he had to let it go on, for Jack's sake, he told himself, his vision blurring through tears.

The only problem was Polly, standing in the doorway, screaming at him to make it stop. He tried to explain what was happening, but it was no good. She ran to the bed, gathered Jack up into her arms, and carried him from the room. Caleb sat there, appalled at what he had done. At what he had failed to do. The terror wasn't Jack's alone, he felt. It was his nightmare too.

Throughout the day Caleb struggled with his fears, barely able to keep his mind focused on his students. Their demands oppressed him, their need for reassurance wore him down. He grew more irritable and short-tempered, so that for the final session of the day, forewarned by the morning's students, fewer than half the afternoon group turned up. Afterwards, he sat alone for an hour in his office, trying to make sense of what was happening to him.

The persistence of Jack's nightmare scared him and his need to make sense of it had become an obsession. He had come to feel connected to it in some way, to believe that the key to deciphering it lay somewhere in his own past.

All day he'd dredged his subterranean memories but had come up empty. As he left the building after 6:00pm, he wondered if in fact he was afraid to probe too deeply. Maybe there was something there he wasn't ready to deal with, some secret he didn't want to discover about himself.

He stopped in the Joiner's Arms on the way home, but found neither relief nor pleasure in the two pints of Three Cliffs Gold he drank, nor in the company of the few regulars who acknowledged his presence but who, faced with his patent desire for isolation, left him to his fretful ponderings.

Jack was watching TV in the living room when Caleb got home. He glanced in at his son then walked by the door and on through to the kitchen. Polly was reading a book at the kitchen table, sipping a glass of red wine. She looked up as he came in and managed an uneven smile. "You okay?" she said.

Caleb shrugged, took a glass from the wall unit and poured himself some wine. "How is he?"

"Okay, I think. Keeps asking about you."

"What's that?" he asked, meaning the book.

She showed him the cover. It was called *Children's Minds*. "Picked it up in town today. Thought it might help us figure out what's going on with Jack."

"And does it?"

"It helps me."

"I'm going to sit with him tonight," Caleb said. "Watch him. I'll try to wake him before it takes hold."

Polly frowned. "You really think that will help him?"

"As much as that book."

She got up from the table and took his hand. "Caleb, can you be honest with me?"

"I thought I was."

"About Jack, I mean. About why he's so afraid for you."

"Jack's not afraid of me," Caleb said, agitated.

"That's not what I said," Polly said, confused. "Jack's afraid for you – not of you. Why? Have you told him something? Something you're not telling me?"

Her questions shook him, filled him with doubt. "Don't – don't be stupid."

"I'm not," Polly said, her voice rising. "I'm scared for our son and I'm worried about you. You're not yourself, Cale. Something's eating you up."

"Please, Polly," Caleb said, trying to hold himself together. "Don't presume you know what's going on in my head. Can you do that? Is it asking too much?" He didn't wait for an answer but hurried upstairs where he stripped off his clothes and took a long, almost scalding shower, as if to burn away the stain of some long forgotten sin.

Later, Caleb apologised to Polly and told her he'd look at the book she'd bought. Maybe it would help him understand what Jack was going through. After dinner, he went to his son's room. Jack was already tucked up in bed, and despite the broad smile that crossed his face, Caleb could see none of his usual vitality and zest for life.

"Mum said you're going to stay."

He stood by the edge of the bed, feeling a sudden, intense pang of guilt. "That's right," he said. "Keep the bad dreams away."

"Are you going to read to me?"

Caleb saw *The Wind in the Willows* on the night table. He shook his head. "Not tonight."

"D'you read it when you were a boy?"

"Yes, though I'd forgotten most of it until I started reading it to you."

"D'you forget your dreams too, Dad?"

Caleb stared at his son, not sure how to respond. He wanted to say the right thing, but he no longer knew what that was. "Most of them."

"Did you dream about—"

"Ssshhh, Jack. Go to sleep."

Jack was silent a moment, his face troubled. Then, as if having plucked up the courage, he said, "Will I die if I dream at thirteen o'clock?"

Caleb leaned over the bed and took hold of Jack's hand. "No," he said, squeezing. "There's no such time as thirteen o'clock."

Jack nodded but seemed unconvinced. He reached up and kissed his father's cheek. "I'm okay, Dad, really," he said, but Caleb saw a wariness in his eyes.

"I hope so, son," he said, letting Jack's hand fall. He moved to the window and sat in the armchair, watching as Jack turned on his side to face him. He'd brought Polly's book upstairs, but after flicking through the first few pages, he let it fall to the floor and focused his attention on his son.

He woke that night with the sound of screams still echoing in his head. Violent tremors shook his body as he crouched in the shadows, clenching his teeth to still their relentless chatter.

A sickly, cloying dread hung in the air, and his flesh recoiled from its touch. Through the fog of dreams that swirled all round his semi-conscious mind, he recognized Polly's voice, splintered to a thin, fragile whisper "Caleb," she was saying, "what happened to you? Where have you been?"

The stench of foam was in his nostrils, the taste of salt on his lips. "Poh-Polly?" he groaned.

"Jesus Cale." Her arms were around him and he felt the heat from her body seep into his cold, damp flesh. "It's okay, you had a nightmare."

He saw the darkness outside the kitchen window. He was crouched on the opposite side of the room, the slate tiles wet beneath him, and the distant pounding of surf reverberating in his head. Cyril cowered behind Polly, as if wary of him. "How did I get here?" he asked.

Polly shook her head, her face drained of colour in the pale light. "Something woke me and you weren't there. I was going to Jack's room when I heard you cry out down here."

"This can't happen, Polly," he said. "I – I can't let it happen to him."

"What can't happen, Cale?" Her grey eyes searched his face. He felt cut off from her, drifting beyond her zone of familiarity." What are you talking about?" she said.

He wondered at her inability to comprehend the vague shapes and shadows that flowed around him. Nothing he saw reassured him, not even her face. Her lips were moving but the words were drowned by the sound of the blood rushing through his brain. Someone had been outside, watching the house. Was he still there, waiting? For Jack?

"Listen to me," he said, trying to warn her, but there was something else too, something he needed to know. The shadows beyond Polly were melting into the floor.

"It's all right, Cale. It's over."

She didn't get it. The dream was there, but all scrambled in his mind. He'd seen this before. Years ago, he thought, when he was a child. The same nightmare Jack was having. A pitiful cry came from elsewhere else in the house.

"Oh please no," Polly whispered, rising to her feet.

Instinctively, he grabbed her hand and said, "What time is it?"

"It's Jack," she said, pulling away from him, heading towards the stairs.

He realized what it was she'd heard. Jack was screaming upstairs. He struggled to get up from the floor. Heart pounding ferociously, he forced himself to look at his watch. It was twelve forty-five. Bad memories stirred inside him.

Caleb looked out through the crack in the curtains, at the three-quarter moon hanging over Three Cliffs Bay and the mist rising silently up over the fields towards Penmaen.

He leaned back in the armchair. Jack was sleeping. Polly had phoned the doctor again that morning, asked him to refer Jack to a child psychologist. Caleb knew it would do no good but he hadn't stopped her. He'd wanted to tell her that only he could help their son, but fear and a sense of his own weakness, had prevented him from articulating this certainty.

What mattered was the hour in which Jack's nightmare came. The same hour in which it had come to him when he was a boy. The thirteenth hour. How many times had it haunted his sleep thirty odd years ago? That feeling of dread. A sense of being apart from the world, an isolation that had filled him with absolute dread. Lying in bed at night clinging to consciousness, fighting to keep the terror of sleep at bay. At least until the hour was past and even then not letting himself fall all the way, anchoring one strand of thought to the shore of reason.

It had withered inside him, he supposed. Withered but not died. He'd buried it deep down in the darkest recesses of his brain where it had lain in wait all these years until it had sensed the nearness of an innocent mind. The idea of it appalled Caleb. Every fibre of his reason screamed against the possibility. Yet he could no longer deny that his own childhood nightmare had transmigrated into the fertile ground of Jack's unconscious.

All day Caleb had thought about the nightmare, trying to collate his own hesitant memories against Jack's fragmented rememberings of the dream. They had both sensed a presence outside, watching the house. Jack had heard the stranger calling out, but he said it sounded a long way away. Sometimes he was inside the house, in the hall or on the stairs. Jack had never seen the nightmare through to the end, and if Caleb had ever done so, he'd forgotten what he'd seen there.

In the dim light, Caleb glanced at his watch. Eleven thirty. Knowing that Jack would soon begin to dream, he prepared to abandon himself to the lure of sleep. Even as it tugged at his mind, he felt the stirring of a residual fear, urging him to resist.

His eyes flickered open for a moment but darkness breathed over them, drawing them down. The strands of reason stretched one by one and snapped as he hovered a while on the edge of consciousness, before drifting across the border into the deep of dreams.

Nothing moved in the room. The chill cloak of darkness made everything one and the same. Caleb held himself still, waiting. His hands hurt from gripping the arms of the chair and every nerve in his body strained for release.

He listened, trying to shut out the pounding of his heart and the crackling white noise of nameless fears. Until, above the sound of his own terrible thoughts, he heard again a muffled footstep on the stairs. Silence again for a moment, followed by more footsteps, coming closer. He caught his breath as they stopped right outside the door. Where was Cyril, he wondered. Why wasn't he barking ?

His flesh crawled as he waited for the sound of the door handle turning. Instead, the footsteps began to recede. He exhaled slowly, peering into the darkness where he imagined the door should be. He turned on the lamp. Dim light pushed feebly at the shadows, barely strong enough to reveal the open door, the empty bed.

He choked back a cry and rushed out onto the landing. There was still time, he told himself. His breath misted in the chill, salty air. There were damp footprints on the stairs. Following them down, he felt the fear clawing at his back, wrapping him in its clammy embrace.

The wet prints marched along the hall through the kitchen, to the open back door. A shroud of mist hung over the garden. Caleb hesitated, his arms braced against the doorframe. His son was out there. "Jack," he whispered, despairingly. "Please Jack, come home."

Hearing the dog bark out there, he forced himself to move, out across the crisp grass that crunched underfoot. He went through the gate at the bottom of the garden, then turned and saw the house rising up out of the moon-yellowed mist.

He felt a terrible loneliness and could barely keep himself from rushing back towards it. But he caught the sound of a soft voice calling to him.

He hauled himself up over the ditch and ran on through the fields that sloped down into tangled woodland. He could no longer hear Cyril as he beat his way through trees and undergrowth, slipping and sliding on the soft earth, until finally he stumbled out onto the muddy banks of Pennard Pwll.

He followed the stream as it meandered out of the valley into the bay. Above the rustling of the water, he could hear his son calling to him.

Impatient, he stepped into the stream, wading across the gushing, knee-high water. He stumbled over a rock, fell and picked himself up again. "Jack!" he cried, as he struggled up on to a sandbank.

Some distance ahead and to his left he saw the three witch-hat peaks that gave the bay its name clawing the night sky through the mist. Having got his bearings, Caleb raced across the sand towards the sea, energized by the blood pumping through his veins.

The jaundiced mist billowed around him as he splashed into the wavelets lapping the shore.

He waded out deeper, ignoring the current that tugged insistently at his legs. He beat at the mist with his arms, trying to open up a space through which he might spy his son.

The sea was perishing, forcing him to snatch shallow, ragged breaths. One moment it was swirling around his waist, the next it was surging up to his chest. The mist seemed to be thinning out and he caught glimpses of the moon up over Cefn Bryn. A wave swamped him, leaving him treading water. The current began to drag him away from the shore.

"Jack, please," he called frantically, as he tried to keep his head above the surface.

Another wave washed over him and when he came up he could see clearly out into the bay. The sea sank its bitter teeth into his flesh. He was swimming hard now, just to stay afloat. He was growing weaker but still he searched for his son, chopping through the moon-silvered water, all the time following the sound of a voice, his own voice, but distant and younger, calling to him from out of a long-forgotten nightmare.

More water poured into his mouth as he went under again, still fighting. He rose in time to hear a distant church bell strike the hour. At one, there was still hope. At two, it began to fade. He heard the thirteenth strike as a muted sound beneath the surface, a strange echo of the pressure of the sea filling his lungs.

It seems like dawn, or maybe dusk. He has difficulty now, telling the time of day. It seems to be always twilight. But still he waits for them, anticipating the moment, imagining a different outcome this time.

But when they appear in the garden, the desperate longing he feels is as overwhelming as it always was. Jack looks bigger, more filled out. He must be ten, at least. Colour reddens Polly's cheeks again, and the small lines around her eyes signify acceptance more than sorrow. He wonders what that means.

He places a hand on the garden wall and as he does so, the house recedes a little, as if wary of him. He calls out their names and for one second, Jack looks up and stares directly at him. "Jack," Caleb cries out again, waving to him. "I'm here." For another moment, Jack continues to look his way, shielding his eyes from the sun. But then he turns and as Caleb looks down in despair, he sees no shadow on the garden wall, only sunlight falling right through the place where he stands.

JOEL LANE

Still Water

JOEL LANE HAS WRITTEN two collections of weird fiction, *The Earth Wire* and *The Lost District and Other Stories*, as well as two novels, *From Blue to Black* and *The Blue Mask*, and two collections of poems, *The Edge of the Screen* and *Trouble in the Heartland*.

He has edited an anthology of subterranean horror stories, *Beneath the Ground*, and co-edited (with Steve Bishop) the crime fiction anthology *Birmingham Noir*.

The author's recent publications include a weird novella from PS Publishing, *The Witnesses Are Gone*, and an article on supernatural horror maestro Fritz Leiber in the critical journal *Wormwood*. He is currently close to finishing his third novel, *Midnight Blue*.

" 'Still Water' is one of a series of supernatural police stories I've been writing for a long time," explains Lane. "Nine others have been published to date, with three more forthcoming.

"This one draws on memories of rural holidays, combined with recent experience of a blues festival. It also stems from my conviction that sexual love, like religion, appears totally psychotic when viewed from the outside."

I T SEEMED FUNNY at the time, but in retrospect it wasn't funny at all.

A gang of jewel thieves who'd gone missing in Stoke had turned up in the Black Country, hiding in a street with no name. It was the late 1970s, and there were quite a few anomalies in the local street map: remnants of lost districts that didn't belong to anywhere, and the council hadn't given them postcodes or kept track of who lived there.

In this case, it was a string of old railwaymen's houses in the poorest part of Aldridge, uninhabited for thirty years at least. A pearl necklace that had been stolen in Derby turned up in a Walsall pawnshop; we traced it to a prostitute who'd got it from some men living out there. She said it was a derelict house.

At that time, I'd been in the force for a year. I was working from the Green Lane station in Walsall. There wasn't much going on except drunkenness and domestic violence. This was my first taste of organized crime. We planned a nocturnal raid on the ruined cottages, with at least four arrests anticipated. According to the prostitute, the gang was like a family. They shared everything. Some of what she told us didn't end up on the interview record. My superior, DI McCann, had a sense of decency that was unusual for a policeman.

Four cars full of police officers descended on the nameless street shortly before dawn.

The houses were built on either side of a railway bridge that had been condemned in the 1950s, but never demolished. They backed onto a patch of wasteland where old canals had leaked into the soil, giving the landscape a fertile variety of plant-growth and a pervasive smell of stagnant water. It made me think of unwashed skin.

We'd been told to go to the third house. It looked just like the others, uninhabited and impossible to inhabit. Black lichen and moss caked the crumbling brick walls; the windows were boarded up, the front door covered with rotting planks. Some tree-dwelling bird called to us mournfully in the night.

Behind the house, the marshy ground and thick brambles made an approach difficult. The rear windows were unprotected, though no light was visible through them. What first appeared to be thick curtain was revealed by our torches as a black mould covering the inside of the glass. It was hard to believe that we'd come to the right place.

But in the silence before we broke in, a faint sound reached us. A man's voice, muffled by brick and glass and layers of filth. He was singing: "Baby, You're Out of Time". So was he.

McCann crashed through the back door, and five of us followed him. The rest waited outside. Our torches made crazy snapshots of the interior: rotting wallpaper, a cracked ceiling, broken chairs. Some new-looking food cartons, bottles and candles on a table were the only sign of occupancy. In all probability, this place had never had electricity.

The singing continued in one of the upstairs rooms. Was it a tape recorder? What kind of trap were we walking into?

On the staircase, my foot went through a rotten step and I fell, cursing. When I got up I was alone on the stairs. Ahead of me was only the song. The blues.

Apart from police, there was only one man in the upper room. He was kneeling on a filthy mattress, in front of a small suitcase. The lid was up. The suitcase was full of jewels: pearls, rubies, silver, emeralds. Some were strung or inlaid, some were loose. He was running his hands through them, and singing to himself.

His hair was knotted and filthy; his once-white shirt was streaked with filth and sweat. He didn't look away from his hoard or stop singing, even when McCann clamped the handcuffs on his wrists.

We kept him at the Green Lane station for a week.

His name was Jason Welles, and he was a member of the Stoke gang. An experienced fence, despite being only twenty. Among the station officers he was known as "Mr Pitiful" – and not only because of the singing.

For two days he did nothing but complain that we'd taken his jewels from him, because "She won't come to me if I don't have them. She's an old-fashioned girl. No gifts, no loving." His eyes were a pale, tormented blue.

One night, when I took him his dinner, he remarked to me as calmly as if we'd been talking about her all evening: "That first time, she came out of the wall. Plaster clinging to her like a shroud. I was holding an emerald bracelet, trying to judge its value. She stood there naked and reached out for it. Then she took me into the garden and showed me where her family live.

"I wanted to stay with her, but she said it wasn't time yet. When will it be time?" The last question was asked as if everyone knew the answer but him. I didn't know what to say.

Every attempt to interview him produced the same story. He lived in a twilight world of ghosts and angels, a delusional shell that could have made him a cult leader if he'd had a better haircut.

It seemed likely that the gang's adolescent games with drugs and prostitutes had triggered some kind of buried madness in him. Or else there'd been some hallucinogen in the moulds and lichens that decorated the ruined Aldridge house.

A search of those houses and the surrounding waste ground had yielded no trace of the other gang members. If he didn't tell us where they were, we'd probably never find out.

But how do you interrogate a madman?

I attended three of the interview sessions. Each time, he sang to himself and muttered random nonsense, ignoring our questions. To be fair, we ignored his. His world and ours rarely seemed to touch.

Typically, he'd rock in his chair and run his hands through imaginary jewels – or through the hair of an imaginary woman. He'd sing "Out of Time" or "I Can't Help Myself", then start talking suddenly, as if resuming a conversation we'd interrupted.

The interview tapes and transcripts are doubtless long since thrown away, but I can remember some of his words . . .

"As soon as I saw the house, I knew it belonged to a family. A real family, not like my mum and her boyfriends after my dad went to prison. Nathan, Mark and Rich, they brought call girls into the house, but I knew the family wouldn't like that.

"Then she came to me one night. Wearing a gown of rotting wallpaper that fell from her, and her body glowed brighter than a candle.

"She showed me where her family sleep under the water. And the thin grey tubes they breathe through, like a baby's umbilical cord.

"I gave her jewels to wear in her long dark hair. To hang in the tunnels under the ground.

"The other three guys . . . well, they were just thieves. They had no idea what anything was worth. It was just money to them. Money to spend on cars and clothes and cunt. I let her family take them." He giggled like a child. "Not much left of them after a while.

"Poetic justice. What they had was stolen. But she never stole from me. I gave her everything. I opened her and wrapped her around me.

"They say when you come off, it never lasts. But I know how to make it last forever.

"Then the morning comes, and she's gone. Baby, you're out of time . . . Where are my jewels? The earrings, the bracelets, the necklaces. I need them to give to her. Why have you taken them from me?" He stared angrily at McCann and me. We said nothing. "She can't reach me here. It's too far from the water. You're out of touch, my baby . . .

"Why don't you let her find me? Why'd you put me in a cell with no plaster or wallpaper, so she can't get through? I've nothing to give her now but myself. Why do you always have to break up the family?"

We weren't getting anything useful from him. And he was a liability as a prisoner. He yelled, kicked at the door, wet the bed, needed a suicide watch. We were glad to get rid of him.

The Stoke police thought he was probably unfit to stand trial, but he'd be on a section for quite a while anyway. It was hard to imagine him getting involved in organized crime. He couldn't even feed himself.

While Jason Welles was dreaming in a secure unit somewhere near Stoke, I took my annual leave.

I'd been going out with a girl called Joanna since the previous year, and this was our first holiday together; a self-catering week in Dorset.

The days were close and rainy, so we spent a lot of time in bed. I kept dreaming about Welles reaching up for something he couldn't touch, saying *I opened her and wrapped her around me.* His obsession had convinced me there was something dangerous about love. We split up not long after we came back to Walsall.

Joanna came from Blackheath, and had a rather bleak sense of humour. That was something we shared. She used to repeat bits of Dolly Allen monologues, an elderly comedienne who was well known in the Black Country at that time. Like the story about the vacuum cleaner salesman: *I opened the door, this young fellow in a suit was stood there. He poured a little bag of dirt onto my hall carpet and said "If my vacuum cleaner can't get that dust out of your carpet in one minute, I'll eat the dust." I said, "Here's a spoon, there's no electric in this house."*

One day when the sky was clear, we went for a walk inland. The footpath took us through an abandoned farm. The old farmhouse was in ruins, its roof-beams open to the sky. The sun was burning and we needed shelter, so we slipped into the barn.

Gaps in the roof showed where the rain had got in and rotted the bundles of hay. Something moved at the edge of my vision – a snake or a mouse. Joanna turned to me and we kissed hungrily in the shadows. We made love with some violence, our fingernails and teeth leaving marks in each other. Afterwards, we struggled for breath and held each other more tenderly than we had all week.

At that moment, I recognized the cold fever-smell of stagnant water. Looking over Joanna's shoulder, I saw a barrel standing behind the haystack we'd used as a bed. It was nearly full of water.

In the dim light, I could just see a number of pale tubes hanging down from the water surface. But I couldn't see what they were connected to. I reached over and let my fingertips brush the water. At once, the tubes convulsed. They were connected to long, translucent maggots that jerked in the water. My finger touched one of them. I threw myself backwards and stood there, breathing hard and trying not to vomit.

Joanna started at me as if I'd gone mad. "What's wrong with you?" I gestured at the water-barrel. She turned and stared at the murky surface. "Oh, some rat-tailed maggots. Horsefly larvae. Not very pleasant, are they?" Her biological knowledge was more wide-ranging than mine, as I'd noticed on other occasions. "The long tubes are for breathing. They live in foul water where there's no oxygen. If you see them, you know the water's not fit for anything much."

I'd been back at the Green Lane station for three hours before DI McCann saw fit to tell me the news. "By the way, that nutter of a jewel thief has escaped from the secure unit they were keeping him in. Broke a guard's leg and ran for it. They said he'd been such a good prisoner, they weren't expecting it. You think they'd be used to the insane.

"Anyway, can't imagine he'll come back here. There's nothing for him, now the jewels have been returned to their rightful owners."

I stared at him. "You're joking, aren't you?"

He looked confused.

"Of course he'll come back here. To the house. His woman."

"But that's just madness. There's no woman there."

"To him there is. Look, you interviewed him five or six times. The woman was more real to him than you were."

It took me another ten minutes to persuade McCann to drive out to the railway bridge. Night was falling, and I wished we'd brought more officers along.

This time, we had a key for the back door; but there was no singing inside. The house was empty of life, except for the secondary life of rot and decay.

We used our torches to search the waste ground behind the house. He was where I'd known he would be: in the shallow pond close to the back door. There didn't appear to have been a struggle. He'd used stones to weigh himself down.

When we pulled him out he was curled up, his arms crossed, his knees close to his chest. Like a kid in a school assembly.

Later, we drained the pond and found nothing more, apart from a mass of weeds and insect life. But I wonder about the layers of marsh and silt beneath those houses. How easy it might be to make tunnels, or to close them down.

It's in the nature of life to adapt. If you don't have food, or oxygen, or love, you find a way. It might not be a good way by someone else's standards, but it's a way.

The autopsy confirmed that Jason Welles had died by drowning in shallow, dirty water. The only external damage was some fretting or eroding of the mouth, caused by small fish or water snails.

The only other significant detail had no bearing on the cause of death, and was described by the pathologist as "demonstrating the feverish reproductive activity of aquatic life at certain times of the year".

When they opened up the dead man's body to remove the viscera, they found that the wall of the body cavity was lined with thousands of tiny pearl-white eggs.

JOE HILL

Thumbprint

JOE HILL IS THE AUTHOR of the *New York Times* bestselling novel *Heart-Shaped Box*, the award-winning collection *20th Century Ghosts*, and a comic book, *Locke & Key*. He lives in New England.

"Thousands of American soldiers have served with great honour and decency in Iraq," says the author, "but for whatever reason – some failing in myself, maybe – I don't know how to write about heroes.

"I tend to be drawn to characters who are morally adrift, hurt, troubled people trying to struggle their way back to goodness. People with regrets, people who have made some mistakes that haunt them.

"The crime novelist James Ellroy was once confronted by an angry police officer, who wanted to know why all the cops in his stories were drug-using, bribe-taking, wife-beating bastards. Ellroy stayed cool, and told him, 'Good cops make for bad fiction'. Sounds about right to me."

THE FIRST THUMBPRINT came in the mail.

Mal was eight months back from Abu Ghraib, where she had done things she regretted. She had returned to Hammett, New York, just in time to bury her father. He died ten hours before her plane touched down in the States, which was maybe all for the best. After the things she had done, she was not sure she could've looked him in the eye. Although a part of her had wanted to talk to him about it, and to see in his face how he judged her. Without him, there was no one to hear her story, no one whose judgment mattered.

The old man had served, too, in Vietnam, as a medic. Her father had saved lives, jumped from a helicopter and dragged kids out of the paddy grass, under heavy fire. He called them kids, although he had only been twenty-five himself at the time. He had been awarded a Purple Heart and a Silver Star.

They hadn't been offering Mal any medals when they sent her on her way. At least she had not been identifiable in any of the photographs of Abu Ghraib – just her boots in that one shot Graner took, with the men piled naked on top of each other, a pyramid of stacked ass and hanging sac. If Graner had just tilted the camera up a little, Mal would have been headed home a lot sooner, only it would have been in handcuffs.

She got back her old job at the Milky Way, keeping bar, and moved into her father's house. It was all he had to leave her, that and the car. The old man's ranch was set three hundred yards from Hatchet Hill Road, backed against the town woods. In the fall, Mal ran in the forest, wearing a full ruck, three miles through the evergreens.

She kept the M4A1 in the downstairs bedroom, broke it down and put it together every morning, a job she could complete by the count of twelve. When she was done, she put the components back in their case with the bayonet, cradling them neatly in their foam cut-outs – you didn't attach the bayonet unless you were about to be overrun. Her M4 had come back to the US with a civilian contractor, who brought it with him on his company's private jet. He had been an interrogator for hire – there had been a lot of them at Abu Ghraib in the final months before the arrests – and he said it was the least he could do, that she had earned it for services rendered, a statement which left her cold.

Come one night in November, Mal walked out of the Milky Way with John Petty, the other bartender, and they found Glen Kardon passed out in the front seat of his Saturn. The driver's side door was open and Glen's butt was in the air, his legs hanging out of the car, feet twisted in the gravel, as if he had just been clubbed to death from behind.

Without thinking, she told Petty to keep an eye out, and then Mal straddled Glen's hips and dug out his wallet. She helped herself to a hundred and twenty dollars cash, dropped the wallet back on the passenger side seat. Petty hissed at her to hurry the fuck up, while Mal wiggled the wedding ring off Glen's finger.

"His wedding ring?" Petty asked, when they were in her car together. Mal gave him half the money for being her lookout, but kept the ring for herself. "Jesus, you're a demented bitch."

Petty put his hand between her legs and ground his thumb hard into the crotch of her black jeans while she drove. She let him do that for a while, his other hand groping her breast. Then she elbowed him off her.

"That's enough," she said.

"No it isn't."

She reached into his jeans, ran her hand down his hard-on, then took his balls and began to apply pressure until he let out a little moan, not entirely of pleasure.

"It's plenty," she said. She pulled her hand out of his pants. "You want more than that, you'll have to wake up your wife. Give her a thrill."

Mal let him out of the car in front of his home, and peeled away, tires throwing gravel at him.

Back at her father's house, she sat on the kitchen counter, looking at the wedding ring in the cup of her palm. A simple gold band, scuffed and scratched, all the shine dulled out of it. She wondered why she had taken it.

Mal knew Glen Kardon, Glen and his wife Helen both. The three of them were the same age, had all gone to school together. Glen had a magician at his tenth birthday party, who had escaped from handcuffs and a straightjacket as his final trick. Years later, Mal would become well acquainted with another escape artist who managed to slip out of a pair of handcuffs, a Ba'athist. Both of his thumbs had been broken, making it possible to squeeze out of the cuffs. It was easy to do, if you could bend your thumb in any direction – all you had to do was ignore the pain.

And Helen had been Mal's lab partner in sixth grade biology. Helen took notes in her delicate cursive, using different coloured inks to brighten up their reports, while Mal sliced things open. Mal liked the scalpel, the way the skin popped apart at the slightest touch of the blade to show what was hidden behind it. She had an instinct for it, always somehow knew just where to put the cut.

Mal shook the wedding ring in one hand for a while and finally dropped it down the sink. She didn't know what to do with it, wasn't sure where to fence it. Had no use for it, really.

When she went down to the mailbox the next morning, she found an oil bill, a real estate flyer, and a plain white envelope. Inside the envelope was a crisp sheet of typing paper, neatly folded, blank except for a single thumbprint in black ink. The print was a clean impression, and among the whorls and lines was a scar, like a fishhook. There was nothing on the envelope: no stamp, no addresses, no mark of any kind. The postman had not left it.

In her first glance she knew it was a threat and that whoever had put the envelope in her mailbox might still be watching. Mal felt her vulnerability in the sick clench of her insides, and had to struggle against the conditioned impulse to get low and find cover. She looked to either side but saw only the trees, their branches waving in the cold swirl of a light breeze. There was no traffic along the road and no sign of life anywhere.

For the long walk back to the house, she was aware of a weakness in her legs. She didn't look at the thumbprint again but carried it inside and left it with the other mail on the kitchen counter. She let her shaky legs carry her on into her father's bedroom; her bedroom now. The M4 was in its case in the closet but her father's .45 automatic was even closer – she slept with it under the pillow – and it didn't need to be assembled. Mal slid the action back to pump a bullet in the chamber. She got her field glasses from her ruck.

Mal climbed the carpeted stairs to the second floor, and opened the door into her old bedroom under the eaves. She hadn't been in there since coming home and the air had a musty, stale quality. A tatty poster of Alan Jackson was stuck up on the inverted slant of the roof. Her dolls – the blue corduroy bear, the pig with the queer silver button eyes which gave him a look of blindness – were set neatly in the shelves of a bookcase without books.

Her bed was made, but when she went close, she was surprised to find the shape of a body pressed into it, the pillow dented in the outline of someone's head. The idea occurred that whoever had left the thumbprint had been inside the house while she was out, and took a nap up here. Mal didn't slow down, but stepped straight up onto the mattress, unlocked the window over it, shoved it open, and climbed through.

In another minute she was sitting on the roof, holding the binoculars to her eyes with one hand, the gun in the other. The asbestos shingles had been warming all day in the sun and provided a pleasant ambient heat beneath her. From where she sat on the roof, she could see in every direction.

She remained there for most of an hour, scanning the trees, following the passage of cars along Hatchet Hill Road. Finally she knew she was looking for someone who wasn't there anymore. She hung the binoculars from her neck and leaned back on the hot shingles and closed her eyes. It had been cold down in the driveway, but up on the roof, on the lee side of the house, out of the wind, she was comfortable, a lizard on a rock.

When Mal swung her body back into the bedroom, she sat for a while on the sill, holding the gun in both hands and considering the impression of a human body on her blankets and pillow. She picked up the pillow and pressed her face into it. Very faintly, she could smell a trace of her father, his cheap corner store cigars, the waxy tang of that shit he put in his hair, same stuff Reagan had used. The thought that he had sometimes been up here, dozing in her bed, gave her a little chill. She wished she was still the kind of person who could hug a pillow and weep over what she had lost. But in truth, maybe she had never been that kind of person.

When she was back in the kitchen, Mal looked once more at the thumbprint on the plain white sheet of paper. Against all logic or sense, it seemed somehow familiar to her. She didn't like that.

He had been brought in with a broken tibia, the Iraqi everyone called "The Professor", but a few hours after they put him in a cast, he was judged well enough to sit for an interrogation. In the early morning, before sunrise, Corporal Plough came to get him.

Mal was working in block 1A then and went with Carmody to collect The Professor. He was in a cell with eight other men: sinewy, unshaved Arabs, most of them dressed in fruit-of-the-loom jockey shorts and nothing else. Some others, who had been unco-operative with CI, had been given pink, flowered panties to wear. The panties fit more snugly than the jockies, which were all extra-large and baggy. The prisoners skulked in the gloom of their stone chamber, giving Mal looks so feverish and hollow-eyed, they appeared deranged. Glancing in at them, Mal didn't know whether to laugh or flinch.

"Walk away from the bars, women," she said in her clumsy Arabic. "Walk away." She crooked her finger at The Professor. "You. Come to here."

He hopped forward, one hand on the wall to steady himself. He wore a hospital johnnie, and his left leg was in a cast from ankle to knee. Carmody had brought a pair of aluminium crutches for him. Mal and Carmody were coming to the end of a twelve-hour shift, in a week of twelve-hour shifts. Escorting the prisoner to CI with Corporal Plough would be their last job of the night. Mal was twitchy from all the Vivarin in her system, so much she could hardly stand still. When she looked at lamps, she saw rays of hard-edged, rainbow-shot light emanating from them, as if she were peering through crystal.

The night before, a patrol had surprised some men planting an IED in the red, hollowed-out carcass of a German Shepherd, on the side of the road back to Baghdad. The bombers scattered, yelling, from the spotlights on the Hummers and a contingent of men went after them.

An engineer named Leeds stayed behind to have a look at the bomb inside the dog. He was three steps from the animal when a cell phone went off inside the dog's bowels, three bars of "Oops, I Did It Again." The dog ruptured in a belch of flame, and with a heavy thud that people standing thirty feet away could feel in the marrow of their bones. Leeds dropped to his knees, holding his face, smoke coming out from under his gloves. The first soldier to get to him said his face peeled off like a cheap black rubber mask that had been stuck to the sinew beneath with rubber cement.

Not long after, the patrol grabbed The Professor – so named because of his horn-rimmed glasses and because he insisted he was a teacher – two blocks from the site of the explosion. He broke his leg jumping off a high berm, running away after the soldiers fired over his head and ordered him to halt.

Now The Professor lurched along on the crutches, Mal and Carmody flanking him and Plough walking behind. They made their way out of 1A and into the pre-dawn morning. The Professor paused, beyond the doors, to take a breath. That was when Plough kicked the left crutch out from under his arm.

The Professor went straight down and forward with a cry, his johnnie flapping open to show the soft paleness of his ass. Carmody reached to help him back up. Plough said leave him.

"Sir?" Carmody asked. Carmody was just nineteen. He had been over as long as Mal, but his skin was oily and white, as if he had never been out of his chemical suit.

"Did you see him swing that crutch at me?" Plough asked Mal.

Mal did not reply, but watched to see what would happen next. She had spent the last two hours bouncing on her heels, chewing her fingernails down to the skin, too wired to stop moving. Now, though, she felt stillness spreading through her, like a drop of ink in water, calming her restless hands, her nervous legs.

Plough bent over and pulled the string at the back of the johnnie, unknotting it so it fell off The Professor's shoulders and down to his wrists. His ass was spotted with dark moles and relatively hairless. His sac was drawn tight to his perineum. The Professor glanced up over his shoulder, his eyes too large in his face, and spoke rapidly in Arab.

"What's he saying?" Plough asked. "I don't speak sand nigger."

"He said don't," Mal said, translating automatically. "He says he hasn't done anything. He was picked up by accident."

Plough kicked away the other crutch. "Get those."

Carmody picked up the crutches.

Plough put his boot in The Professor's fleshy ass and shoved.

"Get going. Tell him get going."

A pair of MPs walked past, turned their heads to look at The Professor as they went by. He was trying to cover his crotch with one hand, but Plough kicked him in the ass again and he had to start crawling. His crawl was awkward stuff, what with his left leg sticking out straight in its cast and the bare foot dragging in the dirt. One of the MPs laughed, and then they moved away into the night.

The Professor struggled to pull his johnnie up onto his shoulders as he crawled, but Plough stepped on it and it tore away.

"Leave it. Tell him leave it and hurry up."

Mal told him. The prisoner couldn't look at her. He looked at Carmody instead, and began pleading with him, asking for something to wear and saying his leg hurt while Carmody stared down at him, eyes bulging, as if he were choking on something.

Mal wasn't surprised The Professor was addressing Carmody instead of her. Part of it was a cultural thing. The Arabs couldn't cope with being humiliated in front of a woman. But also, Carmody had something about him that signified to others, even the enemy, that he was approachable. In spite of the 9mm strapped to his outer thigh, he gave an impression of stumbling, unthreatening cluelessness. In the barracks, he blushed when other guys were ogling centrefolds; he often could be seen praying during heavy mortar attacks.

The prisoner had stopped crawling once more. Mal poked the barrel of her M4 in The Professor's ass to get him going again and the Iraqi jerked, gave a shrill sort of sob. Mal didn't mean to laugh, but there was something funny about the convulsive clench of his butt-cheeks, something that sent a rush of blood to her head. Her blood was racy and strange with Vivarin, and watching the prisoner's ass bunch up like that was the most hilarious thing she had seen in weeks.

The Professor crawled past wire fence, along the edge of the road. Plough told Mal to ask him where his friends were now, his friends who blew up the American GI. He said if The Professor would tell about his friends, he could have his crutches and his johnnie back.

The prisoner said he didn't know anything about the IED. He said he ran because other men were running and soldiers were shooting. He said he was a teacher of literature, that he had a little girl. He said he had taken his twelve-year-old to Disneyland Paris once.

"He's fucking with us," Plough said. "What's a professor of literature doing out at 2:00 a.m. in the worst part of town? Your queer fuck Bin-Laden friends blew the face right off an American GI, a good man, a man with a pregnant wife back home. Where do your friends – Mal, make him understand he's going to tell us where his friends are hiding. Let him know it would be better to tell us now, before we get where we're going. Let him know this is the easy part of his day. CI wants this motherfucker good and soft before we get him there."

Mal nodded, her ears buzzing. She told The Professor he didn't have a daughter, because he was a known homosexual. She asked him if he liked the barrel of her gun in his ass, if it excited him. She said, "Where is the house of your partners who make the dogs into bombs? Where is your homosexual friends go after murdering Americans with their trick dogs? Tell me if you don't want the gun in the hole of your ass."

"I swear by the life of my little girl I don't know who those other men were. Please. My child is named Alaya. She is ten years old. There was a picture of her in my pants. Where are my pants? I will show you."

She stepped on his hand, and felt the bones compress unnaturally under her heel. He shrieked.

"Tell," she said. "Tell."

"I can't."

A steely clashing sound caught Mal's attention. Carmody had dropped the crutches. He looked green, and his hands were hooked into claws, raised almost-but-not-quite to cover his ears.

"You okay?" she asked.

"He's lying," Carmody said. Carmody's Arab was not as good as hers, but not bad. "He said his daughter was twelve the first time."

She stared at Carmody and he stared back, and while they were looking at each other, there came a high, keening whistle, like air being let out of some giant balloon . . . a sound that made Mal's racy blood feel as if it were fizzing with oxygen, made her feel carbonated inside.

She flipped her M4 around to hold it by the barrel in both hands, and when the mortar struck – out beyond the perimeter, but still hitting hard enough to cause the earth to shake underfoot – she drove the butt of the gun straight down into The Professor's broken leg, clubbing at it as if she were trying to drive a stake into the ground.

Over the shattering thunder of the exploding mortar, not even Mal could hear him screaming.

*   *   *

Mal pushed herself hard on her Friday morning run, out in the woods, driving herself up Hatchet Hill, reaching ground so steep she was really climbing, not running. She kept going, until she was short of breath and the sky seemed to spin, as if it were the roof of a carousel.

When she finally paused, she felt faint. The wind breathed in her face, chilling her sweat, a curiously pleasant sensation. Even the feeling of light-headedness, of being close to exhaustion and collapse, was somehow satisfying to her.

The army had her for four years before Mal left to become a part of the reserves. On her second day of basic training, she had done push-ups until she was sick, then was so weak she collapsed in it. She wept in front of others, something she could now hardly bear to remember.

Eventually, she learned to like the feeling that came right before collapse: the way the sky got big, and sounds grew far away and tinny, and all the colours seemed to sharpen to an hallucinatory brightness. There was an intensity of sensation, when you were on the edge of what you could handle, when you were physically tested and made to fight for each breath, that was somehow exhilarating.

At the top of the hill, Mal slipped the stainless steel canteen out of her ruck, her father's old camping canteen, and filled her mouth with ice water. The canteen flashed, a silver mirror in the late morning sun. She poured water into her face, wiped her eyes with the hem of her T-Shirt, put the canteen away, and ran on, ran for home.

She let herself in through the front door, didn't notice the envelope until she stepped on it and heard the crunch of paper underfoot. She stared down at it, her mind blank for one dangerous moment, trying to think who would've come up to the house to slide a bill under the door when they could just leave it in the mailbox. But it wasn't a bill and she knew it.

Mal was framed in the door, the outline of a soldier painted into a neat rectangle, like the human silhouette targets they shot at on the range. She made no sudden moves, however. If someone meant to shoot her, they would have done it – there had been plenty of time – and if she was being watched, Mal wanted to show she wasn't afraid.

She crouched, picked up the envelope. The flap was not sealed. She tapped out the sheet of paper inside and unfolded it. Another thumbprint, this one a fat black oval, like a flattened spoon. There was no fishhook shaped scar on this thumb. This was a different thumb entirely. In some ways, that was more unsettling to her than anything.

No – the most unsettling thing was that this time he had slipped his message under her door, while last time he had left it a hundred yards down the road, in the mailbox. It was maybe his way of saying he could get as close to her as he wanted.

Mal thought police, but discarded the idea. She had been a cop herself, in the army, knew how cops thought. Leaving a couple thumbprints on unsigned sheets of paper wasn't a crime. It was maybe a prank, and you couldn't waste manpower investigating a prank. She felt now, as she had when she saw the first thumbprint, that these messages were not the perverse joke of some local snotnose, but a malicious promise, a warning to be on guard. But it was an irrational feeling, unsupported by any evidence. It was soldier knowledge, not cop knowledge.

Besides, when you called the cops, you never knew what you were going to get. There were cops like her out there. People like that you didn't want getting too interested in you.

She balled up the thumbprint, took it onto the porch. Mal cast her gaze around, scanning the bare trees, the straw-coloured weeds at the edge of the woods. She stood there for close to a minute. Even the trees were perfectly still, no wind to tease their branches into motion, as if the whole world were in a state of suspension, waiting to see what would happen next, only nothing happened next.

She left the balled up paper on the porch railing, went back inside, and got the M4 from the closet. Mal sat on the bedroom floor, assembling and disassembling it, three times, twelve seconds each time. Then she set the parts back in the case with the bayonet and slid it under her father's bed.

Two hours later, Mal ducked down behind the bar at the Milky Way to rack clean glasses. They were fresh from the dishwasher and so hot they burned her fingertips. When she stood up with the empty tray, Glen Kardon was on the other side of the counter, staring at her with red-rimmed, watering eyes. He looked in a kind of stupor, his face puffy, his comb-over dishevelled, as if he had just stumbled out of bed.

"I need to talk to you about something," he said. "I was trying to think if there was some way I could get my wedding ring back. Any way at all."

All the blood seemed to rush from Mal's brain, as if she had stood up too quickly. She lost some of the feeling in her hands, too, and for a moment her palms were overcome with a cool, almost painful tingling.

She wondered why he hadn't arrived with cops, if he meant to give her some kind of chance to settle the matter without the involvement of the police. She wanted to say something to him, but there were no words for this. She could not remember the last time she had felt so helpless, had been caught so exposed, in such indefensible terrain.

Glen went on: "My wife spent the morning crying about it. I heard her in the bedroom, but when I tried to go in and talk to her, the door was locked. She wouldn't let me in. She tried to play it off like she was all right, talking to me through the door. She told me to go to work, don't worry. It was her father's wedding ring, you know. He died three months before we got married. I guess that sounds a little, what do you call it, Oedipal. Like in marrying me she was marrying daddy. Oedipal isn't right, but you know what I'm saying. She loved that old man."

Mal nodded.

"If they only took the money, I'm not sure I even would've told Helen. Not after I got so drunk. I drink too much. Helen wrote me a note, a few months ago, about how much I've been drinking. She wanted to know if it was because I was unhappy with her. It would be easier if she was the kind of woman who'd just scream at me. But I got drunk like that, and the wedding ring she gave me that used to belong to her daddy is gone, and all she did was hug me and say thank God they didn't hurt me."

Mal said, "I'm sorry." She was about to say she would give it all back, ring and money both, and go with him to the police if he wanted – then caught herself. He had said "they": "if they only took the money" and "they didn't hurt me." Not "you."

Glen reached inside his coat and took out a white business envelope, stuffed fat. "I been sick to my stomach all day at work, thinking about it. Then I thought I could put up a note here in the bar. You know, like one of these fliers you see for a lost dog. Only for my lost ring. The guys who robbed me must be customers here. What else would they have been doing down in that lot, that hour of the night? So next time they're in, they'll see my note."

She stared. It took a few moments for what he had said to register. When it did – when she understood he had no idea she was guilty of anything – she was surprised to feel an odd twinge of something like disappointment.

"Electra," she said.

"Huh?"

"A love thing between father and daughter," Mal said. "Is an Electra complex. What's in the envelope?"

He blinked. Now he was the one who needed some processing time. Hardly anyone knew or remembered that Mal had been to college, on Uncle Sam's dime. She had learned Arabic there, and psychology too, although in the end she had wound up back here behind the bar of the Milky Way without a degree. The plan had been to collect her last few credits after she got back from Iraq, but sometime during her tour she had ceased to give a fuck about the plan.

At last Glen came mentally unstuck and replied: "Money. Five hundred dollars. I want you to hold onto it for me."

"Explain."

"I was thinking what to say in my note. I figure I should offer a cash reward for the ring. But whoever stole the ring isn't ever going to come up to me and admit it. Even if I promise not to prosecute, they wouldn't believe me. So I figured out what I need is a middle-man. This is where you come in. So the note would say, bring Mallory Grennan the ring, and she'll give you the reward money, no questions asked. It'll say they can trust you not to tell me or the police who they are. People know you, I think most folks around here will believe that." He pushed the envelope at her.

"Forget it, Glen. No one is bringing that ring back."

"Let's see. Maybe they were drunk, too, when they took it. Maybe they feel remorse."

She laughed.

He grinned, awkwardly. His ears were pink. "It's possible."

She looked at him a moment longer, then put the envelope under the counter. "Okay. Let's write your note. I can copy it on the fax machine. We'll stick it up around the bar, and after a week, when no one brings you your ring, I'll give you your money back and a beer on the house."

"Maybe just a ginger ale," Glen said.

Glen had to go, but Mal promised she'd hang a few flyers in the parking lot. She had just finished taping them up to the street lamps when she spotted a sheet of paper, folded into thirds and stuck under the windshield wiper of her father's car.

The thumbprint on this one was delicate and slender, an almost perfect oval, feminine in some way, while the first two had been squarish and blunt. Three thumbs, each of them different from the others.

She pitched it at a wire garbage can attached to a telephone pole, hit the three-pointer, got out of there.

                    *   *   *

The 82nd had finally arrived at Abu Ghraib, to provide force protection, and to try and nail the fuckers who were mortaring the prison every night. Early in the fall, they began conducting raids in the town around the prison. The first week of operations, they had so many patrols out, and so many raids going, they needed back-up, so General Karpinski assigned squads of MPs to accompany them. Corporal Plough put in for the job, and when he was accepted, told Mal and Carmody they were coming with him.

Mal was glad. She wanted away from the prison, the dark corridors of 1A and 1B, with their smell of old wet rock, urine, flopsweat. She wanted away from the tent cities that held the general prison population, the crowds pressed against the chain-links, who pleaded with her as she walked along the perimeter, black flies crawling on their faces. She wanted to be in a Hummer with open sides, night air rushing in over her. Destination: any-fucking-where else on the planet.

In the hour before dawn, the platoon they had been tacked onto hit a private home, set back in a grove of palms, with a white stucco wall around the yard, and a wrought-iron gate across the drive. The house was stucco too, and had a swimming pool out back, a patio and grill, wouldn't have looked out of place in southern California. Delta Team drove their Hummer right through the gate, which went down with a hard iron bang, hinges shearing out of the wall with a spray of plaster.

That was all Mal saw of the raid. She was behind the wheel of a two-and-a-half ton troop transport for carrying prisoners. No Hummer for her, and no action either. Carmody had another truck. She listened for gunfire, but there was none, the residents giving up without a struggle.

When the house was secure, Corporal Plough left them, said he wanted to size up the situation. What he wanted to do was get his picture taken, chewing on a stogie and holding his gun, with his boot on the neck of a hog-tied insurgent. She heard over the walkie-talkie that they had grabbed one of the Fedayeen Saddam, a Ba'athist lieutenant, and had found weapons, files, personnel information. There was a lot of cornpone whoop-ass on the radio. Everyone in the 82nd looked like Eminem – blue eyes, pale blonde hair in a crew cut – and talked like one of the Duke boys.

Just after sunup, when the shadows were leaning long away from the buildings on the east side of the street, they brought the Fedayeen out and left him on the narrow sidewalk with Plough. The insurgent's wife was still inside the building, soldiers watching her while she packed a bag.

The Fedayeen was a big Arab with hooded eyes and a three-day shadow on his chin, and he wasn't saying anything except, "Fuck you" in American. In the basement, Delta Team had found racked AK-47s, and a table covered in maps, marked all over with symbols, numbers, Arabic letters. They discovered a folder of photographs, featuring US soldiers in the act of establishing checkpoints, rolling barbed wire across different roads. There was also a picture in the folder of George Bush, Sr, smiling a little foggily, posing with Steven Seagal.

Plough was worried the pictures showed places and people the insurgents planned to strike. He had already been on the radio a couple times, back to base, talking with CI about it in a strained, excited voice. He was especially upset about Steven Seagal. Everyone in Plough's unit had been made to watch *Above the Law* at least once, and Plough claimed to have seen it more than a hundred times. After they brought the prisoner out, he stood over the Fedayeen, yelling at him, and sometimes swatting him upside the head with Seagal's rolled-up picture. The Fedayeen said, "More fuck you."

Mal leaned against the driver's side door of her truck for a while, wondering when Plough would quit hollering and swatting the prisoner. She had a Vivarin hangover and her head hurt. Eventually she decided he wouldn't be done yelling until it was time to load up and go, and that might not be for another hour.

She left Plough yelling, walked over the flattened gate and up to the house. She let herself into the cool of the kitchen. Red tile floor, high ceilings, lots of windows so the place was filled with sunlight. Fresh bananas in a glass bowl. Where did they get fresh bananas? She helped herself to one, and ate it on the toilet, the cleanest toilet she had sat on in a year.

She came back out of the house and started down to the road again. On the way there, she put her fingers in her mouth, and sucked on them. She hadn't brushed her teeth in a week, and her breath had a human stink on it.

When she returned to the street, Plough had stopped sweating the prisoner long enough to catch his breath. The Ba'athist looked up at him from under his heavy-lidded eyes. He snorted and said, "Is talk. Is boring. You are no one. I say fuck you still no one."

Mal sank to one knee in front of him, put her fingers under his nose and said in Arab, "Smell that? That is the cunt of your wife. I fuck her myself like a lesbian and she said it was better than your cock."

The Ba'athist tried to lunge at her from his knees, making a sound down in his chest, a strangled growl of rage, but Plough caught him across the chin with the stock of his M4. The sound of the Ba'athist's jaw snapping was as loud as a gunshot.

He lay on his side, twisted into a foetal ball. Mal remained crouched beside him.

"Your jaw is broken," Mal said. "Tell me about the photographs of the US soldiers, and I will bring a no-more-hurt pill."

It was half an hour before she went to get him the painkillers, and by then he had told her when the pictures had been taken, coughed up the name of the photographer.

Mal was leaning into the back of her truck, digging in the first aid kit, when Carmody's shadow joined hers at the rear bumper.

"Did you really do it?" Carmody asked her. The sweat on him glowed with an ill sheen in the noonday light. "The wife?"

"What? Fuck no. Obviously."

"Oh," Carmody said, and swallowed convulsively. "Someone said—" he began, then his voice trailed off.

"What did someone say?"

He glanced across the road, at two soldiers from the 82nd, standing by their Hummer. "One of the guys who was in the building said you marched right in and bent her over. Face-down on the bed."

She looked over at Vaughan and Henrichon, holding their M-16s and struggling to contain their laughter. She flipped them the bird.

"Jesus, Carmody. Don't you know when you're being fucked with?"

His head was down. He stared at his own scarecrow shadow, tilting into the back of the truck.

"No," he said.

Two weeks later, Carmody and Mal were in the back of a different truck, with that same Arab, the Ba'athist, who was being transferred from Abu Ghraib to a smaller prison facility in Baghdad. The prisoner had his head in a steel contraption, to clamp his jaw in place, but he was still able to open his mouth wide enough to hawk a mouthful of spit into Mal's face.

Mal was wiping it away when Carmody got up and grabbed the Fedayeen by the front of his shirt and heaved him out of the back of the truck, into the dirt road. The truck was doing thirty miles an hour at the time, and was part of a convoy that included two reporters from MSNBC.

The prisoner survived, although most of his face was flayed off on the gravel, his jaw rebroken, his hands smashed. Carmody said he leaped out on his own, trying to escape, but no one believed him, and three weeks later Carmody was sent home.

The funny thing was that the insurgent really did escape, a week after that, during another transfer. He was in handcuffs, but with his thumbs broken he was able to slip his hands right out of them. When the MPs stepped out of their Hummer at a checkpoint, to talk porno with some friends, the prisoner dropped out of the back of the transport. It was night. He simply walked into the desert, and, as the stories go, was never seen again.

The band took the stage Friday evening, and didn't come offstage until Saturday morning. Twenty minutes after one, Mal bolted the door behind the last customer. She started helping Candice wipe down tables, but she had been on since before lunch, and Bill Rodier said go home already.

Mal had her jacket on and was headed out when John Petty poked her in the shoulder with something.

"Mal," he said. "This is yours, right? Your name on it."

She turned. Petty was at the cash register, holding a fat envelope toward her. She took.

"That the money Glen gave you, to swap for his wedding ring?" Petty turned his shoulder to her, shifting his attention back to the register. He pulled out stacks of bills, rubber-banded them, and lined them up on the bar. "That's something. Taking his money and fucking him all over again. You think I plop down five hundred bucks, you'd fuck me just as nice?"

As he spoke he put his hand back in the register. Mal reached under his elbow and slammed the drawer on his fingers. He squealed. The drawer began to slide open again on its own, but before he could get his mashed fingers out, Mal slammed it once more. He lifted one foot off the floor and did a comic little jig.

"Ohfuckgoddamyouuglydyke," he said.

"Hey," said Bill Rodier, coming toward the bar. He carried a trash barrel in one hand. "Hey."

She let Petty get his hand out of the drawer. He stumbled clumsily away from her, struck the bar with his hip, and wheeled to face her, clutching the mauled hand to his chest.

"You crazy bitch. I think you broke my fingers."

"Jesus, Mal," Bill said, looking over the bar at Petty's hand. His fat fingers had a purple line of bruise across them. Bill turned his questioning gaze back her way. "I don't know what the hell John said, but you can't do that to people."

"You'd be surprised what you can do to people," she told him.

Outside it was drizzling and cold. She was all the way to her car before she felt a weight in one hand, and realized she was still clutching the envelope full of cash.

Mal held it in her hand, against the inside of her thigh, the whole drive back. She didn't put on the radio, just drove, and listened to the rain tapping on the glass. She had been in the desert for two years and she had seen it rain just twice, although there was often a moist fog in the morning, a mist that smelled of eggs, of brimstone.

When she enlisted, she had hoped for war. She did not see the point of joining if you were not going to get to fight. The risk to her life did not trouble her. It was an incentive. You received a two-hundred-dollar-a-month bonus for every month you spent in the combat zone, and a part of her had relished that her own life was valued so cheap. Mal would not have expected more.

But it did not occur to her, when she first learned she was going to Iraq, that they paid you that money for more than just the risk to your own life. It wasn't just a question of what could happen to you, but also a matter of what you might be asked to do to others. For her two hundred dollar bonus, she had left naked and bound men in stress positions for hours, and told a nineteen-year-old girl that she would be gang-raped if she did not supply information about her boyfriend. Two hundred dollars a month was what it cost to make a torturer out of her. She felt now that she had been crazy there, that the Vivarin, the ephedra, the lack of sleep, the constant scream-and-thump of the mortars, had made her into someone who was mentally ill, a bad dream version of herself. Then Mal felt the weight of the envelope against her thigh, Glen Kardon's payoff, and remembered taking his ring, and it came to her that she was having herself on, pretending she had been someone different in Iraq. Who she had been then and who she was now were the same person. She had taken the prison home with her. She lived in it still.

Mal let herself in the house, soaked and cold, holding the envelope. She found herself standing in front of the kitchen counter with Glen's money. She could sell him back his own ring for five hundred dollars, if she wanted, and it was more than she would get from any pawnshop. She had done worse, for less cash. She stuck her hand down the drain, felt along the wet smoothness of the trap, until her fingertips found the ring.

Mal hooked her ring finger through it, pulled her hand back out. She turned her wrist this way and that, considering how the ring looked on her crooked, blunt finger. *With this I do thee wed.* She didn't know what she'd do with Glen Kardon's five hundred dollars if she swapped it for his ring. It wasn't money she needed. She didn't need his ring either. She couldn't say what it was she needed, but the idea of it was close, a word on the tip of her tongue, maddeningly out of reach.

She made her way to the bathroom, turned on the shower, and let the steam gather while she undressed. Slipping off her black blouse, she noticed she still had the envelope in one hand, Glen's ring on the finger of the other. She tossed the money next to the bathroom sink, left the ring on.

She glanced at the ring sometimes while she was in the shower. She tried to imagine being married to Glen Kardon, pictured him stretched out on her father's bed in boxers and a T-shirt, waiting for her to come out of the bathroom, his stomach aflutter with the anticipation of some late night, connubial action. She snorted at the thought. It was as absurd as trying to imagine what her life would've been like if she had become an astronaut.

The washer and dryer were in the bathroom with her. She dug through the Maytag until she found her Curt Schilling T-Shirt and a fresh pair of Hanes. She slipped back into the darkened bedroom, towelling her hair, and glanced at herself in the dresser mirror, only she couldn't see her face, because a white sheet of paper had been stuck into the top of the frame, and it covered the place where her face belonged. A black thumbprint had been inked in the centre. Around the edges of the sheet of paper, she could see reflected in the mirror a man stretched out on the bed, just as she had pictured Glen Kardon stretched out and waiting for her, only in her head Glen hadn't been wearing grey-and-black fatigues.

She lunged to her side, going for the kitchen door. But Carmody was already moving, launching himself at her, driving his boot into her right knee. The leg twisted in a way it wasn't meant to go, and she felt her ACL pop behind her knee. Carmody was right behind her by then and he got a handful of her hair. As she went down, he drove her forward and smashed her head into the side of the dresser.

A black spoke of pain lanced down into her skull, a nail-gun fired straight into the brain. She was down and flailing and he kicked her in the head. That lick didn't hurt so much, but took the life out of her, as if she were no more than an appliance, and he had jerked the power cord out of the wall.

When he rolled her onto her stomach and twisted her arms behind her back, she had no strength in her to resist. He had the heavy-duty plastic ties, the flexicuffs they used on the prisoners in Iraq sometimes. He sat on her ass and squeezed her ankles together and put the flexicuffs on them too, tightening until it hurt, and then some. Black flashes were still firing behind her eyes, but the fireworks were smaller, and exploding less frequently now. She was coming back to herself, slowly. Breathe. Wait.

When her vision cleared she found Carmody sitting above her, on the edge of her father's bed. He had lost weight and he hadn't any to lose. His eyes peeked out, too bright at the bottom of deep hollows, moonlight reflected in the water at the bottom of a long well. In his lap was a bag, like an old-fashioned doctor's case, the leather pebbled and handsome.

"I observed you while you were running this morning," he began, without preamble. Using the word *observed*, like he would in a report on enemy troop movements. "Who were you signalling when you were up on the hill?"

"Carmody," Mal said. "What are you talking about, Carmody? What is this?"

"You're staying in shape. You're still a soldier. I tried to follow you, but you outran me on the hill this morning. When you were on the crest, I saw you flashing a light. Two long flashes, one short, two long. You signalled someone. Tell me who."

At first she didn't know what he was talking about; then she did. Her canteen. Her canteen had flashed in the sunlight when she tipped it up to drink. She opened her mouth to reply, but before she could, he lowered himself to one knee beside her. Carmody unbuckled his bag and dumped the contents onto the floor. He had a collection of tools: a pair of heavy-duty shears, a taser, a hammer, a hacksaw, a portable vice. Mixed in with the tools were five or six human thumbs.

Some of the thumbs were thick and blunt and male, and some were white and slender and female, and some were too shrivelled and darkened with rot to provide much of any clues about the person they had belonged to. Each thumb ended in a lump of bone and sinew. The inside of the bag had a smell, a sickly-sweet, almost floral stink of corruption.

Carmody selected the heavy-duty shears.

"You went up the hill and signalled someone this morning. And tonight you came back with a lot of money. I looked in the envelope while you were in the shower. So you signalled for a meeting and at the meeting you were paid for intel. Who did you meet? CIA?"

"I went to work. At the bar. You know where I work. You followed me there."

"Five hundred dollars. Is that supposed to be tips?"

She didn't have a reply. She couldn't think. She was looking at the thumbs mixed in with his mess of tools.

He followed her gaze, prodded a blackened and shrivelled thumb with the blade of the shears. The only identifiable feature remaining on the thumb was a twisted, silvery, fishhook scar.

"Plough," Carmody said. "He had helicopters doing flyovers of my house. They'd fly over once or twice a day. They used different kinds of helicopters on different days to try and keep me from putting two and two together. But I knew what they were up to. I started watching them from the kitchen with my field glasses, and one day I saw Plough at the controls of a radio station traffic 'copter. I didn't even know he knew how to pilot a bird until then. He was wearing a black helmet and sunglasses, but I still recognized him."

As Carmody spoke, Mal remembered Corporal Plough trying to open a bottle of Red Stripe with the blade of his bayonet, and the knife slipping, catching him across the thumb, Plough sucking on it and saying around his thumb, *motherfuck, someone open this for me.*

"No, Carmody. It wasn't him. It was just someone who looked like him. If he could fly a helicopter, they would've had him piloting Apaches over there."

"Plough admitted it. Not at first. At first he lied. But eventually he told me everything, that he was in the helicopter, that they had been keeping me under surveillance ever since I came home." Carmody moved the tip of the shears to point at another thumb, shrivelled and brown, with the texture and appearance of a dried mushroom. "This was his wife. She admitted it too. They were putting dope in my water to make me sluggish and stupid. Sometimes I'd be driving home, and I'd forget what my own house looked like. I'd spend twenty minutes cruising around my development, before I realized I had gone by my place twice."

He paused, moved the tip of the shears to a fresher thumb, a woman's, the nail painted red. "She followed me into a supermarket in Poughkeepsie. This was while I was on my way north, to see you. To see if you had been compromised. This woman in the supermarket, she followed me aisle to aisle, always whispering on her cell phone. Pretending not to look at me. Then, later, I went into a

Chinese place, and noticed her parked across the street, still on the phone. She was the toughest to get solid information out of. I almost thought I was wrong about her.

"She told me she was a first-grade teacher. She told me she didn't even know my name and that she wasn't following me. I almost believed her. She had a photo in her purse, of her sitting on the grass with a bunch of little kids. But it was tricked up. They used Photoshop to stick her in that picture. I even got her to admit it in the end."

"Plough told you he could fly helicopters so you wouldn't hurt him anymore. The first-grade teacher told you the photo was faked to make you stop. People will tell you anything if you hurt them badly enough. You're having some kind of break with reality, Carmody. You don't know what's true anymore."

"You would say that. You're part of it. Part of the plan to make me crazy, make me kill myself. I thought the thumbprints would startle you into making contact with your handler and they did. You went straight to the hills, to send him a signal. To let him know I was close. But where's your back-up now?"

"I don't have back-up. I don't have a handler."

"We were friends, Mal. You got me through the worst parts of being over there, when I thought I was going crazy. I hate that I have to do this to you. But I need to know who you were signalling. And you're going to tell. Who did you signal, Mal?"

"No one," she said, trying to squirm away from him on her belly.

He grabbed her hair, and wrapped it around his fist, to keep her from going anywhere. She felt a tearing along her scalp. He pinned her with a knee in her back. She went still, head turned, right cheek mashed against the knubbly rug on the floor.

"I didn't know you were married. I didn't notice the ring until just tonight. Is he coming home? Is he part of it? Tell me." Tapping the ring on her finger with the blade of the shears.

Mal's face was turned so she was staring under the bed at the case with her M4 and bayonet in it. She had left the clasps undone.

Carmody clubbed her in the back of the head, at the base of the skull, with the handles of the shears. The world snapped out of focus, went to a soft blur, and then slowly her vision cleared and details regained their sharpness, until at last she was seeing the case under the bed again, not a foot away from her, the silver clasps hanging loose.

"Tell me, Mal. Tell me the truth now."

In Iraq, the Fedayeen had escaped the handcuffs after his thumbs were broken. Cuffs wouldn't hold a person whose thumb could move in any direction . . . or someone who didn't have a thumb at all.

Mal felt herself growing calm. Her panic was like static on a radio, and she had just found the volume, was slowly dialling it down. He would not begin with the shears, of course, but would work his way up to them. He meant to beat her first. At least. She drew a long, surprisingly steady breath. Mal felt almost as if she were back on Hatchet Hill, climbing with all the will and strength she had in her, for the cold, open blue of the sky.

"I'm not married," she said. "I stole this wedding ring off a drunk. I was just wearing it because I like it."

He laughed: a bitter, ugly sound. "That isn't even a good lie."

And another breath, filling her chest with air, expanding her lungs to their limit. He was about to start hurting her. He would force her to talk, to give him information, to tell him what he wanted to hear. She was ready. She was not afraid of being pushed to the edge of what could be endured. She had a high tolerance for pain, and her bayonet was in arm's reach, if only she had an arm to reach.

"It's the truth," she said, and with that, PFC Mallory Grennan began her confession.

NICHOLAS ROYLE

Lancashire

NICHOLAS ROYLE IS THE AUTHOR of five novels (*Counterparts*, *Saxophone Dreams*, *The Matter of the Heart*, *The Director's Cut* and *Antwerp*) and two novellas (*The Appetite* and *The Enigma of Departure*).

He has published around 120 short stories, and to date has one collection to his name, *Mortality*. Widely published as a journalist, with regular appearances in *Time Out* and the *Independent*, he has also edited thirteen original anthologies, including two volumes of *Darklands*, *The Tiger Garden: A Book of Writers' Dreams* and *'68: New Stories From Children of the Revolution*.

Since 2006, Royle has been teaching creative writing at Manchester Metropolitan University. He has won three British Fantasy Awards and the Bad Sex Prize once.

"This was one of those stories that came to me in the space of less than a minute," he recalls, "pretty much in its entirety. It deviated a little from the plan that I started with, but much less so than usual.

"I wrote it for *Phobic*, an anthology published by Comma Press, an independent publisher based in the north-west of England that deserve special credit for their commitment to the short story. They also have a film production arm, via which a young short film-maker is hoping to shoot an adaptation of the story. The setting is based on the house of my very good friends Christine and Paul and their son Jack."

"NELSON, COLNE, DARWEN," said Cassie, reading the names off the road signs. "I remember all these Lancashire towns from Bournemouth," she said.

"Your mam's talking nonsense again," said her husband Paul into the rear-view mirror.

"What are you talking about, Mummy?" asked James, who at ten was the elder of the two. His two front teeth still hadn't closed the gap, freckles scattered across his nose.

"From when I worked in the sorting office in Bournemouth one Christmas," Cassie explained.

"For Christmas . . . yeah . . ." began Ellie, James's younger sister, "I want an iPod Nano. A black one."

Ellie, her naturally streaked hair looking like it needed a good brush, enunciated slowly, as if she still couldn't quite believe she could speak. Or was Paul projecting his own wonder at his daughter's power of speech? She had been able to speak for years, of course, but had indeed been a slow starter.

"You can't have one," said her brother.

"Why not?"

"Because I haven't got one."

"You've got one on your Christmas list. I saw it."

"But I haven't got one yet and you can't get one at the same time as I get one. You have to wait till I've had one for six weeks. Or a year."

"No, I don't. Mummy, do I?"

"That's enough, children," said Cassie, smiling at Paul. "Look at the wonderful scenery. Isn't this lovely? Just imagine. If we'd been driving for half an hour from our old house, we wouldn't even have got beyond the North Circular."

James and Ellie ignored this, bent over PSP and Game Boy respectively, articulating their thumbs in ways their parents had never learned to do. Paul wondered how long it would be before Ellie decided she also had to graduate from a Game Boy to a PSP.

Sunlight flashed across the windscreen, sparkling in a scattering of raindrops and temporarily blinding him.

"Are you keeping your eye on the map?" he asked Cassie.

"Just keep going on the A666," said Cassie. "All the way."

"Right through Blackburn?" he asked, blinking.

"Right on past these dark Satanic mills," she said as they passed another refurbished chimney.

"Mummy?"

"Do you know what I read the other day?" said Paul. "I read that 'dark Satanic mills' was never meant to imply this sort of thing—" he waved his hand at yet another converted mill, "—the industrial revolution and all that. What Blake was really talking about, apparently, were Oxford and Cambridge universities."

"Mummy?"

"What, darling?"

"What does Satanic mean?"

"Oh, really, Paul?" said Paul, pretending to mimic Cassie. "That's fascinating, Paul. Thank you for sharing that, Paul."

"Ask your dad, Ellie. He seems to know all about it." Cassie placed her hand on Paul's leg and smiled at him. "It was fascinating, darling. I didn't know that, actually."

"It's only conjecture. Academic gossip, you know."

"Are we nearly there?" asked James.

"That's a good question," said Cassie, looking at Paul. "*Are* we nearly there?"

"You tell me. You've got the map." Paul's lips straightened into a suppressed smile.

Conversation was soon restricted to the essentials of navigation while they negotiated Blackburn.

"Who are we going to see again?" James asked as they found their way back on to the A666.

"Penny and Howard. Friends of your mam's."

"Howard and Penny, friends of your dad's more like," said Cassie.

"I thought we were going to see Connor," said James.

"We are," said Paul. "Connor is Penny and Howard's son."

"Are those the people we met in the park?" James asked.

"You know they are. Now, shush, matey. I've got to read the signs."

"Your dad needs all his concentration to read the signs. A lot of men find it very, very hard reading signs."

Paul smiled, then frowned at a hidden sign.

"What did that say? Did that say Wilpshire?"

They turned off the A666 and within a couple of minutes pulled up outside a well-kept Victorian semi. Pampas grasses grew in the lawned garden, steps led up to the front door. Paul pulled on the handbrake.

"Paul, I hope this is going to be all right," Cassie said quietly. "I mean, we barely know these people."

"It's a little late for that," Paul answered.

"We've been out with them, what, twice for drinks?"

"You know what they say about pampas grasses, don't you?" Paul muttered.

"What?" came James's voice from the back.

"Never you mind," said Paul. "It'll be fine. Penny's into stained glass, remember. If you run out of things to talk about, just talk about stained glass. Did you know, children, that your mam's in the *Guinness Book of Records* for length of time talking about stained glass."

"What about you and Howard?" asked Cassie with an indulgent smile.

"We'll have something in common. Didn't he say he liked punk and new wave? Late 1970s, 1980s music? In any case, no one expects blokes to talk. We just have to sit there looking like we're not having a shit time. Anyway," he added, "this is for the children, isn't it? They liked Connor when they met him in the park. And it's kind of them to invite us. Perhaps they know what it's like to be new to an area."

At that point, Cassie became aware of the front door opening and Penny and Howard appeared, all smiles. The child, Connor, squeezed between their legs and ran down the path towards them.

"Here goes," she said as she opened the car door.

They got the standard tour.

Downstairs rooms tastefully restored, with an attractive archway ("Looks original. I don't know, maybe 1920s") connecting them. Kitchen long and narrow – "We're going to open it up at the back – here and here – and have lovely big French windows where that corner is," said Penny. "It's lovely how it is," flattered Cassie. "What, all this clinker? Tongue and groove? Ugh." And so it went on. Upstairs, Connor's bedroom ("Is this really my room?" Strange child. Though weren't all children strange, apart from your own, Cassie thought), amazingly tidy for a ten-year-old's; Penny and Howard's room, drawers and wardrobes neatly closed; and a tiny office for Penny ("Oh, you know, PR," she said with a modest, almost dismissive wave of the hand, when asked to remind them what she did) – a filing cabinet, a laptop closed on a little table, a suspiciously tidy desk-tidy, a pile of magazines (*Lancashire Life*, *Closer*, *OK*). And finally the converted attic, double bed, fresh towels. Velux windows – "You can see Blackpool Tower on a good day."

It wasn't a good day.

Back downstairs a bottle of Pinot Grigio was opened for Cassie and Penny, and local beers broken out for the boys.

"Boys," said Penny with a little laugh.

The children had stayed upstairs with Connor.

"Is this Wire?" Paul asked, glancing at the stereo. "Early Wire, by the sound of it."

"Yes, it's *Pink Flag*," said Howard.

"Oh, they're off," said Penny, leaning towards Cassie on the leather sofa and dropping her hand briefly on her knee.

Flashes of red and green lit up the sky outside the window, followed by a bang.

"It's not fireworks night yet, is it?" asked Paul.

"We've not had Halloween yet," Cassie said.

"I remember when fireworks were saved until Guy Fawkes' Night and Halloween was neither here nor there," said Howard.

"Mmm," agreed Paul. "Nice beer," he added, holding his glass up to the halogen lighting to admire its golden-brown colour.

Howard passed him the bottle.

"Pendle Witches Brew," Paul read from the label.

"Pendle Hill's just up the road," Howard offered.

"It's very good of you to invite us over," Paul heard Cassie saying to Penny.

"We know what it's like when you've just moved somewhere new," Penny said in response.

"It was weird that day in the park," Cassie remembered. "You and I met pretty much exactly at the same time as Howard and Paul bumped into each other right over the other side of the park."

"I remember you had Ellie with you in the playground," said Penny, "and I assumed it was just the two of you. Then you told me your husband and son were somewhere kicking a football. And a minute later they turned up – with Howard and Connor."

"What were you doing there anyway," Cassie asked, "so far from home?"

There was a moment's silence. Paul looked up and saw Penny staring into her wine glass.

"We'd been for a walk, hadn't we, darling? In Fletcher Moss Gardens," said Howard.

"Yes, of course," said Penny, getting to her feet. "I'm just going to check on the hotpot."

"Lancashire hotpot!" exclaimed Paul in delight.

"Is there any other kind?"

"So, have you not been here long?" Cassie asked Howard.

"Oh dear, is it that obvious?" Howard said, and Paul saw Cassie colour up. "No, we haven't been here that long, hence the drive down to south Manchester to investigate Fletcher Moss. We're still seeing the sights."

"I think I'll go and see if Penny wants a hand," said Cassie, and Paul raised his glass to his lips to hide his look of dismay.

"Lovely house," he said, his eyes scanning the walls. There was a handful of pictures, but they were beyond bland, the sort of thing you might buy for a fiver in IKEA. "Do you mind?" he asked as he got up and walked over to check out the CD collection.

"Go ahead. A lot of stuff's still in storage. That's just what I couldn't bear to be parted from."

Joy Division, The Cure, Buzzcocks, UK Subs.

"What's your favourite Cure album?" he asked Howard.

"Oh, I don't know. Remind me which ones are up there."

"*Seventeen Seconds, Pornography, Faith, Disintegration . . .*"

"Er, I really don't know. *Disintegration*, perhaps."

"Mm-hmm. 'The Hanging Garden' is an amazing track, isn't it?"

"Fantastic."

Paul moved away from the CD collection and noticed an Ordnance Survey map folded up on the mantelpiece.

"I love OS maps," he said. "May I?"

"Of course."

Paul spread the map out on the coffee table. The conurbations of Blackburn, Accrington and Burnley looked like clots in the green lungs of Lancashire.

"Can you see Barnoldswick?" Howard asked, kneeling down next to Paul. "See how big it is considering it's not even on an A-road? That's because of the Rolls-Royce factory."

"Oh, right."

"All these little villages here—" Howard pointed to the section of the map between Burnley and the moors above Hebden Bridge, "— the roads just run into the hills and stop. Interesting places. Lots of unusual traditions and rituals . . ."

"Really?" Paul was interested, but they heard Penny calling everyone from the kitchen.

The children came running downstairs. Paul caught James and gave him a bear hug. As the boy struggled to get free, Paul ruffled his hair.

"Good kids," Howard said.

"Yeah, we're lucky. They leapt at the chance to come here so they could see Connor again."

Howard's lips stretched over his teeth in an approximation of a smile.

In the converted attic, Paul and Cassie lay side by side. Cassie was reading a Jackie Kay collection; in an effort to meet some new people, she had joined a book club. Paul was making inroads into a thriller by Stephen Gallagher but was finding it hard to concentrate.

"Cassie?"

"Hmm?" Not looking up.

"Don't you think they're a bit odd? Howard and Penny. Don't you think there's something about them that's not quite right?"

"Hmm?"

"I'm serious."

Finally, Cassie looked up. She closed her book but kept her place with a thumb.

"You've had too much to drink."

"I only had two beers."

"That second one was quite strong."

"Do you know what it was called? It was called Nightmare. Can you believe it?"

"Another local brew?" There was a faintly patronizing tone in Cassie's voice, as if she regarded the interest in local beers as endearing, a "boy" thing.

"It's actually from Yorkshire, but Yorkshire's just up the road. Something to do with the Legend of the White Horse."

"I hope it doesn't give you nightmares."

"I felt at times tonight as if I might be having one, actually."

"Was the hotpot a bit too fatty for you?"

"That was all right. It was the warm salad with black pudding I wasn't sure about."

"Faddy. I think Penny and Howard are very nice and they've been very kind."

"There's just something about them. It's hard to put my finger on. Howard thought 'The Hanging Garden' by the Cure was on *Disintegration*, but it's not. It's on *Pornography*."

"Big deal." A little impatience was starting to creep into Cassie's voice.

"But these were CDs he said he couldn't bear to be parted from. I just got the impression they were trying a bit too hard to get us to like them. Or trust them."

"Don't be silly. We just have some shared interests. Like stained glass."

Paul laughed. "I thought you and Penny were never going to shut up about stained glass at the dinner table."

"Common interests, that's all it is. Now do you think we could get some sleep? They said they'd show us a bit of the countryside in the morning."

But sleep was a long time coming, for Paul at least.

* * *

Paul wanted his dream to continue. In fact, he was convinced it would continue with or without him. The question was whether he could remain part of it. His journey towards full consciousness became a struggle between his strong attachment to the dream – the grammar and meaning of which were losing coherence by the second – and his acknowledgement of responsibility. The day, he sensed, was bringing anxiety, though from what quarter he did not know. Within a few more seconds the warp of reality had completely overpowered the weft of the dream and Paul felt a sudden, inexplicable panic. He sat up and hurriedly pulled on his clothes. Cassie woke and asked him what the matter was, but he couldn't bring himself to answer.

Seconds later he was taking the stairs two at a time down to the next floor, where the children had slept in Connor's bedroom. He opened the door. The room was as quiet as the rest of the house. The curtains were still drawn and the room was dark, but he saw instantly that not only was the bed empty, but the two sleeping bags were as well, left untidily where they lay like the discarded casings of chrysalises.

Paul backed out on to the landing and descended swiftly to the ground floor. Marching down the hall as if wading through treacle, he glanced into the living room, which looked no livelier than the bedroom, and approached the closed door that led to the kitchen. He watched as his hand reached out to open it and the next thing he saw was Penny standing at the sink and beyond her were James and Ellie sat at the table eating croissants and *pains au chocolat* with Connor. All three had chocolate rings around their mouths.

Paul felt confused and relieved at the same time. He said hello and accepted Penny's offer of a pot of tea and retreated, saying he would be back down in a minute. As he passed the living room he saw Howard bent over the coffee table studying the map.

"Morning," said Howard.

"Hi."

As Paul climbed the stairs, he tried to calm himself down, as there was clearly no sense in sharing any of this with Cassie. She met him on the first-floor landing and they went back down to the kitchen together.

Once breakfast was over and the children were dressed, everyone moved towards the front door. Paul and Cassie stepped onto the garden path. Paul took the bags to the car, while Cassie waited for the children. He packed the boot and leaned against the car, enjoying the view over the fields and feeling sheepish for his strange behaviour and yet pretty good about everything, considering. He took in a deep breath and let it out slowly, enjoying the purely physical sensation of filling and emptying his lungs. Over there were Blackburn, Accrington and Burnley, yet he could see nothing but green.

Cassie joined him and told him that the children wanted to go in Connor's car.

"Fine," he said and opened the driver's door to get in.

"Their car's around the back," Cassie said.

"No problem. We wait here, yeah?"

Cassie nodded and Paul looked in the rear-view mirror. It didn't matter how much the children might occasionally bicker in the back of the car, when they weren't there he missed them.

Two or three minutes went by and Howard and Penny still hadn't shown up. Paul kept checking the rear-view mirror.

"How long does it take to strap three kids into a car?" he asked. Cassie shook her head.

"Maybe they're arguing over who sits where?" she said. "You know what they're like."

"Not usually when it's someone else's car," said Paul. "I daresay Howard's a safe driver," he added after a moment.

Cassie, who knew what was going through Paul's mind, said, "How do *you* drive when you have someone else's child in the back? Recklessly or even more safely than usual?"

"Yeah, you're right. As usual," he said, with a little smile. "But what's taking them so long?"

They waited a further minute then Paul got out of the car and wandered down to the lane that led to the back of the house. There was no sign of a vehicle making its way down towards him, so he had a quick look back at Cassie sitting in their car and started walking up the lane. He reached a track on the left, which could only be the access to the rear of Howard and Penny's house. Still no sign of their car. He ran down the little track towards the back of their house, which he isolated from its neighbours. There was no car. He looked around wildly, suddenly feeling exactly as he had done upon waking when he had been convinced, for whatever reason, that the children were no longer in the house.

At his feet in the mud was a set of tyre tracks. They led towards the lane and then turned left rather than right.

There had to be another way around to the front of the house. He turned right and ran back to the road, where Cassie was still sitting waiting in the car.

"Have you seen them?" he asked breathlessly as he reached the car.

"What do you mean?"

"The car's gone. They've gone. They've all gone. They've got the children!"

"Maybe they're coming another way round?"

"They're not. They'd have been here by now. They've gone and they've taken the children. I don't know why, but they've taken the children. Oh Jesus Christ!"

They looked at each other and for a moment said nothing. Paul's breath froze in the air in little clouds.

"Call the police," said Cassie. "No, wait. Maybe they're still in the house? They got delayed or they're playing a joke."

"There's no car at the back."

"Let's check the house."

Together they ran up the front path. The door was locked so Paul knocked hard. When no one came he put his elbow through the stained glass and reached inside to open the door. They entered the house. Paul ran upstairs. Cassie checked the living room and the kitchen. Something made her open cupboard doors in the kitchen. The cupboards were empty. There was no food, nor were there any pots and pans other than the ones they had used the night before. She ran into the living room, where she remembered seeing an oak cabinet with closed doors. It too was empty.

"Paul!" she shouted upstairs.

"Cassie!" he shouted from above. "Come up here!"

She ran upstairs.

"Look!" he said.

The filing cabinet in Penny's office was empty. The laptop had disappeared from the table. The desk tidy was as suspiciously tidy as before. In the bedroom that they had said was theirs, the wardrobes contained nothing but a few rattling wire hangers. In Connor's room it was the same story. Drawers filled with stale air. Empty cupboards that they had presumed were stuffed with toys.

No one lived in this house. No one at all.

MARC LECARD

The Admiral's House

MARC LECARD'S CRIME NOVEL, *Vinnie's Head*, came out from St Martin's Minotaur in 2007. It was followed by a second, *Tiny Little Troubles*.

His short stories have appeared in several anthologies and magazines, most recently in *Killer Year: Stories to Die For* and *All Hallows*. He lives in Oakland, California.

"In the town I grew up in there was a house like the house in the story that follows," explains the author, "much older than the surrounding suburban houses, a house with a tremendous presence.

"I used to wonder what went on there, what stories it had to tell. I never heard any, though, and was forced to make up my own."

WE ALWAYS CALLED IT the admiral's house. Easily the oldest house in town, it had been built right on the bay shore, facing the water, back before the suburban grid was laid out and smaller houses came to crowd around it. Broad and comfortable, with a little square turret, it was a classic Victorian "summer cottage", many rooms larger than my parents' house.

While I was growing up it had actually been lived in by an admiral and his family – a handsome wife, a trio of young sons. I knew Dougal, the middle, son from school; we were good, but not close friends. He was athletic and popular, far above me in the high school caste system, though he always treated me well when we met. He even invited me to his graduation party. That pleased me more than I would have thought.

The admiral's house always seemed to me to embody a kind of unattainable perfection – unattainable by me, anyway. The house itself, the tiny perfect crescent of beach, the family so good-looking, so well-mannered, members of a club that had no other local representatives – all this was more than I could hope to live up to.

In the event my life was changed, the course of it set by the terrible thing that took place there.

I never meant to come back to the town where I grew up. It wasn't the kind of place people stayed in or came back to – a faceless suburb, meant for raising children, for leaving as soon as you were able. But I was childless, by choice, and after my wife died I found I couldn't possibly stay where we had lived our life together. So I sold the house, sold my business, and crawled back to my parents' house (they were dead now and the house was empty) to lick my wounds and decide what if anything I wanted to do with the rest of my life.

Being back in my hometown was eerie and oppressive. I had been gone for nearly thirty years. No one I had known growing up still lived there. I walked the streets feeling like a memory fragment, a ghost haunting my own past. Slowly, without realizing it, I became a kind of recluse, avoiding the neighbours, going out after dark if at all. I began to drink too much.

Then at the liquor store one night, stocking up, I finally ran into someone I used to know.

It was Dougal, the admiral's middle son. When I had known him in high school he was a strong, handsome guy, bold without arrogance, friendly and generous. Life had changed him; at first I didn't recognize the haggard, hunched old man ahead of me in line, waiting to pay for his booze. But when he turned to go, something in his profile woke my memory.

"Dougal? Dougal MacAlester?"

His head snapped towards me, eyes round with what looked like fear. In that instant it occurred to me that some terrible illness or mental breakdown accounted for his presence in town. Somewhat like myself.

"Dougal, I'm sorry," I said, "I didn't mean to startle you. Do you remember me? We were in high school together."

Dougal looked back at me, clearly upset. Slowly his features relaxed and I saw that he knew me.

"Sure, John, I remember you. How have you been?" He shook my hand; the bag he was carrying clinked and rattled as he shifted it to his left arm.

We talked easily together as we walked around to the parking lot. I was unreasonably glad to run in to someone I knew. Dougal apparently felt the same.

"Why don't you come over to my place?" he asked as we paused in front of my car. "Have a drink, talk about how it used to be?"

"Sure, I'd like that," I said. "Where are you living now?"

A shifty look came over his face, hesitant and dishonest, not at all the way I remembered him.

"Same place," he said. "Same old place, down by the water, you know. Dad's house. You know where it is."

The admiral's house was as I remembered it, still a window into another era in the bland suburban street. It had a shut-up, neglected air, though, and even in the dark I could see it hadn't been well cared for.

Stepping through the wide door into the foyer was like stepping out onto a stage. Memories began to wash over me, things I hadn't thought about since the day they had happened. It was as if this door had been shut up and never opened since the last time I had been through it.

They were not all pleasant memories. But in a way my real life had begun there.

After letting us in, Dougal began to walk straight through the house, head down, like a man on a mission.

"Dougal, wait," I called out after him. "Let me look at the house. I haven't been here since . . ."

He stopped and looked back at me.

"Since the party?" he asked.

I nodded.

"What do you want to see?" he muttered. "It's all shut up now, anyway. Too much house for one man."

I looked around at the darkened rooms that opened off the foyer, sheets over most of the furniture, a musty, stale smell in the air.

"Are you all by yourself in here?"

"I had someone come in for a while, clean the place," he said, answering the question I hadn't asked. "But I got rid of her. Too much money; it's easier just to keep it closed up."

"You should rent it, live somewhere else, in the city maybe."

Dougal peered at me for a second, as if looking for some hidden meaning in what I had just said. Then he laughed, a short, sharp, barking laugh.

"I have to be here now," he said.

He took me right through the house to the back room, overlooking the water. I remembered it well; a broad, sunny room, the width of the house, windows all around. Many-paned French windows opened onto a broad deck, with a sand beach beyond, the blue stretch of the bay from wall to wall.

Now of course it was black dark outside, just a few lights across the water, and a streak of white moonlight painted over it.

The room was hot after a hot day. The French windows were all shut up, but a screened window to one side let in a little breeze off the water.

Dougal bent over and flicked on one small lamp in the corner; it barely threw enough light to keep us from barking our shins on the furniture as we found chairs and broke open the bottles.

"I don't like a lot of light," Dougal felt the need to explain. "Hurts my eyes."

I was not sorry for the shadows myself.

Dougal ignored me as he focused on removing a bottle of bourbon from the bag, unscrewing the top and pouring the brown liquor into a tall glass with squint-eyed precision. He gulped half the glass in a piece, held still while the bourbon ran into him, then sat back and turned to me.

"It's good to see you here, John. After all these years."

"I never thought I'd be in this house again," I said honestly.

"You remember that party?" Dougal asked. "The graduation party?"

I did. I had every reason to remember it.

"Angus was there," Dougal said. "That was just before Angus shipped out."

I remembered Angus, the oldest brother. He had joined the Marines, came back to dazzle us with his dress uniform, his short hair and iron posture. Then they shipped him to Vietnam. He never came back.

"My poor parents. That took the heart out of them, first Finn, then Angus getting killed," he said. "It was like they became old people over night. Even the admiral.

"But Angus was still with us for the party. That was a great day, up to the end, anyway. The last great day."

"Nothing was ever the same after that, was it?" I said.

Dougal didn't answer. He stared angrily out at the moonlight on the water.

"They're all dead, now, you know. The family," he said. "I'm the last one. This is my house now."

"It's the same with me, Dougal," I said. "Not that my house is anything to compare with this place."

He snorted. "This place. I'd burn it down if I could. I should. Just burn it."

"The admiral's house?" I was shocked. "Why would you even think of doing that?"

"Too much pain," Dougal said. "Too much pain, too many memories."

We sat in the dark, in silence, for a long time. When he spoke again it was as if he was allowing me back in to a conversation that streamed constantly through his head.

"You remember my other brother? Finn?"

Foolishly I had been hoping to avoid talking about Finn. But what else was there to talk about, in that house? I nodded without speaking.

"I never liked Finn," Dougal said.

"I never knew him," I said. "Not really." Finn had been younger than us, the youngest brother. He would have been around sixteen I guess at the time of the party, almost seventeen.

"He was always gunning for me. Nobody else could ever see it, they thought I was imagining it, but he was always trying to needle me, undermine me. I think he wanted to pry me away from dad. Not that dad ever paid much attention to any of us.

"Anyway, I couldn't really stand him. But I would have left it alone if it hadn't been for Jeanne."

"Jeanne Cary?" I asked.

"Uh-huh," Dougal said. "You remember her?"

I nodded; I didn't trust myself to speak.

"Sure you do," Dougal said. "Anyone would remember Jeanne Cary." He fiddled with his glass, filled it up again. "I loved her, you know."

"So did I. Everyone loved her."

"Not like I did. I never loved anyone like that, before or since. My whole soul was bound up in her every movement. I didn't even know I had a soul, before. Jeanne took it and never knew she had it. And she wouldn't have cared if she had known.

"Oh, she was nice enough to me, not a bitch, I mean. Not cruel at all. We even went out for a while, but it wasn't real. It was like she was doing me a favour, to not hurt my feelings. I could tell it didn't really mean anything to her.

"That was not the way she felt about Finn.

"I knew there was something between them, right from the first. Finn was younger than she was, barely a kid. but they had known each other all their lives, since they were little. They had always gotten along, I guess, and as they got older that deepened into something beyond friendship. I could see it; I hated to see it, but I did. That should have been me.

"But what could I say? He was my brother. It wouldn't have done any good anyway. So I kept my feelings to myself.

"But at the graduation party, when I saw her there, laughing, flirting, talking to Finn, I couldn't stand it. There was something around them, a force field, something between them and the rest of the world. They were together, and all the rest of us were out here, on the other side.

"I don't even know if they understood it themselves, in any conscious way. But I could see it. And it made me crazy.

"That day at the graduation party, I kept coming across them. Not in any kind of compromising position, I mean, not making-out or even holding hands. Just standing there, talking. But I could see it, the energy between them, the way they looked at each other. They were together. I couldn't take it."

Dougal paused to take a drink. When he stopped talking you could hear the waves breaking on the beach outside. The bay had always been part of the admiral's house for me, almost an extension of it. There were no lights on the deck, but the moonlight touched up the shape of things and spilled across the water, so that you could see the silhouettes of neighbouring houses, boats tied up nearby, a distant line of houses on the other shore of the cove, hunched up in the dark with a few lights burning.

"You know those islands across the bay?" Dougal asked. "The barrier islands. You can see them easily in daylight, green bars on the horizon. They're only about, I don't know, four miles away." Dougal looked toward the islands, invisible in the dark, sipping at his bourbon.

"I went up to Finn, pointed to those islands.

" 'Think you could swim to those islands?' " I asked him. 'Little brother?'

"He looked at me, a little up and down look like he couldn't believe I was really that lame.

" 'Sure,' he said.

" 'Well come on then.'

" 'What, right now?'

" 'Right now. Unless you think you can't,' I pushed him. 'Unless you don't have it.'

"I knew he was a punk swimmer, no stamina. I also knew that Jeanne was right there, talking to someone else, but well within hearing. She was looking over at us, frowning a little. I knew she was about to come over and come between us, so I pushed Finn harder.

" 'Come on, little brother, if you can,' and I turned and ran and dove into the water, without even taking my shirt off.

"He was right behind me, like I knew he would be.

"We were both a little drunk by then, I guess. We swam out across the cove, into the big part of the bay. It had been a warm day, and the bay was pretty calm, dead still. We tore it up.

"After a while I pulled up and looked behind me. Finn was still coming on, a little further behind now. I could just see the house, and the beach. I couldn't make out the people; I doubt they could see us at all.

"When Finn was almost up to me I took off again.

"The bay's pretty shallow for the most part. In a good low tide you could walk across most of it. But there's one part where the channel comes out from between the islands, where it shelves off, pretty deep. The water gets dark there. You can feel it get colder, deeper, more powerful. You can almost feel that the water is a being, there, a living thing, that knows you're there. Do you know what I mean? It's frightening, sometimes.

"When we got to the deep part I was far ahead of Finn. Then I thought I heard him call out, call my name: 'Dougal!' I stopped swimming, and hung there, paddling, looking back towards him. At first I couldn't see him; I remember thinking he must have gone under. Then his head came up. He was close enough that I could see his eyes, popping out with panic.

" 'Doog!' he yelled, 'Doog! help me!' Then he went down again.

"I just hung there. There was something cold in me, cold and unmoveable, cold and dark like the deep water.

"It's not true what they say about a drowning man goes down three times. Finn never came up again.

"I watched my brother drown, man! I watched my brother drown.

"After a while I swam over to where I saw him last, and dove down. I didn't see anything the first time. Visibility's never very good in the bay, too much mud and sediment stirred up all the time.

"The second time I went down I saw something pale, floating with its arms hanging. Maybe he was dead already, I don't know. I didn't try to find out.

"I came up again, and started yelling and waving my arms. just in case there was anyone around I hadn't noticed, boaters or fishermen; we were way too far from the beach for them to hear us, or even make us out against the water. Then I began to swim back."

*   *   *

The heavy night was heavier now, the darkness thicker. This is why he brought me here, I thought, to make this confession. But there was more to come.

I thought back to Dougal's return, shivering in the stern of the boat that had finally gone out after them, wrapped in a blanket, his long blond hair darkened by the water, hanging down around his face.

They never found Finn's body. People thought it must have been carried out by the tide through the channel and out to sea.

We were quiet for a long while after he told me about Finn. Dougal drank pretty steadily, looking out over the water, his eyes searching for something, as if he were trying to see back through the years to two swimming figures headed for the distant islands.

Finally I couldn't stand it anymore. The silence seemed to pack my head until I thought it would explode.

"Where did you go, Dougal? After that?" I asked him. "I lost touch with you. We all did."

He seemed to travel back a considerable distance before he replied.

"Went away to school," he said eventually. "Far away. I chose the school I went to because it was far away. I thought I would never see anyone from around here again."

"Did you?"

He smiled oddly. "No, not really." He reached for a bottle, knocked it off the table. We were both pretty drunk at this point.

"But something followed me," Dougal said after he had retrieved the rolling bottle and topped up.

"Something? What do you mean?"

"Something. Little things, at first. Little reminders. Just to let me know I wasn't forgotten, wasn't forgiven. Little things like you would hardly notice." He looked over at me in the dark, squinting through the shadows and the whiskey.

"Like when I went to my dorm room, the first time. My roomie hadn't showed up yet; I was there by myself. When I sat down on my bed, to get a feel for the place, it was wet. I pulled the sheets off: it was soaked through, as if someone had turned a hose on it."

"A practical joke? People do terrible things to freshmen sometimes."

"Maybe. But it was salt water. You could smell it. And not clean salt water. It smelled like the mudflats at low tide, with every dying thing in the universe turning to rotten black mud, bubbling and stinking. It smelled like that.

"I ran out of there.

"But when I went back later, my new roomie was there, unpacking. My bed was dry. I couldn't smell anything.

"That's the way it was. At every important point in my life, every time something was about to happen, to change, to begin, there would be a reminder. I knew it was Finn."

"Finn?"

Dougal nodded. "I knew. Things like that didn't just happen by accident. He was letting me know, telling me it would never be all right.

"When I went to take my bar exam, the first time, for instance. They had those plastic chairs, you remember, with the Formica slab to write on, metal legs. The seats were contoured to fit your ass. But in the seat of my chair there was a pool of water, with a strand of eelgrass floating in it. Eelgrass! I was in the mid-west, miles inland. How did eelgrass get on my chair? How did he know which chair I was going to pick?

"Things like that kept happening. They fucked me up, threw me off my stride. I failed that bar exam, you know. The second time, too. I gave up after that. I knew Finn would never let me pass it.

"Some mornings I'd wake up wet and chilled, as if I'd slept outside all night. The sheets lay on me thick and heavy, like wet sailcloth. Everything smelled of mud and death.

"Then I knew he'd been there, with me, all night."

Dougal's lost his mind, I thought, lost his mind from guilt and drink and sorrow. My own grief woke up and opened up a pit in me. I poured whiskey into it. Maybe losing your mind, I thought, wasn't the worst thing that could happen.

"Little things like that," Dougal went on. "He was always with me. Isn't that what they say? 'I am with you always,'" he laughed derisively.

"But I tried to get on, you know? I kept trying to live my life."

"You can get used to anything," I lied.

"Not this. I began to brace for it. I tried to be ready for it. But it always seemed to take me by surprise.

"I got married at one point," Dougal said, as if he couldn't believe it. "To Marcie, someone I worked with, a great woman. We were pretty happy together at first. I couldn't believe Finn would let it happen. I kept waiting for something to go wrong, for him to show himself, but nothing happened. I actually began to think it was over, that he was satisfied somehow, and would leave me alone now. That by falling in love and getting married I had atoned, or balanced things in some way.

"But I was wrong. He was just waiting, waiting for things to get good for me, so that when he ruined them there would be something to lose, something that would hurt.

"Marcie and I did the whole married thing – car, house in the 'burbs. No kids, thank god, but we talked about having them, made plans.

"Then, after about a year, I began to smell that smell, that evil low-tide reek, everywhere. I tried to scrub it out of the house. I became a fanatic, cleaning everything constantly. My wife thought I'd lost my mind.

"I began to find things, too. Between the pages of a book, there'd be a piece of marsh grass, still damp. And there was sand everywhere all of a sudden, gritty underfoot. Sand in my bed. That smell. We were still in the mid-west, I was determined never to go back to the coast, never to smell salt water again, never see anyone I knew from here. But it all came to me.

"Then, I started hearing him."

"Finn? Did he speak to you? What did he say?"

"Not words. That might have been better. It couldn't have been worse. What I heard was breathing, someone breathing. But not regular breathing – gasping, gurgling, choking – the sounds of someone trying to breathe under water. It got so it was the background music to everything I did.

" 'What are you always listening for?' my wife would ask me. It aggravated her. I never listened to *her,* she said, right before she left me. She said she wanted to be with someone who was actually *there* all the time, who wasn't always sitting there wishing he were anywhere else, listening to things no one else could hear.

"There was more to it than that, of course. You fill in the gaps. But the upshot of it was that we got divorced. I left town, bummed around a while. That's when I started drinking, seriously, I mean.

"I stopped hearing the breathing after the divorce. Everything stopped. But I knew he was just waiting for me to settle down, to get happy again. So I kept moving, kept drinking.

"I lived that way for years.

"Then my mom died, down in Florida. Dad had died the year before – I missed the funeral. When I went down there to take care of things, I found out we still had this house – they couldn't bear to sell it, and had rented it out when they moved to Florida. So I came back here to get rid of it.

"That was a mistake. I knew as soon as I walked in the door that I would never leave here again. Finn wanted me here. All of his persecution had this one end, to drive me back to this house.

"And here I was.

"I would sit here and drink, like this, night after night. I would sit here and yell at the water, challenge him.

" 'Come on out, Finn! Here I am! I'm waiting for you!' "

"Then, finally, he came up out of the water and showed himself to me."

I shuddered; in spite of everything Dougal had told me up to now, I wasn't ready for this.

"You saw him?"

Dougal nodded. "I still see him."

"When does this happen?" I asked, "on the anniversary of his death or something?"

"Oh, no." He shook his head. "Every night."

I glanced out the window at the moonlit deck. "Are we waiting for him now? Tonight?"

Dougal nodded. "He should come soon. He comes around this time. Every night. You'll see."

After that first time, Dougal told me, he had kept the curtains drawn. "But I knew he was out there. I could feel him, smell him. Hear him, too, feeling along the glass, looking for a way in."

It was late now, and in the heavy stillness of that summer night you could hear everything: insects chirring, a distant speedboat gunning through the darkness, out of sight across the bay, the waves shushing in on the beach, lapping against the bulkhead.

Then there was a sound that cut across the regular rhythm of the waves, a slopping, wallowing sound. Dougal stopped talking; his face fell apart, as if someone had just cut the strings that held it together. A rotten, low-tide stench filled the room, getting stronger and stronger until I could barely breathe.

Deep in the shadows, I saw something lying on the deck; I was sure it hadn't been there earlier.

Then whatever it was stood up. It stumbled across the deck and pressed itself against the glass.

"He wants to come in," I said, surprised at the sound of my own voice in the still room.

"I won't let him in," Dougal said. "I'll never let him in."

The figure felt its way along the windows until it reached the far railing of the deck. You could hear the soft pat of its hands against the glass, hear the slight creaking of the window-frames as it pressed against them.

It was too dark to see clearly. I got no more than a glimpse of white flesh through the window, flesh too white to be living, and somehow soft, corrupt, swollen.

I saw the palms of its hands against the glass.

It was appalling. I shut my eyes, and shielded them with an open hand, the way you do against sun-glare, to make sure, I guess, that no image of that thing could get through, light or no light.

When I opened my eyes again it had gone, though I thought I could make out a dim form moving slowly towards the end of the dock. Another minute and something clambered down the pilings and slipped into the bay water.

We sat there in silence for a long time. Dougal's breathing was rough and uneven, as if he'd just run up a flight of stairs. I had to consciously keep myself from holding my breath. I didn't want to draw the dense, rotten miasma of salt marsh and mudflat that filled the room into my lungs.

"You saw that?" Dougal asked after a while.

"Yes," I admitted. "I saw it. How do you know it's Finn?"

"It's Finn. No doubt about that."

"What does he want?"

"This is what he wants. He wants me to remember. He doesn't want me to forget. He doesn't want me to have any more happiness, any more life, than he does."

I thought of Dougal, sitting here in the dark, night after night, waiting for his dead brother to visit him.

"Are you afraid? Do you think it's trying to get in to do you harm?"

Dougal shook his ruined head. "Oh no. He can't harm me. He hasn't the power to hurt me, physically. That's why I opened the curtains, to confront him, to show him I'm not afraid of him. That way he can't hurt me."

I looked around the empty house, its shut-up rooms smelling of mildew, stuffy, peeling walls, the whole house falling apart. I looked at Dougal, his body destroyed by alcohol, his life reduced to a nightly vigil of horror and guilt.

"I think I'd better go," I said. Dougal nodded, never taking his eyes off the window, staring out over the bay.

"He won't come back now," Dougal said. "Not tonight."

"Good night, Dougal," I said. I couldn't think of anything else to say.

Dougal just sat there, silently, cradling a bottle in his lap, staring out at the water.

I let myself out.

Dougal had done all the talking, but I had had something I meant to tell him. In the event I never came out with it. That was just as well.

I didn't have the heart to tell him that I had married Jeanne Cary. I thought he had enough to bear without that.

I drove her home the night of the graduation party. She had been planning on getting a ride from Finn, or Dougal. Otherwise I might not have met someone like her. I comforted her. No, it wasn't like that. But when we met again, there was an opening, an emotional contact already made. We started from there. One thing, as they say, led to another. We spent some good years together before I had to watch her die of cancer. Now that was over and I was back where it all started.

I wouldn't have minded seeing her again, but that was not given to me.

Driving back home along the shore road, I stopped just before the road bends away from the water and looked back towards the admiral's house. On the far point I could just make out the looming shape of it, shadows hovering over a spark of yellow light, the small table lamp burning at the back of the room overlooking the deck. I knew now why Dougal hadn't lit the other lamps.

I knew Dougal was still sitting there, drinking and staring out at the bay. I also knew that one night, when he felt he had waited long enough, been punished enough, Dougal would get up and open the door.

I opened all the windows of my car to let the warm summer night air chase out the heavy, rotten stink of low tide mud that had followed me from the admiral's house and filled the car interior to choking. By the time I pulled up in front of my house I couldn't smell it any more.

TONY RICHARDS

Man, You Gotta See This!

TONY RICHARDS BEGAN his career writing for classic anthologies such as *The Pan Book of Horror Stories* and *The Fontana Book of Great Ghost Stories*. Since then, he has gone on to see six books and more than seventy short stories in print.

Widely travelled, he often sets his fiction in locations that he has visited. His latest novel, *Dark Rain* – the first of a projected series set in the fictional town of Raine's Landing, Massachusetts – is published by Eos/HarperCollins. He lives in north London with his wife.

As for the origin of the apocalyptic story that follows, Richards reveals: "I did go to see the last big Monet exhibit at the Royal Academy, and this is the result."

SEE, THERE'S THIS THING about Jer.

There was a Monet exhibition in our city once. I and Kara – my then girlfriend – trooped through with the rest. Gazed upon the garden scenes and renderings of fog-bound London. Were awed by the way the paintings changed with age and failing eyesight. Loved it. But . . .

There is something more than love, in art. I found that out right at the end.

The exhibit reached its conclusion, you see, in a big square room that just contained one painting. A triptych, they called it. Three almighty canvases put together to form one.

It was water lilies, of course. Took up an entire wall.

And there were benches in front of it, so I just sat down. And then allowed my mind to fall forward into that weightlessness of pastel colour.

I didn't realize Kara had gone wandering back to see the scenes near Tower Bridge again.

When she tapped my shoulder, asked me if I'd been sitting here all this time, more than half an hour had passed.

I had gone completely elsewhere. I'd been lost. Blissfully so.

And Jer would *never* understand that.

Jerry Mulligrew – almost like the jazz saxophonist – my oldest and closest friend. Thirty-four, but looking rather younger. Pony-tailed and scrawny. Avoider of honest labour, as, for the most part, was I. Connoisseur of soft and medium-soft drugs. Lover of heavy metal. Expert puller of the student babes at our local bar – thus proof that earnest eyes, a winning smile and a quick sense of humour compensate for what I'd call weasely looks and dubious dress-sense.

Jer just wasn't into beauty of that kind. It was a concept, he often told me, which had had its day. All of that was misty-eyed stuff, far removed from actual life. We were in the Cyber Age now, and that kind of beauty was old hat.

"And we should replace it with what?" I'd ask him.

"Wonderment, man. Just . . . infinite possibilities. There ain't nothin' we can't do."

We both lived on Packwell Street, me in a pokey one-bedroom apartment that had had its rent fixed twenty years ago, Jer a couple of blocks down in the loft room of a long established squat. If you walked past late at night, you could see the glow of his three state-of-the-art home computers through the window, like some other-worldly glow.

Seeing as he hadn't held down a job since the original George Bush, you might ask how he managed to afford them.

Don't ask.

And . . . when Old Man Hubert died, it was rather like that thing Dorothy Parker said when Calvin Coolidge – I *think* it was Calvin Coolidge – did the same. "How can they tell?"

No one could remember when they had last seen him. He'd had his groceries delivered, and he'd never ventured out. He was almost like a mythic figure to most people on the street. He'd lived in the big house at the very end of Packwell, where the street met the hill, rose for a few blocks, and then gave way to shabby-looking woods. Huge house. Old house. Cupolas and stuff. It was surrounded by an iron fence, and all the drapes were permanently closed.

What did he do there?

"He's supposed to be a painter," Ray the Bartender informed us one time.

"No shit? He has opening nights and stuff?"

Ray shrugged. "Never heard of any. Never seen anything by him. S'far as I know, he never even tries to sell his paintings. The word is he's got inherited money."

I exchanged glances with Jer, but he just shook his head.

"No way, dude," he said once Ray had moved off. "I'm not into that art-stuff, but I respect all creators. In a way, I'm one myself. He's old anyhow. We'll leave it till he's dead."

And now he was.

One day, a hearse simply appeared at the end of the road, but with no limousines following it. A coffin was brought out, and loaded in, and then driven away. The front door was padlocked and the windows boarded up. No moving truck appeared.

When I saw Jer that afternoon, his thumbs were pricking, like the witches in *Macbeth*. He was all keyed up. Then he looked down at my ankle, remembered that I'd twisted it last night – on a loose paving-slab, extremely drunk; he'd had to help me stagger home. And groaned.

"Ah, what the hell?" he philosophized. "It'll probably be months before some lawyer gets around to having the place emptied. We can be in and out as much as we like, take a little at a time. Like – shoplifting, you know? There must be God-knows-what in there."

He was off towards the house alone an hour after darkness fell. Sitting in front of my TV, feeling pretty sorry for myself, I could imagine him prying back the boards.

An hour and a *half* after darkness fell, my phone went. It was Jer, on the cell phone he had bought from Ray a month back.

"Man, you gotta get up here!"

"What are you talking about, bro?"

"Man, you gotta *see* this!"

I felt myself go slightly red. "I'm a cripple, for chrissake! I can't go doing B-and-E in my condition!"

"You get up here right now, man, or you'll forever kick yourself. I shit you not even slightly. This has to be seen to be believed."

What did? I next asked him.

But he told me that he could not even describe it. He gave me details of how to get in.

I was cursing as I limped up the gradient. Two things, apart from the discomfort, really bothered me. First, Jerry often took some kind of upper before heading out on such a venture, to heighten his senses and make his reactions quick. I wondered if his wild excitement was simply the product of some chemical, and nothing more.

Secondly – and this one, honestly, had been nagging away at the back of my mind ever since that talk with Ray – if Old Man Hubert had been a painter, then what was he painting with the drapes all drawn?

The door might be padlocked, but the metal gates had been left open – forgotten about, presumably, when the hearse had driven out through them. I went down the shadiest side of the house, brushing past a row of trees, and there was the small side window, just as Jer had described, with two-thirds of the boards pulled away. There was an overturned bucket to heft myself up from, otherwise I don't think I'd have made it. But my ankle was still hurting like hell by the time I was inside.

"Jer?" I whispered.

A small flashlight came on.

I couldn't see Jerry behind it, but could hear the tremolo in his voice.

"C'mon man! Follow me! You gotta see this stuff!"

He sounded like a little kid who'd just found a dead squirrel.

I hobbled along behind him, painfully aware that if Five-O showed up now I didn't have a chance of running. And I prayed that there weren't any stairs involved.

There weren't.

We went down a corridor into the pitch-black centre of the house. Through a door, which Jer told me to close.

Once I did, a switch clicked – and I was temporarily blinded.

"Jesus!" I swore quietly. "You could have warned me."

"Power's still on. Everything's still on. Seems like most people don't even know Old Hubert's dead."

Or was even alive, I realized.

"So, what's this boundless treasure-trove you're so eager to show me?"

I was aware, by now, of the heavy smell of oil paint in the large, windowless room. And there was an easel propped against the far wall. Different colours spattering the floor. This was where the man had worked.

"That's the crazy thing, dude," Jerry now informed me. "All the rest of the stuff in this place? It's in the plastic-dolphin, souvenir-of-Seaworld category. And this old cat had *money*? But the stuff in here . . ."

Framed canvases were stacked, facing inwards, thirty or forty deep, against the two side-walls. Pile after pile of them. They were ranked according to size. None of them as big as the Monet triptych,

but there were some very large ones. There were also dozens as small
as an edition of *Hustler*.

More than a thousand in all, I took a quick guess. The smell of oil
paint had grown so strong, now, it was starting to make my head reel.

Why might Hubert paint all these, simply to keep them here and
face them inwards?

But then, why would Van Gogh want to go and cut off his own
ear?

"Jer," I said to my friend. "I thought you weren't into paintings."

"Usually no, but—"

"Are they valuable?" I cut in.

"I'd suppose so, dude. I can't imagine anybody not wanting to buy
them. Take a look."

And he turned one of the largest ones to face me.

The truly weird thing was, when I'd gone into that blank at the
Monet exhibit, I'd at least still been aware what I was looking at.
A pond. And lilies.

But I have simply no idea, to this day, what was actually depicted
on the canvas that Jer showed me. Except that I'm sure it wasn't
abstract.

A pastoral scene? A garden? A house? Cityscape? Night sky?

I just don't know.

What were the main colours used?

So far as I can remember, *all* of them.

Jerry shook me rather annoyedly.

"Hey, man!"

"Wh—"

I looked away, with difficulty.

"Dave? I've been talking to ya, like, the last five minutes. You been
dropping too many painkillers?"

I looked back at the painting.

Jerry shook me again.

I didn't even say "wh—" this time. Didn't look around. He had to
physically put a hand to my face, turn it.

"Dude, what are you *on* tonight?"

I shook my head, trying to clear it. "Nothing," I replied, trying to
hide my own confusion.

Something in me screamed out not to look back at the painting.

"Ain't it great?" Jer was enthusing by this time, though. "And
they're all like this, all the ones I've looked at, anyhow. And I don't
normally dig this kind of stuff, but these are . . . such amazing use of
colour! Hubert was a *genius!*"

He set the painting back in place, face inwards. I felt a massive sense of relief.

Now, however, Jerry switched into full Scheming Mode.

"We can't just move them all at once." His tone had become staccato. "What I say is this. We take a half dozen of the smallest ones—"

"*You* take them. I'm a cripple."

"And we show them around some galleries and stuff, and get some valuations. Man, the ones I've seen aren't even signed. I could say that I did them myself."

Which made me wonder if the art world was quite ready for someone like Jerry Mulligrew.

"And if it turns out they're worth something, yeah? We can borrow Ray's pickup and load it up. We might be sitting on a goldmine here, bro!"

He chose five, in the end, of the little ones he liked the best. Helped me through the window, but then let me limp back home myself.

What had happened back there? Just what had I seen? Colours flashed behind my eyelids, every time I blinked.

There was two-thirds of a bottle of generic vodka waiting for me when I got indoors. I finished the lot during the next couple of hours. Don't remember going to bed.

It was noon the next day when I awoke. I was woken by the phone.

"Dude?"

My tongue just about managed, "Hi, Jer."

"You've gotta get over here!"

"The house again?"

"No, man. April's!"

April was a waitress he'd been dating – if you could call what Jer did that – for the past couple of weeks. She lived a couple of blocks crosstown, on Miller Drive.

"What's up?"

"I'm, like, scared man. She is really out of it. I think she's gone and done some bad stuff."

"Call an ambulance, then."

"Man, get your *butt* here!"

The hangover drew attention from the pain in my ankle, at least. I went up the short flight of steps to the front door of April's tiny but incredibly neat dwelling. Went to press the buzzer, but the door was off its latch.

I found them both in the elevator-sized living room, April sat cross-legged, and Jer hunkered over her, every contour of his body a map of concern.

Her pretty, fine-boned face was entirely slack. A trail of saliva depended from her painted lower lip into her lap. A pool was forming.

She didn't seem to blink at all. Her pale blue eyes – were they reflecting something?

"She was like this when I found her," Jerry said, his face screwed up with inner pain.

And it was a familiar one. People like us, with acquaintances like ours? Once every so often, a pal, a girlfriend winds up in this state and finishes up in ER. Quite *literally* finishes, from time to time.

He'd just never believed it would happen to someone like April. Yes, she did a little blow, like any normal person. But nothing else that either of us knew about.

She was facing something that was propped against her armchair. I couldn't see it from this angle.

"Tell me what happened?" I asked.

"Man, I dropped around to see her last night, after . . . you know! We smoked some, then fooled around a little. I even brought her a gift. Came back here 'bout ten this morning, and she was like this. Her *skin's* cold, man, like she's been sitting here all night!"

There were no spoons, candles, or tin foil near her. I inspected her arms, found no tracks.

Then I looked at what she was looking at.

Jerry . . . shook me.

"Dude, what the hell are you doing?"

I had to force myself to look away.

"That's the gift?"

"I thought, why not? We've got plenty of them to spare."

"Jer, there's something wrong with these paintings."

"Say what?" And, incredulous, he almost laughed. "Man, they're just so great. They're . . . beautiful. See? I said it. I acknowledged the existence of your kind of beauty."

"Jer, they—"

"It's gotta be some pills or something," he was babbling away, though. "Pharmaceutical smack or something. Man, if I get my hands on whoever gave her *that* stuff—"

And he would not be told otherwise. He took her in a cab to the local ER in the end, bumming ten off me towards the fare.

I followed them out, refusing to glance back.

April was in a coma, though the people at the hospital could not discover why. It was not drugs. I went to see her the next day. Swore I could see flecks of surplus colour in her open, staring eyes.

The thing that keeps people like Jer going and makes survivors of them – it is their ability to just move on. It's not that he didn't care. Far from it. It's just that he realized, without having to vocalize it, that continued existence depends on – do I really have to use that old "moving shark" metaphor?

Over the next couple of days, he hauled the five paintings – he'd taken April's back – around some dozen galleries.

"What is with it with these fools?" he now complained. "They're supposed to be businessmen, and all they do is gawk? I couldn't get a price-tag out of one of them! And for such beautiful paintings!"

And I finally realized what this was. It was all to do with – immunity. Resistance levels.

A disease goes around, see? A plague. And most people succumb. But a few just have something natural in them that subdues the sickness, makes it less effective.

So it was with Jer. He'd always been aloof towards fine paintings. Totally immune to artistic beauty. And so, when the bug had struck, it had affected him to a degree – but had not felled him completely like the rest of us, apparently.

"Jer—" I tried to tell him for the dozenth time.

But he still wasn't prepared to listen. Maybe that was a part of the paintings' limited effect on him.

When he went home, he looked annoyed enough to do something exceptionally stupid.

Which bothered me enough to go around at ten o'clock and check up on him.

The door wasn't locked. The pungent aroma of California Gold hit me as I went into the hallway.

There were no lights on in Jer's living room. Just the glow of those three screens. That was strong enough to pick out, on the little dining table, an open jar of pharmaceutical coke and a half-empty bottle of bourbon.

Jer was hunkered over the screen of the middle computer, and there was a scanner humming beside him, and several wooden picture frames lay scattered on the floor.

His back was in the way, so I could only see the edges of the image on his screen. It was enough.

It didn't mesmerize me, this time. Maybe you needed the whole picture for that.

"Jer, what are you doing?" I asked.

When he turned towards me, I could see how out of it he was. His face like a plastic mask in the weird light. His pupils too large, his thin lips twitching. He tried to smile, but it came out as something else entirely.

"They're so beautiful, dude," he informed me, like a stuck record. "Beauty like I've never seen in my entire life. If those asses at the galleries won't show them – well, the whole world ought to see them. That's what art's about, right? It belongs to everyone. The entire world."

His e-mail page was now up on the screen. He turned back to it, and started making attachments.

What the—?

"Jer, no!"

And I started lunging forwards.

He had clicked on SEND before my hand could reach him. I stopped, feeling a lot more than helpless, letting my arms drop down to my sides.

"The whole world, man," Jer was mumbling to himself again. "The entire teemin' world."

It is two days later, by this time. And everything has changed.

No planes pass overhead any longer. There are far fewer cars, no trains. The mail hasn't come. The mart down the road is running at half-staff, and running out of supplies. There are hardly any trucks at all.

Not everyone has a computer, of course. Most of those people are just wandering around, trying to figure what the hell is going on.

Sooner or later, most of *them* go into a loved one's place of work, or an offspring's bedroom. And they do not re-emerge.

This morning, a fire started up near the centre of town. And is still spreading. I can see the vast plume of smoke from my window. And I keep on wondering. Those people in front of their screens down there – do they even move when the flames start to consume them? Chill thought.

The power hasn't gone out yet. Emergency measures, I suppose. I wish it would. Although that might change nothing. It took only the space of one night to put April in a coma. And it's now been forty or so hours for most people.

I ought to go see if she's come around, but cannot bring myself, since I suspect the worst.

Jer dropped round about an hour back. He still doesn't seem to realize what's going on.

As I said, maybe that's a side-effect of his partially-immune reaction to the paintings.

He told me six more times how very beautiful they were.

There's looting.

I keep thinking of places that I've only ever seen on the TV. Craggy places. Dusty places. Places where there is not so much as an electrical wire, but people live there.

They don't even know it, but they've just inherited the earth. Does an absence of technology make one meek in any sense?

Someone just got shot, down at the corner. Is the fire heading this way? God, I wish the power would go out, even though that idea rather frightens me.

Maybe I should try to get away from here, though how or where I simply do not know.

Maybe – better, easier – I'll just go back to the old house, back to that paint-redolent room. Turn one of the canvases around.

And get lost.

The same way everything is lost now.

Beautiful!

DAVID A. SUTTON

The Fisherman

DAVID A. SUTTON IS A RECIPIENT of the World Fantasy Award, The International Horror Guild Award and twelve British Fantasy Awards for editing magazines and anthologies. His first professional anthologies were *New Writings in Horror & the Supernatural* (two volumes) and *The Satyr's Head & Other Tales of Terror*. More recently he has edited *Phantoms of Venice*, which was reprinted in paperback by Screaming Dreams in 2007, and *Houses on the Borderland*, a selection of novellas from The British Fantasy Society.

He has also been a genre fiction writer since the 1960s. Some early stories appeared in the horror small press in the 1970s, including *World of Horror*, *Dark Horizons* and *Cthulhu*, while respected editor Hugh Lamb selected stories for two anthologies, *The Taste of Fear* and *Cold Fear*. Since then his fiction has appeared in *More Ghosts & Scholars*, *Kadath*, *The New Lovecraft Circle*, *Gothic*, *Final Shadows*, *Skeleton Crew*, *The Merlin Chronicles*, *The Mammoth Book of Best New Horror*, *The Mammoth Book of Werewolves*, *When Graveyards Yawn*, *The Black Book of Horror*, *Dead Ends* and *Subtle Edens: The Elastic Book of Slipstream*.

His debut short story collection, *Clinically Dead & Other Tales of the Supernatural*, appeared from Crowswing Books.

"In writing 'The Fisherman', I wanted to evoke characters on the edge of their own sense of reality and toiling with loss, real and imagined," explains the author. "The lonely ocean in the far west of Wales, and what might lurk in it, seemed a good metaphor to use around these characters.

"The words from Coleridge and listening to David Bedford's music inspired by 'The Rime of the Ancient Mariner' gave me added impetus in creating the atmosphere for this story."

WHEN STEPHANIE FIRST SAW HIM, his eyes were wild yet unfocused. She found out why later.

She and Rod were waiting outside the holiday cottage in Pembrokeshire; the keys were promised any minute. In front of them huddled the building that had been converted from a farm structure into holiday lets. Not strictly cottages as advertised, but she was not going to quibble. Behind them crouched the tiny inlet of Nolton Haven and the swell of St Bride's Bay beyond. Stephanie had turned to watch the waves that caroused so very close to the dwellings. The beach itself was hidden from her viewpoint, below the shelf of land they were standing on. The twin biceps of the cliffs on either side hugged the bay close. Rugged and yet secure, she thought.

As she watched a seagull lazily ascend in the middle distance, a dark shape suddenly appeared out of the ground.

"*Oh!*" she said, starting back and colliding with her husband as he peered into a room through one of the windows.

Rod pivoted around quickly, recovering his balance and hers in turn. A few yards away an old man in oilskins was rising up as if he was emerging from the rough green turf that separated the promontory of land from the beach. They would later discover the foot-worn steps that allowed beachcombers to negotiate the ten-or-so-foot drop to the pebbles and sand.

"*Yea, slimy things did crawl with legs,*" the old man said as he climbed the top of the rise and walked with a determined pace towards the couple. "*Upon the slimy sea.*"

Stephanie edged closer to Rod and put her arm around his waist. He could feel her shudder. The old man was very close to them now, had entered their personal space, and she could see his red and watery eyes close up – eyes that had been staring out to sea for too many years. A seafarer's eyes, focusing not on her, but distantly, or even inwardly perhaps.

"*Get away you old fool!*" A middle-aged woman had rounded the corner of the holiday lettings, bearing their key. The old man turned to face her and his eyes hardened to marble, but he walked off towards the cliff path without saying anything further.

"Mrs Rollason," Rod introduced her to Steph. "Stephanie, my wife."

"He's all right," Mrs Rollason said. "Gilbert wouldn't hurt a fly I daresay, but he's not quite right, if you know what I mean." She smiled hopefully and handed Rod the key to their accommodation. "Nice to meet you, Stephanie. I'm Joan. I've put a loaf of bread and some butter and milk in the fridge for you both, start you off. The beach shop sells groceries if you don't want to go into Broad Haven right away. If you need anything else in the meantime, please come over to the farmhouse. Either Ted or me'll always be around."

Stephanie nodded in acknowledgment, but was distracted as she watched the old man labouring up the steep coastal path that navigated the cliffs out of Nolton Haven. "Does he live around here?" she asked, hoping he did not. The man had given her quite a jolt.

"Up there," Joan nodded towards the highest visible point of the cliff. At the top, surrounded by gorse, was a small, once white-painted wooden building. It did not look much to live in. "His wife was drowned off the beach, quite a few years ago now, and he's out day and night looking for her, so they say. He's harmless enough. Needs help of course, but won't take it. Stubborn old fool."

"What on earth was he jabbering about?" Rod asked. "Sounded familiar."

"Oh, he's always saying some poetry or other. Now you two newlyweds enjoy your honeymoon and forget about old Gilbert, won't you."

When the farmer's wife had gone, Stephanie snatched the key from Rod and opened the door to Swift Cottage. *A single-bedroom holiday cottage with all the modern conveniences*, she recalled the brochure. The roof space above the living room was open to the rafters, one of the charming features advertised. But the furniture was a bit tatty and the kitchen units, cooker and fridge had all seen their best days some years before.

"You told her we were on our honeymoon?" Stephanie asked as she walked around the living room, her fingers lightly caressing an elaborately decorated earthenware ewer and bowl on an old side-board.

"Well, no," Rod answered, lowering his head to come through the door from the kitchen, where he had been examining the contents of the fridge. "But I didn't disabuse her if that's what she thinks. I just told her we were recently married."

And so they were, but their honeymoon had actually been taken in Turkey earlier in the year and had turned out disastrously. The honeymoon holiday from Hell had nearly wrecked the marriage. They were still trying to get their money back from the tour company, as well as their fractured relationship from each other.

During the holiday, Stephanie had discovered that she did not really know Rod very well at all. So much for whirlwind romances. She loved him still, but the comforting ache of new love had dissipated. She tried to recapture the emotion, yet it eluded her like a favourite piece of music that on subsequent hearing no longer has the passion to arouse. On their honeymoon she found Rod quarrelsome and bad-tempered, and he took his frustrations out on her, instead of the holiday rep.

Nothing went right and, to try to salve the wounds caused by the various holiday brochure failures and their constant arguments, she had suggested on their return that they squeeze their bank account a little more, on the promise of actually getting some compensation, and go away again, for a few days while summer was still hanging on in England. Rod managed to wangle some more leave from the office and she walked another tightrope of self-certificated sick leave. It might be her last before her employer had to let her go.

"Oh, well, this might as well be our honeymoon! The Turkish one definitely wasn't! In fact, Rod," she said eagerly, throwing her arms around his neck and draping herself onto him, "let's *call* this our real honeymoon, eh? Try to forget about the . . . about the . . ."

"The—?" he began before he clocked her little jest. They kissed, Rod tasting the smear of lipstick she wore. He lifted her and carried her to the sofa, which creaked of old springs as he lowered her onto it. They began removing one-another's clothes and Rod's hands caressed her.

His middle finger found its way inside her and she groaned. As her heart beat faster with her arousal, she wondered if the ache of new love was returning. Then she remembered the old man. Pushing Rod up off her, her eyes looked serious for a moment. "Close the curtains will you, Rod," she asked.

He stood up and did so. "In case mad Gilbert peeks in?" he guessed. "Maybe we should pay him a neighbourly visit after, invite him down to dinner?"

"Fuck off." She reached up and pulled his belt free from his jeans as if cracking a whip. "Now fuck."

The seaward facing window of the wooden house that crowned the top of the cliffs gazed blankly across St Bride's Bay, the grey water reflected back upon itself. Inside, a shape moved across the window-pane, an eye's pupil milked by a cataract. The dwelling and its single occupant were as old and weathered and colourless as the sea.

Gilbert pulled up his chair and watched through the salt-rimed glass. Cradled in his hands a mug of hot water in which was dissolved an Oxo cube. Down below, the waves, ever eager to smother the sand, were elbowing close to the land, lifting the stern of his little dinghy where it was moored on the beach. It would soon be dark and he would venture down to the surf and the shadows, and the silver light from the moon. Once again row out on the tide, undisturbed in his search.

Tonight, as ever, he would unleash the boat and make his way to where the two walls of the cliffs hugged around Nolton's bay like protective arms. Out he would go, to where the wide sea spanned to the horizon and the gentle slop of the waves was omnipresent, but muted, so that the sound of the oars could be heard as they sliced and skated the slack ocean. Tonight would be a reprise of many such nights. A habit only curtailed when winter storms blew in, and sea spray mixed with driving rain dashed his tiny vessel with salty fury. Then he would have to curtail his repetitive and fruitless forays.

Watery runnels formed in his glazed, despairing eyes like salt waves bridling across reddened sand, and dripped in a silent cataract down a face as craggy and dark as the grey cliffs. Out there . . . somewhere . . . his beautiful lost Siren.

There seemed to be few tourists here, fewer beachcombers or sun worshippers.

Stephanie and Rod were walking arm-in-arm along the road to the pub up the hill. From up here Stephanie could see a small caravan park nestling in the valley, from which there was little sign of movement, even though summer still had a few throes to throw. She conceded to herself that the beach was a small one by any standards and that the sea was probably too inconsiderate for swimming.

The little bay, hemmed in as it was by high cliffs, allowed the tide too much wilful leeway; delightful rock pools at low tide, but precious little sand to sit on once the sea had ridden in at high tide. The bay had a wild charm but also, she thought, an aura of loneliness. As they walked she watched a lone fulmar skim the cliff's face, wheeling slowly this way and that, its wings as stiff as an aircraft's. The solitary bird evoked the sense of an ancient landscape, one so untenanted that it was a simple matter to believe that they were the first humans to reach this shore since some Celtic tribe harvested the fish here a millennia ago.

Dusk was arriving with the cold breeze off the sea. "Hug me," Stephanie said, wishing she did not always have to ask.

As he did so, Rod turned his attention to the pub. They climbed the steps that wove through the beer garden to its entrance. "Hope the food's hot."

Stephanie wished he were not so easily distracted; she would have liked more of his attention devoted to her. But not wanting to dampen things with an unguarded comment, she said instead, "I should think they get plenty of business from the caravan park." As they entered the lounge, the dining area was surprisingly unoccupied. "Or maybe not." If a pub's busy at mealtimes, she tended to think, its food was likely to be more agreeable.

"It's only," Rod glanced at his watch, "six-thirty. Oh, well, let's see what's on the menu."

They found a small table in a cosy corner by a window and ordered some wine and a meal. While they waited, Stephanie watched the rollers through the window, forever surging for access to the land, but somehow blocked at the last second by a hidden influence, and rippling back. The quickening mass of the ocean was darkening, the surf tracing ragged luminescent curves against the shore.

If she gazed seaward long enough something might take hold in her, she thought, until each gleaming breaker arrives with the impression that the sea is some surly spirit, rising swiftly, disgorging some half-sensed emotion on what was left of the beach. And that ill-natured spirit's jetsam was inside her already. Despite their earlier lovemaking, she did not feel anything much except a formless dissatisfaction.

Rod sat silently beside her, also gazing westwards, until there was nothing but blackness outside, the sea a memory of salt and the tang of seaweed. Then someone switched on the pub's exterior lights, which illuminated the picnic tables in the beer garden and two spiky Cordylines in tubs. Stephanie perked up, trying to imagine that Rod was thinking about the two of them and not his work.

The food finally arrived, and she almost balked at the size of the battered cod and mound of chips on both their plates. "We certainly won't go hungry tonight!" Smiling she brightened as she unwrapped the knife and fork from the red paper napkin and wove her head from side to side as if she did not quite know where on the plate to begin demolishing her meal. "We can find the shops tomorrow and stock up the fridge."

"Maybe we'll eat out more – I wouldn't want you slaving in that excuse for a kitchen every evening." He despatched several french fries. "I've heard there's a couple of very good restaurants in Solva."

"*Expensive* restaurants, Rod." She had also read the tourist information brochure the Rollasons had left in the cottage. "If you'll recall, we just gave a small fortune to that package tour company." It felt good to be chatting amiably.

"Which we *will* get back . . . eventually."

"If you say so. But, really, I don't *mind* self-catering." She prodded her fish and began to eat, and they lapsed into silence for a few minutes.

Later they both sat on bar stools with a glass of brandy each, to finish the evening. The pub's restaurant had not filled up significantly, and most of the clientele appeared to be locals. Among them Rod noticed the farmer who they had rented the cottage from at the other end of the bar. "Evening Mr Rollason," he said, raising his glass.

He did not mean the gesture in any other way than friendly acknowledgment, but the man raised his pewter pot also, saying, "Thanks, most obliged to you. I'll have a pint. Beth?" he called to the barmaid. "Put another one in there when you're ready."

"*Nice one,*" Stephanie said under her breath as the farmer moved down the bar and sat closer to them. She could imagine the state of both men in an hour or two's time, after performing one-upmanship with several more rounds of drinks.

Rod ignored her comment, paying for the drinks and turning his attention to their companion. "Seems quiet," he said to the farmer. "Here. For the time of year," he added.

Rollason took a long gulp of his fresh pint. "Welsh Tourist Board," he said as if that explained everything. "Still, the cottages help, as the farm don't pay these days."

Stephanie thought Rod must have been thinking about the un-populated-looking caravan park and the empty seats in the pub, not the farmer's holiday lets. "Well, it's a lovely place, Mr Rollason," she stated. "Very quiet. I like that." She added, "We're hoping to do some walking, forget about the car for a bit."

"Ted's the name. Yes. You've got some good walking hereabouts, if you've a mind." Just then, his attention was caught by a rough-looking figure of a man who was leaving the pub, having put his head around the door and decided against entering. He snorted into his drink. Stephanie followed his glance and recognized the man passing along outside one of the windows.

"Oh, that old man." She turned to face Mr Rollason. "Your wife told us a bit about him this afternoon. The one who lives at the top of the cliff?"

"Ay, that was 'im." He drained the rest of his pint, keeping whatever thoughts he had to himself for the time being. "I'll take another one in there, Beth, if you please."

Rod sipped his brandy. "His wife drowned, we gather, and it's sent him a bit over the edge."

The farmer glanced sideways at their two unfinished glasses and thought better of offering to buy a round. "Some say," he said conspiratorially, leaning in Rod's direction, "that it was 'im that did it. That it weren't no accident."

"Ahh," Rod said. "The plot thickens!"

Rollason ignored his quip.

Stephanie said, "That's terrible. That's murder." She shivered, in spite of the warmth in the lounge bar. Then she thought about it a bit more. "No, they'd have had their suspicions and arrested him by now, surely?"

"They?" Rollason queried.

"The police, of course," Stephanie replied. Who on earth did he think she meant?

The farmer downed most of his pint in one go, before turning to them both. "Has a boat, he does. You might have seen it on the beach. They say he took her out in it one night and only he came back."

"But it could easily *have* been an accident—" Stephanie rationalized, but Rollason was quick to reply.

"Never found the body, see." Both she and Rod waited as he sipped the remains of his beer. She sensed he had a piece of evidence, a clincher he craved to impart, but wanted to milk the moment. Finally he said, "The tides, y'see, hereabouts. They always bring what's lost back to us." His implication was clear. Drowned bodies float back. Perhaps ones weighted down do not.

Stephanie raised her glass and allowed the dregs of the liquor to inflame her throat and chest. The shivers were on her as soon as she pictured the old man's face, his eyes. That old man, lurking up the cliff in his hut, his secrets wrapped about him like dark green kelp. She would make sure the cottage was locked up tight tonight.

Rollason carefully placed his tankard on the bar and, remembering that he was, to all intents and purposes, supposed to be an ambassador for Welsh tourism, said with a smile, "Don't mind them tales though. Gilbert's been living here quite a few years since it happened and nobody else has disappeared! Thanks again for the drink, I'll wish you goodnight."

Shortly after he left, Rod and Stephanie also started for home. They sauntered down to the sands for a quick walk before bed. The tide was a gentle caress, chuckling over pebbles before drawing back to reveal flat sand gleaming under a risen moon. Out in the bay the water was more agitated, as if tumbling over submerged rocks.

"Look out there," Rod said, pointing. Stephanie stared across the bay, but her eyes had not yet adapted fully to the darkness of the sea. There appeared to be ripples, or many circles of dimpled water, as if the sea itself was agitated. "Something's out there. Fish," he said, stopping to watch. "Swimming into the shallow water. Something big's herding them."

Stephanie could see the phenomenon now, frantic little blips on the surface, as what might have been the fins of fish riding about one another in their haste to escape some predator. Beyond them the sea was calmer, no sign of anything big, like a shark, say. "It's impossible to see exactly—"

"Quiet," Rod said. "Wait." As if not talking would mean whatever it was would come to the surface and show itself clearly. "There's something out there," he repeated in a whisper.

Why would he want to dramatize things? Stephanie asked herself. Yet the gentle, insistent lapping of the tide started to put her on edge. "What is it? A boat?" she asked. "I can't see *anything*."

Then a silver shape surfaced from the agitated black swell. It floundered. The sea decided to roughen up a bit and the rising water cut off her brief sighting. Whatever it was, the object was too large for a bird, too slim for a boat, too streamlined for flotsam.

"*Yes!*" she cried involuntarily as the moon highlighted whatever it was again. The roiling fish were racing away now, back out to sea beyond the arms of the cliffs. The moonlight was rippling on the shape, silvering it, modifying both its real colour and its true outline.

"*Quiet*," Rod insisted. He gave Stephanie an indecipherable look in the dark, and she felt someone step on her grave. Why was he trying to frighten her?

They both gazed, frozen in place by some unsettling emotion whose source eluded Stephanie. Maybe it was the stories about Gilbert and his drowned wife that had allowed vague uncertainties to invade her thoughts. Whatever the strange fancy was, she knew that Rod was experiencing a similar emotion too, though he would deny it if asked.

Moored offshore, the old man's boat bobbed as if it, too, was fearful of whatever had been chasing the fish. Stephanie allowed her concentration to lapse, hoping that a less creepy mood might intervene. Further along the beach, up the rise in the dunes were the barn-converted cottages. There were welcoming lights in some of the windows, suggesting neighbourly occupants.

"A dolphin perhaps?" Rod asked himself out loud. "Most likely."

His words drew Stephanie's attention back to the deeper water and, as a wave seemingly sloughed off a temporary skin, she glimpsed it again. This time there was a more obvious movement, almost a gesture.

"It has arms," she said. "I saw one of them waving."

"Don't be stupid," Rod said. There was not simply disapproval in the sound of his voice, but anger too. "Who on earth would swim at night, in that?" He knew plenty of brave or foolhardy friends who would, but was not going to admit it to Steph. "Got to be a dolphin. Manoeuvring a shoal of fish."

Stephanie resumed her silent watchfulness. She must have been confused. Rod was probably correct. Nobody would swim in the surf off Nolton's beach at night, not perhaps since Gilbert's wife went missing. Not in any event; the currents might be tricky.

Stephanie kept watch intently for a few minutes more as the rollers relentlessly arched up the beach. Her eyes were beginning to ache with trying to distinguish the dolphin from the waves that intermittently allowed a peep into their troughs. Wanting desperately for it to be a dolphin. There was nothing, though, nothing more to be seen. The creature had swum back out to sea in search of that elusive shoal.

Yet, lingering in her mind's eye was that half-seen shape, and it gave her the shudders just imagining what might still be out there somewhere in the depths, if it was not a cetacean. Rightly it must be something with flippers, a shark even, or a dead boat's hull surfacing, spars waving as the sea drove it.

"Well it's gone." Rod said aggressively, as though disgruntled at not being able to make a positive identification. Stephanie slipped her arm under his and tugged gently against his resistance. They turned their backs to the sea and headed to their accommodation. He turned his head back briefly, paused, took a deep breath.

Breasting the dunes using the half-hidden steps that the old man had climbed that afternoon, both of them turned to face the bay again. The moon was a fat crescent, very bright. The extra height furnished them with little more in the way of visibility, however.

Gilbert's dinghy continued to rock to and fro, the only motion besides the restlessness of the tides.

Rod was stroking Stephanie's back, but not affectionately. Unconsciously he was urging whatever had been out in the bay to reappear. The mystery of it aggravated him. Stephanie knew he did not enjoy ambiguities. She could sense his dissatisfaction, but could do nothing about that. In any case, it was hardly worth losing much sleep over.

Except . . . the sighting had left her rather uncertain. As if she had glimpsed something that she should not have.

Gilbert swore and stomped along the beach, his waders grinding on newly deposited seashells. As he skirted the rocky inlet, he opened his flies to relieve himself. The urine gleamed bright yellow in the moonlight and hissed as the swirls and eddies took it. He swore again and spat, the wedge of phlegm phosphorescent as it hit the surf.

"Tonight. *Tonight . . . Tonight.*" He mumbled to himself as he sloshed through the shallows to where his boat was tied up. The vessel tugged on its rein, a frisky horse, anxious for the ride. He felt the vibration in the painter surge through his fingers as he untied it. That urgent, persistent pull. As if the boat knew something . . . He let the line drop into the swell, releasing his watery stallion. As the hull rode the shallows, he stepped aboard and fixed the oars.

Then he began to row, the wooden craft breasting the waves. His strength was transmitted to the timbers and, as if they were extensions of some strangely articulated arms, the oars rowed and rowed.

Tonight . . .

Beyond the cliffs, the sea swell lifted the puny craft and dropped it again, but Gilbert stood up nevertheless as he cast his fishing net overboard. "I'll give an almighty haul," he muttered to the waves. "I cut it loose once." He sat, rowed a few strokes to allow the net to drift on its floats. "I won't next time. *I won't.*" He huddled himself against the sharp and persistent breeze, hugging his waterproofs tight around him.

The sea sensed his presence and the water grew more restless. The moon brightened as luminous drifts of cloud hurried out of the way. Selenitic light shimmered on his oilskins and lit up the boat's cracked paintwork. His eyes roamed to the heavens. "*The water, like a witch's oils, burnt green, and blue, and white.*"

He waited as the boat nodded in acknowledgment of the waves. The moon's argent haloes existed for the brief life of the swell and were a second later lost and another created. Then there was the tug, the net pulling against the boat's prow. Instinctively he moved hand over hand, reeling in. The drag of the mesh was steady at first, as if what was netted was somehow comforted, embraced by the nylon lattice. But then whatever was hidden in the waves began making furious water.

"Coming to bed?" Rod's call from the small bedroom sounded muffled, sleepy.

"Mmm. In a minute." Stephanie moved the closed curtains aside and peeped out. There was the cove, glittering under the high moon.

The surf was rougher now, endless waves poised constantly, on the edge of breaking, gathering their brawn from tideless deeps. She cupped her hands to the glass to eliminate the glare of a table lamp and then she saw the rowing boat coming ashore.

She was holding her breath as she watched a hunched, black-clad, wetly luminous figure haul the dinghy out of the water. Across the thwarts of the boat a fishing net dragged, as if the ocean's hand had gripped the tangled nylon fibres and held them.

She knew who it was. He fell, slipped on seaweed or net or through old-age, and a muffled curse rang out loud in the night. He struggled to his feet, hauling himself up using the boat and it wallowed, daring him to try again as he lost his footing once more. He was acting in a panic now and began dragging on the net while still prostrate in the shallows. Quickly the motion of hand-over-hand in time with yelled words, repeated over and over:

"Tonight! Tonight!"

And some thing was dragged into the shallow water, a shape that flopped, not struggling, as if unsure whether dry land offered more safety than the sea. On the shining sand at Gilbert's feet, luminescent plaits of water . . . and this . . . ?

Stephanie pressed her face closer to the glass, fascinated and terrified at the same time. In the net . . . bilious white, flesh that might have been partly consumed by some predator. She tried to imagine it had arms, the waving arm she had seen earlier. Gilbert reached out his hand and began tenderly to untangle the wrinkles of the net. *No* . . . she mouthed the word silently. He stood and moved in front of her line of sight and bent over the shape on the beach. There was a cry, an echo of which reverberated around the cliffs. An inconsolable cry. Stephanie squeezed her eyes hard shut and, when she next opened them, the old man was trudging for the rocks and the cliff footpath that led to his house.

Once more she tried to focus on the beach. The rising shallows served to shadow whatever had been in the net. It may have been dead or half-alive. Certainly not a thrashing beast anxious to escape its doom on the shore. But there was something still in the water, not moving much. The fishing net both obscuring and trapping its quivering. A dolphin she thought. It must be.

Rod's resonant and irritated sigh dragged her away from the window. Partly that, but mostly because she was frightened her imagination might make her go down to the beach . . .

*   *   *

"No dolphins around here miss," the young man said, shaking his head. "They're all over the other side of the bay. This spot's a problem for 'em." He nodded out towards St Bride's Bay. "Too hemmed in 'ere."

Well there was one last night, Stephanie thought, still assuring herself it had been a cetacean that the old man had caught in his net.

She had risen at first light, leaving Rod flaked out still, and was taking a walk along the beach, to make certain herself that the creature had not died in the shallows. The man had been descending the coastal path and she decided to engage him in conversation. After the usual niceties, she had asked about the dolphin. She had not mentioned Gilbert and his moonlight trip into the bay.

"I don't think I've seen a dolphin round this beach, since . . ." He tailed off as the clap of wood against wood carried down from the cliff.

Stephanie jumped at the sound.

"Gilbert." The young man explained. "That'll be him, lives up there." He gestured at the cliff.

"He's a bit simple, isn't he?" she asked. She did not want to talk about Gilbert, but perhaps this was as good an opportunity as any to mention about him catching something big in his net.

"He's not right," the man agreed. "But there's reasons."

"I heard his wife drowned," Stephanie prompted.

He did not need much encouragement and was soon talking. "People say Gilbert was a fisherman for forty years. He went to the Far East to live for a time and brought a pretty wife back with him, younger than he was. Indonesian. He was well into middle age by then and a grim sort. He'd lived too long alone, some said, and the first time the village saw his new bride the talk started. The first time I clapped eyes on her was almost the last." He smiled oddly.

"I'd been away working in Tenby for the summer and when I came back to Nolton I saw her – she was a cracking girl, hope you don't mind me sayin'. It was in the beach shop over there," he pointed to the caravan park. "Chatted her up a bit I did, until Gilbert turned up. Didn't know it was his missus at the time, I just assumed she was on holiday. He let me have a piece of his mind, I can tell you. After that he kept her mostly confined to barracks like, alone with him up there."

"I've been told a story that she might have been done away with," Stephanie coaxed.

"Well there was no witnesses to what happened, not here in the dark. Nolton's a quiet place. They never found her, that's the point, I'd say."

"Yes, I heard." She continued, "Bodies turn up when they drown, but hers didn't."

The young man nodded. "Ah . . . whether it's guilt at what he done, or sadness for his loss, Gilbert's never been right since. He takes that old wreck of a dinghy out at night, searchin' for her. One of these days it'll be him that doesn't come back." He paused, thinking. "P'raps that's what he's hoping for."

Stephanie ran her hand along the gunwale of Gilbert's boat, the flaking pale blue paint raking against her fingers. The fishing net was still strewn down the beach, a coiled nylon snake. There was no body of any description in its folds.

"Gilbert's story has become a bit of a local legend, a ghost story, if you like, miss," the man remarked. "It's whispered that his dead wife swims out there in the surf, trying to get her revenge on Gilbert. And that people might see her on a moonless night." He laughed. "Maybe that's what you saw last night, miss."

Stephanie started and looked sharply at her companion. "A dolphin. It was definitely a dolphin." And it *wasn't* a moonless night, she thought to herself.

They returned to the beach that night. They had enjoyed their day walking some of the public footpaths and bridle-ways inland, and she had been pleased for once not to have the constant sound of the sea in her ears.

Rod had wanted a quick drink at the pub and straight back to the cottage, but Stephanie was in a curious mood and almost insisted they take a stroll along the strand before they return.

The moon was hidden in its entirety by a dense eiderdown of grey cloud, transforming the beach into a dark sheet and the rocks to hunched figures swirled by inky water. Stephanie scanned the little inlet, from the horizon beyond the cliffs, to the eddies near the shore, but it was so dark tonight, she imagined that the dolphin, if he came back at all, would be indistinguishable from the water.

"Are you all right?" Rod asked tentatively, stopping, taking her hands in his.

She was surprised and pleased with his attention. "Yes, why d'you ask?"

He did not reply immediately. She saw what might have been concern in his eyes.

"It's just that . . . The old man," she said. "I saw him again last night, in his boat. He'd netted a dolphin . . . I think."

"So?" Rod put his arm around her waist and they continued their stroll. "I mean, was it dead or something?"

The waves calmly washed the sand near their feet, drawing close and then back. "No, I don't know. I'd like to know for sure."

They had walked as far as Gilbert's boat and used it to sit on. The craft had been dragged farther up the beach and rested solidly in soft dry sand, but the fishing net still lay neglected, strewn between the dinghy and the shallows.

Rod looked around. "Well, I can't see anything dead lying here. When they strand on a beach they usually attract a lot of attention." He turned to his wife, cupped her chin tenderly and kissed her. "It must have escaped. Or Gilbert let it out of his net."

Stephanie nodded, but she was unable to mould her thoughts into coherent words that Rod would understand. Her feelings were ephemeral, insubstantial, as hazy as the ghostly light upon the water.

Before long the surf was riding higher and wrestling roughly with the sand. The sky was beginning to clear as a strong breeze came off the sea and the moonlight gleamed wetly on the waves. The fish were scurrying again and Stephanie hoped that the dolphin might return, to reassure her that it was still alive.

"Brrr. Winter must be coming early." Rod wrestled with himself. "Maybe we'd better—"

"*Look*," Stephanie hissed, pointing. "*What's that?*" Goosebumps travelled up her bare arms, more through a sudden fright than the chill wind.

Near the cliff-face one of the hunched black rocks was rising, moving towards them. The light from the moon threw the features into shadow, but Rod recognized its gait almost straight away.

"Gilbert. It's Gilbert."

He passed close by them, and Stephanie could swear his wild glare revealed that he was somehow aware that she had been watching him the other night. Yet, he did not acknowledge them or glance back in their direction as he circuited his boat and continued along the beach.

"Ay, difficult waters tonight!" he shouted to himself. Swinging from one hand was a bottle of some sort. Stephanie guessed he was drunk. He wove across the strand and stumbled into the shallows, ankle-deep, knee-deep. Pausing for a breath, he arched his arm and threw his bottle as far as he could. There was a distant hollow plop of sound. Then, ludicrously, he began to wade out after it.

Stephanie never thought she would be so close to a scream. She knew Rod was immune to the atmosphere. Just the old man, drunk and half-mad and mourning his wife all these years, or plagued by guilt at a terrible crime to which he was unable to confess. But there was more to it. More *she* was aware of. Not *aware* exactly, a kind of impression that remained half-acknowledged by the conscious brain, but the substance of which her deeper psyche struggled to communicate.

She realized she need not fear Gilbert. He was too feeble and shrivelled. Too old, with his scruffy oilskins, his unpleasant face with its dark wiry bristling beard. The fuzzy uneasiness that she had thought might be because of him was something else entirely. As she watched him slouching away in the shallows, she felt the boat beneath her grind on pebbles. Rod jumped up, but Stephanie was thrown backwards into the craft and her thoughts were diverted.

All around now the rising tide was sweeping relentlessly up the beach. The sea swirled, dark fingers of water weaving like snakes into the shallow gutters circling beached rocks. Rod felt water melt into his socks as it surged over his boots and he began to run for higher ground. He grabbed the tough tussocks of marram grass and hauled himself up the dunes, off the beach, and kneeling, turned to reach down for Stephanie's hand.

But she had not followed him. Puzzled, he stood up and peered left and right along the shore. Maybe she had made a run for the rocks, silly girl. He would have to wade in now to help her avoid a soaking. But he could not see her clambering onto the rocks.

"*Steph!*" There was no longer any beach to speak of, the sea had swamped nearly all of it. Sloshing inelegantly was Gilbert's boat, heading out on the bay, preceded by the drift of net draped over the prow.

Stephanie struggled to sit up, her right hand and forearm tangled in the net. The boat wobbled about and made her queasy. How *foolish*, she said to herself. Then the boat surged forward, the net tightening, the nylon cutting into her arm.

She felt the dinghy being dragged by the net. She was unable to sit up properly, so she threw herself over on to her front to try to loosen the fibres with her free hand. The boat wallowed heavily and took on some water. Pulling at the mesh awkwardly with her left hand, Stephanie wondered what was tautening the swathes of it in the deep water under the boat. The dinghy was shunting the incoming waves, bludgeoning itself against them, raising white spumes over the prow. Spray cascaded over her, soaking her blouse, chilling her skin.

The moon gleamed on the water as she grappled with the raw nylon, and overboard she saw silver filaments dapple the swell. Like little silver fish, she thought, their fins skipping to the surface.

The danger she was in did not make itself apparent until that moment. She saw the erratic movements of the silver fish and the looming presence of the cliffs at either side of the bay. The open sea was very close. She struggled frantically with the mesh, tearing at it with her lacerated free hand.

Briefly, she stopped her labours to take on reserves of air, her chest heaving in panic. Out to sea the fish were gaining ground, leaving her and the boat behind. Yet still the tangled net pulled the craft against the tide. And there now, she saw. A hump of water, breaking over . . . a shape so sinuous in the swell that it might have been made out of the ocean water itself.

Stephanie was overcome with a strange composure, as if some nymph of the sea were hypnotizing her. The dinghy was awash and might stay afloat only a few minutes longer. Her knees and lower legs were submerged in the chill brine. Time was pausing for her to ready herself, and she felt she was ready. She was calm, waiting.

Out on the flowing water was the thing she had seen before. No, not a dolphin. Nor was it Gilbert's wife, she was long gone. Wavering arms surfaced, seeming to beckon. Was this what the old man had really been fishing for? Was it from this that he sought revenge for his loss? The boat's prow dipped into a trough and did not recover. Not far away, Stephanie watched the sea creature dip too and she knew that she was next.

He had to wade in chest-deep and swim, then catch hold of the stern. He howled Stephanie's name and the word fell flat across the ice cool water. Hauling himself up, the boat's stern went down although the resistance was still firm.

"Fucking stupid old man!" Rod's shout was swallowed by the waves. He hauled on the boat. "It's me, Steph, it's *me*!" The greedy water lugged the boat as Rod lugged back. Unexpectedly, the remnants of the net untangled themselves from within the dinghy and fishtailed over the side. "Got you now . . ." He began to make headway towards the shore, turning the craft around so that he could drag it by the prow.

Stephanie rolled over and sat up. She turned to look out to sea. Gilbert's net was swirling, billowing as if it had become a jellyfish. And farther out, a silvery-black shape spread its arms and dived into the deeps.

The boat scraping on pebbles brought her back, alone, from the arms of St Bride's Bay.

* * *

She did not pretend to know what had happened. She felt sure she had heard Rod call out to her from the water. Sure it had been his hands that had righted the dinghy and saved her. But, of course, she could never be sure.

She saw Gilbert alive the next day, walking on the beach, so at least he had not drowned from his foolish wading into the sea. She walked past him, still numb from the police questions and a sleepless night. Stephanie wanted to thrash an explanation out of his senile face but thought, whatever he said, she would not have been able to piece together the facts.

All she could think was that something, some *being*, had surfaced out of the sea off Nolton Haven. A malign apparition. The old man went fishing there, married to the waves as much as he had been married to his wife. Perhaps he had drowned her, or perhaps one stormy night she had taken the boat and saw something . . . never to return.

Pondering this, the hard ball of pain in her belly intensified. She cupped her hands around her abdomen, held her breath, wondered why the sense of loss was centred there. A heavy stone of hurt, curled up inside her. An anguish that might, in the end, reach her mind and end the numbness.

Gilbert searched endlessly for an answer. Stephanie felt that she would not. Perhaps he came close enough the other night. He nearly netted whatever it was that wallowed and hissed amongst the swell of the deep sea along the beach. And Stephanie felt that if she had been in his position, and had seen what the old man knew was there, she too would set a nightly tryst with the night dark sea. Peering into the kingdom of underwater moonlight and racing surf. An insane and possibly futile pursuit for a lost love, or something that might replace it. Casting her net, trying to catch that elusive dream.

REGGIE OLIVER

The Children of Monte Rosa

REGGIE OLIVER LIVES NEAR Aldeburgh, Suffolk, with his wife, the artist and actress Joanna Dunham (who starred in, among other films, *The House that Dripped Blood*). He has been a professional playwright, actor, and theatre director since 1975.

Besides being a writer of original plays, he has translated the dramatic works of Feydeau, Maupassant and others. *Out of the Woodshed,* his biography of the author of *Cold Comfort Farm,* Stella Gibbons, was published by Bloomsbury in 1998. His other publications include three volumes of ghost stories: *The Dreams of Cardinal Vittorini, The Complete Symphonies of Adolf Hitler* and *Masques of Satan.* He has written about horror fiction for such journals as *Supernatural Tales, All Hallows, Weirdly Supernatural* and *Dark Horizons,* in which "The Children of Monte Rosa" was first published.

"I have trouble sleeping in strange houses," Oliver reveals, "and in these moments of insomnia, unfamiliar memories swarm up unbidden from the subconscious to claim my attention. On one such occasion, while staying for the first time at my stepdaughter's, I suddenly recalled a strange expatriate couple that my parents and I met while on holiday in Portugal.

"It was a brief encounter, and I do not think that they were quite as odd as the de Walters in the following story, though they may have been. The memory began to crystallize into a narrative, along with some thoughts I had been having about childlessness and the alienating effects of living away from one's native land.

"With this was blended another random childhood memory of visiting Mr Potter's Museum of Curiosities, at Bramber in Sussex, which featured glass cases full of stuffed toads playing cricket and the like. Created as an amusing Victorian diversion, it struck me as being somewhat sinister."

I T WAS MY MOTHER who first noticed Mr and Mrs de Walter as they strolled along the promenade. She had a talent for picking out unusual and interesting looking people in the passing crowd and often exercised this gift for my amusement, though mainly for my father. He was a journalist who was always going to write a novel when he could find the time.

My parents and I had been sitting in a little café on the front at Estoril where we were on holiday that year. In 1964 it was still unusual to see English people in Portugal, particularly in the north, and the couple my mother pointed out to us were so obviously English. "They're probably expatriates," she said. As I was only eleven at the time I had to have the term explained to me.

They must have been in their late sixties, though to me at the time they simply looked ancient. They were of a similar height but, while she was skeletally thin, he was flabby and shapeless in an immaculate but crumpled white linen suit. He wore a "Guards" tie – this observation supplied by my father – and a white straw Panama with a hatband in the bacon-and-egg colours of the MCC, which I, a cricket enthusiast, identified myself. A monocle on a ribbon of black watered silk hung from his neck. He had a clipped white moustache and white tufted eyebrows that stood out from the pink of his face. His cheeks were suffused with broken veins that were capable of changing the colour of his complexion with alarming rapidity.

His wife was also decked out in the regalia of antique gentility. Her garments were cream-coloured, softly graduating to yellow age at their edges. Their general formlessness seemed to date them to the flapper era of the 1920s, an impression accentuated by her shingled Eton Crop which was dyed a disconcerting shade of blue. Her most eccentric item of dress was a curious pair of long-sleeved crocheted mittens from which her withered and ringed fingers seemed to claw their way to freedom. The crochet work, executed in a pearl-coloured silky material, was elaborate but irregular, evidently the work of an amateur, making them resemble a pair of badly mended fishermen's nets.

My mother, who was immediately fascinated, was seized by an embarrassing determination that we should somehow get to know them. I have a feeling she thought they would make "good copy" for my father's long-projected novel, or a short story at least. My father and I went along with her plans, not because we approved them but because we knew that resistance was useless.

We were staying at the Grande, one of the big old Edwardian hotels on the seafront, but my mother noticed that "the ex-pats", as she was now calling them, often took a pre-dinner aperitif on the terrace of the Excelsior, a similar establishment adjacent to ours. Accordingly, one evening we went for a drink at the Excelsior, positioning ourselves at a table near to where my mother had seen the expatriates drinking.

For once, everything went according to my mother's plan. The couple arrived shortly after we had, sat down and ordered their drinks, gin and Italian vermouth, a fashionable pre-war cocktail. ("Gin and It," my mother whispered to us, "it's too perfect!") My mother, who had been an actress in her youth, was the possessor of a very audible voice, so our conversation was soon overheard.

Presently we saw that the lady was coming over to us. She seemed to hesitate momentarily, looming over us, before saying: "I couldn't help noticing that you were speaking English." Her mouth was gashed with a thin streak of dark red lipstick, of a primeval 1920s shade.

So we joined them at their table, and they introduced themselves as Hugh and Penelope de Walter. I was a well-behaved boy at that time and, being an only child, had no siblings with whom to fight or conspire, so I think I made a favourable impression. Besides, because I had either inherited or acquired by influence my mother's appetite for human oddities, I was quite happy to sit there with my *sumo d'ananas* and listen to the grown-ups.

The de Walters were, as my mother had correctly surmised, expatriates, and they had a villa at Monte Rosa, a village in the foothills above Estoril.

De Walter had been in the wine trade, hence his acquaintance with Portugal, and, on retiring in the 1950s had decided that England was "going to Hell in a handcart", what with its filthy music, its even filthier plays and the way the working classes generally "have the run of the place these days". De Walter conceded that Salazar, the then-dictator of Portugal, "might have his faults, but at least he runs a tight ship". I had no idea what this meant, but it sounded impressive, if a little forbidding.

Their life at the Villa Monte Rosa – so named because it was the grandest if not the oldest dwelling in their village – was, they told us, more serene and civilized than any they could have hoped to afford in

Worthing or Eastbourne. I wondered, though, if it were not a little lonely for them among all those foreigners, but said nothing.

I think it was after a slight lull in the conversation that the de Walters turned their attention on me. In answer to enquiries I told them where I was presently at school and for which public school I was destined. De Walter nodded his approval.

"I'm a Haileybury man myself," he said. "Are you planning to go to the 'varsity after that?"

I looked blank. My father came to my aid by informing me that "the 'varsity" meant Oxford or Cambridge. I said I hoped so without really knowing what was meant.

"Never got to the 'varsity myself," said de Walter. "I was due to go up in '15, but a certain Kaiser Bill put the kibosh on that."

The First World War was ancient history to me – a series of faded sepia snapshots of mud-filled trenches and Dreadnoughts cutting through the foggy wastes of the North Sea, a tinkle of "Tipperary" on a rickety church piano. Trying to imagine a young de Walter going to war all those years ago silenced me.

"Do you have children yourself, Mr and Mrs de Walter?" my mother asked.

There was an unpleasant little silence. My father, who was frequently embarrassed by my mother's forthrightness, passed a hand through his thinning hair, a familiar gesture of nervous exasperation. The broken veins in de Walter's face had turned it a very ugly shade of dark purple. Mrs de Walter seemed about to say something when her husband restrained her by tightly grasping one of her stick-like arms.

"No," said de Walter in a lower, firmer voice than we had hitherto heard. "We have not been blessed with that inestimable privilege." There was another pause before he added: "We couldn't, you see. War wound."

With Old World courtesy, he cut off my mother's abject apologies for raising the issue. "Please, dear lady," he said, "let us say no more on the subject." Soon we were discussing the present state of English cricket in which de Walter took a passionate interest, even if he could not quite grasp that Denis Compton was no longer saving England from the defeat at the hands of the Australians, or some people whom he called "the fuzzy-wuzzies".

My father, an enthusiast whose information was rather more up-to-date, was able to correct some of de Walter's misapprehensions, while Mrs de Walter told my mother how she had all her clothes made up and sent over to Portugal by her dressmaker in England.

Everything passed off so amicably that we found ourselves being asked to take lunch with the de Walters the following day at the Villa Monte Rosa.

The next day a taxi delivered us to a pair of rusty wrought-iron gates in the pleasantly unspoilt hill village of Monte Rosa. The gates were situated in a high stone wall that surrounded what looked like extensive grounds; a drive from the gates curved into the leafy obscurity of palm and pine trees, and other overgrown vegetation.

We were about to push open the gate when down the drive came a wiry middle-aged woman in overalls. Her head was tied up in a bandanna and she had a narrow, deeply lined face, the colour and consistency of an old pigskin wallet. Silently she shook our hands with an attempt at a smile on her face, then gestured us to follow her up the drive.

The grounds were not well kept, if they were kept at all, but we saw enough of them to guess that they had once been laid out and planted on a lavish scale. Once or twice through some dense and abandoned screen of leaf I caught a glimpse of a lichened piece of classical statuary on a plinth. Then we turned a corner and had our first sight of the Villa Monte Rosa.

It looked to me like a miniature palace made out of pink sugar. Both my parents were entranced by it, but, as they told me later, in slightly different ways. To my father, the ornate neo-Baroque design evoked a vanished world of elegant Edwardian hedonism. Had it been only a little more extensive, it could have passed for a small casino. To my mother, this rose-coloured folly encroached on all sides by deep, undisciplined vegetation, was a fairy-tale abode of the Sleeping Beauty. She said it reminded her of illustrations by Edmond Dulac and Arthur Rackham in the books of her childhood.

The de Walters were there to greet us on the steps that led up to the entrance portico. Lunch, simple and elegant, was served to us on the terrace by the woman who had escorted us up the drive. She was their housekeeper and her name was Maria. The terrace was situated at the back of the villa and looked down a gentle incline towards the sea in the distance. What must once have been a magnificent view was now all but obscured by the pine trees through which flashes of azure tantalized the spectator.

Mrs de Walter informed us proudly that the Villa Monte Rosa had been built in the 1890s by a Russian Prince for his ballerina mistress. It might not have been true, but it was plausible.

The conversation did not greatly interest me. It consisted largely of a monologue on wine from de Walter, who obviously considered himself an aficionado. Though my father knew more than enough to keep up with him, he had the journalist's knack of displaying a little judicious ignorance. My mother and Mrs de Walter, who appeared to have less in common, sporadically discussed the weather and the flowers in the garden of the Villa Monte Rosa.

After lunch, Maria wheeled out a metal trolley on which a large selection of ports and unusual liqueurs were displayed. De Walter proposed a tasting to my parents and then turned to me.

"Why don't you go and explore the grounds, young feller? We won't mind. We'll hold the fort for you here, what? All boys like exploring, don't they? Eh?" This project appealed to me and was acceptable to my parents.

"Don't get lost!" said my mother.

"It's all right," said de Walter with a raucous laugh. "We'll send out search parties if you do!"

So I walked down the shallow steps of the terrace and into the gardens of the Villa Monte Rosa. After crossing a small oval lawn with a lily pond at its centre, I took a serpentine path that led down through shrubberies. Great tropical fronds stooped over me. The gravel path was riven with weeds, and more than once I tripped over a thin green limb of vegetation that had clawed its way across it in search of nourishment. I imagined myself to be an archaeologist uncovering the remains of a lost civilization.

It is often a great shock to find one's fantasy life confirmed by reality. I came down into a dell to find a structure consisting of a statue in a niche above a stone basin in the shape of a shell. It looked like the fountain at the gate of some ancient city. The statue was of a naked woman, lichened and weather-worn, holding a jar, tilted downwards, from which, water had once fallen into the basin which had been dry for a long while. The figure, I now think, was probably modelled on Ingres' *La Source*, which made it mid- to late-nineteenth century in origin. On its pedestal was carved the word DANAIDE. This meant something to me even then. I knew from the simple gobbets of Greek prose that I was beginning to study that the Danaids, because they murdered their husbands, had been condemned to fill leaky vessels for all eternity in Hades, the Land of the Dead.

I stared for a long time at this ancient conceit, turning its significance over in my mind, but coming to no conclusion, until eventually I decided to follow the path around it and travel further down the slope. After a few minutes I came to another clearing, where I received my second and more prodigious shock.

Within a little amphitheatre of box and yew, both rampant and un-pruned, was a hard floor of grassless grit in which was built out of smooth, dressed stones a low circular wall that I took to be the mouth of a well. On the wall sat a pale, fair-haired boy of about my age. He wore grey flannel shorts and a white flannel shirt, of the kind I was made to wear out of doors in the summer at my school. We stared at each other for a long while. To me he was horribly unexpected.

One reason why I spent so long looking at him was that I could not quite make out what I was seeing. He was a perfectly proportioned flesh-and-blood boy in all respects but one. He seemed smaller than he should be, not by much, but by enough to make him seem deformed in some subtle way. As he sat on the wall, his feet dangled a foot or so above the ground when they should have touched it, but he was not dwarfish. His legs were not bowed or stunted; his head was not too big for his body. Apart from the extreme pallor of his skin and hair, he was, I suppose, rather a handsome boy. I could have gone closer to him to confirm my suspicions about his size, but I did not want to.

"Hello," I said, then recollecting that the boy, his appearance notwithstanding, was almost certainly Portuguese, I said: "*Bom Dir.*"

"You're not *Portugoose*, are you?" said the boy. "You're English."

"Yes," I said. He had a voice like mine. He belonged to the middle classes. He asked me my name. I told him and he said his name was Hal.

"Hal what?" I asked.

"Just Hal."

"What are you doing here?"

"What are *you* doing here?"

I told him and then I said it was his turn to tell.

"I come here sometimes," he said.

"Do Mr and Mrs de Walter know?"

"*Of course*, they do, you ass," said Hal. "Anyway, what's it got to do with you? Mind your own beeswax!" *Mind your own beeswax*. It was a piece of slang I had heard once or twice at my school, but even there it had seemed dated, culled perhaps from a reading of *Billy Bunter* or *Stalky & Co.*

Hal asked me about my school, in particular about games. I boasted as much as I could about my distinctly average abilities and my exploits in the third eleven at cricket. He kept his eyes fixed on me, but I wondered how much he was taking in.

He said: "When I grow up I'm going to be a cricketer, like Wally Hammond."

"Who's Wally Hammond?" I asked.

"Crikey, don't you know who Wally Hammond is? You are of blockheads the most crassly ignoramus."

"Is he a cricketer?"

"Is he a cricketer? Of course he's a cricketer, you utterly *frabjous* oaf! Don't you know anything?"

As I was one of those boys who had learned by heart the names of the entire England cricket team, together with their bowling and batting averages, I took great offence at this. Later in our conversation I slipped in a reference to Geoffrey Boycott.

Hal said: "Boycott what?" I did not reply, but I felt vindicated.

It was not long after this that I began to feel that my company was no longer a pleasure to Hal. Something about his eyes was not quite right. They seemed to be darker than when I had first seen them – not only the irises and pupils, but the whites had turned a greyish colour. Perhaps it was a trick of the fading light that may also account for the fact that he was beginning to look even smaller.

Suddenly he said: "Who are you anyway?"

"Who are you for that matter, and what are you doing here?" I said, taking a step towards him.

"Go away!" he shouted. "Private Property!"

The sound of his cry rang in my ears. I turned from him and ran up the path to the top of the slope. When I had reached it, I turned again and looked back. Hal was still sitting there on the lip of the old well, his heels banging against the stones. He was facing in my direction but I could not tell whether he was looking at me or not. The light, which was not quite right in that strange garden, had turned his eye sockets into empty black holes. I turned again and ran. This time I did not look back.

For some time I found that I was lost. In that dense foliage I could not tell which way was the sea and which way the Villa Monte Rosa. I remember some agonizing minutes during which I could not stop myself from going round in a circle. I kept coming back to the same small stone statue of a cat crouching on a plinth. It was perhaps the tomb of a pet, but there was no inscription. I began to panic. The cat looked as if it were about to spring. I decided that the only way of escape was to ignore the paths and move resolutely in one direction.

Surprisingly enough this worked, and in a matter of minutes I found I was walking across the little lawn towards the terrace where my parents were. I was about to set foot on the steps to the terrace when I saw Mrs de Walter at the top of them, scrutinizing me intently. She came down to meet me.

"So you've found your way back," she said. "We were beginning to wonder if you were lost.

I shook my head. She laid her thin hand lightly on my shoulder.

"Did you meet anyone on your travels?" she asked. It was a curious way of expressing herself and I was wary. "You did, didn't you?"

I nodded. It seemed the course of least resistance.

"A little boy?"

I nodded again.

"An English little boy?"

I gave her the same response. The pressure of her hand on my shoulder became so great that I imagined I could feel the bones in her fingers through my thin shirt, or was it the cords of her strange crocheted mittens? She said: "We won't mention the little English boy to anyone else, shall we? Not even our parents. This shall be our personal secret, shan't it?"

I was quite happy to agree with this suggestion, because I had a feeling that my parents would not believe me if I did tell them about Hal.

"Come!" said Mrs de Walter. "I want to show you some things which will amuse you. This way!" Her hand now pressed firmly against my left shoulder blade, she guided me anticlockwise around the villa to a part of it which I had not seen – a long low structure with tall windows abutting onto the main building.

"We call this the orangery," she said. "But it's many years since anyone grew oranges here." She took out a key and turned it in the lock of a door made from grey and wrinkled wood to which a few flakes and blisters of green paint still adhered.

"Who is Hal?" I asked Mrs De Walter.

"Come inside," she said. "There are some things here which I'm sure will amuse you."

We entered a long, dingy space feebly lit by the tall dirty windows that faced onto the garden. At the far end of the orangery was a curtain of faded green damask drawn across a dark space, and along the wall which faced the windows was ranged a series of rectangular glass cases set on legs at a height convenient to the spectator.

"These are bound to amuse you," said Mrs de Walter. "All boys like you are amused by these." Her insistence on my reaction was beginning to make me nervous.

At first I thought that the glass cases simply contained stuffed animals of the kind I had seen in museums, but when I was placed firmly in front of one I saw that this was not quite so. There were stuffed animals certainly, but they were all mice, rats and other rodents, and they had been put into human postures and settings.

The first tableau depicted the oak-panelled parlour of an old-fashioned inn. A red squirrel in an apron was halfway through a door bearing a tray of bottles, glasses and foaming tankards of ale. At a table sat four or five rats and a white mouse. Playing cards were scattered over the table and on the floor. The white mouse was looking disconsolately away towards the viewer while the rats seemed to be gloating over the piles of coin that had accumulated on their side of the table. The white mouse wore an elegant embroidered sash of primrose-coloured silk, while perching on one of the finials of his chair-back was an extravagantly plumed hat. The setting and costume accessories suggested the Carolean period. Two moles wearing spectacles and Puritan steeple hats were watching the proceedings with disapproval from a corner table. It was clear that the rats had gulled the wealthy but innocent young mouse out of his cash at cards.

The tableau looked as if it had been made in the Victorian era and had, I am sure, been designed to amuse, as Mrs de Walter kept reminding me, but there was something dusty and oppressive about the atmosphere it evoked. Perhaps it was the implied moralism of the display, a sort of rodent "Rake's Progress" that disheartened me.

In the second case the scene was set outside the inn. The two moles were now observing the action from an open first floor casement window to the right of the inn sign that bore the image of a skull and a trumpet. On the road in front of the inn, a brawl was taking place between the white mouse and one of the rats. Both were being urged on by groups of their fellow rodents, the mice being smaller obviously, but more elegantly equipped with plumed hats and rapiers swinging from their tasselled baldrics. The rats had a proletarian look about them and had leather rather than silk accoutrements.

The third tableau was set in a forest clearing where the mouse and his comrades had just ambushed the rat with whom he had been brawling in the previous scene. The mouse was plunging a rapier into the belly of the rat, which was now in its death throes. I was slightly surprised by the graphic way in which the creator of these scenes had shown the blood. It surrounded the gaping wound, which the mouse had created. There was a dark, viscous pool of the stuff on the yellow soil beneath its body, and great splashes of it on the mouse's white fur. One could just see the faces of the two moles peeping out from a dense belt of undergrowth to one side.

The final glass case depicted a courtroom, presided over by an owl judge. Other participants were all rodents of one kind or another. The white mouse, his coat still faintly stained with blood, stood in the spike-hedged dock between two burly ferret policemen. A rat in a wig was interrogating one of the moles, whose head was just visible above the wooden sides of the witness box. The entire jury was composed of rats and, as if to confirm the inevitable outcome of the trial, I noticed that a small square of black cloth already reposed upon the owl's flat head.

"I thought these would amuse you," said Mrs de Walter who was standing behind me. I started. In my absorption I had quite forgotten her presence. Amused was not the word, but I was held by a morbid fascination. These scenes with their lurid subject matter and their dusty gallows humour were redolent of long-forgotten illustrated books and savage Victorian childhoods.

"Ah! But you haven't seen behind the curtain, have you?" said Mrs de Walter with a dreadful attempt at a roguish smile. It was then that I became very much afraid. I can only account for the suddenness of my panic by the fact that uneasiness had built it up inside me over the course of the afternoon, that it had reached a critical mass and was now in danger of erupting into sheer terror. One thought dominated: I must not see behind the curtain, and yet, at the same time, I knew I could not look away.

Mrs de Walter appeared to take all this in, but she showed neither concern nor indifference to my state of mind, only a kind of intense curiosity. She bent down and looked directly into my eyes.

"I wonder if you should see this one. It might shock you." She approached the curtain and put one hand on it so that in an instant she could pull it aside. There was a pause before she asked me a question. "Are you by any chance a pious sort of a boy?"

For several seconds I simply could not grasp what she meant. Of course I understood the word "pious". It was the name of a recent Pope; monks in the Middle Ages were pious; but I had never heard it applied to a living human being, let alone myself. I said I didn't know. She smiled.

"All right," she said, "the tiniest peep, then," and she flicked aside the curtain. It was only a few seconds before she released the curtain and all was hidden again, but my impressions, though fragmentary, were all the more vivid for that.

It was a glass case like the others, but the scene within it was very different. I remember the painted background of a lurid and stormy sky, torn apart by zigzags of lightning. Against them the three crosses on a grey mound stood out strongly. I cannot say too much, but it was my impression that the three toads had still been alive when they were nailed to the wood.

I can remember nothing after that until Mrs de Walter and I found ourselves on the terrace again. I saw a table strewn with little glasses and open bottles full of strange-coloured liquids. Mr de Walter and my parents appeared to be having a lively discussion about race.

"I've knocked about the world a bit in my time," de Walter was saying, "and I've met all sorts, I can tell you. And of all the peoples I have met, the best, for all their faults, are the English. 'Fraid so. Modesty forbids and all that, but facts is facts. Next best are the Germans. Now, I know what you're going to say, and I'd agree, your bad German is a Hun of the first water – dammit, I should know! – but your good German is a gentleman. Your Frenchie is an arrogant swine; your Arab is a rogue, but at least he's an honest rogue, unlike your Turk. Don't waste your time with the Swiss: they all have the mentalities of small town stationmasters. Nobody understands the Japs, not even the Japs. But your absolute shit of hell in my experience is the Bulgarian. Scum of the earth; sodomites to a man; rape a woman soon as look at her, but not in the natural way of things if you understand me."

"Hugh!" said Mrs de Walter reproachfully, indicating my presence.

"What about the Portuguese?" said my mother quickly, in an attempt to smother any further revelations about the Bulgarians. "You must like the Portuguese. We've found them to be absolutely charming."

"Your *Portugoose* is not a bad fellow, I grant you," said de Walter rather more thoughtfully than before, "but he's a primitive. You've seen the folk around here – dark, squat little beggars, stunted by our standards. Well, there's a reason for that in my opinion. It's because they're the direct descendants of the original Iberian natives. There's been no intermingling with Aryan races, not even the Romans when they invaded, or the Moors for that matter. They're like another species. I call them the Children of the Earth."

My parents did not know how to respond to this without either compromising themselves or causing offence, so there was a silence. It was broken by de Walter's suggestion that he take us on a tour of the house.

The rooms were luxuriously furnished in an opulent Edwardian style with heavy brocades and potted palms. On side-tables of dark polished wood were ranged treasures of the kind that used to be called "curios" – ostrich eggs mounted in silver, meerschaum pipes whose bowls were shaped like mermaids or wicked bearded heads, little wild animals carved in green nephrite by Fabergé. On a side-table was a gold cigarette case of exquisite workmanship with the letter "E" emblazoned in diamonds upon it. De Walter opened the case for us. Resting in its glittering interior was a charred and withered tube of white paper that might once have been a cigarette.

"I'd blush to tell you how I got hold of this little item, or what I paid for it," he said. "This case once belonged to a very beautiful and tragic lady, the Empress Elizabeth of Austria. And that little scrap of paper was the last cigarette she ever smoked. I have the documents to prove it. She was assassinated, you know. Stabbed by an Italian anarchist in Switzerland of all places. Ghastly people, the Italians: blub over a bambino while holding a knife to your guts under the table."

The books that lined the whole of one wall of what he called his "saloon" were nearly all leather-bound and had curious titles which I did not recognize. They were not like the miscellaneous collection of classics and popular novels to be found in our house.

"Here's something that might amuse you, old man," said de Walter to my father, pulling out a gilt-tooled volume in red leather. "*Crebillon Fils*. The engravings are contemporary."

I saw my father open the book at random. The right-hand page was an engraved illustration of some sort, but he shut it too rapidly for me to see what it was.

My eye was attracted to a group of silver-framed photographs on a bureau. Several of them featured younger versions of the de Walters, which showed that they must once have been elegant if not exactly handsome. Others were of strangers, presumably relatives or friends, usually formal portraits, and of these one stood out. It was an old photograph, pre-war at a guess, of a bald man with a short nose, determined mouth and a fierce stare. He looked straight out menacingly at the camera and, it would seem, at us. It was like no photograph I had ever seen before.

"Know who that is, young feller-me-lad?" De Walter asked me.

"*I* do," said my mother with evident distaste.

"Yes," said de Walter, sensitive to her reaction but unruffled. "He had a certain reputation. The Great Beast, and all that. Queer chap, but he knew a thing or two. Know what he said? Remember this, young 'un. 'Resolute imagination is the key to all successful magical working.' That's what he said. Well, Crowley had the imagination all right. Trouble was, he lacked the resolve. Drugs and other beastliness got in the way. I'm afraid he wasn't quite a gentleman, you see.

"I visited him once or twice during his last days in Hastings. He was in a bad way because the drugs had caught up with him, as they always do. Ghastly, but useful. Got some handy stuff out of him, about the *homunculus*. Ever heard of that, little man?" he said with a wink. I said I hadn't.

"It means 'little man', little man. Except he doesn't come out of a mother's tummy, he comes out of an egg. But it's a special alchemical egg." I was baffled, but I took comfort from the fact that my parents seemed to be equally puzzled. De Walter went on: "Making the egg. That's the hard part. Now, here's another. Have you heard of a *puerculus*, my boy?" And he winked again. I shook my head. "Well now, use your nous. *Puer* in Latin means—?"

"Boy."

"Good. Right ho, then. So if *homunculus* means little man, then *puerculus* means—"

"Hugh, dear, hadn't we better be getting on?" said Mrs de Walter.

"Ha! Yes! Call to order from the lady wife!" De Walter led us out of the room and down a whitewashed corridor towards a stout ironbound oak door with a Gothic arch to it quite unlike the others in the house.

"Now then," said de Walter, putting his hand on a great black key that protruded from the door's lock, "my grand finale. The wine cellars! This way, boys and girls!"

My mother, who had become increasingly nervous throughout the trip, suddenly burst into a stream of agitated speech: "No really, that's awfully kind of you, but we must be on our way. Do forgive us. It's been really delightful, but there's a bus from the village in ten minutes – I consulted the man, you see – which we will just be able to catch. Thank you so much, but—"

"Enough, dear lady, enough!" said de Walter. He seemed more amused than offended, though even then I recognized the amusement of the bully who has successfully humiliated his victim.

When we were safely on the bus, among a troupe of uniformed schoolchildren and three black-clad old women who were carrying cages of hens into Estoril, my mother said: "Never again!"

My father, whose courteous soul, I thought, might have been offended by our hastily-contrived departure, said nothing. I think he even nodded slightly.

*   *   *

One Sunday morning, a year or so after our holiday in Portugal, my parents and I were sitting over breakfast in the kitchen. Sunday papers were, as usual, spread everywhere.

One of my father's indulgences, excused on the grounds of professional interest, was to take a large number of the Sunday papers, including the less "quality" ones, like *The People* and the *News of the World*. I noticed that my father always picked up the latter first and often read it with such avid attention that my mother had to address him several times before he would comply with a simple request, like passing the butter. I had no interest in newspapers at that time and frequently, with my mother's permission, took a book to the breakfast table.

On this occasion I happened to notice my father turn a page of the *News of the World* and give a sudden start. My mother asked if anything was the matter. "I'll tell you later," he said and left the kitchen, taking the paper with him.

When, later that morning, I found the *News of the World* abandoned in the sitting room, I noticed that the centre pages were missing. However, my father had failed to observe that among the exciting list of contents to be found on the front page were the words: HORROR AT THE VILLA MONTE ROSA.

I forget how I managed to get hold of another copy of that paper, but I did that day, and I made sure that my parents did not know about it. These little discretions and courtesies were part of the fabric of our life together.

Across the centre page spread was sprawled the familiar headline: HORROR AT THE VILLA MONTE ROSA.

Much of the space was occupied by a large but fuzzy photograph, probably taken with a long lens from a nearby vantage point, of three people being escorted down the drive of the villa by several Portuguese policemen. Two of them I could clearly make out. They were Mr and Mrs de Walter, their expressions stony and sullen. The third, a woman in an overall, had bowed her head and was covering her face with both hands. I guessed this to be their housekeeper, Maria, an assumption that was confirmed by the text.

The article itself was short on detail, but long on words such as "horror", "gruesome", "grisly" and "sinister". The few clear facts that I could ascertain were as follows. Over the course of about eight or nine years a number of boys, all Portuguese, aged between ten and twelve had disappeared from the Monte Rosa district.

The last boy to vanish, from the village of Monte Rosa itself, had been seen on the day of his disappearance in the company of the de

Walters' housekeeper, Maria. A police search of the Villa Monte Rosa and its grounds resulted in the discovery not only of the boy's corpse "hideously mutilated", according to the article, but the remains of over a dozen other children. Most of these had been found "at the bottom of a disused well in the grounds".

The de Walters, said the article, had "been unable to throw any light on these horrific discoveries", but were still helping the authorities with their investigations.

Some weeks later I confessed to my mother that I had read the article. Her only comment was that I had had a lucky escape, but I am not sure if she was right. The de Walters would not have touched me, and Hal, whom I had met by the well, had not been one of the boys who were killed because they were all Portuguese. Hal, you see, had been English like me and not a *Portugoose*.

I am writing this now because I have been told to, by my wife and the others. Not that I have any complaint against her. We have been married for over twenty years. We have no children; that inestimable privilege had been denied us, and adoption would have been impossible. I could not have taken an alien being into my house. But we have plenty of occupation, my wife and I. We are great collectors; in fact, I am a dealer in antiques and am recognized as something of an expert on Lalique glass.

One afternoon, about three months ago – I think it was three months, it may have been two, or perhaps even less – we were in Bath. Naturally, we did our rounds of the antique shops. There is a little place in Circus Mews, not far from the Royal Crescent, which we often visit, rather shabbier than the rest; at least not tarted-up in some awful way. I won't say we pick up bargains there because the owner knows his stuff, but he has a way of discovering rare and unusual items that I find enviable.

It was a bright summer day, and shafts of sunlight were penetrating the windows of his normally rather gloomy establishment. That is how I believe I had a sense of what was ahead of me even before we opened the door to the shop.

As soon as I was inside, I saw it.

It was one of Mrs de Walter's glass cases of stuffed animals, the second one of the series I had called in my mind "The Rodent's Rake's Progress", and it was exactly as I had remembered it. In fact, it surprised me that it did not seem smaller to me, now that I was myself older and larger.

The scene, as you remember, is set outside the inn with the sign of the Skull and Trumpet. There were the brawling mice and rats in the foreground, and – yes! – the Puritan moles in steeple hats are peering out of a diamond-leaded casement on the first floor to the right of the inn sign. There are windows to the left, but these are not open. And yet – this is something I cannot remember seeing before – there is something behind those windows, and it is not another rodent.

It is the pale head-and-shoulders of a boy in a white flannel shirt, a boy no more than six inches high. I cannot see him too clearly through the little leaded panes of glass, but I think I know him.

I swear that the head moved and turned its black eyes upon me.

They tell me of course this is rubbish, and I want to believe them.

NEIL GAIMAN

The Witch's Headstone

NEIL GAIMAN WAS BORN in Portchester, England, and he now makes his home in America, in a big dark house of uncertain location where he grows exotic pumpkins and accumulates computers and cats.

He is one of the most acclaimed comics writers of his generation, most notably for his epic World Fantasy Award-winning *Sandman* series (collected into various volumes) and his numerous graphic novel collaborations with artist Dave McKean (*Violent Cases*, *Black Orchid*, *Signal to Noise*, *Mr Punch*, *The Day I Swapped My Dad for Two Goldfish* and *The Wolves in the Walls*).

He is the author of such bestselling novels as *Good Omens* (with Terry Pratchett), *Neverwhere*, *Stardust*, *American Gods*, *Coraline*, *Anansi Boys*, *Odd and the Frost Giants*, *Interworld* (with Michael Reaves) and *The Graveyard Book*.

Angels & Visitations: A Miscellany is a collection of his short fiction that won the International Horror Guild Award, despite not having any horror in it. Or hardly any. It was followed by *Smoke and Mirrors*, *Adventures in the Dream Trade*, *Fragile Things* and *M is for Magic*.

He created the BBC mini-series *Neverwhere* (with Lenny Henry) and scripted the English-language version of *Princess Mononoke*, an episode of *Babylon 5* ("Day of the Dead"), Dave McKean's *MirrorMask* and Robert Zemeckis' 3-D epic *Beowulf* (with Roger Avary). Mathhew Vaughn's movie *Stardust* and Henry Selick's *Coraline* are adapted from his work.

Prince of Stories: The Many Worlds of Neil Gaiman by Hank Wagner, Christopher Golden and Stephen R. Bissette was published in 2008.

"I owe this story's existence to my daughter Maddy," explains Gaiman. "We were on holiday. I don't do holidays well, so I started to write a short story. I was about a page into it and decided it wasn't working and to abandon it and do something else when Maddy sat down on the deck chair next to me and asked what I was doing.

"So I read her what I'd written, and she asked what happened next. I had no choice, and carried on writing. Which means I also owe her *The Graveyard Book*, of which this story turns out to be chapter four . . ."

T HERE WAS A WITCH BURIED at the edge of the graveyard, it was common knowledge. Bod had been told to keep away from that corner of the world by Mrs Owens as far back as he could remember.

"Why?" he asked.

"T'aint healthy for a living body," said Mrs Owens. "There's damp down that end of things. It's practically a marsh. You'll catch your death."

Mr Owens himself was more evasive and less imaginative. "It's not a good place," was all he said.

The graveyard proper ended at the edge of the hill, beneath the old apple tree, with a fence of rust-brown iron railings, each topped with a small, rusting spear-head, but there was a wasteland beyond that, a mass of nettles and weeds, of brambles and autumnal rubbish, and Bod, who was a good boy, on the whole, and obedient, did not push between the railings, but he went down there and looked through. He knew he wasn't being told the whole story, and it irritated him.

Bod went back up the hill, to the abandoned church in the middle of the graveyard, and he waited until it got dark. As twilight edged from grey to purple there was a noise in the spire, like a fluttering of heavy velvet, and Silas left his resting-place in the belfry and clambered headfirst down the spire.

"What's in the far corner of the graveyard," asked Bod. "Past Harrison Westwood, Baker of this Parish, and his wives Marion and Joan?"

"Why do you ask?" said his guardian, brushing the dust from his black suit with ivory fingers.

Bod shrugged. "Just wondered."

"It's unconsecrated ground," said Silas. "Do you know what that means?"

"Not really," said Bod.

Silas walked across the path without disturbing a fallen leaf, and sat down on the stone bench, beside Bod. "There are those," he said, in his silken voice, "who believe that all land is sacred. That it is sacred before we come to it, and sacred after. But here, in your land, they bless the churches and the ground they set aside to bury people in, to make it holy. But they leave land unconsecrated beside the sacred ground, Potters Fields to bury the criminals and the suicides or those who were not of the faith."

"So the people buried in the ground on the other side of the fence are bad people?"

Silas raised one perfect eyebrow. "Mm? Oh, not at all. Let's see, it's been a while since I've been down that way. But I don't remember anyone particularly evil. Remember, in days gone by you could be hanged for stealing a shilling. And there are always people who find their lives have become so unsupportable they believe the best thing they could do would be to hasten their transition to another plane of existence."

"They kill themselves, you mean?" said Bod. He was about eight years old, wide-eyed and inquisitive, and he was not stupid.

"Indeed."

"Does it work? Are they happier dead?"

Silas grinned so wide and sudden that he showed his fangs. "Sometimes. Mostly, no. It's like the people who believe they'll be happy if they go and live somewhere else, but who learn it doesn't work that way. Wherever you go, you take yourself with you. If you see what I mean."

"Sort of," said Bod.

Silas reached down and ruffled the boy's hair.

Bod said, "What about the witch?"

"Yes. Exactly," said Silas. "Suicides, criminals and witches. Those who died unshriven." He stood up, a midnight shadow in the twilight. "All this talking," he said, "and I have not even had my breakfast. While you will be late for lessons." In the twilight of the graveyard there was a silent implosion, a flutter of velvet darkness, and Silas was gone.

The moon had begun to rise by the time Bod reached Mr Pennyworth's mausoleum, and Thomes Pennyworth (HERE HE LYES IN THE CERTAINTY OF THE MOFT GLORIOUS REFURRECTION) was already waiting, and was not in the best of moods.

"You are late," he said.

"Sorry, Mr Pennyworth."

Pennyworth tutted. The previous week Mr Pennyworth had been teaching Bod about Elements and Humours, and Bod had kept forgetting which was which. He was expecting a test but instead Mr Pennyworth said, "I think it is time to spend a few days on practical matters. Time is passing, after all."

"Is it?" asked Bod.

"I am afraid so, young Master Owens. Now, how is your Fading?"

Bod had hoped he would not be asked that question.

"It's all right," he said. "I mean. You know."

"No, Master Owens. I do not know. Why do you not demonstrate for me?"

Bod's heart sank. He took a deep breath, and did his best, squinching up his eyes and trying to fade away.

Mr Pennyworth was not impressed.

"Pah. That's not the kind of thing. Not the kind of thing at all. Slipping and fading, boy, the way of the dead. Slip through shadows. Fade from awareness. Try again."

Bod tried harder.

"You're as plain as the nose on your face," said Mr Pennyworth. "And your nose is remarkably obvious. As is the rest of your face, young man. As are you. For the sake of all that is holy, empty your mind. Now. You are an empty alleyway. You are a vacant doorway. You are nothing. Eyes will not see you. Minds will not hold you. Where you are is nothing and nobody."

Bod tried again. He closed his eyes and imagined himself fading into the stained stonework of the mausoleum wall, becoming a shadow on the night and nothing more. He sneezed.

"Dreadful," said Mr Pennyworth, with a sigh. "Quite dreadful. I believe I shall have a word with your guardian about this." He shook his head. "So. The humours. List them."

"Um. Sanguine. Choleric. Phlegmatic. And the other one. Um, Melancholic, I think."

And so it went, until it was time for Grammar and Composition with Miss Letitia Borrows, Spinster of this Parish (WHO DID NO HARM TO NO MAN ALL THE DAIS OF HER LIFE. READER, CAN YOU SAY LYKEWISE?). Bod liked Miss Borrows, and the cosiness of her little crypt, and that she could all-too-easily be led off the subject.

"They say there's a witch in uncons– unconsecrated ground," he said.

"Yes, dear. But you don't want to go over there."

"Why not?"

Miss Borrows smiled the guileless smile of the dead. "They aren't our sort of people," she said.

"But it *is* the graveyard, isn't it? I mean, I'm allowed to go there if I want to?"

"That," said Miss Borrows, "would not be advisable."

Bod was obedient, but curious, and so, when lessons were done for the night, he walked past Harrison Westwood, Baker, and family's memorial, a broken-headed angel, but did not climb down the hill to the Potters Field. Instead he walked up the side of the hill to where a picnic some thirty years before had left its mark in the shape of a large apple tree.

There were some lessons that Bod had mastered. He had eaten a bellyful of unripe apples, sour and white-pipped, from the tree some years before, and had regretted it for days, his guts cramping and painful while Mrs Owens lectured him on what not to eat. Now he waited until the apples were ripe before eating them, and never ate more than two or three a night. He had finished the last of the apples the week before, but he liked the apple tree as a place to think.

He edged up the trunk, to his favourite place in the crook of two branches, and looked down at the Potters Field below him, a brambly patch of weeds and unmown grass in the moonlight. He wondered whether the witch would be old and iron-toothed and travel in a house on chicken legs, or whether she would be thin and sharp-nosed and carry a broomstick.

And then he was hungry. He wished he had not devoured all the apples on the tree. That he had left just one . . .

He glanced up, and thought he saw something. He looked once, looked twice to be certain. An apple, red and ripe

Bod prided himself on his tree-climbing skills. He swung himself up, branch by branch, and imagined he was Silas, swarming smoothly up a sheer brick wall. The apple, the red of it almost black in the moonlight, hung just out of reach. Bod moved slowly forward along the branch, until he was just below the apple. Then he stretched up, and the tips of his fingers touched the perfect apple.

He was never to taste it.

A snap, loud as a hunter's gun, as the branch gave way beneath him.

A flash of pain woke him, sharp as ice, the colour of slow thunder, down in the weeds that summer's night.

The ground beneath him seemed relatively soft, and oddly warm. He pushed a hand down and felt something like warm fur beneath him. He had landed on the grass-pile, where the graveyard's gardener threw the cuttings from the mower, and it had broken his fall. Still, there was a pain in his chest, and his leg hurt as if he had landed on it first, and twisted it.

Bod moaned.

"Hush-a-you-hush-a-boy," said a voice from behind him. "Where did you come from? Dropping like a thunderstone. What way is that to carry on?"

"I was in the apple tree," said Bod.

"Ah. Let me see your leg. Broken like the tree's limb, I'll be bound." Cool fingers prodded his left leg. "Not broken. Twisted, yes, sprained perhaps. You have the Devil's own luck, boy, falling into the compost. 'Tain't the end of the world."

"Oh, good," said Bod. "Hurts, though."

He turned his head, looked up and behind him. She was older than him, but not a grown-up, and she looked neither friendly nor unfriendly. Wary, mostly. She had a face that was intelligent and not even a little bit beautiful.

"I'm Bod," he said.

"The live boy?" she asked.

Bod nodded.

"I thought you must be," she said. "We've heard of you, even over here, in the Potter's Field. What do they call you?"

"Owens," he said. "Nobody Owens. Bod, for short."

"How-de-do, young Master Bod."

Bod looked her up and down. She wore a plain white shift. Her hair was mousy and long, and there was something of the goblin in her face – a sideways hint of a smile that seemed to linger, no matter what the rest of her face was doing.

"Were you a suicide?" he asked. "Did you steal a shilling?"

"Never stole nuffink," she said, "Not even a handkerchief. Anyway," she said, pertly, "the suicides is all over there, on the other side of that hawthorn, and the gallows-birds are in the blackberry-patch, both of them. One was a coiner, t'other a highwayman, or so he says, although if you ask me I doubt he was more than a common footpad and nightwalker."

"Ah," said Bod. Then, suspicion forming, tentatively, he said, "They say a witch is buried here."

She nodded. "Drownded and burnded and buried here without as much as a stone to mark the spot."

"You were drowned *and* burned?"

She settled down on the hill of grass-cuttings beside him, and held his throbbing leg with her chilly hands. "They come to my little cottage at dawn, before I'm proper awake, and drags me out onto the

Green. 'You're a witch!' they shouts, fat and fresh-scrubbed all pink in the morning, like so many pigwiggins scrubbed clean for market day. One by one they gets up beneath the sky and tells of milk gone sour and horses gone lame, and finally Mistress Jemima gets up, the fattest, pinkest, best-scrubbed of them all, and tells how as Solomon Porritt now cuts her dead and instead hangs around the washhouse like a wasp about a honeypot, and it's all my magic, says she, that made him so and the poor young man must be bespelled. So they strap me to the cucking-stool and forces it under the water of the duck pond, saying if I'm a witch I'll neither drown nor care, but if I am not a witch I'll feel it. And Mistress Jemima's father gives them each a silver groat to hold the stool down under the foul green water for a long time, to see if I'd choke on it."

"And did you?"

"Oh yes. Got a lungful of water. It done for me."

"Oh," said Bod. "Then you weren't a witch after all."

The girl fixed him with her beady ghost-eyes and smiled a lopsided smile. She still looked like a goblin, but now she looked like a pretty goblin, and Bod didn't think she would have needed magic to attract Solomon Porritt, not with a smile like that. "What nonsense. Of course I was a witch. They learned that when they untied me from the cucking-stool and stretched me on the green, nine-parts dead and all covered with duckweed and stinking pond-muck. I rolled my eyes back in my head, and I cursed each and every one of them there on the village green that morning, that none of them would ever rest easily in a grave. I was surprised at how easily it came, the cursing. Like dancing it was, when your feet pick up the steps of a new measure your ears have never heard and your head don't know, and they dance it till dawn." She stood, and twirled, and kicked, and her bare feet flashed in the moonlight. "That was how I cursed them, with my last gurgling pond-watery breath. And then I expired. They burned my body on the green until I was nothing but blackened charcoal, and they popped me in a hole in the Potter's Field without so much as a headstone to mark my name," and it was only then that she paused, and seemed, for a moment, wistful.

"Are any of them buried in the graveyard, then?" asked Bod.

"Not a one," said the girl, with a twinkle. "The Saturday after they drownded and toasted me, a carpet was delivered to Master Porringer, all the way from London Town, and it was a fine carpet. But it turned out there was more in that carpet than strong wool and good weaving, for it carried the plague in its pattern, and by Monday five of them were coughing blood, and their skins were gone as black as mine when they hauled me from the fire. A week later and it had taken most of the village, and they threw the bodies all promiscuous in a plague pit they dug outside of the town, that they filled in after."

"Was everyone in the village killed?"

She shrugged. "Everyone who watched me get drownded and burned. How's your leg now?"

"Better," he said. "Thanks."

Bod stood up, slowly, and limped down from the grass-pile. He leaned against the iron railings. "So were you always a witch?" he asked. "I mean, before you cursed them all?"

"As if it would take witchcraft," she said with a sniff, "to get Solomon Porritt mooning round my cottage."

Which, Bod thought, but did not say, was not actually an answer to the question, not at all.

"What's your name?" he asked.

"Got no headstone," she said, turning down the corners of her mouth. "Might be anybody. Mightn't I?"

"But you must have a name."

"Liza Hempstock, if you please," she said tartly. Then she said, "It's not that much to ask, is it? Something to mark my grave. I'm just down there, see? With nothing but nettles to show where I rest." And she looked so sad, just for a moment, that Bod wanted to hug her. And then it came to him, and as he squeezed between the railings of the fence. He would find Liza Hempstock a headstone, with her name upon it. He would make her smile.

He turned to wave goodbye as he began to clamber up the hill, but she was already gone.

There were broken lumps of other people's stones and statues in the graveyard, but, Bod knew, that would have been entirely the wrong sort of thing to bring to the grey-eyed witch in the Potter's Field. It was going to take more than that. He decided not to tell anyone what he was planning, on the not entirely unreasonable basis that they would have told him not to do it.

Over the next few days his mind filled with plans, each more complicated and extravagant than the last. Mr Pennyworth despaired.

"I do believe," he announced, scratching his dusty moustache, "that you are getting, if anything, worse. You are not Fading. You are *obvious*, boy. You are difficult to miss. If you came to me in company with a purple lion, a green elephant, and a scarlet unicorn astride which was the King of England in his Royal Robes, I do believe that it is you and you alone that people would stare at, dismissing the others as minor irrelevancies."

Bod simply stared at him, and said nothing. He was wondering whether there were special shops in the places where the living people gathered that sold only headstones, and if so how he could go about finding one, and Fading was the least of his problems.

He took advantage of Miss Borrow's willingness to be diverted from the subjects of grammar and composition to the subject of anything else at all to ask her about money – how exactly it worked, how one used it to get things one wanted. Bod had a number of coins he had found over the years (he had learned that the best place to find money was to go, afterwards, to wherever courting couples had used the grass of the graveyard as a place to cuddle and snuggle and kiss and roll about. He would often find metal coins on the ground, in the place where they had been) and he thought perhaps he could finally get some use from them.

"How much would a headstone be?" he asked Miss Borrows.

"In my time," she told him, "They were fifteen guineas. I do not know what they would be today. More, I imagine. Much, much more."

Bod had fifty-three pence. It would, he was quite certain, not be enough.

It had been four years, almost half a lifetime, since Bod had visited the Indigo Man's tomb. But he still remembered the way. He climbed to the top of the hill, until he was above the whole town, above even the top of the apple tree, above even the steeple of the ruined church, up where the Frobisher Vault stood like a rotten tooth. He slipped down into it, and down and down and still further down, down to the tiny stone steps cut into the centre of the hill, and those he descended until he reached the stone chamber at the base of the hill. It was dark in that tomb, dark as a deep mine, but Bod saw as the dead see and the room gave up its secrets to him.

The Sleer was coiled around the wall of the barrow. It was as he remembered it, all smoky tendrils and hate and greed. This time, however, he was not afraid of it.

Fear me, whispered the Sleer. *For I guard things precious and never-lost.*

"I don't fear you," said Bod. " Remember? And I need to take something away from here."

Nothing ever leaves, came the reply from the coiled thing in the darkness. *The knife, the brooch, the goblet. I guard them in the darkness. I wait.*

In the centre of the room was a slab of rock, and on it they lay: a stone knife, a brooch, and a goblet.

"Pardon me for asking," said Bod, "But was this your grave?"

Master sets us here on the plain to guard, buries our skulls beneath this stone, leaves us here knowing what we have to do. We guards the treasures until master comes back.

"I expect that he's forgotten all about you," pointed out Bod. "I'm sure he's been dead himself for ages."

We are the Sleer. We Guard.

Bod wondered just how long ago you had to go back before the deepest tomb inside the hill was on a plain, and he knew it must have been an extremely long time ago. He could feel the Sleer winding its waves of fear around him, like the tendrils of some carnivorous plant. He was beginning to feel cold, and slow, as if he had been bitten in the heart by some arctic viper and it was starting to pump its icy venom through his body.

He took a step forward, so he was standing against the stone slab, and he reached down and closed his fingers around the coldness of the brooch.

Hish! whispered the Sleer. *We guards that for the master.*

"He won't mind," said Bod. He took a step backward, walking toward the stone steps, avoiding the desiccated remains of people and animals on the floor.

The Sleer writhed angrily, twining around the tiny chamber like ghost-smoke. Then it slowed. *It comes back*, said the Sleer, in its tangled triple voice. *Always comes back.*

Bod went up the stone steps inside the hill as fast as he could. At one point he imagined that there was something coming after him, but when he broke out of the top, into the Frobisher vault, and he could breathe the cool dawn air, nothing moved or followed.

Bod sat in the open air on the top of the hill and held the brooch. He thought it was all black, at first, but then the sun rose, and he could see that the stone in the centre of the black metal was a swirling red. It was the size of a robin's egg, and Bod stared into the stone wondering if there were things moving in its heart, his eyes and soul deep in the crimson world. If Bod had been smaller he would have wanted to put it into his mouth.

The stone was held in place by a black metal clasp, by something that looked like claws, with something else crawling around it. The something else looked almost snake-like, but it had too many heads. Bod wondered if that was what the Sleer looked like, in the daylight.

He wandered down the hill, taking all the short-cuts he knew, through the ivy tangle that covered the Bartleby's family vault (and inside, the sound of the Bartlebies grumbling and readying for sleep) and on and over and through the railings and into the Potter's Field.

He called "Liza! Liza!" and looked around.

"Good morrow, young lummox," said Liza's voice. Bod could not see her, but there was an extra shadow beneath the Hawthorn tree, and, as he approached it, the shadow resolved itself into something pearlescent and translucent in the early-morning light. Something girl-like. Something grey-eyed. "I should be decently sleeping," she said. "What kind of carrying on is this?"

"Your headstone," he said. "I wanted to know what you want on it."

"My name," she said. "It must have my name on it, with a big E, for Elizabeth, like the old queen that died when I was born, and a big Haitch, for Hempstock. More than that I care not, for I did never master my letters."

"What about dates?" asked Bod.

"Willyum the Conker ten sixty-six," she sang, in the whisper of the dawn-wind in the hawthorn bush. "A big E if you please. And a big Haitch."

"Did you have a job?" asked Bod. "I mean, when you weren't being a witch?"

"I done laundry," said the dead girl, and then the morning sunlight flooded the wasteland, and Bod was alone.

It was nine in the morning, when all the world is sleeping. Bod was determined to stay awake. He was, after all, on a mission. He was eight years old, and the world beyond the graveyard held no terrors for him.

Clothes. He would need clothes. His usual dress, of a grey winding sheet, was, he knew, quite wrong. It was good in the graveyard, the same colour as stone and as shadows. But if he was going to dare the world beyond the graveyard walls, he would need to blend in there.

There were some clothes in the crypt beneath the ruined church, but Bod did not want to go down to the crypt, not even in daylight. While Bod was prepared to justify himself to Master and Mistress Owens, he was not about to explain himself to Silas; the very thought of those dark eyes angry, or worse still, disappointed, filled him with shame.

There was a gardener's hut at the far end of the graveyard, a small green building that smelled like motor oil, and in which the old mower sat and rusted, unused, along with an assortment of ancient garden tools. The hut had been abandoned when the last gardener had retired, before Bod was born, and the task of keeping the graveyard had been shared between the council (who sent in a man to cut the grass, once a month from April to September) and local volunteers.

A huge padlock on the door protected the contents of the hut, but Bod had long ago discovered the loose wooden board in the back. Sometimes he would go to the gardener's hut, and sit, and think, when he wanted to be by himself.

As long as he had been going to the hut there had been a brown working man's jacket hanging on the back of the door, forgotten or abandoned years before, along with a green-stained pair of gardening jeans. The jeans were much too big for him, but he rolled up the cuffs until his feet showed, then he made a belt out of brown garden-twine, and tied them around his waist. There were boots in one corner, and he tried putting them on, but they were so big and encrusted with mud and concrete that he could barely shuffle them, and if he took a step, the boots remained on the floor of the shed. He pushed the jacket out through the space in the loose board, squeezed himself out, then put it on. If he rolled up the sleeves, he decided, it worked quite well. It had big pockets, and he thrust his hands into them, and felt quite the dandy.

Bod walked down to the main gate of the graveyard, and looked out through the bars. A bus rattled past, in the street; there were cars there and noise and shops. Behind him, a cool green shade, over-grown with trees and ivy: home.

His heart pounding, Bod walked out into the world.

Abanazer Bolger had seen some odd types in his time; if you owned a shop like Abanazer's, you'd see them too. The shop, in the warren of streets in the Old Town – a little bit antique shop, a little bit junk shop, a little bit pawnbroker's (and not even Abanazer himself was entirely certain which bit was which) brought odd types and strange people, some of them wanting to buy, some of them needing to sell. Abanazer Bolger traded over the counter, buying and selling, and he did a better trade behind the counter and in the back room, accepting objects that may not have been acquired entirely honestly, and then quietly shifting them on. His business was an iceberg. Only the dusty little shop was visible on the surface. The rest of it was underneath, and that was just how Abanazer Bolger wanted it.

Abanazer Bolger had thick spectacles and a permanent expression of mild distaste, as if he had just realized that the milk in his tea had been on the turn, and he could not get the sour taste of it out of his mouth. The expression served him well when people tried to sell him things. "Honestly," he would tell them, sour-faced, "It's not really worth anything at all. I'll give you what I can, though, as it has sentimental value." You were lucky to get anything like what you thought you wanted from Abanazer Bolger.

A business like Abanazer Bolger's brought in strange people, but the boy who came in that morning was one of the strangest Abanazer could remember in a lifetime of cheating strange people out of their valuables. He looked to be about seven years old, and dressed in his grandfather's clothes. He smelled like a shed. His hair was long and shaggy, and he looked extremely grave. His hands were deep in the pockets of a dusty brown jacket, but even with the hands out of sight, Abanazer could see that something was clutched extremely tightly – protectively – in the boy's right hand.

"Excuse me," said the boy.

"Aye-aye Sonny-Jim," said Abanazer Bolger warily. *Kids*, he thought. *Either they've nicked something, or they're trying to sell their toys.* Either way, he usually said no. Buy stolen property from a kid, and next thing you knew you'd an enraged adult accusing you of having given little Johnnie or Matilda a tenner for their wedding ring. More trouble than they was worth, kids.

"I need something for a friend of mine," said the boy. "And I thought maybe you could buy something I've got."

"I don't buy stuff from kids," said Abanazer Bolger flatly.

Bod took his hand out of his pocket and put the brooch down on the grimy counter-top. Bolger glanced down at it, then he looked at it. He took an eye-piece from the counter-top and he screwed it into his eye. He removed his spectacles. He turned on a little light on the counter and examined the brooch through the eyeglass. "Snakestone?" he said, to himself, not to the boy. Then he took the eyepiece out, replaced his glasses, and fixed the boy with a sour and suspicious look.

"Where did you get this?" Abanazer Bolger asked.

Bod said, "Do you want to buy it?"

"You stole it. You've nicked this from a museum or somewhere, didn't you?"

"No," said Bod flatly. "Are you going to buy it, or shall I go and find somebody who will?"

Abanazer Bolger's sour mood changed then. Suddenly he was all affability. He smiled broadly. "I'm sorry," he said. "It's just you don't see many pieces like this. Not in a shop like this. Not outside of a museum. But I would certainly like it. Tell you what. Why don't we sit down over tea and biscuits – I've got a packet of chocolate chip cookies in the back room – and decide how much something like this is worth? Eh?"

Bod was relieved that the man was finally being friendly. "I need enough to buy a stone," he said. "A headstone for a friend of mine. Well, she's not really my friend. Just someone I know. I think she helped make my leg better, you see."

Abanazer Bolger, paying little attention to the boy's prattle, led him behind the counter, and opened the door to the storeroom, a windowless little space, every inch of which was crammed high with teetering cardboard boxes, each filled with junk. There was a safe in there, in the corner, a big old one. There was a box filled with violins, an accumulation of stuffed dead animals, chairs without seats, books and prints.

There was a small desk beside the door, and Abanazer Bolger pulled up the only chair, and sat down, letting Bod stand. Abanazer rummaged in a drawer, in which Bod could see a half-empty bottle of whisky, and pulled out an almost-finished packet of chocolate chip cookies, and he offered one to the boy; he turned on the desk light, looked at the brooch again, the swirls of red and orange in the stone, and he examined the black metal band that encircled it, suppressing a little shiver at the expression on the heads of the snake-things. "This is old," he said. "It's—" *priceless*, he thought, "—probably not really worth much, but you never know." Bod's face fell. Abanazer Bolger tried to look reassuring. "I just need to know that it's not stolen, though, before I can give you a penny. Did you take it from your mum's dresser? Nick it from a museum? You can tell me. I'll not get you into trouble. I just need to know."

Bod shook his head. He munched on his cookie.

"Then where did you get it?"

Bod said nothing.

Abanazer Bolger did not want to put down the brooch, but he pushed it across the desk to the boy. "If you can't tell me," he said, "You'd better take it back. There has to be trust on both sides, after all. Nice doing business with you. Sorry it couldn't go any further."

Bod looked worried. Then he said, "I found it in an old grave. But I can't say where." And then he stopped, because naked greed and excitement had replaced the friendliness on Abanazer Bolger's face.

"And there's more like this there?"

Bod said, "If you don't want to buy it, I'll find someone else. Thank you for the biscuit."

Bolger said, "You're in a hurry, eh? Mum and dad waiting for you, I expect?"

The boy shook his head, then wished he had nodded.

"Nobody waiting. Good." Abanazer Bolger closed his hands around the brooch. "Now, you tell me exactly where you found this. Eh?"

"I don't remember," said Bod.

"Too late for that," said Abanazer Bolger. "Suppose you have a little think for a bit about where it came from. Then, when you've thought, we'll have a little chat, and you'll tell me."

He got up, and walked out of the room, closing the door behind him. He locked it, with a large metal key.

He opened his hand, and looked at the brooch and smiled, hungrily.

There was a *ding* from the bell above the shop door, to let him know someone had entered, and he looked up, guiltily, but there was nobody there. The door was slightly ajar though, and Bolger pushed it shut, and then for good measure, he turned around the sign in the window, so it said CLOSED. He pushed the bolt shut. Didn't want any busybodies turning up today.

The autumn day had turned from sunny to grey, and a light patter of rain ran down the grubby shop window.

Abanazer Bolger picked up the telephone from the counter and pushed at the buttons with fingers that barely shook.

"Paydirt, Tom," he said. "Get over here, soon as you can."

Bod realized that he was trapped when he heard the lock turn in the door. He pulled on the door, but it held fast. He felt stupid for having been lured inside, foolish for not trusting his first impulses, to get as far away from the sour-faced man as possible. He had broken all the rules of the graveyard, and everything had gone wrong. What would Silas say? Or the Owens? He could feel himself beginning to panic, and he suppressed it, pushing the worry back down inside him. It would all be good. He knew that. Of course, he needed to get out . . .

He examined the room he was trapped in. It was little more than a storeroom with a desk in it. The only entrance was the door.

He opened the desk drawer, finding nothing but small pots of paint (used for brightening up antiques) and a paintbrush. He wondered if he would be able to throw paint in the man's face, and blind him for long enough to escape. He opened the top of a pot of paint and dipped in his finger.

"What're you doin'?" asked a voice close to his ear.

"Nothing," said Bod, screwing the top on the paint-pot, and dropping it into one of the jacket's enormous pockets.

Liza Hempstock looked at him, unimpressed. "Why are you in here?" she asked. "And who's old bag-of-lard out there?"

"It's his shop. I was trying to sell him something."

"Why?"

"None of your beeswax."

She sniffed. "Well," she said, "you should get on back to the graveyard."

"I can't. He's locked me in."

" 'Course you can. Just slip through the wall—"

He shook his head. "I can't. I can only do it at home because they gave me the freedom of the graveyard when I was a baby." He looked up at her, under the electric light. It was hard to see her properly, but Bod had spent his life talking to dead people. "Anyway, what are you doing here? What are you doing out from the grave-yard? It's daytime. And you're not like Silas. You're meant to stay in the graveyard."

She said, "There's rules for those in graveyards, but not for those as was buried in unhallowed ground. Nobody tells *me* what to do, or where to go." She glared at the door. "I don't like that man," she said. "I'm going to see what he's doing."

A flicker, and Bod was alone in the room once more. He heard a rumble of distant thunder.

In the cluttered darkness of Bolger's Antiquities, Abanazer Bolger looked up suspiciously, certain that someone was watching him, then realized he was being foolish. "The boy's locked in the room," he told himself. "The front door's locked." He was polishing the metal clasp surrounding the snakestone, as gently and as carefully as an archaeologist on a dig, taking off the black and revealing the glittering silver beneath it.

He was beginning to regret calling Tom Hustings over, although Hustings was big and good for scaring people. He was also beginning to regret that he was going to have to sell the brooch, when he was done. It was special. The more it glittered, under the tiny light on his counter, the more he wanted it to be his, and only his.

There was more where this came from, though. The boy would tell him. The boy would lead him to it.

The boy . . .

And then an idea struck him. He put down the brooch, reluctantly, and opened a drawer behind the counter, taking out a metal biscuit tin filled with envelopes and cards and slips of paper.

He reached in, and took out a card, only slightly larger than a business card. It was black-edged. There was no name or address printed on it, though. Only one word, hand-written in the centre in an ink that had faded to brown: JACK.

On the back of the card, in pencil, Abanazer Bolger had written instructions to himself, in his tiny, precise handwriting, as a reminder, although he would not have been likely to forget the use of the card, how to use it to summon the man Jack. No, not summon. *Invite*. You did not summon people like him.

A knocking on the outer door of the shop.

Bolger tossed the card down onto the counter, and walked over to the door, peering out into the wet afternoon.

"Hurry up," called Tom Hustings, "It's miserable out here. Dismal. I'm getting soaked."

Bolger unlocked the door and Tom Hustings pushed his way in, his raincoat and hair dripping. "What's so important that you can't talk about it over the phone, then?"

"Our fortune," said Abanazer Bolger, with his sour face. "That's what."

Hustings took off his raincoat and hung it on the back of the shop door. "What is it? Something good fell off the back of a lorry?"

"Treasure," said Abanazer Bolger. "Two kinds." He took his friend over to the counter, showed him the brooch, under the little light.

"It's old, isn't it?"

"From pagan times," said Abanazer. "Before. From Druid times. Before the Romans came. It's called a snakestone. Seen 'em in museums. I've never seen metalwork like that, or one so fine. Must have belonged to a king. The lad who found it says it come from a grave – think of a barrow filled with stuff like this."

"Might be worth doing it legit," said Hustings, thoughtfully. "Declare it as treasure trove. They have to pay us market value for it, and we could make them name it for us. The Hustings-Bolger Bequest."

"Bolger-Hustings," said Abanazer, automatically. Then he said, "There's a few people I know of, people with real money, would pay more than market value, if they could hold it as you are—" for Tom Hustings was fingering the brooch, gently, like a man stroking a kitten "—and there'd be no questions asked." He reached out his hand and, reluctantly, Tom Hustings passed him the brooch.

"You said two kinds of treasure," said Hustings. "What's t'other?"

Abanazer Bolger picked up the black-edged card, held it out for his friend's inspection. "Do you know what this is?"

His friend shook his head.

Abanazer put the card down on the counter. "There's a party is looking for another party."

"So?"

"The way I heard it," said Abanazer Bolger. "The other party is a boy."

"There's boys everywhere," said Tom Hustings. "Running all around. Getting into trouble. I can't abide them. So, there's a party looking for a particular boy?"

"This lad looks to be the right sort of age. He's dressed – well, you'll see how he's dressed. And he found this. It could be him."

"And if it is him?"

Abanazer Bolger picked up the card again, by the edge, and waved it back and forth, slowly, as if running the edge along an imaginary flame. "Here comes a candle to light you to bed . . ." he began.

". . . and here comes a chopper to chop off your head," concluded Tom Hustings, thoughtfully. "But look you. If you call the man Jack, you lose the boy. And if you lose the boy, you lose the treasure."

And the two men went back and forth on it, weighing the merits and disadvantages of reporting the boy or of collecting the treasure, which had grown in their minds to a huge underground cavern filled with precious things, and as they debated Abanazer pulled a bottle of sloe gin from beneath the counter and poured them both a generous tot, "to assist the cerebrations".

Liza was soon bored with their discussions, which went back and forth and around like a whirligig, getting nowhere, and so she went back into the storeroom, to find Bod standing in the middle of the room with his eyes tightly closed and his fists clenched and his face all screwed up as if he had a toothache, almost purple from holding his breath.

"What you a-doin' of now?" she asked, unimpressed.

He opened his eyes and relaxed. "Trying to Fade," he said.

Liza sniffed. "Try again," she said.

He did, holding his breath even longer this time.

"Stop that," she told him. "Or you'll pop."

Bod took a deep breath and then sighed. "It doesn't work," he said. "Maybe I could hit him with a rock, and just run for it." There wasn't a rock, so he picked up a coloured glass paperweight, hefted it in his hand, wondering if he could throw it hard enough to stop Abanazer Bolger in his tracks.

"There's two of them out there now," said Liza. "And if the one don't get you, t'other one will. They say they want to get you to show them where you got the brooch, and then dig up the grave and take the treasure." She did not tell him about the other discussions they were having, nor about the black-edged card. She shook her head. "Why did you do something as stupid as this anyway? You know the rules about leaving the graveyard. Just asking for trouble, it was."

Bod felt very insignificant, and very foolish. "I wanted to get you a headstone," he admitted, in a small voice. "And I thought it would cost more money. So I was going to sell him the brooch, to buy you one."

She didn't say anything.

"Are you angry?"

She shook her head. "It's the first nice thing anyone's done for me in five hundred years," she said, with a hint of a goblin smile. "Why would I be angry?" Then she said, "What do you do, when you try to fade?"

"What Mr Pennyworth told me. *I am an empty doorway, I am a vacant alley, I am nothing. Eyes will not see me, glances slip over me.* But it never works."

"It's because you're alive," said Liza, with a sniff. "There's stuff as works for us, the dead, who have to fight to be noticed at the best of times, that won't never work for you people."

She hugged herself tightly, moving her body back and forth, as if she was debating something. Then she said, "It's because of me you got into this . . . Come here, Nobody Owens."

He took a step towards her, in that tiny room, and she put her cold hand on his forehead. It felt like a wet silk scarf against his skin.

"Now," she said. "Perhaps I can do a good turn for you."

And with that, she began to mutter to herself, mumbling words that Bod could not make out. Then she said, clear and loud,

"Be hole, be dust, be dream, be wind

Be night, be dark, be wish, be mind,

Now slip, now slide, now move unseen,

Above, beneath, betwixt, between."

Something huge touched him, brushed him from head to feet, and he shivered. His hair prickled, and his skin was all goose-flesh. Something had changed. "What did you do?" he asked.

"Just gived you a helping hand," she said. "I may be dead, but I'm a dead witch, remember. And we don't forget."

"But—"

"Hush up," she said. "They're coming back."

The key rattled in the storeroom lock. "Now then chummy," said a voice Bod had not heard clearly before, "I'm sure we're all going to be great friends," and with that Tom Hustings pushed open the door. Then he stood in the doorway looking around, looking puzzled. He was a big, big man, with foxy-red hair and a bottle-red nose. "Here. Abanazer? I thought you said he was in here?"

"I did," said Bolger, from behind him.

"Well, I can't see hide nor hair of him."

Bolger's face appeared behind the ruddy man's and he peered into the room. "Hiding," he said, staring straight at where Bod was standing. "No use hiding," he announced, loudly. "I can see you there. Come on out."

The two men walked into the little room, and Bod stood stock still between them and thought of Mr Pennyworth's lessons. He did not react, he did not move. He let the men's glances slide from him without seeing him.

"You're going to wish you'd come out when I called," said Bolger, and he shut the door. "Right," he said to Tom Hustings. "You block the door, so he can't get past." And with that he walked around the room, peering behind things, and bending, awkwardly, to look beneath the desk. He walked straight past Bod and opened the cupboard. "Now I see you!" he shouted. "Come out!"

Liza giggled.

"What was that?" asked Tom Hustings, spinning round.

"I didn't hear nothing," said Abanazer Bolger.

Liza giggled again. Then she put her lips together and blew, making a noise that began as a whistling, and then sounded like a distant wind. The electric lights in the little room flickered and buzzed. Then they went out.

"Bloody fuses," said Abanazer Bolger. "Come on. This is a waste of time."

The key clicked in the lock, and Liza and Bod were left alone in the room.

"He's got away," said Abanazer Bolger. Bod could hear him now, through the door. "Room like that. There wasn't anywhere he could have been hiding. We'd've seen him if he was."

"The man Jack won't like that."

"Who's going to tell him?"

A pause.

"Here. Tom Hustings. Where's the brooch gone?"

"Mm? That? Here. I was keeping it safe."

"Keeping it safe? In your pocket? Funny place to be keeping it safe, if you ask me. More like you were planning to make off with it – like you was planning to keep my brooch for your own."

"Your brooch, Abanazer? *Your* brooch? Our brooch, you mean."

"Ours, indeed. I don't remember you being here, when I got it from that boy."

"That boy that you couldn't even keep safe for the man Jack, you mean? Can you imagine what he'll do, when he finds *you* had the boy he was looking for, and *you* let him go?"

"Probably not the same boy. Lots of boys in the world, what're the odds it was the one he was looking for? Out the back as soon as my back was turned, I'll bet." And then Abanazer Bolger said, in a high, wheedling voice, "Don't you worry about the man Jack, Tom Hustings. I'm sure that it was a different boy. My old mind playing tricks. And we're almost out of sloe gin – how would you fancy a good Scotch? I've whisky in the back room. You just wait here a moment."

The storeroom door was unlocked, and Abanazer entered, holding a walking stick and an electric torch, looking even more sour of face than before.

"If you're still in here," he said, in a sour mutter, "don't even think of making a run for it. I've called the police on you, that's what I've done." A rummage in a drawer produced the half-filled bottle of whisky, and then a tiny black bottle. Abanazer poured several drops from the little bottle into the larger, then he pocketed the tiny bottle. "My brooch, and mine alone," he muttered, and followed it with a barked, "Just coming, Tom!"

He glared around the dark room, staring past Bod, then he left the storeroom, carrying the whisky in front of him. He locked the door behind him.

"Here you go," came Abanazer Bolger's voice through the door. "Give us your glass then Tom. Nice drop of Scotch, put hairs on your chest. Say when."

Silence. "Cheap muck. Aren't you drinking?"

"That sloe gin's gone to my innards. Give it a minute for my stomach to settle . . ." Then, "Here – Tom! What have you done with my brooch?"

"*Your* brooch is it now? Whoa – what did you . . . you put something in my drink, you little grub!"

"What if I did? I could read on your face what you was planning, Tom Hustings. Thief."

And then there was shouting, and several crashes, and loud bangs, as if heavy items of furniture were being overturned . . .

. . . then silence.

Liza said, "Quickly now. Let's get you out of here."

"But the door's locked." He looked at her. "Is there something you can do?"

"Me? I don't have any magics will get you out of a locked room, boy."

Bod crouched, and peered out through the keyhole. It was blocked; the key sat in the keyhole. Bod thought, then he smiled, momentarily, and it lit his face like the flash of a light bulb. He pulled a crumpled sheet of newspaper from a packing case, flattened it out as best he could, then pushed it underneath the door, leaving only a corner on his side of the doorway.

"What are you playing at?" asked Liza, impatiently.

"I need something like a pencil. Only thinner . . ." he said. "Here we go." And he took a thin paintbrush from the top of the desk, and pushed the brushless end into the lock, jiggled it and pushed some more.

There was a muffled clunk as the key was pushed out, as it dropped from the lock onto the newspaper. Bod pulled the paper back under the door, now with the key sitting on it.

Liza laughed, delighted. "That's wit, young man," she said. "That's wisdom."

Bod put the key in the lock, turned it, and pushed open the storeroom door.

There were two men on the floor, in the middle of the crowded antique shop. Furniture had indeed fallen; the place was a chaos of wrecked clocks and chairs, and in the midst of it the bulk of Tom Hustings lay, fallen on the smaller figure of Abanazer Bolger. Neither of them was moving.

"Are they dead?" asked Bod.

"No such luck," said Liza.

On the floor beside the men was a brooch of glittering silver; a crimson-orange-banded stone, held in place with claws and with snake-heads, and the expression on the snake-heads was one of triumph and avarice and satisfaction.

Bod dropped the brooch into his pocket, where it sat beside the heavy glass paperweight, the paintbrush, and the little pot of paint.

"Take this too," said Liza.

Bod looked at the black-edged card with the word JACK hand-written on one side. It disturbed him. There was something familiar about it, something that stirred old memories, something dangerous. "I don't want it."

"You can't leave it here with them," said Liza. "They were going to use it to hurt you."

"I don't want it," said Bod. "It's bad. Burn it."

"No!" Liza gasped. "Don't do that. You mustn't do that."

"Then I'll give it to Silas," said Bod. And he put the little card into an envelope, so he had to touch it as little as possible, and put the envelope into the inside pocket of his old gardening jacket, beside his heart.

Two hundred miles away, the man Jack woke from his sleep, and sniffed the air. He walked downstairs.

"What is it?" asked his grandmother, stirring the contents of a big iron pot on the stove. "What's got into you now?"

"I don't know," he said. "Something's happening. Something . . . interesting." And then he licked his lips. "Smells tasty," he said. "Very tasty."

Lightning illuminated the cobbled street.

Bod hurried through the rain through the old town, always heading up the hill toward the graveyard. The grey day had become an early night while he was inside the storeroom, and it came as no surprise to him when a familiar shadow swirled beneath the street lamps. Bod hesitated, and a flutter of night-black velvet resolved itself into a man-shape.

Silas stood in front of him, arms folded. He strode forward, impatiently.

"Well?" he said.

Bod said, "I'm sorry, Silas."

"I'm disappointed in you, Bod," Silas said, and he shook his head. "I've been looking for you since I woke. You have the smell of trouble all around you. And you know you're not allowed to go out here, into the living world."

"I know. I'm sorry." There was rain on the boy's face, running down like tears.

"First of all, we need to get you back to safety." Silas reached down, and enfolded the living child inside his cloak, and Bod felt the ground fall away beneath him.

"Silas," he said.

Silas did not answer.

"I was a bit scared," he said. "But I knew you'd come and get me if it got too bad. And Liza was there. She helped a lot."

"Liza?" Silas's voice was sharp.

"The witch. From the Potter's Field."

"And you say she helped you?"

"Yes. She especially helped me with my Fading. I think I can do it now."

Silas grunted. "You can tell me all about it when we're home." And Bod was quiet until they landed beside the church. They went inside, into the empty hall, as the rain redoubled, splashing up from the puddles that covered the ground.

Bod produced the envelope containing the black-edged card. "Um," he said. "I thought you should have this. Well, Liza did, really."

Silas looked at it. Then he opened it, removed the card, stared at it, turned it over, and read Abanazer Bolger's pencilled note to himself, in tiny handwriting, explaining the precise manner of use of the card.

"Tell me everything," he said.

Bod told him everything he could remember about the day. And at the end, Silas shook his head, slowly, thoughtfully.

"Am I in trouble?" asked Bod.

"Nobody Owens," said Silas. " You are indeed in trouble. However, I believe I shall leave it to your foster-parents to administer whatever discipline and reproach they believe to be needed. In the meantime, I need to deal with this."

The black-edged card vanished inside the velvet cloak, and then, in the manner of his kind, Silas was gone.

Bod pulled the jacket up over his head, and clambered up the slippery paths to the top of the hill, to the Frobisher vault, and then he went down, and down, and still further down.

He dropped the brooch beside the goblet and the knife.

"Here you go," he said. "All polished up. Looking pretty."

It comes back, said the Sleer, with satisfaction in its smoke-tendril voice. *It always comes back.*

The night had been long, but it was almost dawn.

Bod was walking, sleepily and a little gingerly, past the final resting place of Harrison Westwood, Baker of this Parish, and his wives Marion and Joan, to the Potter's Field. Mr and Mrs Owens had died several hundred years before it had been decided that beating children was wrong, and Mr Owens had, regretfully, that night, done what he saw as his duty, and Bod's bottom stung like anything. Still, the look of worry on Mrs Owens' face had hurt Bod worse than any beating could have done.

He reached the iron railings that bounded the Potter's Field, and slipped between them.

"Hullo?" he called. There was no answer. Not even an extra shadow in the hawthorn bush. "I hope I didn't get you into trouble, too," he said.

Nothing.

He had replaced the jeans in the gardener's hut – he was more comfortable in just his grey winding sheet – but he had kept the jacket. He liked having the pockets.

When he had gone to the shed to return the jeans, he had taken a small hand-scythe from the wall where it hung, and with it he attacked the nettle-patch in the potter's field, sending the nettles flying, slashing and gutting them till there was nothing but stinging stubble on the ground.

From his pocket he took the large glass paperweight, its insides a multitude of bright colours, along with the paint pot, and the paintbrush.

He dipped the brush into the paint and carefully painted, in brown paint, on the surface of the paperweight, the letters

E H

and beneath them he wrote

WE DON'T FORGET

It was almost daylight. Bedtime, soon, and it would not be wise for him to be late to bed for some time to come.

He put the paperweight down on the ground that had once been a nettle patch, placed it in the place that he estimated her head would have been, and, pausing only to look at his handiwork for a moment, he went through the railings and made his way, rather less gingerly, back up the hill.

"Not bad," said a pert voice from the Potter's Field, behind him. "Not bad at all."

But when he turned to look, there was nobody there.

JOEL KNIGHT

Calico Black, Calico Blue

JOEL KNIGHT WAS BORN in London in 1975, and started writing short fiction eighteen months ago. "Calico Black, Calico Blue" is his first published work, and he is currently compiling a collection of his short fiction.

"The idea for this story came, somewhat incongruously perhaps, while travelling past a construction site in North London," reveals the author. "A building had been semi-demolished, though it was, as I recall, possible to see into several of the remaining rooms. It was, as viewed from top-to-bottom, almost precisely half a house.

"There is, I find, something very evocative about ruins – particularly recent ones."

IT GAVE HIM A BIT of a fright when he saw it. Having had a particularly objectionable day at the office, and navigated his way up three flights of stairs due to the inactivity of the lift, it was, in all honesty, the last thing he had expected to see. It was rested against his front door at a slight angle due to the pile of the doormat: a child's doll; not one of those modern things that cry and need their nappies changing, but a china doll, the kind he always thought of as being quintessential Victoriana. It was wearing a blue calico dress and tiny shoes with tinier buckles. Above painted rosy cheeks its eyes were black and dull. He picked the thing up and held it. There was something strange about the hair: it was very fine, and more akin to the strands of a cobweb than any imitation of a child's head of hair. He brought the doll into the flat and left it on the table in the hall whilst he found pen and paper. With its legs dangling over the edge of the tabletop it did actually look remarkably realistic. He wondered to whom it belonged; obviously to a resident of the flats, or to a younger relative or visitor, as whoever had left it would had to have gained access to the building using the security code. He wrote a very brief message – CHILD'S DOLL FOUND. PLEASE CONTACT DAVID HARNECK. FLAT 12 – leaving his telephone number underneath. On his way to work the following morning, he pinned the note to the board in the entrance hall: the doll itself he had moved to the spare room.

It was a woman's voice. There was a trace of an accent that he could not place.

"You have found my doll?"

The telephone had been ringing as he entered the flat, and he stood in the hallway, slightly out of breath.

"Yes. It was outside my front door," he replied.

"Thank you so much. I have been very worried."

"That's quite alright." He began attempting to manoeuvre himself out of his jacket, whilst balancing the handset between his shoulder and cheek. He was making rather a hash of it.

"I hope she has not caused you any trouble?"

"No, no trouble at all," he replied.

"I will come up for her. I live at number nine."

With no further word he heard a faint click, and then the line was dead. He replaced the handset, and disentangled himself from the jacket, consciously leaving his shoes on. He had barely got to the kitchen to fetch himself a glass of water when the doorbell rang, once, then twice. He moved quickly into the hallway – stubbing the front of his shoe in a bump in the carpet in the process – and opened the front door. There was a woman in the hallway. She was standing a few feet back from the actual doorway at a distance that betrayed possible reticence, apprehension or over-politeness. She showed no sign of exertion, in spite of the fact that, given the amount of time elapsed since the telephone call and the doorbell sounding, she would had to have moved very quickly indeed. Her hands were neatly folded in front of her: her hair very long and dark: her skin pale, and imbued with a slight translucent quality. She was wearing an evening dress that was more than a little ill fitting. She was regarding him with very large eyes. Then she spoke:

"Mr David Harneck?"

"Yes," he replied.

"I believe you have found something of mine," she said.

That accent again: that which he had heard on the phone. He stood looking at her for a few moments, feeling a little out of sorts.

"You've come for the doll?" he said.

"For the doll, yes," she replied.

There was something slightly haughty about her manner, and yet, there was more to it than that. Regal, may have been a more adequate, if potentially over-generous description.

"Do you want to come in for a minute?" he said, instinctively.

"Thank you, no," came the response.

There was something so final about the statement that he knew there was nothing to be done by way of dissuasion.

"I have your doll here," he said. "It's in the spare room, I won't be a moment."

He left her in the doorway and went to retrieve the doll. It was, of course, exactly as he had left it – on top of the bookcase, but faced down, to afford less opportunity for it falling. When he returned to the front door with the doll in one hand he observed that she had moved hardly a muscle. Her eyes glinted when she saw the doll, and in the light from the hallway it seemed her eyes had changed colour, although of this he could not be sure. Her expression – hitherto one of utter earnestness – brightened: the ghost of a smile played across her lips.

"You are really most kind," she said. "She is such a silly thing, quite – but what is the word – strong-willed, is, I think you say."

She took the doll from him and held it, as would a child. It was an odd gesture, and one that did not exactly become a woman in her early thirties, as he presumed her to be. He chose to make light of her utterance about the doll possessing a strong will.

"She often wanders off then, does she?"

"Oh, yes," the woman replied. "She is full of mischief. I sometimes think she is not happy in our family."

To that, he had no response. The woman was obviously a little eccentric, and had carried too many traits – often endearing in a child – into her adult life that were best left behind or outgrown.

"You are most kind," she repeated. "Will you allow me to repay you for your kindness in some way?"

"I can assure you that's not necessary. It was nothing, really.'

"Then, perhaps," she said, "you would come to have a drink with me. I live at number nine. Not this evening, I'm afraid. I am busy this evening, for I have other guests, but shall we say tomorrow?"

He hesitated for a moment, and then something made him acquiesce.

"That would be very pleasant."

He held out his hand. She looked at it, and then turned. She still had the doll in her hand, dangling – though not limply – by her side.

"Come at eight-thirty," she said.

He watched her go, his hand still extended, feeling really rather foolish.

"What is your name?" he said.

But then there was nothing but an empty corridor.

The truth is that, throughout the afternoon of the following day, he seriously considered forgetting the whole thing. It would have appeared terribly impolite not to turn up having agreed to, but there had been something about the woman he had found a little disquieting. All that business with the doll had struck him as more than a bit peculiar: he could have quite done without it. And as for the evening dress, he assumed simply that she had been host to a soirée (she herself admitted that she was entertaining that evening.) But as he sat watching television a few hours after his encounter with her, it had occurred to him that number nine must have been one of the two flats – the other being number eight, by his reckoning – overlooked by his kitchen window. (The architecture of the apartment block was such that his flat formed an L-shape around one side of a central courtyard that only the ground floor flats had access to.) He had looked out of the kitchen window and observed that both flats – eight and nine – were in complete darkness. He thought no more about it at the time, but found it very difficult to get to sleep that night. Thoughts of the woman's skin, and its curious pellucid quality troubled him. He also thought a great deal about what would possess a woman to don an evening dress only to sit around in a darkened flat: and what manner of activity might become such a situation.

Upon leaving work he had all but made up his mind to stay in for the evening. That day was a Tuesday, and he was due to drive up to Manchester the following morning to attend a two-day conference. But something happened on the way home that made him change his mind. It was really rather strange. As he was driving down the Uxbridge Road just past the Shepherd's Bush roundabout he happened to pass an accident, or the aftermath of an accident, to be more precise. A car had mounted the pavement and ploughed straight into a lamppost. The bonnet was shaped like a concertina and steam was rising from the engine. There was a crowd of people gathered around the car, and an ambulance was approaching – its sirens flashing – from the opposite direction in which he himself was travelling. He made to pull over, and as he did so, the crowd around the car parted and he caught a glimpse of something – for he was now moving slow enough to do so – that gave him a bit of a start. It was a pair of bare feet, very pale, sticking out from the underside of the car. The soles of the feet were directly facing him as he looked, and the whole tableau reminded him of the early Renaissance painting with the battle, the fallen soldier and the skewed perspective. The crowd was milling around gesticulating, and a slightly plump ambulance man was approaching wearing a livid yellow visibility jacket.

He drove on, but found himself quite unable to forget what he had seen. It was not the first accident of its kind that he had been partial witness to: it was simply those feet. *Why had the feet been bare?* he kept asking himself. *And to whom did they belong?*

He was still thinking about it when he got home: and indeed, it was only after he had changed out of his work clothes and put on something more casual – having showered and shaved also – that he was able to occupy himself with any other thought. It was at that point that he found himself halfway out of the door, with a bottle of wine (purchased three days earlier, and unopened in the interim) in one hand and his front door key in the other.

He must have passed by the entrance to number nine countless times throughout his residence at the flats, but as he was now a visitor, it somehow afforded him a new perspective. There was no doormat, he observed, and the letterbox appeared to be slightly smaller than usual.

He rang the bell, and from very far away – almost at a distance that should have belied the size of the flat itself – he heard the sound of an electronic buzzer. He had for some reason almost expected the sound of a chime that would have befitted the stateliest of country residences – an entirely fanciful notion – and he could not help thinking that the sound the buzzer made was remarkably squalid.

After a few moments, the door opened, and the woman stood in the doorway. She was wearing a black silk shirt and very tight trousers that were almost riding breeches. Her eyelids looked very sleepy, and he noticed with some distaste that she had already been drinking. Her hair was tangled, and the colour was high in her cheeks.

"Mr David Harneck," she said.

The hallway behind her was completely dark, although he noticed that the wall to her immediate right had quite a considerable crack in it.

"David, please," he said.

"So good. I am glad you could come. Please."

She stood back and to one side a little. He entered the flat and was immediately struck with how very warm it was. He took a few steps forward and she closed the door behind him. He could smell her perfume: it was a strange smell, not entirely unpleasant, though altogether unfamiliar.

"Won't you come into the kitchen?"

He followed her into a room to the left. An overhead light was turned on: the bulb itself appeared to be of inordinately low wattage, given the circumstances.

"You've brought wine. How nice," she said. "Let me get you a glass."

"That would be nice. Thank you."

He looked around. The kitchen appeared filled with relatively modern looking fixtures and appliances. He could not help noticing, however, that there was a fairly substantial looking crack along the far wall. It occupied almost three-quarters of the length, and he thought, suddenly, of structural faults in the building, perhaps even lying dormant in his own property. Then she was there with a glass of wine in an outstretched hand.

"Thank you very much. But, well, I don't even know your name."

"My name is Kaaiija," she said.

He made an attempt to repeat the name, and she shook her head, smiling.

"Kay, ay, ay, eye, eye, jay, ay: Kaaiija," she repeated.

"That's an unusual name," he said.

"It is Estonian."

She raised the glass of wine to her lips. She was drinking red, although the bottle he had brought was white.

"Are you from Estonia?" he asked, he would have admitted, a little gormlessly. History had proven that he was fairly inept at small talk such as this.

"I am from a place called Valetada. It is an island. It is a very traditional place."

She placed particular emphasis on the word traditional, and he wondered if she was referring to some obscure idiom that was lost in translation.

"You have a hint of an accent," he said.

"So do you."

"I can assure you mine is only West London, through and through. Nothing more glamorous than that, I'm afraid."

There was something a little flirtatious in her body language. It was difficult to ascertain whether it was accountable to the drink or some other reason.

"Where is the island you are from?" he asked, somewhat awkwardly.

"You can see it on the map. It is to the west, in the Baltic Sea. Our family home is in the middle of the island."

"I expect it's quite different from the mainland?"

"It is," she said, "as it always has been. We have strong customs and traditional ways, surrounded as we are by water."

"I will profess, I am a little ignorant as to the culture and geography of Estonia," he said.

This was not a lie, but it would have been more truthful for him to have stated that he could not, in fact, distinguish his Latvias from his Lithuanias: the whole Baltic region (with the ignorance particular to many Western Europeans) he associated with cold and dark winters: a hinterland consisting of grey satellite states each one interchangeable from the next, neither Scandinavian nor Eastern European.

"Linguistically and culturally we are, I suppose, closer to the Finns, although—" she added, "—there are differences."

"I suppose things are very different since the fall of the Soviet Union?"

"Yes, though we gained independence long before that."

She raised the wine glass to her lips and took a very delicate sip, not taking her eyes off him for one moment.

"How long have you been over here?"

"It is sometimes difficult for me to remember," she said.

Her expression changed, and for one moment she looked as if plagued by some distant memory, or some occurrence from long ago in her past. Then she looked at him so directly and so intensely that he began to feel quite uncomfortable.

"Shall we go into the living room, David? Shall we?"

"Yes, by all means. I would be interested in seeing the rest of your flat."

Her eyes did not leave him for a second.

"Seeing as we are neighbours," he added.

"Come then. I will show you."

He followed her out of the kitchen into the darkened hallway.

"Will you turn the light out, as you leave?"

"Yes, of course."

He was unsure of her motives in this: was she, in her own way, attempting to create some type of atmosphere, or was it to save on electricity, pure and simple? In order to turn the light off, for some reason, he moved his wine glass into his other hand. His finger flicked the switch, and he noticed that it was slightly tacky, in the way these things get, from cooking vapours and so forth.

The hallway seemed very long. The layout of her flat was notably different from his own, and as he followed, he passed two other rooms, the doors of which were shut.

"Here is the living room," she said.

They were entering a room at the far end of the corridor, from which a pale yellow light emerged. The ceiling seemed very low in comparison to the kitchen, and there were many items of furniture carefully positioned so that, although the room was filled with chairs and tables (and not two but three settees) the impression was still one of balance and proportion.

"Very nice. It's lovely what you've done with the space here," he said.

"It is the living room. The living room is for entertaining."

At this moment, remembering the events of the previous evening – how she had said she had guests – and emboldened, perhaps, by his own nervousness and the first taste of the wine, he ventured a question.

"I remember you saying you had guests last night. Do you entertain often?"

She looked at him as if he had accused her of some small slander.

"Guests? I had no guests last night."

He could offer no rejoinder. He was aware that he had gone a little red.

"Sorry. It's just that—"

The room was very quiet: quiet enough for it to occur to him why it is a custom to have background music playing in such social situations. He could hear the faint ticking of a clock, and then, from somewhere in the flat, in one of the unexplored rooms a sudden thud as if something had fallen.

"—I thought I heard you say yesterday that you were expecting guests?" he finished.

She sat down in an armchair upholstered in purple velvet, and crossed her legs in a very languorous fashion.

"David," she said.

Her legs, he noticed, were really rather short, given her height.

"There were no guests."

He realized that now he was standing inside it, the room was a great deal smaller than he had previously thought. He moved over to the nearest item of furniture – a recliner – and sat down. Whilst placing his wine glass on the floor he couldn't help noticing that the carpet was absolutely covered in hairs: hairs from some domestic animal, one would have thought, though they reminded him – too much – of the doll's hair: the doll he had found outside his flat the previous evening.

"Do you have a pet, Kaaiija? A cat, perhaps?" he asked.

It was a potentially hazardous inquiry: one that called into question his host's domestic pride, yet a question that needed asking, he felt.

"A pet? Why do you ask?"

"I have seen a cat in the building," he lied, thinking about the noise he had heard. "I've often wondered to whom it belonged."

"I have no pets. It would seem unnecessarily cruel to keep an animal living in a flat in the city."

"I quite agree."

He raised the wine glass to his lips and took a sip. There was a very large crack in the ceiling, he noticed. It forked at one end, and the plaster had flaked around it.

"What do you do, David – for a living?" she said.

"I work in market research. Nothing very exciting."

"You are typical English man. You always put yourself down."

She was watching him over the top of her glass, not so much sitting in, as draped across the armchair. Her movements were (perhaps calculably) lithe, and he began to feel that the whole situation was a little absurd. To be frank, he was beginning to feel like the protagonist in some tawdry second-rate erotic vignette. A table light positioned to her right held much of her face in shadow. He could see, from where he was sitting, that she was wearing an amount of make-up that gave her complexion a distinctly greasy quality.

"In what area of market research do you work?" she said.

"Are you familiar with qualitative and quantitative studies?"

She shook her head.

"I work closely with groups of consumers: potential consumers. I find out what makes people buy a certain brand of soap powder, say, or toothpaste."

"Interesting," she said, very slowly. There was absolutely no way of telling from the tone of her voice whether it was a remark that had been intended as facetious.

"And how do you find this information?" she said.

"Well, people fill in surveys. They answer questions, and the results are communicated back to the client. A lot of emphasis is placed on creating brand loyalty."

Her expression betrayed no information whatsoever.

"It's not very interesting," he added. It was a somewhat adolescent thing to say, and as soon as he had said it, he regretted doing so.

"Have you always worked in market research, David?" she said.

"I used to work in advertising. I worked at a small agency, but I left because there was an awful amount of back-stabbing going on."

"Back-stabbing?" she said, her eyebrows raised.

"Not literally, of course," he said. "You know: game-playing. I found it all very oppressive, that's why I got out. There are things I miss, though."

At this point, she placed her wine glass on the tabletop and put both legs – slightly splayed – on the floor. Her face was completely in shadow.

"I knew you were an honest person, David. That is why you return my doll."

He took another drink. He was beginning to feel a little light-headed, though largely from the stuffiness of the room.

"What is it that you do yourself?" he asked.

"I have—" and here she paused, "—a small private income."

He was wishing very much that she would either lean forward or sit back. Looking at her directly was akin to viewing a lunar eclipse.

"You are an honest person," she repeated.

"As I said, it was nothing, really."

"No," she said, abruptly.

She got to her feet and took a few steps towards him. He noticed that one of the buttons on her shirt had come undone. He could see her skin underneath, and it too was marked by a curious translucence. She stood in front of him, not moving. He was completely unsure of what was about to happen. He was unsure as to whether she was about to commence with the removal of all of her clothes, or else begin screaming at the top of her voice.

"I'm sure Marguerite would like to thank you personally for your kindness," she said, in an even monotone.

He cleared his throat gently. The room really was most unpleasantly stuffy, he thought.

"Marguerite?"

"Yes. She would like to thank you personally."

"I don't believe I know any Marguerite," he said.

"Oh, but you have already met her. It is through her, that we meet, David."

"Do you mean—?" he began, but he did not finish his sentence.

She took another step towards him. There was something almost feline about her movements.

"She's waiting," she said.

He got to his feet, the wine glass in one hand.

"Shall we, David?"

"Yes," he said.

She took the wine glass from his hand and placed it on a nearby table. Then she moved towards the doorway, and although she did not actually take his hand, he nevertheless gained the impression that he was being conspicuously led. They had not, by this point, had any form of physical contact, and she was in fact closer in proximity to him now than at any other stage throughout their encounter. Again, he caught her perfume. It was an intoxicating scent, although there was a trace of something else as well. Her hair fell past her shoulders, so very black it seemed to absorb all light. She reached the doorway – he barely a foot behind her – and then turned. He jumped a little: a small sound escaped his throat. Up close, her face had quite an unpleasant aspect. He knew it was not uncommon for women to use a cosmetic concealment to cover any unsightly blemishes on the face, but it appeared that the entirety of Kaaiija's face was slathered in such a substance. Her skin looked very grey, as if she perhaps had some birthmark, or "port wine stain" that covered the majority of her features and sat uneasily with the consistency of the cosmetic. Some of the make-up had got into her hair as well at the edge of the temple. In the yellow light her eyes appeared very dark indeed, almost black.

"You may leave this light on, David," she said.

He had no intention whatsoever of touching anything.

"She waits," she said.

He followed Kaaiija into the hallway. She moved over to the doorway to the left, and from her hip pocket removed a key. In a singularly graceful movement she inserted the key into the lock and gave it a very gentle turn. He heard the small click of the latch. Kaaiija opened the door and felt for the light switch, almost as if she had little or no idea as to its location. From where he was standing he could see nothing of the room's contents.

"I know she would wish to thank you personally," she said.

She entered, and he followed.

The room was full of dolls. There were dolls seated in chairs: dolls positioned on the windowsill: a doll on all fours frozen in the act of crawling across the carpet, its head angled towards the doorway. They were all of a similar kind to the one he had discovered by his front door, yet their clothes and the colour of their hair varied. They did not appear to have been arranged in any obvious manner or formation: in fact, he had the curious sensation that the room had been a hive of activity only moments before their arrival.

"Do you see?" she said. "My perfect, adorable little people?"

"You have so many," he said.

She took a step further into the room and lifted the doll from the floor. She manoeuvred its limbs so that it lay completely flat in her hands, as would a body in a coffin.

"How long have you been collecting?" he asked.

"Oh, nothing so vulgar as collecting," she replied, sounding quite put out. "As with all beautiful things, it is more a question of them finding us, do you not agree?"

She placed the doll in a sitting position on a nearby chair.

"All the world's beautiful things, all great works: we are humbled before them. We have no choice in the matter, I'm afraid," she continued.

She gave a little titter, overtly girlish.

"So it is," she said. "They found me."

He looked about himself. There was a doll by his right foot. He moved his foot cautiously and looked at Kaaiija.

"What is it that they are made of?"

"Many of these are bisque: unglazed porcelain. See, Madeleine has wooden upper arms."

She indicated towards a doll sat at a small table with a teacup in a raised hand. It was the only example, as he could see, of doll-sized furniture in the room. All other fittings – those over which the dolls were arranged – were of normal size. The doll with the teacup was completely bald. The head appeared mottled with dull grey marks.

"Its head—"

"Yes. They are pepper marks. They are impurities found at the time of the firing. Poor thing."

He noted that the room was perceptibly colder than the rest of the flat. He moved away from the doll on the floor.

"Are many of them very old?" he said.

"Nineteenth century. They were made by the great craftsmen: Brémillon, Vrassier. Look here: a Peliebvre Bébé – see her moulded tongue and teeth?"

He did not much like the one to which she was now pointing. Its head was obviously painted as to resemble flesh colour, though it had a distinct bluish quality.

"Their faces are very expressive, aren't they?" he said, meaning quite the opposite.

"They are perfect, adorable little people," she repeated.

She stood regarding them.

"You are obviously very knowledgeable on the subject."

"Not at all," she replied. "I am no expert, simply an aficionado. Many of these have been in my family for quite some years. My father – he was a very well travelled man, although his origins were simple. On Valetada our house stood with nothing but marshland for miles in every direction."

"What line of work was he in, if you don't mind me asking?"

"He was a craftsman. A kind, good man: my father."

"Did he himself make dolls?"

"Not dolls, no."

She bent down and gently drew the doll with the moulded teeth towards her.

"See here: she is a Moulandre and Rasp from Bueurze. Again, bisque. There are so many, David."

She gestured towards the dolls seated on the chairs.

"Wax over Papier-Mâché. Vuissart and Kuennier: they created the most exquisite automated models."

He recognized, then, the doll that he had found by his doorstep. It was positioned on a chair next to another doll whose features were obscured by a small white bonnet. It was wearing the same shoes and the same blue dress, but there was an ugly maroon mark across its face that had not been there previously.

"Can I presume that some of these are automated?"

"Oh, no. Not at all."

"But – the doll—" he said. The room really was very cold indeed, and he felt the prickle of dampness in his armpits, "—it was on my doorstep."

"Like I said. She is full of mischief."

She looked at him for a few seconds without moving.

"Marguerite," she said.

She lifted the doll from the chair and held it towards him, as if indicating that he should take it. He looked at the mark on its face. It ran from the right eye down to the jaw.

"She says she is very grateful to you for helping her find her way home," Kaaiija said, with an expression of intense seriousness. "She is very grateful to you."

He did not know how to respond. In truth, he felt utterly ridiculous.

"Very grateful."

Kaaiija repositioned the doll on the chair. He heard the whisper of the dress fabric against the material on the armrest. She turned towards him, and for one moment her face was full of anguish, as if she were stricken by some deep and private pain.

"We are all so very lonely here, David. Our poor forgotten family."

"I'm very sorry to hear you say that."

"It is the same wherever we go."

She closed her eyes. When she reopened them the expression was gone, and replaced by something akin to hunger. Her eyelids narrowed and she took a step towards him.

"I wish, David, to thank you, as well."

Although he truly had no intention of doing so, there was something about her manner that made him move towards her.

"You are really very kind," she said.

He shivered. Her body was in front of him, and he went to her as if controlled by unseen hands. She put her hands on his body and then her lips were against his, inexpressibly cold. The room was full of her perfume. Their lips touched for only the briefest of moments before they parted. But what happened then was so frightening and so utterly unlike anything that he had ever experienced that he wondered if he had not simply imagined what he saw. What happened was this: as she pulled away her face shifted somehow, and in one fleeting moment he gained the impression of that which lay underneath the make-up being completely beetle-black all over. She looked at him sharply, as if she had sensed his unease.

"So kind," she said.

He took a step away from her, and sensing some obstruction on the ground, looked down to his feet.

His shoes were covered in hair: strands of cobweb-fine hair.

"David," she said.

"Forgive me, but – it's quite late," he replied, though he had in fact lost all sense of time. He was no longer sure what day it was, or if it even mattered.

"It's quite late," he repeated.

"It is late," he heard her say.

He looked at her and saw that her black eyes were glistening greedily. Something in the room moved: a doll seated on the window-sill shifted slightly, and he caught its movement in his peripheral vision. He felt, suddenly, on the edge of something utterly inexplicable. He shifted his feet: the hair sighed lightly around them.

"The dolls' hair—" he said, "—Madeleine, Marguerite – it is very realistic."

"The hair is real. It is all my own."

"But you said they were nineteenth century?"

"It is true," she replied.

He took a further step back. The hairs had amassed around his feet: a number too great to count. The eyes of the doll in the white bonnet rolled over once, the lashes very long and dark.

"Kaaiija," he said.

And then he heard it: the same noise he had heard earlier in the living room, only now the location of its source was evident. Something was moving in the room that lay to the other side of the hallway: something that moved as if taking great pains to conceal that very fact. At once, Kaaiija's expression became utterly vacant.

"My father," she said. "He is awake."

"Your father?" he said, with some alarm. "Forgive me but I thought that you lived alone?"

"Alone?" she replied. "No, not alone."

"In that case I should go. I'm sorry, I had no idea," he gasped.

She took a step towards him.

"Will you not stay, David? My father would love to meet you. I have told him so much about you."

He noticed that the area around her lips was very grey and smeary looking. He raised his fingertips to his own lips and they came away covered in some waxy white substance that had got in under the nails.

"I'm sorry," was all he could say. The thought of meeting the woman's father was not a concept that he could entertain.

"I am sure the two of you will have much to talk about," she said.

"Forgive me, Kaaiija," he replied.

She looked at him very gravely.

"It's *Kaaiija*," she said.

She laid a hand on his, and it was as if there was no movement in her at all: as if she were nothing more than a brittle shop-window dummy. He tried to release his hand from her grip, but he found that he could not. She laughed: a horrid sharp sound.

"David, you look so frightened. You don't have to look as if I were about to eat you."

He went to say her name, but then he stopped. Something was moving in the hallway behind him. It was moving very slowly, but its tread was that of something enormous: a person who may have to lower his or her head by a considerable degree in order to enter a room. He realized too, that the room was now filled with movement. The dolls were awake. The doll with the teacup in its hand was standing up from the table, its petticoat caught above its wooden knees. Its head revolved on its axis with a dull creak: a painted smile upon its lips. The doll with the ugly mark on its face – *his doll, Marguerite,* he thought irrationally – had stretched itself to its full height and was clambering down the side of the armchair in which it had been seated. He watched with mute horror as the doll wearing the white bonnet slowly raised its head and revealed to him the face that lay beneath.

He heard the doll say his name in a voice that was shrill with childlike glee, and then Kaaiija's mouth was full of laughter: her teeth like shards of glass: her face a mask of cracked porcelain. Something loomed above him, its shadow vast, and he understood, with a sudden clarity, that there would be no remains: no, no remains. Not even his pale white feet or small moulded tongue would be spared. He heard a voice utter a word in a language long dead and silent, and then the thing that called itself Kaaiija fell upon him: her eyes black and glassy: her embrace as dark as deepest winter, and from every side: small pairs of eyes watching him, unblinking.

STEVEN ERIKSON

This Rich Evil Sound

STEVEN ERIKSON IS THE PEN-NAME for Steve Lundin. Although born in Toronto, Canada, he grew up in Winnipeg. Erikson began his career as an archaeologist, and worked in this profession for eighteen years.

His first book was a collection of short stories, *A Ruin of Feathers*, published under the Lundin byline in 1991. As Erikson he has published the novels *Gardens of the Moon*, *Deadhouse Gates*, *Memories of Ice*, *House of Chains*, *Midnight Tides*, *The Bonehunters* and *Reaper's Gale* in a projected ten-book series entitled "The Malazan Book of the Fallen" from Bantam/Transworld in the UK and Tor Books in the US. He has also written a number of novellas, published by PS Publishing and Night Shade Books.

"When this story went through its workshop at Iowa, it was received the way most of my stuff was received: no one quite knew what to make of it," admits the author. "Maybe it edged a little too close to genre and made my fellow students uncomfortable. But then, most of my stuff made them uneasy, when even the sniff of genre was not to be found.

"I seem to recall that students started asking questions: 'Is it true it can get cold enough in Canada so that trees explode?' (Yes, black spruce, specifically). 'Can someone actually sleep in a tent when it's that cold?' (Yes, but it's not much fun). 'So, there were wolves, but what about polar bears?' (Sure, plenty, and then I described how the polar bears come through my home city of Winnipeg every spring – all right, I was lying, you'd have to travel about eight hundred miles due north to see something like that in Churchill, Manitoba). Lying? Afraid so, with a straight face at that.

"Anyway, some of the central threads to this story were recounted to me by an old man wintering over in Whiteshell Park. Sometimes, the best thing a writer can do is listen."

I'M NOT AN OLD MAN. Sometimes the tracks old men think along are so deep cut nobody can see where they're going, maybe not even see the tracks themselves. But then I think that maybe there are different kinds of old. People say I should've been born a hundred years ago. Does that make me old in some way? They don't mean harm when they talk like that. It's just that they don't know me. I was in love with this girl, once, back in high school. Her name was Linda, and she was pretty popular, I guess. One day in the lunchroom I got down on one knee and sang for her a love song. One of my buddies had laid a dare on me – they sat at their table laughing and cheering. It was something I wanted to do anyway. No harm in it. The guys thought it was silly, but that's all right, too.

I know people make fun of me. I just look at things different from others. Before I got big I used to get in fights. There's always guys who don't like the way you look at things. They think it makes you weaker than them, maybe, and that's what they were trying to prove by fighting me. By the time I was fifteen they left me alone. They still figured me weak in my head, probably, but my body didn't look weak, not any more.

I'm twenty now, so people have been leaving me alone for about five years. I don't mind. I like being alone. I quit school when I was sixteen, headed out into the bush. I spent the winter in northern Manitoba, nearly froze my feet off. I learned to lay trap lines from this Ojibwa Indian. He didn't know a word of English, except "nineteen seventy". I tried to teach him "nineteen eighty" because that was the year, but I don't think he ever got it. When I got back to Winnipeg I applied for and got a trapping licence and that's what I've been doing ever since, out in Whiteshell Park.

In summers the park is full of people, so I head to Grassy River where it's quieter. But in the winter the only people in the park are rangers and trappers and old people who don't like the city and stay in their cabins. I don't mind running into those people, because we usually look at things the same way, and they don't make fun of me or anything.

This winter I was working Redrock Lake and the Whiteshell River. I'd heard from one of the rangers that Charlie Clark was wintering for the first time up at his cottage on Jessica Lake, so I decided to pay him a visit. Ever since they'd retired, Charlie and his wife had been spending the summers out here. But his wife died last summer, so he was all alone. I knew he'd be glad for some company.

I use a tent, but most trappers got cabins, because the years just pull at you and pretty soon a tent or quincy's too cold. It gets hard checking the lines when all your bones ache. Charlie wasn't a trapper, but I knew he'd understand and put me up for a couple days so I could dry out and get toasty. I'm pretty tough but I don't mind some luxury when I can get it.

Getting to Jessica Lake was easy. The Whiteshell River connects most of the lakes in the park. I broke camp an hour before dawn and walked the river. Winter's the quietest season. You're the only thing moving, the only thing making any sound. You listen to your breath, to the backpack creaking in its straps, to the crunch of your snowshoes. You can sing songs to pass the time and your voice sounds beautiful. And you can think about things, taking all the time you want to, with nobody pushing you for answers. You can think as slow as you like, and the rest of the world, if it cares at all, just waits. No ticking clocks, just shadows all blue and soft and moving slower than you can see.

I reached the park highway by noon. They keep it ploughed for the cross-country skiers who come out from Winnipeg on warm week-ends and for people like Charlie Clark.

I smelled wood smoke long before I saw his cottage. There'd been a cold snap the last couple weeks. No snow, no wind, just that rich silence under a sun-dogged sky. The smoke hung in the air like it had no place to go, smelling bittersweet because it was black spruce. It's not a good wood to burn, since it goes fast and doesn't give off much heat. I figured Charlie was getting low on his wood supply. A few minutes later the cottage came into view, its windows lit.

I gave a shout just to warn him, then turned into the driveway. At the porch I unstrapped my snowshoes. Charlie had come to the window and was now trying to open the frozen door. He had to shove it hard a couple times before it swung free of its frame.

"Goddammit, Daniel, it's good to see you! Get in here!"

"You running low on wood, Charlie?" I asked as I stepped inside and Charlie closed the door behind me.

"Just one pile's getting down," Charlie said. "I cleared some black spruce from out back last summer. Just using it up. How the hell have you been?"

"Good." I took my backpack off, started stripping down some. "Thick pelts this winter."

Charlie shook his head, rubbing his brow. "Animals. They always know when it's gonna be a cold one. They always know, don't they?"

"Sure do," I said. We went into the den and sat down in front of the fireplace. The ranger had told me that Charlie had taken his wife's death pretty hard, and I could see that he didn't look too good. The skin of his face was pasty and yellow. And I saw that a shaking had come to his hands. "How you been, Charlie?" I asked, stretching my feet towards the fire.

"Strange winter, eh?" Charlie looked down, rubbing his forehead again. "I know this sounds funny, but I'm tasting metal these days." He squinted at me. "Can't really explain it, Daniel. But ever since the snows hit for real, I might as well be eating lead ten times a day, from the taste I'm tasting."

I glanced at him, then looked away. He was giving me this real troubled look. I stared at the fire. "Don't know," I finally said. "Maybe it's the lake water."

"Hell no, it isn't like that." He paused. "Had a heart attack last summer, did you know that?"

I shook my head. "Didn't hear anything about it. How bad was—"

"The doctor in the city – I forget his name, he took over when Bill retired, just a kid, really – he's been phoning me about once a week, asking me how I'm doing. So I tell him, but he says it's just psychological. He says there's no way somebody can taste a pacemaker. I suppose he knows what he's talking about." Charlie looked up at me and smiled. "But he was the one making the connection with the wind-up, not me, right? I just said to him, 'I keep tasting metal, Doc. How about that?'"

"And what did he say to that?"

"Psychological, like I told you."

"Oh yeah. Right." I studied the flames, listened to the snapping wood. It was burning real fast, that black spruce. For some reason I wanted it to slow down. It was burning too fast, just eating itself up and hardly any warmth reaching my feet. The way the wood spit out sparks bothered me, too, like words coming so quick all you can do is nod, answering everything "yes" no matter what you hear.

"Young people," Charlie said. "The ones in the city, like that doc." He looked at me. "The city people – can you figure them, Daniel?"

I laughed. "If I could maybe I wouldn't be here."

"You can't figure them, then?"

I shrugged. "They're just different, that's all. Like when things go quiet – they gotta make noise. So when they do something funny everybody laughs real loud, and it's not quiet anymore, and they get comfortable again. And winter, and the bush – well, they don't know what winter is, and they don't like the bush, the way it just swallows their noise. You couldn't laugh loud enough to keep that from happening, I bet."

Charlie was nodding. "Always questions, that's what I notice. Always 'why?' They ask 'why?' and then they answer themselves right away. 'Why? Because.' Just like that. Making everything seem so simple. Know what I mean? And they're always so suspicious, especially about complicated things, like when I say I'm tasting metal. 'Why?' 'Psychological.' Just like that. I was a teacher, did you know that, Daniel?"

"Sure."

"Ten-year-old kids like that question. 'Why?' How old are you, Daniel?"

"Twenty," I said, feeling uncomfortable for some reason, maybe about the way he kept using my name. He made it sound strange, like it wasn't my own. I thought about what I'd said, about city people, and I wondered at how angry I got saying it.

Charlie was talking. "Me and Mary couldn't have kids, did you know that? It was a hard thing for her to accept. I didn't mind. I didn't mind at all. The Lord just didn't see fit, that's all."

The room should have felt cozy, with the bear rug between us and all the knick-knacks crowding the shelves, the mounted jack and the antlers on the walls, the easy chair deep and comfortable. But it didn't feel cozy. I put more black spruce on the fire, then pulled my chair closer to it. "Anybody else drop by?" I asked.

Charlie nodded. "Yeah, the strangest winter. And it's not just the taste in my mouth, either. When it was snowing the ploughs used to come and clear the road a couple times a week. I'd go out and give them a wave, let them know I haven't run out of batteries or something." He laughed. "On the really cold days I flagged them down, gave them a thermos of hot chocolate. And you know, no matter if it was a different driver next week, I always got the thermos back. Sometimes we talked a bit. You know, just to keep the jaws greased. I told them about the buck, the one that comes across the lake every morning, right up to the cabin looking for food. And the very next week one of the drivers drops off two bales of hay. How about that?"

He'd been talking so fast I wondered if I'd missed something. "Charlie, what buck?"

He looked surprised. "I didn't tell you about the buck?"

"I don't think so."

Charlie's gaze returned to the fire. "Hasn't snowed in weeks. The ploughs stopped coming. Sometimes I swear I can hear them, way off down the road, so I go out, right? I go out and wait, figuring they're coming to check up on me. But they must be doing something else, cause they don't come. I can hear them, all right. They must be busy, right?"

"Sure." I stood. "Listen, I'm gonna get some other wood, if that's all right?"

"Fine. You go right ahead and get it, Daniel. That's fine by me. I got some birch out back."

"Great," I said.

Outside, I stood in front of the woodpile, holding Charlie's axe in my hands. I listened to the silence beyond the sounds of my breath. The muscles around my neck felt tight. I let the quiet sink into me, studied the grey trees beyond the clearing. Without leaves the trees all seemed to be standing alone, each one cut off from the others. The snow beneath them was like empty space, as if the roots and earth had been wiped away, leaving nothing behind.

My feet began to tingle. My toes had been frozen so many times there wasn't much feeling left in them anyway. All I had to do, I knew, was to get moving, but I just kept standing there, and the cold started working its way up my legs the way it does – picking out little areas, making them feel sort of wet, exposed. Then the feeling goes and there's just an empty patch. My knees went, then my thighs.

Behind me the backdoor opened. "Hey, Daniel?" The spell, or whatever it was, broke. I turned around. Charlie was standing just inside the door, clouds of vapour around his legs.

"Just thinking," I said to him, smiling.

"Thought you froze right up!" Charlie said, laughing. "Hurry up back inside. I got hot chocolate brewing."

"Right," I said, turning back to the woodpile. I began pulling out birch logs. To split them all I had to do was let the axe fall of its own weight – the logs seemed to almost jump apart. But the moving around brought the feeling back to my legs.

I piled wood on the back porch, then brought an armload inside. Charlie was in the kitchen, standing by the stove.

"They must be pretty busy, right?" he asked, stirring Fry's cocoa into a pot of simmering milk.

"Who?"

"The guys who clear the roads, like I was saying before. There's lots of side roads that probably need work, ones they couldn't get around to earlier, right? Can you believe this cold snap? All night long I can hear trees cracking. Exploding, you know? It's an eerie sound, all right. Can't say I like it. Do you like it, Daniel? I've been getting up at dawn and I make some coffee and sit in the rocker so I can look out over the lake.

"That's how I first saw the buck, looking out over the lake. He comes from the far side, every morning. Stumbling through the deep snow. Uses a different trail every time. Can you figure that?"

Charlie poured us cups of hot chocolate. We returned to the den. I set my cup down on the mantle and went to bring in the birch. The echo of the axe splitting the wood kept going through my head, making me think of what Charlie had been saying about exploding trees.

I stoked the fire, then sat down again. "That doc in the city," I said, "he's still phoning you every week?"

Charlie rubbed his face, then licked his lips. "I unplugged the phone. He kept saying the same old thing, over and over again." He leaned towards me and gestured for me to get closer. "Tell me, do you think my tongue's turning blue?" He poked out his tongue.

I looked at it, then sat back. "Hard to tell," I said. "Don't think so."

"I think so," Charlie said.

The heat coming from the birch logs made me push my chair back. I thought about the nights I'd spent alone, wrapped in my Woods arctic sleeping bag, watching my breath lay a sheet of ice on the nylon ceiling above me. I'd be filled with the silence, so filled and warm, with my thoughts going slow as they like to do. Then crack! A tree would explode. I'd jump, stare into the darkness, my heart pounding. Black spruce. It's the black spruce that explodes.

"I hope the ploughs come back," Charlie said. "We're running low on hay." He frowned suddenly. "Oh," he said, "I forgot." He climbed to his feet. "Come on, Daniel, let's look out over the lake."

I followed him to the large frosted window. We stood side by side and stared outward. I could see the buck's trails, shadowed blue. They stopped at a scuffed-up area just below the porch deck, maybe thirty feet away. The scuffed-up area was spattered with frozen blood, and off to one side lay the frosted carcass of the buck, half-eaten.

"Wolves? Jesus, nobody's seen a wolf in this park for years."

Charlie asked, "Did you see the Northern Lights last night?"

"I'm usually asleep by seven," I said.

"From horizon to horizon, I've never seen them so big. They made a sound like, like wind on sand, falling all around. All around. It's so beautiful, Daniel. There's no real way to describe it, is there?"

"Not really. You're right in that." But I knew that sound, the voice behind the silence, the voice that pushed the silence into me. And I knew what that voice said, the single word over and over again. Alone, alone, alone.

"Only," Charlie continued, "only, there'd be this falling from the sky, right? And all these streams of colour. And deep in the forest, deep in the forest, Daniel. The trees kept on shattering. As if, for just last night, for just those few hours when I was standing out there, the world was made of glass. The thinnest glass. And the trees reaching upward. I don't know." Charlie turned to me, a terrible frown on his lined face. "Maybe the trees were made of glass, too. But all gnarled and bubbled and black. Trying to join the sky, but too rough." He turned back to the window. "Too rough. Just no way they could make it. They were reaching up, to where the colours played. Reaching. Then snapping. Like gunshots. I tell you, in certain lights you can see it – the blue on my tongue. Then the glass in the sky shattered, and there was this falling. Endless falling."

I nodded. "Like the world was made of glass." His words had left a pain inside me, a deep, spreading pain. "Too rough," I said, "wanting to play with the colours, all the colours. But too rough." The voice whispered its word in my head, and it hurt me.

"That buck," Charlie said, "he was so strong, so healthy. All his life. You could see that. He – I built this cabin with my own hands, Daniel, did you know that? He was strong, healthy. He'd been through hard times lately, but he was all right. Four wolves. I watched it all happen. That buck, running across the lake, full bore. I was sitting in this rocker, this one right here. They took him not twenty yards from here – you can see where he first went down. I'd been thinking about getting my bear rifle, but it was already too late. That's the way it looked anyway. But the buck," he shook his head, "that buck, he just got up and kept coming. You can see it – he dragged those wolves ten, fifteen yards. Dragged all of them."

"Son of a bitch," I said.

"He'd been so strong, all his life. He dragged them all right, but in the end it didn't matter. It didn't count for nothing. I just sat here, all this morning, watching them wolves eating. Funny, they kept walking around and around him, not knowing what to do, really. What to do with it all."

I stared at the carcass, at the gnawed ribs and purple ice-flecked meat. "They'll be back for more," I said. "They earned it."

"I'm thinking, Daniel, the same things over and over again. Funny how that happens, eh? I'm thinking about my rifle, and that taste filling my mouth. Metal. He'd been so strong, cut down just like that. And I'm thinking about this window, this one right in front of us, Daniel. Two panes each a quarter inch thick. How everything happened in absolute silence. And the only sound I knew, I know, is something I feel more than hear. It's probably psychological, eh, Daniel? But there's this tingling, like glass chimes, and there's this humming – both coming from my chest. It's fading, I think, Daniel."

I shook my head, again and again, but he wasn't paying any attention to me. I didn't even know what I was saying no to, but in my head a voice kept asking, "Why?" Why? And Charlie, he kept answering me, he kept saying "Because, Daniel. Only because. Just because."

"The strangest winter," Charlie said. "No way to explain it, any of it. My tongue turning bluer and bluer, getting stained deeper and deeper every time, the doc telling me it's psychological – what the hell is that supposed to mean?"

We stood there for a long time, staring at the carcass. I wanted to cry, I wanted to shut my ears, stop the silence outside, never again let it in. But the tracks were cut too deep inside me. I'm not an old man. I don't think I'm very smart as far as young people go. I was never good at things they're good at. I'm not brave, and I'm sorry for that. I really am. I left Charlie that afternoon. I ran from him, across the lake, using one of the buck's trails. I pitched my tent on the other side of Jessica Lake. I could've gone farther but I didn't. I know it wasn't a tree shattering that woke me that night, made me jump up, staring into the darkness, heart pounding. I know that it wasn't a tree, and I'm sorry. Truly sorry.

GLEN HIRSHBERG

Miss Ill-Kept Runt

BOTH OF GLEN HIRSHBERG'S first two collections, *American Morons* and *The Two Sams* won the International Horror Guild Award and were selected by *Locus* as one of the best books of the year.

He is also the author of a novel, *The Snowman's Children*, and a five-time World Fantasy Award finalist. Currently, he is putting the final touches to two new novels and a new collection.

With Dennis Etchison and Peter Atkins, he co-founded the Rolling Darkness Revue, a travelling ghost story performance troupe that tours the West Coast of the United States each October.

His fiction has appeared in numerous magazines and anthologies, including multiple appearances in *The Mammoth Book of Best New Horror*, *The Year's Best Fantasy and Horror*, *Dark Terrors*, *Inferno*, *The Dark*, *Trampoline* and *Cemetery Dance*. He teaches writing and the teaching of writing at Cal State San Bernardino.

"Like many of my stories, this one springs perversely from a happy memory," Hirshberg reveals. "Much as my more talkative, squirmier brother and I got on each other's nerves during car trips, we both always looked forward to the annual summer driving vacation, and especially the drives deep into the night, when it was cool outside and the traffic was non-existent and we could lie side by side in the way-back of the station wagon and watch the dark drop down on us . . ."

> "*My mother's anxiety would not allow her to remain where she was . . . What was it that she feared? Some disaster impended over her husband or herself. He had predicted evils, but professed himself ignorant of what nature they were. When were they to come?*"

> —Charles Brockden Brown, *Wieland*

CHLOE COMES CLINKING out the front door into the twilight, pudding pop in one hand and a dragon in the other. The summer wind sets her frizzy brown hair flying around her, and she says, "Whoa," tilting up on one foot as though anything less than an F5 twister, a tag team of grizzly bears, a fighter jet could drag her and the fifteen pounds or so of bead necklace around her neck off the ground. The plastic baubles and seashell fragments and recently ejected baby teeth bump along her chest as she tilts, then straightens.

"I told you to get in pyjamas," says her father from the side of the station wagon, where he's still trying to wedge the last book and pan boxes into the wall of suitcases and cartons separating the front seat from the way-back, where Chloe and her brother the Miracle will be riding, as always.

"These *are* pyjamas," Chloe says, lifting the mass of beads so her father can see underneath.

Sweating, exhausted before the drive even starts, her father smiles. Better still, the Miracle, who is already stretched in the way-back with his big-kid feet dangling out the open back door and his Pokémon cards spread all over the space Chloe is supposed to occupy, laughs aloud and shakes his head at her. In Chloe's world, there are only a few things better than pudding pops and beads. One of them is her older brother noticing, laughing. The baby teeth on her newest necklace are mostly for him; she actually thinks they look blah, too plain, also a little bitey. But she'd known he would like them.

"Miss Ill-Kept Runt," her brother says, and goes back to his cards.

She's just climbing into the back, enjoying the Miracle's feverish sweeping up of cards, his snapping, "*Wait*" and "*Don't!*" at her, when her mother emerges from the empty house. Freezing, Chloe watches her mother tighten the ugly grey scarf – it looks more like a dishrag – around her beautiful dark hair, linger a last, long moment in the doorway, and finally aim a single glance in the direction of her children. Chloe starts to lift her hand, but her mother is hurrying around the side of the station wagon, eyes down, and Chloe hears her drop into the passenger seat just before her father wedges the Miracle's feet inside the car and shuts the way-back door.

"Stan," her mother says, in her new, bumpy voice, like a road with all the road peeled off. "Let's just *go*."

It's the move, Chlo. That's what her father's been saying. For months, now.

Her father's already in the driver's seat and the station wagon has shuddered to life under Chloe's butt and is making her necklaces rattle when her mother's door pops open, and all of a sudden she's there, pulling the back door up, blue-eyed gaze pouring down on Chloe like a waterfall. Chloe is surprised, elated, she wants to duck her head and close her eyes and bathe in it.

"Happy birthday," her mother says, bumpy-voiced, and reaches to touch her leg, then touches the Miracle's instead. He doesn't look up from his cards, but he waves at her with his sneaker.

"It's not my birthday yet," Chloe says, wanting to keep her mother there, prolong the moment.

Her mother gestures towards the wall of boxes in the back seat. "We'll be driving most of the night. By the time I see your face again, it will be." And there it is – faint as a fossil in rock, but there all the same. Her mother's smile. A trace, anyway.

It really has *been the move*, Chloe thinks, as her mother slams the door down like a lid.

"Say goodbye to the house," her father says from up front, on the other side of the boxes. Chloe can't see him, and she realizes he sounds different, too. Far away, as though he's calling to her across a frothed-up river. But right on cue, she feels the rev, *rrruummm, rruummm;* it's reassuring, the thing he always does before he goes anywhere. She bets he's even turned around to give her his *go!* face, forgetting there's a wall of cardboard there.

Then they are going, and Chloe is surprised to find tears welling in her eyes. They're not because she's sad. Why should she be, they're moving back to Minnesota to be by Grammy and Grumpy's, where they can water-ski every day, Grumpy says, and when Chloe says, "You can't water-ski in winter," Grumpy says, "Maybe *you* can't."

But just for a moment, pulling out of the drive, she's crying, and the Miracle sits up, bumping his big-kid head against the roof and squishing her as he turns for a last look.

"Bye, house," she says.

"Pencil mouse," says the Miracle, and Chloe beams through her tears. It's her own game, silly-rhyme-pencil game, she made it up when she was three to annoy her brother into looking at her, and it mostly worked. But she couldn't ever remember him *playing* it.

"Want to do speed?" she says, and the Miracle laughs. He always laughs now when she says that, but only because their father does. Her father has never said what's funny about it, and she doesn't think the Miracle knows, either.

"*Play* speed," he answers, grinning, maybe to himself but because of her, so that doesn't matter. "In a minute." And he glances fast over his shoulder towards the wall of boxes and then turns away from her again temporarily.

But Chloe has noticed that his grin is gone. And when she settles onto her shoulder blades and stretches out her legs to touch the door while her head brushes the back of the back seat, she realizes she can hear her mother over the rumbling engine, over the road bumping by.

"*Oh, freeze*," her mother is whispering, over and over. Or else, "*cheese*." Or "*please*."

It isn't the words, it's the whispering, and Chloe realizes she knows what her mother's doing, too: she's hunched forward, picking at the hem of her skirt on her knees, her pale, knobby knees.

Knees? Is that what she's saying? No. *Please.*

"Bye, trees," Chloe whispers, watching the familiar branches pop up in her window to wave her away. The blue pine, the birch, the oak where her father *thinks* the woodpecker always knocks, the black-branched, leafless fire-trees the crows pour out of every morning like spiders from a sac. After the fire-trees comes the open stretch of road with no trees. The trees after that are ones she doesn't know, at least not by name, not to say hello or wave goodbye. Then come brand new trees.

"*Please*," comes her mother's voice from the front seat.

"Dad, Gordyfoot," the Miracle all but shouts.

"Right," comes her father's answer, not as shiny as usual but just as fast. Seconds later, the CD's on, and Chloe can't hear her mother any more.

Fire-trees, Chloe is thinking, dreaming. *Fire on a hillside with no grass, in a ring of stones, but not warm enough. No matter how close she wriggles, she can't get close enough, she's been out on this mountainside with the grey rocks and grey snakes for too long, and this cold is old, so old, older than daylight, older than she is, she could jump into the fire and never be warm . . .*

Jerking, Chloe struggles up onto her elbows, almost laughing. She has never been camping, not that she can remember, the snakes she knows are green and slippy-shiny except when they're dead and the crows have been at them, and the only cold she's felt the last few months is the lily-pond water from the Berry's backyard.

On the CD, Gordyfoot is singing about the Pony Man, who'll come at night to take her for a ride, and out the window, the sky's going dark fast with the sun gone. Chloe thinks it's funny that the Miracle asked for this CD, since he says he *hates* Gordon Lightfoot now. But she also understands, or thinks she does. It's hard to imagine being in the way-back, in the car with her parents, and listening to anything else. They keep the entire Gordon Lightfoot collection up there. Also, if the CD wasn't on, they'd have to listen to their mother. *Freeze. Please. Pencil-bees.*

For a while – long enough to get out of their neighbourhood and maybe even out of Missouri, half a CD or more – Chloe watches the wires in her window swing down, shoot up, swing down, shoot up. It's like starting and erasing an Etch a Sketch drawing, the window fills with trees and darkening sky and the thick, black lines of wire, then *boop* – telephone pole – and everything's blank for a second and then fills up again. Gets erased. Fills up again. Gets erased. Abruptly, it's all the way dark, and the wires vanish, and Venus pounces out of the sky. It's too bright, has been all summer, as though it's been lurking all day just on the other side of the sunlight.

With the Miracle coiled away from her and his head tilted down, she can see the semi-circle scar at the base of his neck, like an extra mouth, almost smiling. Chloe has always thought of that spot as the place where the miracle actually happened, though she's been told that's just where the clip to stop blood flow went. The real scar is higher, under the hair, where part of her brother's skull got cut open when he was five years old. Of course, she'd been all of a week old at the time and doesn't remember any of it. But she loves the story. Her mother curled on the waiting room couch where she'd been ever since she'd given birth to Chloe, expecting the doctors to come at any moment and tell her that her son was dead. Her mother erupting from that couch one morning and somehow convincing the surgeons who'd said the surgery couldn't work that it *would* work, just by the way she said it. By the way she seemed to *know*. And it had worked. The pressure that had been building in the Miracle's brain bled away. Two days later, he woke up himself again.

"What?" he says now, turning around to glower at her.

"Speed, speed, speed," she chants.

He glowers some more. But after a few seconds, he nods.

"Yay," says Chloe.

They can barely see the playing cards, which makes the game even more fun. Plus, the piles won't stay straight because of all the vibrations, which frustrates the Miracle but makes Chloe laugh even more as their hands dart between each other's for cards and tangle up and slap and snatch, and finally the Miracle's laughing, too, tickling her, Chloe's shrieking and they're both laughing until their father snarls, "*Kids, Goddamnit,*" and both of them stop dead. Her father sounds growly, furious, nothing like he usually sounds.

Because he's trapped up there with Mom, Chloe thinks, and then she's horrified to have thought that, feels guilty, almost starts crying again.

"Sorry," she whimpers.

"Just . . . sssh," her father says.

It's the move, Chloe thinks, chants to herself. She lies back flat, and the Miracle stretches as much as he can stretch beside her.

"The Pony Man" is on again, so the same CD has played through twice, but only Chloe seems to have noticed. She's listening very closely, like the song says, so she'll hear the Pony Man if he comes. But all she hears is their station wagon's tires *shushing* on the night-time road, which she imagines to be black and wet, like one of those oil puddles birds get stuck in on nature shows. She's fairly sure she can hear her father's thumbs, too, drumming the beat on the steering wheel, and if she closes her eyes, she can see his stain-y SHOW ME! shirt and the wonderful, white prickles around his happy mouth. He has told Chloe he's secretly a cat, and the prickles are whiskers he keeps trimmed so Mom won't know.

He's been shaving more closely lately, though. Smiling less.

Then she realizes she can hear her mother, crying now. Even the cry is new, a low-down bear-grunt, and Chloe turns towards the Miracle's back and pokes it.

"Tomorrow I'll be half as old as you," she whispers. The Miracle doesn't respond. So she adds, "The next day, I'll be *more* than half."

The Miracle still doesn't respond, and she wonders if he's sleeping. His back is hard and curved like an armadillo shell.

"Catching up," she tries, a very little bit louder, and as she speaks she glances into the seatback above her head, as though she could see through it, through the cartons to her parents. As though they could see her.

"You'll never catch up," the Miracle murmurs, just as quiet, and Chloe thinks she sees his head tilt towards the front, too.

"I can if you wait."

"Will you just go to *sleep*?" he hisses, and Chloe startles, squirms back. The Miracle's whole body drums to the road or the steady beat of her father's thumbs. But when he speaks again, he's using his nice voice. "It'll make the drive go faster."

Chloe almost tells him she doesn't want it to go faster. She likes the way-back, always has. Shut in with her brother, Gordyfoot's voice floating over and among them, her parents close but not with them, the stars igniting and the hours stretched longer and thinner than hours should be able to go. Silly Putty hours.

Chloe doesn't remember falling asleep, has no idea how long she sleeps. But she dreams of bird-feet hands. Hands, but the fingers too thin, yellow-hard. *Her* hands? *Reaching through the bars towards the frantic, fluttering thing, all red and beating its pathetic little wings . . .*

A bump jolts her awake, or else the *cold*, that *old* cold, she almost cries out, wraps herself in her own arms, blinks, holds on, drags her brain back to itself. *Air-conditioning, it's just her father blasting the air-conditioning to stay awake, it's not in her chest, there are no hands in her chest.* Chloe's eyes fly all the way open, and just like that, she knows.

She *knows.*

They're not my parents.

She knows because "The Pony Man" is on again, the CD repeating, *how many times, now*? She knows because her father *isn't* tapping the steering wheel, which he always does, always always *always*, especially to Gordyfoot. She knows because her mother would never let it get this cold, her mother can't stand the cold, they always wind up fighting about it on night-drives and then swatting each other off the temperature controls and laughing and sometimes, when they think Chloe and the Miracle are sleeping, talking love-talk, very quietly.

They are talking now, but not that way. And in their changed voices. Her mother's bumpy, grunty and low. Her father's a snarl. Someone else's snarl.

Most of all, she knows because her mother's eyes – her *real* mother's eyes – are *green*, not blue. She very nearly screams, but jams her fist in her mouth, holds dead still. But the realization won't go away.

They aren't my parents.

It's ridiculous, a bird-feet hands dream. She wiggles furiously, trying to shake the realization loose.

But in the front seat, the new people – the ones that were her parents – are grunting. Snarl-whispering. And Chloe's mother's eyes are green.

At least "The Pony Man" finally goes off. But the next song is the "Minstrel of the Dawn" one. Another song about someone coming.

Stupid, Chloe insists her to herself. *This is stupid*. She feels around for the snack bag her father has let the Miracle stow back here, even though they've already brushed their teeth. The spiny, sticky carpet of the way-back scratches against her palms, and the engine shudders underneath her. Her hand smacks down on the paper bag, which makes a little *pop*. Chloe quivers, holds her breath, and up front, the grunting and the whispering stop.

Chloe doesn't move, doesn't breathe. Neither does anyone else in the car. They are four frozen people hurtling through the empty black. Even the CD has gone silent – because her parents have shut it off, Chloe realizes. It is so quiet inside the car that she half-thinks she can hear the cornfields passing, the late-summer stalks looming over the road like an army of aliens, an invasion that didn't come but grew, their bodies grasshopper-thin, leaves heavy, fruit swollen fat and dangling.

"Chlo?" says her not-father, in his almost-snarl.

Nearly faint from holding her breath, Chloe says nothing. After a second, she hears rustling, but whether from the corn or up front, she can't tell.

"See?" her mother whispers. "I told you. I told you, I told you, I—"

"Oh, for Christ's sake," says her father. "Five years of this. *Five years*. You can't really bel—"

"But I can. And so do you. You always have."

"Just shut up, Carol."

"He's coming."

"Carol—"

"He's coming. Face it. Face it. He's—"

"*Shut up!*"

The CD blares to life, and Chloe almost bangs her head against the seatback in surprise. Her breathing comes in spasms, and she can't get it calm. "The Pony Man" is playing again. *Why,* she wonders? *And why is she minding, anyway? According to her mom and dad, this is the first song she ever knew. The one they sang her to sleep with when she woke up screaming when she was a baby.*

Then Chloe thinks, *Shut up?* Her fingers grab so hard at the carpet that she pulls some out, little quills like a porcupine's. *When has her father ever said that, to anyone?*

And why is her mother laughing?

If that is laughing. It's mostly grunt. Panic breathing.

What Chloe wants to do, right now, is wake the Miracle. She can't believe he isn't awake already, but he hasn't stirred, still lies there with his back curved away and his scar smiling at her. If she wakes him, she knows, she'll have to tell him. Explain, somehow. And she's worried they'll hear.

Instead, she lifts herself – so slowly, as silently as she can, matching her movements to the *shush* of the tires – onto her elbows again. Turns over onto her stomach. Raises her head, then raises it more. Until she's above the seatback.

She's hoping she can see. *One good glimpse*, she thinks. *Then she'll know. Then she can decide what to do.*

But her father has packed the boxes too tight. There aren't even cracks between them. The only empty space is at the very tiptop. Pushing all the way up, Chloe straightens, and her beads *clank*.

This time, she very nearly throws herself out the back window. She's ready to. If they turn . . . if they pull to the shoulder and stop . . . she'll grab the Miracle and yank him awake, and they'll *run*.

But the car neither stops nor slows. The CD player continues to blare. The "Minstrel of the Dawn", who'll say your fortune when he comes. If her parents are talking, they're whispering so low that Chloe can't hear them. Apparently, they haven't realized she's moving around. Not yet.

Stretching, gripping her beads to keep them still, Chloe tries to get her eyes level with the opening at the top of the boxes. The little crack. But all see can see is the dark inside dome-light, the tiniest sliver of windshield, at least until a truck passes going the other way, its lights flooding the car and shooting shadows across the ceiling, but the shadows could be corn, seatbacks, surely her parents aren't that thin or that long. It's all Chloe can do to keep from burying her head between her knees in the tornado-position they taught her in kindergarten.

The words are out of her mouth almost before she's thought them or had time to plan.

"I have to go to the bathroom."

For a second, she just sits, horrified, clutching her beads.

But she had to. She needs to see. She's smushing her beads against her chest and holding her breath again, as though any of that matters now.

There is no response. Nothing at all. The car plunges on into the dark, and out her window the corn stalks twist their grasshopper-shoulders to squirm even more tightly together, denying any glimpse of field or farmhouse behind them, so that Chloe's vision is blocked on three sides. The only way she can see is behind, the road that leads back to the home they've left.

"I have to go to the bathroom," she says again, meaning to be louder but sounding smaller.

This time, though, the CD shuts off, and that silence wells up from the floorboards. Chloe has begun to cry again, and this makes her angry. *It's stupid*, she thinks, *this is stupid. Or the world is a nightmare.* Either way makes her angry.

Then comes the sigh, long and explosive, from the front seat.

"I thought I told you to *go*," growls not-Dad.

"Sorry," Chloe says. "I did."

All too soon – sooner than she thought possible, and she's seen no exit sign or prick of gas station light penetrating the leafy, squirmy blackness of the fields around her – Chloe feels the car start to slow, hears the CLICK-*click*, CLICK-*click* of the station wagon's blinker. In her mind, she can see it so clearly, that little green triangle-eye winking at her from the dashboard. "*It's where I keep the frog,*" her father has always said, patting a spot right above the blinking turn-signal, and they'd watch it blink together, and he'd say, "*Ribbit*" in time with the clicking. Until now.

It happens all at once, the corn parting like a curtain and the station appearing, its light so bright that Chloe's eyes water and she has to look away. The Miracle mumbles and rolls over. The light sweeps across the old-mannish wrinkle on his forehead as he dreams. Chloe knows that wrinkle like she knows the frog in the dashboard, her father's cat-whiskers, "The Pony Man". A wave of affection so wide and deep rushes through her that it is all she can do not to throw her arms around her brother's neck and bury her face there.

Then, all at once, she goes rigid again. She hasn't heard any doors opening, they've barely stopped moving. But the silence has gone just that imperceptible bit more still. Her parents – *both of them* – are out of the car.

Chloe whirls just in time to see the face fill the back window, black and scarved, too big, the doors yawn open and she can't help it, she scurries back, pinning herself against the seat and the boxes with her hands raised and her mouth open to scream.

But her mother is already gone, stalking across the blacktop towards the light, the mini-mart inside the station. She doesn't look back, doesn't wave Chloe on or call to her. But for one moment, the set of those shoulders – the stoop and shake of them – is almost enough.

That is my mother, Chloe thinks. *That is my mother crying.*

She is half out of the car before she realizes she has no idea where her father is. Whirling, she bangs her head hard against the top of the door, expecting him to be right on top of her, with new long arms that open like wings and bird-feet hands. At first, she still doesn't see him, and then she does.

He's at the edge of the lot, right on the lip of the road where the cornfield devours the light. Like her mother, he has his back to her, and abruptly Chloe wants nothing more than to call out, lure him here. *He and Mom have been fighting,* she thinks, rubbing the back of her head, making herself breathe. *That's all it is. It's the move, Chlo. Ribbit.*

Something red flickers in his fingers. Chloe has leapt from the station wagon and is backing across the tarmac after her mother before she realizes it's a cigarette. Fast on the heels of that realization comes another. *She has never seen her father with a cigarette before. But he's been smoking lately. That's what that smell has been.*

Stopping by one of the silent pumps, Chloe bathes in the bright light, willing herself to cut it out. Beyond her father, the cornstalks, barely visible, wiggle their leafy antennae in the not-breeze, rattle their bulgy, distended husks. By tomorrow – maybe by the next time she wakes – her family will be at their new house. By tomorrow afternoon, she will be on Grumpy's boat, the rubber boots on the red kid-skis gripping her ankles and the Donald Duck lifejacket wrapping her in its sloppy, damp embrace.

Inside the station, she spots her mother crouching by the peanut butter cheese crackers. She is in profile, but the scarf hides just enough so that Chloe can't see her eyes.

"Going to the bathroom," she says. Her mother doesn't turn.

She dawdles a moment in the candy aisle, running a finger across the silvery *Chunky* wrappers, the boxes of ten-cent Kisses along the bottom shelf. She has almost reached the bathroom when her mother says, "Need help, sweetie?"

Chloe wants to dance, turn around and race at her mother and jump into her arms. Then she does turn, and something prickly and *old*-cold rolls over under her ribs.

Her mother's face, smiling softly down. Tears streaming from her blue eyes.

"No, thank you," Chloe whispers, and shuts herself in.

The toilet has poop in it, and a mound of tissue. Chloe doesn't actually have to go. Sinking into a huddle by the door in the ugly yellow light, she tries to hold her breath, but her chest prickles and she bursts out coughing. Crying again.

She can't stay here, the smell is too much. But she doesn't want to go back out. She's terrified to think what else might have changed by the time she opens the door. Each new breath of putrid air triggers a cough, each blink fresh tears.

Run, she thinks. *Sneak past the Kisses, bolt out the door, find a way to Grumpy's.*

Except that the only place to run is into the corn. In the dark. Chloe can't imagine doing that.

And then she realizes she doesn't want to. She already knows the safest place. The only place that hasn't changed, that's still hers. She needs to get back to the way-back, where the Miracle is.

She has just gotten the heavy door partway open when she hears them. Bumpy-voiced Mom, growly Dad, whispering just out of sight in the next aisle.

"You see?" her father is saying. Halfway snarling.

Her mother sobs.

"I told you."

"You did. It's true."

"You dreamed it, Carol. And no wonder. I mean, those nights. When we both really thought we were going to lose him . . ."

"But we didn't," Chloe's mother whispers, her voice seeming to twitch back and forth now. Chloe's mother/changed-mother/Chloe's mother.

"Because of you," her father whispers. "Because of your unshakable hope."

"Because of *him*. Because he came. Because he—"

"Because of *you*. You saved him, Carol. You saved your son. You do see that now. Right?"

Soft sob. Silence.

Then footsteps. Chloe pushes hard at the door, but by the time she gets out and hurries down the candy aisle after them, they are already at the pumps, arms around each other, halfway to the car. Her father goes straight to the driver's side, dropping his cigarette to the tarmac. It is her mother who waits by the way-back doors and touches Chloe's hair as she climbs in beside her brother.

"Is it my birthday yet?" Chloe asks, not quite looking at her mother's eyes. She doesn't want to see anymore. Doesn't want to think.

She hears her mother gasp, glance at her watch. "Not yet," she whispers. "Oh, shit, not yet."

The door drops down, and the car starts, and up front her parents are snarling and whispering again. Chloe crouches low, curls into a ball with her knees just touching her brother's back. If he wakes and feels that, he'll be furious. But if she's sleeping when he does, he won't mind. *Sleep,* she commands herself. Pleads with herself. *Sleep.*

She dreams cold. Old-cold. Green eyes. Bird-feet hands that aren't her hands—weren't—aren't—reaching for the beating-wing bird. Straw into gold, hillsides of stone. Old stone. Grasshopper-cornstalk squeezing in the window, slithering through it, crouching over her in the empty dark with its antennae brushing her face, and its husks, its dozens of husks hard and bumping against her chest, her legs. Those hands prying into the cage, reaching through the bars. Ribs. Towards the red and beating thing.

Chloe wakes to a silent car, bright sunlight. She is flat on her back, but she can feel the Miracle's heat against her forearm. He is moving now, stretching. Out the window, there are trees overflowing with green, shading her from the brilliant blue overhead. Minnesota lake trees. Somewhere close, there's a hum. Motorboat hum. Chloe is halfway sitting up when she hears them.

"You'll see," says her father, sounding tired. But only tired. And happy, almost. Sure, in the way he somehow still hasn't learned not to be, that the worst is behind him.

He pulls open the back door, arms wide, and it's him, her CatDad with his whisker-face, and she sits all the way up – just to revel in it, just to watch it all land – and he staggers back. Staring.

Revel? That's what *it's* doing, anyway, Chloe knows. The cold one inside her. The one moving her arms, blinking her eyes. Making her watch.

Vaguely, glancing towards her brother, Chloe wonders whether she really did figure it all out, or if the knowledge just came with the intruder. The cold one with the bird-feet hands, practically dancing down her ribs under her skin in his glee. Now she really does know. She knows how this happened. She knows when the cold one first appeared in her mother's hospital room. Her mother, whose eyes have always been blue, it's this *other's* mother that confused her.

Anyway, she knows what the cold one promised. She knows what he got her mother to offer in exchange.

"Where is she?" Chloe's father is murmuring, hovering right outside the way-back door and waving his hands as though trying to clear a fogged windshield, while out the side window, her mother stands rooted, hands over her mouth, shuddering and weeping. There is something almost comforting about it, about both her parents' reaction. At least they can tell. At least she really was *her*. There really was a something named Chloe.

I'm right here, she wants to scream. *Right here*. But of course, the cold one won't let her. He's having way too much fun.

Her father is on his knees, now, just the way the cold one likes him. Murmuring through his tears. Through his disbelief, which isn't really disbelief anymore. *So delicious when they understand,* the cold one tells her, in his inside ice-voice. *When they can't stop denying. Can't stop pleading. Even when they already know.*

So pathetic, her father looks down there. Hands going still. Head flung back in desperation. Or resignation. "Please," he says. "What have you done with my daughter?"

JOE R. LANSDALE

Deadman's Road

JOE R. LANSDALE IS THE AUTHOR of thirty novels and many short stories and articles. His latest works include the novels *Lost Echoes*, *Leather Maiden* and *The Sky Dome Ripped*, the collection *The Shadows Kith and Kin*, the anthology *Retro-Pulp Tales* and a graphic adaptation of Robert E. Howard's *Pigeons from Hell* for Dark Horse Comics.

His story, "Bubba Ho-Tep", was filmed by Don Coscarelli in 2002 and is considered a cult classic.

Lansdale has received numerous awards and recognition for his work, including the Edgar Award, seven Horror Writers Association Bram Stoker Awards, the World Horror Convention Grand Master Award and the Grinzani Prize for Literature.

" 'Deadman's Road' was inspired by a trip I took with my wife and daughter," explains the author. "As we were driving, we passed a sign that said DEADMAN'S ROAD.

"The story jumped almost full-blown into my head, and I knew I wanted to use my Reverend character from *Weird Tales* although, for some reason, I forgot his last name and gave him another.

"It was a fun story to do, and I saw it as a kind of modern gassed-up version of an old pulp tale."

T HE EVENING SUN had rolled down and blown out in a bloody wad, and the white, full moon had rolled up like an enormous ball of tightly wrapped twine. As he rode, the Reverend Jubil Rains watched it glow above the tall pines. All about it stars were sprinkled white-hot in the dead-black heavens.

The trail he rode on was a thin one, and the trees on either side of it crept towards the path as if they might block the way, and close up behind him. The weary horse on which he was riding moved forward with its head down, and Jubil, too weak to fight it, let his mount droop and take its lead. Jubil was too tired to know much at that moment, but he knew one thing. He was a man of the Lord and he hated God, hated the sonofabitch with all his heart.

And he knew God knew and didn't care, because he knew Jubil was his messenger. Not one of the New Testament, but one of the Old Testament, harsh and mean and certain, vengeful and without compromise; a man who would have shot a leg out from under Moses and spat in the face of the Holy Ghost and scalped him, tossing his celestial hair to the wild four winds.

It was not a legacy Jubil would have preferred, being the bad man messenger of God, but it was his, and he had earned it through sin, and no matter how hard he tried to lay it down and leave it be, he could not. He knew that to give in and abandon his God-given curse, was to burn in Hell forever, and to continue was to do as the Lord prescribed, no matter what his feelings towards his mean master might be. His Lord was not a forgiving Lord, nor was he one who cared for your love. All he cared for was obedience, servitude and humiliation. It was why God had invented the human race. Amusement.

As he thought on these matters, the trail turned and widened, and off to one side, amongst tree stumps, was a fairly large clearing, and in its centre was a small log house, and out to the side a somewhat larger log barn. In the curtained window of the cabin was a light that burned orange behind the flour-sack curtains. Jubil, feeling tired and hungry and thirsty and weary of soul, made for it.

Stopping a short distance from the cabin, Jubil leaned forward on his horse and called out, "Hello, the cabin."

He waited for a time, called again, and was halfway through calling when the door opened, and a man about five foot two with a large droopy hat, holding a rifle, stuck himself part of the way out of the cabin, said, "Who is it calling? You got a voice like a bullfrog."

"Reverend Jubil Rains."

"You ain't come to preach none, have you?"

"No, sir. I find it does no good. I'm here to beg for a place in your barn, a night under its roof. Something for my horse, something for myself if it's available. Most anything, as long as water is involved."

"Well," said the man, "this seems to be the gathering place tonight. Done got two others, and we just sat asses down to eat. I got enough you want it, some hot beans and some old bread."

"I would be most obliged, sir," Jubil said.

"Oblige all you want. In the meantime, climb down from that nag, put it in the barn and come in and chow. They call me Old Timer, but I ain't that old. It's 'cause most of my teeth are gone and I'm crippled in a foot a horse stepped on. There's a lantern just inside the barn door. Light that up, and put it out when you finish, come on back to the house."

When Jubil finished grooming and feeding his horse with grain in the barn, watering him, he came into the cabin, made a show of pushing his long black coat back so that it revealed his ivory-handled .44 cartridge-converted revolvers. They were set so that they leaned forward in their holsters, strapped close to the hips, not draped low like punks wore them. Jubil liked to wear them close to the natural swing of his hands. When he pulled them it was a movement quick as the flick of a hummingbird's wings, the hammers clicking from the cock of his thumb, the guns barking, spewing lead with amazing accuracy. He had practised enough to drive a cork into a bottle at about a hundred paces, and he could do it in bad light. He chose to reveal his guns that way to show he was ready for any attempted ambush. He reached up and pushed his wide-brimmed black hat back on his head, showing black hair gone grey-tipped. He thought having his hat tipped made him look casual. It did not. His eyes always seemed aflame in an angry face.

Inside, the cabin was bright with kerosene lamplight, and the kerosene smelled, and there were curls of black smoke twisting about, mixing with grey smoke from the pipe of Old Timer, and the cigarette of a young man with a badge pinned to his shirt. Beside him, sitting on a chopping log by the fireplace, which was too hot for the time of year, but was being used to heat up a pot of beans, was a middle-aged man with a slight paunch and a face that looked like it attracted thrown objects. He had his hat pushed up a bit, and a shock of wheat-coloured, sweaty hair hung on his forehead. There was a cigarette in his mouth, half of it ash. He twisted on the chopping log, and Jubil saw that his hands were manacled together.

"I heard you say you was a preacher," said the manacled man, as he tossed the last of his smoke into the fireplace. "This here sure ain't God's country."

"Worse thing is," said Jubil, "it's exactly God's country."

The manacled man gave out with a snort, and grinned.

"Preacher," said the younger man, "my name is Jim Taylor. I'm a deputy for Sheriff Spradley, out of Nacogdoches. I'm taking this man there for a trial, and most likely a hanging. He killed a fella for a rifle and a horse. I see you tote guns, old style guns, but good ones. Way you tote them, I'm suspecting you know how to use them."

"I've been known to hit what I aim at," Jubil said, and sat in a rickety chair at an equally rickety table. Old Timer put some tin plates on the table, scratched his ass with a long wooden spoon, then grabbed a rag and used it as a pot-holder, lifted the hot bean pot to the table. He popped the lid of the pot, used the ass-scratching spoon to scoop a heap of beans onto plates. He brought over some wooden cups and poured them full from a pitcher of water.

"Thing is," the deputy said, "I could use some help. I don't know I can get back safe with this fella, havin' not slept good in a day or two. Was wondering, you and Old Timer here could watch my back till morning? Wouldn't even mind if you rode along with me tomorrow, as sort of a backup. I could use a gun hand. Sheriff might even give you a dollar for it."

Old Timer, as if this conversation had not been going on, brought over a bowl with some mouldy biscuits in it, placed them on the table. "Made them a week ago. They've gotten a bit ripe, but you can scratch around the mould. I'll warn you though, they're tough enough you could toss one hard and kill a chicken on the run. So mind your teeth."

"That how you lost yours, Old Timer?" the manacled man said.

"Probably part of them," Old Timer said.

"What you say, preacher?" the deputy said. "You let me get some sleep?"

"My problem lies in the fact that I need sleep," Jubil said. "I've been busy, and I'm what could be referred to as tuckered."

"Guess I'm the only one that feels spry," said the manacled man.

"No," said, Old Timer. "I feel right fresh myself."

"Then it's you and me, Old Timer," the manacled man said, and grinned, as if this meant something.

"You give me cause, fella, I'll blow a hole in you and tell God you got in a nest of termites."

The manacled man gave his snort of a laugh again. He seemed to be having a good old time.

"Me and Old Timer can work shifts," Jubil said. "That okay with you, Old Timer?"

"Peachy," Old Timer said, and took another plate from the table and filled it with beans. He gave this one to the manacled man, who said, lifting his bound hands to take it, "What do I eat it with?"

"Your mouth. Ain't got no extra spoons. And I ain't giving you a knife."

The manacled man thought on this for a moment, grinned, lifted the plate and put his face close to the edge of it, sort of poured the beans towards his mouth. He lowered the plate and chewed. "Reckon they taste scorched with or without a spoon."

Jubil reached inside his coat, took out and opened up a pocket knife, used it to spear one of the biscuits, and to scrape the beans towards him.

"You come to the table, young fella," Old Timer said to the deputy, "I'll get my shotgun, he makes a move that ain't eatin', I'll blast him and the beans inside him into that fireplace there."

Old Timer sat with a double barrel shotgun resting on his leg, pointed in the general direction of the manacled man. The deputy told all that his prisoner had done while he ate. Murdered women and children, shot a dog and a horse, and just for the hell of it, shot a cat off a fence, and set fire to an outhouse with a woman in it. He had also raped women, stuck a stick up a sheriff's ass, and killed him, and most likely shot other animals that might have been some good to somebody. Overall, he was tough on human beings, and equally as tough on livestock.

"I never did like animals," the manacled man said. "Carry fleas. And that woman in the outhouse stunk to high heaven. She ought to eat better. She needed burning."

"Shut up," the deputy said. "This fella," and he nodded towards the prisoner, "his name is Bill Barrett, and he's the worst of the worst. Thing is, well, I'm not just tired, I'm a little wounded. He and I had a tussle. I hadn't surprised him, wouldn't be here today. I got a bullet graze in my hip. We had quite a dust up. I finally got him down by putting a gun barrel to his noggin' half a dozen times or so. I'm not hurt so bad, but I lost blood for a couple days. Weakened me. You'd ride along with me Reverend, I'd appreciate it."

"I'll consider it," Jubil said. "But I'm about my business."

"Who you gonna preach to along here, 'sides us?" the deputy said.

"Don't even think about it," Old Timer said. "Just thinking about that Jesus foolishness makes my ass tired. Preaching makes me want to kill the preacher and cut my own throat. Being at a preachin' is like being tied down in a nest red bitin' ants."

"At this point in my life," Jubil said. "I agree."

There was a moment of silence in response to Jubil, then the deputy turned his attention to Old Timer. "What's the fastest route to Nacogdoches?"

"Well now," Old Timer said, "you can keep going like you been going, following the road out front. And in time you'll run into a road, say thirty miles from here, and it goes left. That should take you right near Nacogdoches, which is another ten miles, though you'll have to make a turn somewhere up in there near the end of the trip. Ain't exactly sure where unless I'm looking at it. Whole trip, travelling at an even pace ought to take you two day."

"You could go with us," the deputy said. "Make sure I find that road."

"Could," said Old Timer, "but I won't. I don't ride so good anymore. My balls ache I ride a horse for too long. Last time I rode a pretty good piece, I had to squat over a pan of warm water and salt, soak my taters for an hour or so just so they'd fit back in my pants."

"My balls ache just listening to you," the prisoner said. "Thing is, though, them swollen up like that, was probably the first time in your life you had man-sized balls, you old fart. You should have left them swollen."

Old Timer cocked back the hammers on the double barrel. "This here could go off."

Bill just grinned, leaned his back against the fireplace, then jumped forward. For a moment, it looked as if Old Timer might cut him in half, but he realized what had happened.

"Oh yeah," Old Timer said. "That there's hot, stupid. Why they call it a fireplace."

Bill readjusted himself, so that his back wasn't against the stones. He said, "I'm gonna cut this deputy's pecker off, come back here, make you fry it up and eat it."

"You're gonna shit and fall back in it," Old Timer said. "That's all you're gonna do."

When things had calmed down again, the deputy said to Old Timer, "There's no faster route?"

Old Timer thought for a moment. "None you'd want to take."

"What's that mean?" the deputy said.

Old Timer slowly lowered the hammers on the shotgun, smiling at Bill all the while. When he had them lowered, he turned his head, looked at the deputy. "Well, there's Deadman's Road."

"What's wrong with that?" the deputy asked.

"All manner of things. Used to be called Cemetery Road. Couple years back that changed."

Jubil's interest was aroused. "Tell us about it, Old Timer."

"Now I ain't one to believe in hogwash, but there's a story about the road, and I got it from someone you might say was the horse's mouth."

"A ghost story, that's choice," said Bill.

"How much time would the road cut off going to Nacogdoches?" the deputy asked.

"Near a day," Old Timer said.

"Damn. Then that's the way I got to go," the deputy said.

"Turn off for it ain't far from here, but I wouldn't recommend it," Old Time said. "I ain't much for Jesus, but I believe in haints, things like that. Living out here in this thicket, you see some strange things. There's gods ain't got nothing to do with Jesus or Moses, or any of that bunch. There's older gods than that. Indians talk about them."

"I'm not afraid of any Indian gods," the deputy said.

"Maybe not," Old Timer said, "but these gods, even the Indians ain't fond of them. They ain't their gods. These gods are older than the Indian folk their ownselfs. Indians try not to stir them up. They worship their own."

"And why would this road be different than any other?" Jubil asked. "What does it have to do with ancient gods?"

Old Timer grinned. "You're just wanting to challenge it, ain't you, Reverend? Prove how strong your god is. You weren't no preacher, you'd be a gunfighter, I reckon. Or, maybe you are just that. A gunfighter preacher."

"I not that fond of my god," Jubil said, "but I have been given a duty. Drive out evil. Evil as my god sees it. If these gods are evil, and they're in my path, then I have to confront them."

"They're evil, all right," Old Timer said.

"Tell us about them," Jubil said.

"Gil Gimet was a bee-keeper," Old Timer said. "He raised honey, and lived off of Deadman's Road. Known then as Cemetery Road. That's 'cause there was a graveyard down there. It had some old Spanish graves in it, some said conquistadors who tromped through here but didn't tromp out. I know there was some Indians buried there, early Christian Indians, I reckon. Certainly there were stones and crosses up and Indian names on the crosses. Maybe mixed breeds. Lots of intermarrying around here. Anyway, there were all manner people buried up there. The dead ground don't care what colour you are when you go in, 'cause in the end, we're all gonna be the colour of dirt."

"Hell," Bill said. "You're already the colour of dirt. And you smell like some pretty old dirt at that."

"You gonna keep on, mister," Old Timer said, "and you're gonna wind up having the undertaker wipe your ass." Old Timer cocked back the hammers on the shotgun again. "This here gun could go off accidentally. Could happen, and who here is gonna argue it didn't?"

"Not me," the deputy said. "It would be easier on me you were dead, Bill."

Bill looked at the Reverend. "Yeah, but that wouldn't set right with the Reverend, would it Reverend?"

"Actually, I wouldn't care one way or another. I'm not a man of peace, and I'm not a forgiver, even if what you did wasn't done to me. I think we're all rich and deep in sin. Maybe none of us are worthy of forgiveness."

Bill sunk a little at his seat. No one was even remotely on his side. Old Timer continued with his story.

"This here bee-keeper, Gimet, he wasn't known as much of a man. Mean-hearted is how he was thunk of. I knowed him, and I didn't like him. I seen him snatch up a little dog once and cut the tail off of it with his knife, just 'cause he thought it was funny. Boy who owned the dog tried to fight back, and Gimet, he cut the boy on the arm. No one did nothin' about it. Ain't no real law in these parts, you see, and wasn't nobody brave enough to do nothin'. Me included. And he did lots of other mean things, even killed a couple of men, and claimed self-defence. Might have been, but Gimet was always into something, and whatever he was into always turned out with someone dead, or hurt, or humiliated."

"Bill here sounds like he could be Gimet's brother," the deputy said.

"Oh, no," Old Timer said, shaking his head. "This here scum-licker ain't a bump on the mean old ass of Gimet. Gimet lived in a little shack off Cemetery Road. He raised bees, and brought in honey to sell at the community up the road. Guess you could even call it a town. Schow is the way the place is known, on account of a fella used to live up there was named Schow. He died and got ate up by pigs. Right there in his own pen, just keeled over slopping the hogs, and then they slopped him, all over that place. A store got built on top of where Schow got et up, and that's how the place come by the name. Gimet took his honey in there to the store and sold it, and even though he was a turd, he had some of the best honey you ever smacked your mouth around. Wish I had me some now. It was dark and rich, and sweeter than any sugar. Think that's one reason he got away with things. People don't like killing and such, but they damn sure like their honey."

"This story got a point?" Bill said.

"You don't like way I'm telling it," Old Timer said, "why don't you think about how that rope's gonna fit around your neck. That ought to keep your thoughts occupied, right smart."

Bill made a grunting noise, turned on his block of wood, as if to show he wasn't interested.

"Well, now, honey or not, sweet tooth, or not, everything has an end to it. And thing was he took to a little gal, Mary Lynn Twoshoe. She was a part Indian gal, a real looker, hair black as the bottom of a well, eyes the same colour, and she was just as fine in the features as them pictures you see of them stage actresses. She wasn't five feet tall, and that hair of hers went all the way down her back. Her daddy was dead. The pox got him. And her mama wasn't too well off, being sickly, and all. She made brooms out of straw and branches she trimmed down. Sold a few of them, raised a little garden and a hog. When all this happened, Mary Lynn was probably thirteen, maybe fourteen. Wasn't no older than that."

"If you're gonna tell a tale," Bill said, "least don't wander all over the place."

"So, you're interested?" Old Timer said.

"What else I got to do?" Bill said.

"Go on," Jubil said. "Tell us about Mary Lynn."

Old Timer nodded. "Gimet took to her. Seen her around, bringing the brooms her mama made into the store. He waited on her, grabbed her, and just threw her across his saddle kickin' and screamin', like he'd bought a sack of flour and was ridin' it to the house. Mack Collins, store owner came out and tried to stop him. Well, he said something to him. About how he shouldn't do it, least that's the way I heard it. He didn't push much, and I can't blame him. Didn't do good to cross him Gimet. Anyway, Gimet just said back to Mack, 'Give her mama a big jar of honey. Tell her that's for her daughter. I'll even make her another jar or two, if the meat here's as sweet as I'm expecting.'

"With that, he slapped Mary Lynn on the ass and rode off with her."

"Sounds like my kind of guy," Bill said.

"I have become irritated with you now," Jubil said. "Might I suggest you shut your mouth before I pistol-whip you."

Bill glared at Jubil, but the Reverend's gaze was as dead and menacing as the barrels of Old Timer's shotgun.

"Rest of the story is kind of grim," Old Timer said. "Gimet took her off to his house, and had his way with her. So many times he damn near killed her, and then he turned her loose, or got so drunk she was able to get loose. Time she walked down Cemetery Road, made it back to town, well, she was bleeding so bad from having been used so rough, she collapsed. She lived a day and died from loss of blood. Her mother, out of her sick bed, rode a mule out there to the cemetery on Cemetery Road. I told you she was Indian, and she knew some Indian ways, and she knew about them old gods that wasn't none of the gods of her people, but she still knew about them.

"She knew some signs to draw in cemetery dirt. I don't know the whole of it, but she did some things, and she did it on some old grave out there, and the last thing she did was she cut her own throat, died right there, her blood running on top of that grave and them pictures she drawed in the dirt."

"Don't see how that done her no good," the deputy said.

"Maybe it didn't, but folks think it did," Old Timer said. "Community that had been pushed around by Gimet, finally had enough, went out there in mass to hang his ass, shoot him, whatever it took. Got to his cabin they found Gimet dead outside his shack. His eyes had been torn out, or blown out is how they looked. Skin was peeled off his head, just leaving the skull and a few hairs. His chest was ripped open, and his insides was gone, exceptin' the bones in there. And them bees of his had nested in the hole in his chest, had done gone about making honey. Was buzzing out of that hole, his mouth, empty eyes, nose, or where his nose used to be. I figure they'd rolled him over, tore off his pants, they'd have been coming out of his asshole."

"How come you weren't out there with them?" Bill said. "How come this is all stuff you heard?"

"Because I was a coward when it come to Gimet," Old Timer said. "That's why. Told myself wouldn't never be a coward again, no matter what. I should have been with them. Didn't matter no how. He was done good and dead, them bees all in him. What was done then is the crowd got kind of loco, tore off his clothes, hooked his feet up to a horse and dragged him through a blackberry patch, them bees just bustin' out and hummin' all around him. All that ain't right, but I think I'd been with them, knowing who he was and all the things he'd done, I might have been loco too. They dumped him out on the cemetery to let him rot, took that girl's mother home to be buried some place better. Wasn't no more than a few nights later that folks started seeing Gimet. They said he walked at night, when the moon was at least half, or full, like it is now. Number of folks seen him, said he loped alongside the road, following their horses, grabbing hold of the tail if he could, trying to pull horse and rider down, or pull himself up on the back of their mounts. Said them bees was still in him. Bees black as flies, and angry whirling all about him, and coming from inside him. Worse, there was a larger number of folks took that road that wasn't never seen again. It was figured Gimet got them."

"Horse shit," the deputy said. "No disrespect, Old Timer. You've treated me all right, that's for sure. But a ghost chasing folks down. I don't buy that."

"Don't have to buy it," Old Timer said. "I ain't trying to sell it to you none. Don't have to believe it. And I don't think it's no ghost anyway. I think that girl's mother, she done something to let them old gods out for awhile, sent them after that bastard, used her own life as a sacrifice, that's what I think. And them gods, them things from somewhere else, they ripped him up like that. Them bees is part of that too. They ain't no regular honey bee. They're some other kind of bees. Some kind of fitting death for a bee raiser, is my guess."

"That's silly," the deputy said.

"I don't know," Jubil said. "The Indian woman may only have succeeded in killing him in this life. She may not have understood all that she did. Didn't know she was giving him an opportunity to live again . . . Or maybe that is the curse. Though there are plenty others have to suffer for it."

"Like the folks didn't do nothing when Gimet was alive," Old Time said. " Folks like me that let what went on go on."

Jubil nodded. "Maybe."

The deputy looked at Jubil. "Not you too, Reverend. You should know better than that. There ain't but one true god, and ain't none of that hoodoo business got a drop of truth to it."

"If there's one god," Jubil said, "there can be many. They are at war with one another, that's how it works, or so I think. I've seen some things that have shook my faith in the one true god, the one I'm servant to. And what is our god but hoodoo? It's all hoodoo, my friend."

"Okay. What things have you seen, Reverend?" the deputy asked.

"No use describing it to you, young man," Jubil said. "You wouldn't believe me. But I've recently come from Mud Creek. It had an infestation of a sort. That town burned down, and I had a hand in it."

"Mud Creek," Old Timer said. "I been there."

"Only thing there now," Jubil said, "is some charred wood."

"Ain't the first time it's burned down," Old Timer said. "Some fool always rebuilds it, and with it always comes some kind of ugliness. I'll tell you straight. I don't doubt your word at all, Reverend."

"Thing is," the deputy said, "I don't believe in no haints. That's the shortest road, and it's the road I'm gonna take."

"I wouldn't," Old Timer said.

"Thanks for the advice. But no one goes with me or does, that's the road I'm taking, provided it cuts a day off my trip."

"I'm going with you," Jubil said. "My job is striking at evil. Not to walk around it."

"I'd go during the day," Old Timer said. "Ain't no one seen Gimet in the day, or when the moon is thin or not at all. But way it is now, it's full, and will be again tomorrow night. I'd ride hard tomorrow, you're determined to go. Get there as soon as you can, before dark."

"I'm for getting there," the deputy said. "I'm for getting back to Nacogdoches, and getting this bastard in a cell."

"I'll go with you," Jubil said. "But I want to be there at night, I want to take Deadman's Road at that time. I want to see if Gimet is there. And if he is, send him to his final death. Defy those dark gods the girl's mother called up. Defy them and loose my god on him. What I'd suggest is you get some rest, deputy. Old Timer here can watch a bit, then I'll take over. That way we all get some rest. We can chain this fellow to a tree outside, we have to. We should both get slept up to the gills, then leave here midday, after a good dinner, head out for Deadman's Road. Long as we're there by nightfall."

"That ought to bring you right on it," Old Timer said. "You take Deadman's Road. When you get to the fork, where the road ends, you go right. Ain't no one ever seen Gimet beyond that spot, or in front of where the road begins. He's tied to that stretch, way I heard it."

"Good enough," the deputy said. "I find this all foolish, but if I can get some rest, and have you ride along with me, Reverend, then I'm game. And I'll be fine with getting there at night."

Next morning they slept late, and had an early lunch. Beans and hard biscuits again, a bit of stewed squirrel. Old Timer had shot the rodent that morning while Jubil watched Bill sit on his ass, his hands chained around a tree in the front yard. Inside the cabin, the deputy had continued to sleep.

But now they all sat outside eating, except for Bill.

"What about me?" Bill asked, tugging at his chained hands.

"When we finish," Old Timer said. "Don't know if any of the squirrel will be left, but we got them biscuits for you. I can promise you some of them. I might even let you rub one of them around in my plate, sop up some squirrel gravy."

"Those biscuits are awful," Bill said.

"Ain't they," Old Timer said.

Bill turned his attention to Jubil. "Preacher, you ought to just go on and leave me and the boy here alone. Ain't smart for you to ride along, 'cause I get loose, ain't just the deputy that's gonna pay. I'll put you on the list."

"After what I've seen in this life," Jubil said, "you are nothing to me. An insect . . . So, add me to your list."

"Let's feed him," the deputy said, nodding at Bill, "and get to moving. I'm feeling rested and want to get this ball started."

The moon had begun to rise when they rode in sight of Deadman's Road. The white cross road sign was sticking up beside the road. Trees and brush had grown up around it, and between the limbs and the shadows, the crudely painted words on the sign were halfway readable in the waning light. The wind had picked up and was grabbing at leaves, plucking them from the ground, tumbling them about, tearing them from trees and tossing them across the narrow, clay road with a sound like mice scuttling in straw.

"Fall always depresses me," the deputy said, halting his horse, taking a swig from his canteen.

"Life is a cycle," Jubil said. "You're born, you suffer, then you're punished."

The deputy turned in his saddle to look at Jubil. "You ain't much on that resurrection and reward, are you?"

"No, I'm not."

"I don't know about you," the deputy said, "but I wish we hadn't gotten here so late. I'd rather have gone through in the day."

"Thought you weren't a believer in spooks?" Bill said, and made with his now familiar snort. "You said it didn't matter to you."

The deputy didn't look at Bill when he spoke. "I wasn't here then. Place has a look I don't like. And I don't enjoy temptin' things. Even if I don't believe in them."

"That's the silliest thing I ever heard," Bill said.

"Wanted me with you," Jubil said. "You had to wait."

"You mean to see something, don't you, preacher?" Bill said.

"If there is something to see," Jubil said.

"You believe Old Timer's story?" the deputy said. "I mean, really?"

"Perhaps."

Jubil clucked to his horse and took the lead.

When they turned onto Deadman's Road, Jubil paused and removed a small, fat Bible from his saddlebag.

The deputy paused too, forcing Bill to pause as well. "You ain't as ornery as I thought," the deputy said. "You want the peace of the Bible just like anyone else."

"There is no peace in this book," Jubil said. "That's a real confusion. Bible isn't anything but a book of terror, and that's how God is: terrible. But the book has power. And we might need it."

"I don't know what to think about you, Reverend," the deputy said.

"Ain't nothin' you can think about a man that's gone loco," Bill said. "I don't want to stay with no man that's loco."

"You get an idea to run, Bill, I can shoot you off your horse," the deputy said. "Close range with my revolver, far range with my rifle. You don't want to try it."

"It's still a long way to Nacogdoches," Bill said.

The road was narrow and of red clay. It stretched far ahead like a band of blood, turned sharply to the right around a wooded curve where it was a dark as the bottom of Jonah's whale. The blowing leaves seemed especially intense on the road, scrapping dryly about, winding in the air like giant hornets. The trees, which grew thick, bent in the wind, from right to left. This naturally led the trio to take to the left side of the road.

The farther they went down the road, the darker it became. By the time they got to the curve, the woods were so thick, and the thunderous skies had grown so dark, the moon was barely visible; its light was as weak as a sick baby's grip.

When they had travelled for some time, the deputy said, obviously feeling good about it, "There ain't nothing out here 'sides what you would expect. A possum maybe. The wind."

"Good for you, then," Jubil said. "Good for us all."

"You sound disappointed to me," the deputy said.

"My line of work isn't far from yours, Deputy. I look for bad guys of a sort, and try and send them to Hell . . . Or in some cases, back to Hell."

And then, almost simultaneous with a flash of lightning, something crossed the road not far in front of them.

"What the hell was that?" Bill said, coming out of what had been a near stupor.

"It looked like a man," the deputy said.

"Could have been," Jubil said. "Could have been."

"What do you think it was?"

"You don't want to know."

"I do."

"Gimet," Jubil said.

The sky let the moon loose for a moment, and its light spread through the trees and across the road. In the light there were insects, a large wad of them, buzzing about in the air.

"Bees," Bill said. "Damn if them ain't bees. And at night. That ain't right."

"You an expert on bees?" the deputy asked.

"He's right," Jubil said. "And look, they're gone now."

"Flew off," the deputy said.

"No . . . no they didn't," Bill said. "I was watching, and they didn't fly nowhere. They're just gone. One moment they were there, then they was gone, and that's all there is to it. They're like ghosts."

"You done gone crazy," the deputy said.

"They are not insects of this earth," Jubil said. "They are familiars."

"What," Bill said.

"They assist evil, or evil beings," Jubil said. "In this case, Gimet. They're like a witch's black cat familiar. Familiars take on animal shapes, insects, that sort of thing."

"That's ridiculous," the deputy said. "That don't make no kind of sense at all."

"Whatever you say," Jubil said, "but I would keep my eyes alert, and my senses raw. Wouldn't hurt to keep your revolvers loose in their holsters. You could well need them. Though, come to think of it, your revolvers won't be much use."

"What the hell does that mean?" Bill said.

Jubil didn't answer. He continued to urge his horse on, something that was becoming a bit more difficult as they went. All of the horses snorted and turned their heads left and right, tugged at their bits; their ears went back and their eyes went wide.

"Holy Hell," Bill said, "what's that?"

Jubil and the deputy turned to look at him. Bill was turned in the saddle, looking back. They looked too, just in time to see something that looked pale blue in the moonlight, dive into the brush on the other side of the road. Black dots followed, swarmed in the moon-light, then darted into the bushes behind the pale, blue thing like a load of buckshot.

"What was that?" the deputy said. His voice sounded as if it had been pistol-whipped.

"Already told you," Jubil said.

"That couldn't have been nothing human," the deputy said.

"Don't you get it," Bill said, "that's what the preacher is trying to tell you. It's Gimet, and he ain't nowhere alive. His skin was blue. And he's all messed up. I seen more than you did. I got a good look. And them bees. We ought to break out and ride hard."

"Do as you choose," the Reverend said. "I don't intend to."

"And why not?" Bill said.

"That isn't my job."

"Well, I ain't got no job. Deputy, ain't you supposed to make sure I get to Nacogdoches to get hung? Ain't that your job?"

"It is."

"Then we ought to ride on, not bother with this fool. He wants to fight some grave crawler, then let him. Ain't nothing we ought to get into."

"We made a pact to ride together," the deputy said. "So we will."

"I didn't make no pact," Bill said.

"Your word, your needs, they're nothing to me," the deputy said.

At that moment, something began to move through the woods on their left. Something moving quick and heavy, not bothering with stealth. Jubil looked in the direction of the sounds, saw someone, or something, moving through the underbrush, snapping limbs aside like they were rotten sticks. He could hear the buzz of the bees, loud and angry. Without really meaning to, he urged the horse to a trot. The deputy and Bill joined in with their own mounts, keeping pace with the Reverend's horse.

They came to a place off the side of the road where the brush thinned, and out in the distance they could see what looked like bursting white waves, frozen against the dark. But they soon realized it was tomb-stones. And there were crosses. A graveyard. The graveyard Old Timer had told them about. The sky had cleared now, the wind had ceased to blow hard. They had a fine view of the cemetery, and as they watched, the thing that had been in the brush moved out of it and went up the little rise where the graves were, climbed up on one of the stones and sat. A black cloud formed around its head, and the sound of buzzing could be heard all the way out to the road. The thing sat there like a king on a throne. Even from that distance it was easy to see it was nude, and male, and his skin was grey – blue in the moonlight – and the head looked misshapen. Moon glow slipped through cracks in the back of the horror's head and poked out of fresh cracks at the front of its skull and speared out of the empty eye sockets. The bee's nest, visible through the wound in its chest, was nestled between the ribs. It pulsed with a yellow-honey glow. From time to time, little black dots moved around the glow and flew up and were temporarily pinned in the moonlight above the creature's head.

"Jesus," said the deputy.

"Jesus won't help a bit," Jubil said.

"It's Gimet, ain't it? He . . . it . . . really is dead," the deputy said.

"Undead," Jubil said. "I believe he's toying with us. Waiting for when he plans to strike."

"Strike?" Bill said. "Why?"

"Because that is his purpose," Jubil said, "as it is mine to strike back. Gird your loins men, you will soon be fighting for your life."

"How about we just ride like hell?" Bill said.

In that moment, Jubil's words became prophetic. The thing was gone from the gravestone. Shadows had gathered at the edge of the woods, balled up, become solid, and when the shadows leaped from the even darker shadows of the trees, it was the shape of the thing they had seen on the stone, cool blue in the moonlight, a disaster of a face, and the teeth . . . They were long and sharp. Gimet leaped in such a way that his back foot hit the rear of Jubil's animal, allowing him to spring over the deputy's horse, to land hard and heavy on Bill. Bill let out a howl and was knocked off his mount. When he hit the road, his hat flying, Gimet grabbed him by his bushy head of straw-coloured hair and dragged him off as easily as if he were a kitten. Gimet went into the trees, tugging Bill after him. Gimet blended with the darkness there. The last of Bill was a scream, the raising of his cuffed hands, the cuffs catching the moonlight for a quick blink of silver, then there was a rustle of leaves and a slapping of branches, and Bill was gone.

"My God," the deputy said. "My God. Did you see that thing?"

Jubil dismounted, moved to the edge of the road, leading his horse, his gun drawn. The deputy did not dismount. He pulled his pistol and held it, his hands trembling. "Did you see that?" he said again, and again.

"My eyes are as good as your own," Jubil said. "I saw it. We'll have to go in and get him."

"Get him?" the deputy said. "Why in the name of everything that's holy would we do that? Why would we want to be near that thing?

He's probably done what he's done already . . . Damn, Reverend. Bill, he's a killer. This is just as good as I might want. I say while the old boy is doing whatever he's doing to that bastard, we ride like the goddamn wind, get on out on the far end of this road where it forks. Gimet is supposed to be only able to go on this stretch, ain't he?"

"That's what Old Timer said. You do as you want. I'm going in after him."

"Why? You don't even know him."

"It's not about him," Jubil said.

"Ah, hell. I ain't gonna be shamed." The deputy swung down from his horse, pointed at the place where Gimet had disappeared with Bill. "Can we get the horses through there?"

"Think we will have to go around a bit. I discern a path over there."

"Discern?"

"Recognize. Come on, time is wasting."

They went back up the road a pace, found a trail that led through the trees. The moon was strong now as all the clouds that had covered it had rolled away like wind blown pollen. The air smelled fresh, but as they moved forward, that changed. There was a stench in the air, a putrid smell both sweet and sour, and it floated up and spoiled the freshness.

"Something dead," the deputy said.

"Something long dead," Jubil said.

Finally the brush grew so thick they had to tie the horses, leave them. They pushed their way through briars and limbs.

"There ain't no path," the deputy said. "You don't know he come through this way."

Jubil reached out and plucked a piece of cloth from a limb, held it up so that the moon dropped rays on it. "This is part of Bill's shirt. Am I right?"

The deputy nodded. "But how could Gimet get through here? How could he get Bill through here?"

"What we pursue has little interest in the things that bother man. Limbs, briars. It's nothing to the living dead."

They went on for a while. Vines got in their way. The vines were wet. They were long thick vines, and sticky, and finally they realized they were not vines at all, but guts, strewn about and draped like decorations.

"Fresh," the deputy said. "Bill, I reckon."

"You reckon right," Jubil said.

They pushed on a little farther, and the trail widened, making the going easier. They found more pieces of Bill as they went along. The stomach. Fingers. Pants with one leg in them. A heart, which looked as if it had been bitten into and sucked on. Jubil was curious enough to pick it up and examine it. Finished, he tossed it in the dirt, wiped his hands on Bill's pants, the one with the leg still in it, said, "Gimet just saved you a lot of bother and the State of Texas the trouble of a hanging."

"Heavens," the deputy said, watching Jubil wipe blood on the leg filled pants.

Jubil looked up at the deputy. "He won't mind I get blood on his pants," Jubil said. "He's got more important things to worry about, like dancing in the fires of Hell. And by the way, yonder sports his head."

Jubil pointed. The deputy looked. Bill's head had been pushed onto a broken limb of a tree, the sharp end of the limb being forced through the rear of the skull and out the left eye. The spinal cord dangled from the back of the head like a bell rope.

The deputy puked in the bushes. "Oh, God. I don't want no more of this."

"Go back. I won't think the less of you, 'cause I don't think that much of you to begin with. Take his head for evidence and ride on, just leave me my horse."

The deputy adjusted his hat. "Don't need the head . . . And if it comes to it, you'll be glad I'm here. I ain't no weak sister."

"Don't talk me to death on the matter. Show me what you got, boy."

The trail was slick with Bill's blood. They went along it and up a rise, guns drawn. At the top of the hill they saw a field, grown up, and not far away, a sagging shack with a fallen down chimney.

They went that direction, came to the shack's door. Jubil kicked it with the toe of his boot and it sagged open. Once inside, Jubil struck a match and waved it about. Nothing but cobwebs and dust.

"Must have been Gimet's place," Jubil said. Jubil moved the match before him until he found a lantern full of coal oil. He lit it and placed the lantern on the table.

"Should we do that?" the deputy asked. "Have a light. Won't he find us?"

"In case you have forgotten, that's the idea."

Out the back window, which had long lost its grease paper covering, they could see tombstones and wooden crosses in the distance. "Another view of the graveyard," Jubil said. "That would be where the girl's mother killed herself."

No sooner had Jubil said that, then he saw a shadowy shape move on the hill, flitting between stones and crosses. The shape moved quickly and awkwardly.

"Move to the centre of the room," Jubil said.

The deputy did as he was told, and Jubil moved the lamp there as well. He sat it in the centre of the floor, found a bench and dragged it next to the lantern. Then he reached in his coat pocket and took out the Bible. He dropped to one knee and held the Bible close to the lantern light and tore out certain pages. He wadded them up, and began placing them all around the bench on the floor, placing the crumpled pages about six feet out from the bench and in a circle with each wad two feet apart.

The deputy said nothing. He sat on the bench and watched Jubil's curious work. Jubil sat on the bench beside the deputy, rested one of his pistols on his knee. "You got a .44, don't you?"

"Yeah. I got a converted cartridge pistol, just like you."

"Give me your revolver."

The deputy complied.

Jubil opened the cylinders and let the bullets fall out on the floor.

"What in hell are you doing?"

Jubil didn't answer. He dug into his gun belt and came up with six silver-tipped bullets, loaded the weapon and gave it back to the deputy.

"Silver," Jubil said. "Sometimes it wards off evil."

"Sometimes?"

"Be quiet now. And wait."

"I feel like a staked goat," the deputy said.

After a while, Jubil rose from the bench and looked out the window. Then he sat down promptly and blew out the lantern.

Somewhere in the distance a night bird called. Crickets sawed and a large frog bleated. They sat there on the bench, near each other, facing in opposite directions, their silver loaded pistols on their knees. Neither spoke.

Suddenly the bird ceased to call and the crickets went silent, and no more was heard from the frog. Jubil whispered to the deputy.

"He comes."

The deputy shivered slightly, took a deep breath. Jubil realized he too was breathing deeply.

"Be silent, and be alert," Jubil said.

"All right," said the deputy, and he locked his eyes on the open window at the back of the shack. Jubil faced the door, which stood halfway open and sagging on its rusty hinges.

For a long time there was nothing. Not a sound. Then Jubil saw a shadow move at the doorway and heard it creak slightly as it moved. He could see a hand on what appeared to be an impossibly long arm, reaching out to grab at the edge of the door. The hand clutched there for a long time, not moving. Then, it was gone, taking its shadow with it.

Time crawled by.

"It's at the window," the deputy said, and his voice was so soft it took Jubil a moment to decipher the words. Jubil turned carefully for a look.

It sat on the windowsill, crouched there like a bird of prey, a halo of bees circling around its head. The hive pulsed and glowed in its chest, and in that glow they could see more bees, so thick they appeared to be a sort of humming smoke. Gimet's head sprouted a few springs of hair, like withering grass fighting its way through stone. A slight turn of its head allowed the moon to flow through the back of its cracked skull and out of its empty eyes. Then the head turned and the face was full of shadows again. The room was silent except for the sound of buzzing bees.

"Courage," Jubil said, his mouth close to the deputy's ear. "Keep your place."

The thing climbed into the room quickly, like a spider dropping from a limb, and when it hit the floor, it stayed low, allowing the darkness to lay over it like a cloak.

Jubil had turned completely on the bench now, facing the window. He heard a scratching sound against the floor. He narrowed his eyes, saw what looked like a shadow, but was in fact the thing coming out from under the table.

Jubil felt the deputy move, perhaps to bolt. He grabbed his arm and held him.

"Courage," he said.

The thing kept crawling. It came within three feet of the circle made by the crumpled Bible pages.

The way the moonlight spilled through the window and onto the floor near the circle Jubil had made, it gave Gimet a kind of eerie glow, his satellite bees circling his head. In that moment, every aspect of the thing locked itself in Jubil's mind. The empty eyes, the sharp, wet teeth, the long, cracked nails, blackened from grime, clacking against the wooden floor. As it moved to cross between two wads of scripture, the pages burst into flames and a line of crackling blue fulmination moved between the wadded pages and made the circle light up fully, all the way around, like Ezekiel's wheel.

Gimet gave out with a hoarse cry, scuttled back, clacking nails and knees against the floor. When he moved, he moved so quickly there seemed to be missing spaces between one moment and the next. The buzzing of Gimet's bees was ferocious.

Jubil grabbed the lantern, struck a match and lit it. Gimet was scuttling along the wall like a cockroach, racing to the edge of the window.

Jubil leaped forward, tossed the lit lantern, hit the beast full in the back as it fled through the window. The lantern burst into flames and soaked back, causing a wave of fire to climb from the thing's waist to the top of its head, scorching a horde of bees, dropping them from the sky like exhausted meteors.

Jubil drew his revolver, snapped off a shot. There was a howl of agony, and then the thing was gone.

Jubil raced out of the protective circle and the deputy followed. They stood at the open window, watched as Gimet, flame-wrapped, streaked through the night in the direction of the graveyard.

"I panicked a little," Jubil said. "I should have been more resolute. Now he's escaped."

"I never even got off a shot," the deputy said. "God, but you're fast. What a draw."

"Look, you stay here if you like. I'm going after him. But I tell you now, the circle of power has played out."

The deputy glanced back at it. The pages had burned out and there was nothing now but a black ring on the floor.

"What caused them to catch fire in the first place?"

"Evil," Jubil said. "When he got close, the pages broke into flames. Gave us the protection of God. Unfortunately, as with most of God's blessings, it doesn't last long."

"I stay here, you'd have to put down more pages."

"I'll be taking the Bible with me. I might need it."

"Then I guess I'll be sticking."

They climbed out the window and moved up the hill. They could smell the odour of fire and rotted flesh in the air. The night was as cool and silent as the graves on the hill.

Moments later they moved amongst the stones and wooden crosses, until they came to a long wide hole in the earth. Jubil could see that there was a burrow at one end of the grave that dipped down deeper into the ground.

Jubil paused there. "He's made this old grave his den. Dug it out and dug deeper."

"How do you know?" the deputy asked.

"Experience . . . And it smells of smoke and burned skin. He crawled down there to hide. I think we surprised him a little."

Jubil looked up at the sky. There was the faintest streak of pink on the horizon. "He's running out of daylight, and soon he'll be out of moon. For a while."

"He damn sure surprised me. Why don't we let him hide? You could come back when the moon isn't full, or even half full. Back in the daylight, get him then."

"I'm here now. And it's my job."

"That's one hell of a job you got, mister."

"I'm going to climb down for a better look."

"Help yourself."

Jubil struck a match and dropped himself into the grave, moved the match around at the mouth of the burrow, got down on his knees and stuck the match and his head into the opening.

"Very large," he said, pulling his head out. "I can smell him. I'm going to have to go in."

"What about me?"

"You keep guard at the lip of the grave," Jubil said, standing. "He may have another hole somewhere, he could come out behind you for all I know. He could come out of that hole even as we speak."

"That's wonderful."

Jubil dropped the now dead match on the ground. "I will tell you this. I can't guarantee success. I lose, he'll come for you, you can bet on that, and you better shoot those silvers as straight as William Tell's arrows."

"I'm not really that good a shot."

"I'm sorry," Jubil said, and struck another match along the length of his pants seam, then with his free hand, drew one of his revolvers. He got down on his hands and knees again, stuck the match in the hole and looked around. When the match was near done, he blew it out.

"Ain't you gonna need some light?" the deputy said. "A match ain't nothin'."

"I'll have it." Jubil removed the remains of the Bible from his pocket, tore it in half along the spine, pushed one half in his coat, pushed the other half before him, into the darkness of the burrow. The moment it entered the hole, it flamed.

"Ain't your pocket gonna catch inside that hole?" the deputy asked.

"As long as I hold it or it's on my person, it won't harm me. But the minute I let go of it, and the aura of evil touches it, it'll blaze. I got to hurry, boy."

With that, Jubil wiggled inside the burrow.

In the burrow, Jubil used the tip of his pistol to push the Bible pages forward. They glowed brightly, but Jubil knew the light would be brief. It would burn longer than writing paper, but still, it would not last long.

After a goodly distance, Jubil discovered the burrow dropped off. He found himself inside a fairly large cavern. He could hear the sound of bats, and smell bat guano, which in fact, greased his path as he slid along on his elbows until he could stand inside the higher cavern and look about. The last flames of the Bible burned itself out with a puff of blue light and a sound like an old man breathing his last.

Jubil listened in the dark for a long moment. He could hear the bats squeaking, moving about. The fact that they had given up the night sky, let Jubil know daylight was not far off.

Jubil's ears caught a sound, rocks shifting against the cave floor. Something was moving in the darkness, and he didn't think it was the bats. It scuttled, and Jubil felt certain it was close to the floor, and by the sound of it, moving his way at a creeping pace. The hair on the back of Jubil's neck bristled like porcupine quills. He felt his flesh bump up and crawl. The air became stiffer with the stench of burnt and rotting flesh. Jubil's knees trembled. He reached cautiously inside his coat pocket, produced a match, struck it on his pants leg, held it up.

At that very moment, the thing stood up and was brightly lit in the glow of the match, the bees circling its skin-stripped skull. It snarled and darted forward. Jubil felt its rotten claws on his shirtfront as he fired the revolver. The blaze from the bullet gave a brief, bright flare and was gone. At the same time, the match was knocked out of his hand and Jubil was knocked backwards, onto his back, the thing's claws at his throat. The monster's bees stung him. The stings felt like red-hot pokers entering his flesh. He stuck the revolver into the creature's body and fired. Once. Twice. Three times. A fourth.

Then the hammer clicked empty. He realized he had already fired two other shots. Six dead silver soldiers were in his cylinders, and the thing still had hold of him.

He tried to draw his other gun, but before he could, the thing released him, and Jubil could hear it crawling away in the dark. The bats fluttered and screeched.

Confused, Jubil drew the pistol, managed to get to his feet. He waited, listening, his fresh revolver pointing into the darkness.

Jubil found another match, struck it.

The thing lay with its back draped over a rise of rock. Jubil eased towards it. The silver loads had torn into the hive. It oozed a dark, odoriferous trail of death and decaying honey. Bees began to drop to the cavern floor. The hive in Gimet's chest sizzled and pulsed like a large, black knot. Gimet opened his mouth, snarled, but otherwise didn't move.

Couldn't move.

Jubil, guided by the last wisps of his match, raised the pistol, stuck it against the black knot, and pulled the trigger. The knot exploded. Gimet let out with a shriek so sharp and loud it startled the bats to flight, drove them out of the cave, through the burrow, out into the remains of the night.

Gimet's claw-like hands dug hard at the stones around him, then he was still and Jubil's match went out.

Jubil found the remains of the Bible in his pocket, and as he removed it, tossed it on the ground, it burst into flames. Using the two pistol barrels like large tweezers, he lifted the burning pages and dropped them into Gimet's open chest. The body caught on fire immediately, crackled and popped dryly, and was soon nothing more than a blaze. It lit the cavern up bright as day.

Jubil watched the corpse being consumed by the biblical fire for a moment, then headed towards the burrow, bent down, squirmed through it, came up in the grave.

He looked for the deputy and didn't see him. He climbed out of the grave and looked around. Jubil smiled. If the deputy had lasted until the bats charged out, that was most likely the last straw, and he had bolted.

Jubil looked back at the open grave. Smoke wisped out of the hole and out of the grave and climbed up to the sky. The moon was fading and the pink on the horizon was widening.

Gimet was truly dead now. The road was safe. His job was done.

At least for one brief moment.

Jubil walked down the hill, found his horse tied in the brush near the road where he had left it. The deputy's horse was gone, of course, the deputy most likely having already finished out Deadman's road at a high gallop, on his way to Nacogdoches, perhaps to have a long drink of whisky and turn in his badge.

MARK SAMUELS

A Gentleman from Mexico

MARK SAMUELS IS THE AUTHOR of two short story collections, *The White Hands and Other Weird Tales* and *Black Altars*, as well as the novella *The Face of Twilight*. His tales have appeared in both *The Mammoth Book of Best New Horror* and *The Year's Best Fantasy and Horror*, and a third collection, *Glyphotech*, is due from PS Publishing. He recently completed another novella, *The Dead Underground*, and is now working on a dynastic weird novel set in London's Highgate area.

"One of the inspirations for this tale was the disappearance of Ambrose Bierce in Mexico sometime in 1914," explains Samuels, "a mystery that, to this day, has not been satisfactorily explained. Better to have drowned in the delicious brandy at the capital's Café Gambrinus than face Pancho Villa's firing squad.

"But it was not my intention to write more fiction concerning the Ambrose Bierce mystery, since great writers, such as Carlos Fuentes, have already done so. So I required a different angle.

"What if an author who was long dead reappeared in Mexico rather than disappeared there? And what if his reappearance suggested that his fiction was bleeding over into reality and transforming it? I had the theme. Now I needed the correct author. Really, the choice was obvious."

Barlow, I imagine, can tell you even more about the Old Ones.
—Clark Ashton Smith to August Derleth,
13 April, 1937

V ÍCTOR ARMSTRONG WAS RUNNING LATE for his appointment and so had hailed a taxi rather than trusting to the metro. Bathed in cruel noon sunlight, the green-liveried Volkswagen beetle taxi cruised down Avenida Reforma. In the back of the vehicle, Armstrong rummaged around in his jacket pocket for the pack of Faros cigarettes he'd bought before setting off on his rendezvous.

"*Es okay para mí a fumar en tu taxi?*" Armstrong said, managing to cobble together the request in his iffy Spanish.

He saw the eyes of the driver reflected in the rear-view mirror, and they displayed total indifference. It was as if he'd made a request to fold his arms.

"*Seguro.*" The driver replied, turning the wheel sharply, weaving his way across four lines of traffic. Armstrong was jolted over to the left and clutched at the leather handle hanging from the front passenger door. The right-hand seat at the front had been removed, as was the case with all the green taxis, giving plenty of leg-room and an easy entrance and exit. Like most of the taxi drivers in Mexico City, this one handled his vehicle with savage intent, determined to get from A to B in the minimum possible time. In this almost permanently gridlocked megalopolis, the survival of the fastest was the rule.

Armstrong lit up one of his untipped cigarettes and gazed out the window. Brilliant sunshine illuminated in excruciating detail the chaos and decay of the urban rubbish dump that is the Ciudad de México, Distrito Federal, or "D.F." for short. A great melting pot of the criminal, the insane, the beautiful and the macho, twenty-five million people constantly living in a mire of institutionalized corruption, poverty and crime. But despite all this, Mexico City's soul seems untouched, defiant. No other great city of the world is so vividly alive, dwelling as it does always in the shadow of death. Another earthquake might be just around the corner, the Popocatéptl volcano might blow at any hour, and the brown haze of man-made pollution might finally suffocate the populace. Who knows? What is certain is that the D.F. would rise again, as filthy, crazed and glorious as before.

They were approaching La Condesa, a fashionable area to the north of the centre that had attracted impoverished artists and writers ten years ago, but which had recently been overrun with pricey restaurants and cafes.

Armstrong had arranged to meet with an English-speaking acquaintance at the bookshop café El Torre on the corner of Avenida Nuevo León. This acquaintance, Juan San Isidro, was a so-called underground poet specializing in sinister verse written in the Náhuatl language and who, it was rumoured, had links with the *narcosatá-*

nicos. A notorious drunk, San Isidro had enjoyed a modicum of celebrity in his youth but had burnt out by his mid-twenties. Now a decade older, he was scarcely ever sober and looked twice his actual age. His bitterness and tendency to enter into the kind of vicious quarrels that seem endemic in Latin American literary circles had alienated him from most of his contemporaries.

Armstrong suspected that San Isidro had requested a meeting for one of two reasons; either to tap him for money, or else to seek his assistance in recommending a translator for a re-issue of his poetical work in an English language edition in the United States. It was highly unlikely that San Isidro was going to offer him a work of fiction for one of his upcoming anthologies of short stories.

The taxi pulled up alongside the bookshop.

"*¿Cuánto es?*" Armstrong asked.

"*Veintiún pesos*" The driver responded. Armstrong handed over some coins and exited the vehicle.

Standing on the corner outside the bookshop was a stall selling tortas, tacos and other fast food. The smell of the sizzling meat and chicken, frying smokily on the hob, made Armstrong's mouth water. Despite the call of "*¡Pásele, señor!*", Armstrong passed by, knowing that, as a foreigner, his stomach wouldn't have lasted ten minutes against the native bacteria. Having experienced what they called "Montezuma's Revenge" on his first trip to D.F. a year ago, there was no question of him taking a chance like that again.

Across the street an argument was taking place between two drivers, who had got out of their battered and dirty cars to trade insults. Since their abandoned vehicles were holding up the traffic, the rather half-hearted battle (consisting entirely of feints and shouting) was accompanied by a cacophony of angry car-horns.

El Torre was something of a landmark in the area, its exterior covered with tiles, and windows with external ornate grilles. A three-storey building with a peaked roof, and erected in the colonial era, it had been a haunt for literati of all stripes, novelists, poets and assorted hangers-on, since the 1950s. During the period in which La Condesa had been gentrified some of El Torre's former seedy charm had diminished and, as well as selling books, it had diversified into stocking DVDs and compact discs upstairs.

Part of the ground floor had been converted into an expensive eatery, whilst the first floor now half-occupied a cafe-bar from where drinkers could peer over the centre of the storey down into the level below, watching diners pick at their food and browsers lingering over the books on shelves and on the display tables. As a consequence of these improvements, the space for poetry readings upstairs had been entirely done away with, and Juan San Isidro haunted its former confines as if in eternal protest at the loss of his own personal stage.

As Armstrong entered, he glanced up at the floor above and saw the poet already waiting for him, slumped over a table and tracing a circle on its surface with an empty bottle of Sol beer. His lank black hair hung down to his shoulders, obscuring his face, but even so his immense bulk made him unmistakable.

Armstrong's gaze roved around and sought out the stairway entrance. He caught sight of the only other customer in El Torre besides himself and San Isidro. This other person was dressed in a dark grey linen suit, quite crumpled, with threadbare patches at the elbows and frayed cuffs. The necktie he wore was a plain navy blue and quite unremarkable. His shoes were badly scuffed and he must have repeatedly refused the services of the D.F.'s innumerable *boleros*. They keenly polished shoes on their portable foot-stands for anyone who had a mere dozen pesos to spare. The man had an olive complexion, was perfectly clean-shaven, and about forty years old. His short black hair was parted neatly on the left-hand side. He had the features of a *mestizo*, a typical Mexican of mingled European and Native Indian blood. There was something in the way that he carried himself that told of a gentleman down on his luck, perhaps even an impoverished scholar given his slight stoop, an attribute often acquired by those who pore over books or manuscripts year after year.

He was browsing through the books on display that were published by the likes of Ediciones Valdemar and Ediciones Siruela that had been specially imported from Spain. These were mostly supernatural fiction titles, for which many Mexican readers had a discerning fondness. Armstrong was glad, for his own anthologies invariably were comprised of tales depicting the weird and uncanny, a market that, at least in the Anglophone countries, seemed to have self-destructed after a glut of trashy horror paperbacks in the 1980s. But these were not junk, they were works by the recognized masters, and a quick glance over the classics available for sale here in mass-market form would have drawn the admiration of any English or American devotee.

Here were books by Arthur Machen, Algernon Blackwood, M. R. James and Ambrose Bierce, amongst dozens of others. Most striking however, was the vast range of collections available written by H. P. Lovecraft. The browsing man in the dark suit picked up one after the other, almost reluctant to return each to its proper place, although if his down-at-heel appearance were an indication, their price was surely beyond his limited means. New books in Mexico are scarcely ever cheap.

Armstrong looked away. He could not understand why this rather ordinary gentleman had stirred his imagination. He was, after all, merely typical of the sort of book-addict found anywhere and at any time. Meanwhile Juan San Isidro had noticed Victor's arrival and called down to him.

"¡Ay, Víctor, quiero más chela! Lo siento, pero no tengo dinero."

Armstrong sighed, and made his way up the stairs.

When they were eventually sitting opposite one another, Armstrong with a bottle of Indio and San Isidro with a fresh bottle of Sol, the Mexican switched from Spanish to English. He was always keen to take whatever opportunity he could to converse in the language. A huge bear of a man, he'd recently grown a shaggy goatee beard and the T-shirt he wore bore the logo of some outlandish band called Control Machete, whose music Armstrong did not know and did not want to know. Years ago Armstrong had foolishly mentioned San Isidro's literary efforts to the publisher of a small press imprint in California who was looking for cosmic or outré verse. The result had been a chapbook with a selection of San Isidro's Aztec-influenced work translated into English, and thereafter Armstrong had never been able to entirely shake off his "discovery".

"So," San Isidro said, "how are things with you? Still editing those *antologías?*"

"There's scarcely any money in them Juan," Armstrong replied, "unless I've managed to wrangle something original out of Steve King, the publishers want to nail my balls to the wall."

"You know him? King? Do you think he'd give me a loan? He's very rich, no? Help out a struggling brother artist?"

Armstrong tried not to smile inappropriately. He could only imagine how quickly San Isidro would piss away any handouts he'd receive on booze. No one other than their agents, accountants, lawyers or publishers milks cash-cow authors.

"He's a busy man. I don't think he'd appreciate my . . ."

"You mean he's a *pinche cabrón*. Keeps his money up his *culo* where no one else can get at it. That's why *todos los gringos* walk around with their legs apart, like cowboys, no? All those dollar bills stuffed in there."

Armstrong was relieved to be British. Even liberal Americans who came south, seeking to atone for the recent sins of NAFTA and a long history of land grabbing, were objects of ridicule here. They might get away with such conscience posturing in the north, in cities like Monterrey that were closer to the border and which looked to rich US States like Texas for inspiration, but in Mexico D. F. *gringos* are only ever *pinches gringos* and no amount of self-loathing or atonement on their part could ever erase the fact. The British, on the other hand, despite their Imperial past, were redeemed by virtue of having given the Beatles and association football to the world.

"Why did you want to see me, Juan?" Armstrong asked, taking out his packet of *Faros* and putting them on the table. His companion looked at the cheap brand with amused contempt. Nevertheless, this attitude did not stop him from smoking them.

"I want you to take a look at some *cuentos*," San Isidro replied, puffing away on the cigarette he'd taken. "Read them and make me an offer. They're in your line of work."

He delved into a shoulder bag lying underneath the table and took out a pile of papers, individuated into sections by rubber bands, and handed them over.

"I thought you didn't write short stories." Armstrong said.

"I didn't write them. I'm acting as the exclusive agent. They're in English, as you see, and they're the type of horror stories you like. I handle all his stuff," San Isidro replied.

"Who's this author," Armstrong said, looking at the top sheet, "Felipe López? I can't say I've heard of him."

"*El señor López* has only been writing for a couple of years. He's my personal discovery, like you discovered me, no? *Es un autor auténtico*, not some hack. *Mira al cabellero* down there, the one who's looking through the books? That's *el señor López*. He doesn't want to meet you until you've read his stuff. I told him I knew you, and that you weren't the same as all those other *culeros* who'd rejected him."

So that man in the crumpled grey suit was San Isidro's first client, Armstrong thought. He hesitated for a moment but then relented. At least this man López had the appearance of being literate.

"Alright," Armstrong said, "I'll take them away with me and call you once I've read them. I can't promise anything though."

"Why not sit here and read them now, *compañero*? I tell you, these things are a gold mine. We can have a few more *chelas* while I wait for you to finish. He also does his own proofreading, so you won't need to *trabajar mucho* yourself."

"Short stories," Armstrong riposted, "are fool's gold, Juan. I told you, there's no real money in them anymore. Have another on me if you like, but I've got to go. I'll be in touch."

With that closing remark Armstrong stood up, left a hundred pesos note on the table, and made his exit. He didn't notice whether or not *el Señor López* saw him leave.

Over the next few days Armstrong almost forgot about the stories by Felipe López. He hated being asked to read fiction by an unknown author that had been praised by one of his friends. All too often he had to prick their enthusiasm, usually fired by beer and comradeship rather than from an objective assessment of literary merit. And San Isidro had never acted as an agent for anybody before; he was far too consumed by his own literary ambitions. So it appeared obvious to Armstrong that San Isidro was paying back a favour of some sort. Though it seemed unlikely given the down-at-heel appearance of López, but perhaps it was a case of San Isidro owing him money.

Armstrong was staying close to Cuauhtémoc metro station in an apartment owned by Mexican friends of his. The couple, Enrique and María, were in London for a few weeks, staying in his flat there in an exchange holiday. It was something they did every other year to save on hotel bills. There were only three days left before they were due to cross each other high over the Atlantic in flights going in the opposite direction. Enrique and María were both involved in publishing themselves, and he'd struck up a friendship with them in 1995 whilst attending a fantasy and horror convention held in San Francisco.

Since he was staying in an apartment belonging to friends, Armstrong paid little attention to the telephone, as he knew he'd just be taking messages for his absent hosts. Anything desperately important that needed to be passed on to them would be left on the answering machine. When he got around to checking it, there were three messages, two for Enrique and María, and one for him. It was left by Juan San Isidro.

"*Oye, ¿qué onda?* Man, don't fuck me over. Have you read *los cuentos?* I think not. Otherwise you'd be chasing my ass like a *puto*. You don't leave Mexico until I hear from you, *¿te queda claro?*"

Despite his reluctance, Armstrong didn't see any alternative but to look the stories over. He took them out onto the little balcony overlooking the *privada* in which the apartment was situated. It was pleasantly warm outside in the evening, being October, and since the only traffic passing below consisted of pedestrians it was easy to concentrate. He sat down on the chair he'd moved out there, put the papers that he'd retrieved from his suitcase on his lap, and looked them over.

San Isidro had given him four stories, the longest of which was the third at around 40,000 words.

Armstrong had seen this type of story on dozens of occasions in the past, usually sent for his consideration by "fan authors" who were obsessed with the life and works of H. P. Lovecraft. Most of these pastiches contained long lists of clichéd forbidden books and names of unpronounceable entities to be incorporated into the so-called "Cthulhu Mythos". As he turned the pages of the first of López's tales though, he was surprised to discover that they did not also contain the other feature associated with Lovecraft fan pastiches – there were no obvious grammatical, spelling or common textual errors. The work had already been gone over by an author with a keen eye for copy-editing.

Additionally, it had to be the case that Felipe López was fluent in English to the degree of being able to pass completely for a native. The text contained no trace of any Spanish language idioms indicating his Mexican nationality. Indeed, López even favoured the British spelling of certain words, rather than that used in the United States, in exactly the same fashion as Lovecraft himself had done.

Despite his disdain for pastiche, Armstrong kept reading. Eventually, to his surprise, he found that López's mimetic skills were so expert that he could almost believe that he was reading a previously undiscovered work written by Lovecraft himself. The story had the exact same sense of nightmarish authenticity as the best of the Providence author's tales. By the time he'd finished reading the first story, Armstrong was in a state of dazed wonder. Of course he realized, on a professional level, that the thing had no commercial potential. It smacked far too much of an in-joke, or a hoax, but it was nevertheless profoundly impressive in its own right.

He began to wonder what this López person might be able to achieve were he to wean himself from the Lovecraft influence and produce fiction utilizing a distinct authorial voice. It might result in another modern-day writer of the order of Thomas Ligotti.

Armstrong was dimly aware of the telephone ringing in the background. He ignored the sound, allowing the answering machine to deal with whoever it was. He supposed that it could be San Isidro again and that it might have been better to pick up, but he was too eager to discover whether the story he'd just read was a fluke or not. Since the mosquitoes were now busy in the night air, he took the manuscripts inside and carried on reading.

*   *   *

Whoever had left the weird message on Enrique and María's answering machine was obviously some crank, thought Armstrong. He played it back again the morning after it was recorded.

There was click on the line and the sound of unintelligible voices conferring amongst themselves and then a jarring, discordant muttering in English. The voice had a Mexican accent but was unknown to Armstrong. It said, "*He belongs to us. His products belong to us. No one will take him from us.*"

That was all.

After listening to the message one more time, Armstrong wondered if it were not simply San Isidro playing a joke on him, pretending to be another rival party involved with the works of Felipe López. Perhaps he thought the idea of some competition might spur Armstrong to a quick decision. If so, it was an unnecessary ploy.

After having read the second of López's tales he was convinced that the author had unmatched imagination and ability, despite being almost ruinously handicapped by his slavish mimicry of Lovecraft's style and themes. However, there was more than enough pure genius in there to convince Armstrong to take the matter further. If he could meet with López in person, he was determined to press upon him the necessity of a last revision of the texts – one that removed entirely the Cthulhu Mythos elements and replaced the florid, adjective-ridden prose with a minimalist approach.

When he telephoned Juan San Isidro it was no surprise that the poet-turned-agent was deeply suspicious about Armstrong's insistence that he must meet López alone.

"You want to cut me out of the deal, *¡estás loco!* Forget it, man. Now you know *que es un maestro, lo quieres todo para ti.*"

"I only want to suggest a few changes to the texts, Juan. Nothing sinister in that, really. You'll get your commission, I'll not cheat you, believe me."

Their conversation went round in circles for ten minutes before Armstrong eventually convinced San Isidro that he had no underhand motive with regards to López's work. Even so, Armstrong realized that there was something more going on between the two of them than the usual protective relationship between an agent and his client. Nevertheless, he successfully elicited a promise from San Isidro that he would ensure López met with him alone in the Café la Habana on La Calle de Bucareli at 2:00 p.m. that same afternoon.

The Café la Habana was a haunt for distinguished old men who came to play chess, smoke their pipes or cigars and spend the better part of the afternoon dreaming over coffee or beer. It had a high ceiling and was decorated with framed photographs of Havana from the time before Castro's revolution. Many Communist exiles from Batista Cuba came here, having fled persecution, and its fame dated from that period. The number of exiles had dwindled as the years passed, but it still had a reputation amongst all those who championed leftist defiance. The place had a long pedigree, having been a favourite meeting place, in even earlier decades, of those Spanish Republican refugees who'd settled in D. F. after escaping the wrath of General Franco's regime.

Armstrong sat in a corner, lingering over a glass of tequila with lime, when López walked in. He was half an hour late. His lean form was framed in the doorway by the brilliant sunshine outside. López cast his glance around the place before spotting Armstrong and making for the table at which he sat.

López had changed his dark grey suit for a cream-coloured one, and this time he was wearing a matching Panama hat. He gave a nod of recognition towards Armstrong as he approached.

Before he sat down he shook Armstrong's hand and apologised in English. "I hope that you will excuse my tardiness Mr Armstrong, but the truth is that I was distracted by a particularly fascinating example of eighteenth-century colonial architecture whilst making my way over here."

Armstrong did not reply at once. He was taken aback by López's accent. Unless he was mistaken, it was pure, authentic New England Yankee. There was not a trace of Mexican in it.

"No need to apologise," Armstrong finally said, "can I get you a drink; some beer or tequila perhaps?"

"Thank you but no. I never partake of alcoholic beverages, even for the purposes of refreshment. However, a cup of coffee, perhaps a double espresso, would be most welcome."

Armstrong ordered López's coffee and asked for another tequila with lime to be brought to their table.

"I liked your tales very much, it was quite an experience reading through them I can tell you. Of course they're overly derivative, but I imagine that you could easily tone down all the Lovecraftian elements . . ."

"I'm afraid, Mr Armstrong," López said, with a chill tone entering his voice, "that alterations of any sort are completely out of the question. The stories must be printed as written, down to the last detail, otherwise this conversation is simply a waste of my time and your own."

The drinks arrived. López calmly began to shovel spoonful after spoonful of sugar into his cup, turning the coffee into treacly, caffeine-rich syrup. Armstrong looked at him incredulously. Now he understood what was going on. San Isidro was definitely having a joke at his expense. He must have coached this López character, telling him all about H. P. Lovecraft's mannerisms and . . . to what end?

"Why are you persisting with this absurd Lovecraft impersonation?" Armstrong blurted out, "It's ridiculous. San Isidro put you up to it I suppose. But what I can't figure out is why, so let me in on the joke."

López looked up from his coffee and his eyes were deadly serious. And here it comes, boy and girls, thought Armstrong; here comes the line we've all been waiting for:

This is no joke Mr Armstrong, far from it, for I am in reality Howard Phillips Lovecraft of Providence, Rhode Island.

"Surely the only rational answer has already suggested itself," López replied, very calmly and without any melodrama, "you are in fact sitting across the table from a certifiable lunatic."

Armstrong leaned back in his seat and very carefully considered the man opposite. His manner betrayed no sign of humour and he spoke as if what he'd suggested was an established truism.

"Then despite your behaviour, you know that you're not really Lovecraft?" Armstrong said.

"Howard Phillips Lovecraft died in agony on the morning of Monday 15 March 1937 in Providence's Jane Brown Memorial Hospital. I cannot be him. However, since Tuesday 15 March 2003, I have been subject to a delusion whereby the identity of Lovecraft completely supplanted my own. I currently have no memories whatsoever of having once been Felipe López of Mexico City. His family and friends are complete strangers to me. Meanwhile everyone Lovecraft knew is dead. I have become an outsider in this country and in this time. Unless one accepts the existence of the supernatural, which I emphatically do not, then only the explanation I have advanced has any credence."

Armstrong was taken aback by these remarks. This was like no madman he'd heard of – one who was not only able to recognize his derangement, but who also was totally a slave to it. It was more like some bizarre variant of a multiple personality disorder.

"What did the doctors here have to say?" Armstrong asked.

"They did their best, but with no appreciable effect, let alone any amelioration, upon my malady. They tended to agree with my analysis of the situation." López said, after taking a sip of his coffee.

"What about López before this happened? Did he have any interest in Lovecraft prior to your – umm – alteration? I can't believe something like that would come out of nowhere."

It was annoying, but Armstrong found himself questioning López as if he were actually addressing Lovecraft inhabiting another body.

"Quite so. I have discovered that López was a fanatical devotee of Lovecraft's life and work. Moreover, he was one of that rather contemptible breed of freaks who adhere to the outlandish belief that, rather than writing fiction, Lovecraft had unconscious access to ultra-mundane dimensions. The group to which he belonged, who styled themselves "The Sodality of the Black Sun", advocated the piteous theory that Lovecraft was an occult prophet instead of a mere scribbler. This indicates to me a brain already on the brink of a potential collapse into total chaos. You see before you the inevitable consequence."

There are a lot of sad crazies out there, thought Armstrong, who believe in nothing except the power of their own imaginations to create whatever they want to create from a supposedly malleable reality. A whole bunch of them had doubtless fastened upon Lovecraft's mythos for inspiration, but he doubted that any others had wound up like Felipe López.

"Well," Armstrong said, "I don't know what to make of all this. But surely one consideration has occurred to you already? If you really were Lovecraft, you'd know certain things that only he could possibly have known."

"An ingenious point," said López, "but with all his contemporaries in the grave, how then to verify that information? Mr Armstrong, I must remind you that the idea of Lovecraft's consciousness not only surviving the death of his physical form, but also transferring itself to another body, is patently ridiculous. I make no such claim."

López stared at him wordlessly and then, having finished the dregs of his coffee, got up and left.

When Armstrong arrived back at Enrique and María's apartment, he found the door already ajar. Someone had broken in, forcing their entrance with a crowbar or similar tool judging by the splintered wound in the side of the door's frame. He was relieved to find that the intruders had not torn the place apart and seemed to have scarcely disturbed anything. When he examined his own room however, he noted at once that the López manuscripts were missing.

He unmistakably remembered having left them on his bedside table. However, in their place, was a note left behind by whoever had stolen them. It read:

DO NOT MEDDLE IN OUR AFFAIRS AGAIN,
LEST THE DARKNESS SEEK YOU OUT.

Obviously, this was a targeted burglary by the people who'd left that answering machine message warning him off having dealings with López. They must have wanted to get hold of the López stories extremely badly. Whoever they were, they must have also known that San Isidro had passed them to him, as well as knowing that Armstrong had an appointment with López, thus giving them the perfect moment to strike while he was out.

It was difficult to figure out what to do next. Everyone in Mexico City realizes that to call the police regarding a burglary has two possible outcomes. The first is that they will turn up, treat it as a waste of their time and do nothing. The second is that things will turn surreal very quickly, because they will casually mention how poorly paid police officers are, and, in return for a "donation", they are able to arrange for the swift return of your goods with no questions asked. Given that the burglary was not the work of organized crime but some nutty underground cult, Armstrong thought better of involving the police.

Great, thought Armstrong, now I'm in trouble not only with the local branch of occult loonies, but with San Isidro and López for having lost the manuscripts. The first thing to do was give San Isidro the bad news. Since a matter of this delicate nature was best dealt with face-to-face, Armstrong decided to make his way over to the poet's apartment, after he'd arranged for someone to come over and fix the door.

A cardinal, though unspoken, rule of travelling by metro in Mexico City is not to carry anything of value. If you're a tourist, look like a tourist with little money. The security guards that hover around the ticket barriers are not there just for show. They carry guns for a reason. D. F. is the kidnapping capital of the world. Armstrong had always followed the dress-down rule and, although he stood out anyway because he was a pale-skinned *güerito*, he'd encountered no problems on his travels.

The stations themselves were grimy, functionalist and depressing. Architecturally they resembled prison camps, but located underground. Nevertheless Armstrong enjoyed travelling by metro; it was unbelievably cheap, the gap between trains was less than a minute, and it was like being on a mobile market place. Passengers selling homemade CDs would wander up and down the carriages, with samples of music playing on ghetto blasters slung over their shoulders. Others sold tonics for afflictions from back pain to impotence. Whether these worked or not there was certainly a market for them, as the sellers did a brisk trade.

One of the carriages on the train that Armstrong took must have been defective. All its lights were out and, curiously, he noticed that when anyone thought to board it anyway they changed their minds at once and preferred to either remain on the platform or else rush over into one of the adjacent carriages instead.

Armstrong alighted at Chapultepec station, found his way through the convoluted tunnels up to the surface and turned left alongside the eight-lane road outside. The noise of the traffic blocked out most other sounds, and the vehicle fumes were like a low-level grey nebula held down by the force of the brilliant afternoon sunshine. People scurried to and fro along the pavement, their gazes fixed straight ahead, particularly those of any lone women for whom eye-contact with a *chilango* carried the risk of inviting a lewd suggestion.

A long footbridge flanked the motorway, and was the only means of crossing for pedestrians for a couple of miles or so. At night it was a notorious crime spot and only the foolhardy would cross it unaccompanied. However, at this time of the day everyone safely used it and a constant stream of people went back and forth.

Juan San Isidro's apartment was only five minutes' walk from the bridge, and was housed in a decaying brownstone building just on the fringes of La Condesa. Sometimes Armstrong wondered whether the poet was the structure's only occupant, for the windows of all the other apartments were either blackened by soot or else broken and hanging open day and night to the elements.

He pushed the intercom button for San Isidro, and, after a minute, heard a half-awake voice say, "*¿Quién es?*"

"It's me, Victor, come down and let me in, will you?" Armstrong replied, holding his mouth close to the intercom.

"Stand in front where I can see you," the voice said, "and I'll give you *mis llaves*."

Armstrong left the porch, went onto the pavement and looked up. San Isidro leaned out of one of the third-floor windows, his lank black hair making a cowl over his face. He tossed a plastic bag containing the keys over the ledge, and Armstrong retrieved it after it hit the ground.

The building had grown even worse since the last time he'd paid a visit. If it was run-down before, now it was positively unfit for human habitation and should have been condemned. The lobby was filled with debris, half the tiles had fallen from the walls and a dripping water pipe was poking out from a huge hole in the ceiling. Vermin scurried around back in the shadows. The building's staircase was practically a deathtrap, for if a step had not already collapsed, those that remained seemed likely to do so in the near future.

As Armstrong climbed he clutched at the shaky banister with both hands, his knuckles white with the fierce grip, advancing up sideways like a crab.

San Isidro was standing in the doorway to his apartment, smoking a fat joint with one hand and swigging from a half-bottle of Cuervo with the other. The smell of marijuana greeted Armstrong as he finally made it to the third floor. Being continually stoned, he thought, was about the only way to make the surroundings bearable.

"*Hola, compañero,* good to see you, come on inside."

His half-glazed eyes, wide fixed smile and unsteady gait indicated that he'd been going at the weed and tequila already for most of the day.

"This is a celebration, no? You've come to bring me *mucho dinero*, I hope. I'm honoured that you come here to see me. *Siéntate, por favor.*"

San Isidro cleared a space on the sofa that was littered with porno magazines and empty packets of Delicados cigarettes. Armstrong then sat down while San Isidro picked up an empty glass from the floor, poured some tequila in it and put it in his hand.

"*Salud,*" he said "to our friend and saviour Felipe López, *el mejor escritor de cuentos macabros del mundo, ahora y siempre.*"

"I want you to tell me, Juan, as a friend and in confidence, what happened to López and how he came to think and act exactly like H. P. Lovecraft. And I want to know about the people that are after him. Were they people he knew before his – um – breakdown?" Armstrong said, looking at the glass and trying to find a clean part of the rim from which to drink. At this stage he was reluctant to reveal that the López manuscripts had been stolen. San Isidro was volatile, and Armstrong wasn't sure how he might react to the news.

San Isidro appeared to start momentarily at the mention of "H. P. Lovecraft", but whether it was the effect of the name or the cumulative effect of the booze and weed, it was difficult to tell.

"So he told you, eh? Well, not all of it. *No recuerda nada de antes,* when he was just Felipe López. *No importa qué pasó antes,* sure, there was some heavy shit back then. *Si quieres los cuentos, primero quiero mucho dinero.* Then maybe I'll tell you about it, eh?"

"I'll pay you Juan, and pay you well. But I need to understand the truth," Armstrong replied.

What San Isidro told Armstrong over the next half hour consisted of a meandering monologue, mostly in Spanish, of a brilliant young *gringo* who had come to Mexico in the 1940s to study Mesoamerican anthropology. This man, Robert Hayward Barlow, had been Lovecraft's literary executor. Armstrong had heard the name before, but what little he knew did not prepare him for San Isidro's increasingly bizarre account of events.

He began plausibly enough. Barlow, he said, had taken possession of Lovecraft's papers after the writer's death in 1937. He had gone through them thereafter and donated the bulk to the John Hay Library in Providence, in order to establish a permanent archival resource. However, he was ostracized by the Lovecraft circle, a campaign driven by Donald Wandrei and August Derleth, on the basis that he had supposedly stolen the materials in the first place from under the nose of the Providence author's surviving aunt.

However, what was not known then, San Isidro claimed, was that Barlow had kept some items back, the most important of which was the *Dream Diary of the Arkham Cycle*, a notebook in long-hand of approximately thirty or so pages and akin to Lovecraft's commonplace book.

It contained, so San Isidro alleged, dozens of entries from 1923 to 1936 that appeared to contradict the assertion that Lovecraft's mythos was solely a fictional construct. These entries were not suggestive by and of themselves *at the time they were supposedly written*, for the content was confined to the description of dreams in which elements from his myth-cycle had manifested themselves. These could be accepted as having no basis in reality had it not been for their supposedly *prophetic* nature. One such entry San Isidro quoted from memory. By this stage his voice was thick and the marijuana he'd been smoking made him giggle in a disquieting, paranoid fashion.

"*A dream of the bony fingers of Azathoth reaching down to touch two cities in Imperial Japan, and laying them waste. Mushroom clouds portending the arrival of the Fungi from Yuggoth.*"

To Armstrong, this drivel seemed only a poor attempt to turn Lovecraft into some latter-day Nostradamus, but San Isidro clearly thought otherwise. Armstrong wondered what López had to do with all of this, and whether he would repudiate the so-called "prophecies" by sharing Lovecraft's trust in indefatigable rationalism. That would be ironic.

"How does all this tie in with López?" Armstrong asked.

"In 1948," San Isidro slurred, "there were *unos brujos, se llama-ban La Sociedad del Sol Oscuro*, cheap *gringo* paperbacks of Love-craft were their inspiration. They were interested in revival of worship for the old Aztec gods before they incorporated Cthulhu mythology. The gods of the two are much alike, no? *Sangre, muerte y la onda cósmica*. They tormented Barlow, suspected that's why he came to Mexico, because of the connection. Barlow was a *puto*, he loved to give it to boys, and soon they found out about the dream-diary. That was the end. Blackmail. He killed himself in 1951, took a whole bottle of seconal."

"But what about López?"

"They had to wait *cincuenta años para que se alinearan las estrellas*. Blood sacrifices, so much blood, the police paid-off over decades. But it was prophesized in his own dream-diary: *el espléndido regreso*. Even the exact date was written in there. López was the chosen vessel."

"How do you know all this, Juan?"

"I chose him from amongst us, but I betrayed them, the secret was passed down to me, and now I need to get out of this *pinche* country *rápido*, before *mis hermanos* come for me. López, he wants to go back to Providence, one last time," San Isidro giggled again at this point, "though I reckon it's changed a lot, since he last saw it, eh? But, me, I don't care."

He's as insane as López, Armstrong thought. This is just an elaborate scheme cooked up by the two of them to get money out of someone they think of as simply another stupid, rich foreigner. After all, what evidence was there that any of this nonsense had a grain of truth in it? Like most occultists, they'd cobbled together a mass of pseudo-facts and assertions and dressed it up as secret knowledge known only to the "initiated". Christ, he wouldn't have been surprised if, at this point, San Isidro produced a *Dream Diary of the Arkham Cycle*, some artificially-aged notebook written in the 1960s by a drugged-up kook who'd forged Lovecraft's handwriting and stuffed it full of allusions to events after his death in 1937. They'd managed to pull off a pretty fair imitation of his stories between themselves and whoever else was involved in the scam. The results were certainly no worse than August Derleth's galling at-tempts at "posthumous collaboration" with Lovecraft.

At last, as if San Isidro had reached a stage where he had drunk and smoked himself back to relative sobriety, he lurched up from the easy chair in which he'd been sitting. He ran his fingers through his beard, stared hard at Armstrong and said, "We need to talk business, how much are you going to give me?"

"I'll give you enough to get out of Mexico, for the sake of our friendship," Armstrong replied, "but I can't pay for the stories, Juan. Anyway, someone has stolen them."

Probably you or López, he thought cynically.

The only reaction from San Isidro was that he raised his eyebrows a fraction. Without saying a word he went into the kitchen next door and Armstrong could hear him rattling around in some drawers.

"If you're going to try to fleece me," Armstrong said, raising his voice so that he could be heard in the adjacent room, "then you and López will have to do better than all this Barlow and the 'Sodality of the Black Sun' crap."

When San Isidro came back into the room, his teeth were bared like those of a hungry wolf. In his right hand he was clutching a small calibre pistol, which he raised and aimed directly at Armstrong's head.

"*Cabrón, hijo de puta, di tus últimas oraciones, porque te voy a matar.*"

Sweat broke out on Armstrong's forehead. His thoughts raced. Was the gun loaded or was this only bravado? Another means of extorting money from him? Could he take the chance?

Just as Armstrong was about to cry out, everything went black. Despite the fact that it was the middle of the afternoon, with brilliant sunshine outside, the room was immediately swallowed up by total darkness. Armstrong could not believe what was happening. He thought, at first, that he had gone blind. Only when he stumbled around in the inky void and came right up against the window did he see the sunlight still outside, but not penetrating at all beyond the glass and into the room.

Outside, the world went on as normal. Armstrong turned back away from the window and was aware of a presence moving within the dark. Whatever it was emitted a high-pitched and unearthly whistle that seemed to bore directly into his brain. God, he thought, his train of reasoning in a fit of hysterical chaos, something from Lovecraft's imagination had clawed its way into reality, fully seventy years after the man's death.

Something that might drive a man absolutely insane, if it was seen in the light.

Armstrong thought of the hundreds of hackneyed Cthulhu Mythos stories that he'd been forced to read down the years and over which he'd chortled. He recalled the endless ranks of clichéd yet

supposedly infinitely horrible monstrosities, all with unpronounceable names. But he couldn't laugh now, because the joke wasn't so
funny anymore. So he screamed instead—

"Juan! Juan!"

Armstrong bumped into the sofa in a panic, before he finally
located the exit. From behind him came the sound of six shots, fired
one after the other, deafeningly loud, and then nothing but dead,
gaunt silence. He staggered into the hallway and reached the light
outside, turned back once to look at the impenetrable darkness
behind him, before then hurtling down the stairs. He now gave
no thought, as he had done when coming up, as to how precarious
they were. He did, however, even in the grip of terror, recall that the
building was deserted and that no one could swear to his having been
there.

After what had happened to him, Armstrong expected to feel a sense
of catastrophic psychological disorientation. Whatever had attacked
San Isidro, he thought, carrying darkness along with it so as to hide
its deeds, was proof of something, even if it did not prove that
everything San Isidro had claimed was in fact true.

At the very least it meant that "The Sodality of the Black Sun" had
somehow called a psychic force into existence through their half-
century of meddling with rituals and sacrifices. Armstrong had no
choice but to discount the alternative rational explanation.

At the time when day had become night in San Isidro's apartment
he had been afraid, but nothing more, otherwise he was clear-headed
and not prone to any type of hysterical interlude or hallucinatory
fugue. Rather than feeling that his worldview had been turned
upside-down however, he instead felt a sense of profound loneliness.
What had happened had really happened, but he knew that if he tried
to tell anyone about it, they would scoff or worse, pity him, as he
himself would have done, were he in their position.

Enrique and María returned to their apartment on schedule and
Armstrong told them of his intention to remain in Mexico City a
while longer. They noticed the curious melancholy in him, but did
not question him about it in any detail. Nor would he have told them,
even if prompted.

Armstrong moved out the next day, transferring his meagre
belongings to a room in a seedy hotel overlooking La Calle de
Bucareli. From there he was able to gaze out of a fifth-floor window
in his *cuartito* and keep watch on the Café la Habana opposite. His
remaining connection to the affair was with Felipe López, the man

who had the mind of Lovecraft, and he could not leave without seeing him one last time.

He had no idea whether San Isidro was alive or dead. What was certain was that it was inconceivable that he attempt to make contact with him. Were San Isidro dead, it would arouse suspicion that Armstrong had been connected with his demise, and were he alive, then Armstrong had little doubt that he'd want to exact revenge.

Days passed, and Armstrong's vigil yielded no results. There was no sign of López and he had no way of contacting him directly, no phone number, and no address. He was fearful that the Mexican police might call upon him at any instant, and scanned the newspapers daily in order to see if there were any reports mentioning San Isidro. He found nothing at all relating to him and recalled what he'd been told about the authorities having been paid off with blood money over decades.

When Armstrong left his room it was only to visit the local Oxxo convenience store in order to stock up on *tortas de jamón y queso, Faros, y tequila barato*. The last of these items was most important to him. He spent most of the time pouring the tequila into a tumbler and knocking it back, while sitting at his pigeon-shit stained window, hoping to see López finally enter the Café la Habana in search of him. All he saw was the endless mass of frenzied traffic, drivers going from nowhere to anywhere and back in a hurry, oblivious to the revelation that separated him from such commonplace concerns, and which had taken him out of the predictable track of everyday existence.

And then, twelve days after he'd rented the room in the hotel, he finally saw a slightly stooped figure in a grey suit making his way towards the Café la Habana. It was López; there could be no doubt about it.

López was seated in a table in the corner of the Café, reading a paperback book and sipping at a cup of coffee. As Armstrong approached he saw that the book was a grubby second-hand copy of *Los Mitos de Cthulhu por H. P. Lovecraft y Otros*. The edition had a strange green photographic cover, depicting, it appeared, a close-up of a fossil. López immediately put down the volume once he caught sight of Armstrong.

"San Isidro seems to have disappeared off the face of the earth," he said, "I've been endeavouring to contact him for the last two weeks, but all to no avail. I admit to feeling not a little concern in the matter. Have you crossed paths with him of late?"

Armstrong could not take his eyes off the man. Could "The Sodality of the Black Sun" have succeeded? Was the creature that conversed with him now actually the mind of Lovecraft housed in the body of some Mexican occultist called López? God, what a disappointment it must have been for them, he thought. What irony! To go to all that trouble to reincarnate the consciousness of the great H. P. Lovecraft, only to find that after his return he denied his own posthumous existence! But why keep such a survival alive, why allow the existence of the last word on the subject if it contradicted their aims? It made no sense.

"I'm afraid," said Armstrong, "that San Isidro has vanished."

"I don't see . . ." said López.

"Not all of Lovecraft came back did it? I don't think they salvaged the essence, only a fragment. A thing with his memories, but not the actual man himself. Some sort of failed experiment. You're the one who's been leaving me those warning notes, aren't you?" Armstrong said, interrupting.

"You presume too much, Mr Armstrong," replied López, "and forget that I have not, at any stage, asserted that I believe myself to be anything other than the misguided individual called Felipe López."

"That's just part of the deception!" Armstrong said, getting to his feet and jabbing his finger at López, "that's what you *know* Lovecraft would have said himself!"

"How on earth could I be of benefit to the designs of an occult organization such as The Sodality of the Black Sun if I deny the very existence of supernatural phenomena? You make no sense, sir."

López's lips had narrowed to a thin cruel line upon his face and he was pale with indignation. His voice had dropped to a threatening whisper.

Everyone in the Café la Habana had turned around to stare, stopped dreaming over their pipes, newspapers and games of chess, and paused, their attention drawn by the confrontation being played out in English before them.

"The Old Ones are only now being born, emerging from your fiction into our world," Armstrong said. "The black magicians of The Sodality of the Black Sun want literally to become them. Once they do, the Old Ones will finally exist, independent of their creator, with the power to turn back time, recreating history to their own design as they go along."

"You, sir," said López, "are clearly more deranged than am I."

"Tell me about the notebook, Lovecraft, tell me about your *Dream-Diary of the Arkham Cycle*," Armstrong shouted.

"There is no record of such a thing," López replied, "there are no indications that such an item ever existed amongst Lovecraft's papers, no mention of anything like it in his letters or other writings, no evidence for . . ."

"Tell me whether history is already beginning to change, whether the first of the Old Ones has begun manipulating the events of the past?"

As Armstrong finished asking his question he saw a shocking change come over López's features. Two forces seemed to war within the Mexican's body and a flash of pain distorted his face. At that moment the whites of his eyes vanished, as if the darkness of night looked out through them. But then he blinked heavily, shook his head from side to side, and finally regained his composure. As he did so, his usual aspect returned. The change and its reversal had been so sudden that, despite how vivid it had been, Armstrong could have just imagined it. After all, his nerves were already shredded, and he jumped at shadows.

"I can tell you nothing. What you are suggesting is madness," López said, getting to his feet and picking up the copy of the book on the table. He left without looking back.

Armstrong did not return to London. He acquired a certain notoriety over the years as the irredeemably drunk English derelict who could be found hanging around in the Café la Habana, talking to anyone who would listen to in his broken Spanish.

However, he was never to be found there after nightfall or during an overcast and dark afternoon. At chess, he insisted on playing white, and could not bear to handle the black pieces, asking his opponent to remove them from the board on his behalf.

TOM PICCIRILLI

Loss

TOM PICCIRILLI LIVES IN Colorado where, besides writing, he spends an inordinate amount of time watching trash cult films and reading Gold Medal classic *noir* and hardboiled novels. He is a fan of Asian cinema, especially horror movies, bullet ballet, pinky violence, and samurai flicks.

Piccirilli is the author of twenty novels including *The Cold Spot*, *The Midnight Road*, *The Dead Letters*, *Headstone City*, *November Mourns* and *A Choir of Ill Children*. A four-time winner of the Bram Stoker Award, he has also been nominated for the World Fantasy Award, the International Thriller Writers Award and Le Grand Prix de L'Imaginaire.

As the author reveals: "With 'Loss', I wanted to take some of my deepest fears and seamiest emotions and filter them through a tale so offbeat and darkly humorous that I couldn't help but grin at the worst side of myself.

"Loneliness, jealousy, self-pity – they all rear their heads here. It's easier to take stock of your character flaws and twist them into engaging, quirky source material when you've got a house full of the dead and a literate monkey in the mix."

THE LAST TIME I SAW the great, secret unrequited love of my life, Gabriella Corben, was the day the talking monkey moved into Stark House and the guy who lied about inventing aluminium foil took an ice-pick though the frontal lobe.

I was in the lobby doing Sunday cleaning, polishing the mahogany banister and dusting the ten Dutch Master prints on the walls. At least one of them appeared authentic to me – I'd studied it for many hours over the last two years. I thought it would be just like Corben to stick a million-dollar painting in among the fakes, just to show he could get away with it. I imagined him silently laughing every time he saw me walking up from my basement apartment with my little rag and spritz bottle of cleaner, ready to wash a masterpiece that could set me up in luxury for the rest of my life.

And it was just like me to keep wiping it down and chewing back my petty pride week after week, determined to drop into my grave before I'd pull it from the wall and have it appraised. The chance to retire to Aruba wasn't worth knowing he'd be snickering about it for the rest of his life.

I stared at myself in the buffed mahogany and listened to Corben and Gabriella arguing upstairs. I couldn't make out their words from four flights away. He played the tortured artist well, though, and could really bellow like a wounded water buffalo. He roared and moaned and kicked shit all around. He used to do the same thing in college. I heard a couple of bottles shatter. Probably bourbon or single malt scotch. They were props he occasionally used in order to pretend he was a hard drinker. The journalists and television crews always made a point of saying there was plenty of booze around. I had no doubt he emptied half the bottles down the sink. I knew his act. I'd helped him develop it. For a while it had been mine as well.

Now Gabriella spoke in a low, loud, stern voice, firm but loving. It hurt me to hear her tone because I knew that no matter how bad it got with Corben, she would always stand by him and find a way to make their marriage work.

I kept waiting for the day when his hubris and self-indulgence finally pushed him into seeking out even more dramatic flair and he actually struck her. I wondered if even that would be enough to drive her away. I wondered if I would kick in his door and beat the hell out of him for it, and in a noble show of compassion I would let his unconscious body drop from my bloody hand before breaking his neck. I wondered if she would gaze on me with a new understanding then and fall into my arms and realize we were meant to be together. I often wondered why I wasn't already in long-term therapy.

They owned the top floor of the five-storey building. They'd had a fleet of architects and construction crews come in and bang down walls and shore up doorways and put in flamboyant filigreed arches. In the end they were left with sixteen rooms. I'd been inside their place but never gotten a grand tour. I'd mostly stuck to the bath-rooms and fixed the toilet when it broke. I imagined the library, the den, the sun room, the bedroom. I didn't know of sixteen different types of rooms. Was there a ballroom? A music room? A solarium? I had a passkey to all the apartments in Stark House, even theirs, but I'd somehow managed to resist the temptation to comb through their home.

The other four storeys were inhabited by elderly, faded film and television stars, one-hit pop song wonders, and other forgotten former celebrities who'd become short-lived cultural icons for reasons ranging from the noble to the ludicrous. They were mostly shut-ins who every so often would skulk about the halls for reasons unknown or appear, momentarily, in their darkened doorways, maybe give a wave before retreating.

We had the guy who'd invented aluminium foil. We had a lady who'd given mouth-to-mouth to a former president's son after a pile-up on I-95 and saved his life. We had a performance artist/environmentalist who'd appeared on national television after soaking in a tub of toxic waste in front of the Museum of Modern Art twenty years ago. He was still alive even though there was only about forty per cent of him left after all the surgery. He rolled around the corridors with half a face, tumour-packed, sucking on an oxygen tube.

Corben shouted some more. It sounded like he said, "Radiant Face". It was the title of his first book. He was going through his bibliography again. I sat on the stairs and lit a cigarette. The old loves and hates heaved around in my chest. I looked around the lobby trying to figure out why I was doing this to myself. Why I was no smarter than him when it came to bucking fate.

Our story was as flatly clichéd and uninteresting as it was honest and full of bone and pain. To me, anyway. Corben and I had been childhood best friends. We'd gotten our asses kicked by neighbourhood thugs and spent two nights in jail trying hard to act tough and be strong and not huddle too closely together. We nearly sobbed with relief the afternoon they let us out. We'd encouraged each other as neophyte novelists and helped one another to hone our craft. I'd taken thirty-seven stitches in bar fights for him, and he'd broken his left arm and gotten a concussion for me. We aced entrance exams to the same Ivy League University.

It was a righteous partnership that went south our junior year in college. We were both getting drunk a lot around then. It had something to do with an older woman, perhaps. I had the memory blocked, or maybe it just bored me too much too care anymore, but I couldn't recall the details. Perhaps she was mine and he took her away, or maybe she was his and wound up on my arm or in my bed. However it played out it released a killing flood of repressed jealousy and animosity from both of us and we didn't see each other again for thirteen years.

We settled in to write our novels. His career caught on with his second book, a thriller about a father chasing down the criminals who stole the donated heart on ice the guy needed for his son's transplant. I liked the book in spite of myself. When it sold to the movies it became a major hit that spawned several sequels. He ripped himself off with a similar novel that dealt with a mob hit-man chasing a crippled girl who needed to get to the hospital within thirty-six hours to get the operation that might let her walk again. It aced the bestseller list for six months. Corben got a cameo in the movie version. He was the kindly doctor who sticks the little metal prod in the girl's foot and makes her big toe flinch.

My own books sold slowly and poorly. They received a generous amount of praise and critical comments, but not much fanfare. I brooded and got into stupid scrapes trying to prove myself beyond the page. I couldn't. Corben assailed me in every bookstore, every library, every time I checked the bestseller list. I wrote maudlin tales that sold to literary rags. I won awards and made no money. I took part-time jobs where I could find them. I delivered Chinese food. I taught English as a second language, I ran numbers for a local bookie until he got mopped up in a state-wide sting. I kept the novels coming but their advances and sales were pitiful.

There were women but none of them mattered much. I never fell in love. I wrote thrillers, I wrote mysteries featuring my heroic PI King Carver. I didn't copy Corben but I was surprised at how similar our tastes and capabilities were. I thought my shit blew away his shit.

Thirteen years went by like that, fast but without much action. I lucked into the job as a manager/handyman of Stark House. I lived in Apartment "A", a studio nearest the basement. So near it was actually *in* the fucking basement. It was the basement. I hadn't sold a novel in almost two years. I kept writing them and sending them to my agent. The rejection letters grew shorter and more tersely formal as time went on. I'd lost what little momentum I might've ever had. Eventually all the manuscripts came back and I stacked them on the floor of my closet hoping I might one day have the courage to burn them.

Maybe I had been waiting for Corben, or maybe he'd been waiting for me.

We used to walk past Stark House when we were kids and discuss the history of the building. It had always accommodated misfits of one sort or another. There were rumours about it a little more cryptic and wondrous than the rumours about every other building.

In the late nineteenth century it had been owned by a family of brilliant eccentrics who'd turned out scientists, senators, and more than a few madmen. A number of murders occurred on the premises. Local legends grew about the shadow men who served the politicians. They said the Stark family carried bad blood.

In the early twentieth century the place had been converted to apartments and became home to a famous opera singer, a celebrity husband and wife Broadway acting team, and a bootlegger who'd made a fortune from prohibition. They said there were secret walls. I searched but never found any. The place still called to life a certain glamour nearly lost through time. The wide staircase bisecting the lobby gave the impression of romantic leading men sweeping their lovers upstairs in a swirl of skirts, trains, and veils. The original chandelier still hung above as it had for over a hundred years and I waited for the day it tore from its supports and killed us all.

I knew Corben would eventually try to buy the building. I was lucky to have gotten in before him. Even his wealth couldn't purchase Stark House outright. When he and I finally met face to face again after all those years, neither one of us showed any surprise at all. We didn't exchange words. We shared similar blank, expressionless features. He must've mentioned something to his wife later on because I caught her staring at me on occasion, almost as if she had plenty of questions for me but didn't want to trespass on such a mystery-laden history.

It made perfect sense to me that I would fall in love with Gabriella Corben virtually the moment I met her.

Upstairs, Corben screamed, "Wild Under Heaven! Ancient Shadows!" I never quite understood what kind of point he was trying to make when he ran through his list of titles. Gabriella spoke sternly and more stuff got knocked over. I heard him sob. It gave me no pleasure hearing it. Finally a door slammed and another opened. The corners of the building echoed with the small sounds of the lurking outcast phantoms slinking in and out of shadow. The old-fashioned elevator buzzed and hummed, moving between the second and third floors. I heard footsteps coming down the stairs, and she was there.

I briefly glanced at Gabriella Corben and gave a noncommittal grin. She moved halfway down the staircase and sat in the middle of the carpeted step, her elbows on her knees, watching me. She wouldn't discuss their argument and wouldn't mention him at all. She never did.

My hidden unrequited love was a secret even from her. Or perhaps not. She was perceptive and understanding and probably knew my heart as well as she understood her husband's, which might've been entirely or might've been not at all. He and I still weren't that different. He was up there screaming out loud and I was down here braying inside.

I went about my business. I did my work. I waited for her to say what she wanted to say and I willed the muscles in my back not to twitch.

I knew what I would see if I dared to look over my shoulder. A woman of twenty-five, comfortable beneath the finish of her own calm, with glossy curling black hair draped loosely to frame her face. Lightly freckled from the summer sun, her eyes a rich hazel to offset the glowing brown of her skin. Her body slim but full, her presence assured. I caught a whiff of her perfume combined with the heady, earthy scent of her sweat beneath it. I must've looked like a maniac, polishing one foot of banister over and over, so damn afraid to turn around.

Where she went a kind of light travelled. She carried it with her. It lifted my heart and left me stunned. It was a feeling I wasn't accustomed to and for a long while I fought against it. I had learned to live with resentment instead of romance. It was my preferred state of being until she came along. Now I burned in silence.

She said, almost sleepily, "You ever wonder what it would be like if you could dig down through all the layers of polish, the paint and wax, peeling back the years, say going in a half-inch deep, to a different time, and see what life here might've been like back then?"

A half-inch deep. Probably eighty years. "I suspect you'd find a lot of the same."

"Really?"

"Life wasn't so different. Maybe you wouldn't trip over a guy who sat in toxic waste in front of the MOMA, but there'd be somebody comparable, I bet."

"What could be comparable to that?"

I shrugged. "A lunatic juggling hand grenades. A World War I vet used to panhandle out front here back in the 1920s, and if he didn't make enough coin he'd chase people around with a bayonet. He spooked the neighbours on the other side of the street by flipping around one of those German hand grenades."

She waited but that was all I knew about it. Most tales about real people only had a modicum of interest to them, and no real ending. I didn't want to lose her attention and said, "There's always been plenty of crazy."

"I think you're right. How about the rest of it?"

"The rest of it?"

"Life. Lots of happiness? Beauty? Romance?"

"Sure. This lobby is so nice that there's been a lot of weddings performed right here, at the foot of the stairwell. The publicity shots were gorgeous. They'd have horse and carriages lined up out in the street, and after the ceremony the wedding party would hop in, ride over to Fifth Avenue and down past St Patrick's Cathedral. If the families of the bride or groom had enough pull, they could get the cardinal's okay to have the church bells ring as the carriages went by."

"That must've been lovely."

Dorothy Parker and one of her lovers used to drunkenly chase each other through the halls of Stark House in the raw, but that didn't quite have the right kind of romance I was going for. "A couple of silent film stars met on the fifth floor back in the 1920s. They split their time between Los Angeles and New York and lived next door to each other for a couple of years before ever meeting."

"Which apartments?"

By that she meant, *Which of my rooms?* "I don't know."

"Okay, go on."

"When they did run into each other here it was supposedly love at first sight. They got engaged a week later. The press went nuts with it. They made five movies together too."

"I think I heard about that. Didn't they commit suicide? Jumped off the roof?"

I was hoping to skip that part. Corben had told her more about the place than I thought he might. Or should've. Or maybe she'd been talking to some of the other tenants, though I couldn't figure out which of the shut-ins might actually chat with someone else.

"Yeah, when sound came in. They both sounded too Brooklyn, and no matter what they did they couldn't get rid of the accent."

"Death by Brooklyn," she said. "How sad." She put her hand on the banister and floated it down inch by inch until she'd almost reached the spot I was polishing. She tapped it with her nail. The length of her nail, a half-inch, eighty years. "I've heard there's been even more tragedy as well."

"Of course. Plenty of births, you get plenty of deaths."

"And not all of it by natural means certainly."

"Why do you want to hear about this stuff?" I asked. For the first time I looked directly at her, and as usual, the lust and the ache swept through me. She pulled a face that meant that Corben had been talking up the house history and she wanted a different viewpoint.

"Murder's pretty natural," I told her. "I don't know if that guy ever bayoneted anyone or if the hand grenade ever went off, but there's been a few grudges that ended with a knife or a handgun. One guy pushed his brother down the elevator shaft, and one of the scientists blew himself and his dog to hell mixing up some concoction."

"Scientists?"

"Some scientists used to live here."

"And their dogs."

"Well," I said, "yeah."

"Oh, I see." She chewed on that for a while. I moved up a couple steps, working the banister, easing a little closer. I could see her reflection in the shine. I fought down the primitive inside me trying to get out. Maybe I shouldn't have. Maybe she was just waiting for me to carry her down the stairs. But I didn't make the move.

Gabriella said, "Have you ever considered doing a book about it? The building?"

I didn't want to admit the truth, but she had a way of cooling the endless blazing rage inside me. My loud thoughts softened and quieted, even while I went slowly crazy with wanting her. "Yes, when I was a kid. I've always been intrigued by the building. There's always been a lot of talk, a lot of rumours."

"But you don't want to write one anymore?"

"No."

"Why not?"

It was a good question, and one I wasn't prepared to answer. It took me a while to say anything. "I have my own stories to share, I suppose. I don't need to tell this place's legends and lessons. And it doesn't need me to tell them anyway."

I turned and she smiled at me a little sadly.

I knew then exactly what Corben was doing and what was now ripping him up inside. The damn fool was trying to write a book about Stark House.

A minute later the front door was awash with a blur of black motion, and Gabriella and I wheeled and moved down the stairs together, as one, like I'd seen in a dozen classic films I could name.

Our bare arms touched and I tamped down the thrill that flared through me. She placed a hand on my wrist and my pulse snapped hard. It was odd and a bit unsettling to know that such small, commonplace human actions could still send me spiralling toward the edge. I hadn't realized I was quite so lonely until that moment.

And there it was, the first sighting of Ferdinand the Magnifico, looking dapper as hell in his old world Victorian-era black suit, lace tie. And this too, our initial meeting with the monkey, Mojo, leashed to his master by a sleek length of golden chain, who hopped around doing a dance in his little jacket and cap while holding his cup out. This also wasn't exactly the grand romance I'd been hoping for, but I'd take whatever I could get.

"Halloo!" Ferdi shouted. Behind him scattered out on the sidewalk stood crates, boxes, and a small assortment of furniture. He must've hired some cheap uninsured movers who would only carry your belongings curb to curb.

Mojo jumped back and forth as far as his chain would allow. Gabriella smiled and said, "Are you certain you can bring an animal like that into this building?"

"Animal!" Ferdi cried. "This is no animal, madam! I assure you! This is my partner, Mojo, a gentle soul no different than you or I, with a heart filled with benevolence and an obligation only to make children laugh!"

She ignored the side of his trunk that stated in bold yellow letters FERDINAND THE MAGNIFICO, and asked, "And just who are you?"

"I am Ferdinand! And this is our new home! Today we move into Apartment 2C of the Stark Building!" He glanced at me, but, like all men, he couldn't keep his eyes off Gabriella for longer than that.

"Nice to meet you, Mr Ferdinand."

"Just Ferdinand, madam! Are we neighbours? Say it is so!"

"Just Gabriella, Ferdinand," she said. "And it is so, we're neighbours. And this is Will."

"Well then, as you say!"

I bit back a groan. He was the kind of person who shouted everything with a joyous cry. If the decibel level didn't get you, the enthusiasm might. The monkey looked more like my kind of person. He grinned when you looked at him but otherwise just kind of held back, watching and waiting to see what might be coming his way. Printed on the monkey's little hat was the name MOJO. A button pinned to his fire engine red jacket read THE WORLD'S ONLY TALKING/WRITING CHIMP. There was a pad with a pen attached by a string in a small bag around his neck.

Mojo pressed his tin cup out to Gabriella. He was insistent. She gestured that she had no cash on her and I pulled a quarter out of my pocket and snapped it off my thumbnail into his cup. I expected him to say thank you, seeing as he was a talking monkey, but Mojo only hopped twice, squeaked, took off his hat and bowed.

"If he talks, why does he have a pad and pen?" she asked.

"He prefers to write!"

"I see," she said. She shot me a look. "Just like Will."

A reference to me, not to her bestselling author husband. It took me back a step. Of course, she was also likening me to a chimp, so maybe it wasn't quite the compliment I had wanted it to be.

"Well hello, Mojo," she said, "how are you today?"

Mojo went, "Ook."

Ferdi lifted his arms and clapped happily. "You see! He says he is fine!"

Gabriella laughed pleasantly and tried again. "It will be very nice having you in the building, Mojo, I hope we'll become great friends."

Mojo did a dance, held out his tin cup, and went, "Ook ook."

Ferdi said, "Bravo, Mojo! As all can clearly hear, you have told them you are delighted to be a new neighbour to such gracious and wonderful people!"

"Why doesn't he write us a note instead?" I said.

"I'm sure he soon shall! But at the moment he is enjoying this conversation so much, he has no need to give letters!"

Gabriella gave me the look again and this time I returned it. We were compatriots, we were sharing a moment. She was laughing and I was smiling. That was good enough. I drew another quarter out of my pocket and tossed it into the monkey's cup. If nothing else, he was a smart chimp. He'd already taken me for half a buck.

"Are you with the circus?" I asked.

"No, nor any carnival! We are our own pair, a team! We have toured Central Europe, throughout Asia, New Zealand, and South Dakota! And now, we arrive here!"

"I'll help with your belongings," I said.

"Wonderful!"

Gabriella swept out past us heading for the door, and the over-whelming urge to touch her rose up in me and made me reach for her, maybe to grab her elbow and turn her to face me, so that I might finally find the courage to say something real and true to her, about myself or about Corben, or perhaps about nothing at all. Just a chance to spend more time with her, even if it was only a few more minutes. When you got down to it I was as needy as Corben, and maybe even worse.

But my natural restraint slowed me down too much, and even before I managed to lift my hand she was already out of reach.

My last image of her: a gust of wind whirling her hair into a savage storm about her head while she eased out the front door silhouetted in the morning sun, her skirt snapping back at me once as if demanding my attention, a curious expression of concern or perhaps dismay on her face – perhaps the subtle after effect of her argument with Corben, or maybe even considering me, for the first time, as a potential lover – moving across the street against traffic. A taxi obscured her, the door finished closing, the chimp chittered, and my secret love was gone.

I thought Ferdi and Mojo might have some friends or fans from New Zealand to help them move in, but they had no one but me. Luckily, they didn't have that much stuff. Mojo really did have monkey bars, a collapsible cage that when put together took up an entire room of the three-bedroom apartment. It was probably my duty to call the landlord and squeal on them. No pets were allowed, much less restricted exotic animals, but I liked the action they brought with them, the energy. Let somebody else rat them out.

We carried everything up the stairs rather than futzing with the tight elevator. It took less than two hours for Ferdi and me to get everything inside and set up.

Ferdi handed me twenty dollars as a tip, but the monkey danced so desperately and kept jabbing his cup at me with such ferocity that I finally gave him the crumpled bill. Ferdi had a real racket going, and I wondered if I could talk him into being my new agent. I could just see him giving hell to my editors, the monkey using his little pen to scribble out clauses on bad contracts. Ferdi asked me to stay and share a bottle of wine with him, but I had a story I wanted to finish.

When I got back to my place I sat at my desk staring at the screen at some half-composed paragraphs that made virtually no sense to me. Being with Gabriella had inspired me, but now the words ran together into phrases that held no real resolve. I didn't know my own themes anymore.

I sat back and stared up at he shafts of light stabbing down across my study, feeling the weight of the entire building above me – all the living and the dead, the bricks and mortar of history growing heavier every year. A hundred and forty years worth of heritage and legacy, chronicles and sagas. Soon they might crush me out of existence. Maybe I was even in the mood for it.

I had a stack of unopened mail on my bed. I tore into an envelope containing a royalty check for $21.34. I started to crumple it in my fist, but I needed the money. I decided that no matter how Mojo might push me, I wasn't going to give it to him. I picked up an unfinished chapter of my latest novel and the words offended me. I tossed the pages across the room and watched them dive-bomb against the far wall. There wasn't even enough air in here for them to float on a draft. I wondered if Corben was still up there howling. I wondered if Gabriella had returned to him yet or if she was out in the city enjoying herself, taking in enough of the living world for both of them. For all three of us. The claustrophobia started to get to me and I decided to go walk the building.

I hadn't gotten twenty paces from my apartment door when I spotted a man laid out on the tiled floor of the lobby – a shallow red halo inching outward – with an ice-pick in his forehead that vibrated with every breath he took.

I'd never seen him in the light of day, but I thought it was the guy who'd invented aluminium foil. I couldn't believe he was still alive. Blood and clear fluids lapped from his ears. A wave of vertigo rippled through me and I bit down on my tongue and it passed. I bent to him and had no idea what to do. He was finished, he had to be finished because there was three inches of metal burrowed into his brain, but he was wide-eyed and still staring at me with great interest. He licked his lips and tried to move his hands.

"Jesus holy Christ . . ." I whispered. I didn't have a cell phone. I started to turn and run for my apartment when he called my name.

"Will."

It was astonishing he could actually see. Death was already clouding his eyes and gusting through his chest. His voice had been thickened by it. It was a sound I'd heard several times before. He sounded exactly like my father when the old man had about three minutes left to go. There was no point in leaving him now. I kneeled at his side. "I'm here."

"I lied," he said.

"About what?"

"I didn't invent aluminium foil. Aluminium foil was first introduced into the industry as an insulating material. It later found diverse applications in a variety of fields."

"What?"

"It can be used instead of lead and tinfoil in other specified applications. The aluminium foil thickness ranges from 0.0043 millimetres to 0.127 millimetres. It comes with a bright or dull finish and also with embossed patterns—"

"Shhh."

"Foils are available in thirty-three distinct colours. In 1910, when the first aluminium foil rolling plant was opened in Kreuzlingen, Switzerland, the plant, owned by J. G. Neher & Sons stood at the foot of the Rhine Falls and captured the falls' energy. Neher's sons together with Dr Lauber – oh, Dr Lauber! Dr Lauber! – discovered the endless rolling process and the use of aluminium foil as a protective barrier."

The ice-pick had ripped through his memories. Even if he hadn't invented aluminium foil, he sure knew a hell of a lot about it. I couldn't quite figure why his head was full of all this, but it was probably no worse than thinking about stealing Dutch Master prints and heading to Aruba. I wondered what I would be spouting on about in my last minute if someone stuck a blade into my brain.

I should've offered up some kind of soothing words to send him on his way, but he looked animated and eager to chat despite the fact that his brains were leaking out of his ears and tear ducts. I should've asked him who had done this to him. Instead I said, "Why the hell would you lie about a thing like that?"

"I wanted to meet girls. Forgive me!"

In the hierarchy of sins I thought that lying about inventing aluminium foil in order to meet chicks – which in itself wasn't particularly immoral – just didn't rate very high on the damnation scale. I figured if a priest had been handy, he would've given dispensation without much of a problem.

"You're forgiven," I said. "Who did this to you?"

"Dr Lauber! Dr Lauber!"

"Tell me who—"

"God, the things I've done. I once struck my mother. I ran over a dog, someone's pet. I broke the hearts of my own children. I hurt a woman, she bled. I shall surely go to hell. Please, Dr Lauber!"

"Shhh."

"Dr Lauber!"

"Close your eyes."

He finally did and died that instant.

The cops questioned me full-tilt boogie. They came around in three teams of two. I got the Officer Friendlys, the hair-trigger hardcase growlers, and the plaintive guys who just sort of whined at me and wanted me to admit to murder. I told them his last words and they thought maybe he had ratted out the almighty and vengeful aluminium foil powers that be. They quizzed each other about the name Dr Lauber. They all said it sounded familiar, maybe a hit-man working for the syndicate. Maybe a plastic surgeon who'd gone out of his tree.

I suspected that if anybody Googled the name they'd find him to be the man who'd discovered the endless rolling process with the sons of J. G. Neher.

The whiners took me down to the station and put me in a holding room with a big mirror, where I stared at myself and whoever was behind it and started to re-evaluate the cops in my novels. I'd been trying way too hard. I'd been breaking my ass creating brilliant detectives who solved crimes with the sparsest clues. But these guys were never going to figure out who'd killed the aluminium foil liar, not unless somebody confessed out of hand just to stop all the bitching.

Eventually they cut me loose and I wandered the streets. I was the guy who had to clean up all the blood off the lobby floor back at Stark House. I didn't want to go back yet. I'd seen death before but not murder. I'd written about it and I recognized how far off I'd been from what it really felt like to be in the presence of homicide.

A certain sense of guilt lashed me as I thought about how close I'd come to walking in on the man being attacked. Maybe two minutes, maybe less. Perhaps I could've prevented it. If only I'd moved a little faster. If only I'd run out into the street to see what could be seen. Maybe I would've spotted a killer rushing away or hailing a cab.

I stopped into a bookstore and bought Corben's latest novel. His dedication read: TO ALL THOSE WHO LOVE THE MYSTERIES OF LIFE AND DEATH AS MUCH AS I DO. It was followed by AND TO MY WIFE.

Not even her name, her lovely name. The bastard pasted her in there as an afterthought. How could she read that and not be appalled? How could he expect her not to be upset? I didn't understand it and knew I never would.

I read the first ten pages leaning against the window of a nearby bodega, and read another twenty walking back to Stark House. I sat outside on the front steps for a half-hour and let the paragraphs slide by under my gaze. I didn't know what the hell I was reading. I was too full of my own anger and past to even see the words. I flipped the pages by rote. I looked at the dedication again and tried to see the substance and meaning behind it. Corben didn't love the mysteries of life. I wasn't sure he loved anything at all. I left the book there and went inside.

The cops had put up little orange cones around the murder scene, with yellow tape cordoning the area off. The tape didn't say POLICE LINE, DO NOT CROSS so I tore it down and got my mop, gloves, scouring pads and sanitizers out of the closet. It took me two hours to do an even halfway decent job of it. I had thought it would take longer. There was still a bad stain. I kept having to stop when my hands started to shake. I didn't know if it was because of all the blood or because I'd been so wrapped up in my own problems that I hadn't seen someone else's desperate loneliness. I'd thought I had it bad, but Jesus, dying with the dry facts of aluminium foil on your lips because you wanted to get laid, it was a whole other level of heartbreak.

Ferdinand the Magnifico and Mojo put on little shows for the neighbourhood kids in the garden behind the building. It wasn't much of a garden, but by East Side standards it was practically the Congo. The monkey grunted with certain inflections and Ferdi appeared to honestly believe Mojo was chattering like he was playing Bridge with the Ladies Auxiliary Club. Mojo went "Ook" and Ferdi, with childish glee, raised his arms out and said, "You see there, clear as the chimes of St Patrick's! He said, 'I love you'. You heard it yourself! Did you not?" The kids said that they could. They giggled and clapped and tossed pennies and nickels. They chased the chimp and then ran away when the chimp chased them. It brightened the place up.

I didn't quite get how Ferdi made enough to pay Manhattan rent while nickel and diming it, but maybe he had tours booked. He could've really cleaned up in South Dakota. It seemed possible. For all I knew Mojo'd sold out Fourth of July at Madison Square Garden.

I'd used three different bleaches and detergents doing additional clean-up work over the course of a week but still hadn't managed to get all the blood out of the tile in the lobby. It had become ingrained, as deep as the aluminium foil liar's guilt.

Something had happened to me that day. My usual brooding and pathos took a left turn into a darker, calmer sea of purpose. I had the increasingly powerful feeling that my life held a greater intent and meaning now, though I didn't know what the hell it might be. I watched the front door. I waited for more murder. I could feel it hovering nearby in every hall. I thought about all the lies I had told to get laid, and wondered if they'd come back to haunt me in the end. What would be my last words? And would they sound dreadfully strange to whoever might be there holding my hand?

The media caught wind that Corben lived in the building and the camera crews started floating around. He showed up on television and made up stories about how close he'd been with the aluminium foil guy. He claimed to have a theory about the killer and said he was working closely with the NYPD to solve the case. They asked if he was afraid of potential retribution. He claimed to own a derringer that he always kept on his person. A lovely reporter asked if he had it on him at the moment. He dared her to frisk him. I watched his last couple of novels bullet up the bestseller lists.

My agent kept calling trying to get me to ride his coattails, or more appropriately the murderer's coattails. He said I should be doing whatever I could to get my last few titles out to the reporters. I should carry my novels around with me, stick them in front of the cameras. I asked him if he knew how stupid that might make me feel. He asked me if I knew how stupid he felt representing an author who still couldn't garner more than a five grand chump change advance after publishing a dozen books. It put things into perspective but I still didn't go around clothes-lining the reporters and shoving my novels under their noses. My agent quit calling.

My sleep filled with mad laughter and shouting. Some of it was my own. I occasionally startled myself awake making noises. I started smoking more. I wrote more and deleted more. I painted the foyer and caught up on all the minor fix-it stuff that I'd let slide the last several days. I got a closer look at some of my neighbours.

I finally met the lady who had an affair with a famous televangelist's wife and was now something of a lesbian icon. She mildly flirted with me and prompted me to tell her how pretty she was. She seemed insecure and irritable. She told me she wasn't a lesbian at all but had just been fooling around with the wife for the fun of it, but she couldn't admit it in public anymore because of all the money she was making lecturing to various lesbian organizations. She had the televangelist's show playing on a high definition TV screen with the surround sound turned way up. He seemed to be preaching from every corner of the apartment. It was spooky. I fixed her broken toilet handle and blew out of there.

The toxic waste guy said the old-fashioned elevator didn't accommodate his wheelchair. He was right. The chair was old and wide and well lived in. He'd been in the building the entire time I'd been there. He was proud of his tumours and tried to show them to me as often as he could, turning his melted, half-eaten face this way and that so it would catch the light from the corridor lamps. He was so pale I could see the blood pulsing underneath his skin. I wondered how long it had been since he'd been outside in the sun. I removed one of the side rails in the elevator and it was a tight fit but his chair squeezed in. We tested it together. His oxygen tube hissed into the hole that used to be his nose. The tank clanked loudly whenever the chair went over a bump. I could just imagine it breaching and the explosion taking out the whole floor. He said thank you and rolled back to his apartment and shut the door.

The former child actor turned gay porno star turned sex therapist daytime talk show host cancelled after three months now retired after writing his autobiography wherein he named names, was sued, counter-sued and won big cash off a couple of closeted politicians outed and forced to resign needed a couple of his electrical outlets rewired. He interviewed me like I was a guest on his show, asking me a lot of pointed questions about the murder. He wanted to know how finding a corpse had transformed me. I told him I hadn't found a corpse, that the man was still alive when I got there. He wanted to know how I'd been transformed by the discovery of a dying man with an ice-pick in his forebrain. He wanted to know what I heard, what I smelled, if there had been any aftertaste to the incident. He licked his lips when he said it. He kept looking to one side like he saw an audience there staring at him. I knew he was working on more of his memoirs. When he got to this chapter he'd say that he'd found the aluminium foil liar and the dying man had spoken profound and wondrous lessons of good will.

A couple more days drifted past. I felt eyes on me and found myself constantly looking over my shoulder and checking down the ends of dark hallways. Muffled voices followed me but that was nothing new, muffled voices follow everybody in old apartment houses.

Except I kept hearing my name, or thought I did. For some reason, it made my scalp tighten.

The morning came when I awoke to a knocking – twin knockings – on my basement door. I figured it was the cops doing a follow-up, but instead there was Ferdinand with Mojo, both of them grinning. They were each holding a bunch of paperbacks.

"You are the wonderful writer called Will Darrow!"

"I'm Will Darrow anyway," I told him.

"But why, why did you not let me know this the very day we were introduced? I await the next emergence of your tough guy character, stories of the brutal but heroic King Carver!"

That took me back hard. Mojo pulled on his chain and tugged Ferdi into my apartment. They may have been the first guests I'd ever had inside the place. I said, "You've read my books?"

"Yes, all of them! Will you please sign, yes?"

Mojo extended a novel out to me. It had a cover I'd never seen before, printed in a language I didn't know. Portuguese, maybe?

Neither my agent nor my publisher had ever mentioned selling those sub-rights. Or any. My breath caught in my chest and I tried not to think about how much money folks might be skimming. The monkey wouldn't let go of the book. Ferdinand said, "Mojo, give! For signing! He will return it to you!"

A couple of the other books were in the same language, and two more were in a different one. Maybe Swedish. Danish? I had no idea. The rage climbed the back of my neck but there was also a strange sense of pride coming through, knowing people in other countries were reading my work. My hands were icy. I couldn't remember how to spell my name and just scribbled wavy lines inside the books.

"I ask now when shall I be able to tell my friends a new King Carver adventure shall soon be theirs?"

I didn't know what to say. My agent had sent all my recent manuscripts back. I tried to keep faith. "I don't know, Ferdi. But I'll let you know as soon as I finish a new one, all right?"

"That will be stupendous! Will it not, Mojo?"

Mojo went, "Ook."

"You hear, he says—"

"Uh huh."

"—he shall effort to have patience but he excitedly waits for more King Carver!"

"Uh huh."

"Tell me now, how is Miss Gabriella?"

It was the first time I was aware that I hadn't seen her since that day he'd moved in two weeks earlier. A minor twinge of alarm sang through me. "I don't know, Ferdi, it's been a while."

"If you see her, please say that I have inquired about her health!"

"I'll do that."

I handed him the signed books back and Mojo got mad and started hopping and banging his fists against his knees until Ferdi gave him one of the titles. Mojo immediately quieted, opened the book, and his mouth started moving, as if he really could read.

The cops eventually came around again. All three teams, about two hours apart from one another. The nice guys weren't so nice this time. The hardasses not as hard. The whiners still tried to plead with me to tell the truth and come clean about croaking the old man with an ice-pick. I stuck firm to my story. Nobody hit me with a phone book or a rubber hose. No one asked any new questions or seemed to have any other leads besides me. I started to get a clue as to why there were so many television shows about unsolved crimes. They asked if

Dr Lauber had shown up yet, if I'd seen some guy with a stethoscope and a doctor's bag creeping around the building. Maybe doing illegal abortions in the neighbourhood. I blinked and reminded them that abortions weren't illegal. They discussed this amongst themselves for a bit. They invited my opinion but I chose to stay out of it. I stared at them and they stared at me.

I waited to catch sight of Gabriella. I did everything I could do in order to hang around the fifth floor. Fixing hall lights, bracing the handrails, polishing the footboards and wainscoting, polishing the floors. I put an ear to Corben's door and listened for their voices. I heard nothing. There were no more arguments. He'd quit calling out his bibliography. For all I knew they were vacationing in Monaco.

It's sometimes a curse to have an imagination that can draw up detailed visuals. I thought of them entwined after having just made love, now feeding each other wine and caviar. I hated caviar the one time I tried it, but when I thought of romance that's what came to mind. The window open and a cold breeze pressing back the curtains. Moonlight casting silver across the dark. The sheets clean but rumpled. Her crossing the room with a hint of sweat carried in the niche at the small of her back, slowly dripping over the curve of her *derriére*. When I thought of romance I thought there ought to be some French thrown in there too. The bright flare of the refrigerator opening, her body silhouetted the way it had been the last time I'd seen her. The refrigerator door shutting, night vision lost. Total darkness for a moment and then the pressure of her body easing back into bed.

You didn't need a lover to drive you to the rim, you could do it all on your own.

I wore myself down hoping to escape my dreams. I slept heavily but not well. I wrote a lot but not well. I dropped off with my head against the spacebar.

One morning, I found a note slid under my door.

It went six pad-size pages. It stated, in plainly printed block letters much clearer than my own handwriting:

A MAN MADE OF ALUMINIUM FOIL STEPPED FROM MY CLOSET AND CONFESSED HIS SINS. THEY WERE PLENTIFUL. HIS HANDS ARE RED FROM A WOMAN'S BLOOD. HE IS TERRIFIED BECAUSE HE HAS NOT YET MET GOD, AND FEARS HE NEVER WILL, AND THAT GOD – IF HE EVER EXISTED – EXISTS NO MORE. DR LAUBER, HE SAID, COMMANDS HIS SOUL. THE RHINE

FLOODS ACROSS THE PLANETS. THIS IS NOT THE
AFTERLIFE HE WAS HOPING FOR. AT THE END OF
OUR DAYS WE ALL FULLY EXPECT TO MEET THE
CREATOR, AND, FOR GOOD OR ILL, FOR HIM TO
SPEAK WITH US, EVEN IF ONLY TO JUDGE HARSHLY,
PERHAPS WITH DIVINE HATE. AN AFTERLIFE WITH-
OUT GOD IS ONE WITHOUT PARAMETERS, WITHOUT
CELESTIAL DESIGN. DR LAUBER, THE ALUMINIUM
FOIL MAN SAID, OWNS US ALL, THOUGH SOME OF
US CONTINUE TO ACT AS IF THERE IS SUCH AN AB-
STRACTION AS FREE WILL. I HAVE COME TO THIS
BELIEF MYSELF – THAT NONE OF US ARE FREE – SOME
TIME AGO AS WELL. IT FRIGHTENS ME, IT ALL CHILLS
ME SO. WHAT SAY YOU?

The note was signed: MOJO.

You couldn't be better off dead. You were already a phantom in
this city. The world spun by filled with the vacuous and the caustic
and the fearful. They hunched down inside their coats and disappeared before you really knew they were there. They muttered to
themselves and turned away from bright lights and loud noises. I'd
raised my voice only once on the street in the past month, and that
was hailing a cab. Sometimes I wondered if I'd even know it when my
heart quit beating.

The 1976 one-hit-wonder lady who sang "Sister to the Swamp"
knocked on my apartment door and asked if I'd repair the broken
showerhead in her bathroom. She still had an enormous afro and
wore the kind of silky, streaming dress that she'd worn on Soul Train
during the disco years. I got my toolbox and followed her upstairs.
She had the gold record mounted on the wall near the window so that
the sunlight would send a molten yellow across the room. Everywhere I looked were photos of her with politicians, sports legends,
and other musicians popular at the time.

When she spoke I heard very little beside the lyrics to "Sister to the
Swamp". The heavy bass rhythm of the song pumped through my
head. I got into the tub and worked the showerhead until I got it
fixed. When I finished, the 1976 one-hit-wonder lady was at the
window staring at the rush of foot traffic on the sidewalks below. She
held one hand up to the glass like she was trying to find her way
through without breaking it. She wanted to go outside. She wanted
to sing for the people. I'd seen that haunted need in her eyes and the
eyes of the other shut-ins for a couple of years now. I wanted to ask

her why she didn't just step outside and do her thing. But even I knew it was impossible. Time had moved on without her and she wouldn't be able to get back up to speed. Her photos and her gold record and the lyrics to her one song were all she had left now. She'd chosen that path and it would have to be enough for her. She said nothing more to me and I grabbed my toolbox and got out of there, back into the world. It felt very much the same on one side of the door as the other.

I got downstairs into my place and sat in front of the computer screen willing the words to come. They wouldn't. Every time I thought of King Carver in Danish a flutter of nausea worked through my guts.

I shut my eyes. I let my fingers move across the keypad on their own. I started typing. Corben and I used to clown around with automatic writing back in college. I did it every now and again when I wanted to clear my mind. I forced my focus to some far corner of my brain and left it there. The typing grew louder.

My hands pounded away. I wondered who the hell was writing Mojo letters to me and why. There had been a craftiness to the note, a kind of witty petulance. It seemed a direct insult to the aluminium foil guy. Someone had done his online research on Dr Lauber. But to what end? And why send it my way? And why pose as the monkey? A thin shard of fear scraped inside me, and my hands seized for a moment. What if the note had come from the ice-pick killer? Who even used an ice-pick any more *except* for killers? This was the fucking age of refrigerator door ice-cube makers, baby. Sweat broke across my upper lip. What if the note had really come from Mojo? The paper was the size of the sheets on the chimp's little pad. Why hadn't I seen Gabriella in over a week? My focus snapped back into the keyboard and I felt my fingers type her name. GABRIELLA. What kind of a damn fool dedicates a book as a codicil to his wife, and does so by simply calling her *My wife*? My thoughts twisted to Corben's book on Stark House. What had he learned about this place that I should know? How far along was he? Who would he dedicate this one to? What if the chimp were dancing up behind me right now with an awl in his little monkey fist?

I opened my eyes and turned around. I was alone. My face dripped sweat. I checked the clock. I'd written for twenty minutes. I scanned the computer screen. Much of it was gibberish with a few random whole sentences found in the muck. I spotted DEATH TO KING CARVER in there among a kind of repetitive bitter ranting about lack of royalties and stolen foreign translations. I'd fallen back into some of the same old traps. It was bound to happen. A few maudlin phrases cropped up. I wrote COME GET ME, FUCKER and had a partially completed scene of a disembowelling. A filleting blade eased through flesh. There were slithering intestines and someone trying to hold together his fish-white belly with his fingers. I was getting the feeling that my mental state might currently be a bit skewed. WHERE HAS HE HIDDEN MY LOVE? Deep among the mire stood out SHE SPEAKS.

It took some of the edge off but not nearly enough. I deleted the file and stared at the blank monitor willing some kind of answers that refused to appear. It didn't matter much. I didn't even know what questions I was asking. I wasn't even sure I wanted to try writing another novel. There didn't seem to be much point anymore. I wasn't as wrecked about not giving a damn as I thought I would be.

I picked up the Mojo note and read it again. I wondered if a man made of aluminium foil might be preparing to step from my closet as well. Why should Dr Lauber command anybody's soul?

I hadn't talked to Corben on any kind of a significant level in fifteen years. If we passed each other in the halls we would nod and do no more. I had the phone numbers of everyone in the building. I grabbed the phone and called the apartment. I hoped Gabriella would answer. My back teeth hurt because I was clenching my jaws so tightly. Like a love-struck teenager, I thought I might hang up the moment she answered. The phone rang ten times, twelve, thirteen times. Maybe they really were in Monaco.

I hung up and then gave it another dozen rings.

Finally Corben picked up, and with an exasperated growl said, "Who is this?"

"I'm coming up," I told him.

I tossed the phone down and moved out the door on a near-run.

I got to his apartment and we both took an extra moment for what was coming. I stood on one side listening at the door, and I knew he was standing on the other side, his eye to the peephole. We both waited. I had no idea what we were waiting for. I started forward and before I could knock he flung the door open so hard I heard the doorstop snap.

His face, once bordering handsome, had grown into a collision of sharp edges. His high cheekbones were barely covered with flesh. He looked like he'd been ill for days. His jaw line angled back severe as a hatchet. I hadn't seen him for several weeks and I could tell he hadn't been eating. His eyes were feverish, planted too deeply in his head, and he didn't seem able to completely close his mouth. His upper canines prodded his lower lip. I could smell the sourness of his breath beneath the mint mouthwash. His rapid breathing rustled loudly from him.

A lot of the old pain and jealousy sped through my blood. My pulse stormed along. I could feel the veins in my wrists clattering. I wondered if I was as ugly to him as he was to me.

"Where's Gabriella?" I asked.

The question hit him like a rabbit punch. I don't know what he'd been expecting but it sure wasn't that. His face folded into nine variations of anger, indignity, and confusion before it settled into outright surprise. It suited him just swell.

He couldn't come up with anything better than, "What?" and he hated himself for it. He got grounded again and the peevish tone thrummed into his voice once more. "Who are you to ask that?"

"Who the hell would I have to be? Where is she?"

"She's not here."

"That doesn't answer my damn question. Where is she?"

His resentful front began to fall apart even faster. He couldn't maintain his outrage. I watched it crack to pieces and the sight startled me. We were getting down deep where the nerve clusters were always on fire for one reason or another. The venom began to seep from me but I held onto that desperate need to see her. He detected it in me and almost took a kind of pity as he said, "She's gone."

"What?"

"It's true."

I took a lunging step toward him and caught hold of myself in time. I looked over his shoulder and hoped he was lying, but I couldn't feel her presence in the slightest. I couldn't smell her perfume, I got no sense of her at all.

"Gone where?"

"I don't know, Will."

The way he said my name tightened my chest. It was almost a whimper, an appeal to friendship. The sound of his own voice angered him and I watched his thin face harden further, his shoulders straightening. I took another step until we were toe to toe. "What the hell are you saying?"

"She hasn't been home since the day the old man was killed in the lobby."

"That was over two weeks ago!"

He steeled himself. "Yes."

"Have you called the police? Filed a missing persons report?"

"No."

"Why not?"

He didn't answer. His eyes softened and he dropped his gaze. He fell back a few steps like he was aiming his ass for the rich leather wraparound sofa I saw in his living room, but he began to stumble. I actually had to reach out and grab his arm to keep him from going over. I shook him hard once but he still looked dazed. The cops should've been called in long before this, but I didn't push the point because I'd lost just about all my confidence in the police anyway.

Corben said, "I can't speak to you now."

"You damn well better."

"I can't. Later. Why don't you come up tonight for a drink? It's been a while since we've talked." He slowly closed the door in my face. I had no idea how I'd gotten out into the hall.

I had three cards from the three teams of cops. I picked up the one from the whiners and started to phone them, but before I tapped out all seven numbers I hung up. I was already a second-rate suspect in a cooling murder case. How smooth would it go down with the police if I called them about Gabriella? They'd question Corben and he was a New York celebrity, a personal friend of the mayor and the governor. He'd slick it over if he wanted, and they'd just have even more reason to presume me guilty of something. I couldn't waste the time. I had to find her. I had to make him crack. I felt it was something I had to do. Something only I could do. Audacity is sometimes its own reward.

Leave it to Corben to call a decade and a half "a while". I decided to play along.

A few hours later we sat in his living room drinking bourbon. From the stink of his breath I could tell he'd been at it for a while before I got there. We skipped fifteen years and anything of substance. I wanted to let my gaze roam his apartment. I'd been in the place many times before. Whenever a toilet clogged. Whenever the garbage disposal backed up. I'd cleaned up Corben's shit for two years, but I'd never been a guest and I'd never spent a minute taking in the personality of his apartment. I wanted to look at the photos with him and movie stars, on the sets of his films. I wanted to get up and hold all his rare nineteenth-century first editions. There were many paintings, mostly small originals done by artists who resided in the world's greatest museums. His tastes were similar to mine and I knew I would find many wondrous, beautiful, awe-inspiring aspects to his home.

But I simply sat and looked at him and waited.

He started off with trivial matters. We discussed our latest works – I mentioned the last manuscript I'd finished and made enough misleading comments for him to think it was still under consideration at my publisher. This one was a grand family drama delving into such an assortment of relationships and secrets and personal mysteries that I had no idea what the hell the story was about. He mentioned his latest bestseller, the one I'd bought and left on the front stoop. He didn't talk about the Stark House book.

He was splitting his attention between our conversation and writing in his head at the same time. He was letting his mind wander the building. The slightest noise made him snap his chin aside. The muscles in his legs jumped. He was trying to kill his interest with booze. He wouldn't be able to stand it much longer.

I started in where I'd left off earlier. "Why didn't you call the police?" I asked.

"We had argued that morning—"

"I know. I heard you."

It did something to him. It got down beneath the layers of his created persona and dragged up his real self. I got a view of my old pal again, the kid he was back in the day before we blew our friendship. He was just a scared boy, alone without his mothering wife to lead him safely through the extent of his own life. He'd been coddled for so long that he'd lost any kind of veneer. His hard shell had cracked badly over the years of his success, and it had let in all his insecurities and reservations and doubts. No wonder he screamed out his titles when he was losing a fight. He couldn't apologise and he couldn't debate. It was all he could defend himself with.

It's sometimes a curse to have an imagination that can draw up detailed visuals, and when you got down to it, he was better at it than me. He had a worse affliction to bear.

"Why are you writing about this building?" I asked.

He reared in his seat but the bravado wasn't there anymore. "She told you that?"

"Not outright. We were talking that day and I got a hint of what you were doing. So why are you doing it?"

He poured himself more bourbon. His hands trembled badly but not out of fear. At least not merely out of fear. Gabriella had been his buffer between him and the rest of the world, and without her he was being rubbed raw. "You know why."

"No, I don't."

"You do!" He sank back into his seat, all knife edges and points. If he moved too quickly he'd slash open a cushion. He frowned and his eyes were already so deep in his skull that they nearly disappeared altogether. He studied me, unsure of just how far to go. Finally his voice leaked words. They fell from his lips so softly I missed them.

"What?"

He said, "You've seen those who share the house with us."

"Seen who?"

"Those who stalk these halls."

"The toxic waste guy bothering you?"

He lashed out and sent a vase sailing across the room where it crashed against the far wall. "You know of whom I speak!"

When his speech patterns grew more gentrified I knew he must be really upset. I tried not to let it get too good to me, but it did. I felt a warmth bloom in my guts. Corben was actually nervous, but not about losing his wife. He'd had dinner at the White House and given signings and speeches to crowds numbering in the thousands, but right here in his own living room he sat trembling before something he couldn't even name.

"What congress have you had with them?" he asked.

I couldn't help it. I burst out laughing. I hadn't laughed in so long that once I got rolling I had a difficult time stopping. Maybe if I'd had more recent congress it wouldn't have been so funny. Corben stared at me in shock. It got me going even harder. Then I thought of Gabriella and the noise died in my throat.

"I came to talk about Gabriella, not any of your nonsense."

"It's not nonsense and you know it!" He reached for something else to throw but there was nothing handy so he hurled his glass. It bounced off the sofa and landed right side up on the floor without breaking. "We heard the stories about this place when we were children."

"We heard stories about every building in the city. The only reason you're so scared of this one is because you live here now. If you were over in Trump Tower you'd be acting the same way."

He shot to his feet, grabbed another glass, poured more bourbon and splashed some on the floor. He hadn't been able to hold his liquor in college and wasn't doing any better now. His voice was already losing its sharpness. "You mock me."

"I ought to mock you just for saying 'you mock me', asshole. People really let you get away with talking like that?"

He ignored me. He'd started to slip away. "I can't rest. They don't let me sleep. They work their way into the pages and ruin whatever

I'm writing. Isn't it the same way with you? Tell the truth. How can you find clarity with all the noise? All the tension and weight of their bearing and closeness."

Even if I had the pity to spare I wouldn't throw any his way. "You've got a beach house out in Southampton, a mansion in Beverly Hills, and a villa in Italy, right? So why don't you leave and go spend some time someplace else? Take a trip right after you tell me where your wife is."

"I can't leave, Will. I'm not sure I can ever leave here again. Stark House won't let me go."

"What happened to Gabriella?"

He dropped back into his chair and sat there blankly, withdrawing further into himself, gulping his drink. The ice rattled loudly. He snorted like a pig. A part of me wanted to beat the hell out of him and force him to talk, but I knew it wouldn't do any good. I wasn't going to get any answers from him. He was willing himself to shut down.

"Lay off the sauce," I told him. "I want you clear-headed. I've got more questions and you're going to answer them. We'll talk again soon."

"What was her name?" he asked.

"Who?"

"The one you took away from me in college. Mary? Maggie? Melanie?"

"I don't remember."

"She visits me too," he said. "She's dead but she asks about you. She doesn't remember your name either."

The next afternoon, on the second floor, I saw a young handsome man and a beautifully delicate woman walking up the corridor, holding hands. I'd never seen them before. He was in a tux and tails, and she wore a lace dress that looked straight out of the 1920s. They came toward me and the hair on the back of my next rose. A warm, comforting draft swept across my throat. They both smiled and nodded to me. I couldn't quite get my lips to work but I managed to nod back. I wanted to ask if they'd seen Gabriella but the words wouldn't form. They went to the stairway and began to move down it. I held myself in check for about three seconds and then started after them. I knew what I would see by the time I got there. No one would be on the staircase.

I was wrong. They were still slowly proceeding down it. They murmured back and forth. He said something and she tittered mellifluously. It was a warm and enduring sound. They walked across the lobby floor and out the front door onto the street. Something touched my ankle and I nearly yelped.

Mojo stood at my foot and said, "Ook." The chain that had connected him to Ferdi was gone. He held a piece of paper up to me. I took it.

It was blank.

He chittered and grinned and shoved his cup out against my shin. I tossed him a quarter and he danced back to Apartment 2C.

I went downstairs and stood out on the stoop listening to the world chase itself. Four rapes and two murders had happened in a five-block radius of the building in the last month. There were plenty of suspects but no leads.

I should be looking for Gabriella. I should be beating the piss out of Corben. But I went back to the screen and forced out more sentences. What I wasn't making up I was dredging up. I called up my most shameful moments and laid them on my characters. They all loved Gabriella, they all wanted to smash her husband. I made apologies too late. It was a third-rate redemption at best. I waited for a man made of aluminium foil to climb out of the closet. When it happened I didn't want to jump out of my skin.

I started awakening in the middle of the night to see my old man sitting at the foot of the bed. He always faced away from me, but I recognized his shape, the heft of his hand. When I dared to call to him he hitched his shoulders and began to turn to face me. It was a turn never completed.

Of course he couldn't face me, he was dead. He's been dead most of my life. He wouldn't even recognize me now. I was nine the last time he saw me. Now I look just like the way he did. The heft of my hand is the same. Imagine him now, finding himself at the foot of a stranger's bed, a man he's never met before, who might call out to him, "Dad?" No wonder he vanishes. If it was me, looking back at me, seeing me, a live me facing me, plaintively urging some unknown request of me, I'd run too.

Who the hell wouldn't.

The phone rang and no one was there. It happened more and more.

I kept bleaching the bloodstain and finally it faded enough so folks could walk over it again. I got another royalty check, this one for $12.13. In a moment of spite I grabbed the end of it and flicked my lighter. The corner started to brown but I dropped it before there was any real damage. There was no point in ruining what little of mine they were actually sending through. I should be happy the Danes or the Portuguese or whoever the fuck were reading my books. We all make our deals with the Devil.

A private investigator hired by the parents of one of the rape victims came around asking questions. He eyed me up good. A handyman with no set hours, no clock to punch. He'd asked around and found out about the murder. He tried to brace me and I held onto my dwindling cool. He lacked subtlety and hoped to push my buttons, whatever they were. He ran out scenarios where I couldn't get laid so I waited in dark hallways and leaped down onto teenage girls. I let him talk the talk because it was for a good cause. I wanted him to hunt down the bastard in the area.

I awoke to laughter outside the basement window. Mojo pressed his face to the glass and waved to me. I saw the feet of boys and girls go by. A breeze blew the stalks of weeds and wildflowers against the pane. I got dressed, took the back door, and went out to the garden.

Ferdi and the kids were following Mojo around, all of them in a line and sort of dancing the Conga. They went around and around while I watched. Mojo's little bag around his neck, stuffed with the pad and pen on a string, bounced as he jumped onto the vines and the lower limbs of a couple of gnarled trees bursting up from brick.

I turned and saw a man with eyes like a dull metal finish. He whispered something I didn't understand. It wasn't English. I thought maybe it was German. My stomach tightened but I could feel myself smiling. The mysteries of life and death, baby, and everything in between.

A sweet moist aroma wafted from him, and suddenly I knew what the Rhine Falls must smell like.

"Nobody uses ice-picks anymore," I said. "So he lied. So what? He just wanted to meet girls."

Dr Lauber held his hands up to show me they were empty. He seemed eager to explain to me that his intent was friendly and forgiving. He said something else I couldn't understand. I approached and the sunlight shimmered off him.

I said, "It wasn't you?"

Dr Lauber firmed his lips. He shook his head. He reached out to touch me but the touch never came. He had a lot more he wanted to say. The words poured out of him. He had admissions and apologies and declarations to make. We all did. I knew I would die before making all of mine too. It seemed nobody could do any differently. I listened, thinking about Gabriella. By the time the chain of children came around again he was gone.

Mojo skipped by and then the kids, one after the other. As Ferdinand the Magnifico was about to pass, I reached out and grabbed hold of his coat sleeve.

He stopped and faced me. "My good friend, the wonderful writer Will Darrow! Is it not a glorious day!"

"Why'd you do it, Ferdi?" I asked. "Why'd you kill the aluminium foil guy?"

Our eyes locked and I watched the real person slip out from beneath the costume of his caricature. I saw a sorrow and a resolve there that I hoped I would never have to experience. A strength that had been thoroughly hidden and an anguish that would never depart but had been recently muted. He was trying to regain his soul.

He spoke in a quiet voice for the first time since we'd met. "He murdered my wife in Denmark fourteen years ago. You don't need to know the details."

He was right. I didn't.

I knew he'd told me the truth. We can go our whole lives believing we'll recognize the cold hard truth when we hear it, but when it finally arrives it's like nothing that's ever come before. It strikes a chord that's never been hit, and my head somehow rang with it. Ferdi waited for me to make a move. He appeared ready for any judgment.

The aluminium foil liar had told me he'd done terrible things. He had struck his mother. He had broken the hearts of his children. He had made a woman bleed. He didn't think he deserved to be forgiven.

I shrugged and let go of Ferdi's sleeve. He nodded with a slightly accepting, thankful smile. I lit a cigarette and he rushed to catch up to the kids, and the dance continued around the garden.

I saw someone crouched at the foot of my bed. It was my old man again, facing away from me like always. He held his fist up, and in it was clutched a note. I threw the covers aside and walked to him. Maybe now he would talk to me.

But he couldn't turn around, no matter how close I came. Of course he couldn't face me, he was dead. Without looking at me, he stuck his arm out and offered me the note.

It was five pages long and read:

WE HAVE COME TO A SPOT WHERE THE TISSUE IS THINNEST AND ALREADY TORN. IT IS A DESTINY FEARED AND WORSHIPED. THERE ARE THOSE WHO DESIRE AND CANNOT OWN, THOSE WHO DIE IN NEED. THE HEART SWELLS AND FAILS. I HAVE SEEN HER, IN

THE DEPTHS OF THIS HOUSE, IN THESE ROOMS, LOST AND AT A LOSS BUT STILL RETAINING THAT LUMINES- CENCE OF LIFE. SHE IS LIGHT ITSELF TO SOME. WE CANNOT AFFORD THIS LOSS. SHE HAUNTS THE HALLS EAGER TO REACH OUT TO US AS WE PASS. CAN YOU MAKE SENSE OF IT? I HAVE TRIED BUT I AM INDISPOSED BY THE PART I MUST PLAY. SURELY YOU HAVE HEARD HER IN YOUR DREAMS? YOUR NAME CALLED. HOW BRIGHT SHE IS IN THE DARK PLACES. SHE SPEAKS OF YOU STILL. SHE UNDERSTANDS YOUR LOVE. IT IS NOT TOO LATE.

MOJO

When I looked up again my old man was gone. There was a knock at the door. I opened it and there stood Mojo, smiling, holding his cup, his little hat askew. I looked out into the lobby for Ferdinand, but he was nowhere in sight.

I glanced down at the chimp and said, "Okay, Mojo, fess up. I need to hear it. If you really know how to talk, buddy, then now's the time. It'll be our secret, I swear. But this is important. What happens next is going to change the course of a life or two around here, I think." I went to one knee and got in close. He cocked his head and did a dance and put a paw out to touch my nose. "So I want to hear it from your own lips. Talk to me. Did you see it happen? Did you see Corben kill Gabriella?"

Mojo went, "Ook."

I stared at him and he stared at me.

I nodded and said, "Fuck all, that's good enough for me," and went to confront my oldest friend, my only enemy.

I was wired and hot and ready to break bones, but when he opened the door all my rage left me. Almost all of it.

He hadn't shaved or eaten in days. He'd been steadily losing weight and his sternum stuck out like a spike. His eyes had sunken in even further, his lips crusted and yellow, and his breath stank like hell. He hadn't quit the sauce. His sweat was stale and smelled like whisky and disease. There was a time I would've gloated and been filled with a sick joy. Now I just wanted to know what had happened to his wife.

"I want to talk to you," I said.

"All right."

We sat in his living room again. He hadn't opened a window in ages. The dust swirled in the rays of the sun lancing down through his windows. He'd been drinking too much but I didn't know what else to do for him, so I mixed him a screwdriver. At least he'd get a little orange juice in his system. He looked just a little closer to death than the aluminium foil guy had with the ice-pick vibrating in his head.

His eyes kept wandering to a spot on the wall behind the couch. I couldn't help riffing on Poe's "Cask of Amontillado" and "The Black Cat". But he wasn't checking the place where he'd might've stuck Gabriella's corpse and sealed it over with stucco. He wouldn't keep her so close at hand. He was writing behind his eyes.

"I know you killed her," I said.

"You're a fool."

"The monkey saw you do it."

It made him open his mouth so wide that the hinges of his jaw cracked. "What?"

"Mojo told me what you did."

"The chimp . . . ?"

"You shouldn't have left any witnesses. You didn't think the world's first talking writing monkey would tell somebody? He knows his business. Knocks 'em dead in South Dakota."

"I was wrong. You're not merely foolish. You're insane."

The word caught in his throat. He almost didn't get it out. It wasn't an easy one for him to say aloud. I usually had a hard time with it too. Anyone who spends that much time inside his own head had to be extra cautious of tossing words like crazy and insane around. But in this building, in this city, on this day and during this particular conversation, it seemed even more reckless than usual.

"Where is she?" I asked.

He finished his screwdriver and set the glass aside. "Visiting her mother in Poughkeepsie."

I took it in and felt a clash of relief and disbelief. "That's not what you told me. You said you didn't know."

He made an effort to appear embarrassed. Instead he just looked cornered but sly. "I didn't want to admit to it."

"Cut the horseshit."

"You say that to me after telling me about talking monkeys?"

"That's right, I say it to you, asshole."

Corben refused to keep his mind on Gabriella. I backed away a step. His gaze slid over me. It slid over everything. He couldn't keep his focus on any one spot or idea. It was more than just the writing going on in his head. He was tumbling around inside Stark House without moving. I'd never seen him like this before – lost and at a loss. I stopped trying to control the conversation. I would allow him to take the lead.

We sat there and I finally looked all around the place, letting myself take in his riches and treasures. I went for room to room. Holy shit, there really was a solarium. The beauty and the effort and love that Gabriella had put into her home. How could a man not think it was enough? Are any of us ever satisfied? I wondered if I would have so easily been led down the wrong path if I'd had his successes. Become so self-absorbed, so unappreciative. I supposed it could happen to anyone.

We stayed like that for a half an hour. I thought he'd forgotten about me, so entwined by himself. I didn't mind waiting. I sat down and felt comfortable in his chair, noting all the small details and touches that were of Gabriella.

"Stark House is haunted," Corben said.

"Maybe," I told him.

His upper lip drew back in a wild leer. He ran a hand through his hair and I realized how thin and grey it had gone. He looked around like he wanted to start kicking shit again. He flung the empty screwdriver glass. It shattered against one of his rare paintings. "How can you say that? How can you still be unsure? You must feel it, Will. Every moment of the day! I can't write anymore. There's no need. The books write themselves. There's always someone else at the keyboard. Even now. Right now, this very minute, in my office. Go look if you don't believe me."

"I believe you," I said.

"I accept my sins and vices, I do, sincerely," he said sounding wholly insincere. "I've done terrible things, every man has, but . . . but this – I have seen them in the corridors, in the doorways, in my bed – my God, they stare at me. They're the damned. The forsaken."

I shrugged again. I was doing it a lot. "Everyone is, more or less. We muddle through. So what?"

"Doesn't it fill you with black terror?"

"No." I lit a cigarette, got up, and walked around the room.

"How can it not?"

"Why should it?"

Corben glanced up and we went deep into each others eyes. I knew he'd crossed the line. I knew it with all my heart. He'd killed Gabriella, just to see what it felt like. We'd been reading stories about such men since we were kids: the ones who thought they were too good for moral law. He wanted to feel blood run just so he could write about it. And now it was writing itself without him.

I knew something else. He really had loved her – more than anything, more than he could possibly love anything in this life – except for himself and his art. He'd cast himself in the role of villain of his grandest dramatic work. The one that needed no author. He'd learned what he hadn't really wanted to know, and it was destroying him. He'd gone bony but soft.

"Where is she?" I asked.

"I already told you. Stop asking me!"

"What did you do to her?" I asked. "Where did you leave her?"

"You've no right to question me like this!"

I moved in on him. Two great forces worked through me at once – a jealous rage and a wild desire to shove aside the wasted years and have my friend back again. I wanted to save him and I wanted to crush him.

I swallowed heavily and said, "I heard you two arguing that morning. What were you fighting about?"

"I don't have to tell you anything."

"See, now there's where you're wrong."

I hadn't gone soft. I was all nerve-endings and adrenaline. I had dreams I needed to pursue. I still had to learn French. I'd make another stab at trying caviar. I had to track down my foreign rights and royalties. I had to find my love. "Where is she?"

"She's my wife! Who the hell do you think you are?"

"What did you do to her!"

Corben glowered at me, the corners of his lips turned up as if silently asking why I hadn't discovered her body yet, why I hadn't already smashed him to pieces and rammed a steak knife into his belly. Like all of us, he wanted to live and he wanted to die. His need was so apparent it invigorated and disgusted me. I made a fist and drew it back and willed all my hatred, remorse, and broken potential into it. My blood and bone, our lost friendship, our endless understanding of one another. It was no different than any other time I made a fist. Or smiled. Or wrote. Or made love. Or polished the banister.

I dropped my arm to my side, and he cried out, "She's at her mother's house in Poughkeepsie! It's the truth! It's the truth!"

"You're lying."

"She left me!"

"She would never do that."

"She did!"

"You're lying."

"Am I? Maybe I am. Your voice, Will, it sounds so much like mine."

"No, it doesn't."

"Am I only fighting with myself? Sometimes I think I may be the only one alive in this building. I sit here and can almost start believing that you and all the others are only figments, phantoms, that all of you are—"

"Yeah?" I said. I got up close. "Tell me. You ever think that maybe *you're* the only one who's dead?"

The thought had never crossed his mind, but now it did. It hit him like I'd never seen anything hit him before. His eyes widened and his breathing grew shallow. He started floundering in his seat, his hands flapping uselessly. I got another glass and gave him a tall one of straight vodka. He chugged it down until the glass rattled against his teeth.

He stared at me and I stared at him. After a while I got up and left him there alone, receding deeper into shadows of his own making. His eyes implored me as if I could, or ever would, have the capacity to save him. Now as he began fading beyond even my memory until he too had almost completely vanished. I turned around once before I got to his door, and he was nowhere.

Maybe we were both already dead.

There had been a night a few months ago when he and I passed each other on the stairway, and I'd thought that I shouldn't turn my back on him. That he might, right then, decide to draw the derringer he supposedly always kept on his person and pop me twice in the back of the head. The thought had been so strong that I'd watched him carefully as we went by, my hand on a small screwdriver in my pocket, thin enough to slip between his ribs and puncture his heart. We moved on in opposite directions, wary, but alive.

Or so I'd thought. But now, I wasn't so sure.

Perhaps Corben had murdered Gabriella and hidden her under some alleyway garbage not far from Stark House. Maybe he'd tossed her body in the East River or buried her deep in the garden beneath the wildflowers or beneath the brick. Or maybe she actually was up in Poughkeepsie, at home with her mother, calming herself before a time when she might be willing to return to the building and make amends. With him, or only with herself. The dead roam here the way they roam everywhere else – intact, lost and at a loss. The living were no different. I was no different.

She might eventually come back, for her belongings if not for him. To say goodbye to me if no one else. She might appear in the garden one morning, joining in when the children and Ferdi and Mojo danced together. There were more chances and choices than I'd ever believed in before.

Gabriella might call me tomorrow evening and ask me to come fix her kitchen tap, and I will find her there alone on the fifth floor. She'll have a bottle of wine and a jar of caviar. I won't make faces chewing down the crackers. The window will be open and a cold breeze will press back the curtains. Moonlight will cast silver across the dark. The sheets will be clean but rumpled. I'll do my best to speak French. Total darkness for a moment and then the pressure of her body easing against mine.

Whatever the truth, I would wait for her.

Because, I've been told, she speaks of me still.

She understands my love.

I burn silently. It is not too late.

CHRISTOPHER HARMAN

Behind the Clouds: In Front of the Sun

CHRISTOPHER HARMAN'S FIRST story appeared in 1992. Since then his work has been published in *All Hallows*, *Ghosts and Scholars*, *Enigmatic Electronic*, *Dark Horizons*, *Kimota*, *Supernatural Tales*, *New Genre*, *The Year's Best Fantasy and Horror*, *Acquainted with the Night* and *Strange Tales Volume II*.

He is currently working on a novel, although short stories remain his primary interest. He lives in Preston, England, and is a librarian.

"I wanted to write a supernatural story based around a familiar artefact," Harman says about the following tale, "and chanced upon some intriguing possibilities in *Miller's Antiques Price Guide*.

"At first I had in mind something in the tradition of M. R. James, but by the time I'd finished the first draft of the story it had gone to places I hadn't originally envisaged, not least the imaginary northern city in which it is set.

"In the past I've often been drawn to rural settings, however, the fun I had wandering the city in this tale has led to a couple of subsequent and longer stories in similar environments, which I hope will appear one day."

PROFFIT'S ARMS FIRMLY ENCIRCLED the bulky contents of the black plastic bag for the whole of the journey across the city. The driver had been visibly curious, but had refrained from questioning him. That suited Proffit, preoccupied as he was with his own internal dialogue, in which he argued with himself that this latest purchase was a good deal and not a dud. More than that, it seemed a portent of a better future. Not that the present is all that bad, he thought as the driver slowed and prepared to double park briefly.

The house was one of a row of Victorian buildings facing the park. Ironwork and window mouldings were testament to a prosperous past. Now, if anyone could be bothered, the brickwork needed pointing, and the window frames several fresh coats of paint. Litter choked basement railings.

Dashes of curtain colour, plantless plant-pots and space-filling ornaments were all that distinguished Proffit's building from its neighbours, on one side three floors of dentists and on the other a firm of insurance brokers behind smeared windows. Beneath a sparse wig of aerials Proffit's ersatz family peeped at him from the windows of his rooms on the third floor.

Proffit pushed open the cab door and placed the bag carefully on the pavement, before getting out himself. Having spent enough that afternoon without parting with more, Proffit fed the exact fare into the cabby's hand. The cab screamed off at speed, the driver making a point, Proffit supposed, unless he were anxious to reacquaint himself with the city's busier thoroughfares, whose clamour, heard from this enclave, was a seditious murmur.

Inside the house Proffit was only mildly out of breath by the time he'd reached the top of the stairwell, the item being more awkward than heavy to carry. Entering his flat, he was presented with the problem of where to place the thing amongst his growing collection. In the living room alone every spare surface was lumpy with china and ceramics, a broken Ormolu clock, an ivory chess set, a pile of 1970s box games. Only the walnut coffee table before the second-hand sofa was clear.

The black polythene covered the great roundness like silk. Proffit unknotted the chicken-neck twist of plastic and a whispering crackle welcomed his delving hands. With care, he lifted out the globe and transferred it reverently to the table. He switched on the ceiling light, and the reflected room thrust out over the road. The globe's ghost twin hovered, a dark moon over the park opposite.

Hitherto, the thrill of finding, the bargaining and the moment of possession had been succeeded by an anticlimactic slump in his mood. Not this time.

The globe was clasped at its poles by a plain brass meridian half-ring. Spinning it produced a frail, but strangely eager, squeal, as of something surprised at its own resurrection.

This wasn't Earth, far, perhaps literally far, from it. Bass-relief mountain ranges crossed oceans of red that faintly stained Proffit's fingers where he'd touched. To most of the surface, black oil paint had been applied with a palette knife, in a scale-like effect; Proffit had no idea what physical feature this represented. Zephyrs presided, three or four in each hemisphere; thin rather than plump, their sexlessness assured by discreetly raised bony thighs. They had ashen curls, and cruel teardrop eyes. Cheeks were puffed out roundly in their haggard faces, and from their pursed lips issued burst-pillow effects of crimson feathers. Their fists terminated in black talons.

The woman had asked for twenty pounds in the squashed confines of Cuttings Curios. Fifteen, returned Proffit, with a shrug that said, *Doing you a favour love – I mean – look at it*. And she had looked, her upper lip pulled fastidiously out of true. She'd capitulated to Proffit's offer, cast a cloud of black plastic in his direction, and as good as stood back. People were funny, Proffit reflected.

He stretched. Half a day trawling the charity shops and market stalls had left him pleasurably fatigued. He was hungry though, and for more than the dry and curling morsels in the fridge. Food; he resented the way it spirited away his limited funds, then itself. Objects remained. *Even so*, his stomach protested, aloud.

Three streets away the basement restaurant bore the weight of a dozen perpetually darkened floors. Proffit told the waiter not to stint on peppers and chillies; without them food tasted of nothing to him. Afterwards he went to the video store and hired a war film.

Back in his flat, whenever Proffit had to avert his eyes from the screen, they met the blood-red deserts of the globe. Worst of all was the soldier dealing out his intestines, like a magician casting forth cloth sausages from a top hat. Something like this just might have interested Proffit's charges, when blackboard battles never had.

The film over, Proffit reached for the globe and pushed along its horizontal axis. Shades of blacks, browns and reds smeared, then blurred and seemed to rise off the surface in an effect like encompassing dirty cloud. An arbitrary god, Proffit stopped its whirl. A bit of investigating might unearth a value, failing that he'd make one up; experts did it all the time. Proffit yawned off any other bright ideas. Bed first. Should I attend for work in the morning? The option was no longer available to him, but surveying his narrow kingdom, from the wide throne that was his threadbare sofa, it still gave him pleasure to answer in the negative.

Not a traveller he. Never a hankering to set foot on the foreign fields he'd chalked too many times onto a blackboard. Not a flyer either.

Madness to be in this miles high tube. But flying troubles him now at a basement level. More immediate is the likelihood that one of the passengers in the front rows of the plane is going to turn and see him, pyjama-ed and prone in the brass-framed bed at the rear.

Proffit minimizes himself beneath the covers as the hostess stops just beyond where his feet make twin-peaks of the blanket. "We'll arrive shortly," she says. Her voice has a slight buzz as if it were a discreet tone in the ambient sound of the engine. She's a star he cannot name. She glows like sun-washed terracotta. "'kay," he says meekly, snuggling, arranging the flies of his pyjama bottoms as he knows he'll have leave the refuge of his bed soon.

In the porthole, the stars are so close he can see flames. He corrects himself: they aren't stars, they're planets on fire. Noticing a sensation of inexorable turning, he looks out of the round window to his right.

The black blind is pulled most of the way down, its lower edge bowed in a curve. Only it's not a blind, it's the southern pole of the Earth. He hadn't realized they'd gone so high. The Earth is massive, the plane a hollow pin in comparison, and he a pinprick of blood inside it.

No sense of motion now. The circumference of the black disc is out of sight. It's a target seeking its arrow. He'd never have guessed the Earth's shadowed side could be this dark.

There's a change in the note of the engine. A sick, floating sensation inside Proffit.

A clunking beneath him – landing gear? Not long after, a jolt and rattle as of colossal crates. A sense of motion again, fast but gradually decelerating.

All the lights are out in the cityscape, at the edge of what Proffit assumes is the vast apron of an airport. If landing lights of other runways exist they are comprehensively concealed by multitudes.

The plane has stopped. Voices make thunder against which are lightning solo cries of triumph and anguish. Proffit notices pools of elegantly licking flame. A body rolls, clothed in fire; some think kicking will douse it. To others, the plane offers a distraction. They crush forward. They have upraised pikes and spears-a forest of them. Proffit is dismayed at the horde surrounding the plane. There is a tattered banner marked by a huge black blot.

Despite the peril presented, the door has been opened. The passengers are impassively filing out. "Come on," the hostess calls to him, a tease in her voice. Then she is gone. The lights in the cabin go out, a prompt that he is to follow. Faint firelight from outside suffuses the interior

He'll stay here, that's what he'll do. Responding to his thoughts, the door shuts, subduing the massed voices. But what now? Proffit fingers his blanket as if the stitching encodes an escape-plan.

The plane is an oven building heat.

A toddler begins to wail. Wait a second, the child isn't outside in the maelstrom of violence – it's in here. It must have been left behind, either by accident of design. Whatever the reason, the toddler's harsh thin wailing isn't fearful. Proffit ponders nervously. The child hasn't the years to have accumulated such hate and aggression. Proffit thinks any object might serve as a focus for that savage crying.

He wishes he were outside.

Against the diminishing pattern of headrests, a flaw appears, low in the aisle. An audible intake of breath isn't Proffit's. A vagueness due to the haze of smoke, but there is no mistaking the little, wizened face beneath the mop of hair. It takes another breath, and another. It's not hyperventilating – or playing the Big Bad Wolf. Another breath and its cheeks bulge. Proffit screams helplessly, his face masked by his hands against the heat, the brightness . . .

He was half out of bed in the tight embrace of his twisted duvet, his own cry in his ears. His own bed, no sign of a brass frame. A big rectangle replaced the tiny porthole. A good thing dream fires didn't scorch or blind.

Shouts outside – an inadequate re-enactment of that wild populace.

The carpet was cool, dry land against Proffit's feet. The dream was floating off satisfactorily on an inner sea.

Down in the street a brawl. A youth was puzzled by the blood on his fingers. Two others grappled, their trainered feet doing complex dance-steps over glass shards. Another beckoned with upturned waggling fingers for anyone, just anyone to . . . Another hung ape-like from the park gates; with the bottle in his free hand he toasted the world. Ancient schoolyard scraps played around the action. Not intending to resume his peacemaking role now, Proffit shoved down the sash window on the few inches it had been open. A scratching remained.

He couldn't pinpoint its source with any certainty, but a hollowness in the sound was suggestive of an enclosed space. A rodent in the walls meant a pest problem shared by other residents, in which case they could band together and find the elusive landlord and insist he remedy the problem. Listening carefully, Proffit scowlingly realized the problem was his alone.

He padded out of the bedroom, hesitated a moment on the threshold of the living room. He went in.

He orbited the globe until he'd satisfied himself the scratching came from the inner surface and not the outer. Those scales of black paint were reminiscent of roofs, vastly out of scale in terms of the dimensions of the planet depicted, but maybe representative of an endless city, swirling around every space not occupied by mountain and desert.

The scratching had stopped; he couldn't help but think his sound-less presence had brought this about. He disrupted the outer-space silence with his breaths and considered the matter.

Anything sealed live inside the globe, deliberately or not, perhaps at the time of its fashioning, should have died long since. But what if an insect, or grub, had mindlessly, and to its cost, chewed its way in – or found some pre-existing and overlooked chink? And then grown to a size preventing its egress from the point of entrance, or via any other minuscule exit? Perhaps the recent scratching had been a final paroxysm of effort to escape its paper and card prison, culminating in its death?

Proffit waited; moments later, hearing nothing more from the globe, he returned to his bedroom. He mulled over whether to leave the door ajar, so to hear the scratching should it recommence, or close it to block out that very eventuality. He closed it, against the possibility of the scratching thing escaping and making its presence known to him face to face with bites or stings.

A pattering daylight awoke him. He went into the living room. Nothing within the tapestry of rain sounds. The inhabitant of the globe must be dead, or in a similar dormant state. He pressed his ear against the globe; it felt like cold hard earth. Blood pumping in his inner ear imitated a pounding furnace at a planet's core. He tapped lightly with a knuckle. Nothing responded. A dead planet.

The clutter of furniture and collectibles rekindled the crazed multitudes in his dream. Getting rid, selling with any luck, would clear the flat – as well as his head. He'd start with the globe, but it had to be far less of a mystery first.

The city's wet streets oppressed, from bowed doorsteps, basement railings and gurgling drains, to the high peaks and sagging valleys of the upper world of slate roofing. The rain fizzed on his face, formed tears. Windows, opaque with rain, were blind to his passing, as were huddle-rushing fellow pedestrians.

Proffit splashed through growing puddles, dodged through the white fog pumped from cars. Blotches and veins glowed darkly in brick and stone. He passed the sooty prison-house of Grundy Secondary Modern; its railings, like the raised spears in his dream, dared him to return.

Where the road crossed the canal he viewed the rear of the terrace, reflected in the slick black length pitted with rain. In that murky compressed perspective was the back of number seven. Esther and he had listened morosely on many a night to the rats scuttling at the water's edge. He guessed she still did. Unable to think of a pretext for visiting now, Proffit moved on.

The streets deepened beneath the piled-high architecture of the powers running the city. Old stone was gnawed and dark-stained by rain. High up, cloud mingled with mock-battlements and limp flags. Down below, Proffit felt of no more worth than the ones darkly housed in doorways, and as vulnerable while he was out here.

The city library was a temporary escape from the city. Today was the first time in a while that Proffit was here with a purpose, other than seeking shelter from Harrowby's current two-note weather system; cloudy, cloudy with rain.

The reference department was a series of slant-ceilinged groins in the roof of the building. *The Compendium of Maps and Globes* and several similar works contained nothing resembling Proffit's globe. He waylaid an employee who'd fined him with relish on numerous occasions in the lending department below. She disappeared into a staff enclave behind the enquiry desk and returned with a pile of small periodicals.

Charts! the title proclaimed with enthusiasm, *The Journal of Maps and Atlases*. In the flyleaf of the topmost copy was a list of minor deities, each accompanied by a photograph and the attribute with which he or she held sway in that particular domain of cartography. The economically named Humphrey Humphries was one such; his face and high forehead poked through a halter of neatly trimmed white hair. The "Historical maps" editor was accessible to ordinary mortals via an electronic mail address, which Proffit took down.

Home again, Proffit cranked up the assemblage that was his computer. His e-mail account hadn't lapsed despite two or three months of neglect. He entered the address, the subject (bizarre globe inquiry), then struggled to convey the appearance of the globe in words. He was on surer ground with the zephyrs, describing them as "mean-looking infants", "bags of bones with jazz trumpeters' cheeks". No name or maker's mark on the globe, and his other "extensive researches" had proved fruitless. Any other lines of inquiry would be gratefully received. Proffit thanked Humphries in anticipation and signed off.

Glad to put the matter aside, Proffit restlessly thumbed the TV remote. Mayhem on various scales; bombs in hotter climes, a soap opera family bickered, a cat and dog fought in primary colours. The globe at the corner of his eye was like a persistent fault in his vision

Light had shrivelled to nothing over the park when he returned to his computer. He hadn't expected a reply so soon, but was unduly frustrated as his negative expectation was confirmed.

Prawn crisps, a whisky nightcap then bed. No dreams please, he asked of the silence.

Either the baby crying next door or the scratching from the living room awoke him – perhaps both. Shouts now, a male voice – angry. A door slammed. The scratching was louder, as if to be heard over the competing noise, or even drawing sustenance from it.

So the thing inside the globe survived; a big beetle perhaps? Proffit got out of bed and went into the living room.

The globe looked like solid rock rather than segments of stiff paper ("gores" as he'd learned from his limited studies) covering a sphere of air. Light from the bedroom swathed the western hemisphere in sunshine. The scratching was more pronounced, eager, as if the occupant of the globe were invigorated by Proffit's presence, rather than cowed to the listening silence of the night before.

Next door a glass smashed amidst the shouts of the parents. What were their names? All smiles on the stairs, in the laundry room. The baby ceased suddenly to cry. The adult voices were accusatory. A door shut them away; noisy toys put away for the night. *Scratch, scratch.*

It's getting through, Proffit thought, stepping back. A tiny movement in a join between gores. The end of something sharp protruded minutely, in time with the scratches. No beetle this. Bits of paint and paper fluttered to the floor. Proffit wasn't going to wait for the creature inside to discover him.

He opened the front door of his flat. Back in the living room he warily picked up the globe. Leaving the flat he wondered if the globe were heavier now than when he'd carried it from the shop. Near the stairwell was a small back window. Proffit worked quickly. The talon, for he was convinced that was what it was, had sliced a slit between gores. A bird? That conjecture alone was enough to have him flinching from a desperate flourish of wings. He was a planet himself the way the core of him thudded. The window swung outward from hinges running along the top. Not wasting another second he squeezed the globe through the gap.

It plummeted, a dark star. The night obscured it, cushioning to a soft crumple its impact with the ground. Proffit strained to see it – then it rolled, minus its brass stand and meridian half-circle, into a wedge of moonlight between the dustbin enclosure and a decrepit bench.

The globe and Proffit were as still as each other. A flickering hope in Proffit was doused as the globe shuddered. The jabbing action was evident again, the thing inside seemingly energized in anticipation of the completion of the task it had set itself.

And something broke through. A dark sinewy growth from the seed of the globe. At the end of the growth, cilia waved, then scrabbled blindly on the broken concrete, then became still. Proffit gasped at the sight of the little hand. Suddenly, from this anchorage, the globe moved in a series of fast wide arcs.

The rent in the globe widened. The birth continued with the bulb of a head, narrow shoulders. The globe was shook wildly back and forth for several more seconds, before flying off from the body it had contained.

Bad dream: any moment now the black night would collapse on him, reduce him to nothingness until morning. Or he'd awake. The cold window ledge, the grit on it, defied his wish.

He looked down again. A creature snuffled the ground as if searching for a scent. Proffit dreaded whose. He was still – an insect in amber. Below a face rose, pinched, snub-nosed. It was looking at the sky, not for him. It grinned with satisfaction. Then the grin vanished, focus in the eyes, business to see to. Baby-like, it toddled rapidly away on all-fours into the shadows.

Proffit quietly closed the window. The creature must have been folded like linked playing cards to fit inside the globe. Diminutive, simian in the cast of its bony limbs, and those pale wedges of flesh flopping at its shoulders . . .

Proffit was alert for its reappearance. When he detected renewed movement, out in the darkness, it was at eye level.

Beyond a crumbling wall and a wide dingy plot of broken bricks and weeds was a towering black edifice, daubed with graffiti, its window apertures all brick-filled. Something moved fitfully up the black geometry of the superfluous fire escape. Such was the nimbleness of its ascent, it seemed barely in contact with the steps. Higher and higher until the top-most portion of the fire escape forced a halt. Proffit had room for a new trajectory of astonishment as the figure bobbed out from the protection of the fire escape to cling to adjacent brickwork. And then it rose again, finding adequate handholds in the interstices of the blackened and mouldering brick courses, yet seeming hardly to require them, for the rapid folding in and out of the appendages at its shoulders seemed as necessary in keeping the mite aloft. Wings, Proffit thought, why prevaricate? The narrow summit of the building had an overhang; the child-thing, as unthinkingly as an insect, fluttered out and ascended, as if assisted by a current of air, to finally stand on the small platform of flat roof.

And there, from the way its arms reached skywards, it aspired to greater heights.

The window buzzed faintly. Proffit put his ear to the glass. Cold thrilled through him, further evidence that he wasn't in some outpost of dreamland.

Words caused the sympathetic vibration in the glass. Proffit pushed open the window the better to hear.

Instantly, he flung himself against the adjacent wall. The window crashed back into its frame. Had the thing heard? After several moments Proffit dared to look again.

Still there. The noise hadn't distracted it. Too bad he'd let that high, rusty and oddly demanding voice, unmediated by glass, assault his ears. A summoning and an entreaty, directed at the pale tumours of the clouds, or whatever they might conceal.

Proffit returned to his flat. He didn't sleep, unless the blackness he stared into for an eternity was that condition. Maybe he had slept, and the voice was the leavings of a dream. He wished it would stop; he wished its alien, implacable words, heard through so many thicknesses of bricks and mortar, were unintelligible to him. *Ready. Ready now. Come. The waiting is over.*

Morning: a threadbare light. On the coffee table were a bowl of crisp crumbs and a smeared whisky glass – but no globe.

The computer's querulous hums voiced Proffit's reluctance to face the day. The waiting message scotched Proffit's hopeless hope that the globe had been nothing more than the presiding artefact of an extended dream.

Dear Mr Proffit,
Your globe does seem worthy of investigation. Of course, zephyrs are a commonplace on antique maps and globes, however the ones you describe would appear to be a rum bunch. Are you certain there's no maker's mark? If you would care to send a photograph by post, or via these wondrous contraptions, I will of course respond with all speed.
Sincerely,
Humphry Humphries

The provenance of the globe no longer concerned Proffit. It was out there, like a piece of damp rotting fruit; he only hoped some instinct didn't compel the midget thing to remain near it.

He opened the curtains and the dull light provoked a token squint. With too many clouds to fit comfortably into the sky, some bulged low to blend with the city's misty morning attire. Leached of its colour, a bus passing below seemed like a portion of the road afloat. Two successive shrieks came from the park gates, opened by the keeper.

With the city behaving like its usual self, an interpretation of the night's events came forth. *You threw out the globe, returned to bed and dreamed it out of the window again, but with a weird addendum.* The letterbox rattle concurred with this, and a beige tongue poked fun at any other explanation. But the silence of the flat made his memory of the rasping voice all the more vivid. Proffit decided on a circuitous route to pay the gas bill. Walking, he could corral his thoughts, if not calm them.

Ten minutes later the clouds weren't letting him appreciate the vast freedom of the park; they seemed as inert and solid as a plaster ceiling. A tramp shouted at them, or the chisel-marks that were birds, moving his fist in a stirring motion. Proffit headed to an outlying border of trees and a path that deposited him in narrow streets choked with traffic. Horns were territorial, like bird calls; behind windshields a limited sign-language of waved fists and jabbing fingers. Proffit couldn't see the cause of the gridlock, or why it should provoke this particular ire. There was little to choose between parkland and city pavement; Proffit thought anywhere might feed his tension.

He ate in a cafe window. Outside a skinhead pulled at the tie of a schoolboy, and feinted with his other fist. Passers-by were better placed to intervene, and maybe one did, or said something, for the youth and the boy abruptly ran off in different directions.

Proffit left the cafe and waited with a group at a crossing.

"It's coming," a voice said behind him. All knees and wrist bones, the man sat against the brick division between two shops. The bowed peaked-capped head nodded lower – *Yes, you.* Proffit ignored him. A sad-eyed mongrel licked the black sore on the back of the man's thin trowel of a hand. "Behind the clouds: in front of the sun."

The green man twittered and flashed, legs scissoring. Proffit went with the crossing band, impatience at the man like heartburn.

He paid his bill in the Post Office, then looked at rustic cottages in an estate agent's window. He moved on, and was three streets away.

"It's coming," said a figure set back in an alley. Darkness between the wide brimmed hat and the front complement of the long sandwich board; feet were shod in stumps of darkness. He-she may have been facing away. On the sandwich board a huge black blob, crimson gashed and blistered, dripping red onto the white below.

Proffit breathed in assertively through his nose and advanced on the figure. "What is?"

An arm rose. A match flared, illuminating a scrap of flesh between nose and chin. Smoke billowed as from a vent in a chimney. Proffit stumbled back. "Waste of space," he muttered, though hardly that as the figure backed away, ungainly as one fellow atop another, to slot neatly into a recess in the alley.

Proffit merged himself into the flow on the pavement. The egg-white sun was being bandaged in clouds. He sidestepped into the Regal.

A formulaic thriller though the violence engaged him. His fists clenched with the blows. His body tensed to dodge the gunshot. Horror cinema on the front row as a pair of teenagers consumed each other's faces. Others flicked unidentifiable missiles at the screen.

Proffit left, but the film continued on the street. Shoppers braked on the pavement. Shots; echoes disguised their point of origin so everybody faced all ways. A siren cried. From an upstairs window over shops a woman screamed, perhaps with laughter. Proffit took refuge in the Cancer Shop.

Monica disappeared as soon as she saw him. She returned with a long black trench coat which Proffit, with more politeness than enthusiasm, put on. "Fits like a glove Mr P.," Monica said admiringly. "You look proper distinguished." She said she'd saved it with him in mind. A bargain if you ignored the distant galaxies of impacted dandruff on the shoulders. In her Doc Martens and print frock Monica appeared to have the pick of the stock. Proffit showed one shoulder then the other to the long mirror. The silver buttons were tarnished, and the epaulettes just a little prominent on his shoulders, but yes, he did look like someone to be reckoned with. In fact, a bit of military chic might have encouraged a more studious air in his classes.

With a chilly smile, Proffit said he'd take it. He barely recalled Monica; ex-pupils were merging into composites.

"It'll keep off the rain," she said, keen to keep pleasing him. Bigger, greyer clouds were back, like schoolyard bullies.

"Don't let up do they?" Proffit said.

Back in his flat, relieved to be there, Proffit saw he hadn't logged out of his internet connection. A vague displeasure at the telephone bill left to fatten over several hours was mixed with trepidation at the new message.

Mr Proffit,
Harrowby rang some bells that prompted me to contact a long-standing colleague. I recalled him telling me of a catalogue with a mysterious supplementary list of imaginatively named places, all represented on maps and globes. The seller was one Albert Lostock, a stationer, formerly of your own fair city of Harrowby. To my friend's knowledge none of these globes or maps has ever been documented elsewhere, nor have examples emerged from private collections. Sadly, the fire that apparently destroyed Lostock's shop in 1937 may have robbed us of unique and fascinating items. Send pics soonest, for prompt reply.
Humphrey

Proffit rang the city library that evening. Yes, he was told. Lostock, A. Stationer. 3 Coal Row, Harrowby. Listed in Pigot's Directory of 1936.

Proffit felt comforted. The globe was physically gone, and now given a context and history that further distanced it. With the receiver in his hand he dialled again.

She answered with a clipped "Hello."

"How goes it?" Immediately, the phrase, a punishable offence.

"Fine." Esther was merciful, or sounded so.

"Still chucking?" He knew she'd turned number seven Canal Terrace minimal as soon as he'd left.

"Still hoarding?" A double edge: bottles behind the bookshelves, under the stairs. Funny how drinking had started his collecting. Bottles first, before broadening his scope.

"Hoarding with a purpose," Proffit said, suddenly inspired to add. "Thinking of opening a shop. Antiques." Someone in Esther's presence moved plates carefully; they weren't antique ones, nobody was stepping into Proffit's shoes to that extent. He wasn't going to ask who it was.

"Good luck," Esther said, unconvinced by Proffit's pipedream.

"It's coming apparently."

"Hmm?" A lapse of concentration, then, "What is?"

"That's what *I* said." He let out a chuckle. "People on the street. Doom-sayers." A pause Esther didn't fill. "Actually I'm beginning to believe them."

A sigh in his ear. "I'll have to go now Trevor—"

"One other thing," he began, but no words would serve to introduce that nocturnal adventure. She'd guess it were a stress dream, maybe whisky-fuelled, the zephyr a veritable bottle imp: his problem, no longer hers.

"I'm thinking of leaving the city."

That must have surprised her; it had surprised him as much as the shop idea. "Oh," she said, as if this would be a drastic step even allowing for what had happened between them.

"This city – it's 'doing my head in' as the kids say. The aggression I mean. Complete strangers on the street look like they'd like to knife you. Have you noticed the sirens all day?"

"Cities are tough places, but crime is exaggerated by the media." She sounded like a member of it. "People get paranoid—"

Proffit felt reduced to a trend. Her concern not sufficient to pursue the topic, Esther said she had to be going now.

A stumble of "Byes", a withering "Take care," from Esther.

Proffit slumped on the sofa with a glass of lager. Another glass shattered in the street. As the evening darkened, cries came at intervals too frequent to require investigation from Proffit, or anyone else within earshot; they were all too patently part of the fabric of the city. A madman shouted barely coherent orders in an increasingly hoarse voice as Proffit was preparing for bed. One great explosion, worth a few pages in tomorrow's *Messenger*, made his window brace like old bones stretching. Running steps littered Proffit's dreams, in a chaotic and interminable military deployment.

Proffit groaned, pulled the pillow over his face. He must have slept, and regretted this burdensome wakefulness. The knocking again, like an aural personification of the daylight. His presence was known with a deadly certainty, and nothing less than his presence in the flesh would be acceptable.

Proffit tugged on his clothes, and opened the door. Immediately he could tell the pair before him had nothing to sell and weren't collecting the rent. They smiled at Proffit; apparently he didn't know how lucky he was. Their faces were smeared with earth, or paint, or both

"It's here; it's now." From a slight refinement of feature Proffit guessed the speaker to be a girl. The other nodded, wonder and something of relief in his expression, as if at some point in the past there'd been doubt on some crucial matter, but all was now resolved.

In the gloom of the corridor something about them . . . Proffit folded his arms. "What is?"

"The *new world* of course," she said with a pout and flutter of lashes, as if Proffit were being deliberately obtuse.

"What 'new world'?" He leaned against the jamb, settling in for a debate, getting a better look at them. "I think you'll find there's only this one," he said, unable to prevent a sigh intermingling with the words. They wore combat jackets and jeans, all torn and stained as if they'd been on particularly taxing manoeuvres. Grimy epaulettes on his jacket; murky brass buttons down the front of hers.

"You've got to be ready for the fight," the youth said, half-addressing, through a smile breaking out on his lips, his companion, "Or you'll go under." Barry – '*Baz*' . . . yes. And she was . . . Ann.

Baz smirked. "And you're a good shot, *Sir*."

No, Proffit wasn't, but this world had a mischievous god who had worked in a mysterious way to engineer an outcome that had been a shallowly buried wish. Memories pushed and shoved.

Too many shorts at someone's lunchtime leaving do in the pub behind the school. Proffit staggering into the classroom like he'd been bayoneted. Class 3C primed and waiting. *Today the Great War, the war to end all wars*. Baz burbling away on the back row. A tectonic plate had shifted. Elemental anger. The chalk missile, aimed and not aimed, finding the blue between piggy sporadic lashes. Proffit walking before the governors could push him.

It was a history he wasn't going to allude to for their entertainment.

"Who are we fighting?" Proffit was readying himself for scorn.

"The enemy," she said, "And they're everywhere." Proffit noted with distaste, black deposits at the corners of her eyes. Soap and water wouldn't come amiss, young miss. Had they rolled out of bed only minutes before he had? Puffy faces, pinkly imprinted beneath the dirt, as if they'd slept with their heads on pillows stuffed with cutlery. Proffit felt unnerved as the youth fingered a Swiss army knife hanging from his belt. Finding words to conclude the encounter was suddenly beyond him. Then he thought of one.

Slam was the door's loud monosyllable, into their unwashed and increasingly crazed faces. What had Baz been about to extract from an inner pocket? Both their jackets had been bulky enough to contain arsenals. Proffit was glad of the closed door as a wild violence flew in the cage of him. *Young people today*, the tabloid leader writer trumpeted in his head. Perhaps their enthusiasm for battle would be enacted on the doorsteps of less restrained citizens.

Proffit switched on the computer. It was no surprise, the message waiting for him.

Mr Proffit,
This has come to my attention. Please see attachment for snippet from ADVENTURES IN THE BOOK TRADE by Arnold Durstin (Northern Lines, 1956).

Proffit clicked on the icon.

Albert was a character. His shop was tiny, the catalogue in his head enormous. No kind of businessman, he made a living, though his manner hardly encouraged regular customers. He rather despised humanity en masse. He often opined the world was heading for rack and ruin. In fact he seemed to relish the sorry end he predicted for civilization. He collected, and I fear read, books of a "specialist" nature bearing on the occult. Over a few too many gins one evening he told me of his strange and vivid dreams. He spoke of "flying" over these bizarre and terrible realms. Albert would record them in his notebook on waking. He said that making maps, and latterly globes, of these places was the only means he had of purging them from his head—

Proffit had been aware of the barking for several moments before it became intolerable. He went to the window.
Baz and Ann were with an old man who was walking head down. The old man's dog strained at the end of its lead and yammered at the couple. She was talking as Baz swished at the grass with a long stick.
Proffit returned to the screen.

—I don't believe he sold any, though I believe he tried. He told me he was working on a globe clasped in the grip of a world-spanning city at war with itself. Fire-breathing demons flew over every size and type of conflict, aligning with neither one side or another, but feeding on terror and death—

And not exactly fattening on it, Proffit thought, recalling the grey-shanked zephyrs.
In the park a figure lay on the ground close to where the old man had been. Figures approached, nobody anxious to get there first. Proffit drew a chair up to the window; with tea and toast in hand he had the best seat in the house. It was looking bad. Was that something sticking out of the old boy? A police car and an ambulance entered through the park gates.

Mid-afternoon, Proffit made his way by back streets beneath the grey dunes of the clouds. Muffled cries of pain or pleasure came from a wheel-less, curtained van. A fire was barely contained in the cauldron of a backyard. A crash of glass released from a high room a violent argument, in a language Proffit didn't recognize. Sirens seemed like calls to arms. Sat on a far chimney stack, a misplaced gargoyle hugged its knees. It turned on its axis, a chunky weathercock – then it was no such thing as it became airborne. A bird, Proffit was determined to believe, and not as substantial as it appeared to be.

In the city library, Proffit searched the microfilm of the *Harrowby Messenger* for 1937. It was an hour before he found that which he hardly could have wanted to find.

COAL ROW FIRE MYSTERY

A police spokesman said it was too early to speculate on the cause of the fire at Coal Row, and made no comment on the claims of Mr Ernest Purbright who was one of the first at the scene.

"We couldn't get no further than the hallway. The place was falling apart with smoke and flames everywhere. I saw something at the top of the stairs. I thought it was a monkey, but my workmate said it was a big bird. Whatever it was seemed buoyed up on the smoke; it seemed to have a little pot-belly and weedy arms and legs."

It is believed the body found in the cellar of the house is that of Mr Albert Lostock. The investigation continues.

Proffit returned home on busier streets. It was early evening and street lamps leaked orange; others flickered weakly, or remained unlit in smashed casings. Eyes glanced anxiously or were filled with a furtive hate. Pockets surely bulged with more than the hands they contained. There were scuffles in side-streets.

Glad to be inside again, Proffit looked out. How dense would the clouds need to be before they blocked out daylight completely? A spur of the park looked in danger of being chewed by adjacent office blocks, like blackened tombstone teeth. Tree foliage was the dense coiling black of smoking tyres. Around the crater of the sandpit, grass was grey stubble. Proffit drew the curtains.

Later he opened them again, onto a city like a coastline of black rocks strewn with lit bulbs. Something caught his eye, something so massive the streets it moved along could barely accommodate it. The vehicle, or the load it carried, had a curved upper portion that overlooked roof and chimney. Switchback-style it moved up and down the streets; no deceleration, let alone stops, for road junctions, pedestrian crossings, traffic lights. The monstrous size of the thing must have activated some special dispensation. Proffit would have thought it lost were there not purposefulness in its unhesitating progress. Not so much lost in the city as determined to explore every yard of its network of streets. As if to map it.

As troubling as the vehicle's smooth, almost floating motion, was its disappearance. Either it had gone behind the castellated heights of the city council buildings, or sank into the deep adjacent streets. The city seemed to have darkened while he watched, and fewer street lamps appeared lit than was usual at this time of the evening. The darkest streets seemed the ones the vehicle had passed along – as if it had sucked the dull orange sodium light away leaving black trenches in its wake. The more likely theory soothed a little; those blackened lengths were affected by localized power cuts. Suppose they should spread here? Proffit drew the curtains and searched for candles. He found none, but his dread of sudden darkness receded as the evening progressed, with not a flicker of the living room ceiling light.

There was a message in his e-mail account. He wondered how long this one-sided communication would continue.

My dear Mr Proffit,
I've had a brilliant wheeze. I've decided to bring forward some business I have to do in the north. I feel an examination based on photographic evidence alone will be limited in its usefulness. Look, I won't hear of you making the trip down to the south coast, and I wouldn't countenance the transportation of such a fragile object by even the most ruthlessly efficient mailing company (of which I know of fewer than one). So I suggest a meeting in Harrowby. I have booked into the Railway Hotel for tonight and the night after. This sounds like a fait accompli but you're under no obligation. However I think you can be under no illusion regarding the seriousness with which I take the news of your recent acquisition. No promises, but considerable sums of money are not inconceivable. Don't hesitate to ring the mobile number below. You may of course call. I'll be in room 408.
In anticipation,
Humph.

Darkness, abrupt and shocking. After a death-like instant Proffit's feet were again in touch with the floor. He moved carefully to the curtains and opened them. The computer screen was an impenetrable black; he could hardly believe it had ever been lit up with words. Bed seemed the safest place.

He doubted he was the only one lying awake. Beckoning, urging voices in the street. A vehicle accelerated, skidded; an impact. A sharp tang of sound as a window fragmented.

When he pressed the light switch, Proffit found the power hadn't returned. He got up and felt his way out of the room.

The view from the living room window; he was becoming addicted to it. Discreet crimson glows around the city; flitting figures below. Gun shot barked. Moonlight was painted meanly on the trees of the park. The open space beyond the gates seemed a great blister rather than flat. Was the curve not apparent in daylight because of all the attendant distractions? As he stared, the rise seemed more pronounced. Before the darkness could make it a mound, Proffit closed the curtains against it. The duvet soon covering him was another barrier.

He only drowsed. Where sleep should have taken him there was a shadowed floor; it swelled higher and higher, until it freed itself, and, like a black balloon, floated as free as the walls of his head would allow.

He got up and fetched his portable radio. He desperately wanted its sounds. Re-tuning right across the dial produced coughs and hisses like a premonition of nuclear fallout. He returned to bed.

Dread awoke him, taunted that sleep had been his and was no more. He reached for his alarm clock, squinting to make out the hands. The quality of the light suggested a much earlier hour. But in the dim living room the mantle-piece clock confirmed eight-twenty in the morning. Still no power, so no television, no tea, no toast. He tried the radio but soon switched off the sequence of cracked syllables that were like the calls thrown to the clouds and beyond the other night. The fact that Proffit was experiencing part of a wider privation was of little comfort. Was the Railway Hotel affected? If Humphries had been true to his word, he must be finding Harrowby a poor substitute for the sunny south.

With no allowances for the early hour, the city's repertoire of turmoil was already establishing itself. Esther might retract her complacent words about cities should he be crass enough to remind her of them. He'd drop in; their amicable estrangement was an example to the rest of the city. Besides, wasn't mutual support between friends, ex-lovers, neighbours, desirable, if not essential in these times? Unless the opposite state of affairs was endemic. There was little contact, let alone neighbourliness, between Proffit and his fellow residents. In the passage outside his flat the three other doors might have opened into closets, such was the silence.

Furtive as a spy, Proffit left the building. A harsh chemical in the air hit the back of his nose, and at least had the virtue of waking him fully. Passing cars assisted, blasting their horns at him for no obvious reason. Other cars' wheel-less state left them part-immersed in broken tarmac. On an otherwise dead van a windscreen wiper wagged *No*.

The canal was a ribbon of black gloss paint. On its rubble beach a dummy, or body, lounged. Two crows flop-fluttered together, hopelessly entangled. Rats scampered, busy as clerks preparing for an inspection.

The door of number seven Canal Terrace opened to the limit of the chain. A terrible falling off if this was Esther's new paramour. A sign of the times that such a vested hulk should cower behind a door. Murky the hallway; an odour of over-used cooking oil. A television whisper-hissed.

"Hello – it's Trevor. Esther's 'ex'."

Glimpsing an arm in a sling, a drooping gut, Proffit was appalled. "'Stheroo?'"

Alternatives; Esther and this one, a couple; Esther in the back tied to a chair, the attentions of the vested-one temporarily interrupted; Esther living elsewhere, having moved out at short notice without bothering to tell Proffit. He couldn't believe any of these possibilities. Esther was simply gone, profoundly so.

"'Ckoff," the man said. The door banged shut, lid tight. Proffit returned home.

As if taking advantage of his absence the house had succumbed to the madness. From the five top-floor windows, his included, gargantuan black ropes of smoke rose to flatten against the undersides of the clouds. A dry sob was painful in his throat. Packed into his few rooms was the only future he could envisage. Dentists and patients had vacated the surgery next door and grin-grimaced orange teeth at the show. The insurers had evacuated their building too, and looked hungry, though not, Proffit judged, for the business the fire might have represented. Fellow residents didn't acknowledge him: their fire-lit faces were aghast or elated as at a burning god. Proffit's eyes watered copiously. There was no going in, though he doubted anyone would have tried to stop him.

A rumble of collapsing floors. Perversely, considering the past twenty-four hours or so, no sirens. A suitable end, to walk in, cloth himself in flames, burn to nothing the burden of confusion and dread. But an end for a braver man, and maybe a less curious one. He'd see this through and begin again, as he had only months before. But his thoughts had no emotional impulse. He felt hollow – as eaten away as the inside as the house. But when the metallic sniggering began, anger moved into the void.

The smoke formed a low ceiling over the furnace. A round face, a grimed, grinning urchin's, poked through. There was no way of apprehending that fellow. The fun was his to be had.

Proffit had to tell someone, and only one would understand – Humphries, if he hadn't already vacated his room at the hotel. After Humphries, Proffit would renew contacts with friends and former colleagues. In lieu of the authorities mastering the situation, they'd discuss, exchange information. Abandonment of the city might be the sanest response to the challenges it presented. His own sanity might be questioned if he implicated an old globe in the chaos. No, he'd save talk of the globe for Humphries. The globe would confirm Proffit's identity, and then the expert could take possession of it. Damp and damaged it would be worth pennies – and then only in other cities, not Harrowby, that's if other cities weren't themselves being infected by this one.

Proffit felt the heat of tropical lands as he skirted the building. Amongst the crumbling walls at the back, lidless dustbins on their sides disgorged rubbish. Lids, ideal for shields, Proffit found himself thinking dispassionately.

He found the globe. It was a dead thing. With his fingers encased in the great north south rent, it was like a huge boxing glove.

The street was littered with the detritus of once tepid, routine-driven lives. Broken chairs, bottles, de-limbed dolls, half-consumed packages of fast food, were tokens of lives changed perhaps forever.

Water frothed from a burst water main and pooled in the road. A van passing at speed sprouted great white wings of water. One caught Proffit but he cared little at the drenching.

Viewing the smoking wreck of a car, Proffit wondered how much safer he'd be conveyed on four wheels.

Here was a car, a black one. It might be a cab. And couldn't anything be anything now in this city where the rulebook had been tossed aside? There seemed an intention in the air to return to first principles – or no principles.

The car/cab stopped at his raised hand. Proffit recognized the driver.

"By yourself this time?" the man said. "Should have charged extra for whatever was in that black bag." Wry words, but glaring eyes in the rear-view mirror. He may have been thinking of the omitted tip. Proffit was glad that in the general gloom the cabby hadn't noticed the misshapen globe.

"Railway Hotel," Proffit instructed. " 'Please' " was a nicety, a sign of weakness, he wouldn't display.

A swerving, halting progress along many diversions. Gaps in railings seemed emblematic of iron bars and spears in use elsewhere. A cast-off manhole cover suggested misrule spread to the underside of the city. Birds flew haphazardly, as if the clouds were an unprecedented environment to fly in. Something larger passed over the cab with more purpose. Proffit shrank in his seat as if the metal roof were insufficient protection from the grating giggler. The thing alighted on a skeletal tree to which it, or someone, assigned a bright blazing foliage, an instant before the thing flew off again.

The clamour of approaching sirens shook Proffit to his bones. The muttering driver edged the cab grudgingly left, and two battered ambulances overtook, neck-and-neck, as likely to create emergencies as attend any. People ran in every direction, faces fearful or crazily happy. The red rose emblem on the face of City Hall was being painted black by a man on a rickety platform; he needn't have bothered, as the darkening atmosphere beneath the smoke-fouled clouds was painting quicker.

On the seat next to Proffit the globe felt like a heft of dead flesh. They passed the university hospital. Horseplay on the top floor. The cabby laughed, hands batting the steering wheel. "*Bloody students!*" he shouted over his shoulder. Proffit supposed the white-coated, jeering figure might be one, and he was bloody indeed. So was his colleague. Each held an ankle of a dangling, squirming third. Below, laughing ambulance men tautened a blanket between them and manoeuvred it drunkenly. Proffit turned from the plummeting scream.

A pitched battle on the silvery swirl of lines feeding the railway station. A shape swept overhead; its stubby wings looked barely adequate for the job of keeping aloft the bundle of limbs. Ahead was the Railway Hotel.

The cab braked hard to a rocking sudden standstill. Proffit got out and went around to the driver's door. The driver viewed Proffit's handful of change with contempt, then relented as Proffit thought he might. "Go on then – though I'm thinking money's heading to be a game like everything else."

The façade of the hotel was as lightless as a cliff. The canopy before the entrance hung in rags. Backing away, a cat spat at Proffit.

From a high window opposite the hotel, a child chuckled hoarsely. Proffit's shoes ground glass on the steps rising up to the foyer.

The entrance hall was deserted. Slashed sofas grinned foam. Clothes were frozen in mid-clamber from an abandoned suitcase. There was an opened-out road map with an alternative network of bloodstains. Proffit went to the reception desk and leafed through the visitors' book. The large windows, most divested of their glass, let in sounds of a tumult that appeared to have passed through here – and, Proffit feared, might yet return. The light was gilded with an unnatural sunset.

Here was H. HUMPHRIES, neatly written amongst the previous two days' arrivals.

With each step, the soles of Proffit's shoes peeled away audibly from the sticky carpet. Alcohol fumes sweetened his way past the black mouths of the lifts to a grand switchback stairway.

An anticipatory apprehension invigorated him as he climbed the stairs. Would Humphries be here, and if he were, what could Proffit say when the city was speaking so madly for itself? The globe was an irrelevance. I'm leaving the city, he'd said to Esther, floating an idea he'd not seriously intended to act upon. He felt differently now. From a rural retreat he could have watched the city, or cities, totter in TV news items, and ended the conflict with the OFF on his remote control. But the more he thought of it, the more fantastical seemed any place of repose and peace.

He began to hope Humphries might provide a more balanced perspective. Here was the fourth floor. Past a right-angle another long corridor. All doors were open onto wrecked rooms. How was that avuncular persona, from another world, dealing with this one?

Well enough, Proffit had to concede. Ahead a voice, a plummy, equal-to-anything, voice. Open your eyes Humphries. Proffit ran. It sounded like Humphries was alone and talking into a telephone.

Room 408 coming up. Proffit swung around the door, "Here's the damned . . ."

No lights were on but he could see adequately. It was a large room with two tall windows; one had a single mountain peak of glass. Outside a flash underlit the clouds; a moment later a dull explosion.

No sign of Humphries, though he sounded only a yard or so away.

And he was, in a sense. Profit dropped the globe.

There was a dressing table with a three-leafed mirror. Someone had pulled it away from the wall. In the large central glass Humphries stood bathed in a sunny afternoon. The white hair was a radiant oval frame, from high forehead to chin. No wonder Humphries didn't have a care in the world, for he wasn't exactly in this one. Proffit's hands clasped his mouth; it felt real enough to confirm the reality of everything else. Light spilled from the mirror to the plush patterned carpet; Proffit went to stand in it and face the mirror.

"Course," Humphries was saying into his mobile phone, "I was sceptical from the beginning. And right to be as it turned out. But I had high hopes with this one, this being Lostock's home patch. What . . . ? No I shouldn't think he'll contact me again. Cold feet I expect . . . Oh, maybe some shoddy imitation based on a bit of research – if he'd taken the trouble to make one at all – which I doubt, and which in any case wouldn't have hoodwinked Yours truly . . ."

The person on the other end of the line said something that made Humphries chuckle. The chuckle escalated. Humphries shook as if his torso might lift off from his legs.

Proffit's face contorted. If Humphries had been a bodily presence Proffit would have relished smashing him, pulverizing him – just one more act of violence in a city saturated with it. But all he could do was lift the dressing table chair and swing it with all the force in him, straight into the mirror.

The rain of glass took the day-lit room with it, took away the cruel illusion of a better world elsewhere from which he'd been insidiously sidelined. There had been no bifurcation. There was this city, and no other. Until the authorities took control, individuals like him would have to take matters into their own hands.

The things he could see dipping their curly mops out through the undersides of the clouds could be shot at and brought down. Had nobody thought of that? A savage, incoherent shouting, down in the street. A woman screamed laughter, or for mercy. A flurry of leaderless furious voices grew, then faded.

Proffit didn't doubt he'd find someone who'd know where to obtain a gun. With a sense of purpose burgeoning inside him he left the room.

Along the corridor, down the stairs. He didn't hesitate in the foyer but headed straight through. Determined to engage with it, and not seek the reassurance of its boundary, Proffit went out into the city.

CAITLÍN R. KIERNAN

The Ape's Wife

CAITLÍN R. KIERNAN'S SHORT FICTION has been collected in *Tales of Pain and Wonder*, *From Weird and Distant Shores*, *Wrong Things* (with Poppy Z. Brite), *To Charles Fort, with Love* and *Alabaster*. Her first collection of science fiction stories, *A is for Alien*, is forthcoming from Subterranean Press.

She has also published two collections of "weird erotica", *Frog Toes and Tentacles* and *Tales from the Woeful Platypus*, and her novels include *Silk*, *Threshold*, *Low Red Moon*, *Murder of Angels* and *Daughter of Hounds*.

As Kiernan explains: "Despite the fact that I tend to write open-ended stories that shy away from resolution, that revel in the inexplicable, I often find myself coming to the end of someone else's story, desperately wanting to know "what happens next" and simply wish the story to continue, to see the consequences of the events already set forth by the author.

"Two or three times, this has led me to write my own continuations of stories. I did it first with *Dracula*, when I wrote 'Emptiness Spoke Eloquent', and I've recently written a piece entitled 'Pickman's Other Model', which does the same sort of thing with Lovecraft.

"I'm a great of admirer of *King Kong*, both the 1933 version and Peter Jackson's remake, but, in both instances, I could not help but fixate on what Ann Darrow's life would have been like after what we're shown in the film. Though, in the case of 'The Ape's Wife', I'm also indulging in a bit of alternate reality, positing a rather different outcome to *King Kong* itself.

"Writing the story became a sort of dream-quest for me, tumbling through all the many 'unrealized realities' that might have followed from Ann's time on the island."

NEITHER YET AWAKE nor quite asleep, she pauses in her dreaming to listen to the distant sounds of the jungle approaching twilight. They are each balanced now between one world and another – she between sleep and waking, and the jungle between day and night. In the dream, she is once again the woman she was before she came to the island, the starving woman on that *other* island, that faraway island that was not warm and green but had come to seem to her always cold and grey, stinking of dirty snow and the exhaust of automobiles and buses. She stands outside a lunchroom on Mulberry Street, her empty belly rumbling as she watches other people eat. The evening begins to fill up with the raucous screams of nocturnal birds and flying reptiles and a gentle tropical wind rustling through the leaves of banana and banyan trees, through cycads and ferns grown as tall or taller than the brick and steel and concrete canyon that surrounds her.

She leans forward, and her breath fogs the lunchroom's plate-glass window, but none of those faces turns to stare back at her. They are all too occupied with their meals, these swells with their forks and knives and china platters buried under mounds of scrambled eggs or roast beef on toast or mashed potatoes and gravy. They raise china cups of hot black coffee to their lips and pretend she isn't there. This winter night is too filled with starving, tattered women on the bum. There is not time to notice them all, so better to notice none of them, better not to allow the sight of real hunger to spoil your appetite. A little farther down the street there is a Greek who sells apples and oranges and pears from a little sidewalk stand, and she wonders how long before he catches her stealing, him or someone else. She has never been a particularly lucky girl.

Somewhere close by, a parrot shrieks and another parrot answers it, and finally she turns away from the people and the tiled walls of the lunch room and opens her eyes; the Manhattan street vanishes in a slushy, disorienting flurry and takes the cold with it. She is still hungry, but for a while she is content to lie in her carefully woven nest of rattan, bamboo, and ebony branches, blinking away the last shreds of sleep and gazing deeply into the rising mists and gathering dusk. She has made her home high atop a weathered promontory, this charcoal peak of lava rock and tephra a vestige of the island's fiery origins. It is for this summit's unusual shape – not so unlike a human skull – that white men named the place. And it is here that she last saw the giant ape, before it left her to pursue the moving-picture man and Captain Englehorn, the first mate and the rest of the crew of the *Venture*, left her alone to get itself killed and hauled away in the rusty hold of that evil-smelling ship.

At least, that is one version of the story she tells herself to explain why the beast never returned for her. It may not be the truth. Perhaps the ape died somewhere in the swampy jungle spread out below the mountain, somewhere along the meandering river leading down to the sea. She has learned that there is no end of ways to die on the island, and that nothing alive is so fierce or so cunning as to be entirely immune to those countless perils. The ape's hide was riddled with bullets, and it might simply have succumbed to its wounds and bled to death. Time and again, she has imagined this, the gorilla only halfway back to the wall but growing suddenly too weak to continue the chase, and perhaps it stopped, surrendering to pain and exhaustion, and sat down in a glade somewhere below the cliffs, resting against the bole of an enormous tree. Maybe it sat there, peering through a break in the fog and the forest canopy, gazing forlornly back up at the skull-shaped mountain. It would have been a terrible, lonely death, but not so terrible an end as the beast might have met had it managed to gain the ancient gates and the sandy peninsula beyond.

She has, on occasion, imagined another outcome, one in which the enraged god-thing overtook the men from the steamer, either in the jungle or somewhere out beyond the wall, in the village or on the beachhead. And though the ape was killed by their gunshots and gas bombs (for surely he would have returned, otherwise), first they died screaming, every last mother's son of them. She has taken some grim satisfaction in this fantasy, on days when she has had need of grim satisfaction. But she knows it isn't true, if only because she watched with her own eyes the *Venture* sailing away from the place where it had anchored out past the reefs and the deadly island, the smoke from its single stack drawing an ashen smudge across the blue morning sky. They escaped, at least enough of them to pilot the ship, and left her for dead or good as dead.

She stretches and sits up in her nest, watching the sun as it sinks slowly into the shimmering, flat monotony of the Indian Ocean, the dying day setting the western horizon on fire. She stands, and the red-orange light paints her naked skin the colour of clay. Her stomach growls again, and she thinks of her small hoard of fruit and nuts, dried fish and a couple of turtle eggs she found the day before, all wrapped up safe in banana leaves and hidden in amongst the stones and brambles. Here, she need only fear nightmares of hunger and never hunger itself. There is the faint, rotten smell of sulphur emanating from the cavern that forms the skull's left eye socket, the mountain's malodorous breath wafting up from bubbling hot springs deep within the grotto. She has long since grown accustomed to the stench and has found that the treacherous maze of bubbling lakes and mud helps to protect her from many of the island's predators. For this reason, more than any other, more even than the sentimentality that she no longer denies, she chose these steep volcanic cliffs for her eyrie.

Stepping from her bed, the stones warm against the toughened soles of her feet, she remembers a bit of melody, a ghostly snatch of lyrics that has followed her up from the dream of the city and the woman she will never be again. She closes her eyes, shutting out the jungle noises for just a moment, and listens to the faint crackle of a half-forgotten radio broadcast.

> *Once I built a tower up to the sun,*
> *Brick and rivet and lime.*
> *Once I built a tower,*
> *Now it's done.*
> *Brother, can you spare a dime?*

And when she opens her eyes again, the sun is almost gone, just a blazing sliver remaining now above the sea. She sighs and reminds herself that there is no percentage in recalling the clutter and racket of that lost world. Not now. Not here. Night is coming, sweeping in fast and mean on leathery pterodactyl wings and the wings of flying foxes and the wings of *ur*-birds, and like so many of the island's inhabitants, she puts all else from her mind and rises to meet it. The island has made of her a night thing, has stripped her of old diurnal ways. Better to sleep through the stifling equatorial days than to lie awake through the equally stifling nights; better the company of the sun for her uneasy dreams than the moon's cool, seductive glow and her terror of what might be watching from the cover of darkness.

When she has eaten, she sits awhile near the cliff's edge, contemplating what month this might be, what month in which year. It is a futile pastime, but mostly a harmless one. At first, she scratched marks on stone to keep track of the passing time, but after only a few hundred marks she forgot one day, and then another, and when she finally remembered, she found she was uncertain how many days had come and gone during her forgetfulness. It was then she came to understand the futility of counting days in this place – indeed, the futility of the very concept of time. She has thought often that the island must be time's primordial orphan, a castaway, not unlike herself, stranded in some nether or lower region, this sweltering antediluvian limbo where there is only the rising and setting of the sun, the phases of the moon, the long rainy season which is hardly less hot or less brutal than the longer dry. Maybe the men who built the wall long ago were a race of sorcerers, and in their arrogance they committed a grave transgression against time, some unspeakable contravention of the sanctity of months and hours. And so Chronos cast this place back down into the gulf of Chaos, and now it is damned to exist forever apart from the tick-tock, calendar-page blessings of Aeon.

Yes, she still recalls a few hazy scraps of Greek mythology, and Roman, too, this farmer's only daughter who always got good marks and waited until school was done before leaving the cornfields of Indiana to go east to seek her fortune in New York and New Jersey. All her girlhood dreams of the stage, the silver screen and her name on theatre marquees, but by the time she reached Fort Lee, most of the studios were relocating west to California, following the promise of a more hospitable, more profitable climate. Black Tuesday had left its stain upon the country, and she never found more than extra work at the few remaining studios, happy just to play anonymous faces in crowd scenes and the like, and finally she could not even find that. Finally, she was fit only for the squalor of bread lines and mission soup kitchens and flop houses, until the night she met a man who promised to make her a star; who, chasing dreams of his own, dragged her halfway round the world and then abandoned her here in this serpent-haunted and time-forsaken wilderness. The irony is not lost on her. Seeking fame and adoration, she has found, instead, what might well be the ultimate obscurity.

Below her, some creature suddenly cries out in pain from the forest tangle clinging to the slopes of the mountain, and she watches, squinting into the darkness. She's well aware that hers are only one of a hundred or a thousand pairs of eyes that have stopped to see, to try and catch a glimpse of whatever bloody panoply is being played out among the vines and undergrowth, and that this is only one of the innumerable slaughters to come before sunrise. Something screams and so all eyes turn to see, for every thing that creeps or crawls, flits or slithers upon the island will fall prey, one day or another. And she is no exception.

One day, perhaps, the island itself will fall, not so unlike the dissatisfied angels in Milton or in Blake.

Ann Darrow opens her eyes, having nodded off again, and she is once more only a civilized woman not yet grown old, but no longer young. One who has been taken away from the world and touched, then returned and set adrift in the sooty gulches and avenues and asphalt ravines of this modern, electric city. But that was such a long time ago, before the war that proved the Great War was not so very great after all, that it was not the war to end all wars. Japan has been burned with the fire of two tiny manufactured suns and Europe lies in ruins, and already the fighting has begun again and young men are dying in Korea. History is a steamroller. History is a litany of war.

She sits alone in the Natural History Museum off Central Park, a bench all to herself in the alcove where the giant ape's broken skeleton was mounted for public exhibition after the creature tumbled from the top of the Empire State, plummeting more than 1,200 feet to the frozen streets below. There is an informative placard (white letters on black) declaring it *BRONTOPITHECUS SINGU-LARIS* OSBORN (1933), ONLY KNOWN SPECIMEN, NOW BELIEVED EXTINCT. *So there*, she thinks. Denham and his men dragged it from the not-quite-impenetrable sanctuary of its jungle and hauled it back to Broadway; they chained it and murdered it and, in that final act of desecration, they *named* it. The enigma was dissected and quantified, given its rightful place in the grand analytic scheme, in the Latinized order of things, and that's one less blank spot to cause the mapmakers and zoologists to scratch their heads. Now, Carl Denham's monster is no threat at all, only another harmless, impressive heap of bones shellacked and wired together in this stately, static mausoleum. And hardly anyone remembers or comes to look upon these bleached remains. The world is a steamroller. The Eighth Wonder of the World was old news twenty years ago, and now it is only a chapter in some dusty textbook devoted to anthropological curiosities.

He was the king and the god of the world he knew, but now he comes to civilization, merely a captive, a show to gratify your curiosity. Curiosity killed the cat, and it slew the ape, as well, and that December night hundreds died for the price of a theatre ticket, the fatal price of *their* curiosity and Carl Denham's hubris. By dawn, the passion play was done, and the king and god of Skull Island lay crucified by bi-planes, by the pilots and trigger-happy Navy men borne aloft in Curtis Helldivers armed with .50 calibre machine guns. A tiered Golgotha skyscraper, 102 stories of steel and glass and concrete, a dizzying Art-Deco Calvary, and no resurrection save what the museum's anatomists and taxidermists might in time effect.

Ann Darrow closes her eyes, because she can only ever bear to look at the bones for just so long and no longer. Henry Fairfield Osborn, the museum's former president, had wanted to name it after *her*, in her honour – *Brontopithecus darrowii*, "Darrow's thunder ape" – but she'd threatened a lawsuit against him *and* his museum *and* the scientific journal publishing his paper, and so he'd christened the species *singularis*, instead. She played her Judas role, delivering the jungle god to Manhattan's Roman holiday, and wasn't that enough? Must she also have her name forever nailed up there with the poor beast's corpse? Maybe she deserved as much or far worse, but Osborn's "honour" was poetic justice she managed to evade.

There are voices now, a mother and her little girl, so Ann knows that she's no longer alone in the alcove. She keeps her eyes tightly shut, wishing she could shut her ears as well and not hear the things that are being said.

"Why did they kill him?" asks the little girl.

"It was a very dangerous animal," her mother replies sensibly. "It got loose and hurt people. I was just a child then, about your age."

"They could have put it in a zoo," the girl protests. "They didn't have to kill it."

"I don't think a zoo would ever have been safe. It broke free and hurt a lot of innocent people."

"But there aren't any more like it."

"There are still plenty of gorillas in Africa," the mother replies.

"Not that big," says the little girl. "Not as big as an elephant."

"No," the mother agrees. "Not as big as an elephant. But then we hardly need gorillas as big as elephants, now do we?"

Ann clenches her jaws, grinding her teeth together, biting her tongue (so to speak) and gripping the edge of the bench with nails chewed down to the quicks.

They'll leave soon, she reminds herself. *They always do, get bored and move along after only a minute or so. It won't be much longer.*

"What does *that* part say?" the child asks eagerly, so her mother reads to her from the text printed on the placard.

"Well, it says, 'Kong was not a true gorilla, but a close cousin, and belongs in the Superfamily Hominoidea with gorillas, chimpanzees, orang-utans, gibbons, and human beings. His exceptional size might have evolved in response to his island isolation.'"

"What's a *super* family?"

"I don't really know, dear."

"What's a gibbon?"

"I think it's a sort of monkey."

"But we don't believe in evolution, do we?"

"No, we don't."

"So God made Kong, just like he made us?"

"Yes, honey. God made Kong."

And then there's a pause, and Ann holds her breath, wishing she were still dozing, still lost in her terrible dreams, because this waking world is so much more terrible.

"I want to see the *Tyrannosaurus* again," says the little girl, "and the *Triceratops*, too." Her mother says okay, there's just enough time to see the dinosaurs again before we have to meet your Daddy, and Ann sits still and listens to their footsteps on the polished marble floor, growing fainter and fainter until silence has at last been restored to the alcove. But now the sterile, drab museum smells are gone, supplanted by the various rank odours of the apartment Jack rented for the both of them before he shipped out on a merchant steamer, the *Polyphemus*, bound for the Azores and then Lisbon and the Mediterranean. He never made it much farther than São Miguel, because the steamer was torpedoed by a Nazi U-boat and went down with all hands onboard. Ann opens her eyes, and the strange dream of the museum and the ape's skeleton has already begun to fade. It isn't morning yet, and the lamp beside the bed washes the tiny room with yellow-white light that makes her eyes ache.

She sits up, pushing the sheets away, exposing the ratty grey mattress underneath. The bedclothes are damp with her sweat and with radiator steam, and she reaches for the half-empty gin bottle there beside the lamp. The booze used to keep the dreams at bay, but these last few months, since she got the telegram informing her that Jack Driscoll was drowned and given up for dead and she would never be seeing him again, the nightmares have seemed hardly the least bit intimidated by alcohol. She squints at the clock, way over on the chiffarobe, and sees that it's not yet even 4:00am. Still hours until sunrise, hours until the bitter comfort of winter sunlight through the bedroom curtains. She tips the bottle to her lips, and the liquor tastes like turpentine and regret and everything she's lost in the last three years. Better she would have never been anything more than a starving woman stealing apples and oranges to try to stay alive, better she would have never stepped foot on the *Venture*. Better she would have died in the green hell of that uncharted island. She can easily imagine a thousand ways it might have gone better, all grim but better than *this* drunken half-life. She does not torture herself with fairy-tale fantasies of happy endings that never were and never will be. There's enough pain in the world without that luxury.

She takes another swallow from the bottle, then reminds herself that it has to last until morning and sets it back down on the table.

But morning seems at least as far away as that night on the island, as far away as the carcass of the sailor she married. Often, she dreams of him, gnawed by the barbed teeth of deep-sea fish and mangled by shrapnel, burned alive and rotted beyond recognition, tangled in the wreckage and ropes and cables of a ship somewhere at the bottom of the Atlantic Ocean. He peers out at her with eyes that are no longer eyes at all, but only empty sockets where eels and spiny albino crabs nestle. She usually wakes screaming from those dreams, wakes to the asshole next door pounding on the wall with the heel of a shoe or just his bare fist and shouting how he's gonna call the cops if she can't keep it down. He has a job and has to sleep, and he can't have some goddamn rummy broad half the bay over or gone crazy with the DTs keeping him awake. The old Italian cunt who runs this dump, she says she's tired of hearing the complaints, and either the hollering stops or Ann will have to find another place to flop. She tries not to think about how she'll have to find another place soon, anyway. She had a little money stashed in the lining of her coat, from all the interviews she gave the papers and magazines and the newsreel people, but now it's almost gone. Soon, she'll be back out on the bum, sleeping in mission beds or worse places, whoring for the sauce and as few bites of food as she can possibly get by on. Another month, at most, and isn't that what they mean by coming full circle?

She lies down again, trying not to smell herself or the pillowcase or the sheets, thinking about bright July sun falling warm between green leaves. And soon, she drifts off once more, listening to the rumble of a garbage truck down on Canal Street, the rattle of its engine and the squeal of its breaks not so very different from the primeval grunts and cries that filled the torrid air of the ape's profane cathedral.

And perhaps now she is lying safe and drunk in a squalid Bowery tenement and only dreaming away the sorry dregs of her life, and it's not the freezing morning when Jack led her from the skyscraper's spire down to the bedlam of Fifth Avenue. Maybe these are nothing more than an alcoholic's fevered recollections, and she is not being bundled in wool blankets and shielded from reporters and photographers and the sight of the ape's shattered body.

"It's over," says Jack, and she wants to believe that's true, by all the saints in Heaven and all the sinners in Hell, wherever and whenever she is, she wants to believe that it is finally and irrevocably over. There is not one moment to be relived, not ever again, because it has *ended*, and she is rescued, like Beauty somehow delivered from the clutching paws of the Beast. But there is so much commotion, the chatter of confused and frightened bystanders, the triumphant, confident cheers and shouting of soldiers and policemen, and she's begging Jack to get her out of it, away from it. It *must* be real, all of it, real and here and now, because she has never been so horribly cold in her dreams. She shivers and stares up at the narrow slice of sky visible between the buildings. The summit of that tallest of all tall towers is already washed with dawn, but down here on the street, it may as well still be midnight.

> *Life is just a bowl of cherries.*
> *Don't take it serious; it's too mysterious.*
> *At eight each morning I have got a date,*
> *To take my plunge 'round the Empire State.*
> *You'll admit it's not the berries,*
> *In a building that's so tall . . .*

"It's over," Jack assures her for the tenth or twentieth or fiftieth time. "They got him. The airplanes got him, Ann. He can't hurt you, not anymore."

And she's trying to remember through the clamour of voices and machines and the popping of flash bulbs – *Did he hurt me? Is that what happened?* – when the crowd divides like the holy winds of Jehovah parting the waters for Moses, and for the first time she can see what's left of the ape. And she screams, and they all *think* she's screaming in terror at the sight of a monster. They do not know the truth, and maybe she does not yet know herself and it will be weeks or months before she fully comprehends why she is standing there screaming and unable to look away from the impossible, immense mound of black fur and jutting white bone and the dark rivulets of blood leaking sluggishly from the dead and vanquished thing.

"Don't look at it," Jack says, and he covers her eyes with a callused palm. "It's nothing you need to see."

So she does *not* see, shutting her bright blue eyes and all the eyes of her soul, the eyes without and those other eyes within. Shutting *herself*, slamming closed doors and windows of perception, and how could she have known that she was locking in more than she was locking out. *Don't look at it*, he said, much too late, and these images are burned forever into her lidless, unsleeping mind's eye.

A sable hill from which red torrents flow.

Ann kneels in clay and mud the colour of a slaughterhouse floor, all the shades of shit and blood and gore, and dips her fingertips into the stream. She has performed this simple act of prostration times beyond counting, and it no longer holds for her any revulsion. She comes here from her nest high in the smouldering ruins of Manhattan and places her hand inside the wound, like St Thomas fondling the pierced side of Christ. She comes down to remember, because there is an unpardonable sin in forgetting such a forfeiture. In this deep canyon moulded not by geologic upheaval and erosion but by the tireless, automatic industry of man, she bows her head before the black hill. God sleeps there below the hill, and one day he will awaken from his slumber, for all those in the city are not faithless. Some still remember and follow the buckled blacktop paths, weaving their determined pilgrims' way along decaying thoroughfares and between twisted girders and the tumbledown heaps of burnt-out rubble. The city was cast down when God fell from his throne (or was pushed, as some have dared to whisper), and his fall broke apart the ribs of the world and sundered even the progression of one day unto the next so that time must now spill backwards to fill in the chasm. Ann leans forward, sinking her hand in up to the wrist, and the steaming crimson stream begins to clot and scab where it touches her skin.

Above her, the black hill seems to shudder, to shift almost imperceptibly in its sleep.

She has thought repeatedly of drowning herself in the stream, has wondered what it would be like to submerge in those veins and be carried along through silent veils of silt and ruby-tinted light. She might dissolve and be no more than another bit of flotsam, unburdened by bitter memory and self-knowledge and these rituals to keep a comatose god alive. She would open her mouth wide, and as the air rushed from her lungs and across her mouth, she would fill herself with His blood. She has even entertained the notion that such a sacrifice would be enough to wake the black sleeper, and as the waters that are not waters carried her away, the god beast might stir. As she melted, He would open His eyes and shake Himself free of the holdfasts of that tarmac and cement and sewer-pipe grave. It *could* be that simple. In her waking dreams, she has learned there is incalculable magic in sacrifice.

Ann withdraws her hand from the stream, and blood drips from her fingers, rejoining the whole as it flows away north and east towards the noxious lake that has formed where once lay the carefully landscaped and sculpted conceits of Mr Olmsted and Mr Vaux's Central Park. She will not wipe her hand clean as would some infidel, but rather permit the blood to dry to a claret crust upon her skin, for she has already committed blasphemy enough for three lifetimes. The shuddering black hill is still again, and a vinegar wind blows through the tall grass on either side of the stream.

And then Ann realizes that she's being watched from the gaping brick maw that was a jeweller's window long ago. The frame is still rimmed round about with jagged crystal teeth waiting to snap shut on unwary dreamers, waiting to shred and pierce, starved for diamonds and sapphires and emeralds, but more than ready to accept mere meat. In dusty shafts of sunlight, Ann can see the form of a young girl gazing out at her, her skin almost as dark as the seeping hill.

"What do you want?" Ann calls to her, and a moment or two later, the girl replies.

"You have become a goddess," she says, moving a little nearer the broken shop window so that Ann might have a better look at her. "But even a goddess cannot dream forever. I have come a long way and through many perils to speak with you, Golden Mother, and I did not expect to find you sleeping and hiding in the lies told by dreams."

"I'm not hiding," Ann replies very softly, so softly she thinks surely the girl will not have heard her.

"Forgive me, Golden Mother, but you are. You are seeking refuge in guilt that is not your guilt."

"I am not your mother," Ann tells her. "I have never been anyone's mother."

And then a branch whips around and catches her in the face, a leaf's razor edge to draw a nasty cut across her forehead. But the pain slices cleanly through exhaustion and shock and brings her suddenly back to herself, back to this night and this moment, their mad, headlong dash from the river to the gate. The Cyclopean wall rises up before them, towering above the treetops. There cannot now be more than a hundred yards remaining between them and the safety of the gate, but the ape is so very close behind. A fire-eyed demon who refuses to be so easily cheated of his prize by mere mortal men. The jungle cringes around them, flinching at the cacophony of Kong's approach, and even the air seems to draw back from that typhoon of muscle and fury, his angry roars and thunderous footfalls to divide all creation. Her right hand is gripped tightly in Jack's left, and he's all but dragging her forward. Ann can no longer feel her bare feet, which have been bruised and gouged and torn, and it is a miracle she can still run at all. Now she can make out the dim silhouettes of men standing atop the wall, men with guns and guttering torches, and, for a moment, she allows herself to hope.

"You are needed, Golden Mother," the girl says, and then she steps through the open mouth of the shop window. The blistering sun shimmers off her smooth, coffee-coloured skin. "You are needed

here and *now*," she says. "That night and every way that it might
have gone, but did not, are passed forever beyond even your reach."

"You don't *see* what I can see," Ann tells the girl, hearing the
desperation and resentment in her own voice.

And what she sees is the aboriginal wall and that last line of
banyan figs and tree ferns. What she sees is the open gate and the way
out of this nightmare, the road home.

"Only dreams," the girl says, not unkindly, and she takes a step
nearer the red stream. "Only the phantoms of things that have never
happened and never will."

"No," says Ann, and she shakes her head. "We *made* it to the gate.
Jack and I both, together. We ran and we ran and we ran, and the ape
was right there on top of us all the way, so close that I could smell his
breath. But we didn't look back, not even once. We *ran*, and, in the
end, we made it to the gate."

"No, Golden Mother. It did not happen that way."

One of the sailors on the wall is shouting a warning now, and at
first, Ann believes it's only because he can see Kong behind them. But
then something huge and long-bodied lunges from the underbrush at
the clearing's edge, all scales and knobby scutes, scrabbling talons
and the blue-green iridescent flash of eyes fashioned for night
hunting. The high, sharp quills sprouting from the creature's backbone clatter one against the other like bony castanets, and it snatches
Jack Driscoll in its saurian jaws and drags him screaming into the
reedy shadows. On the wall, someone shouts, and she hears the
staccato report of rifle fire.

The brown girl stands on the far side of the stream flowing along
Fifth Avenue, the tall grass murmuring about her knees. "You have
become lost in All-at-Once time, and you must find your way back
from the Everywhen. I can help."

"I do not *need* your help," Ann snarls. "You keep away from me,
you filthy goddamn heathen."

Beneath the vast, star-specked Indonesian sky, Ann Darrow stands
alone. Jack is gone, taken by some unnameable abomination, and in
another second the ape will be upon her. This is when she realizes
that she's bleeding, a dark bloom unfolding from her right breast,
staining the gossamer rags that are all that remain of her dress and
underclothes. She doesn't yet feel the sting of the bullet, a single shot
gone wild, intended for Jack's attacker, but finding her, instead. *I do
not blame you*, she thinks, slowly collapsing, going down onto her
knees in the thick carpet of moss and ferns. *It was an accident, and I
do not blame anyone . . .*

"That is a lie," the girl says from the other side of the red stream. "You do blame them, Golden Mother, and you blame yourself, most of all."

Ann stares up at the dilapidated skyline of a city as lost in time as she, and the vault of Heaven turns above them like a dime-store kaleidoscope.

Once I built a railroad, I made it run, made it race against time. Once I built a railroad; now it's done. Brother, can you spare a dime? Once I built a tower, up to the sun, brick, and rivet, and lime; Once I built a tower, now it's done. Brother, can you spare a dime?

"When does this end?" she asks, asking the girl or herself or no one at all. "*Where* does it end?"

"Take my hand," the girl replies and reaches out to Ann, a bridge spanning the rill and time and spanning all these endless possibilities. "Take my hand and come back over. Just step across and stand with me."

"No," Ann hears herself say, though it isn't at all what she *wanted* to say or what she *meant* to say. "No, I can't do that. I'm sorry."

And the air around her reeks of hay and sawdust, human filth and beer and cigarette smoke, and the sideshow barker is howling his line of ballyhoo to all the rubes who've paid their two-bits to get a seat under the tent. All the yokels and hayseeds who have come to point and whisper and laugh and gawk at the figure cowering inside the cage.

"Them bars there, they are solid carbon *steel*, mind you," the barker informs them. "Manufactured special for us by the same Pittsburgh firm that supplies prison bars to Alcatraz. Ain't nothing else known to man strong enough to contain her, and if not for those iron bars, well . . . rest assured, my good people, we have not in the least exaggerated the threat she poses to life and limb, in the absence of such precautions."

Inside the cage, Ann squats in a corner, staring out at all the faces staring in. Only she has not been Ann Darrow in years – just ask the barker or the garish canvas flaps rattling in the chilly breeze of an Indiana autumn evening. She is the Ape Woman of Sumatra, captured at great personal risk by intrepid explorers and hauled out into the incandescent light the twentieth century. She is naked, except for the moth-eaten scraps of buffalo and bear-pelts they have given her to wear. Every inch of exposed skin is smeared with dirt and offal and whatever other filth has accumulated in her cage since it was last mucked out. Her snarled and matted hair hangs in her face, and there's nothing the least bit human in the guttural serenade of growls and hoots and yaps that escapes her lips.

The barker slams his walking cane against the iron bars, and she throws her head back and howls. A woman in the front row faints and has to be carried outside.

"She was the queen and the goddess of the strange world she knew," bellows the barker, "but now she comes to civilization, merely a captive, a show to gratify your curiosity. Learned men at colleges – forsaking the words of the Good Book – proclaim that we are *all* descended from monkeys. And, I'll tell you, seeing *this* wretched bitch, I am *almost* tempted to believe them, and also to suspect that in dark and far-flung corners of the globe there exist to this day beings still more simian than human, lower even than your ordinary niggers, hottentots, negritos, and lowly African pygmies."

Ann Darrow stands on the muddy bank of the red stream, and the girl from the ruined and vine-draped jewellery shop holds out her hand, the brown-skinned girl who has somehow found her way into the most secret, tortured recesses of Ann's consciousness.

"The world is still here," the girl says, "only waiting for you to return."

"I have heard another tale of her origin," the barker confides. "But I must *warn* you, it is not fit for the faint of heart or the ears of decent Christian women."

There is a long pause, while two or three of the women rise from their folding chairs and hurriedly leave the tent. The barker tugs at his pink suspenders and grins an enormous, satisfied grin, then glances into the cage.

"As I was saying," he continues, "there is *another* story. The Chinaman who sold me this pitiful oddity of human *de*-evolution said that its mother was born of French aristocracy, the lone survivor of a calamitous shipwreck, cast ashore on black volcanic sands. There, in the hideous misery and perdition of that Sumatran wilderness, the poor woman was *defiled* by some lustful species of jungle imp, though whether it were chimp or baboon I cannot say."

There is a collective gasp from the men and women inside the tent, and the barker rattles the bars again, eliciting another irate howl from its occupant.

"And here before you is the foul *spawn* of that unnatural union of anthropoid and womankind. The aged Mandarin confided to me that the mother expired shortly after giving birth, God rest her immortal soul. Her death was a mercy, I should think, as she would have lived always in shame and horror at having borne into the world this shameful, misbegotten progeny."

"Take my hand," the girl says, reaching into the cage. "You do not have to stay here. Take my hand, Golden Mother, and I will help you find the path."

There below the hairy black tumulus, the great slumbering titan belching forth the headwaters of all the earth's rivers, Ann Darrow takes a single hesitant step into the red stream. *This is the most perilous part of the journey,* she thinks, reaching to accept the girl's outstretched hand. *It wants me, this torrent, and if I am not careful, it will pull me down and drown me for my trespasses.*

"It's only a little ways more," the girl tells her and smiles. "Just step across to me."

The barker raps his silver-handled walking cane sharply against the bars of the cage, so that Ann remembers where she is and when, and doing so, forgets herself again. For the benefit of all those licentious, ogling eyes, all those slack jaws that have paid precious quarters to be shocked and titillated, she bites the head off a live hen, and when she has eaten her fill of the bird, she spreads her thighs and masturbates for the delight of her audience with filthy, bloodstained fingers.

Elsewhen, she takes another step towards the girl, and the softly gurgling stream wraps itself greedily about her calves. Her feet sink deeply into the slimy bottom, and the sinuous, clammy bodies of conger eels and salamanders wriggle between her ankles and twine themselves about her legs. She cannot reach the girl, and the opposite bank may as well be a thousand miles away.

In a smoke-filled screening room, Ann Darrow sits beside Carl Denham while the footage he shot on the island almost a year ago flickers across the screen at twenty-four frames per second. They are not alone, the room half-filled with low-level studio men from RKO and Paramount and Universal and a couple of would-be financiers lured here by the Hollywood rumour mill. Ann watches the images revealed in grainy shades of grey, in overexposed whites and under-exposed smudges of black.

"What exactly are we supposed to be looking at?" someone asks impatiently.

"We shot this stuff from the top of the wall, once Englehorn's men had managed to frighten away all the goddamn tar babies. Just wait. It's coming."

"Denham, we've already been sitting here half-an-hour. This shit's pretty underwhelming, you ask me. You're better off sticking to the safari pictures."

"It's *coming*," Denham insists and chomps anxiously at the stem of his pipe.

And Ann knows he's right, that it's coming, because this is not the first time she's seen the footage. Up there on the screen, the eye of the camera looks out over the jungle canopy, and it always reminds her of Gustave Doré's visions of Eden from her mother's copy of *Paradise Lost*, or the illustrations of lush Pre-Adamite landscapes from a geology book she once perused in the New York Public Library.

"Honestly, Mr Denham," the man from RKO sighs. "I've got a meeting in twenty minutes—"

"*There*," Denham says, pointing at the screen. "There it is. Right fucking *there*. Do you see it?"

And the studio men and the would-be financiers fall silent as the beast's head and shoulders emerge from the tangle of vines and orchid-encrusted branches and wide palm fronds. It stops and turns its mammoth head towards the camera, glaring hatefully up at the wall and directly into the smoke-filled room, across a million years and 9,000 miles. There is a dreadful, unexpected intelligence in those dark eyes as the creature tries to comprehend the purpose of the weird, pale men and their hand-crank contraption perched there on the wall above it. Its lips fold back, baring gigantic canines, eyeteeth longer than a grown man's hand, and there is a low, rumbling sound, then a screeching sort of yell, before the thing the natives called *Kong* turns and vanishes back into the forest.

"Great god," the Universal man whispers.

"Yes gentlemen," says Denham, sounding very pleased with himself and no longer the least bit anxious, certain that he has them all right where he wants them. "That's just *exactly* what those tar babies think. They worship it and offer up human sacrifices. Why, they wanted Ann here. Offered us six of their women so she could become the *bride* of Kong. And *there's* our story, gentlemen."

"Great god," the Universal man says again, louder than before.

"But an expedition like this costs money," Denham tells them, getting down to brass tacks as the reel ends and the lights come up. "I mean to make a picture the whole damn *world's* gonna pay to see, and I can't do that without committed backers."

"Excuse me," Ann says, rising from her seat, feeling sick and dizzy and wanting to be away from these men and all their talk of money and spectacle, wanting to drive the sight of the ape from her mind, once and for all.

"I'm fine, really," she tells them. "I just need some fresh air."

On the far side of the stream, the brown-skinned girl urges her forward, no more than twenty feet left to go and she'll have reached the other side. "You're waking up," the girl says. "You're almost there. Give me your hand."

I'm only going over Jordan
I'm only going over home . . .

And the moments flash and glimmer as the dream breaks apart around her, and the barker rattles the iron bars of a stinking cage, and her empty stomach rumbles as she watches men and women bending over their plates in a lunchroom, and she sits on a bench in an alcove on the third floor of the American Museum of Natural History. Crossing the red stream, Ann Darrow haemorrhages time, all these seconds and hours and days vomited forth like a bellyful of tainted meals. She shuts her eyes and takes another step, sinking even deeper in the mud, the blood risen now as high as her waist. Here is the morning they brought her down from the Empire State Building, and the morning she wakes in her nest on Skull Mountain, and the night she watched Jack Driscoll devoured well within sight of the archaic gates. Here's the Bowery tenement, and here the screening room, and here a fallen Manhattan, crumbling and lost in the storm-tossed gulf of aeons, set adrift no differently than she has set herself adrift. Every moment all at once, each as real as every other, and never mind the contradictions, each damned and equally inevitable, all following from a stolen apple and the man who paid the Greek a dollar to look the other way.

The world is a steamroller.

Once I built a railroad; now it's done.

She stands alone in the seaward lee of the great wall and knows that its gates have been forever shut against her and all the daughters of men yet to come. This hallowed, living wall of human bone and sinew erected to protect what scrap of Paradise lies inside, not the dissolute, iniquitous world of men sprawling beyond its borders. Winged cherubim stand guard on either side, and in their leonine forepaws they grasp flaming swords forged in unknown furnaces before the coming of the World, fiery brands that reach all the way to the sky and about which spin the hearts of newborn hurricanes. The molten eyes of the Cherubim watch her every move, and their indifferent minds know her every secret thought, these dispassionate servants of the vengeful god of her father and her mother. Neither tears nor all her words will ever wring mercy from these sentinels, for they know precisely what she is, and they know her crimes.

> *I am she who cries out,*
> *and I am cast forth upon the face of the earth.*

The starving, ragged woman who stole an apple. Starving in body and in mind, starving in spirit if so base a thing as she can be said to possess a soul. Starving, and ragged in all ways.

> *I am the members of my mother.*
> *I am the barren one*
> *and many are her sons.*
> *I am she whose wedding is great,*
> *and I have not taken a husband.*

And as is the way of all exiles, she cannot kill hope that her exile will one day end. Even the withering gaze of the cherubim cannot kill that hope, and so hope is the cruellest reward.

> *Brother, can you spare a dime?*

"Take my hand," the girl says, and Ann Darrow feels herself grown weightless and buoyed from that foul brook, hauled free of the morass of her own nightmares and regret onto a clean shore of verdant mosses and zoysiagrass, bamboo and reeds, and the girl leans down and kisses her gently on the forehead. The girl smells like sweat and nutmeg and the pungent yellow pigment dabbed across her cheeks.

"You have come *home* to us, Golden Mother," she says, and there are tears in her eyes.

"You don't see," Ann whispers, the words slipping out across her tongue and teeth and lips like her own ghost's death rattle. If the jungle air were not so still and heavy, not so turgid with the smells of living and dying, decay and birth and conception, she's sure it would lift her as easily as it might a stray feather and carry her away. She lies very still, her head cradled in the girl's lap, and the stream flowing past them is only water and the random detritus of any forest stream.

"The world blinds those who cannot close their eyes," the girl tells her. "You were not always a god and have come here from some outer world, so it may be you were never taught how to travel that path and not become lost in All-at-Once time."

Ann Darrow digs her fingers into the soft, damp earth, driving them into the loam of the jungle floor, holding on and still expecting *this* scene to shift, to unfurl, to send her tumbling pell-mell and head-over-heels into some other *now*, some other *where*.

And sometime later, when she's strong enough to stand again, and the sickening, vertigo sensation of fluidity has at last begun to fade, the girl helps Ann to her feet, and together they follow the narrow dirt trail leading back up this long ravine to the temple. Like Ann, the girl is naked save a leather breechcloth tied about her waist. They walk together beneath the sagging boughs of trees that must have been old before Ann's great great grandmothers were born, and here and there is ample evidence of the civilization that ruled the island in some murky, immemorial past – glimpses of great stone idols worn away by time and rain and the humid air, disintegrating walls and archways leaning at such precarious angles Ann cannot fathom why they have not yet succumbed to gravity. Crumbling bas-reliefs depicting the loathsome gods and demons and the bizarre reptilian denizens of this place. As they draw nearer to the temple, the ruins become somewhat more intact, though even here the splayed roots of the trees are slowly forcing the masonry apart. The roots put Ann in mind of the tentacles of gargantuan octopi or cuttlefish, and that is how she envisions the spirit of the jungles and marshes fanning out around this ridge – grey tentacles advancing inch by inch, year by year, inexorably reclaiming what has been theirs all along.

As she and the girl begin to climb the steep and crooked steps leading up from the deep ravine – stones smoothed by untold generations of footsteps – Ann stops to catch her breath and asks the brown girl how she knew where to look, how it was she found her at the stream. But the girl only stares at her, confused and uncomprehending, and then she frowns and shakes her head and says something in the native patois. In Anne's long years on the island, since the *Venture* deserted her and sailed away with what remained of the dead ape, she has never learned more than a few words of that language, and she has never tried to teach this girl nor any of her people English. The girl looks back the way they've come; she presses the fingers of her left hand against her breast, above her heart, then uses the same hand to motion towards Ann.

> *Life is just a bowl of cherries.*
> *Don't take it serious; it's too mysterious.*

By sunset, Ann has taken her place on the rough-hewn throne carved from beds of coral limestone thrust up from the seafloor in the throes of the island's cataclysmic genesis. As night begins to gather once again, torches are lit, and the people come bearing sweet-smelling baskets of flowers and fruit, fish and the roasted flesh of gulls and rats and crocodiles. They lay multicoloured garlands and strings of pearls at her feet, a necklace of ankylosaur teeth, rodent claws, and monkey vertebrae, and she is only the Golden Mother once again. They bow and genuflect, and the tropical night rings out with joyous songs she cannot understand. The men and woman decorate their bodies with yellow paint in an effort to emulate Ann's blonde hair, and a sort of pantomime is acted out for her benefit, as it is once every month, on the night of the new moon. She does not *need* to understand their words to grasp its meaning – the coming of the *Venture* from somewhere far away, Ann offered up as the bride of a god, her marriage and the death of Kong, and the ascent of the Golden Mother from a hellish underworld to preside in his stead.

The end of one myth and the beginning of another, the turning of a page. *I am not lost*, Ann thinks. *I am right here, right now – here and now where, surely, I must belong*, and she watches the glowing bonfire embers rising up to meet the dark sky. She knows she will see that terrible black hill again, the hill that is not a hill and its foetid crimson river, but she knows, too, that there will always be a road back from her dreams, from that All-at-Once tapestry of possibility and penitence. In her dreams, she will be lost and wander those treacherous, deceitful paths of Might-Have-Been, and always she will wake and find herself once more.

CONRAD WILLIAMS

Tight Wrappers

CONRAD WILLIAMS IS THE AUTHOR of the novels *Head Injuries*, *London Revenant* and *The Unblemished*; the novellas *Nearly People*, *Game*, *The Scalding Rooms* and *Rain*, and a collection of short fiction, *Use Once Then Destroy*. As "Conrad A. Williams", he has written the novel *Decay Inevitable*.

He is a recipient of the British Fantasy Award and the International Horror Guild Award and lives in Manchester, with his wife and three sons.

" 'Tight Wrappers' combines two things that I like very much," reveals the author: "first editions and scaffolding. Not the most obvious of bedfellows, but I'm not easily put off.

"There's something beautiful and impossible about the structure of scaffolding; the way it fits together, its geometry and precision. And, like Mantle, my protagonist, once you begin to notice it, you see it everywhere.

"The world of the book collector, with its arcane signs and language, seemed to complement it. Two things we take for granted but, on closer inspection, possess thrilling intricacies . . . well, for people like me, anyway."

M ANTLE HAILED A TAXI on the Edgware Road and piled in. He was breathless and, as always, a little panicky that he'd dropped something, that he was missing some essential part.

"Holland Park," he said, patting the pockets of his raincoat. The hand of another pedestrian, cheated by Mantle's claiming of the cab, slapped against the back window as the taxi moved off, leaving behind an imprint that took some time to fade.

Mantle had stolen the coat from a theme park staff room a couple of decades previously, attracted by the numerous deep pockets, the better for storing his lists, address books, notes and clippings, his maps, an urban *disjecta membra*, the city in leaves. At times he felt as though he were a disorganized filing cabinet on the lam. Occasionally he fell asleep on his bed in his coat. He felt naked without it, or more specifically, that special form of insulation that his papers provided.

The day was a blur in his thoughts, as most were. He struggled to remember what he had breakfasted on, only that it had been in a coffee shop on Old Compton Street, half an eye on the newspaper, his notebook with its codes and descants, the phone in his fist. He had gone on to sell a couple of Fine/Fine Iain Sinclairs, doubles from his own collection, in a sandwich shop at the north side of Blackfriars Bridge before scuttling along the Jubilee Walkway to the National Film Theatre where he met Rob Swaines, his "Southwark Mole". Over the years Rob had fed him some great information on the underground book networks of SE1. He had learned of a Graham Greene first sitting forgotten in a plastic washtub of an Oxfam in Stamford Street, an early Philip K. Dick in a Fitzalan Street squat, a news vendor by the tube station at Lambeth North carried in his pocket a copy of H.G. Wells' *The Island of Dr Moreau* containing an inscription to its recipient from the author not to read it at night.

The rest of the day was a smear of motion, of buses caught at full pelt, of observations written in the corner of a fried chicken cesspit, of phone calls, hot and cold leads, rumours of a Bradbury unclipped *Dark Carnival* in a Battersea pub that came to nothing, hastily scribbled ideas for a book hunt in Edinburgh, catching up with the tracings of his route on the OS maps, marginalia he had forgotten about but that, freshly discovered, sparked more calls, more possibilities; there was no such thing as a closed door in London, he had learned. Every shelf was a display for him; it was just a matter of time before he got round to cherry-picking the best of the best from each one.

He'd received a text from Heaton, his main bloodhound, his *in*, not five minutes previously, alerting him to a rare Very Good/Good in W8. It was pleasing that he was already in the area; if the traffic favoured him he could be on Aubrey Road within minutes. He pulled out his battered Moleskine and slipped off the elastic binding. Inside he flipped through alphabeticized jottings, references to books he had in his sights, rare tomes, the jackets of which he sometimes felt under his fingertips in the moments before he became fully awake. Here was his file on Mick Bett, the thriller writer whose first two novels, *Black Iris* and *One Man on His Own*, published in the early 1960s, had been turned into quirky cult films starring George Kennedy. Bett had killed himself in 1967 when he had become blocked on his third novel, working title *The Mummer*, at a time when the James Bond franchise had hit its stride and a year after Adam Hall's first Quiller novel, *The Berlin Memorandum*, had been turned into a successful film. Mantle wondered if the *Sunday Times* encomium on the front cover of the Pan paperback of *One Man on His Own* ("The best, after Deighton and Le Carré") might have contributed to Bett's decision to leap from the Golden Gate Bridge.

Mantle owned a signed first edition, first printing of *Black Iris* that he had bought at a Brighton book fair in 1976 for a wallet-bruising thirty pounds. The very same book was now worth £7,000. Mantle's assessment of a book's future worth was rarely off the mark. He had no compunction about spending a lot for a Fine/Fine now if his hunch whispered that there'd be a few more noughts on its value a decade hence. Heaton's digging had led to this evening's revelation; a copy of *OMOHO* sitting on a shelf in west London, its spine having probably never known any strain.

The traffic was snarled around Marble Arch; Mantle felt blisters of sweat rise on his forehead. He couldn't relax despite the knowledge that the book, having occupied its place on the Aubrey Road shelf for the last twenty years, wasn't going anywhere in the next ten minutes. His gaze was snagged on a criss-cross of scaffolding clinging to the face of an Edwardian house facing Hyde Park. Light snaked along the tubes and died on the dirty orange plastic netting. The house seemed diminished by the complexity, the aggressive sprawl of the construction. Scaffolding bothered him, it pulled at his vision like a scar.

"What are you reading?" Mantle asked the driver as he shoved the notebook back into its nest. A thrillerfat paperback rested open-bellied on the dashboard. Mantle had learned to quell his disgust at the way other people treated their reading matter, forced into supine positions they did not deserve.

"That Dan Brown guy," the driver said, eventually, predictably. Mantle could dismiss him now. Him and his Very Poor, his Reading Copy. But it was something he had to know. He had to know what was on the cover, what was being sucked up into the eyes. On the tube he would crick his neck to catch a glimpse of any title. He was about to return to his notes, to trace the latest leg of his years-long journey through the capital on his OS map, when the driver came back with a question of his own.

"No," Mantle said, trying to keep the bristling from his voice. "I've never read *The Da Vinci Code*. It's . . . not my thing."

He'd been offered a signed Mint in April, but he wouldn't have forgiven himself, could never have allowed it to rub shoulders with his Lovecrafts and Priests, his M. R.s and his M. Johns. It was snobbery, to be sure, but the very act of collecting, serious collecting, was snobbery anyway. Mantle was too old, too alone to care what anybody thought of him or his obsession. All that mattered to him were the pencil webs he span across his map of London, the treasure he was tracking from Shepherd's Bush to Shoreditch.

The taxi disgorged him on the corner of Aubrey Road. A light rain, so insubstantial as to be barely felt, breathed against him. He looked back at the Bayswater Road and saw it ghosting across the harsh sodium lighting like the sheets of cellophane he wrapped around the jackets of his hardbacks, to further protect them. He darted away from the main drag, patting his pockets, fretting over the corners of reminders, receipts, appointments, all the clues that frothed danger-ously at the lips of his pockets.

He found the address he needed and rapped hard on the front door. He smoothed down his hair and hoped the occupants wouldn't be able to smell his odour, a mix of stale sweat and old paper, not really that bad, but perhaps offensive to those who were not used to it.

A well-dressed woman with professionally styled hair answered the door. She was in her late fifties, it seemed to Mantle, although the way she was turned out made her appear quite a bit younger. Her expression was cold; she was chewing something, a chicken leg, nub of white gristle gleaming, clutched in her hand. He cursed himself. She had been drawn from dinner. She wanted him gone; no amount of charm would work now.

"I apologise for disturbing your dinner," he said.

"Quite all right," she snapped. "What is it?"

"A book."

"A book?" Now her expression did change, to one of bafflement.

"My name's Henry Mantle. I'm a collector, a diviner of text. I've got friends call me Sniffer."

"You've got friends," she said.

Mantle's smile faltered as he wondered if she were belittling him, but he pressed on. "Anyway, I understand you have a copy of Mick

Bett's novel, *One Man on His Own*, published in 1962. I'd like to make you an offer for it."

A further change. The woman, consciously or not, closed the door a fraction. "How did you know I had that?"

"A receipt in a ledger in a Bloomsbury hotel. A book fair in the 1980s. A purchase traced to you."

"But this is . . . this is invasive," she said.

"Not at all, Mrs Greville," he said. "I can assure—"

"How do you know my name?" Needle in the voice now. An aspect of threat.

"The receipt. The book fair."

"I'm sorry, but I don't like this. Please leave."

She was making to shut the door and in his desperation he shot out his hand to block it.

"I'll give you £1,200," he said. "In cash, right now, if you say yes."

She paused, just as it seemed her anger would overflow and she would start shouting. The breath seemed knocked from her. Mantle refrained from smiling; he knew he had won.

"Twelve hundred? For a *book*?"

"I'm a big fan of his work. And copies – nice, well-looked after copies – are scarce."

She seemed to change her mind about him. Maybe she was thinking of all the other unread copies of books on her shelves, perhaps the result of buying sprees by a dearly departed, or something inherited that she couldn't be bothered to take to the charity shop. She drew the door open wider and ushered him in, insisting sharply that he could have five minutes of her time, no more.

He barely took any notice of the hallway he was walking along; the smell of books was in his nostrils. He patted his pockets, felt the comforting scrunch of bus tickets, pencilled symbols and hints, directions and directives etched on paper napkins, beer coasters, cigarette packets. His whole life was in these pockets; he couldn't bear to throw anything away. He supposed it described a weakness in him, a form of psychosis, but he was helpless. He felt emboldened by these layers, these graphite and ink ley-lines. His wallet was fat underneath all of this. He ached for something to happen.

She introduced him to a room whose darkness was penetrated only by a soft, low lozenge of orange light; a cat was curled around the base of the lamp, glancing up unimpressed at Mrs Greville's guest.

"Here's the book," she said, reaching up to tip a volume into her left palm.

He winced as she handled the book. She wouldn't pass it to him quickly enough, and kept hold of it, turning it around in her fingers as if searching for some clue as to why it was worth what he had offered. She gave him a look; her tongue worked at some shred from her rapidly cooling and forgotten dinner.

"You know, this was my husband's, my late husband's, favourite novel. I really don't think I would feel happy letting it go. It's become something to remember him by."

Mantle smiled. He had prepared himself for this. It always happened. "I fully understand. I'm willing to go to sixteen hundred. Which is way over the odds for a book of this sort."

He could see her scrutinizing him, wondering if she could wring out another hundred, wondering how to play the game. But she didn't know anything. She was sold.

"I suppose there's no point in hanging on to the past," she said. "My Eddie would want his books to be appreciated by readers rather than gather dust on the shelf."

Mantle pursed his lips. His mobile phone went off, vibrating against his leg.

"Then you'll take the sixteen hundred?"

"I will," said Mrs Greville, in a voice of almost comical reluctance.

She passed him the book once the bills were in her hand. He was hastily wishing her good night, wrapping the book in a brown paper bag after a swift, expert appraisal of its jacket, boards and copyright page. "Very fine, very fine," he said, his little joke, his signature.

He barely heard Mrs Greville asking if there was anything else he'd like to look at. He fumbled the phone from his pocket and barked his name before the answering service could kick in.

There was no reply, just the sound of air rushing down the line, as if the caller had contacted him from a tunnel, or a windswept beach. There was a pulse to the wind; he was put in mind of the white noise of shortwave signals on his old radio.

"Hello?" he said, his voice thick in his throat. He heard the faint echo of his own greeting, that occasional anomaly of mobile phones. It sounded as though, for a second, he was talking to himself. He might as well have been; nobody replied.

That radio. He wondered where it was now. It had been his father's, but Mantle had spent more time than he twisting its knobs and dials. He would zone in on the pulses and bleats of what he had believed were signals of intent from distant aliens, try to decipher their insistent tattoo. A few months later, after the violent death of his father, he believed they were the frantic, distorted echoes of his last breaths; scorched, impatient, encoded with a meaning he could not extract.

His father had worked as a builder's mate, hod-carrying, mixing cement, making the bacon butty runs. One night he had met a girl in a pub and smuggled her into the site after closing time. Mantle had dramatized what might have happened on many occasions, running sequences and dialogue through his mind like a writer planning a passage in a novel. There were never any happy endings.

He lights cigarettes for them; she tastes the sticky residue of whisky and Guinness on the filter. She watches him lark around, his steel toe capped boots crunching through glass and plaster; the odd, metallic skitter as he kicks a nail across the floor. In here are great mounds of polythene wrap, packaging for fixtures and fittings, looking to her drink-addled mind like greasy clouds frozen into stillness.

He's opened the windows. Outside, the sky is hard with winter. *Goodbye cruel world* as he lurches into the night. A breath catches in her throat. She rushes to see. *Tricked you. Step into my office.* He's giggly, foolish, reckless. Unlike the man who skulks at home, the taciturn man, incapable of tenderness, of affection. The scaffold bites into the building's face like an insect, all folded, fuddled legs. His steps shush and clump on the wood. The angles of metal look cold enough to burn. *Come inside*, she says. She's nervous. This is an unknown, unknowable world to her. It's a sketch of a home. There is no comfort here. She unbuttons her blouse, lets him see the acid white bra, the curve of what it contains. *Come inside.*

Fumbling. Stumbling. An accident. A flame from a match, from the smouldering coals of the cigarettes. A fire leaps, too swift and strong to stamp out. A drunken attempt. The surge of molten plastic. In the flickering orange dark, before she runs to escape, she sees him twisting in the suffocating layers, wrapping himself in clear, wet heat as it melts through his flesh. His fingers fuse together as he tries to claw it from his face. He stands there, silently beseeching, loops of his own cheeks spinning from his hands. The black fug from burning plastic funnels out of him and he staggers to the window, toppling on to that cold, black edifice.

He sees one now. Like an exoskeleton. A riot of violent shapes. His father had never been a great reader, unless you counted the *Sun*, which was never off his dashboard. He had always snorted his derision whenever he found Mantle leafing through an Ian Serraillier, or a David Line. There was always something else to do, in his opinion, as if reading for its own sake, and reading fiction especially, was a waste of time. The scaffolds were erected – that arcane, mysterious practice – and dismantled. They were the means to deliver repair, but Mantle could not, would not see that in them. Whenever he chanced upon them, he saw only his father cooling on the duckboards, black sheaves lifting from his face.

Bitterly, Mantle closed his phone and assessed the road. He couldn't see any taxis but the bus stop across the way was busy; there'd be a ninety-four along any moment. He joined the queue and extracted the book from his pocket. He sucked in its brittle breath and traced the tightness of the head, the embossing of the title and author on the front cover. Twice what he'd paid would have still been a modest price. Quickly, before the cold air, or the pollution, or his excitement could have any adverse effect on the pages, he slid it back into the brown bag. Books and brown paper, well, there was a perfect marriage. Yet an increasingly unlikely one, in the bookshops he haunted throughout the capital. Flimsy plastic bags, one molecule thin it seemed, were used to package books these days. He'd talked to some of the booksellers, suggested returning to paper, that the books might sweat under plastic, that they could be damaged, but had only ever received blank looks. He liked the snug way the brown paper folded against, *into* the book it was protecting, as opposed to the slip and slide of the plastic, as if it were trying to shun what it sheathed. It was too much like smothering.

A sudden gust of wind; a smack and clatter in the deep dark behind him. He flinched. Nobody else seemed to notice. He stared again at the scaffolding as it snaked up the face of the church. The light was good enough only to see a treacly gleam trace the geometry of the struts and tubes and platforms. It waxed across the netting, creating the impression of a series of rhomboid mouths opening and closing against the night. Mantle mimicked them.

The bus arrived; he boarded, feeling the air condense at his back as if someone were hurrying to catch the bus before it departed, but when he glanced back there was nobody. The doors cantilevered shut. On his way home he noticed so many houses and shops masked by aluminium that he had to reach up to his own face to check it wasn't similarly encumbered.

Mantle's flat: bookshelves everywhere. He had the spaces above the doors adapted to take C format paperbacks. There was shelving in the bathroom, although he had spent a fortune on air-conditioning to ensure that the steam from the shower and bath were negated to ensure his books remained in pristine condition. The floor was a maze of literary magazines, reviews, photocopies of library archive material, letters from booksellers.

He unwrapped the Bett and placed it next to *Black Iris*. The covers hissed together as if sighing with contentment. A completeness there. A job done. He could imagine Mick Bett himself nodding his appreciation. Here was somebody who cared as much for the decent writer of bestsellers – and there were some around – as the leftfield scribes, the slipstreamers, the miserablists. There were writers he adored who had never sold well when people like Jeffrey Archer, Dan Brown, Martina Cole were coining it. Forget clitfic, or ladlit, this was shitlit. He'd rather stick with an arresting, original writer who deserved greater exposure, a writer who cared about the craft, a writer who lived for it – an Ursula Bentley, a Christopher Burns, a Robert McLiam Wilson – than some charlatan who could hardly write his or her own name, but whose name was gold because of some other supposed talent: Rooney, Jordan, Kerry fucking Katona.

He drew a bath and pulled a bottle of Magners from the fridge. Food was nothing more than a thought. Already he was considering the following day; Heaton had mentioned possibilities in Crystal Palace: an 1838 Elizabeth B. Barrett, *The Seraphim and Other Poems*, with an inscription. You were looking at 2.5K plus for that. He took the drink over to his desk and looked out at the city. Books under every roof. Most of them forgotten, badly looked after, unread. He felt the weight of all his own literature bristling behind him, smelled that all-pervading tang of ancient pages.

Something shimmered under the caul of city light. The reflections of red security lamps crept along the wet scaffolds like something alive, determined. Mantle was suddenly shocked by the mass of spars and supports cluttering the skyline. It seemed as if the whole of London was crippled, in need of Zimmer frames and callipers. The night breathed through it all, a carbonized, gasping ebb and flow. A miserable suck, a terrible fluting. He thought he saw something move through the confusion, shadow dark, intent, clumsy. Before it merged with a deeper blackness, right at the heart of the scaffold, he saw, thought he saw, deceleration, the wrap of a hand around a column, black fingers that did not shift until his eyes watered and he had to look away.

Mantle remembered his bath and stood up sharply, knocking over his drink and bashing his knee into the underside of his desk. His foot skidded on the open pages of a magazine and he went down awkwardly, an arm outstretched to stabilize himself serving only to swipe a cairn of novels to the floor. Pages riffled across his line of sight, a skin of words in which to wrap his pain. They wouldn't leave him alone, even after he had managed to wrestle a way into sleep.

His alarm didn't so much wake him as rescue him from a desperate conviction that he was about to suffocate. He felt as though he were in the centre of a world of layers, and all of them were trying to iron him flat, as if he were some crease that was spoiling the uniformity of his dreamscape. He wore a tight jacket that was like a corset, pinning his gut back. The city was similarly constricted; he couldn't see brick or stone for the weight of aluminium, slotted with mathematical precision into every available square metre of space. It caused him to feel sick at his own softness; he felt arbitrary, ill-fitting. The books he was carrying seemed to sense his otherness and kept trying to squirm from his grasp. Pages fluttered. He felt the bright sting of a paper cut in his finger. Blood sizzled across onionskin. He gazed at his hands and saw how the print from the books had transferred to his flesh, a backwards code tattooed on every inch. He was ushered into a series of ever-narrowing streets by faces smudged into nonsense by the speed he was moving at, or the lack of oxygen reaching his brain. A building up ahead stood out because of the presence of an open door, a black oblong of perfection among the confused angles. He was fed through it. Shapes, presumably people, gestured and shrugged and pointed. He was shown a gap in the heights, a section of hammer-beam that had rotted and was being prepared for repair. Ladders and platforms were arranged around the workstation like props in a play.

He was cajoled and prodded up the ladder until he reached the ceiling. He was manhandled into the slot, he screamed as his neck was twisted violently to accommodate the rest of his body. Great cranes positioned at either end of the hammerbeam slowly rotated a mechanized nut, the size of a dinner plate. The two ends of the hammerbeam were incrementally forced together. Pressure built in his body; he felt blood rush to his extremities. He bellowed uncontrollably, a nonsense noise, a plea. He felt bones pulverizing, unbearable tensions tearing the shiny tight skin of his suit, his stomach. At the last moment, as breath ceased, he saw himself burst open, everything wet in him raining to the floor. It looked like ink. It looked like a river of words.

Coffee. It burned his lip but he was grateful for anything that reminded him he was still alive. His fingers shook a little as he replaced the cup in its saucer. Heaton's last text was burned into his thoughts, helpfully chasing away the remnants of the dream. He spread out a fan of notes on the table, sucking up the gen on this new quarry. Tucked away in a Stoke Newington studio flat was a Mint/ Mint of Bryce Tanner's first novel, *Noble Rot*, published by Faber in 1982. According to Heaton, the studio had been abandoned by the occupant, some failed venture capitalist who had needed a temporary base while he searched for his Hoxton warehouse. Rumour was he'd drowned himself in one of the reservoirs in N16. The flat had been left as it was while his nearest and dearest were sought, a process taking longer than had been expected. Armed with a hammer, Mantle had cased the building an hour previously, and had been encouraged by the lack of humanity; the building seemed little more than a shell giving the come-on to the wrecking ball and the softstrip crews. The jitters Mantle was suffering on the back of his dream, and a need to be sure of what he was about to do, had driven him away in search of caffeine. Now, sitting on a hard metal chair outside a deli in Church Street, the call of the book too great to resist any longer. He tossed a handful of coins into his saucer and retraced his steps to the High Street. A block sitting back off that busy main drag contained more boards than glass in its window frames. Mantle negotiated the buckled front door and the inevitable climb up the stairs. Broken glass was scattered across every landing; dead insects provided a variety to the crunch under his shoes. The door he needed was padlocked – cheaply – and his hammer dealt with it after a couple of blows. Inside he paused in case his attack had brought any remaining residents to investigate, but either the building was deserted or apathy reigned. It didn't matter – he wasn't going to be disturbed.

The studio was well maintained, leaning towards minimalism but with enough books, CDs and DVDs to suggest that it was a life choice that wasn't being taken seriously. There was nothing to suggest that its inhabitant was likely to take his own life, but Mantle was no psychologist. He didn't care one jot. All that mattered to him was that couple of pounds of paper and board.

He located the book almost immediately. It seemed to call to him from among all the dog-eared paperbacks. It had presence, *gravitas*. He slid it clear from the shelf and hefted it reverentially.

The book turned to ash in his fingers.

He stood there for a while, as the air seemed to darken around him, his mouth open, trying to keep himself together. The notes in his pocket lost their insulating properties. He was in a cold room, bare but for a bucket filled with a dried meringue of shit.

The boards across the window had collapsed; wind flooded in. He moved towards it, the flakes in his hand rising up like angered insects. Scaffolding bit deep into the pebble-dashed skin of the block.

Through the shapes it created he could almost imagine he could see the muscular City architecture, the Gherkin, the old Nat West tower and, further afield, Canary Wharf. The aircraft warning lights they pulsed might shine in the tubing outside this very window, but also, deep within him, matching the insistent thrum of his own heart. He heard the creak of the broken door behind him and he acted upon it, not wanting to turn to see what had followed him up here. Falteringly, he clambered out on to the platform and edged along it until he had reached the end. His hands, coated with the dust of a book he could still smell, clawed at the brackets that kept the entire structure married to the block. They were so cold they scorched his skin.

He heard something struggle out of the window frame and on to the duckboards. Whatever it was had no grace, no balance. Its weight sent stresses and strains along the planks to his own feet, lifting them a little. The song of the wood might have been the keening that played in his throat. He smelled the high, narcotic smell of burned plastic. There were no books. There were no notes. No text messages. No Heaton. No wallet filled with cash. No Mrs Greville. No Mick Bett. No Gherkin. No past, no future. No nothing. Mantle's love of books was desperate, a wish never to be fulfilled. He reached up to his eyes and pressed his fingers against the dry membrane that filmed them. Pockets of interior colour exploded. He could never know what it meant to be able to read a story, no more than he would ever learn what colour his own eyes were.

The lie these books contained. The fictions. It had a face, it had a fury. They infected your life, it was a contagion. You built up your own monster from the deceptions you invented. And Mantle was all about deceit. He'd managed the most horrid of them all, tricking himself. It was second nature, now. The blind leading the blind. Fear unfolded in every pore of his being. Nevertheless, he turned to confront what had chased him all this way, all these years. Not being able to see him gave Mantle a Pyrrhic victory of sorts. He was able to smile, his mouth finding an unusual cast even as the sum of his trickery leaned in close. The hand over his mouth was little more than crisped talons. He felt as if he were becoming infected by that alien flesh, growing desiccated, so sucked dry of moisture that his face might disintegrate. His chest muscles ruptured with the strain of trying to draw a breath. Millions of capillaries burst, flooding his inner sight with red. He heard the stutter and gargle of his own breath, or of the thing silencing him. White noise. Explosions of crumpled paper. In extremis, he managed to kiss the hand, to reach out and hold tight, to imagine that this was the hug he had craved for so long.

KIM NEWMAN

Cold Snap

AS KIM NEWMAN EXPLAINS: "I wrote 'Cold Snap' for my recent collection *Secret Files of the Diogenes Club*, published by Chris Roberson's MonkeyBrain Books as a follow-up to *The Man from the Diogenes Club*. The earlier collection assembles a run of stories I've been doing about Richard Jeperson – mostly set in the 1970s, and featuring Richard and his supporting cast coping with various supernatural or extranormal troubles.

"*Secret Files* dips back further into the history of the Diogenes Club, which I depict in this series as a long-standing British institution, and collects stories about men and women who worked with the Club before Richard came along.

"My initial plan for 'Cold Snap' was simply to have Richard Jeperson at least represented in the new book to provide continuity with *The Man from the Diogenes Club*. However, as it turned out, I also saw an opportunity to draw together threads from other stories in the *Secret Files*, thus converting a linked series of stories into something vaguely like a novel by revealing that elements of this plot have been percolating for over a century.

"Given that my fictions all tend to be interrelated in some way, I also cast around fairly widely for characters to take part in a large-scale crisis. Naturally, you're encouraged to seek out the other books and stories to learn more about the various folks who crop up here – though I've cross-referenced a few things that are (as of writing this) not yet published or finished, so it might take a while to follow every lead.

"For the later lives of some of these folks, see *Life's Lottery* (Keith Marion), *Jago* (Susan Rodway, Anthony Jago), *Seven Stars* (Geneviève, Maureen Mountmain), 'Mother Hen' (Mr & Mrs Karabatsos), *Bad Dreams* (Ariadne), *The Quorum* (Derek Leech), 'Going to

Series' (Myra Lark), 'Organ Donors' (Constant Drache), 'Swellhead' (Sewell Head). For an alternative encounter with the Cold, see *Doctor Who: Time and Relative*. I will eventually reveal more about the Chambers family and Louise Teazle (though, for now, you can find one of her children's books online).

"However, that's all in the future for the people you meet here. Again, you're best off having read the earlier stories in the series, but the following 'Prologue' (original to this printing) should stand as the equivalent of those 'previously . . .' montages they use on TV shows when the ongoing plots get tangled . . ."

PROLOGUE

IN THE MID-NINETEENTH CENTURY, Mycroft Holmes and others as yet unidentified found the Diogenes Club, ostensibly a club for the most unsociable men in London. It is actually a cover for a body charged with handling delicate and often supernatural matters of state. Among its most notable operatives are Charles Beauregard, who succeeds Mycroft as Chair of the Club's Ruling Cabal, and Geneviève Dieudonné, a long-lived vampire lady; in another continuum (the *Anno Dracula* series), they are lovers – here, they are unaware of each other until the 1930s (for *that* story, see "Sorcerer Conjurer Wizard Witch" in Marvin Kaye's forthcoming *A Book of Wizards*).

The Club serves Britain's interests – and, often, humanity's – in a series of crises kept out of the history books: including an incursion from faerie in the 1890s ("The Gypsies in the Wood"), a rise of the Deep Ones in the 1940s ("The Big Fish"), a railway disaster which threatens the world in the 1950s ("The Man Who Got Off the Ghost Train"), a timeslip on the South Coast caused by the psychic dreamer Paulette Michaelsmith in the 1970s ("End of the Pier Show") and the centuries-spanning "Duel of the Seven Stars" (*Seven Stars*).

In 1903, an ab-human entity comes close to committing the most colossal crime ever contemplated – the murder of space and time. No fewer than fifteen of the world's premier magicians, occult detectives, psychic adventurers, criminal geniuses and visionary scientists set aside profound differences and work under Mycroft's direction to avert the rending-asunder of the universe. Yet the only allusion to the affair in the public record is an aside by the biographer of Mycroft's more-famous, frankly less perspicacious brother, concerning the "duellist and journalist" Isidore Persano, found "stark staring mad with a match box in front of him which contained a remarkable worm said to be unknown to science."

In the 1920s, Diogenes Club members Edwin Winthrop and Catriona Kaye encounter a shape-shifting creature who takes the default form of Rose Farrar, a long-missing little girl. It is taken into custody by the Undertaking, a rival organization to the Club who maintain the Mausoleum, a prison/storehouse for unique and dangerous individuals and objects. (*See*: "Angel Down, Sussex".)

Later, Catriona conducts a murder investigation, which prompts Charles Beauregard, the Chair of the Ruling Cabal of the Diogenes Club, to take covert steps to end the careers of the Splendid Six, a collection of arrogant and self-involved aristocratic adventurers whose number includes Richard Cleaver (aka "Clever Dick"), a child prodigy. (*See*: "Clubland Heroes".)

In the 1960s, the position of Great Enchanter – loosely, the commander of forces arrayed against goodness and decency – passes from Colonel Zenf, who had succeeded Isidore Persano, to Derek Leech, an entrepreneurial, Mephistophelean fellow who springs out of the mud of Swinging London and amasses a great deal of temporal power. Leech's history can be found, between the lines, in "Sorcerer Conjurer Wizard Witch", "Another Fish Story", "Organ Donors" and *The Quorum*.

A foundling of the World War II, Richard Jeperson is raised by the men and women of the Diogenes Club to become the successor to Charles Beauregard and Edwin Winthrop. With his allies Fred Regent, a former policeman, and Vanessa, a mystery woman, he has fought evil and investigated strangenesses throughout the late 1960s and early 1970s. Their adventures are recounted in *The Man from the Diogenes Club*.

A legacy is passed down among the Chambers family – who have certain abilities after nightfall, and have waged their own night-time wars. From the 1920s to the 1960s, Jonathan Chambers wore goggles and a slouch hat and operated as the scientific vigilante "Dr Shade" in partnership with the ladylike "Kentish Glory", while his sister Jennifer practised unorthodox medicine. Jonathan's son Jamie is, as yet, unsure of his inheritance.

Now, it's the summer of 1976. Great Britain swelters under the Heat Wave of the Century . . .

I

"Nice motor," said Richard Jeperson, casting an appreciative eye over Derek Leech's Rolls Royce ShadowShark.

"I could say the same of yours," responded Leech, gloved fingertips lightly polishing his red-eyed Spirit of Ecstasy. Richard's car was almost identical, though his bonnet ornament didn't have the inset rubies.

"I've kept the old girl in good nick," said Richard.

"Mine has a horn which plays the theme from *Jaws*," said Leech.

"Mine, I'm glad to say, doesn't."

That was the pleasantries over.

It was the longest, hottest, driest summer of the 1970s. Thanks to a strict hosepipe ban, lawns turned to desert. Neighbours informed on each other over suspiciously verdant patches. Bored regional television crews shot fillers about eggs frying on dustbin lids and sunburn specialists earning consultancy fees in naturist colonies. If they'd been allowed anywhere near here, a considerably more unusual summer weather story was to be had. A news blackout was in effect, and discreet roadblocks limited traffic onto this stretch of the Somerset Levels.

The near-twin cars were parked in a lay-by, equidistant from the seemingly Mediterranean beaches of Burnham-on-Sea and Lyme Regis. While the nation sweltered in bermuda shorts and flip-flops, Richard and Leech shivered in arctic survival gear. Richard wore layers of bearskin, furry knee-length boots with claw-toes, and a lime green balaclava surmounted by a scarlet Andean bobble hat with chinchilla earmuffs – plus the wraparound anti-glare visor recommended by Jean-Claude Killy. Leech wore a snow-white, fur-hooded parka and baggy leggings, ready to lead an Alpine covert assault troop. If not for his black Foster Grants, he could stand against a whitewashed wall and impersonate the Invisible Man.

Around them was a landscape from a malicious Christmas card. They stood in a Cold Spot. Technically, a patch of permafrost, four miles across. From the air, it looked like a rough circle of white stitched onto a brown quilt. Earth stood hard as iron, water like a stone . . . snow had fallen, snow had fallen, *snow on snow*. The epicentre was Sutton Mallet, a hamlet consisting of a few farmhouses, New Chapel (which replaced the old one in 1829) and the Derek Leech International weather research facility.

Leech professed innocence, but this was his fault. Most bad things were.

Bernard Levin said on *Late Night Line-Up* that Leech papers had turned Fleet Street into a Circle of Hell by boasting fewer words and more semi-naked girls than anything else on the news-stands. Charles Shaar Murray insisted in *IT* that the multi-media tycoon was revealed as the Devil Incarnate when he invented the "folk rock cantata" triple LP. The Diogenes Club had seen Derek Leech coming for a long time, and Richard knew exactly what he was dealing with.

Their wonderful cars could go no further, so they had to walk.

After several inconclusive, remote engagements, this was their first face-to-face (or visor-to-sunglasses) meeting. The Most Valued Member of the Diogenes Club and the Great Enchanter were expected to be the antagonists of the age, but the titles meant less than they had in the days of Mycroft Holmes, Charles Beauregard and Edwin Winthrop or Leo Dare, Isidore Persano and Colonel Zenf. Lately, both camps had other things to worry about.

From two official world wars, great nations had learned to conduct their vast duels without all-out armed conflict. Similarly, the Weird Wars of 1903 and 1932 had changed the shadow strategies of the Diogenes Club and its opponents. In the Worm War, there had almost been battle-lines. It had only been won when a significant number of Persano's allies and acolytes switched sides, appalled at the scope of the crime ("the murder of time and space") planned by the wriggling mastermind ("a worm unknown to science") the Great Enchanter kept in a match-box in his waistcoat pocket. The Wizard War, when Beauregard faced Zenf, was a more traditional game of good and evil, though nipped in the bud by stealth, leaving the Club to cope with the ab-human threat of the Deep Ones ("the Water War") and the mundane business of "licking Hitler". Now, in what secret historians were already calling the Winter War, no one knew who to fight.

So, strangely, this was a truce.

As a sensitive – a Talent, as the parapsychology bods had it – Richard was used to trusting his impressions of people and places. He knew in his water when things or folks were out of true. If he squinted, he saw their real faces. If he cocked an ear, he heard what they were thinking. Derek Leech seemed perfectly sincere, and elaborately blameless. No matter how furiously Richard blinked behind his visor, he saw no red horns, no forked beard, no extra mouths. Only a tightness in the man's jaw gave away the effort it took to present himself like this. Leech had to be mindful of a tendency to grind his teeth.

They had driven west – windows rolled down in the futile hope of a cool breeze – through parched, sun-baked countryside. Now, despite thermals and furs, they shivered. Richard saw Leech's breath frosting.

"Snow in July," said Leech. "Worse. Snow in *this* July."

"It's not snow, it's *rime*. Snow is frozen rain. Precipitation. Rime is frozen dew. The moisture in the air, in the ground."

"Don't be such an arse, Jeperson."

"As a newspaperman, you appreciate accuracy."

"As a newspaper *publisher*, I know elitist vocabulary alienates readers. If it looks like snow, tastes like snow and gives you a white Christmas, then . . ."

Leech had devised *So What Do You Know?*, an ITV quiz show where prizes were awarded not for correct answers, but for matching whatever was decided – right or wrong – by the majority vote of a "randomly-selected panel of ordinary Britons". Contestants had taken home fridge-freezers and fondue sets by identifying Sydney as the capital of Australia or categorizing whales as fish. Richard could imagine what Bernard Levin and Charles Shaar Murray thought of that.

Richard opened the boot of his Rolls and hefted out a holdall which contained stout wicker snowshoes, extensible aluminium ski-poles and packs of survival rations. Leech had similar equipment, though his boot-attachments were spiked black metal and his ruck-sack could have contained a jet propulsion unit.

"I'd have thought DLI could supply a Sno-Cat."

"Have you any idea how hard it is to come by one in July?"

"As it happens, yes."

They both laughed, bitterly. Fred Regent, one of the Club's best men, had spent most of yesterday learning that the few places in Great Britain which leased or sold snow-ploughs, caterpillar tractor bikes or jet-skis had either sent their equipment out to be serviced, shut up shop for the summer or gone out of business in despair at unending sunshine. Heather Wilding, Leech's Executive Assistant, had been on the same fruitless mission – she and Fred kept running into each other outside lock-ups with COME BACK IN NOVEMBER posted on them.

Beyond this point, the road to Sutton Mallet – a tricky proposition at the best of times – was impassable. The hamlet was just visible a mile off, black roofs stuck out of white drifts. The fields were usually low-lying, marshy and divided by shallow ditches called rhynes. In the last months, the marsh had set like concrete. The rhynes had turned into stinking runnels, with the barest threads of mud where water usually ran. Now, almost overnight, everything was deep-frozen and heavily frosted. The sun still shone, making a thousand glints, twinkles and refractions. But there was no heat.

Trees, already dead from dutch elm disease or roots loosened from the dry dirt, had fallen under the weight of what only Richard wasn't calling snow, and lay like giant blackened corpses on field-sized shrouds. Telephone poles were down too. No word had been heard

KIM NEWMAN

from Sutton Mallet in two days. A hardy postman had tried to get through on his bicycle, but not come back. A farmer set off to milk his cows was also been swallowed in the whiteness. A helicopter flew over, but the rotor blades slowed as heavy ice-sheaths grew on them. The pilot had barely made it back to Yeovilton Air Field.

Word had spread through "channels". Unnatural phenomena were Diogenes Club business, but Leech had to take an interest too – if only to prove that he wasn't behind the cold snap. Heather Wilding had made a call to Pall Mall, and officially requested the Club's assistance. That didn't happen often or, come to think of it, ever.

Leech looked across the white fields towards Sutton Mallet.

"So we walk," he said.

"It's safest to follow the ditches," advised Richard.

Neither bothered to lock their cars.

They clambered – as bulky and awkward as astronauts going EVA – over a stile to get into the field. The white carpet was virginal. As they tramped on, in the slight trough that marked the rime-filled rhyne, Richard kept looking sidewise at Leech. The man was breathing heavily inside his polar gear. Being incarnate involved certain frailties. But it would not do to underestimate a Great Enchanter.

Derek Leech had popped up apparently out of nowhere in 1961. A day after Colonel Zenf finally died in custody, he first appeared on the radar, making a freak run of successful long-shot bets at a dog track. Since then, he had made several interlocking empires. He was a close friend of Harold Wilson, Brian Epstein, Lord Leaves of Leng, Enoch Powell, Roman Polanski, Mary Millington and Jimmy Saville. He was into *everything* – newspapers (the down-market tabloid *Daily Comet* and the reactionary broadsheet *Sunday Facet*), pop records, telly, a film studio, book publishing, frozen foods, football, road-building, anti-depressants, famine relief, contraception, cross-channel hovercraft, draught lager, touring opera productions, market research, low-cost fashions, educational playthings. He had poked his head out of a trapdoor on *Batman* and expected to be recognized by Adam West – "it's not the *Clock King*, Robin, it's the English *Pop King*, Derek Leech". He appeared in his own adverts, varying his catch-phrase – "if I didn't love it, I wouldn't . . ." eat it, drink it, watch it, groove it, use it, wear it, bare it, shop it, stop it, make it, take it, kiss it, miss it, phone it, own it. He employed "radical visionary architect" Constant Drache to create "ultra-moderne work-place environments" for DLI premises and the ranks upon ranks of "affordable homes for hard-working families" cropping up at the edges of conurbations throughout the land. It was whispered there were private graveyards under many a "Derek Leech Close" or "Derek Leech Drive". Few had tangled with Derek Leech and managed better than a draw. Richard counted himself among the few, but also suspected their occasional path-crossings hadn't been serious.

They made fresh, ragged footprints across the empty fields. They were the only moving things in sight. It was quiet too. Richard saw birds frozen in mid-tweet on boughs, trapped in globules of ice. No smoke rose from the chimneys of Sutton Mallet. Of course, what with the heat wave, even the canniest country folk might have put off getting in a store of fuel for next winter.

"Refresh my memory," said Richard. "How many people are at your weather research station?"

"Five. The director, two junior meteorologists, one general dogs-body and a public relations-security consultant."

Richard had gone over what little the Club could dig up on them. Oddly, a DLI press release provided details of only *four* of the staff.

"Who's the director again?" he asked.

"We've kept that quiet, as you know," said Leech. "It's Professor Cleaver. Another Dick, which is to say a *Richard*."

"Might have been useful to be told that," said Richard, testily.

"I'm telling you now."

Professor Richard Cleaver, a former time-server at the Meteorological Office, had authored *The Coming Ice Age*, an alarmist paperback propounding the terrifying theory of World Cooling. According to Cleaver, natural thickening of the ozone layer in the high atmosphere would, if unchecked, lead to the expansion of the polar icecaps and a global climate much like the one currently obtaining in Sutton Mallet. Now, the man was in the middle of his own prediction, which was troubling. There were recorded cases of individuals who worried so much about things that they made them happen. The Professor could be such a Talent.

They huffed into Sutton Mallet, past the chapel, and went through a small copse. On the other side was the research station, a low-lying cinderblock building with temporary cabins attached. There were sentinels in the front yard.

"Are you in the habit of employing frivolous people, Mr Leech?"

"Only in my frivolous endeavours. I take the weather very seriously."

"I thought as much. Then who made those snowmen?"

They emerged from the rhyne and stood on hard-packed ice over the gravel forecourt of the DLI weather research facility. Outside the main doors stood four classic snowmen: three spheres piled one upon another as legs, torso and head, with twigs for arms, carrots for noses and coals for eyes, buttons and mouths. They were individualized by scarves and headgear – top hat, tam o'shanter, pith helmet and two toy bumblebees on springs attached to an Alice band.

Leech looked at the row. "Rime-men, surely?" he said, pointedly. "As a busybody, you appreciate accuracy."

There were no footprints around the snowmen. No scraped-bare patches or scooped-out drifts. As if they had been grown rather than made.

"A frosty welcoming committee?" suggested Leech.

Before anything happened, Richard *knew*. It was one of the annoyances of his sensitivity – premonitions that come just too late to do anything about.

Top Hat's headball shifted: it spat out a coal, which cracked against Richard's visor. He threw himself down, to avoid further missiles. Top Hat's head was packed with coals, which it could sick up and aim with deadly force.

Leech was as frozen in one spot as the snowmen weren't. This sort of thing happened to others, but not to *him*.

Pith Helmet, who had a cardboard handlebar moustache like Zebedee from *The Magic Roundabout*, rose on ice-column legs and stalked towards Leech, burly white arms sprouting to displace feeble sticks, wicked icicles extruding from powdery fists.

Tam and Bee-Alice circled round, making as if to trap Richard and Leech in the line of fire.

Richard got up, grabbed Leech's arm, and pulled him away from Pith Helmet. It was hard to run in polar gear, but they stumped past Tam and Bee-Alice before the circle closed, and legged it around the main building.

Another snowman loomed up in front of them. In a postman's cap, with a mailbag slung over its shoulder. It was a larger and looser thing than the others, more hastily made, with no face coals or carrot. They barrelled into the shape, which came apart, and sprawled in a tangle on the cold, cold ground – Richard felt the bite of black ice through his gauntlets as the heel of his hand jammed against grit. Under him was a dead but loose-limbed postman, grey-blue in the face, crackly frost in his hair. He had been inside the snowman.

The others were marching around the corner. Were there people inside them too? Somehow, they were frowning – perhaps it was in the angle of their headgear, as if brows were narrowed – and malice burned cold in their eye-coals.

Leech was on his feet first, hauling Richard upright.

Snow crawled around the postman again, forming a thick carapace. The corpse stood like a puppet, dutifully taking up its bag and cap, insistent on retaining its identity.

They were trapped between the snowmen. The five walking, hat-topped heaps had them penned.

Richard was tense, expecting ice-daggers to rip through his furs and into his heart. Leech reached into his snowsuit as if searching for his wallet – in this situation, money wasn't going to be a help. A proper Devil would have some hellfire about his person. Or at least a blowtorch. Leech – who had recorded a series of anti-smoking adverts – managed to produce a flip-top cigarette lighter. He made a flame, which didn't seem to phase the snowmen, and wheeled around, looking for the one to negotiate with. Leech was big on making deals.

"Try Top Hat," suggested Richard. "In cartoon terms, he's obviously the leader."

Leech held the flame near Top Hat's face. Water trickled, but froze again, giving Top Hat a tear-streaked, semi-transparent appearance. A slack face showed inside the ice.

"Who's in there?" asked Leech. "Cleaver?"

Top Hat made no motion.

A door opened, and a small, elderly man leaned out of the research station. He wore a striped scarf and a blue knit cap.

"No, Mr Leech," said Professor Richard Cleaver, "I'm in here. You lot, let them in, now. You've had your fun. For the moment."

The snowmen stood back, leaving a path to the back door. Cleaver beckoned, impatient.

"Do come on," he said. "It's fweezing out."

Richard looked at Leech and shrugged. The gesture was matched. They walked towards the back door.

The last snowman was Bee-Alice. As they passed, it reared up like a kid pretending to be a monster, and stuck out yard-long pseudo-pods of gleaming ice, barbed with jagged claws. Then it retracted its arms and silently chortled at the shivering humans.

"That one's a comedian," said Cleaver. "You have to watch out."

Leech squeezed past the Professor, into the building. Richard looked at the five snowmen, now immobile and innocent-seeming.

"Come on, whoever you are," urged Cleaver. "What are you waiting for? Chwistmas?"

Richard slipped off his sun-visor, then followed Leech.

II

"You in the van, wakey wakey," shouted someone, who was also hammering on the rear doors. "The world needs saving . . ."

"Again?" mumbled Jamie Chambers, waking up with another heat-headache and no idea of the time. Blackout shields on the windows kept out the daylight. Living in gloom was part of the Shade Legacy. He didn't even need Dad's night-vision goggles – which were around here somewhere – to see well enough in the dark.

He sorted through stiff black T-shirts for the freshest, then lay on his back and stuck his legs in the air to wriggle into skinny jeans. Getting dressed in the back of the van without doing himself an injury was a challenge. Sharp metal flanges underlay the carpet of sleeping bags, and any number of dangerous items were haphazardly hung on hooks or stuffed into cardboard boxes. When Bongo Foxe, the drummer in Transhumance, miraculously gained a girlfriend, he'd tactfully kicked Jamie out of the squat in Portobello Road. The keys and codes to Dad's old lair inside Big Ben were around somewhere, but Jamie could never get used to the constant ticking. Mum hated that too. Between addresses, the Black Van was his best option.

"Ground Control to Major Shade," called the hammerer, insistent and bored at the same time. Must be a copper.

"Hang on a mo," said Jamie, "I'm not decent."

"Hear that, Ness?" said the hammerer to a (female?) colleague. "Shall I pop the lock and give you a cheap thrill?"

One of the few pluses of van living, supposedly, was that gits like this couldn't find you. Jamie guessed he was being rousted by gits who could find *anybody*. For the second time this week. He'd already listened to Leech's twist, Heather Wilding. This'd be the other shower, the Diogenes Club. One of the things Jamie agreed with his father about was that it made sense to stay out of either camp and make your own way in the night.

Even parked in eternal shadow under railway arches, the van was like a bread oven with central heating. The punishing summer continued. After seconds, his T-shirt was damp. Within minutes, it'd be soaked and dried. This last six weeks, he'd sweated off pounds. Vron was freaked by how much his skeleton was showing.

He ran fingers through his crispy shock of raven hair (natural), checked a shaving mirror for blackheads (absent), undid special locks the hammerer oughtn't have been able to pop, and threw open the doors.

A warrant card was held in his face. Frederick Regent, New Scotland Yard (Detached). He was in plainclothes – blue jeans, red Fred Perry (with crimson sweat-patches), short hair, surly look. He couldn't have been more like a pig if he'd been oinking and had a curly tail. The girlfriend was a surprise – a red-haired bird with a *Vogue* face and a *Men Only* figure. She wore tennis gear – white plimsolls, knee-socks, shorts cut to look like a skirt, bikini top, Cardin cardigan – with matching floppy hat, milk-blank sunglasses (could she see through those?) and white lipstick.

"I'm Fred, this is Vanessa," said the Detached man. "You are James Christopher Chambers?"

"Jamie," he said.

Vanessa nodded, taking in his preference. She was the sympathetic one. Fred went for brusque. It was an approach, if tired.

"Jamie," said Fred, "we understand you've come into a doctorate?"

"Don't use it," he said, shaking his head. "It was my old man's game."

"But you have the gear," said Vanessa. She reached into the van and took Dad's slouch hat off a hook. "This is a vintage 'Dr Shade' item."

"Give that back," said Jamie, annoyed.

Vanessa handed it over meekly. He stroked the hat as if it were a kitten, and hung it up again. There was family history in the old titfer.

"At his age, he can't really be a doctor," said Fred. "Has there ever been an Intern Shade?"

"I'm not a student," he protested.

"No, you're one of those dropouts. Had a place at Manchester University, but left after a term. Couldn't hack the accents oop North?"

"The band was taking off. All our gigs are in London."

"Don't have to justify your life-choices to us, mate. Except one." Fred wasn't being quite so jokey.

"I think you should listen," said Vanessa, close to his ear. "The world really does need saving."

Jamie knew as much from Heather Wilding. She'd been more businesslike, drenched in Charlie, her cream suit almost-invisibly damp under the arms, two blouse buttons deliberately left unfastened to show an armoured white lace foundation garment.

"The other lot offered a retainer," he said. "Enough for a new amp."

"We heard you'd been approached," said Vanessa. "And were reluctant. Very wise."

Wilding hinted Transhumance might be signed to a Derek Leech label. They didn't only put out moaning hippie box sets and collected bubblegum hits.

"You won't need an amp in the ice age," said Fred. "They'll be burning pop groups to keep going for a few more days."

"Yeah, I'm already shivering," said Jamie, unpicking wet cotton from his breastbone. "Chills up my spine."

"All this heat is a sign of the cold, they say."

"You what?"

Fred cracked a laugh. "Trust us, there could be a cold spell coming."

"Roll on winter, mate."

"Careful what you wish for, Jamie," said Vanessa.

She found his Dad's goggles in a box of eight-track tapes, and slipped them over his head. He saw clearly through the old, tinted glass.

"Saddle up and ride, cowboy," she said. "We're putting together a posse. Just for this round-up. No long-term contract involved."

"Why do you need me?" he asked.

"We need *everybody*," said Fred, laying a palm on the van and wincing – it was like touching a griddle. "Especially you, shadow-boy. You've got a licence to drive and your own transport. Besides standing on the front lines for democracy and decent grub, you can give some of your new comrades a lift to the front. And I don't mean Brighton."

Jamie didn't like the sound of this. "What?" he protested.

"Congratulations, Junior Shade. You've got a new backing group. Are you ready to rock and – indeed – roll?"

Jamie felt that a trap had snapped around him. He was going into the family business after all.

He was going to be a doctor.

III

Inside the research station, crystals crunched underfoot and granulated on every surface. White stalactites hung from doorframes and the ceiling. Windows were iced over and stunted pot-plants frost-bitten solid. Even light bulbs had petals of ice.

Powdery banks of frost (indoor rime? snow, even?) drifted against cabinets of computers. Trudged pathways of clear, deep footprints ran close to the walls, and they kept to them – leaving most of the soft, white, glistening carpet untouched. Richard saw little trails had been blazed into the rooms, keeping mainly to the edges and corners with rare, nimbler tracks to desks or workbenches. The prints had been used over again, as if their maker (Professor Cleaver?) were leery of trampling virgin white and trod carefully on the paths he had made when the cold first set in.

The Professor led them through the cafeteria, where trestle tables and chairs were folded and stacked away to clear the greatest space possible. Here, someone had been playing – making snow-angels, by lying down on the thick frost and moving their arms to make wing-shapes. Richard admired the care that had been taken. The silhouettes – three of them, with different wings, as if writing something in semaphore – matched Cleaver's tubby frame, but Richard couldn't imagine why he had worked so hard on something so childish. Leech had said he didn't employ frivolous people.

If anything, it was colder indoors than out. Richard felt sharp little chest-pains when he inhaled as if he were flash-freezing his alveoli. His exposed face was numb. He worried that if he were to touch his moustache, half would snap off.

They were admitted to the main laboratory. A coffee percolator was frosted up, its jug full of frothy brown solid. On a shelf stood a goldfish bowl, ice bulging over the rim. A startled fish was trapped in the miniature arctic. Richard wondered if it was still alive – like those dinosaurs they found in the 1950s. Here, the floor had been walked over many times, turned to orange slush and frozen again, giving it a rough moon-surface texture. Evidently, this was where the Professor lived.

Richard idly fumbled open a ringbinder that lay on a desk, and pressed his mitten to brittle blue paper.

"Paws off," snapped Cleaver, snatching the file away and hugging it. "That's tip-top secwet."

"Not from me," insisted Leech, holding out his hand. "I sign the cheques, remember. You work for me."

If Derek Leech signed his own cheques, Richard would be surprised.

"My letter of wesignation is in the post," said Cleaver. He blinked furiously when he spoke, as if simultaneously translating in Morse. Rhotacism made him sound childish. How cruel was it to give a speech impediment a technical name that sufferers couldn't properly pronounce? "I handed it to the postman personally. I think he twied to deliver it to you outside. Vewy dedicated, the Post Office. Not snow, nor hail, and so on and so forth."

Leech looked sternly at the babbling little man.

"In that case, you'd better hand over all your materials and leave this facility. Under the circumstances, the severance package will not be generous."

Cleaver wagged a shaking hand at his former employer, not looking him in the eye. His blinks and twitches shook his whole body. He was laughing.

"In my letter," he continued, "I explain fully that this facility has declared independence from your organization. Indeed, fwom all Earthly authowity. There are pwecedents. I've also witten to the Pwime Minister and the Met Office."

Leech wasn't used to this sort of talk from minions. Normally, Richard would have relished the Great Enchanter's discomfort. But it wasn't clear where his own – or, indeed, anybody's – best interests were in Ice Station Sutton Mallet.

"Mr Leech, I know," said Cleaver, "not that we've ever met. I imagine you thought you had more important things to be bothewing with than poor old Clever Dick Cleaver's weather wesearch. Jive music and porn and so forth. I hear you've started a holiday company. Fun in the sun and all that. Jolly good show. Soon you'll be able to open bobsled runs on the Costa Bwava. I'm not surprised you've shown your face now. I expected it and I'm glad you're here. You, I had planned for. No, the face I don't know . . . don't know at all . . . is *yours*."

Cleaver turned to Richard.

"Richard Jeperson," he introduced himself. "I'm from . . ."

". . . the *Diogenes Club*!" said Cleaver, viciously. "Yes, yes, yes, of course. I see the gleam. The wighteous gleam. Know it of old. The insuffewability. Is that fwightful Miss Cathewina Kaye still alive?"

"Catriona," corrected Richard. "Yes."

Currently, Catriona Kaye was Acting Chairman of the Ruling Cabal of the Diogenes Club. She had not sought the position. After the death of Edwin Winthrop, her partner in many things, no one else had been qualified. Richard was not yet ready to leave active service, and had a nagging feeling he wouldn't be suited to the Ruling Cabal anyway. There was talk of reorganizing – "modernizing" – the Club and some of their rivals in Whitehall were bleating about "account-ability" and "payment by results". If it weren't arcanely self-financing, the Club would have been dissolved or absorbed long ago.

"If it weren't for Cathewina Kaye, and a disservice she did me many many years ago, I might have taken a diffewent path. You know about this, Mr Jeperson?"

A penny, long-teetering at the lip of a precipice, dropped – in slow motion, setting memory mechanisms ticking with each turn.

"Richard Cleaver? Clever Dick. You called yourself Clever Dick. That's who you are!"

"That's who I was . . . until that w-woman came along. She hates people like me . . . like both of you, pwobably . . . she only likes people who are n-normal. People who can't *do* anything. You know what I mean. *Normal*."

He drew out the word, with contempt. Richard remembered a time – at school, as a young man – when *he* might have given the word such a knife-twist. Like Dick Cleaver, he had manifested a Talent early. While Cleaver demonstrated excess brain capacity, Richard showed excess feeling. Insights did not always make him happy. Ironically, it was Catriona – not his father or Edwin Winthrop – who most helped him cope with his Talent, to connect with people rather than become estranged. Without her, he might be a stuttering, r-dropping maniac.

"It was never about who you were, Cleaver," said Richard, trying to be kind. "It was about what you did."

Fury boiled behind Cleaver's eyes.

"*I didn't do anything!* We were the Splendid Six, and she took us apart, one by one, working in secwet with your dwatted Diogenes Club. We were heroes . . . Blackfist, Lord Piltdown, the Blue Stweak . . . and sh-she made us *small*, twied to make us *normal*. I'm the last of us, you know. The Splendid *One*. The Bwightest Boy in the World. The others are all dead."

Cleaver was coming up to pensionable age, but he was as frozen inside as his goldfish – still eleven, and poisonous.

"If I suffered a speech impediment like yours, I'd avoid words like 'dratted'," commented Leech. "All this ancient history is fascinating, I'm sure. I know who you used to be, Professor. I don't hire anyone without knowing everything about them first. But I don't see what it has to do with all this . . . this cold business."

A sly look crept into Cleaver's eye. An I-know-a-secret-you're-not-going-to-like look.

"I wather think I've pwoved my point, Mr Leech. You've wead my book, *The Coming Ice Age*?"

"I had someone read it and summarize the findings for me," said Leech, offhandedly. "Very convincing, very alarming. It's why you were head-hunted – at a salary three times what you got at the Met – to head my weather research program."

What exactly had Derek Leech been doing here? Scientific weather control? For reasons which were now all too plain, Richard did not like the notion of a Great Enchanter with command over the elements.

"I employ the best, and you were the best man for this job. What you did as a schoolboy was irrelevant. I didn't even care that you were mad."

Clever Dick Cleaver sputtered.

"Sorry to be blunt, pal, but you are. I can show you the psych reports. Your insanity should not have hindered your ability to fulfil your contract. Quite the contrary. Derek Leech International has a policy of easing the lot of the mentally ill by finding them suitable positions. We consider it our social service remit, repaying a community that has given us so much."

Richard knew all about that. Myra Lark, acknowledged leader in field of shaping minds to suit the requirements of government and industry, was on Leech's staff. Some jobs you really had to be mad to take. Dr Lark's, for instance.

"Your book convinced me it could happen. World Cooling. And only drastic action can forestall the catastrophe. With the full resources of DLI at your disposal, I was expecting happier results. Not this . . . this big fridge."

Cleaver smiled again.

"If you'd actually wead my book, you wouldn't be so surprised. Tell him, Jeperson."

Leech looked at Richard, awaiting enlightenment.

"Professor Cleaver writes that an imminent ice age will lead to world-wide societal collapse and, in all probability, the extinction of the human race."

"Yes, and . . . ?"

"He does *not* write that this would be a bad thing."

Realization dawned in Leech's eyes. Cleaver grinned broadly, showing white dentures with odd, cheap blue settings.

Derek Leech had given his weather control project to someone who *wanted* winter to come and freeze everything solid. Isidore Persano and his worm would be proud.

"What about the snowmen?" Leech asked.

"I was wondewing when you'd get to them. The snowmen. Yes. I'm not alone in this. I have fwiends. One fwiend, mainly. One big fwiend. I call her the Cold. You can call her the End."

IV

He was supposed to park outside the Post Office Tower and wait for the other recruits. One of the group would have further instructions and, he was promised, petrol money. Jamie was off to the Winter War.

Now he'd (provisionally) taken the Queen's Shilling, he wondered whether the Diogenes Club just wanted him as a handy, unpaid chauffeur, ferrying cannon fodder about. Dad wouldn't have thought a lot of that. Still, Jamie only wanted to dip a toe in the waters. He was leery about the shadow life. The Shade Legacy hadn't always been happy, as Mum would tell him at the drop of a black fedora with razors in the brim. At the moment, he was more interested in Transhumance – especially if they could find a better, preferably celibate drummer . . . and a new bass-player, a decent PA and enough songs to bump up their set to an hour without reprises. Vron had been promising new lyrics for weeks, but said the bloody heat made it hard to get into the proper mood. Perhaps he should scrub Transhumance and look for a new band.

The GPO Tower, a needle bristling with dish-arrays, looked like a leftover design from *Stingray*. The revolving restaurant at the summit, opened by Wedgy Benn and Billy Butlin, stopped turning in 1971, after an explosion the public thought was down to the Angry Brigade. Jamie knew the truth. His father's last "exploit" before enforced retirement had been the final defeat of his long-time enemies, the Dynamite Boys. The Tower was taken over by the now-octogenarian Boys, who planned to use the transmitters to send a coded signal to activate the lizard stems of every human brain in the Greater London area and turn folks into enraged animals. Dad stopped them by setting off their own bombs.

Jamie found a parking space in the thin shadow of the tower, which shifted within minutes. Inside the van, stale air began to boil again. Even with the windows down, there was no relief.

"Gather, darkness," he muttered. He hadn't Dad's knack with shadows, but he could at least whip up some healthy gloom. The sky was cloudless, but a meagre cloud-shadow formed around the van. It was too much effort to maintain, and he let it go. In revenge, the sun got hotter.

"Jamie Chambers," said a girl.

He looked out at her. She was dressed for veldt or desert: leather open-toe sandals, fawn culottes, baggy safari jacket, utility belt with pouches, burnt orange sunglasses the size of saucers, leopard-pattern headscarf, Australian bush hat. In a summer when Zenith the Albino sported a nut-brown suntan, her exposed lower face, forearms and calves were pale to the point of colourlessness. People always said Jamie – as instinctively nocturnal as his father – should get out in the sun more, but this girl made him look like an advert for Air Malta. He would have guessed she was about his own age.

"Call me Gené," she said. "I know your aunt Jenny. And your mother, a bit. We worked together a long time ago, when she was Kentish Glory."

Mum had stopped wearing a moth-mask and film-winged leotards decades before Jamie was born. Gené was much older than nineteen.

He got out of the van, and found he was several inches taller than her.

"I'm from the Diogenes Club," she said, holding up an envelope. "You're our ride to Somerset. I've got maps and money here. And the rest of the new bugs."

Three assorted types, all less noticeable than Gené, were loitering.

"Keith, Susan and . . . Sewell, isn't it?"

A middle-aged, bald-headed man stepped forward and nodded. He wore an old, multi-stained overcoat, fingerless Albert Steptoe gloves and a tightly wound woolly scarf as if he expected a sudden winter. His face was unlined, as if he rarely used it, but sticky marks around his mouth marked him as a sweet-addict. He held a paper bag, and was chain-chewing liquorice allsorts.

"Sewell Head," said Gené, tapping her temple. "He's one of the *clever* ones. And one of theirs. Derek Leech fetched him out of a sweet shop. Ask him anything, and he'll know."

"What's Transhumance?" asked Jamie.

"A form of vertical livestock rotation, practised especially in Switzerland," said Sewell Head, popping a pink coconut wheel into his mouth. "Also a London-based popular music group that has never released a record or played to an audience of more than fifty people."

"Fifty is a record for some venues, pal."

"I told you he'd *know*," said Gené. "Does he look evil to you? Or is Hannah Arendt right about banality. He's behaved himself so far. No decapitated kittens. The others are undecideds, not ours, not theirs. Wavering."

"I'm not wavering," said the other girl, Susan. "I'm neutral."

She wore jeans and a purple T-shirt, and hid behind her long brown hair. She tanned like most other people and had pinkish sunburn scabs on her arms. Jamie wondered if he'd seen her before. She must be a year or two older than him, but gave off a studenty vibe.

"Susan Rodway," explained Gené. "You might remember her from a few years ago. She was on television, and there was a book about her. She was a spoon-bender. Until she stopped."

"It wore off," said the girl, shrugging

"That's her story, and she's sticking to it. According to tests, she's off the ESP charts. Psychokinesis, pyrokinesis, psychometry, telepathy, levitation, clairvoyance, clairaudience. She has senses they don't even have Latin names for yet. Can hard-boil an egg with a nasty look."

Susan waved her hands comically, and nothing happened.

"She's pretending to be normal," said Gené. "Probably reading your mind right now."

Irritated, Susan snapped. "One mind I *can't* read, Gené, is yours. So we'll have to fall back on the fount of all factoids. Mr Head . . . what can you tell us about Geneviève Dieudonné?"

Sewell Head paused in mid-chew, as if collecting a ledger from a shelf in his mental attic, took a deep breath, and began "Born in 1416, in the Duchy of Burgundy, Geneviève Dieudonné is mentioned in . . ."

"That's quite enough of that," said Gené, shutting him off.

Jamie couldn't help noticing how sharp the woman's teeth were. Did she have the ghost of a French accent?

"I'm Keith Marion," said the kid in the group, smiling nervously. It didn't take ESP to see he was trying to smooth over an awkward moment. "Undecided."

He stuck out his hand, which Jamie shook. He had a plastic tag around his wrist. Even looking straight at Keith, Jamie couldn't fix a face in his mind. The tag was the only thing about him he could remember.

"We have Keith on day-release," said Gené, proudly. He has a condition. It's named after him. Keith Marion Syndrome."

Jamie let go of the boy's hand.

"I don't mind being out," said Keith. "I was sitting around waiting for my O Level results. Or CSEs. Or call-up papers. Or . . ."

He shrugged, and shut up.

"We make decisions all the time, which send us on varying paths," said Gené. "Keith can *see* his other paths. The ones he might have taken. Apparently, it's like being haunted by ghosts of yourself. All those *doppelgängers*."

"If I concentrate, I can anchor myself here," said Keith. "Assuming this is the real here. It might not be. Other heres feel just as real. And they bleed through more than I'd like."

Sewell Head was interested for a moment, as if filing some fact nugget away for a future *Brain of Britain* quiz. Then he was chewing Bertie Bassett's licorice cud again.

"He's seen two other entirely different lives for me," said Gené.

"I'm having enough trouble with just this one," commented Susan.

"So's everybody," said the pale girl. "That's why we've been called – the good, the bad and the undecided."

She opened her envelope and gave Jamie a map.

"We're heading West. Keith knows the territory. He was born in Somerset."

Jamie opened the rear doors of the van. He had tidied up a bit, and distributed cushions to make the space marginally more comfortable.

Susan borrowed a fifty pence coin from him and the foursome tossed to see who got to sit up front with the driver. Keith called "owl", then admitted to Gené his mind had slipped into a reality with different coins. Head droned statistics and probabilities but couldn't decide what to call, and lost to Susan by default. In the final, Gené called tails. The seven-edged coin spun surprisingly high – and slower than usual – then landed heads-up in Susan's palm.

"Should have known not to toss up with a telekinetic," said Gené, in good humour. "It's into the back of the van with the boys for me."

She clambered in and pulled the door shut. There was some kicking and complaining as they got sorted out.

Susan gave the coin back to Jamie. It was bent at a right angle.

"Oops," she said, arching her thick eyebrows attractively.

"You said it wore off."

"It did. Mostly."

They got into the front of the van. Jamie gave Susan the map and appointed her navigator.

"She can do it with her eyes closed," said Gené, poking her head through between the high-backed front seats.

"Just follow the Roman road," said Keith.

Susan held the map up the wrong way, and chewed a strand of her hair. "I hate to break it to you, but I'm not that good at orienteering. I can tell you about the three people – no, four – who have owned this map since it was printed. Including some interesting details about Little Miss Burgundy. But I don't know if we're best off with the A303."

Gené took the map away and playfully swatted Susan with it.

"Mr Head," she began, "what's the best route from the Post Office Tower, in London, to Alder, in Somerset?"

"Shortest or quickest?"

"Quickest."

Sewell Head swallowed an allsort and recited directions off the top of his head.

"I hope someone's writing this down."

"No need, Jamie," said Gené. "Tell him, Susan."

"It's called eidetic memory," said Susan. "Like photographic, but for sounds and the spoken word. I can replay what he said in snippets over the next few hours. I don't even need to understand what he means. Now, 'turn left into New Cavendish Street, and drive towards Marylebone High Street . . .'"

Relaying Sewell Head's directions, Susan imitated his monotone. She sounded like a machine.

"One day all cars will have gadgets that do this," said Keith.

Jamie doubted that, but started driving anyway.

V

An hour or so into Professor Cleaver's rhotacist monologue, Richard began tuning out. Was hypothermia setting in? Despite thermals and furs, he was freezing. His upper arms ached as if they'd been hit with hammers. His jaws hurt from clenching to prevent teeth-chattering. He no longer had feeling in his fingers and toes. Frozen exhalation made ice droplets in his moustache.

Cold didn't bother Clever Dick. He was one of those mad geniuses who never outgrew a need for an audience. Being clever didn't count unless the people who he was cleverer than knew it. The Professor walked around the room, excited, impassioned, frankly barking. He touched ice-coated surfaces with bare hands Richard assumed were freezer-burned to nervelessness. He puffed out clouds of frost and delighted in tiny falls of indoor hail. He constantly fiddled with his specs – taking them off to scrape away thin film of iced condensation with bitten-to-the-quick thumbnails, putting them back on until they misted up and froze over again. And he kept talking. Talking, talking, talking.

As a child, Dick Cleaver had been indulged – and listened to – far too often. He'd been an adventurer, in the company of immature grown-ups who didn't take the trouble to teach him how to be a real boy. When that career ended, it had been a mind-breaking shock for Clever Dick. Richard had read Catriona Kaye's notes on the Case of the Splendid Six. Her pity for the little boy was plain as purple ink, though she also loathed him. An addendum (initialled by Edwin Winthrop) wickedly noted that Clever Dick suffered such extreme adolescent acne that he'd become known as "Spotted Dick". Angry pockmarks still marred the Professor's chubby cheeks. As an adult, he had become a champion among bores and deliberately entered a profession that required talking at length about the most tedious (yet inescapable) subject in Great British conversation – the weather. Turned out nice again, eh what? Lovely weather for ducks. Bit nippy round the allotments. Cleaver's bestselling book was impossible to read to the end, which was why many took *The Coming Ice Age* for a warning. It was actually a threat, a plan of action, a promise. To Professor Cleaver, the grip of glaciation was a consummation devoutly to be wished.

Behind his glasses, Cleaver's eyes gleamed. He might as well have traced hearts on frozen glass with a fingertip. He was a man in love. Perhaps for the first time. A late, great, literally all-consuming love.

Derek Leech, who rarely made the mistake of explaining *his* evil plans at length, had missed the point when he funded Cleaver's research. That alarmed Richard – Leech might be many things, but he was not easily fooled. Cleaver came across as a ranting, immature idiot with a freak IQ, but had serious connections. If anything could trump a Great Enchanter, it was the Cold.

"The Cold was here first," continued Cleaver. "Before the dawn of man, she weigned over evewything. She was the planet's first evolved intelligence, a giant bwain consisting of a near-infinite number of ice cwystals. A gweat white blanket, sewene and undying. When the glaciers weceded, she went to her west. She hid in a place out of weach until now. Humanity is just a blip. She'd have come back eventually, even without me. She was not dead, but only sleeping."

"Lot of that about," said Leech. "King Arthur, Barbarossa, Great Cthulhu, the terracotta warriors, Gary Glitter. They'll all be back."

Cleaver sputtered with anger. He didn't like being interrupted when he was rhapsodizing.

"You won't laugh when blood fweezes in your veins, Mr Leech. When your eyes pop out on ice-stalks."

Leech flapped his arms and contorted his face in mock panic.

"How many apocalypses have come and gone and fizzled in this century, Jeperson?" Leech asked, airily. "Four? Five? Worm War, Wizard War, Water War, Weird War, World War . . . and that's not counting Princess Cuckoo of Faerie, Little Rosie Farrar as the Whore of Babylon, the Scotch Streak and the Go-Codes, the Seamouth Warp, *six* alien invasions counting two the Diogenes Club doesn't think I know about, two of my youthful indiscretions you don't think I know you know about, and the ongoing Duel of the Seven Stars."

"Don't the Water War, the Scotch Streak and the Egyptian Stars count as alien invasions?" asked Richard. "I mean, *technically*, the Deep Ones are terrestrial, but your Great Squidhead Person is from *outer* outer space. And the other two bothers were down to un-welcome meteorites."

"You've a point. Make that *eight* alien invasions. The Water War was a local skirmish, though. Extra-dimensional, rather than extra-terrestrial . . ."

Cleaver hopped from one foot to the other. The little boy in him was furious that grown-ups were talking over his head. If he hadn't been chucked off his course in life – by Catriona, as he saw it – he might have been in on the Secret History. The Mystic Maharajah, oldest of the Splendid Six, had carried a spear (well, an athane) in the Worm War. Captain Rattray (Blackfist), another Splendid, emerged from disgrace to play a minor role in the Wizard War. Teenage Clever Dick was too busy squeezing pus-filled blemishes to get involved in that set-to. Child sleuths, like child actors, seldom grew up to be stars. Richard was named after Richard Riddle, the famous Boy Detective of the turn of the century (so was Cleaver, probably). Few knew what, if anything, happened to Riddle in later life.

"You won't listen, you won't listen!"

"Have you considered that the Cold might be extra-dimensional rather than antediluvian?" asked Leech, offhandedly. "Seems to me a bright young man of my acquaintance reported something similar in a continuum several path-forks away from our own. It cropped up there in 1963 or so, during the Big Freeze. Didn't do much harm."

"You can't say anything about her," insisted Cleaver, almost squeaking.

"Interesting that you see the Cold as a her," continued Leech. "Then again, I suppose women have been 'cold' to you all your life. You made a poor impression on Miss Kaye, from all accounts. And she's always been generous in her feelings."

Cleaver's face tried to burn. Blood rose in his blueing cheeks, forming purplish patches. He might break out again.

"I know what you're twying to do, you wotter!"

Leech laughed out loud. Richard couldn't help but join in.

"I'm a 'wotter', am I? A wotten wetched wight woyal wascally wotter, perhaps?"

"You're twying to get me angwy!"

"Angwy? Are you succumbing to woawing wed wage?"

Cleaver couldn't help sounding like a toffee-nosed Elmer Fudd. It was cruel of Leech to taunt him Fourth Form fashion. Richard remembered bullies at his schools. With him, it had been his darker skin, his literal lack of background, the numbers tattooed on his wrist, his longer-than-regulation hair, his *eyelashes* for heaven's sake. He had learned early on to control his temper. If he didn't, people got hurt.

"You missed one off your list of apocalypses," said Cleaver, trying to be sly again. "Perfidious Albion. That was an extwa-dimensional thweat. An entire weality out to oblitewate the world. And we stopped it. In 1926! Not your Diogenes Club or those Undertaker fellows, but us! The Splendid Six! Clever Dick, yes. They first called me that to poke fun, but I pwoved it was a wightful name. I stood with the gwown-ups. Blackfist and Lord Piltdown and the Blue Stweak . . ."

". . . and Aviatrix and the Mystic Maharajah," footnoted Richard.

"Should never have let girls and foreigners in," muttered Cleaver. "That's where the wot started."

"Chandra Nguyen Seth turned out to be Sid Ramsbottom, from Stepney," said Richard. "As British as corned-beef fritters and London fog. Used boot polish on his face for years. He might have been Mystic, but he was no Maharajah."

Cleaver didn't take this in – he was a ranter, not a listener. "Seth and the girl *helped*," he admitted. "The Splendids saved the day. Beat back the Knights of Perfidious Albion. Saved evewyone and evewything. Without us, you'd all be cwawling subjects of Queen Morgaine. I was given a medal, by the pwoper King. I was witten up in *Bwitish Pluck*, for months and months. I had an arch-nemesis. Wicked William, my own cousin. I bested the bounder time after time. Made him cwy and cwy and cwy. There was a Clever Dick Club, and ten thousand boys were members. No g-girls allowed! I was in the Lord Mayor's Show and invited to tea at the palace *twice*. I could have been in your wotten old wars. Won them, even. In half the time. Dark Ones, Deep Ones, Wet Ones, Weird Ones. I could have thwashed the lot of 'em and been home before bed-time. But you couldn't leave me alone, could you? No woom in the Gwown-Ups' Club for Clever Dick. Not for any of the Splendids. That w-w-woman had to bwing us down to her level."

"He means your club now," said Leech. "In some circumstances, I'd agree with him."

"You'd both have to climb a mountain to be on a level with Catriona Kaye."

"Touché," said Leech.

"You're both just twying to change the subject."

"Oh dearie me," said Leech. "Let's talk about the weather again, shall we? It's an endless topic of fascination. I was getting bored with writing heatwave headlines . . ."

Leech's *Daily Comet* had been censured for running the headline SWEATY BETTY over a paparazzo shot of Queen Elizabeth II perspiring (in ladylike manner) at an official engagement.

"How do you think he's done it, Jeperson? Science or magic?"

"No such thing as magic," said Cleaver, quickly.

"Says the boy whose best friend used a *magic diamond* to become hard as nails. What was his name again, Captain . . . ?"

"Wattway!" shouted the Professor, duped into a using a double-r name. When he wasn't angry, he spoke carefully, avoiding the letter "r" if possible. Sadly, Cleaver was angry most of the time. "Dennis Wattway! Blackfist!"

"Not a magic person, then?"

"The Fang of Night was imbued with an unknown form of wadioactivity. It altered Captain Wattway's physiology."

"I could pull a hat out of the air and a rabbit out of the hat, and you'd say I accessed a pocket universe."

"A tessewact, yes."

"There's no 'weasoning' with you. So, Jeperson, what do you think?"

Richard wondered whether he should follow Leech's tactic, getting the Professor more and more flustered in the hope of breaking him down and finding a way to roll back the Cold. It was all very well unless Clever Dick decided to stop trying to impress his visitors and just had the snowmen stick icicles through their heads.

"I assume the phenomenon is localized," said Richard. "Deep under the levels. There must have been a pocket of the Cold. Once it was all over the world, a giant organism – a symbiote, drawing nourishment from the rock, from what vegetation it let live. When the Great Ice Age ended, it shrank, shedding most of its bulk into the seas or ordinary ice, but somewhere – maybe in several spots around the world – it left parcels of itself."

"No, you're wong, wong, wong," said Cleaver, nastily.

"Is that a Chinese laundry?" said Leech. "Wong, Wong and Wong."

"*Wwong*," insisted Cleaver. "Ewwoneous. Incowwect. Not wight."

He sputtered, frustrated not to find an r-free synonym for "wrong".

"The Cold didn't hide below the gwound, but beyond the spect-wum of tempewature. Until I weached out for her."

"I see," continued Richard. "With the equipment generously supplied by your former employer, you made contact with the Cold. You woke up Sleeping Beauty . . . with what? A kiss. No, a signal. An alarm-call. No, you had instructions. What common language could you have? Music, Movement and Mime? Doubtful. Mathematics? No, the Cold hasn't got that sort of a mind. A being on her scale has no use for any number other than 'one'."

Richard looked about the room, at the thickening ice that coated everything, at the white dusting over the ice. Tiny, tiny jewels glittered in the powder. He made a leap – perhaps by himself, perhaps snatching from Cleaver's buzzing mind.

"Crystals," he mused. "'A near-infinite number', you said. Each unique and distinctive. An endless alphabet of characters. Chinese cubed."

Cleaver clapped his hands, delighted.

"Yes, *snowflakes*! I can wead them. It cost a gweat deal of Mr Leech's money to learn how. First, to wead them. Then to *make* them."

"Your bird must think you're a right mug," said Leech, sourly. "She must have seen you coming for a million years."

"Eighteen million years, at my best guess," said Cleaver, smugness crumpling. He didn't like it when his goddess was disrespected.

"How do you make snowflakes?" Richard asked. "I mean, snow is frozen rain . . ."

Cleaver was disgusted, as Richard knew he would be. "You don't know anything! Fwozen rain is *sleet*!"

Leech laughed bitterly as Richard was paid back for his pedantry.

"Snow forms when *clouds* are fwozen," said Cleaver, lecturing. "You need humidity *and* cold. It's vapour to ice, not water to ice. Synthetic snow cwystals have been made in vapour diffusion chambers since 1963. But no one else has got beyond dendwitic stars. *Janet and John* cwystallogwaphy! The colder you get inside the box, the more complex the cwystals – hollow plates, columns on plates, multiply capped columns, isolated bullets, awwowhead twins, multiple cups, skeletal forms. Then combinations of forms. I can sculpt them, shape them, *carve* them. *Finnegan's Wake* cwystallogwaphy! You need extwemes of tempewature, and a gweat deal of electwicity. We dwained the national gwid. There was a black-out, wemember?"

A week or so ago, a massive power-cut had paralysed an already-sluggish nation. Officially, it was down to too many fans plugged in and fridge-doors left open.

"You knew about that?" Richard asked Leech.

The Great Enchanter shrugged.

"He *authowised* it!" crowed the Professor, in triumph. "He had no idea what he was doing. None of the others did, either. Kellett and Bakhtinin. McKendwick. And certainly not your spy, Mr Pouncey!"

Leech had listed the other staff: "two junior meteorologists, one general dogsbody and a public relations-security consultant".

"McKendwick had an inkling. He knew I was welaying instwuctions. He made the Box – the vapour diffusion chamber – to my specifications. He kept asking why all the extwa conductors. Why the *designs*? But he cawwied out orders like a good little wesearch assistant."

Cleaver stood by an odd apparatus that Richard had taken for a generator. It consisted of a lot of blackened electrical coils, bright copper slashes showing through shredded rubber. There was a cracked bakelite instrument panel, and – in the heart of the coils – a metal box the size of a cigarette packet, ripped open at one edge. It had exploded *outward*. The metal was covered with intricate, etched symbols. Line after line of branching, hexagonally symmetrical star-shapes. Representational snowflakes, but also symbols of power. Here, science shaded into magic. This was not only an experimental apparatus, but an incantation in copper-wire and steel-plate, a conjuring machine.

"It's burned out now," he said, slapping it, "but it did the twick. In the Box, I took the tempewature down to minus four hundwed and fifty-nine point seven thwee degwees Fahwenheit!"

Richard felt a chill wafting from the ice-slopes of Hell.

"We're supposed to be impressed?" said Leech.

"You can't get colder than *absolute zero*," said Richard. "That's minus four hundred and fifty-nine point *six seven* Fahrenheit."

"I have bwoken the Cold Bawwier," announced Cleaver, proudly.

"Not using physics, you haven't."

"So what was it, magic?"

Richard wasn't going to argue the point. There weren't instruments capable of measuring theoretically impossible temperatures, but Richard suspected the Professor wasn't making an idle boast. Within his Box, reality had broken down. Quantum mechanics gave up, packed its bags and went to Marbella, and the supernatural house-sat for a while.

"It's where I found the Cold. Minus point zewo six. She was sleeping there. A basic hexagon. I almost missed her. Bweaking so-called absolute zewo was so much of an achievement. McKendwick saw her first. The little lab assistant took her for pwoof we had failed. There shouldn't *be* ordinawy cwystals at minus point zewo six. And she wasn't ordinawy. McKendwick found that out."

Richard assumed McKendrick was the snowman with the tam o'shanter. The others must be the rest of Cleaver's staff. Kellett, Bakhtinin, Pouncey. And whoever the postman was. What about the few other residents of Sutton Mallet? Frozen in their homes? Ready to join the snow army?

"Fwom a hexagon, she gwew, into a dendwitic star, with more stars on each bwanch. A hexagon squared. A hexagon cubed."

"Six to the power of six to the power of six?"

"That's wight, Mr Leech. Amusing, eh what? Then, she became a *cluster* of cwystals. A snowflake. Then . . . whoosh. The Box burst. The power went out. But she was fwee. She came fwom beyond the zewo bawwier. A pinpoint speck. Woom tempewature plummeted. The walls iced over, and the fweeze spwead out of the building. She took the village in hours. She took McKendwick and the others. Soon, she'll be evewywhere."

"What about you?" asked Leech. "Will you be the Snow Queen's 'Pwime Minister'?"

"Oh no, I'm going to die. Just like you. When the Cold spweads, over the whole planet, I'll be happy to die with the west of the failed expewiment, humanity. It's quite inevitable. Hadn't you noticed . . . when you were coming here . . . hadn't you noticed she's gwowing? I think we'll be done in thwee months or so, give or take an afternoon."

Richard whistled.

"At least now we know the deadline," he told Leech, slipping the hypodermic out of his hairy sleeve.

Cleaver frowned, wondering if he should have given so much away. It was too late to consider the advisability of ranting.

Leech took hold of the Professor and slammed his forehead against the older man's, smashing his spectacles. A coconut shy crack resounded. Cleaver staggered, smearing his flowing moustache of blood.

"Yhou bwoke mhy nhose!"

Richard slid the needle into Cleaver's neck. He tensed and went limp.

"One down," said Leech. "One to go."

"Yes, but she's a big girl. What are the snowmen doing?"

Leech looked out of the window, and said, "most have wandered off, but the postman's still there, behaving himself."

"While Cleaver's out, they shouldn't move," Richard said, unsure of himself. "Unless the Cold gets angry."

Richard plopped the Professor in a swivel chair and wheeled him into a corner, out of the way. Leech unslung his giant backpack and undid white canvas flaps to reveal a metal box studded with dials and switches like an old-time wireless receiver. He unwound an electrical cord and plugged it into a socket that wasn't iced over. His bulky gadget lit up and began to hum. He opened a hatch and pulled out a trimphone handset, then cranked a handle and asked for an operator.

"Who else would want a telephone you have to carry around?" asked Richard.

Leech gave a feral, humourless smile and muttered, "Wouldn't you like to know?" before getting through.

"This is DL 001," he said. "Yes, yes, Angela, it's Derek. I'd like to speak with Miss Catriona Kaye, at the Manor House, Alder."

Leech held the trimphone against his chest while he was connected.

"Let's see if Madam Chairman has gathered her Talents," he said. Richard certainly hoped she had.

VI

They were on the road to Mangle Wurzel Country because some paranormal crisis was out of hand. Jamie had a fair idea what that meant.

Growing up as the son of the current Dr Shade and the former Kentish Glory, it had taken several playground spats and uncomfortable parent-teacher meetings to realize that other kids (and grown-ups) didn't know these things happened regularly and – what's more – *really* didn't want to know. After getting kicked out of a third school, he learned to answer the question "what does your Daddy do?" with "he's a doctor" rather than "he fights diabolical masterminds". Since leaving home, he'd seen how surreally out-of-the-ordinary his childhood had been. No one ever said he was expected to take over his father's practice, but Dad taught him about the Shade Legacy: how to summon shadows and travel the night-paths, how to touch people inside with tendrils of velvet black, how to use the get-up and the gadgets. Jamie was the only pupil in his class who botched his mock O Levels because he'd spent most of his revision time on the basics of flying an autogyro.

Jamie thought Mum was pleased he was using the darkness in the band rather than on the streets. He was carrying on the Shade line, but in a different way. His father could drop through a skylight and make terror blossom in a dozen wicked souls; Jamie could float onto a tiny stage in a pokey venue and fill a dark room with a deeper shadow that enveloped audiences and seeped into their hearts. When Jamie sang about long, dreadful nights, a certain type of teenager *knew* he was singing about them. Because of Transhumance, they knew – if only for the forty-five minutes of the set – that they weren't alone, that they had friends and lovers in the dark, that tiny pinpoints of starlight were worth striving for. They were kids who only liked purple lollipops because of the colour they stained their lips, wore swathes of black even in this baking summer, would drink vinegar and lie in a bath of ice cubes to be as pale as Gené, lit their squats with black candles bought in head shops, and read thick paperback novels "from the vampire's point of view". Teenagers like Vron – who, come to think of it, he was supposed to be seeing this evening. If the world survived the week, she'd make him pay for standing her up.

Gené had found Vron's dog-eared *Interview with the Vampire* under a cushion in the back of the van, and was performing dramatic passages. Read out with a trace of (sexy) French accent, it sounded sillier than it did when Vron quoted bits of Anne Rice's "philosophy" at him. Vron wrote Transhumance's lyrics, and everyone said – not to her face – the lyrics needed more work. Bongo said, "You can't rhyme 'caverns of despair' with 'kicking o'er a chair' and expect folk not to laugh their kecks off." About the only thing the band could agree on was that they didn't want to be funny.

So what was he doing on the road? In a van with four weird strangers – weird, even by his standards.

Gatherings of disparate talents like this little lot were unusual. Fred had said they needed "*everybody*". Jamie wondered how far down the list the likes of Sewell Head came – though he knew enough not to underestimate anyone. According to Gené, the Diogenes Club was calling this particular brouhaha "the Winter War". That didn't sound so bad. After the last few months, a little winter in July would be welcome.

Beyond Yeovil, they came to a roadblock manned by squaddies who were turning other drivers away from a "military exercise" barrier. The van was waved out of the queue by a NCO and – with no explanation needed – the barrier lifted for them. A riot of envious hooting came from motorists who shut up as soon as a rifle or two was accidentally pointed in their direction. Even Gené kept mum once they were in bandit country – where they were the only moving thing.

As they drove along eerily empty roads, Susan continued to relay Head's directions. "Follow Tapmoor Road for two and a half miles, and turn *right*, drive half a mile, go through Sutton Mallet, then three miles on, to Alder – and we're there."

Jamie spotted the signpost, which was almost smothered by the lower branches of a dying tree, and took the Sutton Mallet turn-off. It should have been a short cut to Alder, the village where they were supposed to rendezvous with the rest of the draftees in the Winter War. The van ploughed to a halt in a four-foot-deep snowdrift.

The temperature plunged – an oven became a fridge in seconds. Gooseflesh raised on Jamie's bare arms. Keith and Sewell Head wrapped themselves in sleeping bags. Susan's teeth chattered, interrupting her travel directions – which were academic anyway. The road was impassable.

Only Gené didn't instantly and obviously feel the cold.

Jamie shifted gears, and reversed. Wheels spun, making a hideous grinding noise for half a minute or so, then the van freed itself from the grip of ice and backed out of the drift. A few yards away, and the temperature climbed again. They were all shocked quiet for a moment, then started talking at once.

"Hush," said Gené, who was elected Head Girl, "look."

The cold front was advancing, visibly – a frozen river. Hedges, half-dead from lack of rain, were swallowed by swells of ice and snow.

They all got out of the van. It was as hot as it had been, though Jamie's skin didn't readjust. He still had gooseflesh.

"It'll be here soon and swallow us again," said Keith.

"At the current rate, in sixteen minutes forty-five seconds," said Sewell Head.

It wasn't just a glacier creeping down a country lane, it was an entire wave advancing across the countryside. Jamie had no doubt Head knew his sums – in just over a quarter of an hour, an arctic climate would reach the road, and sweep around the van, stranding them.

"We have to go ahead on foot," said Gené. "It's only a couple of miles down that lane."

"Three and a half," corrected Head.

"A walk in the park," said Gené.

"Thank you, Captain Scott," said Susan. "We're not exactly equipped."

"You were told to bring warm clothes."

"Naturally, I didn't believe it," said Susan. "We should have been shouted at."

Jamie hadn't been told. He'd take that up with Fred and Vanessa.

"Fifteen minutes," said Head, unconcerned.

"There's gear in the back of the van," said Jamie. "It'll have to do."

"I'm fine as I am," said Gené. "Happy in all weathers."

Jamie dug out one of his father's black greatcoats for Susan. It hung long on her, edges trailing on the ground. Head kept the sleeping bag wrapped around him, and looked even more like a tramp. He must be glad he came out with his scarf and gloves. Keith found a black opera cloak with red-silk lining, and settled it around his shoulders.

"Careful with that, Keith," Jamie cautioned. "It was the Great Edmondo's. There are hidden pockets. You might find a dead canary or two."

Jamie pulled on a ragged black-dyed pullover and gauntlets. He fetched out a hold-all with some useful items from the Legacy, and – as an afterthought – slung the Shade goggles around his neck and put on one of his Dad's wide-brimmed black slouch hats.

"Natty," commented Gené. "It's the Return of Dr Shade!"

"Sod off, Frenchy," he said, smiling.

"Burgundina, remember?"

The cold front was nearly at the mouth of the lane, crawling up around the signpost. He rolled up the van windows, and locked the doors.

Gené climbed onto the snowdrift, and stamped on the powder. It was packed enough to support her. Bare-legged and -armed, she still looked comfortable amid the frozen wastes. She held out a hand and helped haul Susan up beside her. Even in the coat, Susan began shivering. Her nose reddened. She hugged herself, sliding hands into loose sleeves like a mandarin.

"Come on up, lads, the water's l-lovely," she said.

Jamie, Keith and Head managed, with helping hands and a certain amount of swearing, to clamber up beside the girls.

Ahead was a snowscape – thickly carpeted white, trees weighed down by ice, a few roofs poking up where cottages were trapped. Snow wasn't falling, but was whipped up from the ground by cold winds and swirled viciously. Jamie put on his goggles, protecting his eyes from the spits of snow. The flakes were like a million tiny fragments of ice shrapnel.

Gené pointed across the frozen moor, at a tower.

"That's Sutton Mallet chapel. And, see, beyond that, where the hill rises . . . that's Alder."

It ought to have been an hour's stroll. Very pleasant, if you liked walking in the country. Which Jamie didn't, much. Now, it seemed horribly like a Death March.

Susan, he noticed, stopped shivering and chattering. She was padding, carefully across the powder, leaving deep footprints.

Gené applauded. "Now that's *thinking*," she said.

Jamie didn't know what she meant.

"She's a pyrokinetic, remember?" explained Gené. "That's not just setting fire to things with your mind. It's control over *temperature*. She's made her own cocoon of warmth, inside her coat. Look, she's steaming."

Susan turned, smiling wide. Hot fog rose from her shoulders, and snowflakes hissed when they got near her as if falling onto a griddle.

"Are my ears burning?" she asked.

"Never mind your ears," said Keith. "What about everything else?"

Susan's footprints were shallow puddles, which froze a few seconds after she had made them.

"I'm not a proper pyro," she said. "I don't set fires. I just have a thing with warmth. Saves on coins for the meter. Otherwise, it's useless – like wiggling your ears. It takes me an hour to boil enough water for a cup of tea, and by then I'm so fagged out I have to lie down and it's cold again when I wake up. That's the trouble with most of my so-called Talents. Party pieces, but little else. I mean, who needs a drawer full of bent spoons?"

"I think it's amazing," commented Keith. "Mind over matter. You could be on the telly. Or fight crime."

"I'll leave that to the professionals, like Jamie's Dad. You're not seeing me in a union jack bikini and one of those eye-masks which aren't really disguises."

"You'd be surprised how well those masks work," said Jamie. "When she was Kentish Glory, Mum wore this moth-wing domino. Even people she knew really well didn't clock it was her."

"I like a quiet life," said Susan. "So, enough about me being a freak. Gené, what's your secret?"

The blonde shrugged, teasing. "Diet and lots of sleep."

"Come on, slowcoaches," said Susan, who was getting the hang of it. "Last one there's a rotten . . ."

The snow collapsed under her and she sank waist-deep, coat-skirts spreading out around her.

"Shit," she said. "Pardon my Burgundian."

"Didn't Gené say you could levitate?" said Keith, going to help her.

"She's not the one who knows everything," said Susan. "That was only once, and I was six. I've put on weight since then."

Keith took her hands – "she's all warm!" – and hauled her out of her hole.

"Abracadabra," he said, flapping the cloak.

"It doesn't do to get overconfident," cautioned Gené.

Susan made a rude gesture behind the other girl's back.

Jamie felt something. Deeper than the cold. He looked around. The whirling blizzard was thickening. And something was different.

"Hey, gang," he said. "Who made the snowmen?"

VII

"I *know* the Cold is spreading," Catriona Kaye told Derek Leech. "It's here, in Alder. We're three miles from you. Now put Richard on, would you?"

In the Manor House, the telephone was on a stand near the front door. She had to leave her guests in the drawing room to take Leech's call. The hallway was still cluttered from Edwin's days as Lord of this Manor: hats and umbrellas (and Charles Beauregard's old sword-stick) in a hideous Victorian stand, coats on hooks (she liked to use Edwin's flying jacket – still smelling of tobacco and motor-oil – for gardening), framed playbills from the 1920s, shotguns (and less commonplace armaments) in a locked case. Since Edwin's death, she'd tidied away or passed on most of his things, but here she let his ghost linger. Upstairs, on the landing, his shadow was etched permanently into the floorboards. After a lifetime in service to the Diogenes Club, it was all he had for a grave. She supposed she should throw a carpet over it or something.

As she waited for Leech to pass the phone to Richard, Catriona caught sight of herself in the tall, thin art deco mirror from the Bloomsbury flat she had shared with Edwin. At a glance, she was the girl she recognized – she had the same silhouette as she had in her, and the century's, twenties. If she looked for more than a few seconds, she saw her bobbed hair was ash-grey, and even that was dyed. Her wrists and neck were unmistakably a seventy-six-year-old's. Once, certain Valued Members had been grumpily set against even admitting her to the building in Pall Mall, never mind putting her on the rolls. Now, she was practically all that was left of the Diogenes Club as Mycroft Holmes would have recognized it. Even in the Secret World, things were changing.

"Catriona," said Richard, tinny and distorted as if bounced off a relay station in the rings of Saturn. "How are you? Is the Cold . . . ?"

"In the village? Yes. A bother? No. We've enough lively minds in the house to hold it back. Indeed, the cool is misleadingly pleasant. What little of the garden survived the heat-wave has been killed by snow, though – which is really rather tiresome."

Richard succinctly explained the situation.

"'The planet's first evolved intelligence'?" she queried. "That has a familiar ring to it. I shall put the problem to our little Council of War."

"Watch out for snowmen."

"I shall take care to."

She hung up and had a moment's thought, ticking off her long string of black pearls as if they were rosary beads. The general assumption was that they had been dealing with an unnatural phenomenon, perhaps a bleed-through from some parallel wintery world. Now, it seemed there was an *entity* in the picture. Something to be coped with, accommodated or eliminated.

The drawing room was crowded. Extra chairs had been brought in.

Constant Drache, the visionary architect, wanted news of Derek Leech. Catriona assured him that his patron was perfectly well. Drache wasn't a Talent, just a high-ranking minion. He was here with the watchful Dr Lark, corralling the persons Leech had contributed to the Council and making mental notes on the others for use after the truce was ended. That showed a certain optimism, which Catriona found mildly cheering. She had told Richard's team not to call Leech's people "the villains", but the label was hard to avoid. Fred and Vanessa were still in London, liaising with the Minister.

Anthony Jago, wearing a dog-collar the Church of England said he was no longer entitled to, was Leech's prime specimen – an untapped Talent, reputed to be able to overwrite reality on a large scale. The former clergyman said he was looking for property in the West Country and had taken a covetous liking to the Manor House. The man had an understandable streak of self-regarding megalomania, and Lark was evidently trying to keep him unaware of the full extent of his abilities. Catriona would have been terrified of Jago if he weren't completely trumped by Ariadne ("just Ariadne"). The white-haired, utterly beautiful creature had made her way unbidden to the Club and offered her services in the present emergency. She was an Elder of the Kind. Even the Secret Files had almost nothing on them. The Elders hadn't taken an interest in anything in Geneviève Dieudonné's lifetime, though some of their young – the Kith – had occasionally been problematic.

Apart from Jago, none of Leech's soldiers were in the world-changing (or threatening) class. The unnaturally thin, bald, haggard Nigel Karabatsos – along with his unnaturally small, plump, clinging wife – represented a pompous Neo-Satanic sect called the Thirteen. Typically, there weren't thirteen of them. Maureen Mountmain was heiress to a dynasty of Irish mystics who'd been skirmishing with the Club for over eighty years. Catriona would gladly not have seen the red-headed, big-hipped, big-busted Amazon in this house again (she'd been here when the shadows took Edwin). Maureen and

Richard had one of those complicated young persons' things, which neither cared to talk of and – Catriona hoped – would not be resumed. There were enough "undercurrents" in this Council for several West End plays as it was. Jago and Maureen, comparatively youthful and obnoxiously vital, pumped out more pheromones than a beehive. They took an interest in each other which Dr Lark did her best to frustrate by interposing her body. Leech obviously had separate plans for those two.

The mysterious Mr Sewell Head, the other side's last recruit for the Winter War Effort, was out in a snowfield somewhere with Geneviève's party. Catriona suspected they'd have a hard time getting through. Fair enough. If this council failed, someone needed to be left alive to regroup and try a second wave. Geneviève had Young Dr Shade and the interesting Rodway Girl with her – they had the potential to become Valued Talents, and the Cold Crisis should bring them on. Still, it didn't do to think too far ahead. In the long run, there's always an unhappy outcome – except, just possibly, for Ariadne.

Watching Jago and Maureen flex and flutter, attracting like magnets, Catriona worried that the Club's Talents were relics. Swami Anand Gitamo, formerly Harry Cutley, was only here for moral support. He had been Most Valued Member once, but had lately taken a more spiritual role. Still, it was good to see Harry again. His chanted mantras irritated Jago, a point in his favour. Paulette Michaelsmith had even more obviously been hauled out of retirement. She could only use her Talent (under the direction of others) when asleep and dreaming, and was permanently huddled in a bath chair. Catriona noted Dr Lark wasn't too busy playing gooseberry to take an interest in poor, dozy Paulette. Dr Cross, the old woman's minder, was instructed to ward the witch off if she made any sudden moves. Louise Magellan Teazle, one of Catriona's oldest friends, always brought the sunshine with her – a somewhat undervalued Talent this summer, though currently more useful than all Karabatsos' dark summonings or Jago's reality-warping. It was thanks to Louise that the Cold was shut out of the Manor House. She was an author of children's books, and a near neighbour. In her house out on the moor, she'd been first to notice a change in the weather.

While Catriona relayed what Leech and Richard had told her, Louise served high tea. Paulette woke up for fruitcake and was fully alert for whole minutes at a time.

"This Cold," Drache declared. "Can it be killed?"

"Anything can be killed," said Karabatsos.

"Yes, dear, *anything*," echoed his wife.

"We know very little about the creature," admitted Catriona. "The world's leading expert is Professor Cleaver, and his perceptive is – shall we say – distorted."

"All life is sacred," said Anand Gitamo.

"Especially ours," said Maureen. "I'm a mum. I don't want my girl growing up to freeze in an apocalypse of ice and frost."

Catriona had a minor twinge of concern at the prospect of *more* Mountmains.

"How can all life be sacrosanct when some life-forms are inimical, *hein*?" said Drache. "Snake and mongoose. Lion and gazelle. Humanity and the Cold."

"Tom and Jerry," said Paulette, out of nowhere.

"I did not say 'sacrosanct'", pointed out Anand Gitamo.

"The Cold can die," said Ariadne. Everyone listened to her, even Jago. "But it should not be killed. It can kill you and live, as you would shrug off a virus. You cannot kill it and expect to survive, as you cannot murder the seas, the soil or the great forests. The crime would be too great. You could not abide the consequences."

"But we do not matter?" asked Drache.

"I should miss you," admitted Ariadne, gently. "As you cannot do without the trees, who make the air breathable, the Kind cannot do without you, without your dreams. If the Cold spreads, we would outlive you – but eventually, starved, we would fade. The Cold has mind, but no memory. It would retain nothing of you."

"The world doesn't end in ice, but *fire*," said Jago. "This, I have seen."

"The Old Ones will return," said Karabatsos.

"Yes, dear, *Old*," echoed his wife.

It seemed to Catriona that everyone in this business expected a personal, tailor-made apocalypse. They enlisted in the Winter War out of jealousy – a pettish wish to forestall every other prophet's vision, to keep the stage clear for their own variety of Doom. The Cold was Professor Cleaver's End of the World, and the others wanted to shut him down. Derek Leech, at least, needed the planet to stay open for business – which was why Catriona had listened when he called a truce with the Diogenes Club.

The doorbell rang. Catriona would have hurried back to the hall, but David Cross gallantly went for her. Louise poured more tea.

It was not Geneviève and her party, but Mr Zed, last of the Undertakers. He brought another old acquaintance from the Mausoleum, their collection of oddities (frankly, a prison).

Mr Zed, eyes permanently hidden behind dark glasses, stood in the drawing room doorway. Everyone looked at him. The brim of his top hat and the shoulders of his black frock coat were lightly powdered with snow. Many of the Council – and not only those on Derek Leech's side of the room – might once have had cause to fear immurement in the Mausoleum, but the Undertaking was not what it had been. Mr Zed politely took off his hat and stood aside.

Behind him was a little girl who could have stepped out of an illustration from one of Louise's earliest books. She had an indian braid tied with a silver ribbon, and wore a neat pinafore with a kangaroo pouch pocket. She looked like Rose Farrar, who disappeared from a field in Sussex in 1872, "taken by the fairies". This creature had turned up on the same spot in 1925, and come close to delivering an apocalypse that might have suited Jago's biblical tastes. At least she wasn't playing Harlot of Babylon any more.

"Good afternoon, Rose."

Catriona had not seen the girl-shaped creature since the Undertaking took her off. She still had a smooth, pale patch on her hand – where Rose had spat venom at her.

The creature curtseyed. When she looked up, she wore another face – Catriona's, as it had been fifty years ago. She used the face to smile, and aged rapidly – presenting Catriona with what she looked like now. Then, she laughed innocently and was Rose Farrar again.

The procedure was like a slap.

The thing that looked like Rose was on their side, for the moment. But, unlike everyone else in the room – good, bad or undecided – she didn't come from *here*. If the Cold won, Rose wouldn't necessarily lose a home, or a life, or anything she put value on.

Catriona wasn't sure what Rose could contribute, even if she was of a mind to help. Ariadne, Louise and, perhaps, the Rodway girl were Talents – they could alter reality through sheer willpower. Jago and Paulette were "effective dreamers" – they could alter reality on an even larger scale, but at the whim of their unconscious minds. Rose was a living mirror – she could only change *herself*, by plucking notions from the heads of anyone within reach. She resembled the original Rose because that's who the people who found her in Angel Field expected her to be. She had been kept captive all these years by confining her with people (wardens *and* convicts) who *believed* the Mausoleum to be an inescapable prison – which wasn't strictly true.

"What a dear little thing," said Ariadne. "Come here and have some of Miss Teazle's delicious cake."

Rose meekly trotted over to the Elder's side and presented her head to be stroked. Jago turned away from Maureen, and was fascinated. Until today, he hadn't known there were other Talents in the world. Paulette perked up again, momentarily – the most powerful dreamer on record, now in a room with at least two creatures who fed on dreams.

End of the World or not, Catriona wondered whether bringing all these big beasts together was entirely a bright idea.

"More tea, Cat," suggested Louise, who had just given a steaming cup to the Undertaker.

Catriona nodded.

VIII

Jamie wasn't surprised when the snowmen attacked. It wouldn't be a war if there weren't an enemy.

The frosties waited until the five had tramped a hundred difficult yards or so past them, committing to the path ahead and an uncertain footing. They were in Sutton Mallet. It wasn't much of a place. Two Rolls Royces were parked by the path, almost buried, icicles dripping from the bonnet ornaments. Nice machines. His Dad drove one like them.

"What's that thing called again?" he muttered, nodding at the dancers.

"The Spirit of Ecstasy," said Sewell Head. "Originally, the Spirit of Speed. Designed by Charles Sykes for the Rolls-Royce Company in 1911. The model is Eleanor Velasco Thornton."

"Eleanor. That explains it. Dad always called the little figure "Nellie in Her Nightie". I used to think she had wings, but it's supposed to be her dress, streaming in the wind."

Everyone had fallen over more than once. It stopped being remotely funny. Each step was an uncertain adventure that only Gené was nimble enough to enjoy. Then, even she skidded on a frozen puddle and took a tumble into a drift.

She looked up, and saw the four snowy sentinels.

"What are you laughing at?" she shouted.

At that, the snowmen upped stumps and came in a rush. When they moved, they were localized, roughly human-shaped blizzards. They had no problem with their footing, and charged like touchy rhinos whose mothers had just been insulted by howler monkeys.

"There are people inside," yelled Keith. "I think they're dead."

"They better hope they're dead," said Gené, flipping herself upright and standing her ground, adopting a fighting stance.

The first and biggest of the frosties – who wore a top hat – barrelled towards the Burgundian girl, growing into a creature that seemed all shoulders. She met it with an ear-piercing "ki-*yaaa*" and a Bruce Lee-approved power-kick to the midriff. The topper fell off and the frosty stopped in its tracks, shedding great chunks of packed ice to reveal a well-dressed gent with a deeply-cut throat and a slack mouth. He had bled out before freezing. The snow crawled back up around the corpse, cocooning it with white powder, building layers of icy muscle, growing icicle spines and teeth. It reached down with an extensible arm, picked up its hat, and set it back on its head at a jaunty angle. The coals of its mouth rearranged themselves into a fierce grin.

And the other three – who wore a tartan cap, a jungle hat and two bugs on springs – caught up with their leader. They were swollen to the size of big bruisers.

Jamie looked down at his hands. His gauntlets were mittened with black clouds, containing violet electrical arcs. Out in the open, with snow all around and cold sunlight, there was too little shade. Night was far off. He cast darkstuff at the Scotch Snowman, who was nearest, and sheared away a couple of icicles. They instantly grew back.

He would have to do better.

Fred Astaire Snowman patted its healed-over tummy, and shot out a big fist which clenched around Gené's throat. Astaire lifted Gené off the ground. She kicked, but floundered with nothing to brace against. Jamie saw she had longer, sharper nails than normal – but any tears she made in the snow-hand were healed over instantly. She gurgled, unable to talk.

Comical Bugs Snowman and Jungle Explorer Snowman shifted, in opposite directions. They were forming a circle. A killing circle.

Astaire grew a yard-long javelin of solid ice from its shoulder, and snapped it off to make a stake. It pressed the ice-spear against Gené's ribs, ready to hoist her up like a victim of Frosty the Impaler.

Susan had her eyes shut, and radiated warmth – but not heat. Sewell Head was chattering about snowmen in fact and fiction, citing pagan precedents, Christmas cake decorations and the Ronettes. Keith wrapped himself in his magician's cape, and rolled his eyes up so that only the whites showed. Jamie supposed he was having a fit.

Gené squeaked a scream out through her crushed throat. Scarlet blood showed on her safari jacket.

He tried to gather more darkness, from inside.

Suddenly, Keith's eyes snapped back – but they were different.

"Don't waste your energy, Shade," he said, in a commanding tone. "Use this."

From the depths of the cloak, Keith produced a thin, diamond-shaped, black object. It was Dennis Rattray's Fang of Night. Jamie had wondered where Dad had put it after taking it from Blackfist. Keith tossed the jewel to Jamie, who caught it and staggered back. The Fang was the size of a gob-stopper, but weighed as much as a cannonball. He held it in both hands. It was like sticking his fingers into a live electric socket.

"Sue," Keith said, "cover Shade's – Jamie's – back. Imagine a wall of heat, and concentrate. Swellhead, give me some dark refraction indices, considering available light, the Blackfist gem and whatever these snow-things are. Today would be a help."

Astonished, Head scrawled sums in the snow with his forefinger.

"Gené, hang on," said Keith. Gené even tried to nod, though her face was screwed up in agony and spatters of her blood stained the snow under her kicking feet.

"Can you feel it, Shade?"

Jamie was seeing a different Keith Marion. And the jewel didn't seem so heavy once he'd worked out how to hold it. Rattray had tapped into its energy by making a fist around it, but Dad said that was what had killed him in the end. There were other ways of using the Fang of Night.

Head put his hand up, and pointed to a formula he had traced.

"Well played, Swellhead," said Keith, patting Head's bald bonce. "Shade, hold the Fang up to your forehead and focus. Aim for the hat!"

Behind him, Susan grunted, and he heard slushing, melting sounds.

"Ugh, disgusting," she said.

Jamie fought an urge to turn and find out what had happened.

"Concentrate, man," insisted Keith. "Gené can't hold out much longer."

Head began to give a figure in seconds, but Keith shut him up.

Jamie held the stone to his forehead. It seemed to fit into the V above his goggles. The dark matter was sucked in through the gauntlets, thrilling into his palms, surging through his veins and nerves, and gathered in his forebrain, giving him a sudden ice-cream migraine. Then, it was set free.

He saw a flash of dark purple. Astaire's top hat exploded in flames that burned black, and the snowman fell apart. Gené was dropped, and pulled out the ice-shard in her chest before she sprawled in the snow. She crab-walked away from the well-dressed, still-standing corpse that had been inside Astaire. Its knees kinked, and it pitched forward.

"Now, turn," ordered Keith. "The others."

Jamie wheeled about. Susan was on her knees, with her arms held out, fingers wide. Scotch Snowman and Explorer Snowman loomed over her, melt-water raining from their arms and chests and faces – the trapped corpses showing through. Susan was running out of charge, though. A slug of blood crawled out of her nose. Angry weals rose around her fingernails.

This time, it was like blinking. He zapped the tartan cap and the solar topee to fragments, and the snowmen were downed. Susan swooned, and Keith was there to catch her, wrapping her in his cloak, wiping away the blood, squeezing her fingers. She woke up, and he kissed her like someone who'd known her longer and better than few hours.

"Excuse me," said Gené, "but I nearly had an icicle through my heart."

Keith looked at her and asked brusquely "you all right?"

Gené eased her bloody jacket out of the way. Her scrape was already healing.

"Seem to be," she admitted.

"Good, now help Shade with the last of them. It's the most dangerous."

Gené saluted.

"Sue," whispered Keith.

"Do I know you?" she asked, frankly irritated. He let her go, and stood up, stiffly. In his cloak, he looked like the commander of a victorious Roman legion. Jamie didn't know where the kid had got it from.

Bugs had either legged it or melted into the ground.

Jamie had purple vision. It was like night-sight, but in the daytime. With the Fang of Night, he could think faster. He didn't feel the cold. He could take anyone, any day of the week. He could only imagine what he would sound like if he used this onstage.

Keith plucked the jewel from his grasp, holding it between thumb and forefinger as if it were radioactive, then magicked it away with a conjurer's flourish.

"You of all people should know to treat those things carefully," said Keith.

For an instant, Jamie wanted to batter the kid's face and take back the jewel. Then, he understood. Use it, but don't let it get its hooks in you. Dad had said that all the time.

"So, which Keith is this?" said Gené, tugging on the kid's wrist-tag. "What school do you go to?"

"School? There hasn't been any school since the Spiders came. Good job too. They don't teach you anything useful. You have to learn survival, and *resistance*, on the job."

This Keith had a firmer jaw, healed-over scars, and a steady, manly, confident gaze. People snapped in line when he spoke and threw themselves under trains if there was a tactical advantage in it.

"He told us about this before we met you," Gené explained. "Some other Keith lives on an Earth overrun by arachnoid aliens. He's a guerrilla leader. He also plays opening bat for Somerset and has three girlfriends. Opinion is split as to whether it's a viable alternate timeline or some sort of Dungeons and Dragons wish-fulfilment fantasy. At the moment, I don't really care."

She kissed Keith on the mouth. He took it as if it were his right, and then started struggling.

"What happened?" he asked, shaking free of Gené. "Who was here?"

Gené let the familiar – the original? – Keith go, and edged away from him. He still looked confused. The other Keith had been useful in a pinch, but Jamie couldn't say he missed him.

IX

Putting Professor Cleaver to sleep hadn't brought back the summer, but did shut him up – which was a relief.

Richard looked through the heavily-frosted window. There was proper snow, now. Precipitation. It dropped like the gentle rain from Heaven, fluttering down picturesquely before being caught in erratic, spiralling winds and dashed hither and yon. The Cold's sphere of influence scraped the upper atmosphere, where it found clouds to freeze.

According to Catriona, the white blanket was gaining pace, spreading across the moors and fields. Soon, the perimeter of exclusion would be breached. So far, three villages had been evacuated on a flimsy cover story. When the Cold gripped fair-sized towns like Yeovil and Sedgwater, the domesticated feline would be well and truly liberated from the portable container.

Cleaver snorted in his sleep, honking through his broken nose. Not content with tying the Professor to a swivel chair, Leech had shoved a sock in his mouth and bound a scarf around his jaws. Richard loosened the gag, so he wouldn't asphyxiate on bri-nylon and his own false teeth.

Leech shot him a pitiful look. He was picking through Clever Dick's papers.

"The man couldn't maintain an orderly file if his soul depended on it," he said, in exasperation. "From now on, every scientist or researcher who works for me gets shadowed by two form-fillers and a pen-pusher. What's the use of results if you can't *find* them?"

"He wasn't working for you," said Richard.

"Oh yes he was," insisted Leech. "He drew his pay-packet and he signed his contract. Derek Leech International *owns* his results. If this Cold creature is real, then we own *her*. The *Comet* has exclusive rights to her story. I could put her in a zoo, hunt her for sport, license her image for T-shirts, or dissect her crystal by crystal to advance the progress of science and be entirely within my legal rights."

"Tell *her* that."

Leech turned a page and found something. "I just might," he said.

He tore out a sheaf of papers covered in neat little diagrams. Richard thought it might be some form of cipher, then recognized the hexagonal designs as snow crystals. Under each was a scrawl – mirror-written words, not in English.

"Backwards in Latin," mused Leech. "Paranoid little boffin, wouldn't you say? This is Cleaver's Rosetta Stone. Not many words, no subtleties, no syntax at all. But he received instructions. He made and used his Box. He broke the Zero Barrier, and violated the laws of physics."

"All because he could grow snowflakes?"

"Yes, and now I *own* the process. There might not be applications yet, but things get smaller. Transistorization won't stop at the visible. Imagine: trademarked weather, logos on bacteria, microscopic art, micro-miniaturized assassins . . ."

"Let's ensure the future of mankind on the planet before you start pestering the patent office, shall we?"

Leech bit down, grinding his teeth hard. Richard thought something had snapped in his mouth.

"You should watch that," he advised.

Leech smiled, showing even, white, perfect gnashers. Richard suspected he had rows of them, eternally renewed – like a shark.

All rooms have ghosts. Acts and feelings and ideas all have residue, sometimes with a half-life of centuries. Richard took his gauntlets off and began to touch things, feeling for the most recent impressions. His fingertips were so numb that the cold shocks were welcome. His sensitivity was more attuned to living people than dead objects, but he could usually read something if he focused. He scraped a brown stain on the wall, and had a hideous flash: Cleaver, with a knife, smiling; a red-haired man in a white coat, gouting from an open throat.

"What is it?" Leech asked.

Richard forced himself to disconnect from the murder. "The staff," he said. "I saw what happened before they were snowmen."

"Where are they, by the way?" asked Leech.

"Wandered off. Didn't seem to be the sorts to listen to reason. I doubt if you can negotiate with them."

The memory flashes floated in his mind, like neon after-images. He blinked, and they began to dispel. Cleaver had made four sacrifices to the Cold. McKendrick, Kellett, Bakhtinin, Pouncey.

"Were the staff dead before or after they got snow-coated?" asked Leech.

"Does it matter?"

"If the Professor killed them to give the Cold raw material to make cat's paws, they were just unused machines when she got them. If they were alive when the Cold wrapped them up, she might have interfaced with minds other than Clever Dick's."

Richard didn't approve of Leech's use of "interfaced" as a verb-form, but saw where he was going.

"He killed them first," he confirmed. Leech didn't ask him how he knew. "They aren't even zombies. The dead people are more like armatures. The only traces of personality they have . . ."

"The hats."

". . . were imposed by Professor Cleaver. I think he was trying to be funny. He's not very good at humour. Few solipsists are."

Richard proceeded to the remains of the Box. The Cold had come through this doorway. He doubted it could be used to send her back, even if it were repaired. Banishing was never as easy as conjuring. Sometimes performing a ritual backwards worked, but not in a language with six planes of symmetry. You would always get hexagonal palindromes.

Pressing his palm to a frost patch on the surface of a workbench, he felt the slight bite of the crystals, the pull on skin as he took his hand away. He didn't sense an entity, not even the life he would feel if he put his naked hand against the bark of a giant redwood. Yet the Cold was here.

"When the Cold broke through the Zero Barrier," said Leech, "the Professor's Box blew up. After that, he couldn't make his little tiny ice sculptures, but they still talked. She turned the others into snowmen, but spared him. How could he make her understand he was a sympathizer?"

Richard thought about that. "He persuaded the Cold he was her High Priest," he said. "And she let him live . . . for a while."

"Cleaver said the Cold was an intelligent form of life," said Leech. "He did *not* say she was *clever*. Imagine: you're utterly unique, near-omnipotent and have endured millennia upon millennia. You wake up and the only person who talks to you – the only person you have *ever* talked to – is Clever Dick Cleaver. What does that give you?"

"A grossly distorted picture of the world?"

"Exactly. Perhaps it's time our Cold Lady heard another voice."

"Voices," said Richard, firmly.

"Yes, of course," said Leech, not meaning it.

Derek Leech was excited, fathoming possibilities, figuring out angles. Letting the Great Enchanter cut a separate deal with the Cold would be a terrible idea. He was entirely too good at negotiating contracts.

"Now," Leech thought out loud, "how did he talk with her?"

Richard remembered the snow angels. He wandered out of the laboratory. Not caring to maintain Cleaver's obsessive little paths, he waded through snow. It drifted over his ankles. From the cafeteria doorway, he looked again at the three angels. They had reminded him of semaphore signals.

"This is how," he said.

Leech had tagged along with him. He saw it at once too.

"See the feet," said Leech. "Not heel-marks, but toe-marks. When kids make snow angels, they lie on their backs. Cleaver lies on his front. You can see where his face fits, like a mould for a mask."

A muffled screech sounded. Back in the laboratory, the Professor was awake.

Richard stepped into the room and knelt by an angel, touching the negative impression of Cleaver's face. He felt nothing. If this had been the connection, it was dead now. The Cold had moved on.

He would have to try outside.

"Leech," he said, "get on your back-pack blower and ring Catriona again. We have to tell her what we're doing, in case it doesn't work. No sense in the next lot making the same mistakes . . ."

A chill rolled down the corridor.

The doorway was empty. Richard saw a white tangle on the floor. Leech's parka. And another further away. His leggings.

Richard's stomach turned over. He was feeling things *now*.

"Leech!" he shouted.

Only the Professor responded, rattling his chair and yelling around his gag.

Richard jogged down the corridor, past more of Leech's discarded arctic gear. He turned a corner. The main doors were open. One flapped in the blizzard.

He made it to the doors and took the full force of the wind in his face.

Leech – in a lightweight salmon suit – had walked a few yards away from the building. He stood in the middle of whirling snow, casually undoing his wide orange knit tie.

One of the snowmen was back. It was Bee-Alice, swollen to mammoth size, twelve or fourteen feet tall, body-bulbs bulging as if pregnant with a litter of snow-babies. Queen Bee-Alice stood over Leech like a Hollywood pagan idol, greedy for human sacrifice.

It should be a summer evening. Daylight lasting past ten o'clock. Plagues of midges and supper in the garden. A welcome cool after another punishingly blazing drought day. Any sunlight was blocked by the Cold, and premature gloom – not even honest night – had fallen.

Leech popped his cat's-eye cufflinks and began unbuttoning his chocolate-brown ruffle shirt. He exposed his almost-hairless chest, clenching his jaws firmly to keep from chattering. He wasn't quite human, but Richard had known that.

This was not going to happen on Richard's watch. Bad enough that the Cold's wake-up call had come from an embittered lunatic whose emotional age was arrested at eleven. If her next suitor were Derek Leech, the death by freezing of all life on Earth might seem a happier outcome.

Richard tried to stride towards Leech, but wind held him back. He forced himself, inch by inch, out into the open, struggling against pellets of ice to take the few crucial steps.

Queen Bee-Alice creaked, head turning like the world before the BBC-TV news. The novelty bumblebees bounced over her, a crown or a halo. She had giant, wrecking-ball fists. Sharon Kellett, junior meteorologist. Two years out of a polytechnic, with a boyfriend in the Navy and a plan to be national weather girl on the television station Derek Leech wanted to start up. She was among the first casualties of the Winter War. Dead, but not yet fallen. Richard ached at the life lost.

Leech shucked his snug-at-the-crotch, flappy-at-the-ankles trousers. He wore mint-green Y-fronts with electric blue piping.

Richard got to the Great Enchanter and crooked an arm around his neck.

"I won't let you do this," he shouted in his ear.

"You don't understand, Jeperson," he shouted back. At this volume, attempted sincerity sounded just like whining. "*I have to.* For the greater good. I'm willing to sacrifice my – or anyone's – life to end this."

Richard was taken aback, then laughed.

"Nice try, Derek," he said. "But it won't wash."

"It won't, will it?" replied Leech, laughing too.

"Not on your nellie."

"I still have to go through with this, though. You understand, Jeperson? I *can't* pass up the opportunity!"

Leech twisted as if greased in Richard's grip, and shot a tight, knuckled fist into his stomach. Even through layers of protective gear, Richard felt the pile-driver blow. He lost his hold on Leech and the Great Enchanter followed the sucker-punch with a solid right to the jaw, a kick to the knee, and another to the goolies. Richard went down, and took an extra kick – for luck – in his side.

"'You rearn now, Grasshopper,'" said Leech, fingers pulling the corners of his eyes, "'not to charrenge master of ancient and noble art of dirty fighting!'"

Leech couldn't help gloating. Stripped to his underpants, whipped by sleet, skin scaled by gooseflesh, his expression was a mask of ugly victory. His exultant, grin showed at least 168 teeth. Was this the Great Enchanter's true face?

"Really think you can make a deal with the Cold?"

Leech wagged his finger. "You're not getting me like that, Grasshopper. I'm no Clever Dick. I'm not going to explain my wicked plan and give you a chance to get in the way. I'm just going to do what I'm going to do."

Richard had a lump in his fist, an ice-chunk embedded with frozen gravel. His eyes held Leech's gaze, but his hand was busy with the chunk, which he rolled in the snow.

"You didn't go to public school, did you, Derek?"

"No, why?"

"You might have missed a trick."

Richard sat up and, with practised accuracy, threw the heavy-cored snowball at Leech's forehead. The collision made a satisfying sound. Richard's heart surged with immature glee and he recalled earlier victories: as an untried Third Form bowler, smashing the centre-stump and putting out the astonished Captain of the First Eleven; on an autumn playground, wielding a horse chestnut fresh from the branch to split the vinegar-hardened champion conker of the odious Weems-Deverell II.

A third eye of blood opened above Leech's raised brows. His regular eyes showed white and he collapsed, stunned. He lay, twitching, on the snow.

Queen Bee-Alice made no move. Richard hoped she was impartial.

Unable to leave even Derek Leech to freeze, Richard picked him up in a fireman's lift and tossed him inside the building – slamming the doors after him. He didn't know how much time he had before Leech's wits crept back.

He took off his furs. Cold bit, deeper with each layer removed. He went further than Leech, and eventually stood naked in the blizzard. Everything that could shrivel, turn blue or catch frost did so. When the shivering stopped, when sub-zero (if not sub-*absolute zero*) windblast seemed slightly warm, he recognized the beginnings of hypothermia. There was no more pain, just a faint pricking all over his body. Snow packed his ears and deafened him. He was calm, light-headed. Flashes popped in his vision, as the cold did something to his optic nerves he didn't want to think about. He shut his eyes, not needing the distraction. There were still flashes, but easier to ignore.

He knelt before Queen Bee-Alice. Some feeling came from his shins as they sank into the snow – like mild acid, burning gently to the bone. His extremities were far distant countries, sending only the occasional report, always bad news. Cleaver had lain face down, but indoors – with no snowfall. Richard lay back, face up, flakes landing on his cheeks and forehead, knowing his whole body was gradually being covered by layer after layer. His hands were swollen and useless. With his arms he shovelled snow over himself. Snow didn't melt on his skin – any body warmth was gone. He fought the urge to sit up and struggle free, and he fought the disorienting effects that came with a lowering of the temperature of his brain. He was buried quickly, as the Cold made a special effort to clump around him, form a drift, smooth over the bump, swallow him.

As his body temperature lowered, he had to avoid surrendering to the sleep that presaged clinical death. His blood slowed, and his heartbeats became less and less frequent. He was using a meagre repertoire of yogic techniques, but couldn't be distracted by the business of keeping the meat machine running.

He opened up, physically, mentally, spiritually.

In the darkness, he was not alone.

Richard felt the Cold. It was hugely alive, and more alien than the few extra-terrestrials he'd come across. Newly-awake, it stretched out, irritated by moving things and tiny obstructions. It could barely distinguish between piles of stone and people. Both were against the nature it had known. It had an impulse to clean itself by covering these imperfections. It preferred people wrapped in snow, not moving by themselves. But was this its genuine preference, or something learned from Clever Dick Cleaver?

"Hello," shouted Richard, with his mind. "Permit me to introduce myself. I am Richard, and I speak for Mankind."

Snow pressed around his face, like ice-fingers on his eyes.

He *felt* tiny crystals forming inside his brain – not a killing flash-freeze, but the barest pinheads. The Cold was inside him.

"You are not Man."

It wasn't a voice. It wasn't even words. Just snowflake hexagons in the dark of his skull, accompanied by a whisper of arctic winds. But he understood. Meaning was imprinted directly into his brain.

To talk with the Cold, it had to become part of him. This was an interior monologue.

"I am Richard," he tried to reply. It was awkward. He was losing his sense of self, of the *concept* of Richard. "I am not Man." *Man* was what the Cold called Cleaver. "I am *another* Man."

To the Cold, the idea of "other" was still fresh, a shock which had come with its awakening. It had only just got used to Man/Cleaver. It was not yet ready for the independent existence of three billion more unique and individual intelligences. As Richard had guessed, it hadn't previously had use for numbers beyond than One/Self. The corpse-cores of its snowmen weren't like Man/Cleaver. They were tools, empty of consciousness. Had Cleaver killed his staff because he knew more voices would confuse his ice mistress? Probably.

What would Leech have said to the Cold? He would try to make a deal, to his own best advantage. Richard couldn't even blame him. It was what he did. In this position, the Great Enchanter might become a senior partner, stifle the Cold's rudimentary mind and colonize it, use it. Leech/Cold would grip the world, in a different, ultimately crueller way. He wanted slaves, not corpses; a treadmill to the inferno, not peace and quiet.

What should Richard say?

"Please," he projected. "Please don't k— us."

There were no snowflakes for "kill" or "death" or "dead". He shuffled through the tiny vocabulary, and tried again. "Please don't stop/cover/freeze us."

The Cold's mind was changing: not in the sense of altering its intention, but of restructuring its internal architecture. So far, in millennia, it had only needed to make declarative statements, and –

until the last few days – only to itself. It had been like a goldfish, memory wiped every few seconds, constantly reaffirming "this is me, this is my bowl, this is water, this is me, this is my bowl, this is water". Now, the Cold needed to keep track, to impose its will on *others*. It needed a more complicated thought process. It was on the point of inventing a crucial mode of address, of communication. It was about to ask its first *question*.

Richard had got his point over. The Cold now understood that its actions would lead to the ending of Man/Richard. It had a sense Man/Richard was merely one among unimagined and unimaginable numbers of others. For it, "three" was already equivalent to a schoolboy's "gajillion-quajillion-infinitillion to the power of forever". The Cold understood Man/Richard was asking to be allowed to continue. The life of others was in the Cold's gift.

"Please don't kill us," Richard repeated. There *was* a hexagram for "kill/end" now. "Please don't."

The Cold paused, and asked "Why not?"

X

It was getting dark, which didn't bother Jamie. He lifted his goggles and saw in more detail. He also felt the cold less. Most of his teammates were more spooked as shadows spread, but Gené was another nightbird. You'd never know she'd come close to having a dirty great icicle shoved all the way through her chest. Perhaps she had a little of the Shade in her. She'd said she knew Auntie Jenny.

Regular Keith was bewildered about what had happened while he was away, and Susan was trying to fill him in. Sewell Head was quoting weather statistics since before records began. It was snowing even harder, and the slog to Alder wasn't going to be possible without losing one or more of the happy little band. Finding shelter was a high priority. They were in the lee of Sutton Mallet church – which was small, but had a tower. The place was securely chained.

"Can't you break these?" Jamie asked Gené.

"Normal chains, yes. Chapel chains, I have a bit of a mental block about. Try the spoon-bender."

Susan stepped up and laid hands on the metal. She frowned, and links began to buckle.

"Where's Head?" asked Keith.

Captain Cleverclogs wasn't with them. Jamie couldn't understand why anyone would wander off. Had the last snowman got him?

"Here are his tracks," said Gené.

"I can't see any," said Keith.

"Trust me."

Jamie saw them too. Sewell Head had gone into a thicket of trees, just beyond what passed for the centre of Sutton Mallet. There were buildings on the other side.

"I'll fetch him back," he said.

"We're not being that stupid, Jamie," said Susan, dropping mangled but unbroken chains. "You go, we all go. No sense splitting up and getting picked off one by one."

She had a point. He was thinking like Dad, who preferred to work alone.

Beyond the trees were ugly buildings. A concrete shed, temporary cabins.

"This is Derek Leech's weather research station," said Gené. "Almost certainly where all the trouble started."

Derek Leech was in the public eye as a smiling businessman, but Jamie's Dad called him "a human void". Jamie had thought Dad a bit cracked on the subject of Derek Leech – like everyone else's parents were cracked about long hair or short hair or the Common Market or some other bloody thing. He was coming round to think more of what his old man said.

"Shouldn't we stay away from here?" cautioned Keith. "Aren't we supposed to join up with folks more qualified than us?"

"You mean grown-ups?" asked Jamie.

"Well, yes."

"Poor old Swellhead'll be an ice lolly by the time you fetch a teacher."

Beside the building was a towering snowman. Bugs, grown to Kitten Kong proportions. The front doors were blown inward and jammed open by snowdrifts. It was a fair guess Head had gone inside. If he could get past the snow-giant, they had a good chance.

"Susan," he said. "Can you concentrate on the snowman? At the first sign of hassle, melt the big bastard."

The woman snapped off a salute. "Since you ask so nicely," she said, "I'll give it a whirl."

"Okay, gang," he said. "Let's go inside."

They sprinted from the thicket to the doors. Bugs didn't make a move, but Keith tripped and Gené had to help him up and drag him.

Inside the building, which was an ice-palace, the wind was less of a problem, and they were protected from the worst of the snow. Overhead lights buzzed and flickered, bothering Jamie's eyes. He slipped his goggles back on.

They found Sewell Head in a room that might have been a mess hall. He was acting as a valet, helping a man dress in arctic gear. Jamie recognized the bloke from the telly. He was the one who said "If I didn't love it, I wouldn't own it." He must love lots of things, because he owned a shedload of them.

"Hi," he said. "I'm Derek. You must be the new Doctor Shade."

Yes, Jamie realized. He must be.

Leech's smile jangled his shadow-senses. The dark in him was something more than night.

"I'm a big fan of your father's," said Leech. "I learned to read from tear-sheets of the newspaper strip they ran about his adventures. Ahh, 'the Whooping Horror', 'the Piccadilly Gestapo'. How I longed for my own autogyro! I have a car just like Dr Shade's. A Shadow-Shark."

Jamie remembered that there had been *two* Rollses in the snow. Whose was the other one?

"Leech," said Gené, acknowledging him.

"Geneviève Dieudonné," said Leech, cordially. "I thought you'd aged hundreds of years and died."

"I got better."

"Well done. Though live through the night before you pat yourself on the back too much. Where's the rest of the army? The heavy mob. Ariadne, Jago, Mrs Michaelsmith, Little Rose? The Cold's already got Jeperson. We need to go all-out on the attack if we're to have a chance of stopping it."

"We're it, right now," said Jamie.

"You'll have to do, then."

Jamie boiled inside at that. He didn't even know the people Leech had listed. Whoever they might be, he doubted they'd have done as well against the snowmen.

"Who might you be, my dear?" Leech said to Susan.

"I might be Susan Rodway. Or Susan Ames. Mum got remarried, and I have a choice."

"I know exactly who you are," said Leech. "Shade, why didn't you say you had her? She's not Rose Farrar or an Elder of the Kind, but she's a bloody good start."

Susan began primping a bit at the attention. Jamie couldn't believe she'd let this hand-kissing creep smarm her up like that. He'd never understand birds.

"Now, Sewell," said Leech, addressing his instant orderly. "Get on the blower and tell Miss Kaye to pull her finger out. The telephone kit is in the laboratory down the hall – the room with the tied-up-

and-gagged idiot in it. It's simple to use. You'll have the specs for it in your head somewhere."

Head meekly trotted out of the room. He was taking orders without question.

Leech looked over the four of them – Jamie, Gené, Susan, Keith.

"Susan," he said, "can you do something about the room temperature?"

Susan, bizarrely, seemed smitten. "I can *try*," she said, and shut her eyes.

A little warmth radiated from her. Some icicles started dripping. Jamie felt his face pricking, as feeling returned.

"Good girl," said Leech. "You, young fellow-me-lad. Any chance of getting some tea going?"

"Give it a try, sir," said Keith, hunting a kettle.

Jamie already resented Derek Leech. For a start, he had released all those triple LPs of moaning woodwind hippies which got played over and over in student common rooms. Even if he weren't the literal Devil, that alone made him a man not to be trusted. But he was magnetic in person, and Jamie felt a terrible tug – it would be easier to go along with Leech, to take orders, to not be responsible for the others. Dad could be like that too, but he always drummed it into Jamie that he should become his own man. Dad didn't even disapprove of him being in a band rather than joining the night-wars – though he realized he'd done that anyway, as well. If he was the new Dr Shade, he was also a different Shade.

It was Leech's world too. If this big freeze was spreading, it was his interest to side with the angels. If everyone was dead, no one would make a deal with him. No one would buy his crappy music or read his raggy papers.

Jamie saw that Gené was sceptical of anything Leech-related, but Susan and Keith were sucked in. Keith had found his grown-up, his teacher. Susan had found something she needed too. Jamie had been revising his impression of her all day. Leech saw at once that she was the most useful Talent in their crowd. Jamie hadn't even noticed her at first, and he had been around Talents all his life. Susan Rodway was not only Shade-level or better in her abilities, but extremely good at keeping it to herself. She kept talking about the things she couldn't do, or making light of the things she could.

Leech had been briefly interested in Jamie, in *Dr Shade* – but he had instantly passed over him, and latched onto Susan.

He realized – with a tiny shock – that he was jealous. But of whom? Susan, for going to the head of the class? Or Leech, for getting the girl's attention? There wasn't time for this.

"What did you say about Richard Jeperson?" Gené asked Leech.

Jamie knew Jeperson was Fred and Vanessa's guv'nor at the Diogenes Club. He tied in with Gené too.

"Mad, definitely," said Leech, with just a hint of pleasure. "Dead, probably. The Cold took him – it's a thinking thing, not just bad weather – and he went outside, naked. He lay down and let himself be buried. I tried to stop him, but he fought like a tiger, knocked me out . . . gave me this." Leech indicated a fresh wound on his forehead.

"Stone in a snowball," he said. "Playground trick."

Gené thought a few moments and said, "We've got to go out and find him. He might still be alive. He's not helpless. He's a Talent too. If he's buried, we can dig him up."

"I think that's a good idea," said Leech.

Anything Leech thought was a good idea was almost certainly good mostly or only for him. But Jamie couldn't see any alternative. He knew that Fred would give him a right belting if he let Jeperson die.

"Okay, I'll go," he said. "Gené, Susan, stay here. Give Mr Leech any help he needs . . ." *That is, keep a bloody eye on him!* Gené, though worried for her friend, picked that up.

Leech was bland, mild, innocent.

"Keith," said Jamie, at last. "Find a shovel or something, and come with me."

Keith, infuriatingly, looked to Leech – who gave him the nod.

"Come on, find someone useful inside you. Let's get this rescue party on the road!"

Keith gulped and said, "O-okay, Jamie."

XI

Derek Leech was on the telephone again. Really, the man had the most terrible manners. He had some minion bother Catriona, then brushed her aside because he wanted to talk with Maureen Mountmain, of all people. Catriona passed the receiver to the woman, who listened – to her master's voice? – and clucked. *Yes, Mr Leech, no Mr Leech, three bags bloody full, Mr Leech* . . . Catriona caught herself: this was no time to be a cranky old woman.

The Cold was getting into the Manor House, overwhelming Louise Teazle's bubble of summer. Frost grew on the insides of the windows. Sleet and snow rattled against the panes.

In the gloom of the gardens, drifts and banks shifted like beasts. Catriona had pain in her joints, and was irritated. She could list other age-related aches and infirmities, exacerbated by the Cold.

Only Rose Farrar and Ariadne were immune. Rose skipped around the drawing room, exhaling white clouds. Ariadne stood by the fireplace – where the wood wouldn't light, and shivers of snow fell on tidy ashes – and smoked a cigarette in a long, elegant holder.

Paulette Michaelsmith shivered in her sleep, and Louise rearranged her day-blanket without any effect. Karabatsos and his wife huddled together. Mr Zed was white. Swami Anand Gitamo chanted mantras, but his nose was blue. Lark and Cross, the white-coats, passed the china teapot between them, pressing their hands against the last of its warmth. Even Anthony Jago, who feared not the ice and fire of Hell, had his hands in his armpits. The house itself creaked more than usual.

"Richard?" exclaimed Maureen. "Are you sure?"

Catriona, who had been trying not to listen, had a spasm of concern. Maureen had blurted out the name in shock. She and Richard had . . .

Maureen hung up, cutting off Catriona's train of thought. The room looked to Maureen for a report.

"Derek needs us all," she said. "He needs us to hurt the Cold."

A lot of people talked at once, then shut up.

"Catriona," said Maureen, fists pressed together under her impressive bosom, "your man Richard Jeperson is lost."

"Lost?"

"Probably dead. I'm sorry, truly. Derek says he tried to reach the Cold, and it took him. It's a monster, and wants to kill us all. We have to hit it with all we've got, now. All our big guns, he says. Maybe it can't be killed, but can be hurt. Driven back to its hole."

A tear dribbled from Maureen's eye.

"Reverend Jago, Lady Elder, Rose . . . you're our biggest guns. Just tear into the Cold. Miss Teazle, work on Mrs Michaelsmith – direct her. Think of the heat-wave. Karabatsos, clear a circle and make a summoning. A fire elemental. The rest of you, pray. That's not a figure of speech. The only way we can beat this thing is with an enormous spiritual attack."

The news about Richard was a terrible blow. Catriona let Maureen go on with her "to arms" speech, trying to take it in. She was not a sensitive in the way any of these Talents were, but she was not a closed mind. And Maureen had said Richard was only *probably* dead.

Mr and Mrs Karabatsos were the first to act. They rolled aside a carpet and began chalking a circle on the living room floor.

"Excuse me," said Catriona. "Is this your house?"

Karabatsos glared at her, nastily triumphant. Catriona would not be looked at like that in her home.

"No need to bother with that," said Anand Gitamo.

"Summoning a fire elemental requires a circle, and a ritual," said Karabatsos. "Blood must be spilled and burned."

"Yes dear, *spilled* and *burned*," echoed his wife.

"In normal company, maybe," said the Swami, sounding more like plain old Harry Cutley. "But we've got extraordinary guests. We can take short cuts. Now, you two sorcerers shut your eyes and think about your blessed fire elemental. Extra-hot and flaming from the Pits of Abaddon and Erebus and all that. Think hard, now think harder. Imagine more flames, more heat, more burning. Take your basic fire elemental, add the Japanese pikadon, the Norse Surtur, Graeco-Roman Haephaestus or Vulcan, the phoenix, the big bonfire at the end of *The Wicker Man*, that skyscraper from *The Towering Inferno*, the Great Fire of London in 1666, enough napalm to deforest the Republic of Vietnam and the eternal blue flame of the lost city of Kôr . . ."

Nigel Karabatsos and his wife shut their eyes and thought of fire.

"Rose dear," said Gitamo. "Peek into those tiny minds."

Rose Farrar caught fire and expanded. She grew into a nine-foot-tall column of living flame, with long limbs and a blazing skull-face. Though she was hard to look at and her radiant heat filled the room, she didn't burn the ceiling or the carpet. She was Fire.

"Reverend Jago," said Gitamo, "would you open the doors. Rose needs to go outside."

The man in the dog-collar was astonished by what the apparent little girl had become. Anthony Jago didn't know whether to bow down before a fiery angel of the Lord or cast out a demon from Hell. His already-peculiar belief system was horribly battered by this experience. Catriona feared no good would come of that.

But, if anything could hurt the Cold, it would be Fire Rose.

Louise Teazle reported that the snow outside was melting. Fire Rose was radiating, beyond the walls.

"No," said Ariadne, snapping her fingers. "I think not."

Fire Rose went out. Spent-match stink filled the room. The little girl, unburned and unburning, sat on the floor exactly as she had been. She was bewildered. No one had ever switched her off like a light before.

Jago was enraged. All the cups, saucers and cutlery on the table near him and all the books on the shelves behind him leaped at once into the air, and hovered like projectiles about to be slung. Catriona had known he was a telekinetic, but this was off the scale. In any other drawing room, parapsychologists like Cross and Lark would be thinking of the book deals and the lecture tour – though, after Fire Rose, this little display scarcely made the needle tick. Jago's eyes smouldered.

Ariadne shook her head, and everything went neatly back to its place. Not a drop of tea spilled or a dust jacket torn. Jago knitted his brows, blood vessels pulsing, but not so much as a teaspoon responded.

Mr Zed took out a gun, caught Ariadne's gaze, then pointed it at his own head. He stood still as a statue.

"If we're not going off half-cocked," said the Elder of the Kind, "let us review our plan of action. In dealing with the Cold, do we really want to do *what Derek Leech says*."

Exactly. Ariadne had said what Catriona felt.

"You can't win a Winter War with fire," she said. "Fire consumes, leaves only ashes."

"Then what?" said Maureen, frustrated, red-eyed. "If not Derek's plan, what? I'd really like to know, ladies. I'm freezing my tits off here."

"There there," said Catriona, touching Maureen's shoulder. "Have faith. He'll be all right."

Maureen didn't ask who she meant.

"He'll see us through," Catriona said.

Richard.

XII

On some other path in life, an expert outdoorsman Keith had loads of survival training in extreme weather conditions. Probably, Keith had to weed out a couple of dozen plonkers who didn't know how to tie their own shoelaces, but he'd found the useful life in seconds. Not a bad trick. While Jamie scanned for tracks or a human-shaped bump in the snow, Keith barked instructions – keep moving, breathe through your nose, turn your shoulder to the wind.

One good thing: in all this mucky weather, Richard Jeperson couldn't have gone far.

Any footprints were filled by new snow. The marks they had made coming from the thicket to the buildings were already gone. Jamie looked for dark traces, the shadows of shadows. It was Dad's game, and he wasn't expert in it yet – but he could usually see shadow-ghosts, if he caught them in time.

He found a discarded fur boot. And another.

A shaggy clump a little past the boots turned out not to be the missing man, but an abandoned coat. A fold of dayglo green poking up from the snow was a cast-off balaclava. Leech had said Jeperson went out naked. That was not true. Jeperson had gone outside, *then* taken his clothes off. Leech wouldn't have got that wrong unless he were deliberately lying. If Jeperson knocked Leech out and left him inside, Leech would not have known what Jeperson did next – but he had said Jeperson took his clothes off, went out and lay down in the show. Had Leech attacked Jeperson, stripped him, and left him to freeze to death, cooking up a story to exonerate himself? Jamie should have checked at once – tried to replay the shadows in the building. He had an inkling it wouldn't have worked. There was something wrong with Leech's shadow.

He hoped Gené and Susan could take care of themselves. Derek Leech was dangerous.

They were near Bugs, the mammoth snowman. It had lost human shape and become a mountain. Novelty insects still bobbed on its summit like the Union Flag on top of Everest.

Jamie saw the shadow lying at the foot of Mount Bugs. A man, stretched out. Jeperson was under here.

He pointed to the spot and told Keith, "Dig there, mate. *There.*"

"Where?"

Keith didn't have the Shade-sight. Jamie knelt and began scooping snow away with gloved hands. Keith used a tray from the cafeteria as a spade, digging deep.

A face emerged, in a nest of long, frozen hair. Thin, blue, hollow-cheeked, jagged-moustached and open-eyed.

"Hello," said Jeperson, smiling broadly. "You must be the new boys."

XIII

Suddenly, Richard felt the cold. Not the Cold – he was disconnected, now. The little crystals were out of his brain. He hoped he had given the Cold something to think about.

"Would you happen to have seen some clothes in your travels?" he asked the two young men. One wore a long dark greatcoat and goggles, the other a red-lined magician's cloak.

They dragged his fur coat along and tried to wrap him in it. What he could see of his skin was sky-blue.

"It's stopped snowing," he observed.

The wind was down too. And sun shone through, low in the West. It was late evening. Long shadows were red-edged.

The Cold was responding to his plea, drawing in its chill. It could live on in perpetuity as a sub-microscopic speck inside a rock, or confine itself to the poles, or go back to the void below absolute zero. Without Cleaver telling it what it wanted, it had its own choices. Richard hoped he had persuaded the Cold that other life on Earth was entertaining enough to be put up with.

Now, he would probably die.

He hoped he had done the right thing. He was sorry he'd never found out who his real parents had been. He wished he'd spent more time with Barbara, but – obviously – he'd been busy lately. His personal life hadn't been a priority, and that was a regret. He could trust Fred and Vanessa to keep on, at least for a while. And, if these lads were anything to judge by, the Diogenes Club, or something like it, would continue to stand against Great Enchanters present and future, and all manner of other inexplicable threats to the public safety.

The boy in the goggles tried rubbing Richard's hands, but his friend – who knew something about hypothermia treatment – told him not to. Friction just damages more blood vessels. Gradual, all-round warmth was needed. Not that there was an easy supply around here.

He tried to think of quotable last words.

Some people came out of the building. Leech, and two women. One flew to him. Geneviève. Good for her. They'd not worked together much, but the old girl was a long-standing Valued Member.

"Richard, you won't die," she said.

"I think I'll need a second opinion," he muttered. "A less optimistic one."

"No, really," she insisted.

Leech hung back, shiftily. Richard expected no more. Geneviève pulled the other woman – a brown-haired girl who kept herself to herself – to help, and got her to press her hands on Richard's chest.

Warmth radiated from her touch.

"That's very . . . nice," he said. "Who are you?"

"This is Susan," said Geneviève. "She's a friend."

Richard had heard of her. Susan Rodway. She was on Catriona's list of possibles.

He felt as if he were sinking into a hot, perfumed bath. Feeling returned to his limbs. He heard hissing and tinkling, as snow and ice melted around them. A bubble of heat was forming. Susan took it slowly, not heating him too fast. His temperature came up like a diver hauled to the surface in stages to avoid the bends.

He tactfully rearranged a flap of fur to cover his loins. Susan's magic warmth had reached there, with an unshrivelling effect he rarely cared to share on such brief acquaintance.

"What did you do?" asked Geneviève. "Are we saved?"

Richard tried to shrug. "I did what I could. I think the Cold is getting a sense of who we are, what we're about and why we shouldn't just be killed out of hand. Who knows what something like that can really feel, think or do? You have to call off the blitzkrieg, though. Any smiting with fire and sword is liable to undo the work of diplomacy and land us back in the big fridge."

Leech was expressionless. Richard wondered how things would be if he'd had his way.

Geneviève looked back and said, "Make the call, Derek."

He made no move. Geneviève stood. Leech nodded, once, and walked back to the building.

"I see you've met Dr Shade and Conjurer Keith," said Geneviève. "They've done all right too."

Susan took her hands away. Richard regretted it, but knew her touch couldn't last. Everyone looked at the huge, liquefying snow-giant as he stood up and got dressed as best he could. Sharon Kellett would be inside that glacier. The others would be strewn around the fields.

This patch of Somerset would be better irrigated than the rest of Britain – for a few days.

"Who else turned up for the ice age?" Richard asked.

"There's a knowledgeable little fellow you don't need to meet just now," said Geneviève. "He didn't even waver, like some folks. Went straight to Leech. He's inside the weather station. At the Manor House, Catriona has a whole tea party. Old friends and new. Including a strong contingent from the Other Side."

"I can imagine."

"Maureen Mountmain's here," she said, pointedly.

Richard was glad to be warned of that potential complication. Geneviève let the point stick with a needling glance.

"It was a ritual," said Richard, knowing how weak the excuse was.

"It was still . . ." she mouthed the word "sex".

Richard knew he was being ribbed. Now they were less doomed, they could start squabbling, gossiping and teasing again.

Leech came back.

"We're invited to supper at the Manor House," he said. "It's only nine o'clock, would you believe it? You'll have to make my excuses, I'm afraid. I have to get back to London. Things to do, people to buy. Give my best to Miss Kaye. Oh, Cleaver's dead. Choked on his false teeth. Pity."

The blotch on his forehead was already gone. Leech recovered quickly.

"See you soon," he said, and walked away.

Richard knew an autopsy wouldn't show anything conclusive. Professor Cleaver would be listed as another incidental casualty.

"I feel much warmer now he's gone," said Geneviève. "Didn't he say something about supper?"

XIV

Most of the company had scurried back to their holes. Catriona was relieved to have them out of the house.

She sat in her drawing room. Paulette Michaelsmith was upstairs, tucked up and dreaming safely. Louise Teazle had walked home to the Hollow, her house on the moor. Geneviève was outside in the garden, with the young people. She was the last of the old ladies.

Ariadne had taken Rose with her. Mr Zed, round weal on his temple, didn't even complain. The Undertakers were a spent force, but even in their prime they couldn't have stood against an Elder of the Kind. Rose would be safe with Ariadne, and – more to the point – the world would be safe from her. Catriona assumed that Ariadne could pack Rose off to where she came from, just as – eighty years ago – Charles Beauregard sent Princess Cuckoo home. However, the Elder might choose to raise the creature who usually looked like a little girl as her own. At this stage of her life, Catriona doubted she'd live to find out. Charles wasn't here. Edwin wasn't here. At times, Catriona wondered if she were really here. She knew more ghosts than living people, and regretted the rasher statements made about spirits of the unquiet dead in books she had published in her long-ago youth. Occasionally, she welcomed the odd clanking chain or floating bed-sheet.

Maureen Mountmain, clearly torn, had wanted to stay and see Richard – she babbled a bit about having something to tell him – but Leech had ordered her to rally a party of Mr and Mrs Karabatsos,

Myra Lark, Jago and leave. Jago, well on the way to replacing Rose as Catriona's idea of the most frightening person on the planet, took a last look around the Manor House, as if thinking of moving in, and slid off into the evening with Maureen's group. They wouldn't be able to keep him for long. Jago had his own plans. Leech had picked up Sewell Head, too – though Catriona had looked over his file, and concluded it would take a lot to lure him out of his sweet shop and away from his books of quiz questions.

On the plus side, the Club had tentative gains. Susan Rodway and Jamie Chambers – the new Dr Shade! – were hardly clubbable in the old-fashioned sense, but Mycroft Holmes had founded the Diogenes Club as a club for the unclubbable. Even Keith Marion, in a reasonable percentage of his might-have-been selves, was inclined to the good – though finding a place for him was even more of a challenge. Geneviève reported that the Chambers Boy showed his father's dark spark, tempered with a little more sympathy than habitually displayed by Jonathan Chambers. Derek Leech must want to sign up Dr Shade. The Shades wavered, leaning towards one side or the other according to circumstance or their various personalities. The boy could not be forced or wooed too strongly, for fear of driving him to the bad. Leech would not give up on such a potent Talent. There might even be a percentage in letting Jamie get close to Leech, putting the lad in the other camp for a while. Susan was reluctant to become a laboratory rat for David Cross or Myra Lark, but was too prodigious to let slip. Without her warm hands, Richard would not have lived through this cold spell. Susan needed help coping with her Talent, and had taken Catriona's card. If Jamie could be a counter for Leech, Susan was possibly their best hope of matching Jago. It chilled Catriona that she could even consider sending a girl barely in her twenties up against an Effective Talent like Anthony Jago, but no one else was left to make the decisions.

She was thinking like Edwin now, or even Mycroft. The Diogenes Club, or whatever stood in its stead, had to play a long game. She had been a girl younger than Susan or Jamie when this started for her. The rector's daughter, not the lady of the manor. At eighteen, with Edwin away at the front, she had been escorted by Charles to Mycroft's funeral. That had been a changing of the guard. Some of the famous names and faces of generations before her own seemed like dinosaurs and relics in her eyes. Even Mycroft's famous brother was a bright-eyed old gaffer with a beaky nose, fingers bandaged from bee-stings and yellow teeth from decades of three-pipe problems. Richard Riddle had been there, with his uncle and aunt. In his

RFC uniform and jaunty eye-patch, the former boy detective was impossibly glamorous to her. She had a better idea than most where he had flown to in 1934, and still expected him to turn up again, with his chums Vi and Ernie.

Charles had pointed out Inspector Henry Mist, Thomas Carnacki, Sir Henry Merrivale, Winston Churchill, General Hector Tarr, John Silence, Sir Michael Calme, Mansfield Smith-Cumming, Margery Device, the Keeper of the Ravens, and others. Now, Catriona knew Geneviève had been there too, spying through blue lenses from the edge of the crowd – Mycroft's most *secret* secret agent and, contrary to the public record, the first Lady Member of the Diogenes Club. After all the fuss, Catriona turned out not to be the first of her sex to be admitted to the Inner Rooms – though she was the first woman to chair the Ruling Cabal.

It had been a busy sixty years. Angel Down, Irene Dobson, the Murder Mandarin, the Seven Stars, the last flight of the Demon Ace, Spring-Heel'd Jack, Dien Ch'ing, the Splendid Six, Weezie's Hauntings, the Rat Among the Ravens, the Crazy Gang, Parsifal le Gallois, the Water War, Adolf Hitler, Swastika Girl, the Malvern Mystery, the Scotch Streak, the Trouble with Titan, Castle De'ath, the Drache Development, Paulette's dream, the Soho Golem, the Ghoul Crisis, the Missing Mythwrhn, and so many others. And now the Cold. There was more to come, she knew. Richard Jeperson's work wasn't done. Her work wasn't done. The Secret Files of the Diogenes Club remained open.

She felt a whisper against her cheek.

XV

The garden was Disneyfied: white pools of melting ice, nightbirds singing. Light spilled onto the lawns from the upstairs windows of the Manor House. Glints reflected in dwindling icicles. Jamie saw activity streaks in the shadows. With the Cold drawn in, the land was healing.

No one had to worry about World Cooling any more.

Richard Jeperson, the Man from the Diogenes Club, tried to explain what he had done. It boiled down to getting the attention of a vast, unknowable creature and asking it very nicely not to wipe out all lifeforms that needed a temperature above freezing to survive. Jamie realized how lucky they had been. Only someone who could ask *very* politely and tactfully would have got a result. A few bumps the other way, along one of Keith's paths, and it could have been Derek Leech under the snow . . .

Leech had left Jamie his card, and he hadn't thrown it away.

Many of the people drawn to the Winter War had melted away like the ice. Some were sleeping over in the house. Jamie's van was parked next to Richard's ShadowShark in the drive.

He sat on a white filigree lawn-chair, drinking black coffee from an electric pot. The hostess, an elderly lady who had not joined them outside, provided a pretty fair scratch supper for the survivors and their hangers-on. Now, there were wafer-thin mints. Gené was in a lawn-swing, drinking something red and steaming that wasn't tomato soup. Richard, still glowing with whatever Susan had fed into him, smoked a fat, hand-rolled cigarette that wasn't a joint but wasn't tobacco either. Considering what he'd done, Jamie reckoned he could demand that the Archbishop of Canterbury and the Prime Minister hand-deliver an ounce of Jamaican, the Crown Jewels and Princess Margaret dressed up in a St Trinian's uniform to his room within the next half-hour and expect an answer of "right away, sir".

"How was your first day on the job?" Gené asked him.

"Job?"

"Your Dad called it a practice. Being Dr Shade."

"Not sure about the handle. I thought I'd just go with 'Shade' for a bit. 'Jamie Shade', maybe? I'd use it for the band, but it sounds too much like Slade."

"I quite like Slade," said Richard.

"You would," said Jamie. "What a year, eh?"

"It has had its meteorological anomalies."

"No, I mean the charts. Telly Savalas, Real Thing, The Brother-hood of Man, Abba, the Wurzels, J. J. Barrie, Demis Roussos . . . 'Brand New Combine Harvester', 'Save Your Kisses for Me', bloody 'No Charge'. It has to be the low-point in music since forever. It's like some great evil entity was sucking the guts out of our sounds. Some *other* great evil entity. You can't blame Leech for all of it. Even he wouldn't touch the Wurzels. Something's got to change. Maybe I'll stick with the band, leave monsters and magic to other folk. Kids are fed up, you know. They want to hear something new. And you lot are getting on."

"Do you feel 'long in the tooth', Geneviève?" Richard asked.

Gené bared teeth that Jamie could have sworn were longer than they had been earlier.

"It's not about how old you are," said Susan, who had been quietly sipping a drink with fruit in it. "It's about what you do."

"Here's to that," said Richard, clinking his glass to hers.

Keith was sitting quietly, not letting on which of his selves was home. The primary Keith had reluctantly given Jamie back the Great Edmondo's cloak and its hidden tricks. He had asked if Dr Shade needed an assistant, and started shuttling through selves when Jamie told him he really needed a new drummer. Now, despite what he'd said, he wasn't sure. Being Dr Shade meant something, and came with a lot of baggage. He half-thought Vron was only with him because of who his Dad was. These people kept calling him "Junior Shade", "Young Dr Shade" or "the New Dr Shade". Perhaps he should take them seriously. He was already a veteran of the Winter War, if something over inside two days counted as a war.

Like Dad, he wasn't much of a joiner. He couldn't see himself putting a tie on to get into some fusty old club. But he played well with others. How randomly had his vanload of raw recruits been assembled? Even Sewell Head, now lost to Leech, had come in handy. Maybe, he'd found his new band. Susan, Gené and Keith all had Talents. Perhaps the old hippie with the ringlets and the 'tache could take the odd guest guitar solo. One thing was for certain, they wouldn't sign with a Derek Leech label.

In the house, the lights went off, and the garden was dark. Jamie didn't mind the dark. From now on, he owned it.

"Catriona's gone to bed," said Richard.

Gené, another night person, stretched out on the grass, as if sunning herself in shadows.

"Some of us never sleep," she said. "Someone has to watch out for the world. Or we might lose it."

"We're not going to let that happen," said Richard.

STEPHEN JONES & KIM NEWMAN

Necrology: 2007

ONCE AGAIN, we remember the passing of writers, artists, performers and technicians who, during their lifetimes, made significant contributions to the horror, science fiction and fantasy genres, or left their mark on popular culture and music in other, often fascinating, ways . . .

AUTHORS/ARTISTS/COMPOSERS

Turkish-born novelist turned *noir* screenwriter **A.** (Albert) **I.** (Isaac) "Buzz" **Bezzerides,** who scripted *Track of the Cat* and *Kiss Me Deadly*, died on 1 January after complications from a fall. He was 98. He later co-created the Western TV series *The Big Valley* (1965–69) starring Barbara Stanwyck.

TV writer and producer **Laurence Heath** died on 9 January, aged 78. He worked on *Mission: Impossible* during the early 1970s, and his other credits include *The Invaders*, *The Magician*, *Murder She Wrote* and the 1978 TV movie *The Beasts Are on the Streets*.

American writer, lecturer and conspiracy theorist **Robert Anton Wilson** died after a long illness from post-polio syndrome on 11 January, aged 74. When his condition became known in 2006, and it was revealed that he had no money for care, an online appeal to fans raised enough to allow him to live out his remaining days in home hospice care. Best-known for his 1970s *Illuminatus!* trilogy (co-written with Robert Shea) – *The Eye in the Pyramid*, *The Golden Apple* and *Leviathan* – Wilson's other books included *Cosmic Trigger: The Final Secret of the Illuminati*, *The Illuminati Papers* and *Masks of the Illuminati*. The original trilogy was adapted as a stage play and premiered in Liverpool in 1977. His *Schrödinger's Cat* trilogy (*The Universe Next Door, The Trick Top Hat* and *The Homing Pigeons*) dealt with quantum mechanics and parallel universes, and he co-edited the anthology *Semiotext(e) SF* with Rudy Rucker and Peter Lamborn Wilson. Wilson's fifteen-year-old daughter, Patricia Luna Wilson, was murdered in 1975, and the family had her brain cryogenically frozen.

Fifty-one-year-old **John W. Brower**, the founder of Minneapolis regional convention Arcana, was found dead in his apartment in early January. He had been suffering from intestinal problems and had died sometime in late December 2006.

British screenwriter and producer **Tudor Gates** died on 14 January, aged 76. Best remembered for his early 1970s lesbian vampire trilogy for Hammer Films – *The Vampire Lovers, Lust for a Vampire* and *Twins of Evil* – he also contributed to the scripts for *Danger: Diabolk, Barbarella* and *The Young The Evil and The Savage* (uncredited), and wrote *Fright* (aka *Night Legs*) plus episodes of TV's *Strange Report* and *Sherlock Holmes and Doctor Watson*. As "Teddy White" or "Edward Hyde" he variously wrote, produced or directed such sexploitation films as *The Love Box, The Sex Thief* (directed by Martin Campbell), *Intimate Games* and *Sex with the Stars*.

Emmy Award-winning composer and orchestrator **Harvey R. Cohen** died of a heart attack on the same day, aged 55. He composed music for such 1990s animated TV shows as *Aladdin, Batman, Casper, Superman, The New Batman Adventures* and *Superman: The Last Son of Krypton*, along with the 1988 movie *Ghost Town*. Cohen also worked on a number of other films, including *DeepStar Six, Wes Craven's New Nightmare, Bicentennial Man, Little Nicky, King Kong* (2005) and *The Shaggy Dog* (2006).

Renowned American author **Daniel Stern** died of complications from heart surgery on 24 January, aged 79. His short stories are collected in *Twice Told Tales, Twice Upon a Time* and *One Day's Perfect Weather*, while his 1968 novel *The Suicide Academy* is set in a world where suicide is encouraged.

Brazilian-born American author **Charles L.** (Louis) **Fontenay** died on 27 January, aged 89. He published his first story in *If* in 1954, and his shorter work is collected in *Here There and Elsewhen, The Solar System* and *Beyond and Now and Elsewhen*. He wrote three SF novels in the 1950s and 1960s (*Twice Upon a Time, Rebels of the Red Planet* and *The Day the Oceans Overflowed*), and returned in the 1980s and 1990s with a series of eighteen children's novellas, the "Kipton Chronicles". His later books include *Target: Grant 1862* and *Modál*.

Bob Carroll Jr (Robert Gordon Carroll, Jr) who, with Madelyn Pugh Davis, wrote all 180 episodes of TV's *I Love Lucy* (1951–57) and various spin-off shows, died on the same day, aged 87.

Sixty-eight-year-old Czechoslovakian pop composer **Karel Svoboda** was found dead at his home from a self-inflicted gunshot wound on 28 January. A former rock singer with the band "Mefisto", he scored numerous films and TV shows, including *Tomorrow I'll Wake Up and Scald Myself With Tea* (based on a SF story by Josef Nesvadba) and the animated TV series *The Adventures of Pinocchio* (1976). His stage musical of *Dracula* sold 250,000 soundtrack albums, and his last major work was a 2006 musical titled *Golem*.

Bestselling novelist and Oscar-winning Hollywood screenwriter **Sidney Sheldon** died of complications from pneumonia on 30 January, aged 89. He began writing at the age of fifty, and his eighteen published novels sold around 300 million copies and were translated into seventy-one languages. He created and produced the TV series *I Dream of Jeannie* (1965–69) and scripted the 1986 vampire episode "Red Snow" for *Twilight Zone*.

Ninety-year-old **Julius Dixson, Sr**, who co-wrote the 1958 pop hit "Lollipop" for The Chordettes, reportedly starved to death in a Manhattan hospital the same day. Staff apparently ignored complaints that he needed his missing dentures to eat. "Lollipop" was covered in Britain by The Mudlarks, where it also went to the top of the charts. Dixson also wrote hits for Bill Haley and The Comets and The Spacemen.

Anthology editor and publisher **Roger P.** (Paul) **Elwood** died of cancer on 2 February, aged 64. Beginning with *Alien Worlds* in 1964 he edited or co-edited more than eighty original SF anthologies, most of which (fifty-five) were published between 1972 and 1977. As a result of this market saturation, he was blamed by many for the collapse of the anthology market, which has continued to this day. In 1975 Elwood founded the Laser Books imprint for romance publisher Harlequin and from 1975–77 fifty-eight books were issued, all with original covers by Frank Kelly Freas. These included first novels by Tim Powers and K. W. Jeter. A committed Christian, he edited SF lines for Pyramid, Bobbs-Merrill and Pinnacle before writing more than thirty "inspirational" novels, many with SF and fantasy elements.

American fan writer, editor and author **Lee Hoffman** (Shirley Bell Hoffman) died of a heart attack on 6 February, aged 74. She published thirty issues of the fanzine *Quandry* (1950–53) and other small press titles, and a collection of essays and articles, *In and Out of Quandry*, was published to commemorate her appearance as Fan Guest of Honor at Chicon IV, the 1982 World Science Fiction Convention in Chicago. Best known as an award-winning writer of Westerns (her novel *The Valdez Horses* was filmed as *Chino*), her SF books include *Telepower*, *The Caves of Karst*, *Always the Black Knight* and *Change Song*. She was married to editor Larry Shaw from 1956–58, and during that period was assistant editor on his magazines *Infinity Science Fiction* and *Science Fiction Adventures*.

American author **Fred Mustard Stewart**, best known for his superior supernatural novel *The Mephisto Waltz* (filmed in 1971), died of cancer on 7 February. His other novels include *Star Child* and *The Methuselah Enzyme*.

Comics artist **Joe Edwards** died of complications from heart problems on 8 February, aged 85. After working for Dell and Timely, he joined MLJ Comics, which subsequently changed its name to Archie. A former animation artist, he drew a number of "funny animal" strips for *Archie Comics* #1 (1942) and went on to illustrate many flagship characters, including "Super Duck", "Captain Sprocket" and, most notably, "Li'l Jinx".

English-born Australian writer **Elizabeth Jolly** (Monica Elizabeth Knight) died of complications from Alzheimer's disease in Perth on 13 February, aged 83. Her "Australian Gothic" novels include *Milk and Honey* and *The Well*, and her short fiction is collected in *Five Acre Virgin*.

Oscar-winning lyricist **Ray Evans** died on 15 February of an apparent heart attack. He was 92. During the 1940s and 1950s with writing partner Jay Livingston (who died in 2001) he was responsible for such hits from the movies as "Buttons and Bows", "Mona Lisa", "Silver Bells", "Que Sera Sera", "Tammy" and "Dear Heart". After their song "G'bye Now" from Olsen & Johnson's Broadway revue *Hellzapoppin'* became a hit in 1941, Evans and Livingston moved to Hollywood three years later, where they were put under contract by Paramount. They were later responsible for the TV themes for *Bonanza* and *Mr Ed*.

British biographer, theatre critic and broadcaster **Sheridan Morley** died in his sleep on 16 February, aged 65. The son of the late actor Robert Morley, he wrote more than thirty books, including biographies of David Niven, John Gielgud, Audrey Hepburn, Elizabeth Taylor and Marlene Dietrich, among others.

Scottish-born SF writer and rare books librarian **David I.** (Irvin) **Masson** died on 25 February, aged 91. In the mid-1960s he had seven stories published in Michael Moorcock's *New Worlds* magazine, and these were collected as *The Caltraps of Time* (1968). A 2003 reprint included three additionally published stories. Masson also contributed regular reviews to *Foundation* in the 1970s.

French editor, translator, author and screenwriter **Patrice Duvic** died on the same day after a long battle with cancer. He was 61. During the 1980s he compiled a number of "Best of" anthologies for Presses Pocket before moving to La Découverte, where he published many important SF novels and launched an impressive paperback horror line. His own novels include *Naissez, nous ferons le'reste* (*Get Born, We'll Take Care of the Rest*), *Poisson-pilote* (*Pilotfish*) and *Autant en emporte le divan* (*Gone With the Couch*), and in 1986 he wrote both the screenplay and novelization of Pierre-William Glenn's film *Terminus*.

Sixty-nine-year-old **Leigh Eddings** (Judith Leigh Schall), who co-wrote bestselling epic fantasy novels with her husband David, died on 28 February after a long illness and a series of strokes. Although she worked on all her husband's novels, it was only from the mid-1990s that she was credited on such books as *Belgarath the Sorcerer*, *Polgara the Sorceress*, *Regina's Song*, *The Elder Gods*, *The Crystal Gorge*, *The Younger Gods* and others.

Emmy-nominated film and TV composer **Robert Prince** (aka "Bob Prince") died on 4 March after a brief illness, aged 78. His credits include *Squirm* and *Claws*, plus episodes of *The Wild Wild West*, *Land of the Giants*, *Rod Serling's Night Gallery*, *The Name of the Game* ("LA 2017", directed by Steven Spielberg), *Mission Impossible*, *Ghost Story*, *The Sixth Sense*, *Wonder Woman*, *The Fantastic Journey*, *Buck Rogers in the 25th Century* ("Space Vampire"), and the TV movies *Gargoyles*, *The Return of Charlie Chan*, *Scream Pretty Peggy*, *The Strange and Deadly Occurrence*, *Where Have All the People Gone*, *The Dead Don't Die* and *Snowbeast*.

Early SF fan **Jack Agnew** died on 5 March, aged 84. With Robert A. Madle he launched the SF specialty book-selling service Fantascience Sales Service in 1946, and two years later with Madle and Al Pepper he co-published David H. Keller's *The Solitary Hunters and The Abyss*, the only book from New Era Publishers.

Elly Bloch (Elly Zalisko), who was married to *Psycho* author Robert Bloch for thirty years until his death in 1994, died in a nursing home in Manitoba, Canada, on 7 March. She was 91.

Librarian **Paul G. Walker**, who published a number of SF stories in *Galaxy* and *The Magazine of Fantasy & Science Fiction* during the 1970s, died on 8 March, aged 64. He also contributed the "Galaxy Bookshelf" review column to several issues of *Galaxy*, and the 1978 book *Speaking of Science Fiction* was based on his interviews with SF writers during that decade.

Ninety-year-old **Joan Temple** (Joan Streeton), the widow of British SF author William F. Temple (who died in 1989), died in Edinburgh, Scotland, on 10 March. She was the inspiration for the main female character "Lena" in her husband's first novel, *Four-Sided Triangle*.

DC Comics writer **Arnold Drake**, who created the Doom Patrol and Deadman, died of pneumonia on 12 March, aged 83. Introduced to DC in the 1940s by his neighbour, Batman creator Bob Kane, Drake wrote for *House of Mystery*, *Tommy Tomorrow*, *Batman* and many other titles before moving briefly to Marvel to work on *X-Men*. He then went to Gold Key Comics, where he wrote for *Twilight Zone* and *Star Trek*. Drake also scripted the 1963 nudie film *50,000 BC (Before Clothing)* and the 1964 cult horror movie *The Flesh Eaters*.

Sportswriter **Charles Einstein**, whose first novel *The Bloody Spur* was filmed by Fritz Lang as *While the City Sleeps* (1956), died on 14 March, aged 80. During the 1950s he published a number of stories in *Saturn*, *Satellite* and *If*, and his 1964 novel *The Day New York Went Dry* was also SF.

The 1950s Universal-International staff composer **Herman Stein**, who often went uncredited, died of congestive heart failure on 15 March, aged 91. He worked for the studio on such films as *The Strange Door*, *Abbott and Costello Meet Dr Jekyll and Mr Hyde*, *Abbott and Costello Go to Mars*, *Creature from the Black Lagoon*, *Revenge of the Creature*, *This Island Earth*, *Tarantula*, *The Creature Walks Among Us*, *Francis in the Haunted House*, *The Incredible Shrinking Man*, *Monster on the Campus*, *The Land Unknown*, *The Monolith Monsters*, *The Thing That Couldn't Die* and *King Kong vs Godzilla*. Stein also contributed music to *Let's Kill Uncle*, *Blazing Stewardesses*, and episodes of TV's *Voyage to the Bottom of the Sea*, *Lost in Space* and *The Time Tunnel*.

Comics artist **Marshall Rogers**, who was best known for his stylish depiction of Batman in *Detective Comics* in the late 1970s, died of a heart attack on 25 March, aged 57. He began his career working on Marvel's black and white comics before moving over to DC Comics where he contributed to such titles as *Mister Miracle*, *House of Mystery*, *The Shadow* and *Weird War Tales*. In the 1980s he worked for Eclipse Comics and then back at Marvel again, where he illustrated *Doctor Strange*, *Spider-Man* and *The Silver Surfer*. Rogers briefly became the artist on the *Batman* daily newspaper strip in 1989, and he returned to DC to illustrate the miniseries *Green Lantern: Evil's Might*, *Batman: Legends of the Dark Knight* and *Batman: Dark Detective*, along with a 1986 graphic adaptation of Harlan Ellison's *Demon With a Glass Hand*.

American author **Leslie [Elson] Waller**, who wrote the novelization of *Close Encounters of the Third Kind*, died on 29 March, aged 83. He published more than fifty books, including a 2001 thriller about the assassination of Princess Diana.

Madelon Gernsback, the daughter of pioneering SF editor Hugo Gernsback, died on the same day, aged 98.

British scriptwriter **Dave [Ralph] Martin**, who co-created the annoying robotic companion "K-9" for BBC's *Doctor Who* ("The Invisible Enemy"), died of lung cancer on 30 March, aged 72. With Bob Baker, he wrote eight episodes of the original show during the 1970s, including "The Hand of Fear", "The Three Doctors" and "The Claws of Axos". His other credits include an episode of *Into the Labyrinth* and the 1986 HTV film *Succubus*.

American screenwriter **A. J. Carothers**, who was a close friend of Walt Disney, died of cancer on 9 April, aged 75. His many credits include the TV movies *Topper Returns* (1973) and *The Thief of Baghdad* (1978).

Influential American writer **Kurt Vonnegut, Jr** died on 11 April from brain injuries sustained in a fall at his New York home several weeks earlier. He was 84. Best known for his 1969 time-travel novel *Slaughterhouse-Five: or, The Children's Crusader: A Duty-Dance with Death*, his other SF works include *Player Piano* (aka *Utopia 14*), *The Sirens of Titan*, *Mother Night*, *Cat's Cradle*, *God Bless You Mr Rosewater: or, Pearls Before Swine*, *Breakfast of Champions: or, Goodbye Blue Monday*, *Slapstick: or, Lonesome No More*, *Hocus Pocus* and *Timequake*. He created the character of failed SF author "Kilgore Trout", who appeared in a number of novels. Vonnegut struggled with depression most of his life and attempted to commit suicide in 1984. His 1991 autobiography was titled *Fates Worse Than Death*.

Thirty-five-year-old Professor **Christopher James** ("Jamie") **Bishop**, the son of author Michael Bishop, was one of thirty-two people shot dead by crazed student Cho Seung-Hui at Virgina Tech university campus on 16 April. The South Korean-born murderer subsequently killed himself in America's worst mass-shooting case.

Bishop, a foreign languages and literature teacher, designed the digital covers for four of his father's books: *Time Pieces*, *Brighten to Incandescence*, *A Reverie for Mister Ray* and the anthology *Passing for Human*.

Eighty-six-year-old American cartoonist **Brant Parker**, who co-created the long-running newspaper strip *The Wizard of Id* with **Johnny Hart**, died on 18 April of Alzheimer's disease and a stroke he had suffered the previous year. Hart died eight days earlier, aged 76.

Emily Sunstein (Emily Weisberg), who wrote the biographies *A Different Face: The Life of Mary Wollstonecraft* and *Mary Shelley: Romance and Reality*, died of complications from autoimmune vasculitis on 22 April, aged 82.

Irish author **Pat O'Shea** (Catherine Patricia Shiels), best known for her young adult fantasy novel *The Hounds of the Morrigan* (1985), died on 3 May, aged 76.

Screenwriter **Bernard Gordon** (Raymond T. Marcus, aka "John T. Williams"), who was blacklisted as one of the "Hollywood Ten" by the House of Un-American Activities in the mid-1950s, died of bone cancer on 11 May, aged 88. His scripts include *Earth vs. the Flying Saucers*, *Zombies of Mora Tau*, *The Man Who Turned to Stone* (all under the pseudonym "Raymond T. Marcus") and *The Day of the Triffids* ("fronted" by producer Philip Yordan). Gordon also produced the Spanish-made *Horror Express*, starring Christopher Lee and Peter Cushing. Some of his writing credits were restored by the Writers Guild of America forty years later, although Gordon remained bitter and led the campaign against director Elia Kazan receiving an honorary Academy Award in 1999.

American young adult author **Lloyd** [Chudley] **Alexander**, best known for his "Chronicles of Prydain" sequence of novels (1964-68) died of lung cancer on 17 May, aged 83. Comprising *The Book of Three*, *The Black Cauldron*, *The Castle of Llyr*, *Taran Wanderer* and *The High King*, the series was based on Welsh mythology, and the first two books were made into an animated film by Disney in 1985. A related collection, *The Foundling and Other Tales from Prydain*, was published in 1970. Alexander wrote more than forty books, including *Time Cat*, *The Marvelous Misadventures of Sebastian*, *Westmark* and *The Golden Dream of Carlo Chuchio*. He was a winner of the Newbery Medal, American Book Award, National Book Award and World Fantasy Award for Life Achievement.

Eighty-five-year-old pianist **Ben Wiseman**, who co-wrote a number of songs for Elvis Presley, including "Follow That Dream", died of complications from a stroke on 20 May.

Walt Disney animator **Art(hur) Stevens** died of a heart attack on 22 May, aged 92. He began his long career at the studio working on *Fantasia* as an "in-betweener". His main animation credits include *Peter Pan*, *One Hundred and One Dalmatians*, *Winnie the Pooh and the Blustery Day*, *It's Tough to Be a Bird*, *Bedknobs and Broomsticks*, *Robin Hood* and *The Rescuers*, which he also directed along with *The Fox and the Hound*. Stevens also co-wrote the story for *The Black Cauldron*, based on the fantasy series by Lloyd Alexander. He retired in 1983.

American music composer and pianist **George Greeley** died of emphysema on 26 May, aged 89. A composer for such TV series as *My Favorite Martian* (including the theme), *My Living Doll*, *The Ghost & Mrs Muir* and *Small Wonder*, he also contributed stock music to such movies as *The 27th Day* and *Screaming Mimi*.

Walter J. (James) "Doc" **Daugherty**, who for many years was the official staff photographer for Forrest J Ackerman's *Famous Monsters of Filmland* magazine, died in his sleep on 14 June, aged 90. The son of silent film actors, Daugherty was chairman of the 1946 World Science Fiction Convention, Fan Guest of Honour at the 1968 Worldcon, and a member of First Fandom.

Seventy-two-year-old Canadian-born science fiction writer, poet and editor **Douglas [Arthur] Hill** was killed on 21 June when he was run over by a double-decker bus while on a pedestrian crossing in North London. He was declared dead at the scene. Hill moved to the UK in 1959 as a freelance writer, and he was associate editor from 1967–68 of Michael Moorcock's *New Worlds* magazine. His nearly seventy books, many for younger readers, include the non-fiction study *The Supernatural* (with Pat Willams), the anthology *Way of the Werewolf*, the "Last Legionary" quartet (*Galactic Warlord*, *Deathwing Over Veynaa*, *Day of the Starwind* and *Planet of the Warlord*), *The Huntsman*, *Exiles from Olsec*, *World of Stiks* and the "Cade" and "Demon Stalkers" trilogies. For very young children he also wrote *Tales of Trellie the Troog*, *The Dragon Charmer* and *Melleron's Monsters*.

Margaret F. Crawford (Margaret Ruth Finn, aka "Garret Ford"), who helped her husband William L. Crawford (who died in 1984) found American small press imprint FPCI (Fantasy Publishing Company, Incorporated) in the 1940s, died of heart failure on 23 June, aged 82. FPCI published around forty books, including the 1945 Robert E. Howard pamphlet *Garden of Fear*, three novels by L. Ron Hubbard (*Death's Deputy*, *The Kingslayer* and *The Triton*) and *The Undesired Princess* by L. Sprague de Camp. The Crawfords also published eight issues of *Fantasy Book*, along with the magazines *Spaceway* and *Coven 13* (later retitled *Witchcraft & Sorcery*).

Author, sculptor and jeweller **Sterling E.** (Edmund) **Lanier**, best-known for his post-holocaust novel *Hiero's Journey* (1973) and its sequel *The Unforsaken Hiero*, died on 28 June at the age of 79. As the managing editor of Chilton Books in the 1960s, he convinced that publisher of primarily automotive manuals to issue Frank Herbert's *Dune*, which had been turned down by every other publisher it was submitted to. Lanier's own SF career began in *Astounding* in 1961 and his "Brigadier Ffellowes" series of stories were collected in *The Peculiar Exploits of Brigadier Ffellowes* and *The Curious Quest of Brigadier Ffellowes*.

Seventy-seven-year-old American author **Fred** (Frederick) [Thomas] **Saberhagen** died after a long battle with prostate cancer on 29 June. Best-known for his robotic "Berserker" SF series, beginning with the eponymously-titled collection in 1967, he made his debut in *Galaxy* in 1961 and published around sixty books, including *The Frankenstein Papers*, *Merlin's Bones*, two collaborations with Roger Zelazny, the "Empire of the East" series, the "Swords" trilogy, "The Book of the Gods" series and his sympathetic "Dracula" sequence. The latter comprised *The Dracula Tape* (1975), *The Holmes-Dracula File*, *An Old Friend in the Family*, *Thorn*, *Dominion*, *A Matter of Taste*, *Séance for a Vampire*, *A Sharpness on the Neck* and *A Coldness in the Blood*. Saberhagen also wrote novelizations of the 1992 movie *Bram Stoker's Dracula* and the TV series *Earth: Final Conflict*.

American movie reviewer **Joel Siegel**, best-known as the lead film critic and entertainment editor for ABC-TV's *Good Morning America*, died after a long battle with colon cancer on the same day, aged 63. Siegel began his career working as a book reviewer for the *Los Angeles Times* and writing gags for Robert F. Kennedy's political campaign.

Pulitzer Prize-winning American composer and conductor **Will Shaeffer** (Willis H. Shaeffer) died of cancer on 30 June, aged 78. His credits include Disney's *The Shaggy Dog* (1959) and *The Aristocats*, TV's *I Dream of Jeannie* and *The Flying Nun*, and such cartoon series as *The Flintstones*, *The Yogi Bear Show*, *Scooby Doo Where Are You?*, *Super Friends* and *The Godzilla Power Hour*.

Prolific American romance author **Ronda Thompson** (Ronda L. Widener), who wrote a number of paranormal romance novels, died of cancer on 11 July, aged 51. Her Regency "Wild Wulfs of London" series comprised *A Wulf's Curse*, *The Dark One*, *The Untamed One* and *The Cursed One*. Her other werewolf books include *After the Twilight*, *Call of the Moon* and *Confessions of a Werewolf Supermodel*.

Screenwriter and novelist **Marc Behm** died on 12 July, aged 82. He worked on the scripts of such movies as *The Return of Dr Mabuse* (1961), The Beatles' *Help!*, *Someone Behind the Door*, *Lady Chatterley's Lover* (1981) and *Hospital Massacre*. His serial killer novel *The Eye of the Beholder* has been filmed twice (1983 and 1999), while another book, *The Ice Maiden*, has a vampire as its central character.

American novelist **Alice Borchardt** (Alice Allen O'Brien), the elder sister of Anne Rice, died of cancer on 24 July, aged 67. Her books included the "Silver Wolf" werewolf series, *The Silver Wolf* (1998), *Night of the Wolf* and *The Wolf Queen*, along with the romantic fantasies *Devoted*, *Beguiled*, *The Dragon Queen* and *The Raven Warrior*.

Former British book dealer and literary agent **Leslie Flood** died of complications from leukaemia in Marbella, Spain, on 1 August. He was 85. A co-founder of the International Fantasy Awards (1951–57), Flood helped shape the Gollancz SF list into the late 1960s as its chief reader. He took over the E. J. Carnell literary agency after John Carnell's death in 1972, where his client list included Brian Lumley. Upon his retirement in 1986 he received a special British Fantasy Award for his services to the genre.

British author **John [Edmund] Gardner**, best known for his series of novels about spy "Boysie Oakes", which started with *The Liquidator* (1964), died of heart failure on 3 August, aged 80. His many other books include fourteen official James Bond continuations (beginning with *Licence Renewed* in 1981), two Bond movie novelizations and two Holmesian novels based around Professor Moriarty.

British science fiction author **Colin Kapp** died on the same day, aged 79. His first short story appeared in *New Worlds* in 1958, and he also contributed fiction to *Analog*, *Galaxy*, *Worlds of If* and *New Writings in SF*. Kapp wrote twelve novels, including *Transfinite Man*, *The Patterns of Chaos*, *Survival Game* and *The Ion War*. Starting with *Search for the Sun* in 1982, he published four books in the "Cageworld" series, and his short puzzle stories are collected in *The Unorthodox Engineers*. His 1962 story "Lambda 1" was adapted for the TV series *Out of the Unknown*. When invited as Guest of Honour to the British National SF Convention in Glasgow in 1980, Kapp famously delivered his speech wearing a space suit.

American country singer, songwriter and record producer **Lee Hazlewood** died of renal cancer on 4 August, aged 78. In 1966 he teamed up with Nancy Sinatra for "These Boots Are Made for Walkin'" and went on to produce nine albums for the singer. Hazlewood's songs have been covered by acts such as Dean Martin, Nick Cave, Megadeth and Primal Scream.

Sixty-seven-year-old German horror author **Jürgen Grasmück** (aka "Dan Shocker") died after a long illness on 7 August. His numerous books (written under more than a dozen pseudonyms) included the long-running "Larry Brent" and "Macabros" series.

Oscar-winning Hollywood comedy writer, producer and director **Melville Shavelson** died on 8 August, aged 90. He scripted the 1945 Danny Kaye fantasy *Wonder Man*.

Italian-born comic book artist **Mike** (Michael Lance) **Wieringo** (aka "Ringo") who worked on DC's *The Flash* and Marvel's *Fantastic Four* and *The Sensational Spider-Man*, died of an aortic dissection on 12 August, aged 44.

British scriptwriter **Clive Exton** (Clive Jack Montague Brooks), died on 16 August, aged 77. He wrote the movies *Night Must Fall* (1964), *10 Rillington Place*, *Doomwatch*, *The House in Nightmare Park* (which he also produced), *The Awakening*, *Red Sonja*, and episodes of *Out of This World* (hosted by Boris Karloff), *Out of the Unknown*, *Survivors* (as "M. K. Jeeves"), *Ghost Story for Christmas: Stigma*, *ITV Playhouse* ("Casting the Runes") and *The Infinite Worlds of H. G. Wells*.

American TV scriptwriter and producer **Max Hodge** died on 17 August, aged 91. The creator of chilly villain "Mr Freeze" for the 1960s *Batman* TV series, he also wrote for *The Wild Wild West*, *Mission: Impossible*, *The Night Stalker* and *Supertrain*, and he was associate producer on *The Girl from U.N.C.L.E.* (1966–67).

SF researcher **Richard A.** (Alan) **Hauptmann** died on 20 August after a long battle with cancer. He was 62. An expert on the works of Jack Williamson, his books include *The Work of Jack Williamson: An Annotated Bibliography and Guide* and *Seventy-Five: The Diamond Anniversary of a Science Fiction Pioneer* (with Stephen Haffner).

Author and stage actor **Denny Martin Flinn**, who co-scripted *Star Trek VI: The Undiscovered Country* with director Nicholas Meyer and wrote the 1995 *Trek* novel *The Fearful Summons*, died of cancer on 24 August, aged 59.

Hungarian-born artist **Attila Hejja** died of a heart attack on 26 August, aged 52. He emigrated to the United States with his family in

1956 and later became the director of Stevenson Academy of Fine Arts. Best known for his Aerospace illustrations for Boeing, Lockheed and General Electric, Hejja also designed the poster for the first *Star Trek* movie and created a series of stamps on space in 1998 for the US Postal Service to commemorate NASA's 40th Anniversary. His work also appeared on more than seventy-five book covers and he produced over twenty-five cover illustrations for *Popular Mechanics* magazine.

American attorney, circuit court judge and SF/mystery writer **Joe L. (Joseph Louis) Hensley** died of complications from leukaemia on the same day, aged 81. His first published science fiction appeared in a 1952 edition of *Planet Stories*. He also wrote the 1976 post-holocaust novel *The Black Roads*, and his short SF stories are collected in *Final Doors*.

Playwright, poet and children's fantasy author **Madeleine L'Engle** [Camp] died on 5 September, aged 88. Best known for her Newbery Award-winning novel *A Wrinkle in Time* (1962), which was initially rejected by twenty-six publishers, her more than sixty other books included *The Young Unicorns*, *A Wind in the Door*, *Dragons in the Waters*, *A Swiftly Tilting Planet*, *Many Waters*, *An Acceptable Time* and the collection *The Sphinx at Dawn*. She was awarded the World Fantasy Lifetime Achievement Award in 1997.

Veteran Walt Disney artist **Ralph Kent**, who designed the first limited edition Mickey Mouse wristwatch in 1965 along with other Disneyland and Walt Disney World souvenirs, died of complications of oesophageal cancer on 10 September, aged 68. Known as "The Keeper of the Mouse", he taught new artists how to draw Mickey and other classic Disney characters before retiring in 2004. He was named a "Disney Legend" the same year.

Bestselling American fantasy author **Robert Jordan** (James Oliver Rigney, Jr) died of complications from the rare blood disease cardiac amyloidosis on 16 September. He was 58. Jordan's first novel, historical family saga *The Fallon Blood* (1980), was written under the pseudonym "Reagan O'Neal", and he used other pen names for his Westerns ("Jackson O'Reilly") and non-fiction ("Chang Lung"). After becoming an editor at Tor Books he wrote a series of "Conan" novels under the Jordan byline: *Conan the Invincible* (1982), *Conan the Defender*, *Conan the Unconquered*, *Conan the Triumphant*, *Conan the Magnificent*, *Conan the Victorious* and the film tie-in *Conan the Destroyer*. *The Eye of the World* (1990) was the first volume in his hugely popular "The Wheel of Time" series, which encompassed twelve fantasy novels and sold more than fifteen million copies in North America alone. He was working on the concluding volume, *A Memory of Light*, at the time of his death.

Hollywood screenwriter **Charles B. Griffith** died on 28 September, aged 77. In 1954 he was introduced to Roger Corman by actor Jonathan Haze and went on to script such early Corman films as *It Conquered the World* (uncredited), *Not of This Earth*, *Attack of the Crab Monsters*, *The Undead*, *A Bucket of Blood*, *Beast from Haunted Cave*, *The Little Shop of Horrors*, *Atlas*, *Creature from the Haunted Sea* and *The Wild Angels*. Griffith's other writing credits include *Death Race 2000*, *Dr Heckyl and Mr Hype*, *Wizards of the Lost Kingdom II*, and the remakes of *Little Shop of Horrors*, *Not of This Earth* (1988 and 1995) and *A Bucket of Blood* (aka *The Death Artist*). As a supporting actor he turned up in *It Conquered the World*, *Attack of the Crab Monsters*, *The Little Shop of Horrors* (in several roles), *Atlas*, *Hollywood Boulevard* and *Eating Raoul*, and he directed *Up from the Depths*, *Dr Heckyl and Mr Hype* and *Wizards of the Lost Kingdom II*. Quentin Tarantino dedicated his recent film *Death Proof* to Griffith.

Archie Comics president and co-publisher **Richard H. Goldwater**, who inherited the company founded in 1941 by his father, John, and business partner Louis Silberkleit, died of cancer on 2 October, aged 71. During his time with the company, Goldwater expanded such character franchises as *Archie*, *Sabrina the Teenage Witch* and *Josie and the Pussycats* into TV series and movies.

Susan Chandler (Susan Schlenker), the second wife of the late SF author A. Bertram Chandler, died in Sydney, Australia, on 5 October. In the mid-1960s the couple collaborated on a story in *Worlds of Tomorrow* and, with Keith Curtis, she co-edited the posthumous Chandler collection *From Sea to Shining Star* (1989).

Community theatre actor, playwright and Sherlock Holmes enthusiast **Richard Valley**, who published, edited and co-founded (with Jessie Lilley) the classic horror and mystery film magazine *Scarlet Street*, died of cancer on 12 October, aged 58. Fifty-five issues of the magazine appeared from 1991–2006.

Simeon Shoul, who was a regular reviewer for *Infinity Plus*, died of a heart attack on 16 October.

Polish novelist, poet and translator **Jerzy Peterkiewicz** died on 26 October, aged 91. His books include the metaphysical fantasy *The Quick and the Dead* and the SF-themed *Inner Circle*.

Seventy-three-year-old **Hank Reinhardt** (Julius Henry Reinhardt), a mediaeval weapons expert who co-edited the 1979 anthology *Heroic Fantasy* with Gerald W. Page, died of an antibiotic-resistant infection developed during heart bypass surgery on 30 October. He was married to Baen Books publisher Toni Weisskopf.

German-born author and screenwriter **Peter Viertel** died of lymphoma in Marbella, Spain, on 4 November, aged 86. His wife, actress Deborah Kerr, died three weeks earlier at the same age. During the 1940s, he was involved with Val Lewton's "B" movie unit at RKO, and co-scripted Alfred Hitchcock's *Saboteur*. Along with books about his friends Ernest Hemingway and John Huston, Viertel worked on the screenplays for *The African Queen*, *Beat the Devil* and *The Sun Also Rises*, and wrote the 1953 novel *White Hunter Black Hunter*, filmed by Clint Eastwood in 1990.

British SF author and photo-journalist **Roger Eldridge** died on the same day, aged 63. His novels include *The Shadow of the Gloom-World* and *The Fishers of Darksea*.

Acclaimed American writer **Norman** [Kingsley] **Mailer** died of acute renal failure on 10 November, aged 84. His books include *The Naked and the Dead*, *The Executioner's Song*, *Ancient Evenings* and *Tough Guys Don't Dance*. The two-time Pulitzer Prize winner's final novel was *The Castle in the Forest* (2007), a psychic biography of Adolph Hitler's early life narrated by one of Satan's underlings. He was working on a sequel at the time of his death. Co-founder of the *Village Voice*, Mailer also wrote, produced and directed for the screen, as well as acting in a number of films. In 2005, the author received a gold medal for Lifetime Achievement at the National Book Awards.

Bestselling novelist and playwright **Ira** [Marvin] **Levin** died of a heart attack in his Manhattan apartment on 12 November, aged 78. Starting out as a TV writer (*Lights Out*; *Alfred Hitchcock Presents*), his debut book, *A Kiss Before Dying*, won the Edgar Allan Poe Award in 1954 for best first novel and was filmed in 1956 and 1991. *Rosemary's Baby*, his second novel, was not completed until fourteen years later and was filmed by director Roman Polanski in 1968. His other novels, *The Stepford Wives*, *The Boys from Brazil* and *Sliver*, were adapted for the screen with less success. Levin's flop macabre play *Dr Crook's Garden* was filmed for TV in 1971 starring Bing Crosby, and his Edgar-winning Broadway hit *Deathtrap* was turned into movies in 1982 and 2007, both starring Michael Caine. He received a Life Achievement Award from The Horror Writers Association in 1997 and was named Grand Master by the Mystery Writers of America in 2003.

Hollywood screenwriter **Lester Ziffren** died of congestive heart failure the same day, aged 101. A former reporter for United Press during the Spanish Civil War, in the early 1940s he contributed to the scripts for *Charlie Chan in Panama*, *Charlie Chan's Murder Cruise*, *Murder Over New York* and *Charlie Chan in Rio*.

American theoretical physicist and SF fan **Sidney** [Richard] **Coleman** died on 18 November from diffuse Lewy Body disease, a rare form of dementia. He was aged 70. In 1956 Coleman co-founded the Chicago specialist press Advent: Publishers, and he contributed book reviews to *The Magazine of Fantasy and Science Fiction* in the 1970s.

Britain's premier anthologist, **Peter** [Alexander] **Haining** (aka "Ric Alexander" and "Richard Peyton"), died of a heart attack while playing football on 19 November, aged 67. Described as "the most prolific anthologist of horror fiction in the world", he compiled his first anthology, *The Hell of Mirrors*, in 1965. He went on to edit more than 130 volumes, including *The Craft of Terror*, *Dr Caligari's Black Book*, *The Evil People*, *The Midnight People*, *The Hollywood Nightmare*, *The Wild Night Company*, *Gothic Tales of Terror*, *The Nightmare Reader*, *The Ghouls*, *Christopher Lee's New Chamber of Horrors*, *The Black Magic Omnibus* (two volumes), *Weird Tales: A Facsimile of the World's Most Famous Fantasy Magazine*, *More Tales of Unknown Horror*, *Zombie*, *Supernatural Sleuths: Stories of Occult Investigators*, *Werewolf: Horror Stories of the Man-Beast*, *Mummy: Stories of the Living Corpse*, *Great Irish Stories of the Supernatural*, *Vampires at Midnight*, *The Armchair Horror Collection*, *Peter Cushing's Monster Movies*, *The Vampire Omnibus*, *The Vampire Hunters' Casebook*, *Scottish Ghost Stories*, *The Mammoth Book of 20th Century Ghost Stories*, *The Mammoth Book of Haunted House Stories* and *The Mammoth Book of Modern Ghost Stories*, among numerous other compilations. A former journalist and editorial director at UK publishing house New English Library, Haining also wrote around ninety non-fiction books and media-related volumes, including *Doctor Who A Celebration: Two Decades Through Time and Space*, *The Doctor Who File*, *The Nine Lives of Doctor Who*, *James Bond: A Celebration*, *The Invasion: Earth Companion*, *M. R. James – Book of the Supernatural*, *Witchcraft and Black Magic*, *The Monster Makers*, *Terror! History of Horror Illustrations from the Pulp Magazines*, *A Sherlock Holmes Compendium*, *The H. G. Wells Scrapbook*, *Sherlock Holmes Scrapbook*, *The Dracula Scrapbook*, *Sweeney Todd: The Real Story of the Demon Barber of Fleet Street* and *The Un-dead: The Legend of Bram Stoker and Dracula* (with Peter Tremayne). In 2001 he was awarded the British Fantasy Society's Karl Edward Wagner Special Award.

American writer **Richard Leigh**, co-author of the 1982 speculative history *The Holy Blood and The Holy Grail*, died of a heart condition in London on 21 November, aged 64. Leigh and Michael Baigent, who unsuccessfully tried to sue Dan Brown's publisher Random House for plagiarism over themes in *The Da Vinci Code*, also collaborated on *The Messianic Legacy*, *The Dead Sea Scrolls Deception* and *Secret Germany*.

Avant-garde German composer **Karlheinz Stockhausen**, who contributed original music to Adam Simon's 2000 documentary about horror films, *The American Nightmare*, died on 5 December, aged 79. His work was acknowledged as influencing John Lennon, David Bowie and Frank Zappa.

Laura Huxley (Laura Archera), the Italian-born widow of writer Aldous Huxley (*Brave New World*), died of cancer in Los Angeles on 13 December. She was 96. In 1968, five years after her husband's death, she published the memoir *This Timeless Moment: A Personal View of Aldous Huxley*.

Iconoclastic American author **Jody Scott** (Joann Margaret Huguelet/Jody Hugelot Scott Wood) died in Seattle on 24 December, aged 84. A former sardine packer, orthopaedist's office assistant, *Circle Magazine* editor (she knew Henry Miller and Anais Nin), artist's model, factory hand, cabbage-puller, softcore movie-maker, bookstore/art gallery owner and headline writer for the *Monterey Herald*, she lived in England and Guatemala for various periods. Her first book was the 1951 crime novel *Cure it With Honey* (aka *I'll Get Mine*), written with George Thurston Leite and published under the pseudonym "Thurston Scott". It was followed some years later by the feminist SF novel *Passing for Human* and its sequel, *I, Vampire*. She was also a contributor to the anthologies *The Best from Fantasy and Science Fiction Eleventh Series*, *Tales by Moonlight*, *Afterlives*, *Heroic Visions II*, *Daughters of Darkness: Lesbian Vampire Stories* and the poetry collection *Now We Are Sick*. Her erotic novel *Kiss the Whip* remains unpublished.

British SF bookseller **Marion Van Der Voort** (Marion Blanchard), who ran The Sign of the Dragon with her husband Richard for thirty-five years, died in Scotland of complications from double pneumonia on 26 December, aged 71.

Seventy-one-year-old screenwriter and advertising executive **Philip B. "Phil" Dusenberry** died of complications from lung cancer on 29 December. With Robert Towne he scripted the 1984 baseball fantasy *The Natural*, and he was also responsible for creating Pepsi's "The Choice of a New Generation" ad campaign.

Scriptwriter and actor **Bill** (William) **Idelson** died of complications from a fall on 31 December, aged 87. He wrote for such TV shows as *The Flintstones*, *The Twilight Zone* ("Long Distance Call", in collaboration with Charles Beaumont), *Get Smart*, *Bewitched* and *The Ghost and Mrs Muir*. His other writing credits include the 1963 movie *The Crawling Hand*. A former child actor, Idelson turned up in episodes of *The Twilight Zone* (his friend Richard Matheson's "A World of Difference"), *Thriller* ("The Twisted Image") and *My Favorite Martian*, and he did voice work for various *Flintstones* cartoons in the late 1970s.

PERFORMERS/PERSONALITIES

Nikki Bacharach, the only daughter of songwriter Burt Bacharach and actress Angie Dickinson, committed suicide by suffocation on 4 January, aged 40. Born prematurely, she had spent many years battling the brain disorder Asperger's syndrome.

Canadian-born Hollywood actress **Yvonne De Carlo** (Margaret "Peggy" Yvonne Middleton), who played the vampiric Lily, the long-suffering wife of Herman Munster in TV's *The Munsters* (1964–66), died of heart failure on 8 January, aged 84. She appeared in the films *This Gun for Hire* (uncredited), *Road to Morocco* (uncredited), *The Ten Commandments* (1956, as Moses' wife), *Munster Go Home!*, *The Power*, *Blazing Stewardesses*, *La casa de las sombras*, *Satan's Cheerleaders*, *Nocturna* (as the bride of John Carradine's Dracula), *The Silent Scream*, *The Munster's Revenge*, *Vultures*, *Play Dead*, *American Gothic*, *Cellar Dweller*, *Mirror Mirror*, *Here Come the Munsters* and *The Barefoot Executive* (1995), along with such TV shows as *The Girl from U.N.C.L.E.*, *Fantasy Island* and *Tales from the Crypt*. In her 1987 book, *Yvonne, An Autobiography*, she claimed affairs with Howard Hughes, Billy Wilder, Burt Lancaster, Robert Stack and Robert Taylor, among others.

Denny Doherty, 66-year-old lead singer and one of the founding members of 1960s folk-pop group the Mamas and the Papas ("California Dreamin'"), died on 19 January in Ontario, Canada. He had been suffering from kidney problems following surgery in December 2006.

Twenty-five-year-old South Korean "K-Pop" superstar **U Nee** (Heo Yoon, aka "Lee Hye-Ryeon") committed suicide by hanging on 21 January. She had been diagnosed with depression. The actress and teen pop star underwent plastic surgery to give her a more westernized appearance. However, when her album sales decreased, she was pushed towards appearing in men's magazines.

Former stripper, showgirl and cult movie actress **Liz Renay** (Pearl Elizabeth Dobbins, aka "Melissa Morgan" and "Liz René") died in Las Vegas of cardiopulmonary arrest and gastric bleeding on 22 January, aged 80. Having initially gained attention as a fashion model and Marilyn Monroe look-alike, her films include *The Thrill Killers*, *The Nasty Rabbit*, *Day of the Nightmare* (uncredited), *Lady Godiva Rides*, *Blackenstein*, John Waters' *Desperate Living*, *Dimension in Fear*, *The Corpse Grinders 2* and *Mark of the Astro-Zombies*. She toured as a stripper with her daughter Brenda (who committed suicide in 1982 on her 39th birthday) and streaked down Hollywood Boulevard at noon in 1974. Renay served a twenty-seven month term in federal prison in 1959 for perjuring herself during the tax evasion trial of her then-boyfriend, Hollywood mobster Mickey Cohen. Her 1992 autobiography was titled *My First 2,000 Men*. She was married seven times, divorced five times and widowed twice.

American character actor **Tige** (Tiger) **Andrews**, who played "Captain Adam Greer" on TV's *The Mod Squad* (1968–72), died of cardiac arrest on 27 January, aged 86. He portrayed the titular character in the 1975 TV movie *The Werewolf of Woodstock*, and also appeared in episodes of *Inner Sanctum* and *Star Trek* (as a Klingon in "Friday's Child"). Andrews is also credited with introducing the song "Mack the Knife" in the original New York production of *The Threepenny Opera*.

TV actor **Lee Bergere** died on 31 January, aged 88. He portrayed Abraham Lincoln in the *Star Trek* episode "The Savage Curtain", and his other credits include episodes of *The Munsters*, *The Alfred Hitchcock Hour*, *The Addams Family*, *My Favorite Martian*, *The Man from U.N.C.L.E.*, *Get Smart*, *The Wild Wild West*, *The Six Million Dollar Man* and *Wonder Woman*, plus the 1989 movie *Time Trackers*.

Ninety-three-year-old American-Italian singer **Frankie Laine** (Francesco Paolo LoVecchio) died of heart failure on 6 February, following hip replacement surgery. He recorded the theme songs for a number of Western movies, including the spoof B*lazing Saddles* and TV's *Rawhide*. During his career, Laine sold around 250 million record albums and performed his signature tune "Mule Train" at the 1950 Academy Awards.

Thirty-nine-year-old former topless dancer, 1993 *Playboy* Playmate of the Year and reality TV star **Anna Nicole Smith** (Vickie Lynn Hogan), who was notoriously married to 89-year-old billionaire J.

Howard Marshall for just fourteen months before his death in 1995, was found unconscious in a Florida hotel room on 8 February and died later that same day of a suspected prescription drug overdose. The self-styled Marilyn Monroe look-alike starred in a number of low-budget movies, including the 2006 SF comedy *Illegal Aliens*, which she also produced. Her 20-year-old son, Daniel Smith, died in similar circumstances in September 2006, while visiting his mother and her three-day-old baby daughter in hospital in the Bahamas. Four different men subsequently claimed to be the father of the girl, named Dannielynn.

Scottish-born stage and screen actor **Ian [William] Richardson** CBE died in his sleep on 9 February, aged 72. One of the great classical actors of his generation, he starred as Sherlock Holmes in two 1983 TV movies, *The Sign of Four* and *The Hound of the Baskervilles*, and portrayed Dr Joseph Bell, who is said to have inspired Sir Arthur Conan Doyle's fictional character, in the 2000–01 TV series *Murder Rooms: Dark Beginnings of Sherlock Holmes*. Richardson was one of the founding members of the Royal Shakespeare Company and his other credits include *Marat/Sade*, *A Midsummer Night's Dream* (1968), *Gawain and the Green Knight* (as the uncredited narrator), *The Woman in White* (both the 1982 and 1997 versions as the same character, Frederick Fairlie), *Brazil*, *Whoops Apocalypse*, *The Phantom of the Opera* (1990), *The Canterville Ghost* (1997), *Dark City*, *A Knight in Camelot* (as Merlin), *Alice Through the Looking Glass* (1998), *The Magician's House*, *Gormenghast*, *102 Dalmatians*, *From Hell*, *Daemos Rising* and the miniseries of Terry Pratchett's *Hogfather* (as the voice of "Death"). Richardson also appeared in episodes of *Chillers* and *Highlander*, and he played the enigmatic Canon Adolphus Black in the 2003 BBC-TV series *Strange*. In addition to his many stage and screen roles, the actor also appeared in one of the American TV mustard commercials as the man in the Rolls-Royce who enquires, "Pardon me, would you have any Grey Poupon?"

The death from congestive heart failure (complicated by lung cancer and emphysema) of 77-year-old Canadian-born actor **Lee Patterson** was announced eight months after it happened on 14 February. Best known for his role as newsman "Joe Riley" on ABC-TV's soap opera *One Life to Live*, Patterson appeared in the movies *Meet Mr Lucifer* (uncredited), *The Spaniard's Curse*, *Jack the Ripper* (1959), *The 3 Worlds of Gulliver* and *The Search for the Evil One*, along with episodes of *The Avengers*, *The Immortal*, *Jason King* and *Zorro* (1991).

American character actor and voice artist **Walker Edmiston** died of cancer on 15 February, aged 81. Best known as the voice of "Ernie the Keebler Elf" in the American TV cookie commercials, his other voice credits include *Time for Beany*, *Top Cat*, *The Flintstones*, *H. R. Pufnstuff* (as "Dr Blinke" and "Orson the Vulture"), the live-action *Star Trek*, *Pufnstuf*, *The Andromeda Strain*, *Sigmund and the Sea Monsters*, *Trilogy of Terror* (as the voice of the Zuni doll), *Wholly Moses!* (as the voice of God), *Transformers*, Disney's *The Great Mouse Detective*, *Dick Tracy* (1990) and various TV series of *Spider-Man*. He appeared in *The Night That Panicked America*, *Scared to Death* (1981) and episodes of *Thriller*, *Get Smart*, *Batman*, *The Monkees*, *The Wild Wild West*, *The Lost Saucer*, *Shazam!*, *Fantasy Island*, *Land of the Lost* (as "Enik" the Sleestak) and *Buck Rogers in the 25th Century*. Edmiston also dubbed the voice (uncredited) of German actor Günter Meisner in *Willy Wonka & the Chocolate Factory*, and he appeared in and wrote the song "There's a Monster in the Surf" for the 1965 cult movie *The Beach Girls and the Monster*.

Tony Award-nominated stage and screen actor **Daniel McDonald** died in New York of brain cancer on the same day, aged 46. His credits include episodes of *Shadow Chasers* and *Freddy's Nightmares*.

American actress **Janet Blair** (Martha Jean Lafferty) died of complications from pneumonia on 19 February, aged 85. After starting her movie career in the 1940s in a number of musicals and comedies, including the 1944 fantasy *Once Upon a Time*, she also appeared in a 1955 TV production of *A Connecticut Yankee* (with Boris Karloff as King Arthur) and *Night of the Eagle* (aka *Burn, Witch, Burn!*, based on the novel *Conjure Wife* by Fritz Leiber). Her other credits include episodes of TV's *The Outer Limits*, *Switch* and *Fantasy Island*.

British TV and stage actor **Derek Waring** (Derek Barton-Chapple) died of cancer on 20 February, aged 79. During the 1960s and '70s he appeared in episodes of *Sherlock Holmes*, *The New Avengers* and *Doctor Who*. Waring was married to actress Dorothy Tutin from 1963 until her death in 2001, and the actor's father, Wing Commander H. J. Barton-Chapple, helped John Logie Baird develop television.

Former 1928 Olympic shot-putting champion turned actor [Harold] **Herman Brix** (aka "Bruce Bennett") died of complications from a broken hip of 24 February. He was 100. After narrowly missing out on the role of Tarazan in the 1930s MGM series, he was chosen by author Edgar Rice Burroughs himself to portray the King of the Jungle in the independent Guatemala-filmed serial *The New Adventures of Tarzan* (1935), which was subsequently reissued as the cut-down feature *Tarzan and the Green Goddess*. He went on to star in such serials as *Shadow of Chinatown* (with Bela Lugosi), *Blake of Scotland Yard*, *The Lone Ranger* (1938), *The Fighting Devil Dogs* and *Daredevils of the Red Circle*. After starring as the Tarzan-like "Kioga" in the 1938 Republic serial *Hawk of the Wilderness*, he took acting lessons and changed his name. Later credits include *The Man With Nine Lives* and *Before I Hang* (both with Boris Karloff), *Island of Doomed Men* (with Peter Lorre), *The Spook Speaks* (a short with Buster Keaton), *The Treasure of Sierra Madre* (with Humphrey Bogart), *Angels in the Outfield* (1951), *Love Me Tender* (with Elvis), *The Cosmic Man* (with John Carradine), *The Alligator People* (with Lon Chaney, Jr) and several episodes of TV's *Science Fiction Theatre*. Brix retired from movies in 1961 after starring in and co-writing *Fiend of Dope Island*. He become a sales manager for a multi-million dollar vending machine company before returning some years later to make a few guest appearances in films and TV shows. His final screen credit was as a laboratory assistant in *The Clones* (1973).

Danish actor and singer **Otto** [Herman Max] **Brandenburg** died on 1 March, aged 72. His song "Journey to the Seventh Planet" was often cut from the American version of the 1963 film of the same title. He played "Hansen" in both TV miniseries of Lars von Trier's *Riget* (aka *The Kingdom*).

Fifty-five-year-old **Brad Delp**, the lead singer with soft rock group Boston, was found dead on 9 May. He had committed suicide. Delp's vocals can be heard on the band's hits "More Than a Feeling" and "Long Time".

Fifty-year-old American stand-up comedian **Richard Jeni** (Richard John Colangelo) committed suicide by gunshot on 10 March. He had been suffering from severe clinical depression. Jeni appeared in a few films, including *The Mask* (1994), and he voiced "The Host" on the *Batman* cartoon episode, "Make 'Em Laugh", the same year.

American actress **Lanna Saunders**, best known for playing "Sister Marie Horton" on NBC-TV's *Days of Our Lives* from 1979–85, died of complications from multiple sclerosis the same day, aged 65. Her other credits include episodes of *The Six Million Dollar Man* and *Fantasy Island*.

Hollywood musical comedy star **Betty Hutton** (Elizabeth June Thornburg) died of colon cancer on 11 March, aged 86. Best known for her 1950 film *Annie Get Your Gun*, she also starred in *The Perils of Pauline* (1947). In 1952 she walked out of her contract with Paramount Pictures and, except for a year-long TV series, rarely worked again.

Austrian-born character actor **Herbert Fux** died on 13 March, aged 79. His many films include *The Invisible Terror, House of 1,000 Dolls* (with Vincent Price), *Gorilla Gang, Island of Lost Girls, Castle of Fu Manchu* (with Christopher Lee), *Mark of the Devil, Eugenie . . . the Story of Her Journey Into Perversion* (again with Lee), *Bite Me Darling, Lady Frankenstein, Hitler's Son* (with Peter Cushing), *Lady Dracula* and *Asterix and Obelix Take on Caesar*. He became a founding member of Austria's Green Party and was a Member of Parliament during the 1980s.

British actor **Gareth Hunt** (Alan Leonard Hunt), who played tough guy "Mike Gambit" opposite Patrick Macnee and Joanna Lumley in *The New Avengers* (1976–77), died of pancreatic cancer on 14 March, aged 64. The nephew of actress Martita Hunt, he also appeared in *Doctor Who* ("Planet of the Spiders"), *Space: 1999, Hammer House of Mystery and Suspense*, the sci-spy spoof *Licensed to Love and Kill* (aka *The Man from S.E.X.*) and *Bloodbath at the House of Death* (with Vincent Price).

Singer **Carol Richards** (Carol June Vosburgh), who recorded "Silver Bells" in 1950 and other Christmas songs with Bing Crosby, died of heart disease and kidney failure on 16 March, aged 84. In the movies she provided the uncredited singing voices for Joan Caulfield, Vera-Ellen, Betta St John and Cyd Charisse (including *Brigadoon*).

Seventy-four-year-old Japanese actor **Eiji Funakoshi** died of a cerebral infarction on his birthday, 17 May. His many credits include *Kaidan Kakuidori, Gamera, The Ghostly Trap* and *Gamera vs. Guillon*.

David Letterman's former sidekick **Calvert DeForest**, who was known on the 1980s NBC-TV talk show (1962–2002) as "Larry (Bud) Melman", died in New York after a long illness on 19 March, aged 85. The cousin of Bebe Daniels and *Star Trek* actor DeForest Kelley, he had small roles in the films *My Demon Lover, Freaked* and *Encino Woman*.

Soul singer **Luther Ingram**, who had a hit with "If Loving You is Wrong (I Don't Want to Be Right)" in 1972, died of heart failure the same day, aged 69. He also wrote the Staple Singers' hit "Respect Yourself".

American character actor **John P. Ryan** died of a stroke on 20 March, aged 70. A discovery of Jack Nicholson's, he was frequently cast by director Bob Rafelson in films. He played protective father "Frank Davis" in the first two films of Larry Cohen's mutant baby trilogy – *It's Alive* and *It Lives Again*. His other credits include *Futureworld*, *Class of 1999*, *Batman: Mask of the Phantasm* and episodes of *Matt Helm*, *Buck Rogers in the 25th Century*, *Faerie Tale Theatre* and *The Adventures of Brisco County, Jr.*

American character actor **Harry Frazier**, best known for his portrayals as Santa Claus on TV and playing King Neptune in *Power Rangers Lightspeed Rescue*, died of complications from diabetes on 26 May, aged 77. His other credits include episodes of *Batman* and *Shelley Duvall's Tall Tales and Legends* ("The Legend of Sleepy Hollow").

Bahamian-born actor **Calvin Lockhart** (Bert Cooper) died of complications from a stroke on 29 March, aged 72. Best remembered as the obsessed werewolf hunter in Amicus' *The Beast Must Die* (aka *Black Werewolf*), he also appeared in *Myra Breckinridge*, *Predator 2* and David Lynch's *Wild at Heart* and *Twin Peaks: Fire Walk With Me*.

British "tough guy" actor **George Sewell**, who portrayed "Colonel Alec Freeman" in Gerry Anderson's SF series *UFO* (1970–71), died of cancer on 1 April, aged 83. His many film and TV appearances include *Deadlier Than the Male* (uncredited), Hammer's *The Vengeance of She*, *The Haunted House of Horror* (aka *Horror House*), *Doppelgänger* (aka *Journey to the Far Side of the Sun*), *Randall and Hopkirk (Deceased)*, *Tales of the Unexpected*, *Hammer House of Mystery and Suspense* ("Mark of the Devil") and *Doctor Who* ("Remembrance of the Daleks").

American character actor **Edward Mallory**, who portrayed "Dr Bill Horton" on the NBC daytime soap opera *Days of Our Lives* for fourteen years, died on 4 April after a long illness. He was 76. Mallory's other credits include episodes of *Men Into Space*, *The Alfred Hitchcock Hour*, *The Man from U.N.C.L.E.*, *Bewitched*, *The Munsters* (including the unaired pilot) and *Automan*.

Barry Nelson (Robert Haakon Nielson), the first actor to play James ("Jimmy") Bond on the screen in a 1954 TV adaptation of *Casino Royale* (opposite Peter Lorre), died on 7 April, aged 89. An MGM contract player in the 1940s, his film credits include *Shadow of the Thin Man*, *A Guy Named Joe*, *Island Claws* and Stanley Kubrick's *The Shining*, along with episodes of *Alfred Hitchcock Presents* (A. M. Burrage's "The Waxwork"), *The Twilight Zone*, *The Alfred Hitchcock Hour*, *Ghost Story*, *Thriller* (1974), *Battlestar Galactica*, *Salvage 1*, *Fantasy Island* and *Monsters* (Michael McDowell's "Far Below").

Emmy Award-winning actor **Roscoe Lee Browne** died of cancer on 11 April, aged 81. A former track champion, college literature instructor and wine-seller, he made his acting debut in the early 1960s and his credits include Disney's *The World's Greatest Athlete* (1973), *Logan's Run* (as the robot "Box"), *Twilight's Last Gleaming*, *Dr Scorpion*, *Night Angel* (aka *Hellborn*), *Moon 44*, *The Beast* (1995) and *Muppet Treasure Island* (uncredited), along with episodes of TV's *The Invaders*, *Planet of the Apes*, *Highway to Heaven* and *SeaQuest DSV*. His rich Shakespearean tones could also be heard in Disney's *Oliver and Company* and *Treasure Planet*, *The Real Ghostbusters*, *Batman: The Animated Series*, *Freakazoid!* and various episodes of *Spider-Man* (as "The Kingpin"). Browne also narrated *Babe*, *Babe Pig in the City*, *Garfield: A Tale of Two Kitties* and *Epic Movie*.

Broadway theatres dimmed their lights in honour of stage and screen singer and actress **Kitty Carlisle** [Hart] (Catherine Conn) who died of congestive heart failure on 17 April following a long battle with pneumonia. She was 96. A former opera singer, Carlisle moved to Hollywood in the early 1930s, where she appeared in the musical mystery *Murder at the Vanities* (Bela Lugosi was in the stage version), The Marx Brothers' comedy *A Night at the Opera* and Woody Allen's *Radio Days*. She was married to composer Moss Hart from 1946 until his death in 1961.

French leading man **Jean-Pierre Cassel** (Jean-Pierre Crochon) died of cancer on 19 April, aged 74. A discovery of Gene Kelly, he was the father of actor Vincent Cassel and the father-in-law of Italian actress Monica Belluci. Cassel's many credits include *Malpertius*, *Superman II* (uncredited), *Alice* (1982), *The Phantom of the Opera* (1992), *Mister Frost*, *The Favour the Watch and the Very Big Fish*, *The Crimson Rivers*, *Asterix at the Olympic Games* and an episode of *The Young Indiana Jones Chronicles*.

Detroit TV horror host **Sir Graves Ghastly** (Lawson J. Deming) died of congestive heart failure in a Ohio nursing home on 24 April, the day after his 94th birthday. Each weekend from 1967–1983 he appeared on WJBK-TV as the vampiric host introducing classic horror movies.

Canadian-born character actor **Roy Jenson**, best known for playing thugs in films like *Chinatown*, died of cancer in Los Angeles the same day, aged 80. In a career that spanned five decades, the former stuntman and double for Robert Mitchum appeared in more than 170 films (often uncredited), including *13 Ghosts* (1960, as a ghost), *Atlantis the Lost Continent*, *Confessions of An Opium Eater* (with

Vincent Price), *Five Weeks in a Balloon*, *Our Man Flint*, *The Ambushers*, *The Helicopter Spies*, *5 Card Stud*, *Nightmare Honeymoon*, *Soylent Green*, *99 and 44/100% Dead*, *Helter Skelter*, *The Car*, *Demonoid*, *Red Dawn*, *The Night Stalker* and *Solar Crisis*. Jenson also turned up in episodes of *Batman*, *Voyage to the Bottom of the Sea*, *The Wild Wild West*, *The Invaders*, *The Man from U.N.C.L.E.* ("The Prince of Darkness Affair"), *Tarzan*, *Star Trek*, *Search*, *Kung Fu*, *Fantasy Island* and *Knight Rider*.

He's no longer working in the lab, late one night . . . Singer **Bobby "Boris" Pickett** (Robert George Pickett), whose spot-on Boris Karloff impersonation sent "Monster Mash" (which he co-wrote in half an hour) to the top of the US music charts in October 1962, died of leukaemia on 25 April, aged 69. The son of a movie theatre manager, Pickett recorded "Monster Mash" with a backing band christened "The Crypt-Kickers" (which included a then-unknown piano player named Leon Russell). When originally released, BBC Radio banned the song for being "offensive" and "unhealthy". The song "was a graveyard smash" again in 1970 and 1973, and formed the basis of the 1967 stage musical *I'm Sorry the Bridge is Out, You'll Have to Spend the Night*. It was filmed in 1995 as *Monster Mash: The Movie* (aka *Frankenstein Sings*) with Pickett playing Dr Victor Frankenstein. He was also in *It's a Bikini World*, *Deathmaster* (uncredited), *Strange Invaders*, *Sister Sister*, *Frankenstein General Hospital*, *Lobster Man from Mars*, *Boogie With the Undead* and an episode of *The Simpsons*. Described as "The Guy Lombardo of Halloween", Pickett's Christmas follow-up single, "Monster's Holiday", reached #30 in December 1962. In 1973, while on a Halloween tour, his bus broke down outside the town of Frankenstein, Missouri.

Veteran American character actor **Dabbs** [Robert William] **Greer** died of a kidney and heart ailment on 28 April, aged 90. Best known for playing "Old Paul Edgecomb" in the 1999 film adaptation of Stephen King's *The Green Mile*, his many other films include *Monkey Business* (uncredited), *House of Wax* (1953), *Invasion of the Body Snatchers* (1956), *Hot Rod Girl* (1956), *The Vampire* (1957), *It! The Terror from Beyond Space*, *Evil Town*, *Sundown: The Vampire in Retreat* and *House IV*, plus episodes of *Dick Tracy*, *Space Patrol*, *Alfred Hitchcock Presents*, *Science Fiction Theatre*, *The New Adventures of Charlie Chan*, *Adventures of Superman*, *The Twilight Zone*, *The Outer Limits*, *The Invaders*, *The Wild Wild West*, *The Ghost & Mrs Muir* (in the recurring role of "Norrie Coolidge"), *Ghost Story*, *Shazam!*, *The Incredible Hulk*, *The Greatest American Hero* and *Starman*.

Eighty-year-old *peplum* muscleman actor and 1950s screen Tarzan **Gordon Scott** (Gordon Merrill Werschkul) died on 30 April of heart failure following post-heart valve surgery complications. Scott was discovered by Hollywood producer Sol Lesser while he was working as a lifeguard at the Sahara Hotel in Las Vegas. His films include *Tarzan's Hidden Jungle*, *Tarzan and the Lost Safari*, *Tarzan and the Trappers*, *Tarzan's Fight for Life*, *Tarzan's Greatest Adventure*, *Tarzan the Magnificent* (with John Carradine), *Goliath and the Vampires*, *Hercules Against Moloch*, *Death Ray* (as super-spy "Bart Fargo") and the TV pilot *Hercules and the Princess Troy*. Scott was married to actress Vera Miles from 1954–59 and spent the final six years of his life living as a "guest" in the spare bedroom of a couple of his fans in Baltimore, Maryland.

Veteran character actor **Tom** (Thomas) **Poston**, best known for his recurring roles as "George Utley" on TV's *Newhart*, died of respiratory failure the same day following a brief illness. He was 85. His credits include William Castle's *Zotz!* and *The Old Dark House* (1963), *The Happy Hooker* and *The Girl the Gold Watch & Dynamite*, plus episodes of *Lights Out* ("Dr Heidegger's Experiment"), *Tom Corbett Space Cadet*, *Thriller* ("Masquerade"), *Get Smart*, *Mork & Mindy* (as neighbour "Franklin Delano Bickley"), *Sabrina the Teenage Witch*, *Touched by an Angel*, *Honey I Shrunk the Kids: The TV Show*, *Dr Quinn Medicine Woman* ("Halloween") and *The Lone Gunman*. He married his third wife, actress Suzanne Pleshette, in 2001.

Zola Taylor (Zoletta Lyn Taylor), a founding member of the 1950s singing group The Platters, died of pneumonia on 30 April, aged 69. The group, whose hits include "Only You", "The Great Pretender" and "Smoke Gets in Your Eyes", appeared in such films as *Rock Around the Clock* and *The Girl Can't Help It*. Taylor was married to doo-wop singer Frankie Lymon from 1959 until his death in 1968, and Halle Berry portrayed her in the 1998 film *Why Do Fools Fall in Love*.

Beefy American character actor **Nicholas Worth** died of heart failure on 7 May, aged 69. He appeared in *Scream Blacula Scream*, *The Terminal Man*, *Coma*, *Don't Answer the Phone!*, *Swamp Thing*, *Invitation to Hell*, *Hell Comes to Frogtown*, *Darkman*, *Dark Angel: The Ascent*, *Plughead Rewired: Circuitry Man II*, *New Eden*, *Hologram Man*, *Timelock*, *Barb Wire*, *Blood Dolls* and *Starforce*, along with episodes of TV's *The Invisible Man* (1975), *The Greatest American Hero*, *Fantasy Island*, *Knight Rider*, *Tarzan: The Epic Adventures*, *Star Trek: Deep Space Nine*, *Sliders*, *The X Files* and *Star Trek: Voyager*.

Tony Award-winning stage and screen actor **Charles Nelson Reilly** died of complications from pneumonia after a long illness on 25 May, aged 76. Best known for his recurring role as "Claymore Gregg" on TV's *The Ghost & Mrs Muir* (1968–70), his other credits include *Charlotte's Web* (1973), *All Dogs Go to Heaven* (and various sequels and spin-offs), *A Troll in Central Park, Babes in Toyland* (1997), *SpongeBob Square Pants* and *Tom and Jerry in Shiver Me Whiskers*, along with episodes of *The Flintstone Comedy Hour* (as the voice of "Frank Frankenstone"), *Spacecats, Amazing Stories*, and *The X Files* and *Millenium* (as author "Jose Chung" in both series). He was also a regular on various game shows on American television in the 1970s and 1980s.

Italian actress **Leonora Ruffo** (Eleonora Ruffo), who played "Princess Deianira" in Mario Bava's *Hercules in the Haunted World*, died on 28 May, aged 72. Her other film credits include *Goliath and the Dragon, Goliath and the Vampires* and *Star Pilot* (aka *2+5: Missione Hydra*).

Prolific French actor and director **Jean-Claude Brialy** died of cancer on 30 May, aged 74. He appeared in the 1962 adaptation of John Dickson Carr's *The Burning Court* (*La Chambre ardente*), *Demon of the Island* and the serial killer comedy *The Monster* (1994).

Lugubrious New Zealand-born British character actor **Gordon** [Massey] **Gostelow** died on 3 June, aged 82. He emigrated to Britain in 1950, where he appeared in Disney's *The Scarecrow of Romney Marsh, Wuthering Heights* (1970), *Merlin of the Crystal Cave* and episodes of TV's *Sherlock Holmes* (1965), *The Saint, Doctor Who* ("The Space Pirates"), *The Rivals of Sherlock Holmes, Return of the Saint* and *The Return of Sherlock Holmes* ("The Sign of Four"). Gostelow was married to actress Vivian Pickles.

Hollywood leading lady **Marla Powers** (Mary Ellen Powers) died of complications from leukaemia on 11 June, aged 75. At the age of eleven she appeared (uncredited) in the 1942 Bowery Boys comedy *Tough as They Come*. Her other films include *The Unknown Terror, The Colossus of New York, Flight of the Lost Balloon, Daddy's Gone A-Hunting* and *The Doomsday Machine*, and she also appeared in episodes of *Thriller, The Man from U.N.C.L.E., The Wild Wild West* and *Bewitched*. Powers later became an author of children's books and taught acting.

Hank Medress, a singer with the Tokens, whose doo-wop vocals were heard on the 1961 hit "The Lion Sleeps Tonight", died of lung cancer on 18 June, aged 68.

Canadian-born WWE wrestling champion **Chris Benoit,** known as the "Canadian Crippler", was found hanged at his Atlanta home on 25 June in what police believe was a double murder-suicide. The asphyxiated bodies of Benoit's wife, Nancy, and 7-year-old son, Daniel, were also found in the house. The 40-year-old wrestler was a former world heavyweight and intercontinental champion. In a bizarre twist, it was revealed that the death of 43-year-old Nancy Benoit was apparently posted on Wikipedia several hours before the bodies were discovered.

Nashville saxophonist **Boots Randolph** (Homer Louis "Boots" Randolph III) died of a cerebral haemorrhage on 3 July, aged 80. Best known for his 1963 hit "Yakety Sax", he also played on tracks by Roy Orbison, Jerry Lee Lewis, Brenda Lee and REO Speedwagon.

British jazz singer, author and scriptwriter **George Melly** died of lung cancer on 4 July, aged 80. A film critic for *The Observer* newspaper in the early 1960s, he scripted the film *Smashing Time* and wrote the long-running *Daily Mail* satirical cartoon strip *Flook* with artist creator "Trog" (Wally Fawkes). He was also the voice of a dwarf in Richard Williams' 1993 animated film *The Princess and the Cobbler* (aka *The Thief and the Cobbler*) starring Vincent Price. Diagnosed with cancer in 2005, Melly refused treatment and, despite also suffering from dementia, continued to perform in public until a month before his death.

Singer **Bill Pinkney**, the last founding member of the original Drifters, died of an apparent heart attack the same day, aged 81. He left the R&B group in 1958 to set up the Original Drifters.

American leading man **Kerwin Matthews** died of a heart attack on 5 July, aged 81. Best remembered as the swashbuckling hero pitted against Ray Harryhausen's stop-motion monsters in the classic *The 7th Voyage of Sinbad*, his other credits include *The 3 Worlds of Gulliver* (again with Harryhausen), Hammer's *The Pirates of Blood River* (opposite Christopher Lee) and *Maniac*, the *Sinbad*-influenced *Jack the Giant Killer*, the European sci-spy adventures *OSS 117* and *Panic in Bangkok*, *Battle Beneath the Earth*, *Octaman*, *Death Takes a Holiday* (1971), *The Boy Who Cried Werewolf* and *Nightmare in Blood*. Matthews also turned up in an episode of TV's *Space Patrol* and a 1958 production of *The Suicide Club*, and he starred in the failed 1960s pilots *Ghostbreakers* and *Dead of Night: A Darkness at Blaisedon*.

Veteran American character actor **Charles Lane** (Charles Gerstle Levison, aka "Charles Levison") died on 9 July at the ripe old age of 102. His numerous credits (often in small or uncredited parts playing crotchety tax inspectors or desk clerks) include *Blonde Crazy, 42nd Street, Gold Diggers of 1933, Twentieth Century, Ali Baba Goes to Town, Professor Beware,* Tod Browning's *Miracles for Sale, Television Spy, Beware Spooks!, The Cat and the Canary* (1939), *The Invisible Woman, I Wake Up Screaming, Tarzan's New York Adventure, Arsenic and Old Lace, It's a Wonderful Life, Mighty Joe Young, The 30 Foot Bride of Candy Rock, It's a Mad Mad Mad Mad World, The Ghost and Mr Chicken, The Gnome-Mobile, The Aristocats, Strange Behaviour* (aka *Dead Kids*), *Strange Invaders, Date With an Angel, The Computer Wore Tennis Shoes* (1995) and he narrated the 2006 animated short *The Night Before Christmas*. A regular on such TV shows as *Petticoat Junction, I Love Lucy* and *The Lucy Show,* Lane also turned up in episodes of *Topper, The Twilight Zone, Mister Ed, Get Smart, Honey West, The Munsters, The Man from U.N.C.L.E., The Wild Wild West, Bewitched, Mork & Mindy, Otherworld* and the 1991 revival of *Dark Shadows*. One of the last survivors of the 1906 San Francisco Earthquake, he was a founding member of the Screen Actors Guild in 1933. In 2005, 30 January was named "Charles Lane Day" by SAG, and that same year he was honoured at the Emmy Awards on the occasion of his 100th birthday.

British actor **Peter Tuddenham** died on the same day, aged 88. Best known as the voice of the computer, "Orac", in the BBC-TV series *Blakes 7* (1978-81) and its 1998 radio spin-off, his other credits include *Tales of the Unexpected* and three episodes of *Doctor Who*.

Sixty-eight-year-old former singer and actor **Rod Lauren** (Roger Lawrence Strunk) was found dead in the parking lot of an inn in Tracy, California, on 11 July. He had apparently committed suicide by jumping from a second-floor balcony. During the 1960s he appeared in such films as *Terrified, The Black Zoo* (as Michael Gough's mute assistant "Carl") and *The Crawling Hand,* along with an episode of *Alfred Hitchcock Presents*. His wife, Philippine actress Nida Blanca, was found stabbed to death in her car in 2001. Lauren returned to the US before charges were filed against him, and he had continued to resist extradition.

Irish-born leading man **Kieron Moore** (Kieron O'Hanrahan) died in France on 15 July, aged 82. After moving to England in 1942 to play "Heathcliff" in a London stage performance of *Wuthering Heights,* he appeared in such films as *Satellite in the Sky,* Disney's live-action *Darby O'Gill and the Little People, Doctor Blood's Coffin, The Day of the Triffids* and *Crack in the World*. On TV he recreated his role for a 1948 production of *Wuthering Heights* and turned up in an episode of *Randall and Hopkirk (Deceased)*.

British stunt co-ordinater **Frank Maher** (Francis James Mahar) died on 21 July, aged 78. His credits include *Children of the Damned*, *One More Time*, and such TV shows as *Danger Man* (aka *Secret Agent*), *The Avengers*, *The Prisoner*, *Space: 1999*, *Blakes 7*, *The Champions* and *Randall and Hopkirk (Deceased)*.

British stand-up comedian turned character actor **Mike Reid** died in Spain of a heart attack on 29 July, aged 67. A former film extra and stunt driver on such films as *Casino Royale*, *Chitty Chitty Bang Bang* and Hammer's *The Devil Rides Out* (aka *The Devil's Bride*), he came to prominence on the 1970s TV series *The Comedians*. Reid's dramatic credits include episodes of *Doctor Who* ("The War Machines" and "Dimensions in Time"), *The Saint* (he also stunt-doubled Roger Moore on the show), *The Champions*, *Department S* and *Worzel Gummidge*. From 1989–2005 he portrayed "Frank Butcher" on the BBC soap *EastEnders*.

French actor **Michel Serrault** died of cancer on the same day, aged 79. His numerous credits include Henri-Georges Clouzot's *Les Diaboliques*, *Malevil*, *Les Fantômes de chapelier* and *Belphégor: Le fantôme du Louvre*.

Late night NBC (1973–82) and CBS (1995–99) TV talk show host **Tom Snyder** died of leukaemia on 29 July, aged 71. He appeared as himself in the 1977 episode of TV's *McCloud*, "McCloud Meets Dracula".

Character actor **James T.** (Thomas) **Callahan** died of oesophageal cancer on 3 August, aged 76. Often cast as a sheriff, he appeared in *Return of the Living Dead III*, the TV movies *She Waits*, Disney's *Mystery of Dracula's Castle* and *The Haunting of Harrington House*, plus episodes of *The Twilight Zone*, *My Favorite Martian*, *The Time Tunnel*, *The Invaders*, *Holmes and Yo-Yo*, *The Hardy Boys/Nancy Drew Mysteries*, *Automan*, *Knight Rider*, *Alfred Hitchcock Presents*, *Highway to Heaven*, *Amazing Stories* and *Medium*.

Forty-year-old Canadian-born scriptwriter and part-time actor **Jacob L. Adams** was found dead at the Los Angeles home of actor Ving Rhames the same day. He was covered in blood and dog bites, but it wasn't clear if he had been killed by the four dogs he had been hired to look after. Adams had small parts in several films, including *Blues Brothers 2000* and the remake of *Dawn of the Dead*, along with episodes of *Babylon 5* and *Earth: Final Conflict*.

American TV legend **Merv**(yn) [Edward] **Griffin** died of prostate cancer on 12 August, aged 82. Having created such popular game shows as *Jeopardy!* and *Wheel of Fortune*, he hosted *The Merv Griffin Show* on CBS-TV from 1962–86. His uncredited voice can be heard as a radio announcer in *The Beast from 20,000 Fathoms*, and he was featured in such films as *Phantom of the Rue Morgue*, *Hello Down There*, *Slapstick (Of Another Kind)*, *The Man With Two Brains* (as the "Elevator Killer"), *Alice in Wonderland* (1985) and Disney's animated *Hercules*. In 1950, his novelty song with Freddy Martin, "I've Got a Lovely Bunch of Coconuts", went to the top of the US charts.

American character actor **Robert Symonds**, the step-father of actress Amy Irving, died of prostate cancer on 23 August, aged 80. His film credits include *The Exorcist*, *Linda Lovelace for President*, *Superstition* (aka *The Witch*), *The Ice Pirates*, *Rumplestiltskin*, *C.H.U.D. II: Bud the Chud* and *Mandroid*. He also appeared in the TV movies *Demon Demon* and *The Legend of Lizzie Borden*, along with episodes of *Future Cop*, *The Six Million Dollar Man*, *Knight Rider*, *Beauty and the Beast*, *Freddy's Nightmares*, *Quantum Leap* and *Star Trek: Deep Space Nine*. Symonds was married to actress Priscilla Pointer, and the couple often worked together.

Mexican actor/wrestler **"Karloff" Legarde** died in Mexico City on 1 September, aged 78. He appeared in the 1960s films *El Asesino invisible*, *Los Endemoniados del ring*, *La Mano que aprieta* and *Santo en la frontera del terror*.

The 1930s child actress **Marcia Mae Jones** (Marsha Mae Jones) died of pneumonia on 2 September, aged 83. Following her film debut in 1926, she appeared in *The Bishop Murder Case* (uncredited), *Dr Kildare's Strange Case*, *Haunted House* (1940), *The Spectre of Edgar Allan Poe* and episodes of TV's *Mr Ed* and *Shazam!*.

Thirty-four-year-old **Jeffrey Carter Albrecht**, a keyboard player with Edie Brickell & New Bohemians, was shot dead on 3 September when he tried to kick down the door of the house next to that of his girlfriend. The neighbour apparently thought that he was being burgled.

British-born stage and screen actor [John] **Michael Evans** died at an assisted-living facility in Woodland Hills, California, on 4 September, aged 87. Best remembered for his role as "Col. Douglas Austin" on *The Young and the Restless* during the 1980s and 1990s, he also appeared in *Time After Time*, *Goliath Awaits* (with Christopher Lee and John Carradine), *The Sword and the Sorcerer* and an episode of TV's *The Man from U.N.C.L.E.* ("The Double Affair", aka *The Spy With My Face*).

Canadian-born character actor **Percy Rodrigues** died of kidney failure on 6 September, aged 89. His credits include *Rhinoceros, The Legend of Hillbilly John* (based on the stories of Manly Wade Wellman), *Invisible Strangler, Galaxina, Heavy Metal, Deadly Blessing, BrainWaves,* the TV movies *Genesis II* and *Perry Mason: The Case of the Sinister Spirit,* plus episodes of *The Wild Wild West, The Man from U.N.C.L.E., Star Trek, Tarzan, The Sixth Sense, The Starlost, Planet of the Apes* and *Gemini Man.* Rodrigues was also the uncredited narrator of the 3-D Michael Jackson short *Captain EO,* shown at Disneyland.

Italian opera singer **Luciano Pavarotti** died of pancreatic cancer on the same day, aged 71. The world's most popular operatic tenor, he can be heard on the soundtracks for *The Witches of Eastwick* and *Fatal Attraction.*

Oscar-winning Hollywood actress and singer **Jane Wyman** (Sarah Jane Fulks [Mayfield]) died on 10 September, aged 93 (or 90, sources vary). The first wife of actor and future US President Ronald Reagan (they divorced in 1948), her film credits include *The Body Disappears, The Lost Weekend* and Alfred Hitchcock's *Stage Fright.* She was in an episode of *The Sixth Sense,* and from 1981–90 she played vineyard matriarch "Angela Channing" on TV's *Falcon's Crest.*

Loretta King, who starred opposite Bela Lugosi in Edward D. Wood, Jr's infamous *Bride of the Monster* (1955), died on the same day, aged around 90. She also appeared in a couple of 1990s documentaries about Wood and Lugosi, and was portrayed by Juliet Landau in Tim Burton's *Ed Wood* (1994).

American comedienne and character actress **Alice Ghostley** died of colon cancer and a series of strokes on 21 September, aged 81. Best known for her role as the accident-prone witch "Aunt Esmeralda" in TV's *Bewitched* from 1969–72, her other credits include the movies *Blue Sunshine* and *Addams Family Reunion* (as "Granny"), the TV productions of *Rodgers and Hammerstein's Cinderella* and *Hallmark Hall of Fame: Shangri-La,* plus episodes of *Dow Hour of Great Mysteries, Get Smart, The Ghost & Mrs Muir, Ghost Story, Kolchak: The Night Stalker, Monster Squad, Tales from the Darkside, Highway to Heaven, Touched by an Angel* and *Sabrina the Teenage Witch.* In 2000 she turned up as "Matilda Matthews" in four episodes of NBC-TV's supernatural soap opera *Passions.*

French mime artist **Marcel Marceau** (Marcel Mangel) died in Paris on 22 September, aged 84. World-famous for his mime persona "Bip", he also appeared in such films as *Barbarella,* William Castle's horror movie *Shanks* and Mel Brooks' *Silent Movie* (in which he spoke the only word of dialogue – "Non"). Michael Jackson reportedly based his famous "Moonwalk" routine on a sketch by Marceau.

Karl Hardman died on the same day, aged 80. In 1968 he helped produce George A. Romero's *Night of the Living Dead*, as well as working in the sound and make-up departments and appearing as the obnoxious "Harry Cooper" in the film. Besides *Night*-related documentaries, his only other credits are the 1996 horror film *Santa Claws* and the BBC series *Clive Barker's A–Z of Horror*. Hardman's wife, Marilyn Eastman, and daughter Kyra Schon, also appeared in Romero's influential zombie film.

Texas-born singer and vocal arranger **Randy Van Horne**, who sang *The Flintstones* and *The Jetsons* theme songs with his ensemble, died on 26 September, aged 83.

Canadian-born actress **Lois Maxwell** (Lois Hooker) died of cancer in Western Australia on 29 September, aged 80. For more than twenty years she was best known for her role as M's flirtatious secretary "Miss Moneypenny" in the James Bond movies *Dr No*, *From Russia With Love*, *Goldfinger*, *Thunderball*, *You Only Live Twice*, *On Her Majesty's Secret Service*, *Diamonds Are Forever*, *Live and Let Die*, *The Man With the Golden Gun*, *The Spy Who Loved Me*, *Moonraker*, *For Your Eyes Only*, *Octopussy* and *A View to a Kill*, along with the Bond spoofs *Operation Kid Brother* (as "Miss Maxwell") and *From Hong Kong With Love* (as "Miss Moneypenny", opposite Bernard Lee's "M"). Maxwell's other film appearances include *A Matter of Life and Death* (uncredited), *Corridor of Mirrors* (which also featured Christopher Lee), *Satellite in the Sky*, *Face of Fire*, *The Haunting* (1963), *Endless Night* and *Eternal Evil* (aka *The Blue Man*). She also supplied the voice of "Lt Atlanta Shore" on Gerry Anderson's puppet TV show *Stingray*, and her other credits include episodes of *One Step Beyond*, *The Avengers*, *Randall and Hopkirk (Deceased)*, *Department S*, *UFO* and the 1987 revival of *Alfred Hitchcock Presents*.

Tony Award-winning American character actor **George Grizzard** died of complications from lung cancer on 2 October, aged 79. Although best known for his stage work on Broadway, he also appeared in the TV movies *The Stranger Within* and *The Night Rider*, along with episodes of *One Step Beyond*, *Thriller* ("The Twisted Image"), *Alfred Hitchcock Presents*, *The Twilight Zone*, *3rd Rock from the Sun* and *Touched by an Angel*.

British stage and screen actor **Rodney Diak** (David Rodney Jones) died of cancer on 6 October, aged 83. His few film credits include

Fire Maidens from Outer Space and *The Flesh and Blood Show*. Queen Elizabeth II's sister, Princess Margaret, once described Diak as "the most handsome actor in Britain" and Dirk Bogarde reputedly vetoed his casting in *A Tale of Two Cities* because he was too good-looking.

Stuntman and actor **Bud Ekins**, best known for the classic motorcycle jump in *The Great Escape*, died on the same day, aged 77. He also worked on such films as *How to Stuff a Wild Bikini*, *Diamonds Are Forever*, *The Thing With Two Heads*, *Earthquake*, *The Towering Inferno*, *Race With the Devil*, *Return from Witch Mountain*, *1941*, *Megaforce*, *Jekyll and Hyde . . . Together Again* and *Black Moon Rising*.

Florida TV horror host **M. T. Graves** (Charles Morrison Baxter) also died on 6 October, aged 82. From 1957 until the early 1960s he hosted the weekly Saturday afternoon horror film show *The Dungeon* on channel WCKT.

Veteran American character actor **Lonny Chapman** (aka "Lonnie Chapman") died of heart disease and pneumonia on 12 October, aged 87. He made his TV debut in *Captain Video* in 1949, and his numerous other appearances include Hitchcock's *The Birds*, *The Screaming Woman*, *Visions*, *Earthquake* (uncredited), *The Witch Who Came from the Sea*, *Terror Out of the Sky* and *Nightwatch* (1997), plus episodes of *One Step Beyond*, *The Alfred Hitchcock Hour*, *Rod Serling's Night Gallery*, *Planet of the Apes*, *The Incredible Hulk* and *Knight Rider*.

Scottish-born leading lady **Deborah Kerr** CBE (Deborah Jane Kerr-Trimmer) died from complications of Parkinson's disease on 16 October, aged 86. After making her film debut in 1941 she appeared in *Black Narcissus*, *King Solomon's Mines* (1950), *The Innocents* (based on the classic ghost story *The Turn of the Screw* by Henry James), *Eye of the Devil* (aka *13*) and the James Bond spoof *Casino Royale.* She mostly stopped acting in 1968 and finally retired altogether in 1986. Kerr held the record for the most Oscar nominations (six) without winning, and she received an Honorary Academy Award in 1994.

Comedian **Joey Bishop** (Joseph Abraham Gottlieb), the last survivor of Frank Sinatra's legendary "Rat Pack", died on 17 October, aged 89. He appeared in a number of films and TV shows, and had an uncredited cameo in a 1967 episode of *Get Smart*.

American-born character actor **Don Fellows** died in London on 21 October, aged 84. He appeared in *Pretty Poison*, *The Omen* (1976), *Twilight's Last Gleaming*, *Licensed to Love and Kill* (aka *The Man* from S.E.X.), Superman II, Raiders of the Lost Ark, Electric Dreams, Riders of the Storm, Haunted Honeymoon and Superman IV: The Quest for Peace, plus episodes of Space: 1999 and Tales of the Unexpected.

South African-born actress **Moira Lister** died in Cape Town on 27 October, aged 84. She moved to England in 1944 and appeared in a number of films and TV shows. Her credits include the 1989 movie of Ten Little Indians, the miniseries The 10th Kingdom, the 2007 TV movie Flood and an episode of The Avengers.

Seventy-three-year-old American singer and actor **Robert** [Gerard] **Goulet**, who portrayed "Lancelot" in the original 1960 Broadway production of Camelot, opposite Richard Burton and Julie Andrews, died of interstitial pulmonary fibrosis on 30 October while awaiting a lung transplant. A Tony Award winner in 1968, he had seventeen albums in the charts from 1962–70. His film credits include the animated Gay Purr-ee, The Daydreamer (with Boris Karloff), Beetle Juice, Scrooged, Mr Wrong, Toy Story 2 and G-Men from Hell (as the Devil). Goulet also appeared in various episodes of Fantasy Island, as well as an Emmy-winning 1966 TV version of Brigadoon and a 1967 adaptation of Carousel.

South African-born soccer star turned actor **Henry Cele** died of complications from a chest infection on 2 November, aged 58. He appeared in Curse III: Blood Sacrifice (aka Panga) with Christopher Lee, and The Ghost and the Darkness.

Hollywood actress **Laraine Day** (Laraine Johnson), who portrayed "Nurse Mary Lamont" in MGM's Doctor Kildare series during the early 1940s, died of cancer on 10 November, aged 87. She also appeared in Tarzan Finds a Son!, Fingers at the Window (with Basil Rathbone), Return to Fantasy Island and episodes of TV's The Alfred Hitchcock Hour, The Sixth Sense and Fantasy Island.

American-born character actor **Al Mancini**, (Alfred Benito Mancini), who worked for many years in Britain, died of complications from Alzheimer's disease on 12 November, one day short of his 75th birthday. A regular on the 1960s BBC satirical TV show That Was the Week That Was, he also appeared in episodes of The Prisoner, Department S, UFO, Jason King, The Protectors, Beauty and the Beast, Monsters (Dan Simmons' "A Shave and a Haircut, Two Bites"), Joan of Arcadia and the TV movies Madam Sin and Baffled!. Mancini's voice was featured in Babe: Pig in the City.

American actor, novelist and screenwriter **Michael Blodgett** died of an apparent heart attack on 14 November, aged 68. After hosting his own TV shows in the LA area, Blodgett starred as "Lance Rocke" in the X-rated cult movie *Beyond the Valley of the Dolls*. His other credits include *The Trip* and *The Velvet Vampire*, and episodes of *The Alfred Hitchcock Hour*, *The Munsters*, *Night Gallery* ("The Dead Man") and *Isis*, while Blodgett's novel *Hero and the Terror* was filmed in 1988 starring Chuck Norris. One of his three wives was actress Meredith Baxter.

Actor **Ronnie Burns**, the adopted son of George Burns and Gracie Allen, died of cancer on the same day, aged 72. He appeared in the 1961 film *Anatomy of a Psycho* before going into real estate investment and raising Arabian horses.

Blonde actress and former model **Sigrid Valdes** (Patricia Olson), best known for playing Colonel Klink's sexy secretary "Hilda" on the CBS-TV series *Hogan's Heroes* (1965–71), died of lung cancer on 14 November, aged 72. In 1970 she married the show's star, Bob Crane, who was found bludgeoned to death eight years later. Valdes' other credits include *Our Man Flint*, *The Venetian Affair* (uncredited) and a two episodes of TV's *The Wild Wild West*.

Veteran character actor **Dick Wilson** (Riccardo DiGuglielmo, aka Richard Wilson), who also appeared as various characters in *Hogan's Heroes*, died on 18 November, aged 91. Best known for appearing as grocery store owner "Mr Whipple" in more than 500 TV commercials between 1964–85 for Charmin toilet paper, the British-born Wilson's other appearances include *Diary of a Madman* (with Vincent Price), *Our Man Flint* (uncredited), *The Ghost and Mr Chicken* (uncredited), Disney's *The World's Greatest Athlete* and *The Incredible Shrinking Woman*, plus episodes of *The Twilight Zone*, *My Living Doll*, *My Favorite Martian*, *The Munsters*, *My Mother the Car*, *The Flying Nun*, *Get Smart*, *I Dream of Jeannie*, *Bewitched*, *Tabitha* and *Fantasy Island*. In a 1975 poll he was voted the second-most-recognizable person in America after President Richard Nixon.

Ottomar Rudolphe Vlad Dracula, Prince Kretzulesco of Transylvania and Wallachia died of a brain tumour on 19 November, aged 67. A former German baker and antiques dealer named Otto Berbig, he was adopted in the 1970s by Ekaterina Olympia Kretzulesco, who believed herself to be descended from Romanian ruler Vlad III of Wallachia (1431–76), who Bram Stoker based his character of Dracula on. Three months earlier, an attempt by the prince to turn his German castle into a vampire-themed attraction ended in bankruptcy, and his property was seized by the bank because of unpaid debts.

Seventy-nine-year-old **Reg Park** (Roy Park), the British-born world championship bodybuilder turned muscleman actor, died after a long battle with cancer in Johannesburg, on 22 November. A former Mr Britain and three-time winner of the Mr Universe title, in the early 1960s he followed Steve Reeves and Mark Forest (Lou Degni) into the role of Hercules in the Italian *peplums Hercules Conquers Atlantis* (aka *Hercules and the Captive Women*), Mario Bava's *Hercules in the Haunted World* (aka *Hercules in the Center of the Earth*, with Christopher Lee), *Hercules Prisoner of Evil*, and the cobbled-together *Hercules the Avenger*. His only other film was *Maciste in King Solomon's Mines* (aka *Samson in King Solomon's Mines*). Park ran a chain of successful personal fitness clubs in South Africa and, during the late 1960s, he worked with Arnold Schwarzenegger, becoming the latter's mentor and inspiration.

Flamboyant motorcycle daredevil **Evel Knievel** (Robert Craig Knievel) died of complications from diabetes and idiopathic pulmonary fibrosis on 30 November, aged 69. He had been in poor health for some years following a liver transplant in 1999 after nearly dying from hepatitis C. George Hamilton portrayed him in the biopic *Evel Knievel* (1971), while Knievel appeared as himself in a 1977 episode of TV's *The Bionic Woman* and the movie *Viva Knievel!*, made the same year.

Character actor **Anton Rodgers** (Anthony Rodgers) died on 1 December, aged 74. A regular face on British TV in the 1960s and 1970s, he appeared in episodes of *One Step Beyond*, *Danger Man*, *Sherlock Holmes* (1965), *Out of the Unknown*, *The Saint*, *The Prisoner* (as a "Number Two"), *The Champions*, *Department S*, *Randall and Hopkirk (Deceased)*, *Jason King*, *The Protectors*, *Orson Welles' Great Mysteries*, *Return of the Saint* and *Zodiac* (as regular "David Gradley"). His other credits include the 1979 TV movie *The Shining Pyramid* and the movies *The Man Who Haunted Himself* and *Scrooge* (1970).

Italian actress **Eleonora Rossi Drago** (Palma Omiccioli) died of a cerebral haemorrhage on 2 December, aged 82. Her many films include *David and Goliath*, *The Red Hand*, *Sword of the Conqueror*, *The Carpet of Horror*, *Hypnosis* (aka *Dummy of Death*), *The Flying Saucer* (1964), *The Bible In the Beginning . . .*, *Camille 2000* and *Dorian Gray* (1970).

American Southern Rapper **Pimp C** (Chad Butler), one half of the hip hop group UGK, was found dead in bed at a West Hollywood hotel on 4 December, aged 33.

Singer **Ike Turner** (Izear Luster Turner, Jr), who discovered and later married Tina Turner before their well-publicized split in the mid-1970s, died of a cocaine overdose on 12 December, aged 76. Best known for such hits as "Proud Mary" and "Nutbush City Limits", he became a cocaine addict and served time in prison before making a successful comeback album, *Here and Now*, in 2001. Ike Turner was portrayed by Laurence Fishburne in the 1993 Tina Turner biopic *What's Love Got to Do With It?*

Native American actor, folk singer and environmental activist **Floyd "Red Crow" Westerman** died from complications of leukaemia on 13 December, aged 71. His credits include *The Doors* (in which he played Jim Morrison's spirit guide), *Atlantis: Milo's Return* and episodes of *McGyver*, *Captain Planet and the Planeteers*, *Murder She Wrote*, *Baywatch Nights*, *Poltergeist: The Legacy*, *Millennium* and *The X Files* (in the recurring role of "Albert Hosteen").

Singer-songwriter **Dan Fogelberg** died of prostate cancer on 16 December, aged 56. His acclaimed soft-rock/country albums included his 1972 debut *Home Free*, the hugely successful *Souvenirs*, *Captured Angel* and *The Innocent Age* (which featured the hits "Leader of the Band" and "Same Old Lang Syne"), the environmental-aware *River of Souls*, and *Full Circle* (2003), which was his first album of original material in nearly a decade.

Busty "B" movie actress **Jeanne** [Laverne] **Carmen** died of lymphoma on 20 December, aged 77. A former chorus girl, model and trick golfer, she was a close friend of Las Vegas mobster Johnny Roselli, Clark Gable, Elvis Presley, Frank Sinatra and Marilyn Monroe, among others. Carmen's film appearances include *The Monster of Piedras Blancas*, *The Devil's Hand* and *The Naked Monster*.

Canadian jazz pianist **Oscar** [Emmanuel] **Peterson** died on 24 December, aged 82. He won seven Grammies, including one in 1997 for Lifetime Achievement.

FILM/TV TECHNICIANS

Steve Krantz (Stephen Falk Krantz), who produced the X-rated cartoon movie *Fritz the Cat* (1972), died of complications from pneumonia on 4 January, aged 83. A former TV writer, he worked with Milton Berle and helped create *Dennis the Menace* and *Bewitched* while head of development at Columbia Pictures Television. His other credits include the 1960s *Spider-Man* TV series, *Heavy Traffic*, *The Nine Lives of Fritz the Cat*, *Cooley High* and a number of miniseries based on books by his wife, bestselling romance author Judith Krantz. As a writer he came up with the stories for Curtis

Harrington's *Ruby* and the *Carrie*-like *Jennifer*, both of which he also produced.

Seventy-two-year-old "Sneaky" Pete (Peter) **Kleinow**, pedal guitarist with country rock band The Flying Burrito Bros, died on 6 January of complications from Alzheimer's disease. In 1974 he became a stop-motion animator on Sid & Marty Krofft's TV series *Land of the Lost*, and he later worked on the visual effects for such movies as *Caveman*, *Spacehunter: Adventures in the Forbidden Zone*, *The Right Stuff*, *The Terminator*, *Gremlins*, *The Return of the Living Dead*, *RoboCop 2*, *Terminator 2: Judgment Day*, *Army of Darkness*, *Nemesis* and *Holes*.

American animation designer, producer and director **Iwao Takamoto**, who helped create such characters as The Flintstones, The Jetsons and Scooby-Doo while working for Hanna-Barbera, died of heart failure on 8 January, aged 81. In a career spanning six decades, he worked on the designs for such Disney classics as *Peter Pan*, *101 Dalmatians* and *Cinderella* and co-scripted and directed the 1973 cartoon version of *Charlotte's Web*. Other credits include *The Addams Family* (1973), *Super Friends*, *Goober and the Ghost Chasers* and *The Robotic Stooges*. At the time of his death, Takamoto (who learned to draw in a Japanese-American internment camp during World War II) was a vice-president at Warner Bros. Animation.

Italian-born producer **Carlo** [Fortunaro Pietro] **Ponti**, the husband of actress Sophia Loren, died in Switzerland of pulmonary complications on 10 January, aged 94. The producer of more than 150 films, his credits include *Ulysses* (1955), *The Ape Woman*, *The Tenth Victim*, *Blow-Up*, *Cinderella – Italian Style*, *Ghosts – Italian Style*, Roman Polanski's *What?*, *Gawain and the Green Knight*, *Flesh for Frankenstein* and *Whisky and Ghosts*.

British-born film production designer **Brian Eatwell** died in Los Angeles on 20 January following a short illness. He was 67. Best remembered for his innovative 1930s Art Deco set designs for *The Abominable Dr Phibes* and *Dr Phibes Rises Again* (both with Vincent Price), his other credits include *The Shuttered Room*, *If . . .*, *Madame Sin*, *Godspell*, *The Man Who Fell to Earth*, *Sgt Pepper's Lonely Heart's Club Band*, *Morons from Outer Space*, *A Connecticut Yankee in King Arthur's Court* (1989) and *The Watcher*.

Mexican film producer **Alfredo Ripstein, Jr** died of respiratory arrest the same day, aged 90. His many film credits include *Swamp of the Lost Monsters*, *The Black Pit of Dr M*, *The Living Coffin* and *Pepito y Chabelo contra los monstruos*.

Set dresser **David Ritchie** was fatally injured on the set of the SF movie *Jumper* in Toronto on 25 January. He was 56. Ritchie's other credits include *X-Men*, *Zoom* and the 1994 TV series of *RoboCop*.

Oscar-nominated costume designer **Donfeld** (Donald Lee Feld, aka Don Feld), who created costumes for the 1970s TV series *The New Adventures of Wonder Woman*, died on 3 February, aged 72. His other credits include *Dead Ringer*, *The New Original Wonder Woman*, *Brainstorm* and *Spaceballs*.

Producer and screenwriter **Charles S.** (Samuel) **Swartz**, who was head of production at Roger Corman's New World Pictures and later co-founder and executive vice-president of acquisition and production at Dimension Pictures, died of pneumonia on 10 February, aged 67. He had been battling brain cancer for several months. Swartz's credits include *It's a Bikini World*, *The Student Nurses*, *The Velvet Vampire*, *Terminal Island* and *Beyond Atlantis*.

British-born special effects supervisor and matte artist **Peter Ellenshaw** (William Ellenshaw), who for more than thirty years worked on numerous classic live-action films for Walt Disney, died in Santa Barbara, California, on 12 February, aged 93. He also contributed to *The Ghost Goes West*, *Things to Come*, *The Man Who Could Work Miracles*, *The Thief of Bagdad* (1940), *A Matter of Life and Death* and *The Red Shoes* (all uncredited), *20,000 Leagues Under the Sea*, *Darby O'Gill and the Little People*, *The Absent-Minded Professor*, *In Search of the Castaways*, *Son of Flubber*, *Mary Poppins* (for which he won an Oscar), *The Gnome-Mobile*, *Blackbeard's Ghost*, *The Love Bug*, *The Island at the Top of the World*, *Bedknobs and Broomsticks*, *The Black Hole*, *Superman IV: The Quest for Peace* and *Dick Tracy* (1990). Ellenshaw painted the first map of Disneyland, which was used on early postcards and souvenir booklets, and he was designated a "Disney Legend" in 1993.

Casting director and Oscar-winning short film producer **Randy Stone** died of heart failure on the same day, aged 48. As head of casting at Twentieth Century Fox Television he was responsible for such shows as *Space: Above and Beyond*, *The X Files* and *Millennium*. His other credits include casting *Jaws 3-D* and he appeared as a flight attendant in *Final Destination*.

Robert Adler, who won an Emmy Award for co-inventing the television remote control with Eugene Polley for Zenith in 1956, died of heart failure on 15 February, aged 93.

Casting executive **Meryl O'Loughlin** (Meryl Abeles) died of complications from ovarian cancer on 27 February, aged 72. She was first credited as a casting director on TV's *The Outer Limits* in 1964 (including the unsold pilot, *The Unknown*), and she also worked on such series as *Fantasy Island*, *Shazam!*, *The Ghost Busters* (1975), *Isis* and *A.L.F.*, along with *Deadly Messages*, *Alice in Wonderland* (1985) and *Tremors II: Aftershocks*.

Sixty-nine-year-old **Jon Lackey**, who created the infamous "carpet monster" for *The Creeping Terror* (1964), died of cancer on the same day. Reputedly, a much better-looking monster was built for the movie, but was stolen a few days before shooting began.

Oscar-nominated production designer, art director, visual consultant and storyboard artist **Harold Michelson** died on 2 March after a long illness, aged 87. His many films (often uncredited) include *Journey to the Center of the Earth*, *The Birds*, *Catch-22*, *Johnny Got His Gun*, *Star Trek the Motion Picture*, *Firestarter* (1984), *The Fly* (1986), *Spaceballs*, *Dick Tracy* and *Matilda*, and he made a brief cameo appearance in *Stephen King's Graveyard Shift*.

Prolific American TV director **Sutton** [Wilson] **Roley** died on 3 March, aged 84. He directed episodes of *Voyage to the Bottom of the Sea*, *The Invaders*, *Lost in Space*, *The Man from U.N.C.L.E.* (including the composite film *How to Steal the World*, created from the series finale), *The Sixth Sense*, *Mission: Impossible*, *Switch*, *Cliffhangers: The Curse of Dracula* and *Shades of LA*, plus the movies *Sweet Sweet Rachel*, *Chosen Survivors* and *Satan's Triangle*.

"B" movie producer and director **Andy** (Andrew) **Sidaris** died of throat cancer on 7 March, aged 76. Although he began his career in TV sports for ABC, he ended up directing Playboy Playmates in such direct-to-video action films as *Malibu Express*, *Do or Die*, *Hard Hunted*, *Fit to Kill* and the two *L.E.T.H.A.L. Ladies* movies. Sidaris also directed episodes of TV's *Gemini Man* and *The Hardy Boys/ Nancy Drew Mysteries*, and he turned up as an actor in *The Bare Wench Project* and its two sequels.

American director **Stuart Rosenberg** died of a heart attack on 15 March, aged 79. His varied credits include the original *The Amityville Horror* (1979) and episodes of TV's *Alfred Hitchcock Presents* and *The Twilight Zone*.

Two-time Oscar-winning British cinematographer and director **Freddie Francis** died of complications from a stroke on 17 March, aged 89. As a camera operator and later acclaimed director of photography, he shot *The Tales of Hoffman* (uncredited), *Beat the Devil*, *Moby Dick* (second unit), *Never Take Sweets from a Stranger*, *The Innocents*, *Night Must Fall* (1964), *The Elephant Man*, *Dune*, *Return to Oz* (uncredited) and the remake of *Cape Fear*

(1991). During the 1960s and '70s he directed a number of low-budget genre films for such companies as Hammer, Amicus and Tyburn (run by his son Kevin). These included *Paranoiac, Nightmare, The Evil of Frankenstein, Dr Terror's House of Horrors, Hysteria, The Skull, The Psychopath, Torture Garden, The Deadly Bees, They Came from Beyond Space, Dracula Has Risen from the Grave, Tales from the Crypt, Legend of the Werewolf* and *The Ghoul* (1975). Among Francis' other credits as a director are *The Day of the Triffids* (uncredited), *The Brain, Mumsy Nanny Sonny and Girly, Trog* (with Joan Crawford), *The Vampire Happening, The Creeping Flesh, Tales That Witness Madness, Son of Dracula* (1974), *Craze, The Doctor and the Devils, Dark Tower,* several episodes of *Star Maidens* (1976) and *Sherlock Holmes and Doctor Watson* (1980), and an episode of the HBO TV series *Tales from the Crypt* ("Last Respects").

Sixty-two-year-old American scriptwriter and producer **Bill** (William N.) **Panzer** died on the same day of a brain haemorrhage after an accident while ice-skating. He produced all five "Highlander" films, *Highlander, Highlander II: The Quickening, Highlander: Endgame,* the *anime Highlander: The Search for Vengeance,* and *Highlander: The Source,* plus the TV series *Highlander, Highlander: The Animated Series* and *Highlander: The Raven.* Panzer also executive produced the 1989 horror film *Cutting Class.*

American writer, producer and director **Burt Topper** (Burton Topper) died of pulmonary failure on 3 April, aged 78. He directed the 1964 film *The Strangler* starring Victor Buono and was a producer on *Space Monster, Wild in the Streets* and *C.H.O.M.P.S.*

Sixty-seven-year-old Canadian film director **Bob** (Benjamin) **Clark** was killed in a car crash with his 22-year-old son, Ariel, on California's Pacific Coast Highway on 4 April. According to police reports, they were killed at 2:30 a.m. when an SUV swerved into the southbound lane. The driver, who didn't have a licence, was arrested on suspicion of driving under the influence of alcohol and gross vehicular manslaughter. Clark's varied credits include *Children Shouldn't Play With Dead Things, Dead of Night* (1974), *Black Christmas* (1974, and the 2006 remake), *Murder by Decree, Porky's* and *Porky's II: The Next Day, Popcorn* and an episode of Steven Spielberg's *Amazing Stories.* At the time of his death, Clark was working on remakes of *Porky's* and *Children Shouldn't Play With Dead Things.*

Oscar-winning Hollywood art director and production designer **George Jenkins** died of heart failure on 6 April, aged 98. His credits include *The Secret Life of Walter Mitty* (with Boris Karloff), *The Bishop's Wife* (1947), *Mickey One*, *Wait Until Dark*, *The Angel Levine*, *Rollover* and *Dream Lover*.

The controversial Chairman and Chief Executive Officer of the Motion Picture Association of America, **Jack** [Joseph] **Valenti** died on 26 April of complications from a stroke he suffered in March. He was 85. In 1968 Valenti helped develop the MPAA's film rating system, which is still in place today, and in 1982 he famously compared the advent of home video recording to the Boston Strangler. He voiced himself in a two-part 1995 episode of the TV cartoon *Freakazoid!*. Valenti was in charge of John F. Kennedy's press detail on 22 November, 1963, when the President was assassinated in Dallas, Texas. He was six cars behind Kennedy's vehicle in the motorcade.

American film and TV director **Curtis Harrington** died of complications from a stroke on 6 May, aged 80. A former film critic (*Films & Filming*, *Films Illustrated* etc.) well-known for his Hollywood parties, he was a close friend and associate of such movie legends as James Whale, Josef von Sternberg and Kenneth Anger. After appearing in Anger's underground film *Inauguration of the Pleasure Dome* and working as associate producer on *Return to Peyton Place*, Harrington carved himself an idiosyncratic career as a talented genre film-maker with such titles as *Night Tide*, *Voyage to the Prehistoric Planet* (credited as "John Sebastian"), *Queen of Blood*, *Games*, *Who Slew Auntie Roo?* (aka *Whoever Slew Auntie Roo?*), *What's the Matter With Helen?*, *The Killing Kind*, *Ruby*, *Usher* (a 2002 short film based on the story by Edgar Allan Poe), and the TV movies *How Awful About Allan*, *The Cat Creature*, *Killer Bees*, *The Dead Don't Die* (based on the story by Robert Bloch) and *Devil Dog Hound of Hell*. He also directed episodes of *Wonder Woman*, *Tales of the Unexpected*, *Logan's Run*, *Darkroom* and *The Twilight Zone* (1987), and made an uncredited appearance in *Gods and Monsters* as a party guest.

Italian exploitation director, writer and editor **Bruno Mattei** (aka "Vincent Dawn") died of a brain tumour in Rome on 21 May, aged 75. After working with Spanish director Jesus Franco, Mattei's film credits (under numerous pseudonyms) include *The Other Hell*, *Zombie Creeping Flesh* (aka *Night of the Zombies*), *The Seven Magnificent Gladiators*, *Rats*, *Robowar*, *Zombi 3*, *Alienators*, *Madness*, *Cruel Jaws*, *Cannibal Ferox 3: Land of Death*, *Cannibal World*, *The Tomb*, *Island of the Living Dead* and *Zombies: The Beginning*, along with numerous soft-core porn titles.

Fifty-seven-year-old **Patrick Stocksill**, the official historian of the Academy of Motion Picture Arts and Sciences, died of complications after a heart-liver-kidney transplant on 24 May. Obsessed with movies, by 1982 Stocksill had more than 10,000 index cards cataloguing Oscar data when he applied for a job at the MPAS. His database was subsequently digitized on to computer. As a perk of the job, he guarded the Oscars at the annual award show, handing out the statuettes to the presenters.

American film-maker and occasional actor **R. Lee Frost** (David Kayne) died on 25 May, aged 71. Under various pseudonyms he directed such titles as *House on Bare Mountain*, *Love Camp 7* and *The Thing With Two Heads*, and he shot additional footage for the Italian documentary *Witchcraft '70* (aka *The Satanists*). Frost also co-scripted *Race With the Devil*.

Scottish-born Canadian "tax shelter" film producer **Peter R. Simpson** died in Toronto of lung cancer on 5 June, aged 64. The founder of Simcom Ltd (later Norstar Filmed Entertainment) in 1971, his many credits include *Prom Night, Curtains, Hello Mary Lou: Prom Night II, Cold Comfort, Norman's Awesome Experience, The Marsh* and *Succubus*. In 1990 he produced and co-directed *Prom Night III: The Last Kiss* (as "Peter Simpson").

Canadian-born **Bill Glen** (William E. Glenn), who directed the 1974 TV movie *House of Evil*, died in Los Angeles on 11 June, aged 74.

British cinematographer **Alex Thomson** (Alexander Thomson) died on 14 June, aged 78. A regular camera operator for Nicolas Roeg before becoming a director of photography in 1968, his many credits include *Scent of Mystery, Dr Crippen, The Masque of the Red Death* (1964), *Fahrenheit 451, Casino Royale* (1967, uncredited), *The Night Digger, Death Line* (aka *Raw Meat*), *Dr Phibes Rises Again, The Man Who Would Be King, The Seven-Per-Cent Solution, Superman* (1978), *The Cat and the Canary* (1979), *Excalibur, The Keep, Electric Dreams, Legend, Labyrinth, High Spirits, Leviathan, Alien³, Demolition Man* and *Hamlet* (1996).

Animal trainer **Moe Di Sesso**, who trained the raven, Jim Jr, in Roger Corman's horror-comedy *The Raven* (1963), died on July 2nd, aged 83. His other credits include *Willard, Ben, The Hills Have Eyes* (1977), *Devil Dog The Hound of Hell, My Stepmother is an Alien* and *Scissors*, along with episodes of *The Bionic Woman* and *3rd Rock from the Sun*.

Australian-born screenwriter, producer and director **Richard Franklin** died of prostate cancer on 11 July, aged 58. Inspired by

Hitchcock's *Psycho*, his credits include *The True Story of Eskimo Nell* (aka *Dick Down Under*), *Patrick*, *RoadGames*, *Psycho II*, *Cloak & Dagger*, *Link*, *F/X 2*, *Running Delilah*, *Visitors* and episodes of TV's *Beauty and the Beast*, *The Lost World* and *Flatland*. He made a cameo appearance in John Landis' *Into the Night*.

Adult film producer and director **Jim Mitchell** (James Lowell Mitchell) died of a heart attack on 12 July, aged 63. With his younger brother, Artie, he formed the pioneering Mitchell Brothers production company in the San Francisco Bay area in the early 1970s. It became one of the most successful "adult entertainment" studios ever with such hits as *Behind the Green Door* and *Resurrection of Eve* (both starring Marilyn Chambers), *Sodom & Gomorrah: The Last 7 Days* and *Beyond De Sade*. Mitchell served six years in prison after killing his brother in February 1991, and a TV film about their life, *Rated X*, was made by Emilio Estevez in 2000.

Hungarian-born cinematographer **László Kovács** (aka "Lester Kovacks") died of cancer on 21 July, aged 74. He relocated to America in 1956 following the Hungarian revolution, and his eclectic credits include *The Incredibly Strange Creatures Who Stopped Living and Became Mixed-up Zombies!!?* (in which he also appears), *The Time Travelers*, *Kiss Me Quick*, *Mantis in Lace*, *Psych-Out*, *Targets* (with Boris Karloff), *Easy Rider*, *Blood of Dracula's Castle* (with John Carradine), *Hell's Bloody Devils*, *Five Easy Pieces*, *Alex in Wonderland*, *Close Encounters of the Third Kind*, *Blow Out*, *The Legend of the Lone Ranger*, *Ghostbusters*, *Sliver*, *Copycat*, *Multiplicity*, *Jack Frost* and *Return to Me*. In 2002 he received the American Society of Cinematographer's Lifetime Achievement Award.

Record producer and business manager **Don Arden** (Harry Levy), the father of Sharon Osbourne, died on the same day, aged 81. Often known as the "Al Capone" of pop, he helped build the careers of the Small Faces, Black Sabbath and the Electric Light Orchestra. He was estranged from his daughter for more than twenty years until they were reunited on the reality TV series *The Osbournes* in 2002.

Carmen Dirigo (Daisy Obradowits), who was the hair and wig stylist at Universal during the 1940s, died on 25 July, aged 99. She began her film career in the mid-1930s, and her many credits for the studio include *House of Dracula*, *The Spider Woman Strikes Back*, *The Cat Creeps*, *The Brute Man* and [Abbott and Costello] *Meet Frankenstein*. She also worked on *A Double Life*, *Secret Beyond the Door . . .*, *Mr Peabody and the Mermaid*, *Two Lost Worlds*, *The*

Vampire (1957), *Diary of a Madman* and the 1971 TV movie *A Taste of Evil*.

Veteran MGM make-up artist **William** [Julian] **Tuttle** died on 27 July, aged 95. During his thirty-five years at the studio, where he became head of the make-up department (1950–69), he worked on such movies as *The Mark of the Vampire* (the bullet hole in Bela Lugosi's head) and *The Wizard of Oz* (both uncredited), *Angels in the Outfield, Brigadoon, Moonfleet, Forbidden Planet, The World the Flesh and the Devil, Tarzan the Ape Man* (1959), the 1960 *The Time Machine* (creating the memorable Morlocks), *Atlantis the Los Continent, The Wonderful World of the Brothers Grimm, The 7 Faces of Dr Lao* (for which he received an honorary Oscar in 1965), *The Glass Bottom Boat, The Venetian Affair, The Power, The Maltese Bippy, What's the Matter with Helen?, Moon of the Wolf, Necromancy, The Night Strangler, So Evil My Sister, The Phantom of Hollywood, Young Frankenstein, Logan's Run, The Fury, Love at First Bite* and ten titles starring Elvis Presley. Tuttle also contributed to several *Twilight Zone* episodes, including "Eye of the Beholder" and "Horror at 20,000 Feet", and *One Step Beyond*, and he appeared in *The Girl from U.N.C.L.E.* episode "The Mother Muffin Affair" featuring Boris Karloff. He was married five times, and his first wife was actress Donna Reed, whom he met at MGM in 1943.

Acclaimed Swedish screenwriter, producer, and film and stage director [Ernst] **Ingmar Bergman** died on 30 July, aged 89. His best remembered film is *The Seventh Seal* (*Det Sjunde inseglet*) in which Max von Sydow's medieval knight plays chess with Death (Bengt Ekerot). Many of his other movies, including *The Face* (aka *The Magician*), *The Virgin Spring* (an Oscar winner), *The Devil's Eye, Through a Glass Darkly* (another Oscar winner), *Persona, Hour of the Wolf, The Magic Flute* and *Face to Face*, contain fantasy elements. He had at least nine children and was married five times.

Legendary Italian director **Michelangelo Antonioni** died on the same day, aged 94. He was best known for his "swinging sixties" thriller *Blow-Up* and the road movie *Zabriskie Point*. Antonioni, who won an honorary Academy Award in 1995 for his life's work, once said: "Actors are like cows. You have to lead them through a fence."

British editor, writer, producer and director **Peter Graham Scott** died on 5 August, aged 83. He directed *The Headless Ghost* and Hammer's *Captain Clegg* (aka *Night Creatures*, with Peter Cushing), and produced *The Curse of King Tut's Tomb* and *The Canterville Ghost* (1986) for TV. Scott's other television credits include an apparently forgotten series, *One Step Beyond* (1948–49), *Tales of Mystery*, *Danger Man* (aka *Secret Agent*), *The Avengers*, *The Prisoner*, *Children of the Stones* and *Into the Labyrinth*.

British TV broadcaster-turned-music entrepreneur **Tony** (Anthony Howard) **Wilson** died of a heart attack on 10 August after a year-long battle with kidney cancer. He was 57. Known as "Mr Manchester" for his support of that northern city's music industry, he founded Factory Records, the label behind such bands as New Order, Joy Division and The Happy Mondays, and set up the legendary Hacienda Club in the late 1980s. He was portrayed by comedian Steve Coogan in the 2002 movie *24 Hour Party People*.

British film producer **Aida Young** (Aida Cohen) died on 12 August, aged 86. She began her career as an uncredited second unit director on such Hammer Films as *Four-Sided Triangle* and *The Quatermass Experiment* and as a production manager for the television series *The New Adventures of Charlie Chan* (1957–58) and *Invisible Man* (1958–59). As a producer, her credits include Hammer's *She* (1965), *One Million Years B.C.*, *Slave Girls*, *The Vengeance of She*, *Dracula Has Risen from the Grave*, *Taste the Blood of Dracula*, *When Dinosaurs Ruled the Earth*, *Scars of Dracula* and *Hands of the Ripper*, along with *The Thief of Baghdad* (1978). She also worked (uncredited) on *Hellbound: Hellraiser II*.

American film editor and producer **Anthony Carras** died of liver cancer on 15 August, aged 86. As an editor for Roger Corman his credits include *A Bucket of Blood* (1959), *Beast from Haunted Cave*, *The Fall of the House of Usher* (1960), *Last Woman on Earth*, *Master of the World*, *Pit and the Pendulum*, *Tales of Terror* and *X: The Man With X-Ray Eyes*. He also edited *The Comedy of Terrors* and *Tarzan and the Great River*. Carras received a co-producer credit on a number of films, including *Bikini Beach*, *Pajama Party*, *Beach Blanket Bingo*, *How to Stuff a Wild Bikini*, *Sergeant Dead Head*, *Dr Goldfoot and the Bikini Machine* and *The Ghost in the Invisible Bikini*, and he co-wrote, produced and directed the 1971 Mexican horror movie *The Fearmaker* (aka *Rancho del miedo*).

Film director **Richard T. Heffron** died on 27 August, aged 76. His credits include *Locusts*, *Futureworld* and the miniseries *V: The Final Battle*.

Costume designer **Jerry Bono**, who worked on the TV series *Star Trek: The Next Generation* and *Star Trek: Deep Space Nine*, died on 31 August, aged 65.

Hollywood dancer and choreographer **Alex Romero** (Alexander Bernard Quiroga) died on 8 September, aged 94. He worked on a number of classic musicals (often uncredited), including *On the Town*, *An American in Paris* and *Seven Brides for Seven Brothers*, as well as *Tom Thumb*, *The Wonderful World of the Brothers Grimm*, *What Ever Happened to Baby Jane?*, *7 Faces of Dr Lao*, *Some Call It Loving*, *Love at First Bite* and *Xanadu*.

Spanish production designer and special visual effects supervisor **Emilio Ruiz del Río** died of respiratory failure in Madrid on 14 September, aged 84. His many credits (often for director Juan Piquer Simón) include *The Blancheville Monster*, *Devil's Possessed* (with Paul Naschy), *Where Time Began*, *Supersonic Man*, *The Humanoid*, *Mystery on Monster Island* (with Peter Cushing and Naschy), *Treasure Island in Outer Space* (aka *Space Island*), *Conan the Barbarian*, *Conan the Destroyer*, *Dune*, *Cat's Eye*, *Red Sonja*, *Slugs* (based on the novel by Shaun Hutson), *The Rift*, *Cthulhu Mansion*, *Acción mutante*, *La Isla del diablo*, *The Devil's Backbone* and *Pan's Labyrinth*.

Film producer **Stanley S. Canter**, whose credits include *Greystoke The Legend of Tarzan Lord of the Apes* and *Tarzan and the Lost City*, died of cardiovascular complications on 12 October. He was 75.

British TV director **Peter Moffatt** died on 21 October, aged 84. He began his career on the 1961 series *Tales of Mystery*, which featured John Laurie as Algernon Blackwood, and also worked on such shows as *Sexton Blake*, *Thriller* (1974), *Doom Castle* and *Doctor Who* (including "The Five Doctors" and "The Two Doctors").

Emmy Award-winning TV producer **Robert F. O'Neill** died of complications from colon cancer on 23 October, aged 86. From the 1960s until the 1970s he produced such shows for Universal Television as *The NBC Mystery Movie*, *Columbo*, *The Sixth Sense*, *The Invisible Man* (1975), *Gemini Man* (he also scripted one episode), *Darkroom* and *Murder She Wrote*, along with the 1970s TV movies *Maneater* and *Live Again Die Again*.

American TV director and producer **Bernard L.** (Louis) **Kowalski** died on 26 October, aged 78. Along with episodes of *The Wild Wild West*, *Mission: Impossible* (which he co-owned), *Blue Thunder*, *Airwolf*, *Knight Rider* and *Baywatch Nights*, and the TV movies *Terror in the Sky* and *Black Noon*, he also directed the feature films *Hot Car Girl*, *Night of the Blood Beast*, *Attack of the Giant Leeches* (aka *Demons of the Swamp*) and *SSSSSSS* (aka *SSSSnake*). Kowalsi began his career as a five-year-old extra in Warner Bros.' "Dead End Kids" movies and was the uncle of Hollywood producer Brian Grazer.

Academy Award-winning film and TV director and producer **Delbert** [Martin] **Mann** [Jr] died of pneumonia on 11 November, aged 87. Mann worked in live television (*Lights Out*, etc.) before getting his big-screen break with *Marty* (1955), which won four Oscars. He never repeated that success, and later credits include such TV films as *Jane Eyre* (1970) and the ghostly *She Waits*.

Italian screenwriter and film director **Ferdinando Baldi** died in Rome on 12 November, aged 80. His many credits include Mario Bava's *Night is the Phantom* (aka *What*, as associate producer "Free Baldwin"), *David and Goliath* and *Treasure of the Four Crowns* (in 3-D!).

Make-up artist **Monty** (Montague) **Westmore** (aka Monte Westmore), a third generation of the family dynasty, died of prostate cancer on 13 November, aged 84. Oscar-nominated for his work on *Hook*, Westmore also contributed to Orson Welles' *A Touch of Evil* (uncredited), *Sex Kittens Go to College* (aka *The Beauty and the Robot*), *What Ever Happened to Baby Jane?*, *Strait-Jacket*, *Doc Savage: The Man of Bronze*, *Lipstick*, *Blood Beach*, *Endangered Species*, *Stand By Me*, *Alien Nation*, *Jurassic Park*, *The Shawshank Redemption*, *Outbreak*, *Se7en*, *Star Trek: First Contact*, *Star Trek: Insurrection* and *How the Grinch Stole Christmas*.

Eighty-eight-year-old Oscar-winning film editor **Peter Zinner** died on the same day, after a long battle with non-Hodgkin's lymphoma. The Austrian-born Zinner began his career as a music editor on such films as *King Kong vs. Godzilla*, *Varan the Unbelievable*, *They Saved Hitler's Brain* and *The Madmen of Mandoras*. As a film editor he cut *In Cold Blood*, the first two *Godfather* films, *Tintorera!*, *The Deer Hunter*, *An Officer and a Gentleman* and the Christian SF film *The Omega Code*.

British TV and film producer **Verity** [Ann] **Lambert** OBE died of cancer on 22 November, just a few days before her 72nd birthday. The first producer of BBC-TV's *Doctor Who* (1963–66), she also worked on *Adam Adamant Lives!*, *Quatermass* (1979), *Jonathan Creek* and the movies *Dreamchild*, *Morons from Outer Space* and *Link*.

British costume designer **Marit Allen** died of a brain aneurysm in Australia on 26 November, aged 66. Her credits include *Don't Look Now*, *Dream Lover*, *Little Shop of Horrors* (1986), *The Witches* (1990), *The Secret Garden* (1993), *Snow White: A Tale of Terror*, *Hulk* (2003) and *Thunderbirds* (2004). At the time of her death she was working on the movie version of *Justice League of America*.

British film producer **Tony Tenser** (Samuel Anthony Tenser), who founded Tigon Films in 1966, died on 5 December, aged 87. During the late 1960s and early 1970s Tigon was third only to Hammer and Amicus for producing horror films in the UK, including *The Sorcerers*, *Curse of the Crimson Altar* (aka *The Crimson Cult*), *The Blood Beat Terror* (aka *The Vampire-Beast Craves Blood*), *Witchfinder General* (aka *The Conqueror Worm*), *Zeta One* (aka *The Love Factor*), *The Body Stealers* (aka *Thin Air*), *The Haunted House of Horror* (aka *Horror House*), *The Beast in the Cellar*, *Blood on Satan's Claw*, *Doomwatch*, *Neither the Sea Nor the Sand* and *The Creeping Flesh*. Tenser's other film credits include *The Black Torment*, Roman Polanski's *Repulsion* and *Cul-de-Sac*, *The Projected Man* and *Frightmare*. He reportedly coined the term "sex kitten" to describe Brigitte Bardot.

Hollywood agent and producer **Freddie Fields** died of lung cancer on 11 December, aged 84. Founder of the powerful Creative Management Associates (CMA), he produced *Lipstick*, *Looking for Mr Goodbar* and *Wholly Moses!*, and executive produced *Poltergeist II: The Other Side* and *Millennium*, the latter based on the SF story by John Varley.

Hollywood film producer **Frank [Warner] Capra, Jr,** the son of the famous film director, died of prostate cancer on 19 December, aged 73. After working his way up from an assistant director to a co-producer with Arthur P. Jacobs on three of the *Planet of the Apes* sequels, he worked on such films as *Marooned*, *Play it Again Sam* and *Firestarter* (1984).

Japanese film and TV director **Tokuzo Tanaka**, best known for his superior contributions to the "Zatoichi" *chanbara* series about the eponymous blind swordsman, died of a haemorrhage on 20 December, aged 87. Mentored by Akira Kurosawa and Kenji Mizoguchi, Tanaka's other credits include the ghost movies *The Snow Woman* (*Kaidan yukionna*) and *The Haunted Castle* (*Hiroku kaibyoden*).

Larry Cassingham (J. Lawrence Cassingham), a civilian radiation expert who developed the first practical portable Geiger counter in the 1940s, died on 23 December, the day after his 89th birthday. During the 1950s, he worked as a technical advisor on such films as *The Brain from Planet Arous*, *Zombies of the Stratosphere*, *The Magnetic Monster* and *The Atomic Kid*.

USEFUL ADDRESSES

THE FOLLOWING LISTING of organizations, publications, dealers and individuals is designed to present readers and authors with further avenues to explore. Although I can personally recommend most of those listed on the following pages, neither the publisher nor myself can take any responsibility for the services they offer. Please also note that the information below is only a guide and is subject to change without notice.

—The Editor

ORGANIZATIONS

The British Fantasy Society (*www.britishfantasysociety.org*) was founded in 1971 and publishes the bi-monthly newsletter *Prism* and the magazine *Dark Horizons*, featuring articles, interviews and fiction, along with occasional special booklets. The BFS also enjoys a lively online community – there is an e-mail news-feed, a discussion board with numerous links, and a CyberStore selling various publications. FantasyCon is one of the UK's friendliest conventions and there are social gatherings and meet-the-author events organized around Britain. For yearly membership details, e-mail: *secretary@britishfantasysociety.org.uk*. You can also join online through the Cyberstore.

The Friends of Arthur Machen (*www.machensoc.demon.co.uk*) is a literary society whose objectives include encouraging a wider recognition of Machen's work and providing a focus for critical debate. Members get a hardbound journal, *Faunus*, twice a year, and also the informative newsletter *Machenalia*. For membership details, contact Jeremy Cantwell, FOAM Treasurer, Apt.5, 26 Hervey Road, Blackheath, London SE3 8BS, UK.

The Friends of the Merril Collection (*www.friendsofmerril.org/*) is a volunteer organization that provides support and assistance to the largest public collection of science fiction, fantasy and horror books in North America. Details about annual membership and donations are available from the website or by contacting The Friends of the Merril Collection, c/o Lillian H. Smith Branch, Toronto Public Library, 239 College Street, 3rd Floor, Toronto, Ontario M5T 1R5, Canada. E-mail: *ltoolis@tpl.toronto.on.ca*

The Ghost Story Society (*www.ash-tree.bc.ca/GSS.html*) is organized by Barbara and Christopher Roden. They publish the excellent *All Hallows* three times a year. For more information contact PO Box 1360, Ashcroft, British Columbia, Canada V0K 1A0. E-mail: *nebuly@telus.net.*

The Horror Writers Association (*www.horror.org*) is a worldwide organization of writers and publishing professionals dedicated to promoting the interests of writers of Horror and Dark Fantasy. It was formed in the early 1980s. Interested individuals may apply for Active, Affiliate or Associate membership. Active membership is limited to professional writers. HWA publishes a monthly online *Newsletter*, and sponsors the annual Bram Stoker Awards. Apply online or write to HWA Membership, PO Box 50577, Palo Alto, CA 94303, USA.

World Fantasy Convention (*www.worldfantasy.org*) is an annual convention held in a different (usually American) city each year, oriented particularly towards serious readers and genre professionals.

World Horror Convention (*www.worldhorrorsociety.org*) is a smaller, more relaxed, event. It is aimed specifically at horror fans and professionals, and held in a different city each year.

SELECTED SMALL PRESS PUBLISHERS

Annihilation Press (*www.annihilationpress.com*), 609 N. Bridge Street, Carbondale, IL 62901, USA.

Burning Effigy Press (*www.burningeffigy.com*), Toronto, Canada. E-mail: *mail@burningeffigy.com*

Cemetery Dance Publications (*www.cemeterydance.com*), 132-B Industry Lane, Unit 7, Forest Hill, MD 21050, USA.

Comma Press (*www.commapress.co.uk*), 3rd Floor, 24 Lever Street, Manchester M1 1DW, UK.

Dark Regions Press (*www.darkregions.com*), PO Box 1264, Colusa, CA 95932, USA.

Delirium Books (*www.deliriumbooks.com*), PO Box 338, North Webster, IN 46555, USA. E-mail: *sales@deliriumbooks.com*

618 USEFUL ADDRESSES

Earthling Publications (*www.earthlingpub.com*), PO Box 413, Northborough, MA 01532, USA. E-mail: *earthlingpub@yahoo.com*

Elastic Press (*www.elasticpress.com*), 85 Gertrude Road, Norwich, UK. E-mail: *elasticpress@elasticpress.com*

Fantagraphics Books (*www.fantagraphics.com*), 7563 Lake City Way N.E., Seattle, WA 98115, USA.

Gray Friar Press (*www.grayfriarpress.com*), 19 Ruffield Side, Delph Hill, Wyke, Bradford, West Yorkshire BD12 8DP, UK. E-mail: *g.fry@blueyonder.co.uk*

The Haworth Press (*www.haworthpress.com*), 10 Alice Street, Binghamton, New York 13904–1580, USA. E-mail: *orders@ haworthpress.com*

Hill House, Publishers (*www.hillhousepublishers.com*), 491 Illington Road, Ossining, NY 10562, USA. E-mail: *peter.hillhouse@ gmail.com*

Humdrumming (*www.humdrumming.co.uk*), 13B Queens Road, Bounds Green, London N11 2QJ, UK.

JnJ Publications (*www.jeffnjoys.co.uk*), 3 Fairy Dell, Marton, Middlesborough TS7 8LF, England. E-mail: *jeff@jeffnjoys.co.uk*

MonkeyBrain Books (*www.monkeybrainbooks.com*), 11204 Crossland Drive, Austin, TX 78726, USA. E-mail: *info@monkey brainbooks.com*.

Mythos Books, LLC (*www.mythosbooks.com*), 351 Lake Ridge Road, Poplar Buff, MO 63901, USA.

Night Shade Books (*www.nightshadebooks.com*), 1423 33rd Avenue, San Francisco, CA 94122, USA. E-mail: *night@.nightshade books.com*

Pendragon Press (*www.pendragonpress.co.uk*), PO Box 12, Maesteg, Mid Glamorgan, South Wales CF34 0XG, UK.

PS Publishing (*www.pspublishing.co.uk*), Grosvenor House, 1 New Road, Hornsea, East Yorkshire HU18 1PG, UK. E-mail: *editor@pspublishing.co.uk*

Rainfall Books (*www.rainfallsite.com*), 22 Woodland Park, Caine, Wiltshire SN11 0JX, UK.

Sabledrake Enterprises (*www.saledrake.com*), PO Box 30751, Seattle, WA 98113, USA. E-mail: *sabledrake@sabledrake.com*

Savoy Books (*www.savoy.abel.co.uk*), 446 Wilmslow Road, Withington, Manchester M20 3BW, UK. E-mail: *office@ savoy.abel.co.uk*

Screaming Dreams (*www.screamingdreams.com*), 13 Warn's Terrace, Abertysswg, Rhymney, Tredegar, Gwent NP22 5AG, UK. E-mail: *steve@screamingdreams.com*

Side Real Press (*www.siderealpress.co.uk*), 34 Normanton Terrace, Elswick, Newcastle Upon Tyne NE4 6PP, UK.

Space & Time (*www.cith.org/s&t_books*) 138 West 70th Street (4B), New York, NY 10023–4468, USA. E-mail: *glinzner@hotmail.com*

Subterranean Press (*www.subterraneanpress.com*), PO Box 190106, Burton, MI 48519, USA. E-mail: *subpress@earthlink.net*

Tachyon Publications (*www.tachyonpublications.com*), 1459 18th Street #139, San Francisco, CA 94107, USA. E-mail: *jill@tachyonpublications.com*

Tartarus Press (*tartaruspress.com*), Coverley House, Carlton-in-Coverdale, Leyburn, North Yorkshire DL8 4AY, UK. E-mail: *tartarus@pavilion.co.uk*

Tasmaniac Publications (*www.tasmaniacpublications.com*), PO Box 45, Hagley. Tasmania 7292, Australia.

Telos Publishing Ltd (*www.telos.co.uk*), 61 Elgar Avenue, Tolworth, Surrey KT5 9JP, UK. E-mail: *feedback@telos.co.uk*

Tightrope Books (*www.tightropebooks.com*), 17 Greyton Crescent, Toronto, Ontario, Canada M6E 2G1.

SELECTED MAGAZINES

Apex Science Fiction & Horror Digest (*www.apexdigest.com*) is a quarterly digest magazine edited by Jason B. Sizemore. Four-issue subscriptions are available from: Apex Digest, PO Box 2223, Lexington, KY 40588-2223, USA. E-mail: *jason@apexdigest.com*

Black Gate: Adventures in Fantasy Literature (*www.blackgate.com*) is an attractive pulp-style publication that includes heroic fantasy and horror fiction. Four- and eight-issue subscriptions are available from: New Epoch Press, 815 Oak Street, St. Charles, IL 60174, USA. E-mail: *john@blackgate.com*

Black Static (*www.ttapress.com*) is a new British magazine devoted to darker fiction. Published bi-monthly, six- and twelve-issue subscriptions are available from TTA Press, 5 Martins Lane, Witcham, Ely, Cambs CB6 2LB, UK, or from the secure TTA website.

Cemetery Dance Magazine (*www.cemeterydance.com*) is edited by Richard Chizmar and Robert Morrish and includes fiction up to 5,000 words, interviews, articles and columns by many of the biggest names in horror. For subscription information contact: Cemetery Dance Publications, PO Box 623, Forest Hill, MD 21050, USA. E-mail: *info@cemeterydance.com*

Dark Discoveries (*www.darkdiscoveries.com*) is a nicely produced quarterly magazine devoted to horror fiction and those who create it.

For submission queries and subscription orders, contact: James R. Beach, Dark Discoveries Publications, 142 Woodside Drive, Long-view, WA 98632, USA. E-mail: *darkdiscoveries@msn.com*

Dark Wisdom: The Magazine of Dark Fiction (*www.darkwisdom .com*) is an attractive-looking magazine published by Elder Signs Press, PO Box 389, Lake Orion, MI 43861-0389, USA. Four-issue subscriptions (US funds only) and submission guidelines are available from the website.

H. P. Lovecraft's Magazine of Horror (*www.wildsidepress.com*) is published by Wildside Press LLC. Single copies or a four-issue subscription are available (in US funds only) from: Wildside Press LLC, Attn: HPL Magazine, 9710 Traville Gateway Drive #234, Rockville, MD 20850-7408, USA. Writer and artist submission queries should be sent to *lovecraft@wildsidepress.com*

Locus (*www.locusmag.com*) is the monthly newspaper of the SF/fantasy/horror field. Contact: Locus Publications, PO Box 13305, Oakland, CA 94661, USA. Subscription information with other rates and order forms are also available on the website. E-mail: *locus@ locusmag.com*

The Magazine of Fantasy & Science Fiction (*www.fandsf.com*) has been publishing some of the best imaginative fiction for more than fifty years. Edited by Gordon Van Gelder, single copies or an annual subscription (which includes the double October/November anniversary issue) are available by US cheques or credit card from: Fantasy & Science Fiction, PO Box 3447, Hoboken, NJ 07030, USA, or you can subscribe online.

Midnight Street: Journeys Into Darkness (*www.midnightstreet. co.uk*) is a horror fiction and interview magazine. Three-issue subscriptions are available from: Midnight Street, 7 Mount View, Church Lane West, Aldershot, Hampshire GU11 3LN, UK. E-mail: *tdenyer@ntlworld.com*

New Genre (*www.new-genre.com*) is published annually in soft-cover book format by editors Adam Golaski (horror) and Jeff Paris (science fiction). Unsolicited submissions are welcomed up to 14,000 words. Unpublished works only, no electronic submissions. Enclose a SAE for reply. Back issues also available. New Genre, PO Box 270092, West Hartford, CT 06127, USA. E-mail: *info@new-genre. com*

PostScripts: The A to Z of Fantastic Fiction (*www.pspublishing. co.uk*) is an excellent hardcover magazine from PS Publishing. Each issue features approximately 60,000 words of fiction (SF, fantasy, horror and crime/suspense), plus a guest editorial, interviews and occasional non-fiction. Issues are also available as signed, limited editions. For more information contact: PS Publishing Ltd., Grosvenor House, 1 New Road, Hornsea, East Yorkshire HU18 1PG, UK. E-mail: *editor@pspublishing.co*

Rue Morgue (*www.rue-morgue.com*), is a glossy bi-monthly magazine edited by Jovanka Vuckovic and subtitled "Horror in Culture & Entertainment". Each issue is packed with full colour features and reviews of new films, books, comics, music and game releases. Subscriptions are available from: Marrs Media Inc., 2926 Dundas Street West, Toronto, ON M6P 1Y8, Canada, or by credit card on the website. E-mail: *info@rue-morgue.com*. *Rue Morgue* also runs the Festival of Fear: Canadian National Horror Expo in Toronto. Every Friday you can log on to a new show at Rue Morgue Radio at *www.ruemorgueradio.com* and your horror shopping online source, The Rue Morgue Marketplace, is at *www.ruemorguemarketplace.com*

SF Site (*www.sfsite.com*) has been posted twice each month since 1997. Presently, it publishes around thirty to fifty reviews of SF, fantasy and horror from mass-market publishers and some small press. They also maintain link pages for Author and Fan Tribute Sites and other facets including pages for Interviews, Fiction, Science Fact, Bookstores, Small Press, Publishers, E-zines and Magazines, Artists, Audio, Art Galleries, Newsgroups and Writers' Resources. Periodically, they add features such as author and publisher reading lists.

Supernatural Tales is a twice-yearly fiction magazine edited by David Longhorn. Three-issue subscriptions are available via post or order through the British Fantasy Society Store (*www.britishfantasysociety.org/store*). Supernatural Tales, 291 Eastbourne Avenue, Gateshead NE8 4NN, UK. E-mail: *davidlonghorn@hotmail.com*

Talebones (*www.talebones.com*) is an attractive digest magazine of science fiction and dark fantasy edited and published two to three times a year by Patrick Swenson. For one and two year subscriptions (US funds only) write to: 21528 104th Street Court East, Bonney Lake, WA 98391, USA. E-mail: *info@talebones.com*

Weird Tales (*www.weirdtalesmagazine.com*) is an updated version of the classic pulp title. Published by Wildside Press LLC, in association with Terminus Publishing Co., Inc. Single copies or a six-issue subscription are available (in US funds only) from: Wildside Press, 9710 Traville Gateway Drive #234, Rockville, MD 20850-7408, USA. Submissions should be sent to *weirdtales@gmail.com* or mailed to Weird Tales, PO Box 38190, Tallahassee, FL 32315, USA. Writers' guidelines are available from the website. For subscriptions in the UK contact: Cold Tonnage Books, 22 Kings Lane, Windlesham, Surrey, GU20 6JQ, UK (*andy@coldtonnage.co.uk*).

DEALERS

Bookfellows/Mystery and Imagination Books (*www.mysteryand imagination.com*) is owned and operated by Malcolm and Christine Bell, who have been selling fine and rare books since 1975. This clean and neatly organized store includes SF/fantasy/horror/mystery, along with all other areas of popular literature. Many editions are signed, and catalogues are issued regularly. Credit cards accepted. Open seven days a week at 238 N. Brand Blvd., Glendale, California 91203, USA. Tel: (818) 545-0206. Fax: (818) 545-0094. E-mail: *bookfellows@gowebway.com*

Borderlands Books (*www.borderlands-books.com*) is a nicely designed store with friendly staff and an impressive stock of new and used books from both sides of the Atlantic. 866 Valencia Street (at 19th), San Francisco, CA 94110, USA. Tel: (415) 824-8203 or (888) 893-4008 (toll free in the US). Credit cards accepted. Worldwide shipping. E-mail: *office@borderlands-books.com*

Cold Tonnage Books (*www.coldtonnage.com*) offers excellent mail order new and used SF/fantasy/horror, art, reference, limited editions etc. Write to: Andy & Angela Richards, Cold Tonnage Books, 22 Kings Lane, Windlesham, Surrey GU20 6JQ, UK. Credit cards accepted. Tel: +44 (0)1276-475388. E-mail: *andy@coldtonnage.com*

Ken Cowley offers mostly used SF/fantasy/horror/crime/supernatural, collectibles, pulps, videos etc. by mail order at very reasonable prices. Write to: Trinity Cottage, 153 Old Church Road, Clevedon, North Somerset, BS21 7TU, UK. Tel: +44 (0)1275-872247. E-mail: *kencowley@blueyonder.co.uk*

Dark Delicacies (*www.darkdel.com*) is a friendly Burbank, California, store specializing in horror books, toys, vampire merchandise and signings. They also do mail order and run money-saving book club and membership discount deals. 4213 West Burbank Blvd., Burbank, CA 91505, USA. Tel: (818) 556-6660. Credit cards accepted. E-mail: *darkdel@darkdel.com*

DreamHaven Books & Comics (*www.dreamhavenbooks.com*) store and mail order offers new and used SF/fantasy/horror/art and illustrated etc. with regular catalogues (both print and e-mail). Write to: 2301 E. 38th St, Minneapolis, MN 55406, USA. Credit cards accepted. Tel: (612) 823-6070. E-mail: *dream@dream havenbooks.com*

Fantastic Literature (*www.fantasticliterature.com*) mail order offers the UK's biggest online out-of-print SF/fantasy/horror genre bookshop. Fanzines, pulps and vintage paperbacks as well. Write to: Simon and Laraine Gosden, Fantastic Literature, 35 The Ramparts, Rayleigh, Essex SS6 8PY, UK. Credit cards and Pay Pal accepted. Tel/Fax: +44 (0)1268-747564. E-mail: *sgosden@netcomuk.co.uk*

Fantasy Centre (*www.fantasycentre.biz*) shop (open 10:00 a.m.–6:00 p.m., Monday to Saturday) and mail order has used SF/fantasy/horror, art, reference, pulps etc. at reasonable prices with regular bi-monthly catalogues. They also stock a wide range of new books from small, specialist publishers. Write to: 157 Holloway Road, London N7 8LX, UK. Credit cards accepted. Tel/Fax: +44 (0)20-7607 9433. E-mail: *books@fantasycentre.biz*

Ferret Fantasy, 27 Beechcroft Road, Upper Tooting, London SW17 7BX, UK. George Locke's legendary mail-order business now shares retail premises at Greening Burland, 27 Cecil Court, London WC2N 4EZ, UK (10:00 a.m.–6:00 p.m. weekdays; 10:00 a.m.–5:00 p.m. Sundays). Used SF/fantasy/horror, antiquarian, modern first editions. Catalogues issued. Tel: +44 (0)20-8767-0029. E-mail: *george_locke@hotmail.com*

Ghost Stories run by Richard Dalby issues semi-regular mail order lists of used ghost and supernatural volumes at very reasonable prices. Write to: 4 Westbourne Park, Scarborough, North Yorkshire YO12 4AT, UK.

Horrorbles (*www.horribles.com*), 6731 West Roosevelt Road, Berwyn, IL 60402, USA. Small, friendly Chicago store selling horror and sci-fi toys, memorabilia and magazines that has monthly specials and in-store signings. Specializes in exclusive "Basil Gogos" and "Svengoolie" items. Tel: 1-708-484-7370. E-mail: *store@horrorbles.com*

Kayo Books (*www.kayobooks.com*) is a bright, clean treasure-trove of used SF/fantasy/horror/mystery/pulps spread over two floors. Titles are stacked alphabetically by subject, and there are many bargains to be had. Credit cards accepted. Visit the store (Wednesday–Saturday, 11:00 a.m. to 6:00 p.m.) at 814 Post Street, San Francisco, CA 94109, USA or order off their website. Tel: (415) 749 0554. E-mail: *kayo@kayobooks.com*

Porcupine Books offers regular catalogues and extensive mail order lists of used fantasy/horror/SF titles via e-mail *brian@porcupine.demon.co.uk* or write to: 37 Coventry Road, Ilford, Essex IG1 4QR, UK. Tel: +44 (0)20 8554-3799.

Kirk Ruebotham (*www.abebooks.com/home/kirk61/*) is a mail-order only dealer, who sells out-of-print and used horror/SF/fantasy/crime and related non-fiction at very good prices, with regular catalogues. Write to: 16 Beaconsfield Road, Runcorn, Cheshire WA7 4BX, UK. Tel: +44 (0)1928-560540 (10:00 a.m.–8:00 p.m.). E-mail: *kirk.ruebotham@ntlworld.com*

The Talking Dead is run by Bob and Julie Wardzinski and offers reasonably priced paperbacks, rare pulps and hardcovers, with catalogues issued occasionally. They accept wants lists and are also the exclusive supplier of back issues of *Interzone*. Credit cards accepted. Contact them at: 12 Rosamund Avenue, Merley, Wimborne, Dorset BH21 1TE, UK. Tel: +44 (0)1202-849212 (9:00 a.m.–9:00 p.m.). E-mail: *books@thetalkingdead.fsnet.co.uk*

Ygor's Books specializes in out of print science fiction, fantasy and horror titles, including British, signed, speciality press and limited editions. They also buy books, letters and original art in these fields. E-mail: *ygorsbooks@earthlink.net*